Hawthorn Academy

COLLECTION

Hawthorn Academy

COLLECTION

KATIE LOWRIE

contents

To Skylar,
Thanks for entering my mind one July day and
helping me achieve my dream.

Author's Note

For any content warnings you may need, please head to my website by scanning the QR code below

P.S. A quick heads up: the vocabulary, grammar, and spelling of The Hawthorn Academy Collection is written in British English.

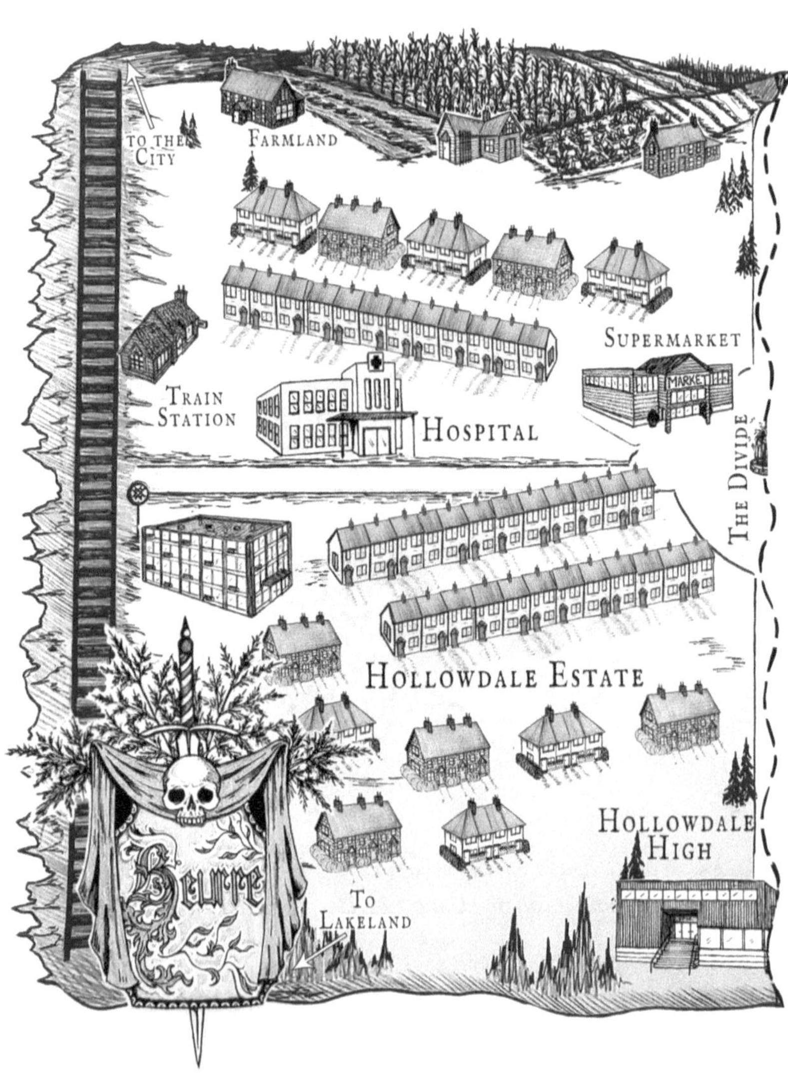

To the City
Farmland
Train Station
Supermarket
MARKET
Hospital
The Divide
Hollowdale Estate
Hollowdale High
Beurre
To Lakeland

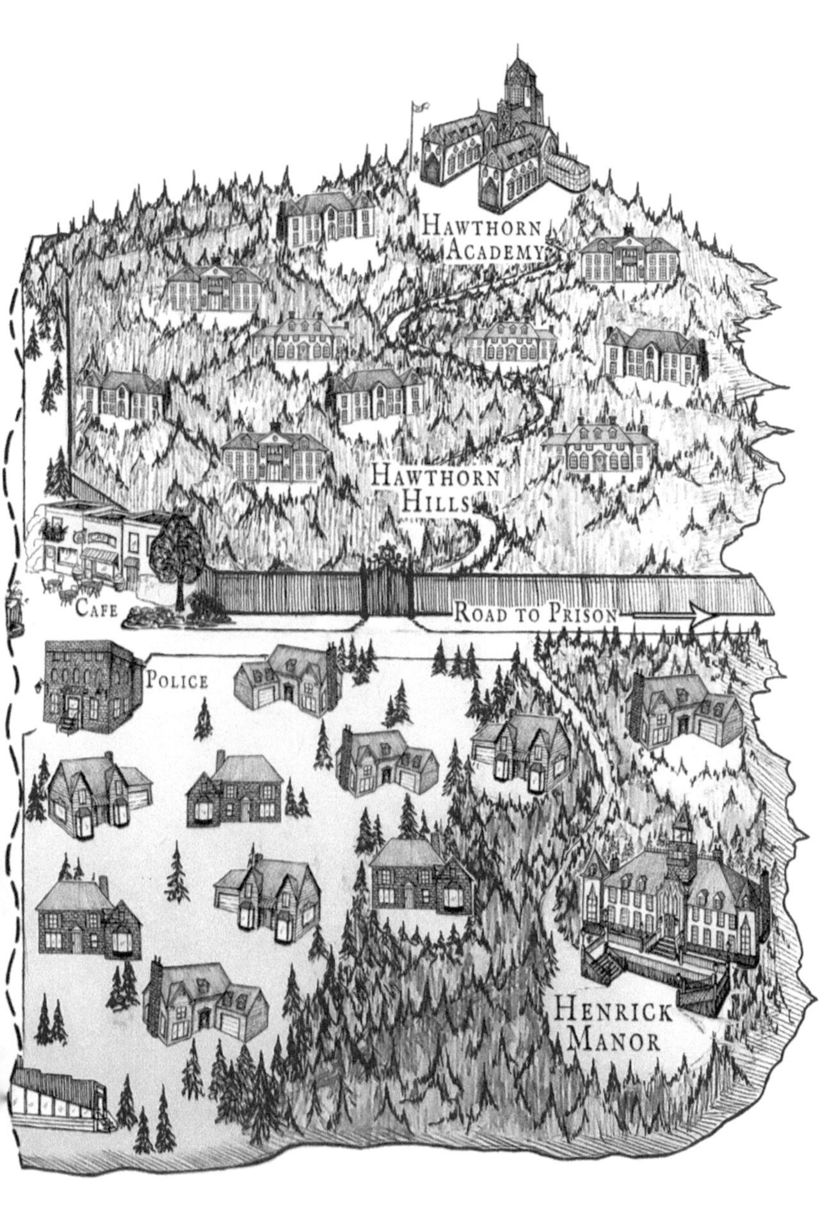

Hawthorn Academy
Hawthorn Hills
Cafe
Road to Prison
Police
Henrick Manor

DISORDER

book one

DISORDER

noun -
a lack of order; disarray; confusion
a deviation from the normal system or order

verb -
to upset the order of; disarrange; muddle
to disturb the health or mind of

Prologue

LOOKING INTO HIS COLD EYES, I could see the true depth of his hate. Could see the contempt he felt towards me, and the disgust on his features only confirmed it.

I knew things had taken a turn for the worse.

That the boy standing across from me was no longer the one I had got to know. No longer the one I thought meant something to me.

Cold. Detached.

His eyes, normally a startling bright blue, had turned a dark indigo filled with anger and loathing.

I could see the exact moment the mist descended. The exact moment his emotions flipped.

A bone-deep shiver ran through me, and it wasn't because of the cold chill in the air.

I wasn't sure what else I could do. Where else I could run. A place where he wouldn't find me again.

Trapped. Alone.

The worst part? I'd been blind to my situation and had walked willingly to my fate.

I was the reason I was here. Every decision, every thought, every moment had led me to the spot I was rooted to, and there was nobody else to blame.

'W-why are you doing this?'

My whisper carried. The high ceiling and the echo of the swimming pool meant he heard me clearly.

Something must have happened to have caused his change. No part of me could accept that this had been coming for longer. No part of me *would* accept it.

The slow smile spreading across his features broke my heart. Shattered it into tiny pieces that clattered to the floor, spilled for all to see.

'You don't belong here, Skylar.' He smirked. 'You never did.'

I crumbled. Tears pricked my eyes, and I tried my hardest to stop them from falling. The second a tear fell, I knew everything would become real. That he truly was looking at me like I was worthless.

I should have known better.

I should have never fallen for the beast, and I most definitely should have never thought of myself as the beauty.

Fairy tales were just that for a reason. Real life was never as satisfying, and there certainly wasn't much truth in happily ever after.

One

EVEN THE BIRDS outside knew the day was different from any other. They'd been outside my bedroom window, incessantly chirping for three hours and, fuck me, I wanted to hurt them.

My first day at Hawthorn Academy, and if I was being completely honest with myself, I was absolutely bricking it. My stomach formed into knots from the moment I woke up and still hadn't untangled itself.

Being a loner, I'd always been, well, alone. I found friends overrated. Or maybe just the idea of friends. But I wasn't always like that. Growing up, I had a couple of friends who lived on the same estate as me. We were mostly friends because we had circumstances in common, rather than personality things. One of the girls, Remi, was a few years younger than me but always acted older, so we never noticed the age difference. Well, until she started befriending the popular girls at school, but that was a whole other story.

The town of Beurre was divided into a rich side and a poor side. Two guesses as to what side I belonged to.

The Hollowdale estate where I lived was where those with less money resided. And most of the time, it didn't bother me. Some people weren't born into money, and that was just how it went. No point in being bitter about it. It was how it was, and I could either fight against it or let it defeat me.

Already, in my sixteen short years of living, I'd found out that in this life all I could rely upon was myself.

God, even my family was a total waste of space. Well, I say family, but really it was just my mum, Cora. I didn't know my dad. He disappeared when I was young. At first, I wished he'd show up on the doorstep and whisk me away to his palace, but he never did. Not that he had a palace. Or maybe he did. Not like I'd know. Whenever I asked about him, Mum would clam up. Which, if you knew my mum, that was the complete opposite of her usual M.O.

'Skylar! Skylar! Get down here at once!' Mum shouted from the kitchen and if I didn't make an appearance downstairs within minutes, she'd send Andy up to get me. Something I definitely didn't want to happen.

Andy was my mum's new, totally useless, husband. He had no job, no money, and absolutely no manners. From the moment I first met him, he gave me an icky feeling. He'd never outright been inappropriate with me, but some of his lewd comments and the way he looked at me made me super uncomfortable. My skin crawled at the way he perused me from head to toe, his beady eyes bugging out of his skull.

'I'll be down in a minute, Mum. Just getting dressed,' I hollered back, hoping she'd hear me and give me a moment. I wouldn't put it past her or Andy to disrespect my privacy and just barge into my bedroom without invitation if given the chance. Mum was always bursting into my bubble without permission, but so far Andy hadn't actually stepped across the threshold of my bedroom. Sometimes, though, I could sense his presence outside my closed door while I changed. A shadow lingering underneath the doorframe. A creak of the floorboards.

I rushed around my room and threw on a vest top and joggers at lightning speed and hot-footed it down the stairs as fast as I could. It was my final day with them, and I wasn't risking shit.

With my head down, I turned the corner into the kitchen without looking where I was going. Stupid of me really, because I nearly walked straight into Andy's chest.

'Shit, sorry!' I said, looking up to see his crooked brown teeth lurking above me, a wicked smile set on his features.

Goosebumps covered my entire body in seconds, and yet, I couldn't look away from his searing gaze. I gulped, willing my reaction to his closeness to go unnoticed. It would only give him a thrill if he knew how uncomfortable he made me, and I refused to give him that satisfaction.

'You should watch where you're going, Sky. You never know who could be around the next corner,' Andy said with a wink. As if he hadn't just lingered in my personal space for longer than needed, he turned around and walked further into the kitchen to sit by my mum, almost making me believe I'd imagined the entire thing.

'Oh, there you are, Skylar! Did you get the shopping I wanted?' Mum asked, her tone one of exasperation.

My eyes went to where she was sitting and I repressed a laugh at her appearance. No point antagonising her over breakfast.

Cora looked old and haggard. Her blonde hair resembled straw, coarse and dry, and it looked to me like she'd taken her makeup tips from the local clown, Bingo, who performed at all the kids' parties. Or I assumed he did. I'd never been lucky enough to have one, and it wasn't like I got invited to many parties growing up. I only knew him because he lived around the corner, offering out pencils instead of candy when the local kids went trick or treating.

Honestly, Mum had looked that way for years. Tired and old. Even though she was only in her thirties.

I tried to find it in myself to have love for her, but I struggled. It always made me feel super shitty, though, as everybody should love their mum, right? It made me wonder if there was something wrong with me, if it was all my fault we never developed a bond. But then I remembered she was a huge narcissist, so that probably had something to do with it.

'Course I did,' I replied with a sigh. 'I put it in the hallway last night when I got home.' I gestured towards the hall, where the carrier bags were in the exact same place I left them the night before. The bags she would've walked past to get to the kitchen and actively chose to ignore.

During the summer holidays, I worked in the local supermarket, so most nights Mum would send me a long list of items she needed me to get for her so I could use my staff discount to make it cheaper. Not that it mattered to her how much the shopping cost, seeing as she had never once paid me for anything I had brought for her.

'Cheers, love. Remind me again why you can't shop for us anymore?' she asked, her over-plucked eyebrow rising slowly. Every time she asked me a question, it was with a tone of disbelief. Like I was going out of my way to be awkward on purpose.

'I've told you so many times, Mum. I'm starting at Hawthorn Academy today. The big elite boarding school on the hill. We definitely spoke about it...' I tapered off mid-sentence when I noticed that neither Mum nor Andy was paying me any attention. The two of them were staring at her phone, probably at some crappy selling page post that was selling a used sofa for pennies. A sofa so cheap because really it belonged in the nearest skip.

'Yeah, yeah, Sky. I remember,' she said, but when she looked up from her phone, her face told me otherwise. Honestly, the woman was constantly attached to that thing like it was another limb. Around a year ago she was adamant that she'd never trade in her trusty Nokia as she "couldn't handle technology like that." Then Andy came along, and voilá, the woman had a brand-new shiny toy she loved more than she loved me.

'What did I even just say, Mum?' I sighed, knowing I'd lost them both. Not that I really had them to begin with. Although sometimes in my head I fooled myself that I was important to her. Being her only child and all.

'School on the hill, Sky. Honestly, I'm just trying to watch this video Leslie sent me and you keep ruining it.'

So, yeah, there she is, ladies and gentlemen. The woman who birthed me.

Leslie was her best friend and just as boring and desperate as her. A match made in heaven if you asked me. The two of them were in constant contact. Pretty sure they even told each other when they were going to the toilet, they were just that close.

'Well, guess I'll be going upstairs to get ready and check my packing.' I looked around the kitchen of the house I'd lived in my whole life, and I knew I wouldn't miss it one bit. The memories weren't exactly horrific or anything, but they weren't particularly stellar either. It was just another place I hated. Another place I was more than ready to escape from.

Mum wasn't abusive. She never laid a finger on me or even threatened to. But she didn't care about me. Not one bit. And as fucked up as it sounded, I couldn't decide what I thought was worse. Because at least if she raised her voice at me, she cared a small iota, right?

I'd always been at the bottom of her list of things to give a shit about. Even our menagerie of pets had always come before me, including the time we had two ferrets named Bert and Ernie. Even when Ernie had nearly bit her finger off, she cooed at him and told him she forgave him.

She hadn't yet forgiven me for the time I ate the last chocolate bar ten years ago.

I was used to it.

I got up from the table, and I could feel Andy's beady gaze regarding me, a thoughtful expression on his face, and I could tell that whatever he was thinking about hurt. I wished I knew the thoughts running through his mind and why he seemed to be aiming them at me.

The fact the man was thinking that hard, in my direction no less, was a major red flag. My mind screamed *"DANGER!"* Yeah, he'd always been a creep, but I'd never felt scared of him before.

But like all moments, the moment passed, and I was left wondering whether I'd imagined it entirely.

By lunchtime, I was changed into something a little more presentable, counting down the minutes until the car arrived. I'd checked and triple-checked my packing and the list of items the Academy required me to bring. Actually, I'd been checking every day for the last two weeks. Nothing could mess up my opportunity, and I didn't want to arrive and realise I'd forgotten something important.

When I received the letter of acceptance, I was a little startled at first. It arrived at the beginning of the summer break, with no postmark. The letter itself was strange, to put it mildly, and even though it had been over a month since I'd received it, I still reread it every now and again to make sure I wasn't reading it wrong. Not that I could read it wrong, but more in the sense that I may have got the intention wrong.

> *Dear Miss Skylar Crescent,*
>
> *It is my pleasure to inform you that you are the recipient of Hawthorn Academy's newly established annual scholarship fund for the next two years. There were many worthy candidates, but after looking through your application thoroughly, we believe you are a perfect fit for our fine establishment.*
>
> *Enclosed is a list of items you will need to bring and a list of those the Academy will provide.*
> *We look forward to seeing you on the first day of term, September 4th, and hope you are pleased about this news.*
>
> *Yours sincerely,*
> *Ms Winifred Hawthorn, Headmistress*

The list of items I had to provide contained obvious items you'd expect to find on a boarding school list, such as toiletries. Then there were some that were a tad more unusual. For example, new lingerie with tags still attached, in one of the school colours. Seeing as the main school colour was a dark bottle green, it was pretty hard to do. Only the fanciest boutique in town had what I was looking for, and I only managed to save up enough the week before. The money I made working wasn't enough to buy expensive, luxury shit. It was barely enough to buy non-expensive shit. Before, my small underwear collection came from the local supermarket. I wasn't sure I wanted to know why my lingerie was of importance to them. I had tried to do some research into the scholarship and the school itself, but my online searches yielded little result. It was like the school was one big secret. All I could find was your generic bullshit about the school, its benefactors, and famous alumni. As if that was enough for anybody to go on.

The whole scenario was strange as fuck because I didn't recall even applying for a scholarship at Hawthorn Academy. When I emailed Ms Hawthorn to ensure that I was the correct recipient, I received a very curt email response that made it clear how stupid she found my enquiry to be. According to her, the name and address being correct on the invitation was confirmation enough it had gone to the correct person. Which made sense to a degree. They knew my full name and address, after all. The scholarship was "newly established," so maybe a teacher at Hollowdale put me forward for it without me knowing.

Guess the scholarship being new explained why I couldn't find much information online about it. Plus, I was so desperate to leave this place that I saw it as a blessing. One of those divine intervention moments where your life changed all because of one letter. One moment in time. One person. Even if I should look more into it, I knew I wasn't going to. The hope the scholarship provided me was enough for me to overlook all the weird shit attached to it.

The list of items the school was providing contained the usual suspects, like pens, paper, that kind of thing, and ones I found very hard to believe. They were providing the school uniform itself, which was fair as uniforms could be pricey, especially ones with fancy blazers. The school was providing me with a laptop and a mobile phone to access the school internet system and complete my assignments. The website didn't have any pricing listed, but from the list of school provided items, I knew it must be a fortune.

Then there was the downright bizarre. The school would provide health check-ups and any protection deemed necessary. What the fuck did that even mean? And why was it of importance to the academy? Then again, rich people had never made much sense to me.

Reading the list once more as I paced my room, I paused when a large thud sounded outside in the hallway. My stomach dropped, and dread filled my gut. I tried to ignore it and continued to read, but there was a feeling gnawing at me. Something telling me that the sound was something to worry about. My bedroom door pushed open, the creak it always made giving it away, and I turned around to find Andy standing at the edge of the threshold, smirking at me.

'Off to your fancy school today, ain't ya?' he asked, his words slurred. The smell of stale beer instantly surrounded me, entered my nose, and clung to my skin. Just one of the many things I looked forward to not having to deal with at Hawthorn.

'Yeah...' I tailed off as he took a step closer to me, entering my personal bubble. I stumbled backwards, the backs of my legs hitting the side of my bed, while trying to smile as if nothing was wrong.

'Guess I won't be eyeing up your young, curvy body for much longer. Pity. You really are quite stunning when you try, Skylar.'

I held back a gag, not wanting to give him the satisfaction. Knowing Andy, he probably thought of his words as a compliment, as something I should be thankful for.

He took another step towards me until he was close enough for me to see the broken capillaries on his nose. All red and irritated, his problem with alcohol on full display for anybody to see.

On his final step, he stumbled and fell forwards. Or at least at first I thought that was what had happened, but when he grabbed me and pulled me tight against him, I knew the stumble was filled with purpose.

His body pressed flush up against mine, the hardness in his joggers causing vomit to rise in my mouth. My heart, and my head, knew this was what he intended to do when he entered my room. A last-ditch attempt to grab me before I left. All those looks over the years culminating in that moment.

His closeness suffocated me. My heart started to beat so fast, I thought it would become visible through my clothes. Fear and anxiety mixed together to create a crescendo of beats.

'M-my mum will wonder where you are,' I said, my stutter showing my surprise. It was rare my stutter came out anymore, especially at home. When I was younger, it was a lot worse, but once my nursery helped with arranging therapy, things had improved. It still lingered under the surface, never fully gone, only showing itself in times of fear or when I was overly anxious. Over-thinking too much about everything.

I didn't even attempt to pull the *"I'll tell Mum"* card with Andy as I knew she wouldn't listen anyway. Or even care. She'd believe him over me any day of the week. She always did.

'Oh, but, Sky, that's where you're wrong,' Andy said, confirming my thoughts. 'I told your mum I was coming up here to talk to ya. You're going to meet a load of fancy wankers at this fancy school, so I told her I'd warn you about them. She doesn't suspect a thing.' The slur of his words made his cockney accent thicker than usual, and it made my skin crawl all the more.

He was telling the truth, too. I could see it in his evil, brown eyes. He'd obviously seen his opportunity and pounced on it, knowing I would leave and wouldn't tell anyone about it.

The smell of stale alcohol lingering on his breath invaded my senses. Revolting, rotting, and putrid. Just like him. His face loomed closer to mine, his eyes making his intentions clear. I tried to turn my face, to look away or shout out, but his hands clamped to my cheeks, keeping my face in place. He kissed me, shoving his tongue deep in my mouth and moving it around violently with no mercy. His tongue slithered around, slimy against mine, and I could taste the beer he'd consumed all morning. Without think-ing, I raised my knee into his crotch, causing him to stumble back-wards, losing his balance. It felt empowering to hurt him, even if only a little.

The knee to the balls seemed to bring Andy to his senses,

grimacing through the pain. He shook his head at me in disappointment.

'You'll pay for that, Skylar, just you wait,' he spat ominously and stormed out of my room.

All I could do was stand still in shock, thinking of all the ways I could rake my tongue to get him off of me. To get the lingering taste of stale beer out of my mouth and out of my brain, forever.

THE LONG, sleek, *expensive* black car arrived at noon.

The driver, a tall, dark-haired man with dark sunglasses on, even though it wasn't overly sunny, handed me a Non-Disclosure Agreement the moment I opened the front door. No greeting. No how do you do? Just a piece of paper thrust into my hands with a fancy-looking fountain pen.

'Er,' I said, looking down at the paper in my hands. 'Thanks?'

'Sign the form please, miss.'

'Okay...' I trailed off before joking, 'I'm not signing my life away, am I?'

'If you could please sign the form please, miss, then we can be on our way.'

'Okay, sure. But *why* am I signing the form?'

'I'm not at liberty to say more until you sign the form.'

I rolled my eyes and read the agreement as thoroughly as I could in the short time I had, then signed on the dotted line.

Pretty sure I hadn't just signed over my firstborn.

Well, fifty percent sure at least.

'Thank you,' he said, taking back the pen and signed form. 'The car is ready for you, Miss Crescent. I'm able to answer any questions you may have on the journey, but I must insist that we leave right this instant.' His voice was a low, tense tone that brooked no argument. I beamed at him, hoping he'd soften at my winning smile, but I barely got a lip twitch back. *Tough crowd.*

'Do I have time to say goodbye to my family?' I asked. The words came out very reluctant. I knew I *should* go and say goodbye to Mum and Andy, even if it mattered to neither of them. If anything, I wanted to make my leaving official.

See you later, wankers. And all that jazz.

'Be quick please, miss. We're on a tight schedule and must be at the Academy for the welcome briefing from Ms Hawthorn at two.'

I nodded at the driver and dashed to the kitchen where I once again found my mum and Andy looking at something fascinating on her phone. Andy acted like what happened upstairs hadn't taken place, and trust me, I wouldn't be the one to remind him.

'The car's here,' I told them. 'I don't know when I'll be home next.'

'That's lovely, sweetheart. Have fun,' Mum said, still looking down at her phone. The only discernible movement came from her hand, which moved quickly, in something that sort of resembled a wave. And I use the term sort of loosely.

You wouldn't have known that her only child was leaving, would you?

Oh fuck it, why did I even bother anymore?

I knew why, though, even if I didn't want to admit it. There was a small part, buried deep down inside of me, that still wished to be loved by its mother. Still wanted to feel wanted. Loved.

And I hated that part of me. That weakness.

I stormed back to the front door, angered at myself for letting my mother's shitty actions affect me again. Taking in a deep breath, I filled my lungs with the cool, fresh September air, and made my way towards the fancy car idling on the street. Towards my new life.

Once inside, the driver handed me an information pack.

'You should have a good read of that, miss,' he mumbled, turning back to the front and arranging his rear-view mirror. 'Tells you all you need to know. I'll answer your questions if I can.'

'Th-thanks.'

Flipping through the pack, nothing looked too out of the ordinary. At first glance, I saw a map of the school and my class schedule. You know. Normal introductory school things. But as I kept flicking through, the last few pages made me pause. It was a social calendar of sorts, with galas and parties listed. But it wasn't on an official school letterhead. It looked haphazard and hastily drawn up. I wondered how it had got in my pack.

I'd never been one to socialise often. It wasn't like I'd attended many parties, and galas in general sounded intimidating to me. My whole life I'd suffered from terrible anxiety. I struggled to even make phone calls to takeaways on the odd occasion I could afford one.

Finally, the car moved away from the only home I'd ever known. I had to remind myself to breathe. In through the nose, out through the mouth. Or wait, was it the other way around?

As I watched my childhood home fade away out of the back window, I smiled. Onwards and upwards to a better life.

Two

HAWTHORN ACADEMY LOOMED at the top of the hill in the wealthy area of town aptly named Hawthorn Hills. It had always seemed elusive to me. I never thought I'd have the chance to find out what happened at the top, but apparently somebody else had a different plan for me.

The car ascended at a snail's speed, so slow that I hyperventilated. Well, maybe that was a bit dramatic. My breathing increased, and my skin prickled with sweat.

The more I worried, the more my anxiety grew as we got closer to the top. Like a thick fog, ready to cloud my vision and leave me sightless.

The nerves overtook me so much that I couldn't even form questions for the driver. When I got in the car, I had so many swirling around in my brain, yet the moment I got inside, they all disappeared. Ran away from me and deserted me in my time of need.

As the car slowly travelled up, block-shaped buildings came into view on the right-hand side of the road and when I looked out the other window, large sports fields were directly in front of me. Being somebody who detested sports, I didn't know much about the school's athletic accolades. Hollowdale, my old school, prided itself on being a sports college. Which translated to a lot of sports, even if you didn't want to take part. I hoped it was different here.

In the far background, there was a long line of trees as far as the eye could see. They moved with the wind, swaying to and fro in a unified frenzy. Red berries covered them, creating an eerie view as they swayed in the wind. The branches seemingly taking on a life of their own. They were pretty, too, in their own way. But mostly eerie.

Questions began to form in my mind the further up the hill we went. Questions I couldn't exactly ask the driver, even if my tongue wanted to speak. Things like: What if I made no friends? Or what if I couldn't keep up academically? Some of the kids would've attended since they were eleven, not to forget that they were very rich, and I had no doubt they had the best private tutors if they were struggling. For all I knew, they could be fluent in frigging Latin!

And I supposed if they were, they'd understand the school motto without having to look it up on an internet search the way I had.

Yep. The school had a motto. A motto that loomed above the car on a sign upon entering the Academy grounds. An idea I always thought was lifted from a movie or a gothic text.

Large and sinister. Welcoming me.

Warning me.

Audentes fortuna iuvat.

Dulce periculum.

Literally translated to English:

Fortune favours the bold.
Danger is sweet.

So yep, that was that.

AFTER THE CAR finally pulled up to the front of the main building, I realised just how big the school really was. Even what I'd seen from the car didn't fully convey the sheer size of the place. How many buildings there really were.

I had always known it was large, but it turned out that what you could see from the bottom of the hill was only the tip of the iceberg. The hill, and the many trees, had hidden so much. I wondered just what else was being hidden in plain sight. Hidden from the town below.

On the front of the main building, a stone gargoyle sat above each corner of the large dark wooden double doors. A shiver ran down my spine at the gothic vibe I got from the building. It was all little turrets and spikes, gargoyles and stained-glass windows. Very picturesque. Very creepy.

The gargoyles' beady eyes looked down on all who entered. Shit, even their sheer presence was menacing and foreboding. A chill crept up my spine, the cold seeping into my bones. *Think happy thoughts. Think happy thoughts.*

Ha. Listen to me. I sounded like a badly written gothic novel. Nothing worse than sounding like *Wuthering Heights*. And trust me, I never wanted to sound like that shit show. It happened to be my least favourite of the classics and that was saying something. Give me *The Old Curiosity Shop* any day.

'We're here, miss,' the driver said, turning around in his seat to look me in the eye. My spider sense was telling me there was so much he wished he could say to me but wouldn't dare to. Or couldn't. Or maybe he merely didn't know where to start because I'd sat in the back of the car acting like a fucking mute even after he told me he'd answer what he could if I asked.

'Thank you. Do I need to grab my bags or...?' I trailed off, uncertain and insecure. It was one of the things I hated most about myself. My inner voice could be strong and feisty; my actual voice, not so much.

'I'll take them and somebody will deliver them to your room after inspection,' he said with a broad smile. He got out of the car and came to open my door for me, giving me my first taste of what it must feel like to have money. Or how I assumed it would feel. Did chauffeurs actually exist outside of fiction?

Taking a giant step, both physically and mentally, I got out of the car. The fresh, brisk September air outside hit me right in the face and I nearly stumbled at the sheer force of it. Great. If I didn't die of embarrassment through existing, maybe I would when I fell over in front of everybody due to the *wind*.

Righting myself to get my balance back, I rubbed my hands down the front of the pinafore dress I chose to wear. It was the nicest thing in my closet, and even though it was thrifted, you couldn't tell.

The main building in front of me beckoned, and I walked towards it, sensing that was where I should go next. A group of four bleached-blonde girls nearby in my peripheral clustered together in a pack. All talking at once, giggling really, and all looking at me. Self-doubt hit me, and shame rose in my cheeks, colouring them in an instant. Their actions, and my reaction to those actions, instantly pissed me off. Why was I letting them get to me already? They had no idea about me, and I knew nothing of them, either.

The only thing I could determine was that they were a similar height and build to each other. You know the "popular" type: slim and petite.

Must be about my age, too.

Wonderful.

Every Academy story I'd read had a grand staircase leading into the school where, usually, the female main character would glance up and see a group of scary, hot guys giving her an ominous look from the top.

I noticed the stairs, but there were no hot guys staring down at me from the top.

Go figure.

No, instead when I looked up, all I could see was a stern-looking woman impatiently waiting for somebody. Pretty sure that *somebody* was me.

I made my way towards her, trying to keep calm and act as if I wasn't about to shit myself any moment. I wasn't wearing a watch, but it hadn't been long since I arrived, so I wasn't quite late yet. I hoped.

'Hello, I'm Skylar Crescent,' I said, holding out my hand to her. I knew instantly that she wouldn't take it, though. A look of impatience mingled with disgust twisted her features, reminding me of a fairy-tale hag of sorts.

'Yes, hello there, Miss Crescent. I'm Ms Hawthorn. Headmistress here at Hawthorn Academy,' she said, her nose upturned and her voice serious.

Everything about this woman was grey. Her eyes, her hair—even the colour of her skin. Maybe she didn't get out much.

'I'm here to welcome you to our fine institution. You are the only recipient of the scholarship fund this year. There is one other recipient of the fund in the year above, who will be along shortly to give you the tour.' The irritation emanated off her in waves, and I swallowed, choosing not to speak and annoying her more.

I smiled, hoping she'd notice and not think I was some uncouth heathen. The look she gave me back told me that my smile wasn't helping matters. If anything, it was making it worse.

'Here she comes now,' Ms Hawthorn said, focused on something over to my left. 'I'm sure you and Miss Luck will get along just fine.'

Just fine didn't exactly sound like a ringing endorsement, did it?

Then she turned around and walked away without so much as a "goodbye." Leaving me there, alone, as I awaited the arrival of somebody called Miss Luck. What were the odds that she lived up to her name and was a lucky person?

As the girl got closer, she wriggled her fingers, and I warmed towards her in an instant. The first thing I noticed about her was her long, dark auburn hair as it swished back and forth in the wind as she walked. At five-foot-five, I'd always been the same height as most other girls my age, but I could already tell that with her, I'd feel like a giant. An inviting enough smile with straight, shiny teeth—too perfect, almost. Little laugh lines lived on either side of her mouth. She was curvy in all the right places and it suited her. I bet she got a lot of attention from the boys here.

'Hey! You must be Skylar, right?' she asked, looking closely at my face, taking it all in. I nodded in response, too nervous to talk just yet. She smiled and said, 'I'm Clover. Yes, I am aware of just how wank my name is. My parents apparently decided from birth that I deserved to be ridiculed.'

She rolled her eyes, and I wasn't sure how to respond. Did I laugh and agree? Did I nod my head, hoping that was the correct response?

'... what do you think?' She watched me expectantly, yet I had no clue how the question started. I'd been off in my own world as usual. I stared blankly back. Way to look like a brain-dead zombie.

Great first impression, Sky.

'I am so s-sorry. I sort of spaced out back there. W-what do I think about what?' I asked, nerves jumbling around in my stomach so bad, I thought I might vomit on the spot. My stutter had started already and I could feel the blush rising on my cheeks. I knew how much I judged people on first impressions, and I felt like I'd messed this one up for myself completely.

'No problem.' Clover laughed and my anxiety wondered whether she was laughing with me, or *at* me. Who fucking knew?

'I was asking if you wanted to see your room first or the rest of the school?'

'I'd love the tour, thank you,' I said quietly. We made eye contact and smiled, the warm feeling returning to my gut. I didn't want to be one of those girls who automatically believed they'd found a new best friend due to a shared look and circumstance, but I thought that maybe I could become friends with the girl. Not straight away, but sometime in the future at least.

'THAT'S THE POOL BUILDING, but I'd avoid going there unless totally necessary,' Clover told me, pointing at a large red brick building on our left. It didn't look like any pool building I'd ever seen. It wasn't sleek and modern like the one at my old school. It was old-fashioned, and the colour made it seem out of place, but the architecture was in line with the rest of the buildings.

So far, Clover had shown me the buildings that held the class-rooms and inside the large main building where the cafeteria and admin offices were. Not that I would call it a cafeteria. It was more like a fancy dining room than anything else.

The school was a lot bigger than I expected, and, even armed with my map, I knew I was going to get terribly lost. Ever since I was young and went on a camping field trip with the school, I'd known I had an awful sense of direction. God forbid if somebody ever handed me a compass and a direction to head in because I would never find my way.

'Why should I avoid the pool?' I asked, the curiosity getting the better of me. It was the first time she'd commented on a building and, call me intrigued, I needed to know why.

'Oh, well, that's where...' Clover stopped herself mid-sentence and scoffed. 'Talk of the devils.'

I turned my head to look in the same direction as her and nearly swallowed my tongue. Three guys were exiting the pool building together, and I shit you not, they looked like gods among men. They were unlike any other teenager I'd ever seen before.

Each of them had wet hair and looked good enough to devour. I had to stop myself from drooling on the spot. The three of them were beyond gorgeous. All tall, tanned, and as rugged as a teenage boy could be.

'W-who are they?' I asked, my stutter rearing its ugly head. But I couldn't help it. The sheer sight of them had caught me off guard. Had caused my heart rate to spike and my body to break out into all over shivers.

'The one with blonde hair and blue eyes is Leo Hawthorn, the oldest of the three, and trust me, he likes to wield the fact that he's a Hawthorn like a weapon. He's in my year.'

She sighed, rolling her eyes, and I thought that maybe there was more to it. I stayed silent, waiting for her to continue, but she stopped talking about him and moved on to the guy standing beside him.

'The one with red hair and a cheeky grin is Griffin, but everybody calls him Griff. He's in your year. I'd be careful with that one if I were you.'

I nodded absentmindedly. Obviously, I was wondering why I should be careful with Griff, but then he caught my eye and focused his cheeky grin in my direction. I had to stop my mouth from opening of its own accord. He winked, and I averted my gaze fast. *Be careful with that one.*

'Last but not least is Oliver Brandon—only call him Ollie if he tells you to, and even then, I probably still wouldn't. He's also in your year and is one of the most sought-after bachelors at this school.' She fake gagged, and if I wasn't sure about there being history between her and those three, then her gesture had all but confirmed it. 'Be careful you don't end up in his eye line. All the girls here would fight for even a speck of his attention. Believe me, you'd do best to stay away from all three of them.'

Clover's eyes locked with mine and somehow managed to convey every emotion at once. Like I could see into her soul and know the seriousness of her words. It was overwhelming, to say the least.

Oliver was by far the hottest guy of the three. My ovaries were screaming just looking at him. He had that whole chiselled jaw thing going on. You know, imagine the character Charles Brandon in the early seasons of *The Tudors*. That was who Oliver reminded me of. He also had something that was uniquely his own, though. Something I couldn't quite put my finger on. He noticed Griff looking over in our direction and turned his head to see what the fuss was about.

Our gazes collided. I gasped at the sheer intensity of it. Like Leo, he had blue eyes, but his hair was the colour of hazelnut. That perfect shade of light brown that looked good enough to eat.

Jesus, Sky, get a grip.

'Is that a bad thing then?' I asked. Clover looked at me perplexed and I added, 'The fact that the other girls want him?' I felt so naïve. At my previous school, I minded my business. I had never needed to know the inner workings of a group of girls before or how they operated.

'Oh, honey. It's a very, very bad thing.' Clover looked at me with sympathetic eyes. I noticed that they were the same shade of green as our uniform, but I didn't want to compliment her on how unique they were in case she thought I was being mean. She'd been nice to me for the few hours I'd known her, and I *definitely* did not want to screw up what could become my first friendship at my new school.

At that moment, I could have sworn that the air around us began to change, and no, it wasn't because the wind had picked up. Well, the wind *had* picked up, but that wasn't why.

No.

It was all because the boys were heading towards us.

Shit.

Clover stood next to me, staring at them as they got closer, then rolled her eyes, her irritation at their existence clear.

I froze. What was I meant to do? Was I even meant to do anything at all?

Should I introduce myself? Stay silent?

Too many variables ran through my head and I could feel the slow simmering burn of a panic attack building. Wires were short-circuiting up there, frazzling. My anxiety always got worse around new people and new situations, and no matter how much I prepped myself during the summer, that feeling hadn't gone away. Black slowly crept in around the edges of what I saw, my vision a pinprick, still fixated on the three boys coming closer. My breathing was so fast, yet I wasn't taking any air into my lungs. The tightness hurt.

My sight cleared to all three of them standing in front of me. Tall, imposing, and dramatic.

Griff glanced at me, his gaze amused, yet assessing. Leo, the rather gorgeous blond one, looked bored by the whole situation. But it was Oliver I focused on. He looked at me with pity shining in his blue eyes, his lips curved up at the edges in a sympathetic smile. Or was it sinister?

I hated not being able to read people that well. It was something I always struggled with. If somebody had a good poker face, then I would never win in life.

'Everything okay here?' Oliver asked, looking at Clover, but we all knew he was talking to me. Or maybe *about* me.

'Sure is. This is the new girl, Skylar. Sky, I already told you who these three are. If you know what's good for you, you'll take whatever they say with a pinch of salt.'

'No need to be like that, Clo. We're all friends here. An introduction is the proper way.' He turned to me with a grin wide on his face. 'I'm Griffin. Call me Griff.'

'Hello,' I mumbled, a small smile playing on my lips at his cheery attitude.

'Don't be fooled by that smile, Sky,' Clover warned, crossing her arms on her chest.

'I'm sure Sky can make up her own mind, can't you?' Griff asked, looking at me. He smiled wide again, and I realised the grin must be his trademark look. He definitely had to know how endearing it was. All straight white teeth and dimples.

'I g-guess,' I said. My breathing sounded like I'd been in a boxing ring for all twelve rounds. That, along with my stutter, I was certain I was making a fool of myself.

'Oh cute, did you hear that, Ollie? She stutters,' Leo said, looking around himself as if he would rather be anywhere else. His tone was filled with derision and clearly he was over the entire situation and wanted it to be finished as soon as possible. He made no eye contact with either me or Clover, preferring to look at the group of four girls who'd laughed at me earlier in the day.

'So she does,' Oliver said, his voice like honey. Sticky and sweet. 'Sky, was it? Nice to meet you. Welcome to Hawthorn Academy. Clover here will make the school rules clear for you, I'm sure. Wouldn't want you to forget any now, would we?'

Oliver smirked in Clo's direction, and something private passed between them. Something I wasn't yet privy to. Maybe never would be.

'Come on, lads,' Oliver said, elbowing Griff in the ribs. 'Let's leave the girls to it.'

The three of them turned and walked away in unison. No more words said. A well-oiled machine, practised and polished to perfection.

I looked at Clover, and her face had gone as red as her hair.

'Those boys will be the death of me, I swear it. Every time I'm near them, I just get so blood-boiling mad! Don't listen to them, seriously. The three of them think they rule this school because their families are rich.'

I laughed. Clover seemed genuine, and I hoped I hadn't blown it by acting a little tongue-tied when the boys came over. Making a friend at Hawthorn was vital if I was going to survive. I'd never been around this many rich kids before, and I hadn't grown up with money. I assumed that if Clover was here on scholarship too, then she understood how I felt. Overwhelmed.

It had only been half a day, and already I needed to process a lot.

'What did they mean by rules?' I asked as Clover led us towards another building.

'Oh, didn't you read through your welcome pack? Duh'—she hit her head playfully—'of course you didn't! Let's go to our room and I'll tell you all about it. I can show you the Hive too. To be honest, it's probably best we talk about all this in private anyway.' Clover's words and tone were light as a feather, but I could feel the heaviness of her statement living beneath the surface.

'Our room?' I asked. It was the part of her sentence that I'd homed in on, happy to hear that I wouldn't be living alone in a strange place.

'Yeah. As the only two scholarship students here, we're sharing a room as our funds only cover the basic necessities or some kind of crap like that. Didn't really listen, to be honest.'

'My letter said that the scholarship fund was newly established?' I asked. 'But you're clearly not new this year?'

'What makes you say that?'

'You seem super familiar with everyone,' I pointed out. 'You knew the guys and that.'

'Oh, well, yeah. I started last year.' She pouted her lips and looked away before returning her face to mine with a large smile. 'Got to know the douchebags pretty quick.'

'Fair,' I said, her explanation making sense. Even if she started last year, that was still pretty new for an establishment that had been around for over one hundred years. 'I'm glad we get to share a room. I was worried I'd be alone and isolate myself away.'

'I'm sure you'll be thankful we're sharing in due course.'

Clover's cryptic answer did nothing for my anxiety, but I attempted a smile, anyway.

Pretty sure it came out as more of a grimace.

Three

OUR ROOM WAS LARGER than my one at home, that was for sure. It may even be bigger than the living room, too.

Most likely one of the largest rooms I'd ever been in, to tell the truth.

It made me wonder how large the other rooms were, and just how expensive they were, if Clover and I needed to share due to budgeting.

On each side of the room, there was a double bed pushed up against the wall, with some space in between for a rug and some bedside cabinets. It was obvious which side of the room belonged to Clover as she had covered the pinboards with pictures and newspaper cuttings. One of the pictures was of Clover and two people I assumed were her parents. They had the same hair colour as her. Plus, their eyes were the same unusual green hue.

'Do your parents miss you?' I asked, pointing at the photograph.

Clover's smile faded and soured.

'They hate that I'm here,' she admitted, twisting a strand of hair around her finger. 'But they also know it's for the best.'

She shrugged and I said no more. I may not always be able to read facial expressions, but I also liked to think I knew when to stop talking.

My eyes went back to taking in everything in the room. There was a little kitchenette in a small space in front of my bed and an en-suite bathroom to the right of the kitchen area. It was more than I hoped for. In my head, I had some awful visions of having to share a bathroom with every girl on the floor and having my clothes stolen—or worse.

The light cream colour of the walls went perfectly with the black furnishings dotted around the room. I loved it. It resembled how I always wanted my bedroom at home to look but never quite achieved. Happiness filled me. I would be living here for the next two years. It was a whole lot better than I imagined it would be. Lying in bed at night, thinking of the academy, I always found it hard to envision it. Whenever I thought about how things would go, it had taken on a mythical quality in my mind. Dream-like and hazy.

Clover flopped down on her bed and sighed extra loud. If the walls were thin between our room and the one next to it, they definitely heard her. Our room was the last one at the end of a corridor, so the bathroom wall was joined to another one, and I supposed the wall behind the built-in wardrobe that took up the wall space at the end of Clo's bed.

I wanted to ask why she'd sighed so deep, but I felt self-conscious about it. I kicked myself for feeling that way. It was stupid, really. At no point during our tour did she give me the impression she'd be judgemental like that, but guess there was no way to know for sure. Like a fish out of water, I hovered. I didn't know the rules and I felt completely out of my comfort zone.

Luckily for me, Clover broke the silence first.

'You can call me Clo, by the way. I know it sounded super shitty and sarcastic coming from Griff, but that's the nickname I answer to.'

I nodded, thankful she'd told me, because I was already thinking of her as Clo in my head, anyway.

'It's the only nickname I can get away with, really. Nobody wants Ver to be their nickname, I can tell you that. The bitches always shortened it to Over, which was highly original as you can imagine.'

Her tone of voice and her open face really were comforting

and a smile broke out across my face. Feeling welcomed here in such a short period of time was more than I could've hoped for. Warmth spread through me and my feet were grounded to the floor, settled and ready to tackle the journey ahead.

'Over,' I said with a laugh. It always amused me the wit of kids and bitches. 'Back at your old school?'

'Right. My old school...' Clover's eyes shifted around the room, no longer looking at me or trying to catch my eye. 'And here, too. Guess it's not that original after all.'

I nodded. Lucky for me, my name couldn't be shortened to anything like that. And shortening it to Sky wasn't exactly going to win them points in the bullying stakes. Not that I'd been bullied at Hollowdale. Just... ignored.

'I need to fill you in on some things, Sky. Things here at Hawthorn, I mean. The girls who go here are twats nearly all the time. Leo and I were friendly when we were younger, and the girls here didn't like that one bit.' Clover looked out the window, her tone softening when she spoke again. 'They call themselves *The Set*.'

She rolled her eyes so hard, I thought they were going to leave her face.

'*The Set*? Original.' I laughed, trying to ease the tension that had seeped into the room. I could taste it. This urgency that hadn't been there before. I knew Clover wanted to tell me more. My brain urged her to tell me more.

'Yeah. There are four of them and they are the biggest bitches I've ever met. I don't use that term lightly. Their names all begin with the same letter like some knock-off *Heathers* shit.'

'So, who are they? What do they do?'

'Well, they can be any age, but it's usually reserved for the upper two years. And when the older two graduate, there are two new members all primed, ready to take their place. It's an old tradition. Passed down through years and years of snobby people who send their children here. Kind of a birthright thing?'

'Right...' I said, wrapping my mind around it.

'So, you have Olivia and Odette. They're in my year. Then

there's Ophelia and Oralie. They're in your year and have only been members for a year. They take it all very seriously. Most of the time, they use their words to keep people in check. They've escalated to *pranks* in the past, though, and believe me when I say that there's nothing harmless about *those*.' Clover's eyes met mine from across the room. 'Read the rules, Sky. I know it sounded like Oliver was making fun when he mentioned the rules, but they really do exist.'

'Where can I find them?' I asked. I couldn't recall seeing them when I flipped through the welcome pack in the car, but I wasn't exactly looking for them either. 'Are they in the pack I got?'

'Of sorts,' Clover replied, getting up a screen on her phone to show me. 'This is Hive. An app the school designed to keep students aware of news, etcetera. Now, it's controlled by *The Set* and—'

I stopped her mid-sentence and asked, 'Let me guess, there's a boy version.'

'Bingo!' Clo said with a laugh. 'And of course it's the three boys I introduced you to earlier.'

'Of course.'

'But let me make one thing clear. The boys will never refer to themselves that way, so probably best not to say it to their faces. It's more something the Os and the rest of the students say, okay?'

'Okay... Is there a fourth I didn't meet?'

'Nope. They decided they didn't like anybody else enough. And with Leo's dad owning the place, not like anybody could say shit against them.'

'So what name do they go by?' I asked, feeling silly. It was a valid question, though in the alternative world I'd found myself in. In the bully academy books I read—and loved—they always had a group name, but, fuck me, it didn't make me feel less stupid.

I fully expected Clover to tell me they were the *Kings* or the *Princes*. Something obvious and stereotypical. There had been a group at my old school that referred to themselves as the *Rebels*, but that wasn't because of money or tradition or anything like that. No. They were just kids with big egos from the poor side of town.

'They call them *The Sect*.'

I could see that Clover was trying her hardest to keep her face semi-straight.

'Apparently, those names have been in place ever since the school opened in 1850. This school has always had some kind of self-opposed royalty. So fucking sad.'

Clover couldn't keep her laughter in any longer. Tears started streaking down her face, a level of hysteria plain to see. At first, it kind of unnerved me. It wasn't *that* funny. But as with all hysteria, I got swept up in its midst.

Obviously, I did what everybody else did when watching a laughter meltdown unfold. I laughed too.

The hardest I'd laughed in a long time. Maybe the hardest ever.

That kind of infectious laughter that made no sense to anybody else, that when you tried to stop, you'd catch one another's eye and start up again.

And it was at that moment, lungs burning in protest, that I felt a genuine connection to Clover. That maybe I would survive my time here with her as an ally. Maybe one day even as a true friend.

We were both here on somebody else's money, trying to get by and doing our best to better ourselves.

My whole life nobody thought I would amount to much. Everybody I knew believed I would work in a supermarket forever, wasting away.

We would see about that.

THE EVENING PASSED, and as it progressed, I found myself falling for Clover. Not romantically. But in that way girls did when they wanted to be friends with somebody and wanted them to love them and befriend them in return. A major girl crush.

'So,' I said around the cheese roll Clover had made for our dinner, 'tell me more about *The Set* and *The Sect*.'

'Well, what d'you wanna know?' she replied, swallowing her bite of food before wiping the back of her hand on her mouth. I smiled at her lack of manners, knowing we were going to get along more and more by the minute.

'The history of it all, I suppose? Must'a started somewhere.'

'Right'—she nodded—'okay. So the school was founded in 1850 by Robert Hawthorn and introduced the groups to keep students in line, but their roles changed over the years, I guess. A scholarship fund was first introduced in the 1950s, and they were used as a way to keep the younger students and any scholarship recipients in line. There hasn't been a scholarship since the early noughties, though.'

'Why's that?'

'No clue. Nobody really talks about it. But we're the first since then. They're used to create order and stop anybody from rising too high above their station in life.'

I rolled my eyes at that as Clover made bunny fingers, clearly as unimpressed as me. The thing was, though, I also fully believed that was why they did it. Rich people definitely had different priorities in life. That was the conclusion I'd come to.

For the last two years of my life, I'd often wondered about how I would afford to keep food in the house or rent paid on time, and then there were these fuckers worried about some eleven to sixteen-year-olds dating somebody in a different pay bracket. Madness.

I glanced at my class schedule while I finished eating. Most of the lessons were in typical subjects like English Literature. Then there were subjects I hadn't ever thought I'd be able to study, such as Philosophy and Ethics. Luckily, because I didn't join at age eleven, the school didn't expect me to study Latin. *Of course they all know frigging Latin.* The language I studied at my old school, French, was listed instead.

'Want me to show you the rules on Hive?' Clover asked, finishing her roll and rubbing her hands together to get rid of any crumbs. She picked up her phone and went back on the app she'd briefly shown me earlier. It was a bright garish yellow with a bee emoji in the top left-hand corner. 'You'll have your own personal log in on your phone. I'll set it up for you. So, you click the bee for the menu to drop down.'

I nodded, watching as she navigated the app. The menu listed her class schedule, test results, and some other things I would need to know. Then she clicked on the section of the menu that said *Other*.

Wording instantly appeared on the page in an elegant script I could barely read.

'Can we get this up on a laptop?' I asked, squinting at the phone in Clo's hand. 'I can barely read it.'

The school had provided me with a phone, laptop, and other necessary supplies like they had said they would, so it made sense to make the most of them. It was strange to own something as expensive as the phone and laptop the school provided, but I wasn't complaining. My mum may have the newest iPhone, but I had been holding on to my trusty Blackberry for years, praying it wouldn't die on me. The phone was so old, they didn't even make it anymore! It's not like I had needed a phone to talk with friends, anyway.

We loaded up the laptop and while we waited, I asked, 'Surely none of these rules are that hard to follow?'

'It's not that they're hard to follow per se. It's more of just what each rule means in actuality.'

Rules of Hawthorn Academy:
As decided by The Sect and The Set.
All students must adhere or face the dire consequences.

I looked at Clover and asked, 'What does it mean by "face the dire consequences"? Sounds like something that would happen in a bad made-for-TV movie.'

I laughed.

She did not.

If anything, her face got even more serious as she said, 'Seriously, Sky, I don't want to be *that* person, but I mean this. You do not want to find out. Do not give them any reason to look at you. They all saw you today and the Os definitely know that the boys spoke to you. Do us both a favour and just stay away.'

'I promise, Clo, I'll try.' Her seriousness put a chill inside of me. We had been joking all day about the other kids that go here and about rich people in general. At no point had she sounded so sombre.

My eyes went back to the page to read the rules.

Rule One: DO NOT approach *The Sect* or *The Set* without being summoned first.
Rule Two: DO NOT look at the above-mentioned groups unless deemed necessary.
Rule Three: DO NOT bring shame upon your family or this fine institution.
Rule Four: NEVER date someone above your class without asking for permission.
Rule Five: NEVER turn down the invitation of somebody from *The Sect* or *The Set*.

We will punish anybody failing to adhere to the above as we see fit.

I got colder after reading each rule. Technically, I had already broken one of them without even meaning to. I had looked at the girls laughing at me, and I had *definitely* looked at the boys before they came over to us. I wondered what they meant by "deemed necessary." How could you know whether to look at them? Who even determined what was necessary or not? Maybe I just ignored them unless they talked to me and looked at me first. That seemed the best bet.

'Clo, what is the punishment for breaking these rules?' I wondered whether it could be as serious as it seemed. Surely not? The students here were aged between eleven and eighteen. Could the punishment really be that severe? The faculty must know about them if these groups have existed for as long as the school itself.

'Well, it totally depends on what rule you break and who you've pissed off. The boys play dirtier than the girls. Remember that. Girls will be blatant and in your face. Boys, they'll ruin your life without you even knowing they lifted a finger.'

'How comforting,' I said in a dry tone. I could feel it in my bones, though, that she wasn't making any of it up. Clover really believed what she was saying. I wasn't saying that it wasn't true, but *c'mon*, maybe it was a slight exaggeration.

'I'm not exaggerating, Sky,' Clo said, her eyes cutting into mine.

Well, there went that theory.

Clo didn't notice my distracted look and continued talking, 'I've heard stories that would make you run far from here. A couple of years ago, somebody upset *The Sect*, and it was horrible. I'm not sure what they did, and I doubt they did anything to justify what happened to them, but they ended up in the hospital. They tried to take their own life. It was dark.'

I gulped.

The air became thick, and suddenly, I found it hard to breathe. I felt like I had earlier, when the boys had approached me. My vision started to fade, black around the edges once again. I couldn't place why my body was betraying me. Why a panic attack had started at Clo's words. Maybe it was from the serious-ness of her tone.

Either way, the last thing I remembered was staring hard at Clover and trying to communicate just how trapped I was feeling in my own body.

Then nothing.

Four

I OPENED MY EYES, expecting to see Clover's scared green ones looking back at me.

That was not what I saw.

At all.

Bright blue piercing eyes were looking down at me instead. I couldn't place them at first, but there was one thing I knew.

You know when you could tell something just by looking into somebody's eyes?

Well, I could tell that these eyes held secrets. Lots of them.

'Hey there, are you okay?' the owner of the eyes asked. I blinked, trying to adjust to my new surroundings. The azure eyes belonged to Oliver, and I was staring into their light.

Wait, am I already breaking rule number whatever?

I hoped not. He looked into my eyes first, not the other way around.

'I-I'm fine, I think.' *Man, I wish my stutter would just piss off.* Although really, I should cut myself some slack. I had passed out and awoken somewhere unfamiliar. 'Where am I?' I asked. I couldn't see around him to figure out where I was.

'You're in the school's hospital wing,' he answered, and all that was occupying my mind was that I really was in an academy novel now. Complete with a wing for ill people.

Wait. An entire wing dedicated to ill students didn't bode well, did it?

'How? What happened?' I had no recollection of the events leading up to that moment, like, at all.

'You passed out. I was about to knock when Clover burst through the door, saying something about how you were acting strange and blacked out,' he said, gazing at me intently. 'So I carried you here, to the hospital wing.'

I nodded. In theory, his story made sense. The last thing I remembered was Clover looking at me funny. I had no idea why he would be outside my room, though. Surely he hadn't been coming to seek *me* out. When we first met earlier that day, he made it clear I was beneath him. Somebody not worth his time.

'T-thanks, I appreciate it. You really didn't have to. Sometimes I get anxiety attacks and feel faint,' I told him, hoping he'd leave now that I'd woken up. Then it hit me. 'Where's Clover? Did she not come with us?'

'Clover's outside the room. I said I'd let her in once you were awake,' he said, his eyes shining with humour.

What a beautiful boy, I thought. I shook my head and laughed out loud.

'A beautiful boy?' he asked, chuckling.

Realising my error, I stopped laughing abruptly. Oliver's lips twitched, but he stopped himself from laughing any more than he already had. I couldn't believe I said that out loud. That I put those words out into the universe where he could hear them. No doubt he thought I had a few screws loose.

'I'm beautiful? Really? You don't think I'm sexy?' The amused look on his face, mixed with the teasing in his tone, made me want to shrivel up and disappear. Looking closely into his eyes, I could see a hint of something else lingering in his gaze. A kind of heat that made me feel a certain way. I imagined how dominant he'd be in private, and I could feel my cheeks going red. No matter what I did, my cheeks always showed my emotions, which caused me some awkward situations in the past.

'I—' I started talking, attempting to prevent him from looking so intently at my cheeks.

He cut me off. 'I'm joking, Sky. I'm glad you've noticed me,' he said, seeming genuinely perplexed, shaking his head, as if he couldn't quite believe somebody like me would think so highly of his looks. Which, let's be honest, was the biggest load of bullshit acting that I'd seen in a while. Maybe ever.

'Everybody notices you, I'm sure. Ever considered that they're too scared to look at you? You know, because of all those rules on Hive?' The moment the words left me, I wished I'd kept my mouth closed. Of all the things I could have said, I had to say something about the rules. About the fact that he and his friends thought they were untouchable. What was wrong with me?

'Maybe you should remember that fear is good. Being scared can ensure you live. That you don't make life-threatening mistakes. Ever considered that, Little One?'

The second those words left his lips, Oliver left the room, taking the heat with him. His words—fuck, the entire conversation—had made me feel frozen inside. Was that a warning or a threat?

***

NOT LONG AFTER Oliver walked out, Clover entered, curious.

'So... What did he say?' she demanded the moment she came into view.

'Nothing much.'

'Nothing much?' she asked, disappointed. 'Why don't I believe you?'

'No idea.' I shrugged, staying tight-lipped. I hadn't even had time to process what happened myself. Not that much *had* happened, but still. Clover meant well—I assumed. Not like I knew the girl well enough yet to truly know her motivations.

Although, a kinship of sorts was building between us, and one day I could see us being the best of friends.

Still, I was wary. I didn't want to give her all my trust and then have it thrown back in my face in the future. I had no idea who I could truly trust, and I wouldn't be stupid and make that big of a decision on my first day.

The sour-faced, miserable-looking nurse approached and Clover stopped the words that were about to leave her lips.

You know when people's lips looked as if they'd been sucking on a sour gobstopper for hours? All pursed and puckered. Well, that was the face on the nurse.

'Can I leave and go back to my room?' I asked her. I really didn't need to be there. My vision had returned to normal and I no longer felt faint.

'You'll leave when I have permission from Master Hawthorn,' she replied, her voice as dull and lifeless as the rest of her. My mind instantly went to Leo, and I wondered why he had anything to do with me getting out of here. My eyes found Clover, questioning, hoping she'd have an answer for me.

Clover just shrugged, though. Maybe it was the way things went at Hawthorn.

I wanted to leave and get settled in my bed and prepared, both physically and mentally, for the next morning. There was to be a huge assembly for the entire school first thing, and attendance was mandatory.

I was already nervous enough, but after my stunt that evening, there would be rumours flying around about the "New Girl" and the reason why she ended up in the hospital wing with Oliver by her side, of all people.

After another hour or so, the sour nurse finally relented. She must have heard from Leo. Or realised that it was absolutely bloody ridiculous to keep me there on the whims of a seventeen-year-old boy. Either way, midnight had long passed and my eyes could barely stay open. The entire day felt like a clusterfuck of emotions. So much had happened in such a short period, yet I'd only been on school grounds for eight hours. Eight hours that felt a hell of a lot longer.

Clover stayed with me the whole time, keeping the conversation flowing. She kept it light and surface level, which I was extremely thankful for, even if I didn't respond to half of what she said.

On our way back to our room, Clover tried to help me figure out where on the property we were. She'd pointed out the hospital wing on her tour, but it wasn't somewhere I thought I needed to become acquainted with, so I'd failed to pay much attention. Apparently, we were now on the second floor walkway that led to the Admin building.

'Are we near the pool house?' I asked, trying to recall the map of the school in my mind. Pretty sure we were on the west side of the campus. 'A—'

'Shh,' Clover whispered, bringing her finger to her lips. 'Be quiet a second.'

She stopped on the spot, and I halted too.

'Can you hear that?'

My ears strained, listening for any sound other than our breathing, but if I was being honest, I couldn't hear a thing.

'What is it?' I hushed out, keeping my voice as low as I could.

'I'm not sure. But it sounded like noises coming from down the hall,' Clover said, nodding in the direction we were headed.

We continued up the corridor on silent feet, listening out for any more noises.

A low moan reached us, and that was when I saw *them*.

Two figures were up ahead, standing so close to one another, they were almost one. I couldn't make out anything but their body shapes. No faces or features.

I put my finger on my lips and gestured to Clo to follow me as I once more tiptoed up the hall, towards the couple.

Like the saying goes, curiosity killed the cat. And often, I acted like the cat. It was as if a compulsion took over me and I had to know what was happening. I knew I should have just continued on my way and gone to bed. *Obviously, I should have done that.* But nope. Instead, I crept closer.

Leo Hawthorn stood beside one of the O girls Clover had told me all about, but I wasn't sure which one. The two of them were definitely kissing—potentially more. Heavy breathing filled the air, and it became obvious they hadn't noticed us.

A gasp came from behind me, but when I turned my head to glance back at Clover, I saw her back as she ran away. She had left me there without an explanation. No words. Nothing.

What the fuck?

Clover's gasp echoed through the hall and the two of them stopped making out to stare at me. The dim lighting of the hallway made it hard to see much, but it was light enough to make out facial expressions. The girl was pissed.

Great.

'What are you doing here, New Girl? Can't you see we're busy?' she spat. The girl had long, ice blonde hair. Perfectly straight, reaching all the way down to her waist. It swished with every word she spoke.

'I-I-I...' I couldn't speak. My tongue became heavy and felt like it was glued to the roof of my mouth. My vision blurred around the edges and moisture slowly covered my body in a thin sheen of sweat. I hated myself at that moment. I hated how weak I felt.

'I-I-I...' she mocked, looking me dead in the eyes. 'Leo, can you hear this shit?'

Her laughter rang out, reaching every corner, as she turned back to face Leo once more.

'Leave her alone, Odette,' Leo snapped. He looked at me, his eyes taking in the full length of my body. He didn't look interested in me. He didn't look disgusted either, though. He was just... looking.

'You're seriously going to take her side?' Odette seethed. 'Honestly, Leo, she's a poor, ugly nobody. Probably riddled with disease, too. She doesn't deserve to even be here.'

Her beautiful features morphed into something evil. Something almost otherworldly, the light hitting her at an angle that only made her look more sinister.

'Get off me,' Leo growled, shoving her from him with such force that she nearly fell over. Luckily, she caught herself in time.

'Go back to your room, Odette. I don't want to see you again tonight.'

'What?' she roared, even more pissed than she was before. 'Are you being serious? Le—'

'Get out!' he said, cutting her off before she could plead her case. 'Leave!'

Odette huffed and turned to storm away. Not before delivering her parting shot to me, though.

'You better watch your back, New Girl. Oh, the things we could do to you.' Her words reminded me of a Seuss poem. Odette continued to laugh like a villain in a second-rate horror film as she disappeared around the corner and out of our view.

Leo watched her go, his expression unchanging. He didn't smile or show that he wanted to exchange pleasantries.

'Ignore her,' he said, nodding down the corridor in the direction Odette stormed off. 'She's a bitch.'

He moved to face me, a blank expression covering his face.

I wasn't panicked before, but the moment he faced me, my heart rate shot up. All I could focus on, all I could think about, was the fact I had broken their stupid rules and would have to face the consequences. Clover made it clear those rules were to be taken seriously.

'O-oh, it's okay. I'm sorry I'm looking at you,' I said.

'Well, you don't seem to be looking away even now that you've realised,' he said, his tone bored, but his eyes lit up, giving away his amusement. My cheeks flushed, his bored low grumble sounding so sensual in the dimly lit corridor. I watched his lips move, but the words weren't computing. My brain was mush, complete goo, as I tried to look away. Tried to control my embarrassment.

'...If you are, come and tell me. Or Oliver,' he said, the smirk fully established on his face. 'He'll want you to tell him about anything the girls do to you.'

'I don't have permission to come talk to you without being summoned first,' I joked, tongue in cheek. An attempt at a joke at least. Not sure if it landed the way I hoped. Leo's face didn't change.

'I'm giving you permission now, aren't I?' He cocked his head, no longer looking as disinterested. 'Don't disappoint me, New Girl.'

'Thanks, I guess...' I mumbled, my sentence trailing off at the end, no idea what else to do or say. I found Leo intimidating. At over six feet tall, he seemed like a giant compared to my five-foot-five—although he made me feel even shorter than that. *Or maybe he just makes me feel small?*

'No problem. I'll see you around,' he said, all of his teeth showing. Sinister, almost. A threat.

Leo's strides were filled with purpose as he walked away. He didn't look back at me once. I did hear a chuckle come from him, though, before he was completely out of my eye line.

I walked back to my room, thinking back over what the fuck had just happened. I would definitely be giving Clover a piece of my mind.

Or maybe I would give her a piece of my mind in my own head.

I didn't want our friendship on the rocks before it ever had the chance to take off.

It took me a while to struggle back to my room. On more than one occasion, I couldn't figure out where the heck I was in the school. I couldn't catch my bearings and kept coming across dead ends and wrong turns.

I hoped dead ends and wrong turns wouldn't become a common occurrence. But knowing my luck, they for sure would be.

Five

THE ASSEMBLY for the entire school was taking place in the large auditorium located in the main building. Once inside the hall, the enormity of the room took my breath away. The ceiling was so high, it reminded me of a cathedral. The stained glass windows probably helped that.

On the wall opposite the entrance, there was a large rectangle stained glass window, the beauty of it shining throughout the entire room. The morning sun coming through created the most beautiful colours on the grey stone floor.

Nobody seemed to pay attention to me or Clover on the surface, but the surrounding whispers sounded like angry bees, buzzing away; the stares as sharp as daggers when we weren't looking. After the run-in with Leo and Odette last night, I didn't want to draw any more negative attention to myself. My gut was sure the girls were already plotting something for me. Something sinister.

'So.' Clover halted once we reached the seating area and said, 'I have to go sit with my year in the last row.' She rolled her eyes, making it clear how unimpressed she was.

'Where do I sit?' I asked her, looking around, not seeing any signs or anything. Guess it was a situation where people just *knew* what to do. Something I wouldn't know being the new girl.

'The last two rows of the stands are for my year, and the two rows before that are for year twelve. Sit in any seat but try to get a seat on the aisle. Means you can make a quick getaway when it's over,' she said as she gave me a slight shove towards the steps and I made my way towards the rows she'd pointed out. I took a seat near the end of the row, leaving the last seat of the row empty. Nobody liked the dickhead who didn't move all the way down a row and expected newcomers to climb over them.

Clover was sitting a few rows behind me, next to Leo of all people, and I could hear the two of them grumbling at one another. No idea what words were being spoken, but it didn't sound friendly, that was for sure.

After a few minutes, I sensed a body dropping into the seat next to me.

'I hope you don't mind me sitting here.'

I groaned inwardly. I recognised that voice. Oliver's voice. Looking at him only confirmed it.

'Sure,' I said with a sigh, knowing that there was nothing I could say or do to change it. A very small part of me didn't want to change it—but I'd keep that to myself. 'Of course I d-don't.'

One day soon, I hoped I could come across as a normal teenage girl and not some tongue-tied loser. Alas, today was not that day.

'Thanks. I feel like we haven't formally introduced ourselves. I'm Oliver Brandon,' he said and held out his hand for me to shake. I sat frozen, uncertain. Had he forgotten yesterday? Or had our conversation in the hospital wing been a part of my imagination? Pretty certain we were introduced yesterday and had multiple run-ins. *Right?*

'I'm Skylar Crescent,' I said as he moved his hand and placed it in mine. What happened next startled me. I shit you not. An electrical current travelled up my arm, starting in my fingertips until it reverberated through my shoulder. Shocked, I darted my hand away. A smug smile covered Oliver's face, the speed of my action amusing him.

'I know who you are,' he said, the condescending tone not lost on me. After a beat, he said, 'Leo told me about last night.'

'He d-did?' I asked, puzzled as to what he meant. Or what part he'd told him about. He'd been there for half of it.

'Leo mentioned he told you to come to me if any of *The Set* bothers you. He said you were worried about punishment for not following the rules, so I wanted to clear it up with you.' His eyes glinted with excitement when speaking of punishment, but the glint disappeared as fast as it came.

'T-thank you. I really appreciate it.' I'd been doing so well in controlling my stammer, but this guy was so hot, he was melting my brain a little. Up close, I could see his blue eyes had flecks of silver running through them. His lips were full, and I really wanted to take a bite out of them. I could feel my face heating. My thoughts were clear on my face for all to see, my pale complexion giving it away. And my thoughts were heading to a really dirty place. Having his hand hold mine even for the briefest moment had me imagining where else he could use his hands.

Get a grip, Skylar.

'You're really cute when you stammer, you know. Makes me wonder how much I could make you stammer with my dick deep inside you.' The casual way in which he spoke made me choke on air. It was so left field, but now those images filled my imagination to the point I couldn't see anything else—the hall no longer registering.

'Err...' I was at a loss for words. I raised my eyebrows, not sure about the correct response. I'd never found myself in a similar scenario before.

I was so lost in Oliver's suggestive look, I didn't notice that Ms Hawthorn had walked to the centre of the stage at the front of the hall.

'Silence, everybody,' she called out, her tone assertive, echoing throughout the hall. Her gaze covered the entire room and with her words, every single student went quiet. A pin could have dropped and everybody would hear. 'Welcome to a new year here at Hawthorn Academy. We have a new scholarship student joining us this year by the name of Skylar Crescent. I hope that everybody will make her feel at home.'

I shrank in my seat, hunching my shoulders to try to make myself as small as possible. I hadn't expected her to name-drop me like that. The way she said it made it sound like a threat, paranoia playing within the deep recesses of my brain.

Oliver nudged me with his elbow and smiled widely. I thought his smirk was sexy as fuck, but wow, his smile was even better than his smirk.

'So, New Girl Skylar, how can I make you feel at home here?' he asked, having come closer to me, entering my space. His words whispered over my ear and made me tingle from head to toe. Goosebumps covered my arms, and I tried to focus on whatever Ms Hawthorn was saying—but I was failing miserably.

Even just sitting next to Oliver made me nervous, and I counted down the minutes, hoping this torture would be over soon.

'Enjoy the first week, students,' Ms Hawthorn said, ending her speech—a speech I'd heard none of. *Hope it wasn't important.*

People moved in their seats and stood to leave.

Thank fuck it was finally over.

But before I could leave in silence, Oliver put a hand on my arm to hold me in place.

'How about you join me tonight for dinner at my table?' he asked, and on noticing my reluctance, he added, 'Bring Clover, too.'

'O-okay,' I said, a rabbit in the headlights. No other words would come to mind. And with that one word, I sealed my fate.

AFTER I AGREED to sit with him at dinner, Oliver didn't utter another word. Just left the hall, leaving me standing there a little shaken up. I had no idea what to expect. Clover and I had eaten breakfast in our room as we'd overslept, and last night I'd missed dinner in the dining hall while lying in a hospital bed and had to make do with some sandwiches the nurse begrudgingly handed out.

Clover met me after the assembly ended and when I asked her what she and Leo had been discussing, her face turned sour.

'Leo's the biggest prick I know.' She pursed her lips together, saying no more on the subject.

Duly noted.

While walking down the corridor to my first lesson here at the academy, I remembered what I agreed to during that brief conversation with Oliver in the assembly.

Here goes nothing.

'Clo,' I mumbled, taking in a big breath to prepare for my next words. Or maybe I was preparing for her reaction to said words. 'Oliver's asked if I'll sit at his table tonight for dinner. He said you can join us if you want to. I may have agreed...' I trailed off when I saw her face. Her green eyes narrowed and her lips puckered, acid dripping from her features.

Clover looked at me like she personally wanted to deliver my death.

She stopped in the middle of the corridor, some poor kid bumping into her back and running off when she glared at him.

'I'm sorry, but what did you just say?' Her voice was ice. 'I thought I just heard you say that you'd agreed to sit with *The Sect* for dinner? But that can't be possible because there is no way you're that fucking stupid. Right?'

I squirmed. I knew she wouldn't take it well, but to drop the F-bomb that early in the day meant she was even madder than I expected.

'I-I must be?' I asked, looking everywhere; anywhere that wasn't Clover.

'Skylar Crescent, didn't I say yesterday to stay away from those boys? Did you not listen to anything I said?' She was shaking her head and giving me a pitying look. I felt embarrassed. I *had* listened to everything she told me, but when Oliver was asking me to join them, I just couldn't stop myself.

'I promise I did, Clo. It is one of the rules, though, and...' I was still looking around and trailed off when I saw Griffin approaching us, waving exaggeratedly at me. So exaggerated that he hit a girl so hard, she stumbled. Even that couldn't stop Griff's cheeky grin, planted firmly on his face, and I couldn't help but smile back at him.

'Yo, girls, what's happening?' he asked loudly and pulled me into an awkward hug that I hadn't seen coming as he trapped my hands between us. He buried his nose into the nape of my neck. 'Damn, New Girl, you smell like girlfriend material.'

He let me out of the hug and all I could do was gape at him. I mean, seriously, did that line ever work on anybody?

'Just ignore him, Sky. The boy doesn't know when to stop.' Clover's bemused face made me smile. Griff seemed to have that effect on people. I always wondered if people who came across as easy-going were actually hiding something darker underneath the surface. Something they wanted to keep hidden so badly that they'd joke about anything, act the fool, so nobody would look deeper.

'A-and what does girlfriend m-material smell like?' I asked, holding back a laugh. My smile stayed firmly in place, though. I felt so much more at ease with him than I did with Oliver or Leo. Within moments of being near him, a warmth entered me and filled me with a sense of joy.

'You,' he whispered, his hand caressing my face. He seemed super proud of his comeback.

I laughed for real then, letting it bark out of me, my smile manic.

'Oh, ha-ha, Griff,' Clover said, her voice anything but amused. 'You are such a wind-up. Leave my girl Sky here alone. She's already sitting at your table for dinner, after all.'

She crossed her arms over her chest, making it clear once again that she thought I'd made a poor decision.

'New Girl, you are in for a treat! Please sit next to me, pretty please,' he said, ignoring Clo's negativity as his eyes met mine and his pleading tone made me laugh a little. I had no romantic attraction to him, but he really was a force. He even batted his eyelids at me, his long eyelashes fluttering with the motion.

Words failed me, but I gave a small nod of the head, agreeing with his request. He pumped his fist in the air and shouted, 'Score!'

The few students left mingling in the hall all turned to stare at the commotion that was Griffin Cooper, and their eyes widened when they realised he was conversing with me. I wondered if he was acting out of character. I also wondered how many of them would've been punished—or already had been—for doing the same thing.

Griff looped his arm through mine, and then Clo's, to walk us to my first class of the day, History. I didn't ask how he knew where I was meant to be. Seemed like a waste of breath, as I knew he probably wouldn't tell me, anyway.

'Here you are, my fair lady,' Griff said, sweeping his arm towards the classroom door and lowering himself into a bow. 'Learning awaits.'

I shook my head and waved bye to him and Clover, who was biting her bottom lip, a mixture of amusement and anger dancing on her face.

The moment I entered the classroom, I spotted a few empty desks. I chose one in the back row and took my school laptop from my bag.

A velvety voice entered my ear.

'Fancy seeing you here.'

Oliver.

'Yes, f-fancy seeing me in class at the school we both attend,' I snapped. My words came out a lot more snarky than I intended, but there was just something about that boy that really put me on edge. One of my flaws was that when my anxiety couldn't handle a situation, it turned me into the biggest brat known to man. *This* was one of those times.

'Whoa,' he said, raising his hands, palms facing forward. 'Slow your horses, New Girl. I meant it in jest. You know, after we sat together for assembly, I didn't realise I'd be seeing you in my first class, that's all. I would have walked you here had I known.'

'Yes, well, Griff walked me here, so no sweat,' I said, looking around the classroom instead of directly at him. Whether I liked it or not, the boy made me sweat.

Oliver visibly bristled at the fact Griff walked me to class, and I felt a little smug about it. He threw himself into the empty seat beside me and I rolled my eyes.

'*Griff* walked you here?' he asked. I couldn't decide if it was the sheer fact that Griff had done something nice for me pissed him off the most. Or the fact he hadn't thought of it himself first.

'Yep. He wants me to sit next to him tonight at dinner, too. Seemed super chuffed to know I was joining you.' Internally, I laughed. On the outside, I remained cool as a cucumber. I just couldn't help myself. Riling up the devil was my idea of fun, clearly.

'You'll do no such thing,' he growled.

Still refusing to look at Oliver, I glanced around the room some more, taking it all in. Everything looked a little different from the classrooms I was used to back at my old school. The technology here surpassed anything they had at Hollowdale High.

At each desk, a student sat with their school issued laptop. A SMART board linked up to a computer took up the majority of the far wall. Honestly, at my old school the teachers were still using dry-erase boards as the school had spent all of their funding on the science labs and the sports programmes.

'I'm sure I read in the rules somewhere that us mere p-peasants can't turn down the invitation of somebody from *The Sect*. Griff asked me to sit with him and I said yes. Pretty simple if you think about it, Oliver.' I shrugged.

I knew I was holding out on a technicality, but fuck him. Sure, it was Oliver who asked me to dinner in the first place, so he probably intended for me to sit with him. But I hated the attitude and bullshit of it all. Yeah, I'd accepted his invitation. But I never specified who I would sit with, and he never specified I had to sit with *him*.

The moment I referred to them as *The Sect*, though, Oliver's face soured. His lips formed into a point, and his eyes darkened.

'Call me Ollie,' he said, his nostrils flaring, his tone deadly.

The teacher arrived, and Oliver said no more.

I remembered what Clover told me: nobody called him Ollie unless he told them they could.

The teacher started the lesson, and I ignored *Oliver* for the rest of the lesson. There was no way I would bow down to him. We weren't friends.

The lesson itself was about the art of warfare.

How fitting.

THE REST of the day flew by and I had made it to the last period without making a total fool of myself, which was a real plus in my eyes.

In every class there was at least one member of *The Set* or *The Sect*. Oliver was in my History class. Griff was in my Philosophy and Ethics class. The two O girls, Oralie and Ophelia, were in English.

It was time for French, the last lesson of the day, and I sighed deeply as I slumped into an empty seat in the back row. In every class, I had taken a seat in the back to stay out of the limelight a little. I'd already heard people whispering about Oliver sitting with me in assembly and him inviting me to dinner. The rumour mill at Hawthorn was similar to my old schools'—filled with half-truths and blatant lies.

I walked into the room and my eyes snapped to the blue ones staring at me from the back row.

Oliver was sitting with Oralie and Ophelia on either side of him, smirking at me. The only available seat in the room was the one next to Oralie, and although I didn't want to sit next to her, I knew they had thrown down the gauntlet so to speak.

I slumped into the chair at the same time a high-pitched voice whined, 'Oh, Ollie. Don't you think you should tell *that* girl not to sit there? She doesn't deserve to sit with us.' Her hand was running up and down his arm, her fingers grazing his skin in a casual way that was completely at odds with the strained look on her face.

'She's a nobody. Did you hear that she interrupted Ode while she was with Leo last night? Bet she's one of those freaks who enjoys watching others get it on.' Oralie joined in.

Ode?

What kind of a shit nickname was *Ode*?

A giggle bubbled out of me—I couldn't help myself. My eyes went to where Oliver was sitting, wanting to see his reaction to the lies Oralie was spouting. His eyes lit up, a dark glint flashing through them before disappearing without a trace. *Is he a voyeur?*

I tried my hardest not to roll my eyes. I *really* did. But some reactions just happen involuntarily.

'Lay off her, girls. I've invited Sky to sit with us at dinner tonight,' he said, his tone harsh.

My heart thudded in my chest. With *us*?

Stupid old me hadn't fully realised that eating dinner with the boys would also mean eating dinner with the girls, too. No wonder Clover had been ready to kill me for accepting the invitation. After what happened the night before and over the course of the morning, it had become clear that Clo was definitely keeping things from me.

I tuned my ears back into the conversation.

'But whyyyyy?' Ophelia's whine reminded me of the whine of a four-year-old meeting Santa at a local mall. One who wanted all the toys but left with none.

I scoffed at her theatrics. Something I was already learning here at Hawthorn was that rich girls were another breed. My old school may have sat dead centre of the 'divide' between the poor side of the town and wealthier side, but nobody acted the way these girls did.

Unfortunately for me, Ophelia heard me.

'What are you scoffing at, you swine?' she spat. *Literally*. Her spit landed right in front of Oliver, drawing my eyes' focus.

I laughed. *Swine?* Was she for real?

'I said, leave her alone, Ophelia!' Oliver raised his voice so loud that the entire class stopped their conversations and turned to face us. Slumping even further down in my chair, I tried to make myself as small and invisible as I could. 'Move now, Oralie. I'm not playing around.'

I was still slowly sinking in my chair as Oliver sat down into the one Oralie had sharply vacated.

'I'm sorry about her,' he said, leaning in to whisper in my ear, his breath causing a chill to run down my spine. 'About both of them, actually.'

I nodded. I just knew I would stutter if I replied to him. My brave behaviour towards him was a thing of the past.

The teacher entered the classroom and assessed the room, his eyes narrowing when they landed on a certain someone.

'Master Brandon,' he called out, his voice deep and booming. 'What are you doing in here?'

'Thought I'd learn some French, sir,' Oliver said, the smirk firm on his face. So sure of himself and filled with an almost egotistical swagger.

'Get out, or I will report you to Ms Hawthorn,' he said, his rotund face turning a shade of red that reminded me of a dark wine that was very popular at the supermarket I worked at.

The more red his face got, the more I genuinely worried he would have an attack of some sort, being both *very* short and *very* large. Nobody else seemed worried about him.

'We both know that isn't exactly a threat, sir,' Oliver said but stood and left the classroom anyway, winking in my direction before disappearing from view.

I rolled my eyes and chuckled lightly, even though he could no longer see me. He had some gall. I'd give him that.

The rest of the lesson passed in a blur. All I could think about was the fact that Oliver wasn't matching up to any of my preconceived ideas about him. Clover had told me to stay away. The rules I'd read on the Hive also made me believe I should steer well clear of him.

But Oliver wasn't acting the way I thought he would. Each new encounter led me to further question my judgement. He'd been a dick yesterday when we first met, then there was the whole hospital wing fiasco. Plus, I still didn't know why he'd been about to knock on my door. He was a flirt in assembly, and every time I recalled that whole stutter/dick line, I flushed the deepest red. Then he was sticking up for me against these girls he'd known for years. None of it added up.

When the last bell of the day rang, I still hadn't figured any of it out. I spotted Clover waiting for me outside in the hallway and I rushed out of the door as quick as I could, grabbing her arm when I passed her, and ran towards our room with her dragging along behind.

'Sky, what the hell's got into you? Why are we moving so fast?'

'I'll explain when we get back to our room. Just hurry!' I pulled her the entire way back, then, once inside, I slammed the door behind us and locked it. I didn't want anyone "accidentally" entering. Or anybody overhearing, either.

Clover sat down on her bed, and I sat on mine, facing her. Trying to catch my breath, I put my hand out to halt any words Clover might speak. Our sprint through the school had once again reminded me I was super unfit. Raking my hands through my hair, I sighed.

'Clo. I think I'm in trouble,' I said, urgency in my tone.

'What do you mean, *in trouble*?' she asked, confused.

'Well, you know how you basically implied that I should avoid the pool building and the boys who occupy it?'

'Yes...' Her eyebrows rose, climbing up her forehead. I was being cryptic, and fancy, to try and quell my nerves at talking to her about it.

'And you know how I agreed to sit with them for dinner tonight?'

'Yes...'

I could hear her getting impatient with me, so I decided to blurt it out, 'Well... I think I'm developing a major crush on Ollie.' I said it super fast, hoping that would make it easier. Like ripping off a Band-Aid or a waxing strip.

Clover gasped when I used his nickname.

'He's been so nice to me today, standing up against the O girls for me. Plus, he may have made a comment this morning about wanting to hear if I stutter with his dick deep inside me.' By the end of the sentence, I was whispering and my face must have been redder than a fire engine. I covered my face with my hands, trying to hide it from her.

Clover's expression turned to one of pity as she made the sign of the cross.

'Oh, honey, no.' Shaking her head, she said, 'You can't feel like that about him. Trust me when I say that he's not a good guy. I know he was there last night and was nice to you today, but I promise you, Sky, he has an agenda. It may not be obvious right now, but he definitely has one. Those boys do nothing without some kind of endgame. Even Griff can be a prick when he feels like it.'

'I know, I know. I don't *want* to feel this way!'

'Maybe we should just eat dinner here, get something delivered to the school gates? I'm just going to put this out into the universe so that when shit comes back to bite you, I can say I told you so, okay?'

I nodded.

Clo looked at me imploringly and said, 'Sky, you know deep down that he's playing you. Or that he has some kind of motive.'

'No. I don't know that for definite. We're going to go eat dinner with them, Clo. I'm not having people talk shit about me on my first full day. Plus, I'm pretty sure the rules say you can't turn down an invitation from them, right?'

'Right,' she said, reluctantly agreeing with me.

Six

THE CAFETERIA, if you could even call it that, resembled a fine dining restaurant rather than any school dining hall I'd ever been in. The sheer size of it was overwhelming. I half expected Oliver and the others to be sitting at some kind of large top table like royalty, but instead they were occupying the large circular table in the very centre of the room. Knights of the Round Table, much?

Clover and I made our way to the table and sat in the two empty seats; me beside Griff like he had requested, with Oliver sitting on my other side. Clover had to sit between Leo and Olivia, and trust me, her face made it clear how pissed at me she was for putting her in that position. With a wince and a shrug, I looked back at her, trying to send my apology telepathically.

Once we sat down, servers flooded over to take our orders, like rain beetles at the first sight of water droplets. I'd never felt so out of place. I glanced at the menu in front of me, but none of it computed. On my way in, I'd spotted a kid eating *snails* as if it were a regular dinner you'd find at any school. Yeah. Any school for the extremely wealthy.

The O girls were doing nothing to hide their feelings about me and Clo sitting with them. They were beyond livid. All four of them kept looking at me and then each other, then Clover, then the boys. It went on for a full five minutes and nobody spoke.

It was awkward as fuck.

'S-so how was everybody's day?' I asked, trying to break the tension seeping into the atmosphere and tainting the air. The moment the words left me, I hoped my chair would dissolve into the tiled floor.

'That stutter is honestly the cutest thing,' Griff said with an overdramatic sigh. 'Don't you agree, Ollie? Damn, Sky. I'm hard just hearing it.' I realised it was his signature grin planted firm on his face, his dimples pressed in and his teeth on show.

Well, *that* broke the tension.

'Oh, shut up, dickhead,' Clover said, trying to contain her laughter. 'Do you think before you speak or does it just come out unbidden?'

'My sweet lucky Clover, has anybody told you you look hot when you're acting all fierce? Don't you agree, Leo?' Griff asked, his eyebrows waggling in Leo's direction, teasing in a way only a true friend could.

'Hmph.' Leo was too busy looking at Odette while she stared back to give Griff a proper answer. I thought I saw her hand moving underneath the table in a suspicious rhythm and my face heated at the implication.

Surely not?

One thing was certain. Rich people acted weird.

'Don't mind him, he knows the truth,' said Griff, nodding. 'My day was perfect. I got my dick sucked in the caretaker's cupboard earlier and I'm hoping I'll get a repeat later.'

I gulped and averted my gaze. I was so out of my league here.

It sounded like a cliché, but I was a virgin. A rather non-experienced virgin at that. My whole life I'd never spent time around people who talked like this; so open and honest with no regard to who could hear them. No care in the world.

'Nobody needs to hear about you getting your dick sucked, Griff. Don't worry, though. I'm sure Oralie will repeat the favour for you for her dessert,' Clover said, her smile dripping poison, giving Oralie a look of pure condescension.

'As if!' Oralie sputtered. 'I wouldn't go near *that* even if you paid me.'

I rolled my eyes, a small giggle leaving my lips, and when I looked to my right, I found myself staring directly into Oliver's azure blue ones. They had a glint of menace, but he covered it up pretty fast and then they just looked bland.

'Nobody would pay for your mouth. More like you'd have to pay them,' Clover smarted back at her.

'I could kiss you, my lady luck!' Griff looked in his element, rubbing his hands together with glee. He reminded me of a bad cartoon villain, and I couldn't help but laugh. He raised his hand in my direction and I gave him a high-five in response. Who was I to turn down the calling of the high-five?

Griff didn't seem so bad. Out of the group at the table, he seemed the most chill one. The one you could have a laugh with. But then Clover's warning from yesterday came back to me, and I had to wonder just what Griff kept hidden.

Finally, the food arrived, and the mood around the table improved by a margin. Other than the odd spurts of banter between Griff and Clover, nobody else said much, though. Food silenced everything and everyone.

Leo and Odette were still touching one another intimately, and I reckoned Clover had considered stabbing him with her steak knife multiple times.

Griff grinned wide and acted like everything happening around the table amused him—it probably did. The O girls were whispering about something the rest of the table weren't privy to. Both Clover's and my names popped up multiple times, so chances were it was something about us.

Then there was Oliver, who had put his hand on my thigh during the main course and was yet to remove it. Both of us were silent, caught up in the moment. His fingers moved in a slow circle, drawing a swirling pattern on my bare skin from where my skirt had risen, his hand touching my bare leg.

Other than the leg touching, he'd made no effort to interact with me. He hadn't spoken to me once. Or to anybody at the table, come to think of it.

I couldn't tell you what I'd expected, but I *had* at least

expected him to converse with me a little. You know, acknowledge my presence with words and not just his hand that was wandering higher up my thigh with each second.

'W-what are you doing?' I whispered as low as I could, turning to face him, not wanting the rest of the table to hear me.

He leaned into me, pressing his mouth flush to my ear. His breath warm as it skated across my skin, causing shivers to erupt all over.

'Don't try and tell me you aren't enjoying it. I can feel the goosebumps. Feel the excitement. You like this just as much as I do.'

'Like what?'

'That we haven't said one word to each other, yet I'm touching you, anyway. Taking what I want.'

I gasped as his hand went higher, touching the outer edge of my underwear, teasing me. Clover raised her eyebrow at me, a silent question. I shook my head at her, hoping I didn't look as flustered as I felt. And boy, did I feel flustered. Oliver spoke the truth. I *was* enjoying this. It felt so naughty and forbidden that he hadn't said a word but pushed my boundaries, regardless.

'You're beautiful. You know that, right?' His tongue briefly grazed my ear before he leaned back in his seat.

Fuck. I was a goner.

The spell between us broke when Griff started shouting while flailing his arms around, 'Yo! Did anybody even hear what I said?'

'Yes. The entire room heard you, Griff,' Clover deadpanned. 'Even Ms Hawthorn in her office three corridors away must have heard you.'

'What shit you chatting now, wanker?' asked Leo as he turned to face the table, looking at everybody in turn. Come to think of it, I couldn't think of a time yet where Leo hadn't seemed bored. But then it hit me. He hadn't seemed bored last night when I'd bumped into him and Odette tangled up in one another's webs. He had been the complete opposite, in fact. His eyes were amused then, and his face had given him away for just a moment.

Like he had a secret only he knew about.

AFTER DINNER ENDED, the girls stormed off as a pack.

Leo wasn't far behind, as he disappeared the second we left the hall, not telling anybody where he was dashing off to. He left without saying a word to anyone.

Oliver whispered that he would see me tomorrow and then also vanished down the corridor, heading in the direction of the pool building. *The Sect* were a part of the school swim team and were the reason the school had so many accolades—probably helped fuel a little of their popularity, too. Leo had a swimmer's body, but if you looked at the other two, I would've sworn they played football or maybe even rugby. Some kind of contact sport, at least.

Griff was the only one who stuck around, and like a gentleman, he walked us back to our room and hugged us both good night, winking before he left. I was softening towards him. He was charming, and he seemed so laid back compared to the other two.

Once settled on my bed, I grabbed my phone to aimlessly scroll through *Hive*. Maybe look at some extra-curricular activities or clubs I could join. Make my time at school even more worthwhile.

'Sky. What the hell was happening during dinner?' Clover pounced the second she got comfortable on her bed, her question shooting from her like she'd been holding it in the whole walk back. 'Don't even think about saying nothing because I swear to you, I am not that dumb.'

'Nothing,' I said, brushing it off, even though my blush probably gave me away that I was bullshitting. 'Seriously.'

She narrowed her eyes, not believing me for a second, and the pressure emanating from her made me feel I needed to say more. I caved, the ice queen look gutting me in the heart. Plus, I didn't want my only friend pissed off at me. Not like I'd had other people fighting over me today trying to become my friend.

'Okay, fine! Oliver may or may not have been touching my leg.'

'I bet he was,' she seethed. 'Be careful, Sky. I don't know why the three of them are acting nice to you.'

I looked at her questioningly. She'd seemed friendly enough with Griff on the walk back and throughout dinner.

'Okay, the two of them,' she clarified, amending her previous statement. We both knew that Leo wasn't acting anything towards me except disinterested.

'Talking of being careful, *Clo*. What exactly did Leo say to you this morning in assembly?'

'Nothing.' She averted her gaze, opened her laptop, and started tapping away at something.

'I'm asking nicely.' I fluttered my eyelashes at her, hoping she'd take pity on me and spill her guts. I could sense that she wanted to talk about it but was scared of something too. Maybe her need to get it out in the open would win out.

'I promise that one day I'll tell you everything, Sky, but today is not that day.'

After I'd read a few posts on Hive and was getting comfortable, I sensed fidgeting on the other side of the room that drew my attention.

'Sky...' Clover looked unsure, words sitting on the tip of her tongue.

'Yeah?'

'Have you ever been in love?'

In the short time I'd known her, I hadn't seen Clover look this shy or self-conscious. She was a badass, and she knew it. But this was a completely new side to her. I scoffed, wanting to make her feel less self-conscious about her question.

'Nope,' I replied, shaking my head. 'I've never even had a boyfriend.'

'Oh... Right.'

'Have you?'

'Have I what?'

'Ever been in love?'

'I thought I was once. But now I realise it was just how it looked in the light of day.' She lay back down on her bed, facing the ceiling. 'Skylar. I think you and I are going to be friends for a long time. Maybe even for life. Something's just clicked, you know?'

'I feel the exact same way,' I replied, my smile taking over my face. It was nice to have a friend.

I wasn't lying, either. Something in my heart knew I'd found a soulmate in Clover. Ride or die. After so many years of being a loner, it felt good to have somebody in my corner. One who wouldn't judge me for the stupid decisions I was no doubt about to make.

Trust me, I knew I would eventually throw caution to the wind in order to find out just what Oliver wanted with me.

There was something drawing me in. Pulling me to him. Two magnets, locked together, the reaction they experienced once they'd found their mate.

Seven

THE NEXT MORNING, I was thrilled I didn't wake up late. That mainly had to do with the fact that Clover had thrown a croissant at my head. She'd woken up early and gone down to grab us some breakfast, but when she tried to wake me, I didn't listen to her shouts—hence the croissant. It seemed like breakfast was more casual than the fine affair dinner had been last night. There was no assembly, either, which was a total plus.

The wind whistled through the trees in the distance, and when I looked out our window, I could see across the campus to the trees that lined the edge of the hill. A chill ran down my spine.

My first lesson of the day was History, a class I knew Oliver was also in, and it filled my stomach with nerves, my anxiety creeping up a notch with every action I took to get ready for my day. A small part of me wanted him to sit with me and give me attention. *Stupid Skylar.*

'Remember,' Clo called from her side of the room, throwing her blazer on. 'Keep to yourself today, Sky. I know you didn't have a bad day yesterday, but trust me when I say that these bitches are probably just trying to lull you into a false sense of security.'

'By bitches you mean the O girls?' I asked her, certain I knew the answer but wanting to hear it leave her lips, mainly to see if it riled her up.

'Of course,' she said as her face flushed. I laughed and when she saw my face, she realised I had been joking. Clover's shoulders deflated as she relaxed a little. 'You got me for a moment there. I genuinely believed you didn't know who I meant.'

'Oh, come off it, Clo. I'm not that dense.' I stopped and quickly added, 'Right?'

'Well...' Clo's smile grew super wide after a few seconds, 'No, you're not.'

'Phew.'

OLIVER DID SIT NEXT to me in History class and I tried my hardest the entire time to pay attention to Miss Woodland and not to anything he tried to whisper to me. And believe me, he was trying to whisper a *lot* of things. *Dirty things.*

Okay, maybe they weren't that dirty. They were phrases like, *I wish I could kiss you all over, see if you taste as good as you smell.* Or there was, *One day soon I'm going to bend you over this desk and fuck you from behind.*

Okay. Maybe it was hard to ignore.

His words were filthy as fuck and all I could do was think about the salacious images he painted in my mind with his words. I had no idea what war the teacher was telling us about. The only war I knew was the one going on between my head and, well, not my heart, that was for sure.

By the time the class ended, I was the colour of a fire engine and I think I may have even foamed at the mouth a little... which really wasn't a good look. I think Oliver also believed I'd turned into a mindless zombie from the way his eyebrow twitched in my direction. I just couldn't wrap my head around it, though. I used to think I could see through bullshit—I'd always seen through my mum and Andy—but with Oliver, I just couldn't figure him out. Was he genuine? Was he interested in me? Or was I a target for some kind of game I didn't know I was playing? I sighed, making a mental note to myself to talk to Clover and find out more about him and the others.

'What're you thinking about?' he asked as we left the classroom and I moved towards my English class. The halls were abuzz with students, but when they saw Oliver coming, they cleared a path for us, like it was second nature to them.

'W-what?' I hadn't fully heard him, too lost in my head.

'What're you thinking about?' he repeated.

'Oh... Things.'

Great answer, Sky.

'By chance do those things have anything to do with what I said in class?'

'N-no,' I sputtered. 'You just caught me off guard, that's all.'

'Sure I did.' His tone was filled with amusement. 'I'm also sure the reason your face is bright red has nothing to do with me either.'

I took a glance to my left, to find him looking so smug, so sure of himself. I knew I had to knock his ego a little, but I wasn't experienced in this kind of psychological warfare. I found it hard enough to not get distracted by his eyes, or his chiselled jawline. Or the way his blazer strained across his broad shoulders. Even just looking at him, I felt myself getting hot. Then the perfect insult hit me.

'Oh, believe me. I was imagining your words...'

Oliver's face lit up, his eyes glinted with mischief, but then I delivered the blow.

Putting emphasis on the first word, I said, '*But* I replaced the thought of you with Griff.'

Take that, I thought, feeling good about myself for the first time in an interaction with him. Every other time we had spoken, I hadn't been thinking fully, totally flustered at the situation.

Oliver didn't seem to find my words funny, though. Instantly his eyes darkened in anger to an indigo instead of their usual light sky blue colour. He grabbed my upper arm tight, stopping me from walking further.

'What did you just say to me?' he rasped. His eyes were hard, with no trace of humour left in them—or on his face for that matter. I'd made him mad, and a small part of me was happy about it. Served him right.

'I was f-fantasising about Griff,' I said. The stutter didn't help me sound certain, but by the look on his face, Oliver only registered the words and not my awkward, stutter-filled delivery.

'Griff?' he questioned, his face growing darker somehow. The pressure from his hand got tighter with each word he spoke. 'You're going to regret saying that, New Girl,' he spat. A tiny fleck of it landed on my cheek, and I tried to stay calm. Letting go of my arm, he turned around and stormed off, leaving me alone in the now empty, silent corridor. I rubbed the top of my arm, trying to soothe the ache, knowing he'd probably left a bruise. *Dickhead.*

There wasn't enough time to stand and think about it as I needed to get to my lesson. My feet moved down the corridor, as I kept my head down low, and I silently slipped into my English classroom, hoping that somehow I had become invisible in the last hour. An empty seat in the back row beckoned me.

Not long after I'd sat down and got comfortable in my chair, Oralie and Ophelia entered the classroom together, staring at me once they spotted me in the back. Instantly they started whispering to each other. I rolled my eyes at their behaviour—even though I knew I shouldn't. I knew I was playing with fire, but I couldn't help myself. I had a gut feeling that the girls definitely took the rules more seriously than the guys did, and I shouldn't be pushing my luck—especially on the second day of term.

'Eurgh, Lia, why on earth is the New Girl looking at us?' Oralie asked, raising her voice to ensure I heard her. That the entire classroom heard her.

'I have no idea, but she better stop right now if she knows what's best for her,' Ophelia answered, looking way too happy for somebody delivering a threat.

'Bitch, don't you remember the rules? I *do not* deem it necessary for you to be looking at us right now,' Oralie snapped at me. 'And trust me, little girl, I will punish you.'

I sank further down into my chair. Inside, I told myself not to listen to her words. They sounded like a budget movie villain's lines that weren't overly thought out. And I knew there was nothing she could really do that would hurt me mentally.

But let's be honest—she *could* do a lot to hurt me *physically*. Teenagers can be cruel, and bullying was rife back in my old school. And from just a couple of days at Hawthorn, I could tell rich girls played even dirtier than those I grew up with.

I watched as Miss Morrison, our English teacher, swept into the room and started playing "Wuthering Heights" by Kate Bush through the whiteboard speakers, and I swear I died inside even more. The song was undoubtedly a tune, but it could only mean one thing; we were about to read *Wuthering Heights*, and I couldn't think of anything worse. The façade of the main building had already reminded me of it. I didn't need to be studying it too. Every teenage fiction book I'd read had some kind of sick fascination with the love story of Cathy and Heathcliff, but honestly, they were both toxic as fuck to one another and she died halfway through the book, so they weren't ever together anyway. Definitely not my idea of a love story.

Miss Morrison announced our new topic for the term, gothic literature, and lazily said, 'Solo reading for the next hour, please. Start the book and highlight any passages of note.'

I opened the book and began reading, hating every second of it. A rustling of pages and students shuffling in their seats filled the room. At least solo reading meant I didn't have to talk to anybody.

Oralie and Ophelia spent the first hour of the double period talking about me and trying to encourage others to do the same. The words, "scum," "slut," and "bitch" were whispered across the room, reaching me every couple of minutes. They were slowly building an audience, too. The girl at the desk next to me kept staring at me before leaning in and murmuring to me that I'd really fucked up by angering *The Set*.

At first, it didn't affect me. They were just trying to make themselves feel better about the fact that Oliver seemed to have taken an interest in me. But after the first hour, it sank in and as the dark cloud of their words hit other students, I could feel myself breathing slower. It was like that first night in my bedroom again. The world blurred at the edges and I didn't dare talk as I knew I would be a stuttering mess, making no sense. The room spun. My vision faltered. In my mind, the chair underneath me melted.

I can't black out here.

The girls would never let me live it down and I had heard nobody talking about my visit to the hospital wing the night before, so maybe Oliver and Leo had kept that tidbit quiet.

Or I just hadn't heard that particular nugget of gossip yet.

An hour of solo reading passed.

Miss Morrison had realised that maybe the class wasn't actually reading the book in their heads and were actually more focused on aiming nasty words and soggy spit wads at me. How original.

'Ophelia, dear,' Miss Morrison called out, surveying the classroom. 'Could you read aloud from the beginning of chapter three?'

'Of course, miss, it'd be my pleasure,' Ophelia said, her tone sickly sweet. Like butter wouldn't melt. Nausea rose in my stomach, and a slight huffing noise left me. What a little kiss arse.

Ophelia started to read out loud, and I followed along in my copy, but after a few pages, she stopped.

'Miss,' she said after a small pause. 'I feel like we should let somebody else read now. I don't want to bore people with my voice.' She tittered, or at least that was the only word I could think of to describe the noise she'd made. All girlish and fake. 'How about we let Skylar read now? She *is* new and I wouldn't want her to feel excluded. She's a Hawthorn girl now, after all.'

Well, fuck me. It was obvious to me that Ophelia knew exactly what she was doing, although I honestly wasn't sure whether the teacher knew that Ophelia was being a bitch to me or whether she genuinely believed she was trying to "help" me. What help would it really be for me to read out loud to a class of pupils I'd barely met?

'Oh, what a lovely, inclusive idea, dear. Skylar, please stand and read to us starting from page thirty-six,' Miss Morrison said, her gaze finding mine. Her smile was encouraging enough and her kind blue eyes looked open and honest.

I knew there was no way out of this. The fact I had to stand made it even worse. All eyes were on me. Even though I was at the back of the classroom, every pupil had turned to face me, their gazes taking me in from head to toe. I prayed I wouldn't stutter my way through it. I wasn't ready just yet for that kind of humiliation, thank you very much. I definitely didn't want to draw even more attention to myself than what had already been thrust upon me by eating dinner with *The Sect* last night.

I stood and raised my book, to read of course, but also to use as a shield so I didn't have to see the entire class looking at me. You would think they'd be looking at their own copies in order to follow along and make notes or some shit—but apparently watching the New Girl flounder was more exciting. Which, yeah, in their position, I would agree. Seeing me falter would be more interesting compared to *Wuthering Heights*.

'"If the little f-fiend had got in at the window, she p-probably would have s-strangled me!"' Aware of my slow pace, I tried to read faster, but the faster I read, the more mistakes I made.

Not like it mattered. The entire class erupted in laughter the second I stuttered over the first word and didn't stop from then onwards. I could hear them repeating my mistakes, emphasising every stutter and trip-up. Every error reverberating through the room, until I couldn't see the words in front of my face any more from the tears blurring my vision.

'Not the w-w-window,' Oralie mocked, nudging Ophelia in the side with her elbow.

I knew miss could hear them, could see them making rude gestures at me, but she never once told them to stop. She'd turned a blind eye to proceedings, sitting at her desk and drinking her coffee with no care. She wasn't going to put a stop to any of it. I was on my own.

Of course, Ophelia and Oralie were jeering the loudest. The whispers surrounded me.

"She should go hide in her room. Nobody wants her here."

"She should go slit her wrists. Not like anybody would miss her."

"She's so ugly, only a blind man would fuck her."

It took everything in me not to let the tears gathering in my eyes fall.

'You can take over reading now, Wesley,' Miss Morrison said, aiming her words at a boy sitting in the row ahead of me. 'Thank you, Skylar.'

I slumped down into my seat, thankful for the reprieve, and kept my head down as I listened to Wesley pick up where I left off.

Finally, the class neared its end, and all I wanted to do was get out of there as quickly as I could and disappear deep into the library where nobody would think to look for me. Thankfully, it was lunch next, followed by a free period, and I was so ready to become invisible.

I looked up as Miss Morrison wrapped up the lesson and I saw Oliver standing in the doorway, leaning against the doorframe in that way popular, hot guys seemed to do *really* well. I shrank even further into my seat. I had no idea how long he'd been standing there, but I reckoned he saw at least some of what Ophelia and Oralie had started. His facial expression gave nothing away, though, and for all I knew, he could be standing there waiting for the girls to go to lunch with him. We hadn't exactly left things on great terms earlier. My arm still smarted from the way he'd gripped it so tight.

The class filed out of the room and I stood slowly, wondering if he would walk away with Ophelia and Oralie when they passed him. I had to admit that I felt a little smug when he paid them no attention at all. I waited until every single student had left the room and Oliver still stood there. He was definitely waiting for me.

'H-how long were you standing there?' I asked.

I vowed one day I would talk to him with no stutter, but once again, it was not that day.

'Long enough,' he said. His clipped answer and tone told me all I needed to know. He'd witnessed what the class had done to me—what they'd been saying to me. He knew how they had all been laughing at me.

'R-right,' I mumbled. 'Well, I'll see you later.' In an attempt to rush around him, I darted right, but he caught my arm before I could get away. I grimaced. It was the exact same part of my arm he'd grabbed in the corridor earlier. Why was he so interested in me, especially after I pissed him off earlier in the day? The dark, twisted look on his face told me he knew how much his tight grip hurt me. Yet he didn't care either way.

He tightened his hold.

'Where d'you think you're going?' he asked or demanded.

'To the l-library.'

'It's lunch time,' he said. 'What are you doing about food? Gotta eat, right?'

'I was going to grab something on my way.'

'I'll join you. I have a free period after lunch, too,' he said, finally loosening his grip around my arm. Oliver's lips rose at the corners, a semi-smile of sorts. One filled with warning.

I nodded, resigned to my fate, and let him drag me along beside him.

It wasn't until a lot later that I realised I'd never told him I had a free period after lunch.

Eight

HEADING STRAIGHT FOR THE LIBRARY, I tried to ignore the imposing figure next to me, but he was hard not to take notice of. I kept trying to walk faster, but with every two strides I took, he only needed one, so there was no way I was going to out-walk him—or outrun him, if I ever needed to.

I also couldn't help but notice how handsome he was. He really had that whole *I'm a good-looking guy and I know it* vibe going on. Oliver was hot, and I'd be lying if I said I couldn't see why all the girls here were hoping to one day "land him." I'd liter-ally heard some girl use that phrase and it still made me die thinking about it.

We headed across the school grounds because even though you'd expect the English classrooms to be near the library, they were actually the furthest away. Ignoring Oliver was difficult when he kept entering my personal bubble.

A quick stop in the hall for lunch and the two of us stayed silent. The tension in the air was palpable, and all I wanted to do was get away. Everybody stared at us, the whispers growing louder each second. In no time at all—that felt like a heck of a lot of time—we got to the front of the line and grabbed some sand-wiches and put them in a to-go bag.

Leaving the hall with our lunch, Oliver asked me, 'You going to tell me what happened back there?'

'Back where?' I asked, pretending I didn't understand the question. Oblivious to the end.

'Pretend you don't know what I'm talking about all you want, New Girl,' Oliver said, shrugging. 'Not like I'm going to give up.'

'I-it was nothing.' I hoped he'd leave my blatant lie alone. It was only my second day, and I didn't want to have the wrath of *The Set* fall on me so soon. It had already started in English and I prayed I wouldn't have to endure that in every class I shared with them. It would make my time here at Hawthorn a lot harder than it needed to be.

'That wasn't nothing, Sky. You were shaking and on the verge of tears when I got there.'

'Seriously, *Oliver*, it was nothing.' I stressed his name, hoping he would take me at my word as I didn't want to rehash any of what had happened to him, of all people. I picked up my pace, but he matched me step for step.

'Thought I told you to call me Ollie?' he asked, his irritation at my refusal clear.

'You did. But I decided not to,' I told him, not completely certain where this badass-ness was coming from. Well, as badass as I could be with my stutter.

'And why is that, New Girl?' he asked, his tone dark.

'Because we're not friends,' I told him. I wasn't sure how he would react, but ever since he'd told me to call him by his nickname, I just couldn't bring myself to. Not even in my head. I'd slipped when talking to Clo one time, but since then, I'd been careful. It was a slippery slope.

Oliver didn't answer.

After what felt like a lifetime but was in actuality probably only a few minutes, we finally made it to the library.

For me, the library gave away the school's age. Large, old, and daunting, it looked to be one of the oldest buildings, and fuck was it impressive. Clover had briefly taken me here during her tour, but we hadn't focused on it for too long. At that point, it wasn't like she'd known how much I loved books.

But I did. I loved reading, and I loved seeing all these books together, just waiting for somebody to pick them up and find the wonder that lived inside their pages. I used to spend all my time at the local library in town—when I wasn't working at the supermarket or at school. It had been my respite when things were hard at home. When things became too much for me to handle. Books were always there, and within the pages of books, I'd found many friends and worlds I would've done anything to visit—I still would if given the chance.

Being older now, I was more likely to read romance books that you wouldn't find in your local library—but I still visited all the same. It was one place I could truly find peace.

Sadly, being in this library with Oliver meant I probably wouldn't get much peace. I knew he hadn't finished asking his questions. He was biding his time. Waiting it out. Then he would pounce, like a beast from the shadows.

I found a table at the very back of the library to sit at, dumping my lunch and my bag filled with my books and laptop down with a thud.

Oliver placed his food and bag down gently and took a seat, meaning I had no choice but to sit next to him.

Well, that was what I told myself, anyway, and I was sticking to it.

We sat next to one another in silence for five minutes—a fucking long time to sit with anybody in uncomfortable silence, believe me. Part of me felt excited, but the majority of me just felt irritated that he was interrupting my peace and not even saying anything.

The silence was obviously affecting Oliver too, as he turned to face me and asked once again, 'What happened in class, Sky?'

'I told you, nothing important.'

'I saw the end. The girls were picking on you. I thought Leo told you to come to me if you had any trouble with them?'

I stayed quiet. Yeah, Leo had said that to me, but I hadn't believed him. I thought he'd been lying or, I don't know, trying to make me feel better or something. I felt stupid saying that out loud, though. I felt stupid saying mostly everything out loud, especially when I stuttered like a little bitch. Plus, it wasn't like I'd had much chance to tell Oliver prior to him asking.

Oliver's face darkened, his eyebrows furrowing, and his mouth as straight as I'd ever seen it. He resembled the Oliver I'd seen leaving the pool house on the day I arrived. When Clover had warned me about them. Shit, had that only been two days ago? I must try to remember that the girl I'd formed a bond with here— make that the only person I'd connected with—made it very clear that I should stay away from *The Sect*. Obviously that included present company. Rule number five could kiss my ass. If he invited me to dinner again, I would refuse.

'Sky, I won't repeat myself. Come to me or Leo or, fuck, even Griff if you need to, okay? Just let us know what's going on and we can sort it.'

'O-okay.'

'Please tell me what happened,' he said. The sincerity in his tone and the pleading look in his eyes made me finally cave. Also, the fact that he had actually said please to me made my heart warm a little.

'I-it was nothing. Oralie and Ophelia thought it would be funny to have me read aloud,' I admitted with a sigh. 'And my stutter definitely makes reading in class hard.'

'They're just mean, rich girls, Sky. I'll talk to them.'

'Please don't,' I whispered. The last thing I needed Oliver to do was talk to them and make them want to hurt me even more than they already did. I wanted to fly under the radar, not become a beacon.

'Fine. But I swear to God, Skylar, if you do not tell me about them in the future, I will spank you so hard, you won't forget again.'

I choked on the bite of sandwich I'd thought it was safe to take.

Oliver had a habit of slipping these dark, flirtatious sentences into conversation and expected me to take them, no questions asked. I blushed at him, which only seemed to make him more smug.

'Y-you wouldn't.' My words sounded a lot more confident than I felt.

'Oh, you'd be surprised at just what I would do to you, New Girl.' His tone was dark and delicious, causing a shiver to run down my spine. 'Ever since I first saw you, I've wanted to get under that skin of yours and see the true you. Figure out exactly what makes you tick.'

His blue eyes stared into mine and it felt to me as if he wanted to see into my soul. *Which was absurd, right?* We'd only known each other for a few days and it wasn't like we'd had any in-depth convos in that time or anything. When I first saw him, the connection between us had sparked to life, but I definitely only felt attraction—not obsession. Oliver seemed the type to obsess over small things. Guess I was one of those *things*.

'I d-don't know why. I'm not important,' I said. My voice quavered, and my true opinion of myself bled through my words. I could feel them in the atmosphere, threatening to choke me with embarrassment. Man, I was pathetic and chances were at this rate anyway, that Oliver would notice pretty soon just how much of a loser I truly was.

'Don't say that,' he said, his tone harsh and abrupt. It surprised me. Fucking *shocked* me, actually. I thought that maybe he'd just agree with me or something. His eyes stared into mine, imploring. 'You are important.'

We both fell silent after that.

We finished our lunch and both started on our homework. It was quite nice to work side by side in silence. Every now and again, I found my gaze wandering in his direction. He really filled the school uniform out nicely. His broad chest and wide shoulders looked so good in his white shirt, and even though he was wearing a bottle green blazer, he was really making it work for him. You know that saying, *"wear clothes and don't let the clothes wear you"*? That sprang to mind whenever I looked at Oliver. And I appreciated it—appreciated him.

But the silence couldn't last forever.

Oliver turned to face me, and the look on his face told me he really didn't want to say the words about to leave his mouth, but he was going to say them anyway.

He sighed and whispered, 'Sky, why don't you think you're important?'

I closed my eyes and did that whole *I wish the ground would swallow me whole* thing, but it didn't work. When I opened them, his face was even closer than it had been, and his eyes were staring into mine. Attempting, but failing, to unravel all of my secrets.

'I never have,' I admitted, realising I needed to give him a little more. 'I guess I never had many friends or family there to t-tell me otherwise. Believe it or not, Oliver, I've always been a bit of a loner.'

I hated focusing on my lack of friends and the fact that my family didn't give a shit about me. My mum may be the worst, but she kept a roof over my head to an extent and she never abandoned me. Even if sometimes I thought my life would have been better if she had.

My dad, on the other hand, I'd never met. He split from my mum when I was a few months old and nobody ever really talked about him much. I knew he existed once upon a time and that he and my mum came from totally different upbringings and backgrounds, but that was all I knew.

Having no friends was another thing entirely. After we hit secondary school, I had nothing in common with the girls I'd grown up around. Especially Remi. The girls were interested in boys and makeup and having the newest clothes and all that kind of material rubbish. I just wanted to read and escape into the book world. I had no time for boys, and makeup and clothes were luxuries I couldn't afford. Before Andy came along, I was lucky if my mum even remembered to fill the fridge with edible items.

Oliver speaking brought me out of my dark thoughts.

'Believe it or not, New Girl, I *can* believe that.' He was laughing—at me or with me, I wasn't completely certain. 'But now you don't have to be. You've made friends with Clover, right?'

I nodded. 'Yeah, she's great.'

'And you're now a part of the inner circle too, what with us inviting you to hang out and all.'

I looked away, the bookshelves suddenly seeming more enticing to me than his mesmerising blue eyes. I could hear an underlying threat hidden underneath his kind words. Why did I get the impression that being a part of the inner circle was the last thing I should want?

'I g-guess.'

'Did you mean what you said earlier?' he asked, changing direction. Confusing me.

He changed the topic so fast, I almost got whiplash turning abruptly to face him once more.

'About w-what exactly?'

'Did you mean what you said about Griff? Imagining him doing the things I whispered to you.' He leaned closer, his words whispered against my ear, and I shivered at the slight touch of his lips.

'No.' I shook my head, both in response to him, but also as an attempt to clear the fog my mind seemed to have clinging to it. 'I just said those things to make you m-mad.'

'Would you believe me if I said it worked?'

'You deserved it, Oliver.'

'*Please*, call me Ollie,' he said, almost pleading with me, and I couldn't help myself from smiling with satisfaction. There wasn't much I could do to piss him off, yet calling him by his full name seemed to work as a treat. I highly doubted that many people ignored him when he gave a direct order, let alone when he asked politely.

'I'll think about it. But I still don't think we're friends.'

I needed to create some distance between the two of us. I could still feel his whisper in my ear. His lips had grazed my cheek and the featherlight touch of it lingered.

The effect he had on me irritated me. Why was I letting him get to me so much?

Aggravated, I stood abruptly, the chair nearly falling to the floor from the shove I gave it. I don't know what it was about Ollie that riled me up so much, but I did know one thing. I couldn't sit there across from him pretending to study any longer.

I had to get away.

Shoulders tense, I spun away from his smirk and stomped off. My mind was buzzing with thoughts just as my body buzzed with restrained emotions, trapping me in my own little world. I wandered deeper into the library, absently headed toward the part I knew no one visited. It would be nice and quiet. Just what I needed.

I quickly found my way to the non-fiction section of the library. No other students were around, and I sighed in relief when I made it to a dead-end. My shoulders rose and lowered again with the motion. It was a deep sigh. I needed to find a history book to complete an assignment, and I didn't want anyone stepping inside my personal bubble.

One time, back when I worked at the supermarket, I'd had an anxiety attack because somebody had come too close to me when I was stocking a shelf. They'd reached across me, innocently enough, yet my heart had stopped and my vision had wavered. How humiliating.

It wasn't until I stopped beside some shelves loaded with thick hardbacks that I sensed someone at my back. I realised immediately it wasn't just anyone who'd followed me back here.

I was just about to turn around when a hard body pressed up against my back. An arm came up on either side of me, caging me in, stopping me from going anywhere.

'Running away, New Girl?'

His words whispered against my neck.

'Leave me alone,' I growled, whipping around to face him, but he moved his hand in order to hold my neck firmly in place.

The only thing I could hear in the silence was our breathing. I swore the people around could hear my breathing throughout the entire library.

Oliver started placing small kisses up and down my neck. I moaned in a mix of frustration and arousal. His hardness pressed into my back and all I could think about was how he must look naked.

He grabbed me by the waist, hard, and flipped me around so we were facing one another.

'God, you don't realise just how fucking sexy you are, Skylar.'

He was *seriously* in my bubble now, those hard muscles tempting me from beneath his shirt. With him so close, I had to tilt my head back to look up at his irritatingly smug face. Eurgh, why did all the hot guys have to be such gorgeous dickheads?

I hated the way my body responded to Ollie, making me fight what seemed to be a natural pull toward him. It would have been so much easier to give in, but I was not about to give him that kind of power over me.

'Tell me to leave then,' he whispered, leaning in even closer, my body lighting on fire at his closeness.

Breathless, I couldn't find the words to tell him to go.

Ollie's grin grew, taking me in with his gaze in a way that made my knees feel weak.

'That's what I thought.' His smile turned sinister. 'You secretly like me being close to you, don't you, New Girl?' His voice dropped in volume as he leaned in closer and took a subtle sniff of my perfume.

I didn't move, staring at him warily, feeling lost in this new situation.

But he was right. There was a part of me that didn't want to run from him anymore.

Then his lips touched mine, devouring them. The action was almost violent. The way he forced my mouth open—the way he used his tongue against mine. All of it. *Pure violence.*

The kiss was anything but sweet and I could feel his hard length pressing up against me, which only made me want it elsewhere. My hormones were racing through the roof and I tried to focus on what was happening, to stay in the moment.

I stopped fighting him, stunned.

Ollie was *kissing* me? Ugh, why did I like it so much? Why did he have to be such a surprisingly good kisser?

I had no strength to push him away. Feeling helpless, I warily allowed him to kiss me, secretly relishing in the way he devoured me like he'd been starving himself for weeks and I was a meal delivered to him by the gods.

One of Oliver's hands was in my hair, gripping it tightly; the other hand squeezed my nipple through my bra. The pain mixed with the pleasure and I moaned even louder. I was so turned on, I couldn't think straight. The way he was making me feel was unlike any way I'd ever felt before. I was riding high, enjoying his attention.

'Fuck,' he groaned.

He stopped the kiss abruptly.

He moved away from me, creating a gap between our bodies. His expression dark, his emotions shutting off in front of me.

'You want to be right here, pressed between me and the book-shelf,' he continued, just as my shoulder blades hit the shelf behind me from the way I was still leaning back from the gap he'd created between us. Yet, my feet wouldn't move. My body wouldn't escape. My attention was riveted on Ollie as his face came too close to mine... again.

'As for me,' he continued talking, 'I want a little more than just this.' He growled, low in his throat, causing my heart to beat twice as fast. 'I'd like to have you a little more pliant. Less resistant. I want to feel you melt against me.'

Once more, his arm darted out and slipped behind my back and pulled me to him, throwing me off-balance. As I fought to gain control of myself, he pressed his lips to mine in a softer but still demanding kiss.

I felt hot by the time his lips broke from mine, pulling back just enough to let us both breathe. Before I could truly recover, he pressed me back against the bookshelf with one arm, the other roaming down my side as his gaze locked with mine.

'Very good, New Girl,' he breathed. 'But now I want more. I want this'—he squeezed my arse hard, nearly bruising it before moving his hand back up, skirting across my hip on its way toward my left breast—'and I want these. I want you to moan as I leave bite marks all over your body. As I draw your nipples into tight, needy little buds.'

His face lowered from mine, giving me a sense of relief that lasted for only a second as I felt his breath on my neck instead. A moment later, he bit my neck, sending another rush of heat through me.

Oh, I hated it. But damn, did it feel so good.

As he nipped at my neck harshly enough to likely leave marks, his hand moved to my nipple, pinching and pulling at it. My resolve to not make a sound wavered as he worked me over, and my hands gripped the bookshelf at the back of my thighs hard as I fought to control myself.

'I've never had sex in a public place like this before,' Ollie muttered against my jaw just below my ear, his hand once more travelling further south. 'What do you think? Could you handle my cock if I stripped you down right now?'

A small squeak left me when his hand went under my skirt, and his fingers curled against my clit, my body shuddering as the need for release skyrocketed. I felt his grin against my throat as he slipped my panties to the side, touching me directly in a way I liked far too much. A way nobody else had before.

As his fingers worked expertly on me inside and out, I wiggled and even let out a few whimpers, but I was too hungry for more to pay it much mind. At least, until he pulled away from me suddenly, leaving the air feeling too cold and empty in his absence.

My fingers involuntarily touched my lips in a daze. I looked around and luckily found myself alone still.

I felt like I was living in my very own twisted tale; left in a library, the feared monster gone, my heart slightly thawing.

As he left, I could only watch him with a swirl of emotions I was pissed at him for leaving me with.

What a dick.

Nine

PHILOSOPHY AND ETHICS was the class I was looking forward to the most. It hadn't been offered back at Hollowdale High. It was yet another advantage the scholarship to Hawthorn could give me. I had to remember that. I couldn't forget that my end goal was to graduate from here with the best grades I could get in order to apply to the best universities. There was no way I was going to waste the opportunity. No matter what happened with deliciously dark boys who pinned me up against library book stacks and then said nothing before they left.

My mind wandered to the way Ollie looked before he stormed away from me. *Tormented.* Out of control.

Griff strode into the classroom, looking like he had no care in the world, which when I thought about it, he probably didn't. Ever since meeting him, I'd never once seen him take anything seriously. He constantly cracked jokes and made everybody around him smile. Or groan—in a heartfelt way.

He fell into the chair on my right, looking at me questioningly. 'Well, well, well, New Girl. What have we here?' His wide smile covered his face. 'You look a little... flushed.'

I wanted to smack him and hide from him simultaneously. I decided not to respond, mostly because I had no idea what to say. I was still processing what had happened with me and Ollie in the library.

Shit.

I was thinking of him as Ollie.

It was official. *I was fucked.*

Griff couldn't see the turmoil going on in my mind, though, as he continued talking and said, 'So, Sky. Would you say the History section or the Science Fiction section is better for hookups? I'm asking for a friend.'

I rolled my eyes at him, trying my hardest not to smile but feeling my lips twitch, anyway. He sure was persistent, though, got to give him that.

'New Girl, I'm messing with you. I give zero shits about you hooking up amongst the library shelves. Actually, I'm sort of cheesed off that I hadn't thought to try it before.'

'C-cheesed off?' I giggled. Then quickly put my hand over my mouth, but the damage was already done.

'Was that a giggle I just heard, New Girl? Damn. I did *not* have you down as a giggler,' he teased, unleashing a bright smile in my direction, and I swear to you, I was almost blinded by his teeth. 'Now you've made me wonder how your giggle would sound with me doing all sorts of naughty shit to you.'

'What is it with you guys and w-wondering how I'll sound when you're inside me?' I asked, definitely raising my voice too loud, but I couldn't help it. First Ollie with my stutter and now Griff with my giggle. These boys were going to be the death of me.

'I'm just messing with you, Sky. We're friends and I just know we're going to be *best* friends. Nothing more,' he said, his eyes matching the sincerity of his words. He had called me by my name, for starters. 'Ollie, I can't vouch for. He definitely wants to know how you'd sound around his dick,' Griff added as an afterthought.

Then I made a noise that I couldn't even find the word for. It was like a mix between a guffaw and a chortle. I covered my mouth again. I needed to try harder to keep a hold of myself.

'I'm sure he doesn't,' I sputtered, whilst trying to stop myself from laughing more. I just couldn't understand it. Even though Ollie *had* just kissed me in the library—a little more than kissed me—I couldn't compute in my mind that he actually *wanted* me.

I was a game to him. Nothing more.

'I'm serious,' Griff said. 'That boy wants you bad. Even threatened me after what you said to him this morning about fantasising about me. Super handy for the ego, love. I knew you wanted a piece of the Griff-man.'

'Please never refer to yourself as the "Griff-man" ever again,' I said. I couldn't stop my laughter now that it was coming full force. A tear escaped from my eye, trailing down my face until I could taste the salt of it on my lips.

'New Girl,' he said, his tone surprised. 'Your stutters disappeared.'

'Oh.' I shook my head in confusion. I hadn't even realised it. The only other person I'd been able to talk to here without a stutter was Clover. She was the *only* person I felt comfortable around, full stop. But there was something about Griff that eased my anxiety. I think it had something to do with the fact that he didn't seem to take anything too seriously. He was full of jokes and had made me smile more than anybody else here. 'I guess your bullshit has made me realise there's no reason to be nervous around you.'

'Should I take that as an insult, New Girl? 'Cause I gotta say, that doesn't sound too flattering.'

'No. You should actually be super happy about it. Means I like you.'

'Well, then!' He slapped his hand to his knee, and I giggled again at his enthusiasm. He smiled, teeth on show, and said, 'You should've just said that.'

I smiled back as the teacher, Mr Sommers, entered the classroom. He was a towering beanpole of a man. Sort of reminded me of the tall one from *Fantastic Mr Fox* by Roald Dahl—one of my favourite stories growing up. Roald Dahl's stories had always fascinated me. For a child with no father and a shit mother, his stories had shown me that there were many children out there suffering at the hands of stupid adults.

In all honesty, I barely paid any attention to the lesson, even though I'd been so excited about it. My mind was still stuck in the library. My time with Ollie replaying in my head on a constant loop. A sick perversion that wouldn't leave me, and every single time, the scene progressed further. Or I did something different, evolving the fantasy into something *more*.

Frustration and stupidity at my actions hit me in a gust of thoughts. I knew Ollie wasn't actually interested in me and that this was surely some big game to them all. The fact that Griff had known what happened when we'd got to class meant that *somebody* had already told him. My money was on Ollie, as nobody else had been there.

And if Ollie had passed it on that fast, then it surely meant nothing to him at all.

I needed to forget it happened. *Easier said than done.*

After classes had ended for the day, I made it back to Clo's and my dorm room in record time.

I desperately needed to talk to Clover, to get her opinion on everything that had happened. It felt like so much had changed since I saw her that morning. Chances were she'd just roll her eyes and tell me I was making a huge mistake by getting involved with any of them in any capacity. Regardless, I wanted to hear it from her lips, anyway. I needed talking down from the ledge I seemed to have found myself teetering on.

Entering our room, I could see Clover sitting on her bed, engrossed in something on her laptop screen. She looked up at me and instantly said, 'Spill.'

'Spill what?' I asked, shaking my head in wonder at how she could tell I had gossip after only looking at me for a second. Was my face that much of a dead giveaway?

'Spill whatever it is you wanna tell me. You look fit to burst. Plus, you made it across campus super fast. I wasn't expecting you back for at least another ten minutes.'

'I can walk fast when I want to.' I shrugged, trying to calm down the thoughts racing through my head. Even I could hear the defensiveness in my tone, though. 'We're not all lucky to have a free period at the end of the day.'

'Just tell me, Sky, and we can sort whatever it is.'

'So…' I took a deep breath. 'I may have kissed Ollie earlier.'

I threw myself onto my bed in a super dramatic fashion, the mattress screaming in protest. I covered my ears, knowing that a squeal was about to come out of Clover's mouth.

In three… two… one…

'You WHAT?' Clover asked, her voice shrill and so loud, I wondered if anybody lingering in the corridor could hear her.

'Well, actually. He kissed me. In the library.'

'With his tongue?' Clover said and started laughing, and I wasn't positive, but I reckoned she was trying to make some kind of *Cluedo* reference. You know, the board game with Miss Scarlett and the rope. A board game of tact, if you knew how.

'Yeah, with his tongue,' I replied, a smile playing on my lips. Even just talking about it caused a visual to materialise in my mind. I could still feel Ollie's lips on mine and his chest pressed up against me. His fingers sliding against me. Touching my bare thigh. Chills covered my arms and I rubbed them to ease the ache.

'Wait a minute!' Clover gasped. 'You're fucking calling him Ollie now, too? Oh hell no, Sky, what on earth are you thinking?'

'Pretty sure I wasn't really thinking.' I pondered for a moment and added, 'Actually, I *was* thinking, but they weren't exactly PG thoughts.'

'You definitely weren't thinking, Skylar. This is going to blow up in your face. You know that, right?' she asked, her face exasperated.

'It might not,' I said, petulant as a child.

'Oh, baby girl, it definitely will,' Clover said and looked at me with pity.

'What makes you so sure?' I asked her, mostly because I wanted to believe that things could work out for me. The way Ollie kissed me was so different from what I'd had before. He kissed me with passion, with no restraint, and by God, the boy could do things with his tongue—and hands.

'I just know, Sky. I know these boys. I've known them forever and not once has Ollie ever taken an interest in any girl. Not being funny, but you're on scholarship here. Did you not read the rules?'

'Course I did. We read them together and scoffed over them, remember?' I asked rhetorically.

'Right. So you'll have remembered rule four. The one that says about dating above your class. And you can bet that you and Ollie dating is something they wouldn't be okay with.'

It surprised me that Clover knew the rules by heart, numbers and all.

'But surely he doesn't have to ask for permission? If he upholds the rules, then surely he can break them? What's the use of being in a position of power if you can't do shit-all to do what you want?'

'Sort of not the point, Sky. The point is, I find all of this highly suspish,' Clover said, her eyebrows knitted together.

'So, w-what, you don't think Ollie could actually fancy me?' I asked, my lip quivering slightly, a little upset by her statement. I didn't want to be that girl, but her words had hit me in my already rather low self-esteem.

'No, sweetie, I don't mean that,' Clover said, throwing a compassionate look my way. My mattress depressed as she sat down beside me and pulled me into a one-armed hug. 'I just mean that it seems funky to me, that's all. On tour day, the boys definitely saw you as a new toy to play with, and now we're meant to just believe that Griff is your friend and that Ollie wants you? I'm sorry, but I don't—I can't.'

'No, I know. I get it. I do. You know them better than I do, after all.' I hugged her back, so glad that I had her on my side. 'I just need to think about all of this logically. Not get caught up in what happened in the past to others. Who knows, it may have meant nothing to him and I'm getting all worked up for no reason.'

'I mean this for your sake. I hope he isn't toying with you. But yeah, girl, keep your guard up just in case it is all bullshit.'

'You're right.'

We dropped the conversation, and Clover moved on to telling me about her day that was totally uneventful compared to mine.

I tuned her out, making encouraging conversation noises every now and again when she needed it, and instead thought of the events of the day. *Fuck me.* I'd known that I fancied Ollie. Who wouldn't, after all? But I also hadn't expected him to do that, and as much as I talked a good-ish game with Clover, I was in way over my head. I didn't want to get my hopes up, but I knew I would, anyway. No matter how much I didn't want to. No matter how much I shouldn't.

'Wait, Sky,' Clo said, breaking her stream of words about what something said during class. 'I heard something about what happened in English.'

'Oh...' I sighed and asked, 'What exactly did you hear?'

'That those absolute bitches picked on you, forced the teacher to pick you to read out loud, and took the piss out of your stutter.'

'Yep. Pretty much sums it all up,' I mumbled as moisture filled my eyes. I'd been trying so hard all day to forget about what had happened. About how it had made me feel. Small. Helpless. An outcast. I knew that if I put too much energy into thinking about it, I would bawl my eyes out all night and not stop. Something I really didn't want to do. I hated crying and was always more likely to cry when angry than when I felt sad. Yeah, messed up, I know, but I'd been that way ever since I was a kid.

'I know this is going to sound so fucking stupid, Sky, but you really need to ignore the O girls. Or at least try and rise above it all. I've been there, and it's shit.'

'Thanks, I think?'

Although Clo's words weren't the best or the most uplifting, they were the truth—her truth. I appreciated that she was trying to help me. I still didn't know the full story of Clover's past, and I could sense that it wasn't the time to ask her about it, but I was aware that shit had gone down in her past between her and *them*. And that one day she would tell me all.

All I could do was try and survive my time at Hawthorn. I mean, it had only been in one class and it hadn't been too bad. I just needed to grow a thicker skin. *Or grow a new, stronger backbone.*

I planned to ignore *The Set* while I tried my best to put the kiss with Ollie behind me. I had to try.

For my sanity.

Ten

THE REST of the school week passed without much to report.

Well, actually, I'm totally bullshitting.

It wasn't completely without drama.

The Set announced on the third day of school—the day after Ollie kissed me in the library—both in the hallway and on the Hive, that I was persona non grata to them and that nobody should enjoy my company or make me feel welcome. What that meant exactly, fuck knows. All I knew was that the rest of the student body helped them in their tirade against me.

Clover declared it all to be bullshit the second Odette announced it and made it obvious that she would stick by me, regardless.

"They're just twats, Sky. Definitely not going to let them decide who I can and can't be friends with. I've got your back."

There was one aspect of it all the O girls couldn't have predicted, though, and that was the fact that both Ollie and Griff ignored *them* now. They sat with me in every class that we shared, and the four of us had taken to sitting with each other at breakfast, lunch, and dinner. I told them they didn't need to, especially as Leo had chosen not to leave the girls and still sat with them. I didn't want either of them to feel as if they were choosing me over one of their longest friends—and over school tradition. From what little they'd told me, I gathered the three of them had been friends since birth. Well, something like that, anyway.

When I mentioned to them they didn't need to choose me, I got two similar, but also completely different, answers.

Griff declared, *'There's nothing those little bitches can do to make me side with them. Gosh, New Girl, what do you take me for? A total dickhead? I'm on your side, Sky.'*

I'd smiled and hugged him when he said that to me. He was slowly growing to be one of my favourite people, not that there were many people fighting for that spot.

When I asked Ollie, he said, *'I'm in the best place for me right now. I'm by your side, Sky.'*

I noticed the "right now" in Ollie's response, but honestly, I couldn't really expect more than that from him. Not like we meant anything to one another. Yeah, there was everything that took place in the library that one time, but nothing had happened, or been said, since. Not one thing said between us about it since. Not the kiss and not the fact he'd left me in the library, alone. Even the flirting and whispered dick lines had died down to nothing.

It made me question every interaction we'd had together. Had I made it all up in my mind? Did he not want to talk about it with me? Or was it meant to add an aura of mystery? *Fuck if I knew.*

I tuned into the conversation happening around me.

'So then I said, you telling me you don't want my d in your v?' Griff laughed. 'Apparently, that was not the right thing to say *at all*. She went and got her brother and told him what I'd said. He was a big motherfucker too.' He was in the middle of telling some story about a girl he tried to pull at a school party a few years back. His stories always made us all laugh. Sometimes with him, and sometimes *at* him.

'Serves you right!' Clover laughed and I could tell she was enjoying the story, even if her expression showed disbelief. Griff had a way of telling a story that gripped you entirely, holding you by the balls until the very last sentence. Even when he wasn't coming across in the best light, you still wanted to give him a hug and keep him safe. Sometimes, the boy was too much of a cheeky dickhead for his own good.

'It doesn't serve me right at all. I didn't even say anything offensive to her!'

'Pretty sure she got offended when you offered to show her your dick, mate,' Ollie said, joining the conversation. A smirk covered his face, amused at Griff's antics.

The four of us were sitting together in the restaurant-like dining hall, waiting for our food to arrive, and I could sense the eyes of *The Set* on us. Leo, however, paid no attention to his surroundings. He looked so bored, and as if he believed he was completely above the hierarchy bullshit the girls were trying to drag the entire school down into. Whether he agreed with them or not, he still chose to sit with them over us. I didn't know him well enough to be upset about it, but none of it made sense to me. Leo was the one who told me to come to him if the girls picked on me. So, why he would now choose them and ignore me, confused me.

Ultimately, though, Leo didn't owe me anything.

'Nah, that wasn't it at all,' said Griff as he shook his head at Ollie's words. 'I technically never offered to show her my dick. Just offered to put it inside her.'

'Bit of a technicality, mate,' Ollie joked at the same time as Clover.

''Cause that's so much better,' she said, wiping tears from her eyes, the story too much for her. It didn't take me long to realise that a lot of Griff's stories revolved around some kind of sexual situation; or something he'd said or done to some girl or another.

'W-well, I'm sure she felt blessed for you to even offer,' I said, joining in with their banter.

'See, Skylar gets it,' Griff said, putting his arm around me, pulling me close. He did this often. Made me feel cared for and happy. 'She's my new favourite. The two of you can piss right off.'

We all reacted to his words at the same time. Clover hit him from his other side. Ollie rolled his eyes, while also looking slightly bemused. I giggled, quickly putting my hand across my mouth in an attempt to stifle the noise.

'Definitely my favourite. Are you sure I can't hear that giggle in a more intimate setting?' Griff let me go and made a love heart with his hands, batting his long, fair eyelashes at me. Pretty sure he waggled his eyebrows, too.

'Oh, stop.' I hit him on the head with a laugh. The whole thing felt good, though. Like I had become a part of something. A part of a real friendship group, with people who laughed together and enjoyed each other's company.

But when will the other shoe drop?

NEARING the end of my second week, I had just got comfortable in my seat next to Griff in Philosophy class when an announcement came over the school speakers.

Would Miss Crescent please make her way to Ms Hawthorn's office. I repeat, Miss Crescent for Ms Hawthorn's office immediately. Thank you.

All eyes in the class turned to me in the back row as I desperately wished to make myself invisible. Luckily for me, the worst of the bullies weren't in the class with me, but there were still some horrible, shitty people in the room.

'Ummm,' said Griff, making the noise a five-year-old did when another kid was in trouble. I jabbed my elbow into his rib. 'Oof, no need to hurt precious cargo, New Girl.'

'Off you go then, Miss Crescent.' Ms Wella smiled at me, her eyes crinkled and kind, and I packed up my table as swiftly as I could. I wondered what it was Ms Hawthorn wanted to talk to me about. I hadn't seen or heard of her since the assembly on the first morning of term. It was as if she was a ghost that had vanished into the ether.

The campus was empty as I made my way across, what with most of the pupils in class and those that weren't in class holed up in the library or the common room. The closer I got to the administration offices, the quieter it became.

I'd become accustomed to the strange school layout, so it didn't take me any time at all to get around anymore. No more getting lost in the corridors, or making wrong turns.

When I reached Ms Hawthorn's office, I knocked on the dark wood door and waited.

'Enter.' Her voice came out muffled through the thick door.

I walked into the room and took in my surroundings. The room was quite large, with dark wood panelling and an enormous fireplace on the left-hand side. Ms Hawthorn's table was directly in front of me, with her seat facing the door and a large black ornate empty chair sitting empty across from her. It looked a lot fancier than any office I'd seen in my old school; but let's be honest, my old school wasn't for the obscenely rich—not entirely. The kids—and the parents—there were lucky if they could afford to pay the bills and buy food. Or at least half of them were.

'Take a seat, Miss Crescent.' Her tone of voice was cold; seemed she hadn't changed her opinion of me in the two weeks I'd been a student here. Her eyes were still focused on her desk, not having raised them to even glance at me.

I took the empty seat in front of her desk, and for at least a minute the two of us existed in silence, as I waited for her to finish reading the paperwork I could only assume was important. She'd called me here, after all. No like I wanted to be in here.

After what felt like an eternity, she finally looked up at me and frowned.

'How are things going for you here at the academy, Miss Crescent?'

'Err, f-fine, thanks, Ms Hawthorn,' I said, wringing my hands together under the table. A habit of mine that would make Lady Macbeth proud.

'I take it you've settled in well to your classes and made some friends?' Her shrewd grey eyes could only be described as looking into my soul. There was something off about this lady, something that made me feel strange deep down, but I couldn't place a finger on what it was that had me feeling so out of sorts.

'Yes, thank you,' I replied, eyeing her warily. 'Clover has been a good friend to me. So has Griff.'

At that, her face soured like she was sucking on a lemon. It made the wrinkles around her mouth even more prominent, even more grotesque.

'Yes, I've heard that Master Cooper has been paying very close attention to you.' Her eyes were intense and focused on mine. A slight flicker of her eyelids had discomfort rushing through me. 'Please remember, Miss Crescent, that we expect you to be on your best behaviour while you are a student at this establishment. I've been hearing some unsavoury things about you.'

Unsavoury? What on earth?

I'd barely done anything wrong since I started. Nothing I could recall, at least.

Confused by her words, the heat of her gaze burning, I maintained eye contact with her, knowing that if I broke it, she would think even less of me than she already seemed to.

'Yes, Ms,' I said in response, trying to sound polite. I didn't want to get on her nasty side, but it seemed as though I may already be there.

'You may return to class. I'll be talking to you soon,' she said in a final, ominous sort of way.

Clearly dismissed, I stood up from my seat.

What a waste of my time.

Ms Hawthorn had already returned to her paperwork and clearly wanted me gone. It made no sense to me why she'd wanted to see me in the first place. Her questions weren't overly important and it wasn't like she'd said anything that couldn't wait. Maybe she just wanted to warn me again about my behaviour. *Odd.*

Leaving the room, I closed the door softly behind me and turned to face the corridor.

'SHIT!' I physically startled, jumping an inch off the stone floor. Ollie stood outside the door leaning on the wall on the opposite side of the hall, a smirk planted on his face. The epitome of cool, calm, and collected.

Oh. And amused.

'Sorry, I didn't mean to scare you,' he said, looking contrite. Or at least, I thought it was a look of contrition. It was always hard to tell whether somebody was being true or if they were genuinely sorry.

'That's okay. What are you d-doing here?'

'I heard the announcement on the Tannoy. Wanted to see what the old bat wanted with you.' He gestured towards the door I'd just closed.

'Oh, well, t-thanks. I guess?'

'So, what did she want?' he asked, looking all sorts of handsome. The dark brown of his hair caught the light, and he brushed it out of his face, messing it up.

He looked so good, my mind was thinking of licking him instead of paying attention to the question he'd just asked.

'Errr...' I trailed off. I'd lost all my brain cells in the last twenty seconds. Ollie's blue eyes were so clear, like the ocean on a summer's day. I could easily get lost in them and never come back up for air.

'You okay?' he asked, looking like he wanted to laugh at me but was reining it in. The wide smile on his face was a rare sight— even his teeth were showing.

'I'm fine.' I smiled back, pushing my hair behind my ears. I tried to stay still and not fidget, but nerves filled me. My stomach a swarm of butterflies and anxiety. It was the first time we'd been alone together since the library. Since the kiss. Since... more.

'So,' he continued, assessing me. 'Are you going to tell me what that cow wanted?'

'She just wanted to know how I was g-getting on. Friends and things.' I shrugged, not sure what else to say. The conversation wasn't exactly in-depth, and there really wasn't much else to elaborate on.

'And what exactly did you tell her?'

'I told her I'd made friends in Clover and Griff.' Our eyes locked together, and his smile dimmed a little, a crease forming at the edge of each eye.

'Are we not friends then, Little One?' he questioned, one side of his mouth tilting upward.

'I don't know,' I whispered, deciding to go with honesty.

It was the most honest I'd been in a while. I didn't know if I would class him as a friend. I'd started to think that maybe we could be friends, but then he went and left me cold and alone in the library like a piece of trash on the side of the road.

'Well, guess I'll just have to do something to change your mind.'

'L-like what?'

'L-like this,' Ollie said, mimicking my stutter. He pushed me against the wall and kissed me.

The kiss was so different from the one he gave me in the library. The kiss was gentle. Sweet. A soft brushing together of lips. His hands softly cupped my face, revering me, like a precious gem; unlike last time when they had roamed all over me.

The kiss ended not long after it started. It was as if we both came to our senses together and remembered we were in the school corridor, out in the open, outside Ms Hawthorn's office.

'What was that for?' I stuttered. I took a step away from him, needing some space. It was rare that I let people into my personal bubble, and even though I wanted Ollie—I *really* wanted Ollie—I also needed to keep my head about me. I couldn't let his chiselled jaw and beautiful eyes pull me in.

'I just needed to do that,' he said, his smile once again wide and carefree. 'I'll see you later.'

He left me standing there, alone once more. But at the end of the corridor, he turned and shouted back to me, 'There's a party. Friday night in the woods. Be there.'

He knew I couldn't turn down that invitation. Not without having *The Set* come after me even harder than they already were, and believe me, they'd started coming for me pretty hard. Every class I shared with them, they had turned all the other students against me.

So far, they had attempted nothing physical. It'd all been words, or mean looks, or gestures across the dining hall, or a classroom. But I knew it was only a matter of time until they escalated.

Bullies and bitches usually do.

Eleven

FRIDAY NIGHT ARRIVED, and we were getting ready to go out. I didn't own many clothes suitable for a party, but luckily Clover had a few pieces I could borrow and although we weren't the same size, we could get away with sharing some items.

'Are we even allowed to party in the woods?' I asked Clo after Ollie invited me to the party in the corridor by Hawthorn's office.

'Technically… No. But none of the faculty ever pays any notice to what the rich kids get up to. After all, the generosity of the school benefactors pays their salaries. Benefactors who are the parents of the shitty rich kid students that go here. The only way they'd get involved is if something bad happened.' Clover's eyes went out of focus for a split second. 'Well, you'd think so anyway,' she muttered, almost too quiet for me to hear.

'Sorry?' I asked, hoping she'd clarify her mutter, but Clover didn't take the bait.

'Oh, nothing. Just me mumbling to myself as usual,' she said, adding an odd 'ha' at the end to sell it as a quirk of hers, but I'd honestly never heard her talking to herself. Of course, that wasn't to say that she didn't when I wasn't around. I did it frequently.

'So, will you come with me?'

'Come with you where?'

'To the party of course.'

'Well, I'm not going to let you make a tit of yourself alone, am I?'

So yeah, Clover had sort of—not really, but kind of—agreed to come to the party with me. Mostly I reckoned she agreed to come because she didn't trust Ollie and wanted to keep an eye on me.

The whole school was buzzing about it. It had been the main conversation topic in the dining hall over last week—I'd also heard a few mentions of it while sitting in class, too.

'Are you sure we need to go tonight? Wouldn't you rather we stay in and just eat pizza?' Clover almost pleaded with me. I understood her qualms. Even shared them. But Ollie *had* asked me to attend, and I couldn't break the rule.

Just one week ago some girl looked at Odette wrong, and the next thing everyone knew, she was suspended for some nonsensical reason.

'You don't need to come with me if you're really against it, Clo,' I said, looking at her across our room. She was sitting on her bed, still in her uniform, procrastinating from getting ready. 'But I would love to have you there with me. You *know* I can't bail.'

'I *know* that and *that* is the only reason I'm coming with you,' Clover said. She pouted, jutting her bottom lip out slightly, and widened her eyes at me.

'Don't give me that look, Clo.' I laughed at her childlike tactics. 'It's making me want to give in and give you your way. But I can't, and if I'm being a little honest here, I don't want to.'

I'd tried to come to terms with the fact that a large part of me really wanted to go tonight. I'd also tried to tell Clover multiple times that I wanted to go in a way that wouldn't cause conflict between us, but I still hadn't found the right words. Clover and I may have grown to be pretty good friends pretty fast, but it had still only been a couple of weeks and I didn't want to rock the boat.

Already dressed and ready to go, I waited on Clover to get ready too. We'd decided that I should wear something a mix between casual and sexy. We went with high-waisted dark denim jeans, a white Bardot crop top, and white plimsolls. My light silvery-purple hair was styled in loose waves that came down just past my shoulders. Before coming here, I'd never made much of an effort with my appearance—except my hair. My hair was something I'd always changed. Changing my hair colour and style always made me feel better when my anxiety became over-whelming. It was something I could do for myself, too; no friends or trips outside of the house needed. Minimal cost if you got the home box dyes.

Clover dressed herself in black skinny jeans, a band shirt, and black Converse. Her auburn hair was tied up in a high ponytail, with two wisps of her fringe hanging down on either side. She looked like a rocker chick, with her eyeliner super thick around her green eyes, making them stand out.

'You look hot!' I raised my eyebrows up and down at her. She chucked a pillow at me.

'Stop it, I look ite.' She waved me off, a small flush on her cheeks. 'You, however, look mighty fine. The boys won't know what to do with themselves.'

Clover grabbed both our phones, putting hers in her pocket before passing mine to me.

'By boys I meant Ollie and Griff, if you weren't sure.'

'You know Leo will totally be into how you look right now,' I replied. I wanted so bad to know more about her history with Leo, and I was sort of hoping that Clover would drink enough tonight for her tongue to loosen to get the goods. Loose lips sink ships, and all that.

'I give zero shits about what Leo thinks,' she said. The bite in her tone shut me up. 'Let's go.'

I opened our door and nearly went head first into a very hard, very muscular chest.

My eyes tracked upward, and I found myself looking into Griff's eyes. I'd never noticed before, but his eyes made me think of a meadow on a summer's day. They were that truly rare colour; blue edges with a green centre. He looked debonair, or in less fancy terms, really fucking hot.

'Whoa. Be careful, Sky,' Griff said. His smile was super wide, the dimples in his cheeks pressed in, his eyes shining bright with amusement. 'You might run into somebody who doesn't want to let you go.'

'Oh, ha-ha.' I faked laughter, smiling back at him. 'Who would that be?'

His expression changed. Like day to night in a millisecond. His eyes darkened, and I worried I'd said the wrong thing.

'There are beasts lurking around every corner, New Girl. Remember that,' he said, his tone one of warning.

'Okay.' I was too stunned to say more.

I looked around us. There was nobody in the halls, and I assumed that was because of the party. From what I'd gathered from Clo, pretty much everybody went. Even the younger years would try and sneak out from their heavily guarded dorms to join in.

Nobody wanted to miss a party.

THE OUTSKIRTS of the woods were only around a five-minute walk from campus, but the clearing holding the party was another fifteen minutes' walk away.

'I didn't realise the surrounding land was this big,' I said after we'd been walking in silence for some time. I would've said anything, just so we weren't quiet anymore. The whistle of the wind through the leaves was disconcerting, to say the least.

'Well, yeah. The school's on the hill too, remember? So all the land up here belongs to the Hawthorn family,' Clover replied.

'I totally forgot Leo's family owned this place. Suppose he's related to Ms Hawthorn?' I asked. I'd never made the connection before.

'Sadly, yes. His aunt,' Griff said, looking at me. 'But nobody ever acknowledges it. Best not to bring it up with him.'

'Pft, yeah, like I even talk to Leo, anyway. He's taken his side,' I said.

He had, after all, hadn't he? He may have told me that first night I could come to him, but absolutely none of his actions afterward had backed up his claim.

'Of course he has because he's a massive cumstain who

should really just piss off,' Clover said, her eyebrows furrowing, her dislike of Leo oozing from every pore.

'A massive cumstain?' I sputtered, laughing at her, raising my eyebrows. She was always so serious but also so comical when it came to talk of Leo. Even when she didn't mean to be. Like how young children acted on a playground with the people they fancied. Pick on them, call them names, all to disguise the fact you like them.

'You know what I mean!' Clo said, joining in the laughter, which stopped abruptly when we came to the dimly lit clearing. Tiny lanterns placed in the trees were giving off little light, creating a seedy effect.

The bass of the music thumped and vibrated through the soles of my shoes as it made its way up my legs, and there were bodies everywhere. Some stood on what looked like a makeshift dance floor, grinding on one another. Others dotted around, standing in friendship groups; talking, playing drinking games or hooking up. It was all happening around us and I felt over-whelmed. I'd never been to a party like this before—I'd never had friends in school that would invite me to anything like this. The popular kids at my old school all went to the field on a Friday night, but I never did. It wasn't my scene—plus, I had to work.

I spotted Ollie across the clearing, standing with Leo, but when he saw we'd arrived, he left Leo's side and came straight over to us.

'You're finally here,' he said, relieved, his eyes taking me in from head to toe. 'You look beautiful.' He kissed my cheek in greeting and then said a quick hello to Clover and Griff. 'Fancy a drink?'

'P-please,' I said, nodding at him. I watched as he headed over to a table set up with bottles of booze covering it, all different types and strengths. I hoped that Ollie didn't get me anything too strong. I'd never been much of a drinker and was so worried that I'd end up drinking too much and embarrass myself. Clover and I ate a big dinner, though, so we wouldn't be drinking on an empty stomach.

'Remember the motto, Sky.' Clover grabbed my attention from Ollie and shook my shoulder. 'Beer before liquor, never sicker.'

'Liquor before beer, in the clear,' we said together, ending the fun phrase Clo had taught me earlier.

I took the drink Ollie offered me on his return and took a tentative sip. The taste of cranberry and vodka hit me. It wasn't overly strong, and it tasted all right, so I continued to sip at it.

'Is this your first party then, New Girl?' he asked.

'Y-yeah. Is it that obvious?' I was worried I'd embarrassed myself already, but even for me that was a bit ridiculous.

'You look nervous,' he said, reaching his hand out to touch my cheek before it slowly trailed down my neck. The touch was soft, sensual, and full of warmth. Light. My breath hitched, my stomach fluttered, and I felt nauseous all at once. All I could think in that moment was I hoped I didn't look as much of a fucking lemon as I thought I did. My face must've stuck in a confused expression because Ollie looked at me and raised his brow in question.

'You okay, Sky?' His eyes rose and his lips formed slowly into a smirk.

I wanted nothing more than for him to kiss me properly, but it wasn't the right time for that.

'O-of course. I'm solid,' I replied, trying to put an airiness into my voice. *Solid? When the fuck have I ever said that before? Ground, swallow me whole.*

'Glad to hear it,' he said, brushing his lips on my cheek in another subtle kiss. I didn't know how to react—he'd never shown me affection in public before, and I didn't want to get too excited in case it meant fuck all to him.

Ollie sauntered to stand behind me, wrapping his arms around my shoulders as he leant his head on top of mine. I was the perfect height for him to do it comfortably. Bewildered by his actions, I had no idea of how to react to any of this.

The whispers of *The Sect* followed me around, and I knew Ollie could be having me on. Playing a cruel joke on me.

I needed to keep my wits about me and not give into him so easily. But damn, his face made that hard to do.

I felt so new to this shit. I had entered a world with multiple rules that I knew fuck all about, and I wasn't sure how to cope with it all without losing myself.

A FEW DRINKS into the evening, I started to feel the effects, to the point where I started seeing two of Ollie. And they were both hot. Even my stutter had taken a leave of absence for the night. *Loose lips sink ships indeed.*

'Want to dance?' Ollie asked, sneaking up behind me as I was sitting on the floor playing *Never Have I Ever* with Griff and Clover. He began rubbing my shoulders, kneading out the knots there.

I looked back and up at him, a wide smile on my lips unbidden, as if I couldn't help being happy in his presence. He moved his hands, so that one was now directly in front of my face, offering to help me stand. I took it, and the force of the pull had me hurtling into him at a faster speed than I expected.

'Whoa, be careful there, little lady. Maybe you should slow down on the drinks,' he said, a caring look in his eyes. I laughed, giddy.

'I'm okay, big boy.' The words left my lips before my mind caught up with them, but the moment it did, I froze, a slow flush creeping onto my cheeks.

Was I at the point of slurring my words? I couldn't be sure. They all sounded perfectly fine to me.

Ollie laughed at me. 'Big boy? I'll prove just how *big* I am one day.' His promised words made my face heat further. He had me running hot and cold all the time, so much, it made me worried I'd get chilblains.

'Come dance,' he demanded. People filled the dance floor, bodies thrummed to the beat, and more couples than not reenacted the opening credits from *Dirty Dancing*, or they were full-on making out with no care about who could see them.

Ollie held me close, and we swayed together.

'We can't slow dance to this,' I told him quietly. The music was upbeat, and it was awkward to step from side to side to it. I'd never been much of a dancer. Rhythm did *not* come naturally to me.

'We can make it whatever we want it to be,' he whispered, his fingers playing with the waistband of my jeans.

'Oh, we can, can we?' I sassed, raising my eyebrows at how casual he was. His fingers continued playing with the top of my jeans before fumbling with the button at the front. 'What on earth are you doing?'

'I know you want me to touch you. You've been giving off signals ever since we first met that you want me,' Ollie said, his hands still travelling around my hip bones, tickling me.

'You seem very sure of yourself. Maybe even a little *too* sure.'

'You're talking a big game, Sky. Let's see if you can walk the walk.' His eyes were wide as his face came closer to mine, leaning down into my bubble.

Lips touched mine. Fingers still reaching, trying to breach my underwear and make their way to the place I wanted them most. To the place he'd touched in the library that day.

That day we'd never spoken of since.

'Can we move into the shadows?' I asked, stopping his hand from moving further, intertwining our fingers.

He didn't say a word in response, but I led him away from the spot on the dance floor and we headed further into the trees. Far enough away that we couldn't be seen, but close enough that we could still feel the bass, the thrum of energy in the air.

Hidden away from the others, I felt bold. My veins on fire, and my mind brave enough to take what it wanted.

I initiated the next contact between us.

Grabbing his face between my hands and pulling it down to my level, I kissed him, as if my life was dependent upon it. Beneath my lips, I felt the moment Ollie snapped—the moment he became an active participant. His soft lips pushed against mine, a small nip of his teeth on my bottom lip sending my mind into overdrive. My hands moved to his chest, roaming, his pecs hard underneath my fingertips, and his abs even harder.

With force, Ollie pushed me into a tree, using his strength to pin me there. Trapped. At his mercy. His hands moved down to my thighs, pushing them, causing my legs to fall apart in a wider stance so he could step between them.

His dick pressed into my right thigh, and all I wanted to do was touch him. My hand moved towards the top of his jeans, but he stopped me by raising my hand to his mouth and biting down on it, hard. *Fuck.* The heady mix of the alcohol and his touch meant I was turned the fuck on. I could feel my wetness, and every move he made, every touch, only made me wetter.

The jean button that had caused him an issue earlier was undone in a flash. The zip came down, fingers now making their way down, down, and into my lace underwear, leaving a trail of heat in every place they touched. My skin on fire, the burn worth it.

Ollie plunged a finger inside of me, hard, and I gasped at the sudden invasion. There had been no build-up. No teasing. Yet I was ready for him, my warmth welcoming him in.

'Your moans are so fucking sexy,' Ollie whispered. His mouth on my ear and his whispers caused goosebumps to rise along my arms.

'Don't stop,' I said, my breath coming out faster.

His finger started moving, building in speed, and when I thought I could take no more, he added another finger.

'You're killing me,' he moaned. 'One day, Sky, I swear, you *will* stutter around my dick.'

My orgasm was building, threatening to push me over the edge, climbing with each stroke of his thumb on my clit, and each time his fingers moved inside of me, it got stronger. I wasn't a stranger to orgasms—I knew how to get myself there—and although it was completely different having Ollie touch me, the sensations inside of me remained the same.

When Ollie bit my bottom lip, his sharp teeth causing blood to rise up and spot on my lip, he added a third finger and my climax hit me in full force. It was like I'd been climbing until there was nowhere else to go. Lightheaded and dazed, I looked into Ollie's burning gaze.

'So fucking hot,' he whispered, almost too quiet for me to hear. My pulse was loud in my ears, drumming away, and I couldn't hear much else, lost in the sensations.

I sighed contentedly. A chill ran up my arms, and the cold became more obvious than it had a moment ago. It crept back in slowly now that I was coming down from the high my body had been on. My mouth felt dry; the aftertaste of blood still coating my tongue. That metallic tang overtaking everything.

Ollie stepped away from me, creating distance between us, and raked his hand through his hair that looked slightly gold in the moonlight. *What a rogue.*

'I'll go get us another drink,' he said and walked away, back towards the clearing where the party was still raging on as if we hadn't slipped away. The two of us weren't missed, that was for sure.

Waiting for him, I lost track of time.

He returned after five minutes, maybe? He had a cup in each hand, both filled with red-purple liquid. Passing me one, he said, 'Here you go, Little One.'

I took the cup, thankful, and gulped down the cranberry juice and vodka concoction inside. The orgasm he'd given me was still moving through my body like little shock waves. Little ripples of emotions I didn't want to face yet, so I drank it all. It was the strongest drink I'd had all night, but also rather sweet tasting—something I could focus on. Ground myself with.

'You'll feel better soon,' he said, breathless, hugging me close once again.

The hug was warm and comforting. I'd never been much of a hugger and I rarely instigated contact with people first. Ollie's arms were no longer bare, but instead were covered by a soft black leather jacket. He must've had it stashed out here somewhere, knowing how cold it would get. I wished I'd thought to do the same thing. An off-the-shoulder crop top was *not* the perfect September attire, especially when on the top of a cold, windy hill in England.

'I know,' I replied, my voice whisper-soft, muffled by his hard chest. 'You're here after all. Nothing bad can happen to me now.'

The last thing I remembered was Ollie's face gazing at me intently. The moonlight hitting one side of his face, almost like a mask, making his features look sinister. Dark.

A hard glint formed in his eyes and they looked darker than they normally were.

Then everything went black.

Twelve

SHIT.

My head was banging. A cacophony of drums played inside my skull, pounding away. Like a truck had hit it, or even maybe a brick repeatedly smashed down onto my skull. Alongside the headache from hell, my mouth was dry, scratched, and tasted foul. *What on earth happened last night?*

It was probably the worst I'd felt in my entire life, and I wasn't even exaggerating—much.

I needed water and some paracetamol stat.

My eyes fluttered open, and I tried to get my bearings without drawing too much attention to myself. I had no idea where the fuck I was, and with little memory of how I got there, it could be anywhere. The room looked familiar in that way dorm rooms do, but it was one I hadn't seen before.

Beads of sweat rose up on my arms, and an all-body chill rushed through me. My anxiety always got worse when unexpected things happened; things outside of my routine or the norm.

This is one hundred percent outside of the norm.

The scent of tobacco and vanilla was strong in the air, and slowly, as my mind caught up to my nose, I realised where I knew that specific smell from. It had been invading my personal bubble ever since school started, no matter that I'd tried to avoid it.

I startled when a door opened nearby.

Looking around again, I noticed the room had an en-suite attached and only one bed. It was a suite more than a room, at least double the size of the one I shared with Clo.

And then there in the doorway of the bathroom stood Ollie.

In a towel.

Looking fine as fuck.

Oh, fucking hell.

Of course it was Ollie's room I was in. Which meant I was lying in Ollie's bed. Ollie's very large super king-sized bed that could definitely have fit an Ollie-shaped body next to my smaller one. The pillow next to me had a head-shaped indent. I had slept next to Ollie. The guy who fingered me up against a tree last night before everything went black.

My cheeks were aflame as I took a quick inventory of my clothes and noticed that I was still wearing my underwear—and nothing else.

Double shit.

Double fuck.

Double everything.

I decided I wouldn't be the one to break the silence and tried to pretend I was still asleep, wrapping myself up in the duvet, all warm and cosy. Like I hadn't noticed where I was. Like I hadn't seen him two seconds ago standing in only a towel, with water droplets still making their way down his abs. His very fine abs.

'I know you're awake, Sky.'

'H-how do you know that?' I asked, keeping my eyes squeezed closed. I wanted to still have some form of deniability.

'I've been beside you all night and your breathing's different when you're asleep,' he replied, his smile reminding me of Griff's. Cheeky and all-knowing.

'Surely, you slept too? How can you be so sure?'

'I didn't exactly sleep, New Girl. Had to stay awake and watch you. Be responsible. You know, make sure you didn't choke on your own vomit and all that good shit,' he said, a smile playing at the corner of his lips.

'What?' I sputtered.

'You don't remember much from last night, do you?' he asked me, but I was pretty sure it was rhetorical, so I chose not to answer. 'Someone drugged you last night.'

He didn't sugarcoat it. Didn't slowly build up to it. Nope. Not Ollie. He just threw the words out there, with no thought to how they would sound. It was almost careless and unfeeling.

'I was what?' I raised my voice at him, my displeasure bleeding into every syllable. Thinking I'd got drunk and not understanding my limits had been bad enough, but to hear that someone drugged me, in such a casual manner, flabbergasted me —so much so, I thought of the word flabbergasted.

'Somebody spiked your drink. You must've accepted one that the girls had tampered with or put yours down at some point,' he told me as if it was the only explanation, no question about it.

'But I didn't,' I said, looking at him head-on for the first time since I woke. 'It was in my hand at all times.'

I knew I didn't let go of it, and I knew I hadn't taken a drink from a stranger. It was something I was super conscious of after reading one too many horror stories online about girls who were date raped.

'I only took drinks from Clover, Griff, or you.'

'You must have done, Sky. There's no shame in it.'

'Ollie, I swear to you I didn't!'

'Well, somehow your drink *was* messed with and I offered to bring you up here and look after you. The faculty's less likely to be monitoring this hall, especially on a Friday night.'

I rolled my eyes, then regretted it two point five seconds later as it made my head pound even more. I believed him about the faculty not monitoring these halls as closely, though. Bet they were paid a fair amount not to. Not that Clover and I had seen them often, but every now and again we would see a caretaker or hall monitor outside our room, making sure that nothing was amiss.

Ollie didn't believe me. I could tell I'd disappointed him in a way that didn't quite make sense to me yet. None of this was making sense to me. All I knew was that I hadn't been careless with my drink like Ollie was implying, yet there was no way to prove it.

Ollie sat on the edge of the bed, facing me, still wrapped in only a towel.

'I need to let Clover know where I am.'

'She knows where you are, New Girl. It took all four of us to get you back here last night,' he said with a lazy smirk.

'The f-four of you?' I asked, puzzled.

'Me, Griff, Clover, and Leo.'

'Oh, right.'

'There was no way I could've done it by myself. You weren't able to control your limbs, and you kept telling me how you wished I *had* found out what your stutter sounds like with my dick inside you.'

You know when you could feel a blush on your face, but you had no idea how to stop it from happening? I covered my burning face with the duvet in shame, even though I had no way of knowing whether he was telling the truth. For all I knew, he could be teasing me on purpose to embarrass me.

'I've never mentioned it before, but you are really quite cute sometimes, Sky.' He chuckled. Even his chuckle sounded X-rated to me.

'Are you trying to make me feel worse?' I shrieked. 'What time is it?'

'Ten. We missed breakfast but, lucky for you, I got Griff to deliver some to us before the buffet closed.'

'Don't really f-feel like eating.' I swallowed hard again, trying to get the lump out of my throat that seemed to have taken root there. 'A drink would be g-great, though.'

Ollie instantly got up and moved to the kitchenette area on the left-hand side of the room, then came back with a glass of water in his outstretched hand. I took it and chugged it down in one go. He instantly took the empty glass from me and refilled it.

I grabbed it, and while taking small sips, I regarded him.

'Thank you. For looking after me, I mean. Not for accusing me of being irresponsible.'

Ollie's eyes warmed. I could swim in the blue of his eyes.

'I'm not a *total* dick, Sky. I wouldn't have left you like that.' He came to lie down beside me, keeping on top of the cover, leaving a small distance between us. 'And we *will* find out who did this to you.'

'Surely there are only four suspects?' It made total sense to me that *The Set* did this, right? I knew I had made no friends outside of Clo and Griff, but drugging somebody was a step further than mean comments during class.

'You think the O girls did this?' he asked, his eyebrow arching. I'd never heard him call them that before. Come to think of it, he'd never really referred to them as anything at all. Even though they'd been the topic of conversation more than once recently, he never said their names. Ollie had never said more than a few words about their actions, choosing to stay silent about their cruelty towards me.

'Who else would?' I asked, feeling like we were going around in circles.

Slowly, the two of us gravitated towards one another on the bed. His breath felt warm on my face, his eyes staring into mine.

'They've m-made it clear that they hate me.'

'Seems bold, even for them,' he said, dismissing me, but he softened the blow of his words by tucking a piece of my hair behind my ear.

'Does it? I heard from Clover that somebody died last year?' I asked, curious, even though I knew I was pushing my luck with him. Not like he was gonna tell me the truth.

'That's nothing for you to worry about,' he said, dismissing me once again. I was about to prod him more, try and get more details from him, but his face told me not to bother. His chiselled jaw was clenched tight, a slight tick of his eye.

I didn't even want to examine what it meant about me, but my God, he looked even hotter when he was angry. I'd always found that in books and films, I was more attracted to the *bad boys*. Those characters who acted like total dickheads, but you couldn't help but want them, anyway. Not that I'd actually met any guy like that before coming to Hawthorn.

'Whatever happened last year has nothing to do with what's happening now. I can promise you that.'

'Yeah?' I asked, my tone unsure.

'Skylar, I swear to you, this is all because the girls are feeling threatened by you. You're beautiful, funny, and everything they wish they could be. You've caught my eye and Griff loves you. Even Leo's got a soft spot for you.'

He was full of shit. That wasn't how it was at all. Yeah, I was friendly with Griff, and Ollie *acted* interested in me, but that could just be because he wanted in my pants. The part about Leo was a stretch, though. The boy barely looked my way, and if he did, I assumed it was only because I was usually sitting next to Clover.

'You're s-such a liar.' I giggled, not believing him.

'Either way, those girls are bitches. Don't let them get to you, no matter what, okay? They're not worth it.' He reached out to trail his finger up and down my arm, causing goosebumps to rise in the places his fingers grazed.

'Bitches with power. The other kids follow them.'

'I'll see what I can do,' he said. His ominous tone gave me pause. I thought he'd already been trying to see what he could do, but maybe the fact that someone drugged me had made him realise this was more serious than some kids taking the piss out of a girl's stutter and family background.

The rest of the day, the two of us stayed in Ollie's room until dinner—in silence, mostly. We watched films and just lay next to one another, not touching, but comfortable in one another's company.

I didn't want to imagine how badly last night could have gone if he hadn't rescued me—hadn't looked after me. He may be a self-entitled dick, but last night, he'd been my saviour.

Okay, yeah, a bit dramatic, Sky.

But still, I couldn't overlook that, no matter how much I probably *should*.

Thirteen

THE THIRD WEEK of term started the same as the two before it, but as the days went by, things kept getting worse and worse.

It all began when Oralie and Ophelia cornered me in the girls' toilets on Tuesday. I'd gone in there to use the facilities, but when I exited the stall, the two of them were standing by the sinks, waiting for me.

'Look who it is, Lee. The trashy, charity tramp,' Ophelia said. Her face was one of disgust with her over-enhanced top lip curled upward, her eyes narrowed into slits.

'Eurgh. What are you looking at, slut?' Oralie asked, equally livid, her face scrunched up.

'I'm just looking ahead?' My words came out as a question when I wanted to sound assertive.

Even though the two of them had been making English class unbearable and were encouraging everybody to pick on me throughout the school day, I usually had either Clover, Ollie, or Griff with me. People would only say so much in front of the guys and nobody had taken anything beyond words yet, but I could feel it brewing. I knew *The Set* wouldn't stop at just slander, and I knew the time would come when things would escalate.

Seems today is that day.

'Nobody wants you here, skank,' Ophelia said as Oralie nodded beside her. They were standing together, a united front;

one with her hands on her hips and the other with her arms crossed across her inflated chest.

'I'm here on scholarship. I didn't even choose to be here,' I said. They knew that, too. I still wasn't sure if I preferred it at Hawthorn over my old school. The only two parts that were a win were my friendship with Clover and the fact I didn't have to live with my mum and Andy anymore. Who, funnily enough, I hadn't heard from since I left. I'd always known they didn't give a shit about me, but it was nice to have it confirmed with their silence.

'We can tell,' Oralie said, looking super smug. 'That you're poor, I mean.'

'You're such a little bitch. I thought at first you were putting the stutter on to get attention, but now it's clear that you're actually a scared, pathetic pussy.'

The two of them advanced towards me in tandem. I would've been impressed if I wasn't so alarmed at the look of menace on their faces.

'Maybe we need to teach you a lesson.'

As soon as Ophelia said those words, Oralie pounced faster than a tiger and grabbed both of my arms and held them behind my back, gripping them tightly in place. Not wanting to waste a golden opportunity, Ophelia punched me in the middle of my face, catching me on the nose, causing blood to gush out.

Shit.

That hurt. A lot.

I couldn't give them the satisfaction of letting them know just how much. Still, Ophelia kept hitting me. Punching me. In the face, the arm, the stomach. Anywhere she could. I fell to the floor, no longer able to hold myself upright, but the two of them proceeded to kick me instead. My stomach was tender, and I knew this was going to bruise like a bitch.

The punching and kicking continued. My vision had blurred after a couple of minutes, my anxiety peaking once again. I *was* getting beat on by two bitches, after all, and neither of them was holding back. All of their anger and frustration aimed at me.

In the distance, I could hear muffled shouting, the noise getting louder by the minute. Getting closer to where we were.

Lucky for me, the girls heard the shouts and realised they were pushing their luck. That they would be discovered soon. Somebody was bound to enter the room. They blinked, looking down at me, taking stock of the situation they'd found themselves in, shocked they'd gone as far as they had.

'Shit,' Ophelia said and hit Oralie on the shoulder. 'This isn't over, charity trash.' Her spit hit my lip, yet I didn't wipe it away. I had a lot more to worry about at this point—like the intense pain in my side and the blood drying on my face.

With one last kick, they hurried out of the room, leaving me sprawled out on the floor, unable to move.

The door didn't fully close behind them as somebody pushed it open, catching it with their foot before it slammed.

'What the fuck?' Clover screamed, her gaze finding me on the floor. Tears filled my eyes at the sight of her. I wanted to tell her what had happened, but the last kick winded me and I was struggling to catch my breath. Clo popped her head outside the door. 'Shit, guys! She's in here!'

Her yell caused both Ollie and Griff to storm into the room, their fury coming off of them in waves.

'Who did this, New Girl?' Griff asked with an urgency that was new for him.

My eyes trailed upwards to glance at Griff, and the look on his face was so unlike the expression he usually wore. There was no hint of a cheeky smile or any dimples, and I didn't want to be Ophelia or Oralie when he caught up with them.

'Leo needs to put them on a fucking leash,' Ollie said, spit spraying from his mouth. He looked so mad. Like a beast, ready to rip the heads off of those responsible for my despair. Even I could admit I was slightly scared of him at that moment. I'd never seen this dark of an expression on his face before, and I was so glad he didn't aim it at me. Ollie looked at Griff. 'Go find Leo and tell him about this.'

Griff was leaning over me, and Clover was hovering nearby,

feeling out of place. When neither of them moved to follow Ollie's instructions, he roared. 'Now!'

Griff stood, leaving the room, but not before he kissed my cheek and whispered some words in my ear. 'We're gonna kick their butts, New Girl.'

Hands helped me into a sitting position, and after a time my breathing returned to normal. Blood was dried on my face, but at least my nose had stopped bleeding, and other than feeling a little swollen when I prodded it, I didn't think it was broken like I'd first feared.

'How are you feeling?' Clover asked. Or more demanded.

I understood it, though. I'd probably be acting the same way if she were in my position. I would hate not knowing whether they hurt her more than the eye could see.

'Sore,' I groaned, gripping my side, trying to alleviate some of the pain there. Lifting my shirt, I could see the bruises already forming. Swirls of pink and red bloomed under my skin. The repeated kicks to my side and stomach were going to leave their mark for a while. 'I wasn't able to s-stop them. Held my arms back.'

'Shh. Let's get you to our room,' Clo whispered.

'No. She'll come back to my room where I can keep an eye on her,' Ollie ordered.

'You've done enough!' Clover spat out. If a look could kill, then Ollie would be dead with the way Clover was looking at him. 'This is *all* your fault.'

'And how do you gather that?' he asked in a clipped tone.

'After the party Friday, after they'd *drugged* Skylar, you knew the girls would escalate.'

'I suggest you stop right there, Clover. Just because you're Sky's best friend doesn't mean I'll let you talk to a member of *The Sect* like that,' Ollie said, his lips forming into a sneer.

Clover's hands clenched at her sides, and I thought I'd have to prevent her from clocking him one. The two of them had been wary of each other before today, but I never thought they'd actually come to blows. Especially over something as stupid as my safety.

'Guys, stop!' I pleaded. 'I just want to g-get off the bathroom floor.'

Clover rushed to help me up, and I used her body to hold myself up. I felt like Quasimodo, all hunched over and standing awkwardly.

'Come on,' Clo said to me, keeping a firm grip on my arm.

The hallway was clear of students when we exited, which was the first bit of luck I'd had all day. No bells had rung while I was in there—not that I heard—but a new period must have started.

Slowly, we made our way across campus with me limping beside Clover. Ollie on the other side of me, staying close just in case I needed him. It surprised me he hadn't demanded that Clover move, but I thought maybe the two of them were trying to be civil just so I would get back to my room and rest.

After what felt like years, we finally made it back to my room. Clearly, by being the one to steer me, she'd got her way and got to decide what room I went to. I just wanted to get into a bed —any bed.

'Do you want to shower?' Clo asked, and I nodded in response. I wanted to wash, but if I was being honest, a shower didn't sound overly appealing. What I really wanted was a long soak in the bath. I was a bath girl through and through, and I would never understand the appeal of showers. Standing up would never seem relaxing to me.

'I could help with that,' Ollie said, without a trace of joking or flirting in his voice. No ulterior motive. I would've been annoyed if Ollie had used a sleazy tone, but luckily for his balls, he sounded like he genuinely wanted to help me. A large part of me wanted him to help—he had the strength to hold me up—but an even larger part of me wasn't ready for that. It was next level shit.

Fuck, the two of us hadn't even spoken about any of the shit we'd done together. And if I was being honest, I'd never been naked in front of a guy, and it was okay to admit to yourself that you weren't at that stage yet mentally.

'I'll do it,' Clover snapped at him. I attempted a shrug, but the movement hurt me too much. I hoped my face conveyed my emotions to let him know I wasn't mad at him, but that I wanted Clo to help me. The narrowing of his eyes told me that maybe my intention had got lost in translation.

Like a lot of things when it comes to Oliver Brandon.

THE SHOWER HELPED me feel slightly more human and once he tucked me into my bed, Ollie left after saying he had some errands to run. I wasn't even going to guess at what those were. Griff arrived shortly after and hugged me so tight, I thought my ribs would bruise alongside everything else.

'Honestly, New Girl, you cannot be going anywhere alone anytime soon. Those girls aren't messing around,' he said in greeting.

'Well, hello to you too!' I said, laughing at his no-nonsense tone. 'You already come with me most places.'

'I mean it, Sky,' he said, sitting down at the bottom of my bed, making sure not to touch me. The use of my name sent a chill down my spine. It wasn't like Griff. 'Until we've sorted this shit out with them, you're not to be alone.'

'Ay, ay, Captain!' I said with a mock salute. 'Did you go speak to them?'

'I hope you kicked their asses, Griff. I don't care if they've got vaginas,' Clo piped up from her spot on her bed, looking so fierce that if I were *The Set*, I'd be terrified. She was *not* playing around.

'Classy, Clo,' Griff said, his smile cheeky, but I also noticed he deflected the question asked. 'So, whores, what are we going to watch tonight?'

'Whores?' I asked, sputtering. The boy was something else. My mouth moved into a lopsided smile at him.

'Is that not what the girls say? Want me to call you sisters or girlies?'

'No!' Clover and I both yelled, shaking our heads at him in amusement.

'Let's pick a film, girlies,' Griff said, defying us as he got up Netflix and started flicking through the options. His watch list killed me. It had some of my favourite films on it and I smiled, wondering if Griff had them on there because he liked them or in order to have a quick "Netflix and chill" film on hand.

'*To all the boys?*' I asked the room and got a resounding 'YES!' from Clover and a, 'Oh, I love a bit of Peter Kavinsky,' from Griff.

'Let's do this,' I said, getting more comfortable in my bed, pulling the duvet up to my chin. Griff settled beside me while making sure he didn't touch my side or hurt me further.

Having friends was such a novelty to me, but if the warm and fuzzy feeling growing in my gut as we ate takeaway pizza and watched films was what it felt like, then I never wanted this feeling to go away.

Fourteen

HEALING after the O girls beat me up was a bitch. It was a couple of days before I was able to get up and walk without wincing at each step. The first few days, the door of my room was constantly revolving. Clover, Griff, and Ollie barely left me alone and one of them was always by my side. Even when I would've rather been left alone.

It took me a week to return to classes, and even then, I still dawdled everywhere. My sides were bruised, but mentally I was okay—and that was what mattered to me. I wasn't going to miss out on my classes because of some stuck-up snooty bitches who thought they had the right to harm me. I couldn't miss any more classes without my grades suffering and Ms Hawthorn forcing me to come into her office to discuss the terms of my scholarship was not something I wanted to do right now. It wasn't something I wanted to do *ever*.

Six weeks later and things were slowly returning to normal. No students were looking at my face with sneering smiles anymore now the bruises had faded—or at least none that I could see. Sure, they were having a field day of murmurs behind my back, though.

'Kant's a bit of an unfortunate name, isn't it,' Griff said, and I nodded, only half listening to whatever it was he was wittering on about. The boy didn't stop talking, and I wondered how he managed to fill his lungs with enough air to keep up his constant stream of babbles.

The two of us had just left our Ethics class and were heading towards the dining hall to grab some lunch. That was one thing I could say about Hawthorn: the food was to die for. Everything from the pastries at breakfast, to the rich pasta dishes at dinner. Even the pizza they sometimes had on the menu was elevated above anything I'd ever tasted before. No thick, greasy, cheese pizza for such a fine establishment.

Griff continued prattling on, and I kept nodding at what I thought were the right moments. The occasional hum seemed to satisfy him. It was in the middle of one of those nods that I bumped into somebody. *Leo*, in fact. And by *bumped* I meant I literally walked straight into him, colliding with a loud thump.

'S-sorry.' Like any Brit that bumped into another person, my first instinct was to apologise profusely. After the third 'sorry' he took pity on me.

'That's okay, Stutter,' he said, his mouth tilting up on one side, the amusement dripping off him. His hair was brushed to one side and I found myself wanting to run my fingers through it to see if it was as soft as it looked. *Down, Sky.*

I blinked at him, processing his words. *Great.* I'd got a cute nickname from Leo. At least it was better than trailer, charity trash, which the O girls were lovingly calling me every time they saw me.

I brushed my hands where we made impact, then realised what I was doing and stopped straight away, resting my hands on his chest near his heart.

'I should really w-watch where I'm going.'

'Must have distracted her with my manliness,' Griff said, his words catching me off-guard. I snorted loudly with laughter, covering my mouth with my hand.

'And she snorts too.' Leo's face became even more amused. 'Stutter, if you ever want to ditch that tool you're currently attached to, I'm available.' His bored tone didn't match his words or the expression on his face in the slightest. He sounded as if he didn't give a fuck about any of it, which only made me wonder more about him.

'If Ollie fucks it up, which, let's be honest, could happen soon, then I'm definitely the next in line. Right, Sky?' Griff asked, his signature grin in place.

'Sure, Griff,' I said to placate him, tapping his shoulder before I pulled at his arm to get him to continue walking with me. Away from Leo's inquisitive gaze.

Leo's tone may be wary, but his eyes were anything but. He was looking for something, and I couldn't quite figure out what.

***

My bump into Leo wasn't the last time I ran into him during the week. I bumped into him again a couple of days later, but sadly, I wasn't with Griff.

Nope. I was with Clover—the girl who hated Leo's guts more than anyone else at school.

Plus, Leo was *not* alone.

The two of us had just left dinner and were making our way back to our dorm when Clo suggested we go a different way. To mix it up a bit.

Going our usual route typically meant we ran into Odette and the other O girls, or people who were only too happy to prove their loyalty to *The Set* and call me names. Some people barged into me, trying to knock me into other people in the hall or into walls.

So I agreed to go a new route.

And that was how Clover and I found ourselves in the hallway that attached the pool house to the hospital wing. We avoided the pool house as a rule, mostly because that was where you could find Leo, Ollie, and Griff when they weren't bugging us. If they weren't with us or in class, then they were at the pool. The three of them were on the swim team and were apparently fantastic to watch, winning the school all kinds of trophies and shit. I was low-key excited to watch a meet. Mainly because I wanted to see those three in speedos. *Sue me.*

The corridor was dimly lit in comparison to the rest of the school. Griff had told me it was because these buildings were some of the oldest and they hadn't installed as many light fittings or some shit like that. The school board had kept it that way too in order to keep the original building's authenticity. And they'd succeeded. It looked exactly how you'd expect it to look. All brick walls, high vaulted arch ceilings, and wooden flooring.

Our conversation topic: the upcoming Parents' Day that Hawthorn threw once a year. The one day where every student could invite their parents to come visit, and then be thankful that they left at the end of it. A day for the parents to meet the teachers and see how their kids were doing. Find out if they were engaging in any extracurricular activities. Find out exactly what they were doing with their twenty thousand a year plus education.

'I'm not asking mine to come.' Clover shook her head as if the thought of her parents coming was too much for her to cope with.

'How come?' I knew little about her parents—not once since we became friends had she mentioned them.

'I don't want to subject them to it. Fuck, Sky, I don't want to subject myself to it either.'

'I get you. I've not invited Mum and Andy either. I'm already the butt of enough jokes. I don't need the two biggest jokes in my life coming here and making things ten times worse.'

And they would make things worse. It was the curse of Andy and Cora. It was what they did no matter the situation.

The thought of them sharing air space with the likes of Ollie and Griff made me shudder. I knew they were my friends, sort of, and that they liked me for me, or at least I assumed they did, but still. Everybody already knew I came here because of the scholarship. Inviting Mum here would only highlight just how little money I came from. It was for the best that they never set foot on Hawthorn grounds.

'Can you hear that?' Clover looked at me, making a shushing motion with her finger, even though she'd just asked me a question. I shook my head. I couldn't hear anything outside of our footsteps. We hadn't passed another student.

Then I heard it. The smooching and smacking sounds of two lips going at it got closer, and eventually we could see the couple up ahead.

Of course. It just *had* to be Leo and Odette. *Again.*

At least Clover didn't instantly run off and leave me standing alone like last time. She continued walking and when we got close enough for them to hear us, Clover coughed while actually covering up a word.

'Skank.'

I wanted to laugh, but the fake cough didn't cover her chosen word at all, so instead I stayed silent. No need to provoke the beast.

The two of them stopped what they were doing. Odette, using reflexes I didn't expect her to possess, reached out and grabbed Clover's arm, gripping tight.

'If you've got something to say, *Over*, I suggest you share it with the class.'

'Get off her! You're hurting her.' I didn't even think before I acted. I just grabbed Odette's hand and yanked it away from Clover as hard as I could. There was no way she was gonna put her hands on my best friend without me getting involved.

She let go, a scowl on her face aimed at me. I'd caught Odette off-guard.

Fuck. I'd caught myself off-guard.

I was certain she had something to do with Ophelia and Oralie attacking me in the toilets, but there was no proof of that. Even though *The Set* didn't have an actual leader, everybody knew Odette classed herself as the one in charge. Probably because she was the one hooking up with Leo, the oldest member of *The Sect*.

'Get your fucking pauper hands off me!' Odette shrieked, looking at Leo. 'Are you not going to say anything?'

Leo stayed silent, raising an eyebrow at her, the slight quirk of his top lip letting us into his mind.

'Really, Leo?' Odette demanded, stomping her foot. 'Again?'

'Stop, Stutter, stop,' Leo said, uninterested, mocking her. He wanted me to stop as much as he wanted to be involved. But that didn't stop Clover from looking over at me, betrayal plain in her features. It was clear she thought I was closer to Leo than I'd let on. The fact he'd made a *cute* nickname for me didn't help my case. I raised my eyebrows at him in warning, but he only smirked in return.

'Are you for fucking real, Leo Hawthorn?' Clover asked, disbelief in her voice.

'What's the matter, Red? Jealous of your new friend?' Leo asked, his tone having lost the disinterest he constantly exuded. It was like he'd come to life. His eyes were sparkling with malice, the darkness simmering just under the surface, wanting to be let free. Leo calling her Red told me more than he'd probably meant to.

One day soon, I would make sure Clover told me more about their history. She'd been disguising just how well they knew one another, and any time I asked, she clammed up, refusing to tell me anything.

'I'd never be jealous of this Barbie. I hope you get chlamydia or worse. Maybe if I'm lucky, your dick will drop off and save the rest of the female population. Oh, wait. They're already safe. The size of your dick won't do them any damage.'

With that, Clover walked off. Stomping down the corridor, without once turning around, away from the bomb she'd just unleashed. Odette was foaming at the mouth, her eyes narrowed on Clover's retreating back.

'Go on, Stutter. Better make sure Red doesn't go find a blade and come back for more,' Leo said, dismissing me, his attention once again returning to Odette, trying to calm her down.

I walked off slowly, trying to make sense of what I just witnessed.

One thing I knew: Leo was playing some kind of game, and I had a feeling it could be a long one.

For the rest of the night, Clover wouldn't talk to me more than to tell me she was going for a shower and then putting on her headphones and getting some essays done. I found the last part highly suspicious, though, as Clover's classes were practical subjects with barely any writing attached, like food tech. If she wanted to block me out, then I'd let her. She wanted to stop me from asking her any probing questions.

I'd respect her wishes for now, but I was getting sick of her trying to block me out. Friendship went both ways, or so I thought, and I'd definitely been a lot more open and forthcoming with her than she ever had with me. I'd told her things about my life before Hawthorn. My lack of friends, my relationship with my mum. I'd even told her about Andy's advances on the day I left. Yet all I'd got from her was that her family fell on hard times a couple of years ago.

That was it. *In six weeks.*

I knew some people found it hard to open up, hard to talk about the deep shit, but I thought I'd made it clear that I was her friend regardless of what had happened. I wouldn't judge her, and it sucked that she thought I might.

I put my headphones in my ears and pulled up Netflix, chose one of my favourite films and pressed play. I barely got through the opening credits before I got a text from an unknown number.

Only Clo, Griff, and Ollie had this number.

STUTTER. KEEP AN EYE ON RED FOR ME. LET ME KNOW IF THE GIRLS BOTHER EITHER OF YOU. SAVE THIS NUMBER. USE IT IF YOU EVER NEED HELP.

Confused by the entire message, I tried to make sense of it in my mind. Leo had my number and had used it to message me... about Clover?

I looked over at Clover and wondered whether I should bother her. Maybe she'd be able to shed some light on why Leo texted me about keeping an eye on her. But knowing Clo, she'd just fob me off again, and I wasn't in the mood to disagree with her.

I texted back one word.

OKAY.

That should be enough. I saved his number under the name Thorn, as in thorn in my side, amusing myself. After all, Clo was saved as Lady Luck and Griff was saved as Hercules—*don't ask*.

I'd debated for some time about what to save Ollie as.

Before the party in the woods, it had been *Ollie*, then after the whole drugging and rescue thing, it had been *Hero*, but that didn't fit him either. After the girls beat me up in the toilets, and he was the most angry I'd ever seen him, I changed it to *Beast*. Mostly because I knew that deep down, lurking under the surface, he could be the worst kind of monster that existed.

And I needed to keep my wits about me around him.

Fifteen

PARENTS' Day was a big deal at Hawthorn Academy. It was a way for the faculty to prove to the rich parents that they were spending their hard-earned cash well and that, if they felt so inclined, they could always donate more—the school would always highly appreciate it.

It was also the event that led into the October break, meaning that some of the students would return home afterward with their parents. I could sense the excitement, so palpable in the corridors, it was close to overwhelming, the atmosphere almost feverish.

'Do we even need to attend if our parents aren't coming?' I asked Clover. All I really wanted to do was spend the day in our room, gorging on sweets and lusting after Ryan Gosling.

'Yep. It's a part of the required social calendar, the one on Hive. You got a copy on your first day, right?' Clover groaned. 'Have to look like they're treating us charity cases well, after all. No preferential treatment here at Hawthorn.'

'True. So do all the parents attend?' I asked, curious.

'If you're asking if Ollie's and Leo's parents are coming, then yeah, they'll be here,' Clo said, only partially answering my question.

'What about Griff's?'

'Oh, er... No,' Clover mumbled, her eyes shifting around the room. It looked like she wanted to say more but had bitten her own tongue to stop herself. Unlike the other things she wasn't telling me, I could understand this one better. Whatever it was wasn't hers to tell, and I could respect Clover for that.

'Fair enough. I'm just glad my mum knows nothing about today.'

And I meant every word. Thank fuck Cora was none the wiser.

THE MAIN HALL had been transformed from its usual plain area into a fete of sorts. An event like that would be better outside, but the weather in England in October could be a little unpredictable, to put it mildly, so I understood why they were holding it indoors instead.

Everywhere I looked, there were tables set up with teachers stood behind them and each department had its own table. Then there was a long table filled with refreshments along the left-hand wall—a bar of sorts. In the centre of the room were the tables we usually ate our dinner from, all arranged with name cards for each student and their parents. *How fun.* A formal situation.

'Thought there'd be more tables,' I mentioned to Clo, looking around the room. 'Bit of a surprise.'

'A lot of the kids are related. Or like mine, their parents aren't coming.'

Huh. Made sense, I guessed. Rich people *were* popping out children in hopes of business and world domination, yet didn't actually *care* about their children for any other reason.

Guess they weren't much different from my parents—although mine definitely didn't have me for world domination.

The two of us began wandering around the room, taking in the parents and kids who were already there.

'I wonder whose parents they are. Must be one of the younger years,' Clo muttered beside me, looking at a tall, thin couple dressed in expensive fabrics standing by the entrance.

'Huh?'

'The couple that just entered... I've never seen them before. Just odd. Thought I knew everyone.' Clo shrugged and I turned my attention back to the band setting up on the stage. 'Oh wow. Now that's a funky outfit.'

I turned to see the person she was talking about and my heart melted. Fully melted, and the pieces puddled together on the floor in a big wet mess. *Shit.*

'Darling!' my mum called across the hall. 'Oh, how lovely you look!'

Of course she was trying to put on her *posh* accent, which, if anything, just made her sound even more common. She even put an emphasis in the middle of the word lovely, and I cringed so hard, I thought it would never stop.

Andy, the slimy toad, stood beside her, and I realised they'd attempted to dress up for the occasion. By that, I meant they'd brushed their hair and worn clothes without stains. Clothes that were obviously cheap that definitely didn't fit in with the surroundings. Mum had even put on a large red fascinator that clashed terribly with her orange V-neck top, and I was pretty sure my shame levels couldn't go any higher.

'Fuck. What are they doing here?' I asked, bewildered.

'That's your *mum?*' Clover asked, sounding as exasperated as I felt.

'Yep.' I popped the P like so many heroines do. 'How did she find out about today?'

'No idea. Sure you didn't mention it to her?' Clo asked.

'Clo. I haven't spoken to her since I started at Hawthorn. I'm surprised the woman even remembers she *has* a daughter.'

Mum and Andy had made their way over to us, waving and grabbing everybody's attention. Luckily for me, the boys weren't here yet, but it was only a matter of time before they arrived too. There was no way to hide my mum from them.

'Oh, Skylar, darling, I am so happy to see you!' Mum practically shouted, making sure that all those around us could hear her. 'Look at you. You look so fancy. I didn't realise this school was so fancy either.'

'You barely listened when I told you about it, Mum,' I said, my tone flat. In one sentence, the woman who birthed me had shown just how little she paid attention to me.

'I would have remembered if you told me about somewhere as grandiose-ly as this. All you told us was you'd be leaving for school and quitting your job at the shop,' she said.

Of course that's all she remembers.

I chose to ignore her use of the word "grandiose-ly". My mum always invented words and threw them into sentences constantly as if they belonged there—an annoying habit of hers.

I wondered how they afforded to keep the roof over their heads seeing as I was gone and couldn't help with the bills. Knowing them, they'd probably just applied for more government benefits.

'H-how did you know to come?' I asked, looking at them in turn, the feeling of incredulity growing. I could feel my anxiety rearing its ugly head, the sweat rising to the surface of my skin, my nerves climbing, worried that Ollie and Griff were about to enter the hall with their parents and see who raised me. They knew I had a poor excuse of a mother, but knowing something and meeting it were two very different things.

'We got an invite from ya in the post,' Andy said, his beady eyes locking on me, causing a wave of nausea to travel through me.

I hadn't really processed what he did to me the last time I saw him. I came straight to Hawthorn and events at school were more pressing and in my face. But seeing him, hearing him talk, made me want to scream. Or run away and not return until after they'd left the grounds. Until they were far, far away from here.

'That wasn't from me,' I said as I looked Mum in the eye.

I felt confident that I knew who it *was* from, though. It had Odette and her clones written all over it. It hadn't been enough to have people bully me. It hadn't been enough to beat me up. No, they needed to humiliate me in front of the entire school, too.

'It had your name on it,' Mum said, looking at me with a question in her eyes. Maybe she thought I was lying in front of Clover.

'It said there'd be free food and drink here, so obviously we had to come.'

Don't get me wrong, I'm always game for free food and drink. Isn't everybody?

But that was the real reason they'd come. Mum hadn't come to see me or to even see the place her only child was living. No. The two of them had come for the free food and booze.

'Mum. Andy. This is my best friend, Clover,' I said, pointing beside me.

'Hello, darling, aren't you just a dream?' Mum smiled, and I could tell she was putting on her charm. It disarmed people, but I hoped Clo would be clever enough to see through the façade.

'Hey. Nice to meet you, Cora,' Clover said before we shared a look. A look that told me she was bullshitting through her teeth.

One thing I loved about the moment was that Clover didn't suck up.

AN HOUR PASSED with Clover and me making awkward small talk with Mum and Andy, showing them around the grounds and telling them about what we were learning. Not that they gave much of a shit, but there were still another few hours until the sit-down meal and we needed to pass the time somehow. The two of them went to grab another drink—probably their fifth of the afternoon.

'I haven't seen the boys yet. Have you?' Clover turned to whisper in my ear once they returned, both of them holding a drink in each hand.

I shook my head, not wanting to say anything more in front of Mum. She was the type of woman who loved gossip and any talk of boys would definitely pique her interest, and one thing I really didn't want her to know was about Ollie. I didn't know what was happening between us—or if *anything* was happening between us —but I definitely didn't want her to know about it.

'Shit, there they are,' Clover said as she looked towards the door. It was like a scene in a film, that part where everybody turned to see who had arrived at a party, or like when Mr Darcy arrived at the Meryton Assembly. Ollie was standing next to a stern-looking man with grey hair and grey eyes, wearing a dark blue suit. Handsome in an older guy kind of way. From the similarities between them, it had to be his father.

Then there was a stunning woman with her arm in Leo's, brown hair flowing to her waist, wearing a classic black dress with black court shoes. She oozed power and money. Leo looked pretty dapper too, to be fair, in a grey suit and white shirt that helped highlight the intensity of his blue eyes.

Clover gasped at the sight of them.

On the other side of Leo stood his father—another stern-looking rich man who reminded me of a king surveying his kingdom. His hair was the same colour as Leo's and you could see the family resemblance instantly. Griff stood on the end, looking carefree as usual. Carefree and alone.

Ollie and his father both looked over at me, and together they started walking in our direction. *Just wonderful.*

'Hey,' Ollie said curtly, giving me a quick head nod. 'Dad, this is Skylar Crescent. Sky, this is my father, Henry Brandon.'

'Hello, girls,' Henry said, smiling, but his eyes assessed everything, surveying the entire room. I felt a sharp nudge in my side that definitely came from an elbow. An exaggerated cough followed.

Here we go.

'Ollie. Mr Brandon,' I said, reluctance in my voice. 'This is my mum, Cora, and my stepdad, Andy.'

Everybody shook hands and acted friendly enough, but I could see the level of disgust in Henry's eyes. He even wiped his hands after shaking Andy's—which yeah, fair—but it still made me feel crappy inside.

The conversation resembled a shitshow from the start.

'How do you know my beautiful Skylar?' Mum asked Ollie with a cheeky wink. 'Got her looks from me, didn't she?' She was surveying everybody gathered with us. Probably attempting to decipher the cumulative wealth standing in front of her.

'We're in class together,' Ollie replied, curt, completely ignoring the second part of Mum's sentence.

'How wonderful,' Mum said with enthusiasm. 'Andy, isn't it just super-duper that our Sky has made such *handsome* friends?'

The emphasis on handsome nauseated me.

'Course it is, hot stuff,' Andy replied, leering at Mum.

Could this get any worse?

He grabbed Mum's bum in full view of everyone. Mortified, my face continued turning a deep shade of red from overheating. Of course shit could always get worse with those two around.

The group of us settled into an uncomfortable silence, nobody knowing what to say or do next.

Somebody was clearly looking out for me as a bell rang out through the hall, letting the room know the sit-down part of the meal would commence shortly.

'I guess we'll see you later,' I said, being careful not to look Ollie in the eye. 'It was nice meeting you, Mr Brandon.'

'Please,' Mr Brandon said, brushing my arm. 'Call me Henry.'

I smiled, and everybody else began to say their awkward as fuck goodbyes. After it was over, we went our separate ways to take our seats. Mum made a big song and dance about finding our seats, meandering slowly through the tables and reading each name card out loud.

I take back what I said. There was no saviour looking out for me. And I knew that, because when we found our seats, they were at the table with Ollie, his dad, Griff, Leo, and his parents.

Go figure.

As EXPECTED, the meal was awkward as fuck. Barely anybody had spoken after I'd introduced Mum and Leo had introduced his parents, Edward and Lottie. Clover sat there next to me in complete silence, only answering when Lottie had asked her a couple of questions about how her baking was coming along and how her grades were.

The band played throughout, and when we finished the meal, Ms Hawthorn walked out onto the stage. Grumbles went out across the hall, as did a few whispers. I noticed Leo's dad sat up taller and looked interested instantly, but then I remembered he owned this place and was related to the woman standing in the centre, ready to address everybody here.

A projector screen appeared behind her, which could only mean we were going to have to sit through some kind of school bullshit propaganda intended to woo the rich people and entice them to donate even more of their enormous fortunes. How exciting.

'Welcome to Parents' Day, where you are once again able to see how your children and protégés are progressing at this fine institution.' Her grey, beady eyes assessed the room, spending a fraction longer on Clover and me. Or maybe on my mum. Or maybe I was just imagining the whole thing, paranoia getting the better of me. Just because I felt disgusted by her didn't mean everybody else felt the same. A shiver ran down my spine at her words. They sounded so false and pretentious. 'The students of A-Level Media Studies have put together this short film for you. I do hope you enjoy it.'

The lights in the hall dimmed, and the projector screen flickered to life. Images of the school were being shown to a bouncy background beat, then a voiceover started.

'Hawthorn Academy was first established in 1850 by Sir Robert Hawthorn, who hoped the future generations would have the best education money could buy. Still today, this fine establishment does exactly what Robert set out to do.'

Exterior shots of the school played, followed by shots of students sitting in classrooms or out on the field playing team sports.

'Recently, the school has restarted the scholarship fund, in order for those less fortunate to benefit from the connections that can be made here and to obtain the best education.'

My stomach dipped as butterflies started to make a home in there. I wanted nothing more than for that section of the tape to be over quickly. I looked at Clover, who seemed to have the same expression on her face as I did on mine. It was clear from the voice speaking that it had been recorded by Ophelia, which definitely didn't bode well for me.

'The scholarship students fit in well and are a welcome addition to Hawthorn Academy. Although, they do seem to be a little too friendly with the elite business world's future leaders.'

Abruptly, the footage changed.

It changed to a shaky, handheld video recording taken on a mobile phone. Whoever was recording giggled, in that way people did when they were trying to stay incognito and were doing something they knew they shouldn't.

Like the fog on my brain was lifting, I recognised just when the footage was from—and where.

It was from the night of the party in the woods. I could see me and Ollie dancing together on the makeshift dance floor. Then I saw me, on the screen, take Ollie's hand and lead him further into the trees, a soft smile on my face. An even wider one on his.

I knew what came next, and I really thought I might be sick from the butterflies swarming in my stomach, thrashing about and jostling the sides.

How dare they film that? How dare they take a private, intimate moment and taint it? Well, as private a moment could be hidden from a crowd of people. How dare they show that to all of these people?

I was livid in an instant. A hot, burning anger travelled through me, threatening to cause a scream to leave my throat unbidden. But tears were forming in my eyes, near to spilling over at any moment. I sat in silence and watched it unfold along with everybody else, too scared to make a noise. To draw more attention to myself.

Once the content of the footage became clear to everybody in the hall, Ms Hawthorn rushed back to the stage and stopped the tape, the screen returning to white once again. As if it hadn't just shown something so cruel.

Whispers.

The entire hall began to talk in whispers that became louder with every moment. I could hear parents commenting on what they'd just seen. Half of them were angry about the party. The other half were only mad that they'd been made to watch it.

Ollie's eyes met mine from across the table. An angry, yet cold stare that made me pause.

He didn't look sad. He looked furious. I couldn't tell whether it was aimed at me because it happened in the first place, or if it was the fact they'd aired it to the entire school. Not like the two of us discussed it after it happened.

To make matters worse, his father was staring me down with a look of clear disdain. I was a rabbit caught in the headlights. I didn't want to leave the hall and let them see that they'd won. Just because I hadn't seen the girls and their parents today didn't mean they weren't in here somewhere, giggling to themselves with glee. Biding their time. Waiting to see what I'd do. How I'd react.

My mum broke the silence at the table in a way only she could.

'Darling, I wouldn't worry,' she said, a smile playing on her bright lips. 'I used to get up to a lot worse when I was at school. Like mother, like daughter, ay?'

I cringed inside. She even had the audacity to throw a wink in my direction as if that softened any of it.

'Ay.' Andy winked at me too. 'Now everybody knows how much of a slut you are, Sky. Can't hide it anymore, sweetheart.' He leered at me, and all I could picture was his face looming closer to mine, his tongue invading my mouth without permission. That rotten, putrid stench of alcohol clinging to his skin. To mine.

Fuck this. I'm out.

'If you'll excuse me, I must go freshen up,' I announced to everybody and nobody. The table all nodded, and every man but Andy stood when I left. Clover quickly followed me, dashing after me as fast as she could while keeping her decorum. As soon as we made it out of the hall, Clover put her arm around me and steered me to the nearest toilets.

'Those little bitches,' Clover spat, her anger for me etched all over her face. 'I promise you, Skylar, we *will* get them back. Maybe not today, but sometime this year, we will.'

I nodded, still too shocked about the change of events to say anything.

'Although...' Clover trailed off, a cheeky prying look appearing on her face. 'You didn't tell me *that* happened with Ollie.'

I covered my face with my palm. I wasn't embarrassed as such, but I could feel a blush forming, starting on my cheeks and bleeding outward to the rest of my face.

'I know,' I whined. 'To be honest with you, I wasn't even sure it actually happened. After they drugged me, I doubted my own memories. Ollie hadn't said a word afterward about it, so I wondered if I'd just had a super feverish dream as I lay beside him in bed.'

My logic made sense, in my head at least. I didn't want to assume that anything I remembered actually happened, so I'd decided it was best to keep it to myself. But apparently that wasn't possible. Everybody knew the truth thanks to the O girls.

After some deep breaths, Clover and I returned to the hall where the parents were saying their goodbyes. It only occurred to me then that my mum, or Andy, could have said anything while I'd been gone.

I didn't look at Ollie. Or Griff or Leo. I just didn't want to know what they were thinking about me. About the whole *Ollie fingered me, pinned up against a tree* scenario we'd all just watched play out. Not like either of us could deny it when there was footage saying otherwise.

Ms Hawthorn joined the group to say her goodbyes. But her focus was solely on her brother, Edward. Things looked tense between them, but that could be a result of my amateur porn clip. The fact Ollie and I were both sixteen definitely made this even worse. For us *and* the school.

'Miss Crescent,' Ms Hawthorn called out, her voice clear yet hushed. 'I expect to see you in my office first thing Monday morning.' Her eyes narrowed when she looked at me and her lips were pursed together.

'Yes, Ms,' I responded, using my best contrite manner. Couldn't wait for that meeting... *Not.*

'It's been nice to meet you, Skylar. Clover,' Lottie Hawthorn said, giving us both a kind smile that reached her eyes, and I could feel it in my bones that at least one person at the table was genuine.

'Skylar. Clover.' Edward nodded at each of us and left with his wife, Leo following closely along behind them.

'It's been a pleasure,' Henry said, his face telling me it had been the complete opposite of a pleasure, but nobody called him out on it. He and Ollie left together, and although I didn't look at him, I could sense Ollie glanced back at me before he left the hall.

That left me, Clover, and Griff standing with my mum, Andy, and Ms Hawthorn. An odd mix of people who didn't all need to stand together any longer.

'Mum, it's been fun,' I lied, hoping she couldn't hear in my voice just how much I wanted her gone. If she knew I wanted her to leave, she'd stay longer just to spite me. She'd done it in the past, so I knew it was something she'd do. 'Glad you could make it, though.'

'Oh, me too, darling. I'm so glad to have found out my daughter is just as much of a skunk as I am,' she said, slurring her words. Pretty sure she meant to call me a skank, but not like I was going to correct her. The copious amounts of free booze she'd drunk today must be finally catching up with her. I hoped they could get out of here before one of them did something terrible. Or both of them.

'Been lovely to meet you two,' Clover said, also lying through her teeth, the pain in her eyes at her words giving her away. 'Have a safe journey home.' As an afterthought she added, 'You have a lift home, right?'

'Yep. The school sent somebody to pick us up and they're

taking us back too,' Andy said. He went to hug me goodbye, but Griff grabbed me out of harm's way and put his hand out for Andy to shake instead.

'It's been real. I'll walk you to your car.'

Honestly, I could kiss him. Instead, I squeezed his shoulder, making it clear I appreciated the way he'd stepped in for me. I'd never told Griff much about my life before Hawthorn, but I reckoned he had an inkling. Especially after today.

He'd been quiet all day, which was unusual for him, taking in his surroundings and listening to the conversations going on around him, but barely joining in.

'I'll meet you two back up at your room.' Griff winked at us, sweeping his arm towards the door, and followed after my mum and Andy. Neither of them walked off in a straight line. *Eurgh*. All I needed now was for them to be sick before reaching the car, and my day of humiliation and shame would be complete.

Luckily for me, roughly an hour later when Griff made it back to our room, he didn't have any puke stories to share with me. I took that as a plus. According to him, they'd got in the car with no real fanfare but had promised to return when next invited.

Believe me, if I have anything to do with it, the two of them will never set foot on school grounds ever again.

Ollie never came to my room to talk to me that night. He didn't even send me a text. Nice to know he cared about me enough to wonder about me, wonder about how I was coping with what had gone down.

Oh, wait.

He didn't.

Sixteen

'NEW GIRL, you're coming to the swim meet tomorrow, right?' Griff asked.

'I didn't know that there was a swim meet tomorrow?' I asked, confused. 'What the fuck even happens at one of those?'

'A lot of races,' he joked. 'You mean Ollie didn't tell you?' His eyes widened dramatically and his mouth fell open in a comedic way. Prick.

'Not being funny, Griff, but Ollie would have to *talk* to me in order to tell me about it.'

'Ouch. Right. I'm sure he's just busy with his dad. You know he's staying at the Hawthorn residence on the grounds tonight along with Leo's parents.'

'Once again, Griff. He'd have to talk to me for me to know shit.'

'Got it. Anyway, there's a swim meet and your boy is going to kill the competition.'

'By *your boy*, do you mean Ollie or you?' I asked, laughing at his use of words. For starters, Ollie was definitely not *my* boy. But if Griff was talking about himself, then I found that quite sweet in a best friend kind of way. He may have originally started to hang out with us to rile the other two boys up, but I genuinely believed that Griff was just as much our friend as he was theirs.

'Oh, definitely me,' he replied. His cocky grin was charming as all get-out. Not for the first time I wished it was Griff I had a connection with, but all I could see him as was a brother. A big-headed, egotistical, older brother who knew what buttons to push and when.

And I wouldn't have it any other way.

THE CONVERSATION with Griff the night before was how I found myself on Sunday afternoon, sitting in the stands of the swimming pool alongside the other students and parents. Clover begrudgingly sat beside me, but only because Griff and I had begged her to come and keep me company. Apparently, she didn't want to witness Leo's smug grin when he won yet again. *The Sect* were the best on the team and I hated to say it, but I was excited to see just how decent they were.

Even if I still thought Ollie was a dickhead. I'd woken up to a text from him that didn't make me feel much warmer towards him.

DON'T BE MAD. WE'LL TALK LATER. I ACTED LIKE A DICK.

With a roll of my eyes, I responded with a quick **K**. After all, everybody knew what a "K" text meant.

'How long does a swim meet last?' I had no idea what to expect. My old school didn't have a swimming pool, therefore, no swim team.

'Too long,' she replied in a weary tone.

Basically, she was no help at all.

The first few rounds of races were for the younger years, and those races made me realise that swimming wasn't my favourite sport to watch. Not that there were many sports I enjoyed watching, but still. I was the kind of girl who would watch the Olympics, and that was about it. Maybe the odd Wimbledon, because you know, tennis could be pretty exciting to watch, and the entire country got behind it every June. Then promptly forgot about it again by July.

Finally, it was time for Ollie and Griff to compete. I knew that Ollie hid a hot body underneath his uniform, but seeing him like this, his chest in all its glory, was truly a sight to behold. A genuine work of art. He had a six-pack, so defined, that the only image going through my mind was that of him with water dripping down into every crease. Don't get me started on his legs. They were long and pure muscle. Even the tiny shorts they wore weren't enough to deter me. It ensured that my mind was now imagining Ollie's dick. He had that V—you know, the one that led to the main event. Ollie was an Adonis, plain and simple, and I had to wipe away some drool before Clover spotted it. It did piss me off a little that I wasn't the only person witnessing this. There were too many eyes on him, and for a split second, I considered stabbing the eyes out of *The Set* just so they couldn't see him.

Despite my best efforts, I've turned into a basic, petty, horny bitch.

Griff stood beside Ollie, and his body was not one to be sniffed at either. He had wide shoulders and I could see that he was sporting a six-pack *and* an Adonis belt. Even if I saw him as a brother, I could still appreciate that he worked hard on his body. All three of them did, spending a lot of their time training in the pool or in the school gym. It had paid off, that was for damn sure.

I couldn't tell you much of the race itself. I didn't know the length they swam or the stroke or anything like that. All I could tell you was that Ollie won. Every single race he competed in, he won by at least an entire second each time. The crowd cheered and hollered as he brought home yet another medal and another trophy for the school. Griff came second, and he seemed super chuffed with the result. His cheeky façade never faltered, his smile constantly in place. He even winked and dabbed in our direction when collecting his medal. *What a loser.*

The last race of the day was Leo's. According to the whispers around me, *his* was the race to watch. Ollie had been amazing, but Leo was something else entirely. A new species, almost. It also helped that Leo had an impressive body. The whole disinterested thing totally worked for him in a competitive setting, too. He stayed calm before the race, and he flew through that water, leaving the opponents in his wake. He was spectacular and I could totally see him one day competing at the Olympics, or something major like that. Leo was just *that* good.

'Fuck me, Clo. Did you see that?' I asked, astonished.

'Yep,' she replied bluntly. She looked so sour on the outside, but she couldn't fool me. I saw her face while he was racing. She was as tense as everybody else here, and I could totally tell her bum cheeks were clenched just as tight as mine from start to finish. 'He's good.'

'Good? Clover, did we just watch the same thing?' I asked in disbelief at her indifference. I couldn't believe she was being such a dick about it all.

After the race, Ollie and Griff went and showered off the chlorine, then came and joined us.

'Did you see how fly I was?' Griff asked the two of us, his dimples pressing in.

'Fly? Who even are you?' I laughed, shaking my head, knowing that Griff was doing his best to get a rise out of us all and be the comedian like usual.

'I was definitely better,' Ollie said, all smug, and you could tell he really believed in his own hype. Which, yeah, he *was* good, but nowhere near as good as Leo.

'Of course you were, handsome,' Griff said, hugging him. He gave him a big kiss on his cheek. Ollie groaned and wiped it away instantly, but that action made Griff even more determined to land more kisses on Ollie. 'You were legiterally perfect.'

'What the fuck is legiterally?' Clover asked, piping up.

'You know. It's a mix of legit and literally. I made it up,' he said, his face bright.

'No way!' I gasped. Arms came around my waist, hugging my back into a hard chest. Instantly, the smell of Ollie's vanilla and tobacco scent I loved so much filled my senses and I breathed it in. I made a note to find out what it was because I wouldn't mind spritzing my clothes with that smell. He turned me to face him, his blue eyes looking into my soul.

Honestly, this boy gives me whiplash.

'I'm sorry, Sky,' he said, his face blank but sincere. 'I should've tried to speak to you last night.'

'You think?' I said, not wanting to make it too easy for him, but knowing I would let him off. 'You could've tried to talk to me.'

'I know, but I didn't know what to say. And then there's my dad.'

'What about your dad?'

'He's a prick. That's all you need to know.'

'Okay...' I knew he was evading my question, but the glint of apology in his eye distracted me from asking more.

'So do you forgive me?'

'Don't do it again, Ollie. It made me feel cheap and unimportant.'

'Promise,' he said, then placed a soft kiss on my forehead. 'Oh, while I remember. I want you to come to my birthday party next Friday night.'

It wasn't a question. It was a demand, slightly softened with a smile.

'It's your birthday next week?' *Shit.* What on earth would I get him, and why had he only just mentioned it?

'On Halloween,' he said, smirking. 'Costume party in the woods.'

'W-wow. Okay,' I said, trying not to focus too hard on the woods part of the sentence. I looked at Clo. 'Guess we need to put on our thinking caps.'

She nodded but didn't look happy about it. I assumed she knew Ollie's birthday was coming up, so not mentioning it was a bit of a dick move. They must have celebrated last year—even if Clo hadn't been invited, she would've heard shit, right?

'Come on, babe. Let's go watch a film and get some pizza in.' Ollie's arm came around my shoulder, pulling me to him as he walked us away from the pool entrance.

'Let's go.' I smiled as the four of us headed off towards Ollie's room. As we walked past the door to the locker room, I spotted Leo standing there, looking straight in our direction.

Dead eyes staring at us, no light in them.

Seventeen

MONDAY MORNING, I made my way to Ms Hawthorn's office. Butterflies sat heavy in my stomach, and I worried about what she would say to me regarding the whole video debacle. All night my nerves were in overdrive. The others tried to take my mind off it all, but nothing they did helped. It pissed me off that Ollie wasn't being summoned into her office. He was as much a part of that video as me.

Ollie and Griff both offered to come with me, put on a united front, but I decided to come alone. I didn't need them fighting my battles for me—well, not all of them anyway.

I knocked on the large wooden door, the sound reverberating throughout the empty hallway. While I waited, my eyes looked around the hallway, and when they landed on the spot Ollie kissed me in, I snapped my gaze away.

Stop thinking about him.

'Come in,' Ms Hawthorn called from the other side of the door.

I took in a deep lungful of air and pushed the heavy door. Or at least it felt heavier than the last time I opened it. Maybe it was my mind that felt heavy.

'Sit,' she said, curt, her face hard.

The chair cushion squished underneath my weight, the legs gave out a groan, and I looked at Ms Hawthorn across the desk. I maintained eye contact for as long as I could, but her stare intimidated me. My eyes flitted down to the table, where they focused on a wood swirl.

'Miss Crescent, you are on your last warning here at the academy.' Her eyes narrowed. 'I will not have you besmirching this fine establishment.'

'I—' I found myself saying the first thing that came to mind, but not knowing where to go with it, my word tapered off.

'If any reports of further misconduct come my way, I must expel you. Do you understand me?' she asked, and I nodded instantly with a gulp. I couldn't get expelled. I couldn't go back to my previous life.

'O-of course. It won't happen again, Ms Hawthorn.'

'See that it doesn't,' she said, dismissing me, her eyes instantly going back to the paperwork in front of her.

I stood and walked out slowly, trying to close the door softly behind me. I wondered if the other girls were being called into her office today, but I highly doubted it.

If they continued to bully me, the school would expel me. Yep, sounded about right.

EVEN A WEEK LATER, I was still feeling a little raw about everything that had happened on Parents' Day. That my mum and Andy had been there to witness my humiliation definitely made it one thousand times worse. Or maybe the humiliation they gave me from being there was worse. Either way, it was all pretty shit.

It was on Sunday night, as Clover and I were sitting in our room in silence, both trying to work on our homework, that Clover turned towards me with a determined look on her face. Things had been tense between us ever since Ollie had invited us to his birthday slash Halloween party.

Clover didn't want to go. And I did.

'Sky, do you really think it's a good idea to go to the Halloween party on Friday?'

I rolled my eyes at her words. We'd been having a variation of the same conversation on and off for what felt like forever. I got her point. The last party in the woods I'd attended I was drugged and recorded. *Not an impressive track record.*

'Honestly, I don't know. But it's Ollie's birthday, and I said I'd be there.'

I smiled, thoughts of Ollie filling my mind. Things were going well between us and I didn't want to snub his birthday party or fuck up the tentative truce we'd come to. Also, everybody knew that Halloween parties were an excuse to dress up as a fantasy, and I had the perfect costume idea for Clover and me.

'Also, not like I can disobey. Ollie invited me and he's a member of *The Sect*, so I can't exactly turn it down without having more mean shit happen to me.' We both knew my excuses were pretty hollow at that point. The girls had backed off after Parents' Day. Believe it or not, they'd got in shit with Ms Hawthorn. It wasn't hard for her to figure out Ophelia's voice on the voiceover, plus the O girls all took media. As far as I knew from what Griff told me, none of them were threatened with expulsion for their actions. Their parents did sign the big checks, after all.

The truth of the matter was I wanted to go to the Halloween party. Yeah, there was a small part of me that knew it could all come crashing down, or that the girls could target me again, but it was a chance I was willing to take. The way Ollie had looked at me this week was real. I could feel it deep down inside of me. And we needed more time alone in a non-classroom setting.

'I get it. I really, *really* do. I've been there, you know. I was in your position once,' Clover said, staring at me intently. I nodded at her, but I was already tuning her out. She meant well, but there were only so many times you could hear your best friend rail on the guy you liked without it pissing you off. 'Last year was really hard for me. I didn't have any friends, and if you think *The Set* is bad this year, they're nothing compared to last year. The two older girls last year made Ophelia and Oralie look like kittens.'

'Right, you mentioned last year before, but, Clo, you've never even told me what happened. Not like they've targeted you this year?'

I had thought about it once or twice. Clover kept hinting at the events of the previous year and how bad school had been for her, but never went into much detail when I asked for more details. Definitely not enough for me to form an opinion. People barely acknowledged her this year, except for when she stuck up for me. I found it hard to believe that their shitty treatment of her stopped overnight. *Something doesn't add up.*

'That's exactly it!' she exclaimed, raising her voice. 'I don't know why it all stopped and I have a terrible feeling about all of this, Skylar. Proper.'

'I know you do. I promise I hear you, Clo. But I can't explain it. I just feel it in my gut. I need to go to this party and I need you there by my side. You're my best friend,' I said, hoping my last sentence would sweeten the deal a little, grabbing her hand in mine.

'I don't want to see Leo,' she rasped, her words filled with so much venom.

I rolled my eyes, hard. It was tiring constantly hearing about Leo and how Clover wanted nothing to do with him. I could see in her eyes, though, that she wasn't giving me the full story. She'd fobbed me off with half-hearted excuses, or she changed the subject to me and Ollie, or even to Griff's jokes, never letting me see the truth. I'd had my suspicions ever since Leo's mum had treated her so kindly. They totally knew one another a lot better than mere acquaintances.

'I know, Clo, and I'm not asking you to.'

'But you are, Sky. Just by wanting to be at the party with Ollie, and Griff, you're asking me to spend time with Leo because at some point you know he'll join us. He'll stand there like the dickhead he is and smirk and judge me with his fucking judging eyes,' said Clo, who, talking of judging eyes, was giving me a very judgemental look.

I couldn't help myself.

I burst into laughter at the way her face had gone as red as her hair. I could feel her anger, but it was also super clear to me that Leo got under her skin because she still had feelings for him.

'Just admit it, Clo. You've got feelings for the guy. Nothing to be ashamed about.'

'That's where you're wrong. Sure, I have feelings for Leo Hawthorn, but you can bet your arse the feelings I have for him are ones born of hatred,' she said vehemently.

I knew that Clo meant her words, I could feel it in the air, but I also knew that she was living in denial. The sexual tension between the two of them was thick and one day they would combust. Something had to give, after all.

'Okay, okay,' I said to placate her. One thing I had learned about having a best friend was that sometimes it was just easier to agree. Easier to have them think you were with them 100 percent even if inside you disagreed with them. 'Course that's what it is.'

'It is, I promise,' she said, a little too indignant, but I didn't push it further. I could tell she was getting close to the end of her patience on the subject—and with me.

'Eurgh, fine! I'll tell you a little. Take this and run with it, 'cause I don't know if I'll talk about it again.'

I nodded straight away, biting my tongue until she stopped talking. I didn't want her to stop before she'd fully opened up.

'Basically, I've known Leo ever since I was really young, but that isn't what's important. What matters is the fact that Leo, Ollie, and sometimes Griff, alongside *The Set*, made my life hell last year. Every single thing I did, they would make it bad. Turn it into something to be ashamed of. They would ruin my food, my exam results, destroy my homework, and constantly write shit about me in the toilets or on the Hive,' she said, looking into my eyes.

I stayed silent, thrilled she was finally talking, and not wanting to do anything to ruin it or throw her off.

'They threw rotten food at me, locked me in the dark caretaker's cupboard, spat at me in class. Literally, they did anything they could to isolate me. I had no friends and nobody to turn to or to keep me sane and tell me that I was worth more than the shit I was getting from them.'

Tears shimmered in her eyes, threatening to fall. Talking about it had brought it all up for her again, and I felt her pain. Felt how much the experience had affected her. The girls had targeted me since the start of the school year, but I had Clover and Griff to help me keep afloat. Their friendship meant that I could keep myself from dwelling on it. I couldn't imagine how I would feel if I was alone. Plus, the start of the school year was less than two months ago.

'That's why I'm finding this U-turn on Ollie's part so hard to understand and come to terms with. Griff too. At least he apologised to me the other night, after Parents' Day. I think the girls showing that footage of you and Ollie really made him see how his actions last year affected me.'

I knew she wanted me to talk, to say something, to agree with her or accept her stance on Ollie and his actions. I wasn't sure what I could say, though. What they'd done to her was beyond shit and shouldn't have happened. But I also couldn't take in everything she said and completely change how I acted around Ollie, Griff, and even Leo because of it.

'I'm glad Griff came to his senses. I get why you feel the way you do, Clo. I promise, I'll be sensible. But c'mon, a Halloween party sounds like exactly what we need right now.'

Clover grumbled, but I thought maybe she sort of agreed with me, even if only slightly.

'Fine. We'll go. But if any funny business takes place, don't say I didn't tell you so!'

'Thank you! You won't regret it,' I squealed, clapping my hands together.

And she didn't. Couldn't say the same about myself, though.

Eighteen

FRIDAY NIGHT ARRIVED and I was terrified.

My friendship with Clover had been tense ever since Monday when we had our mini argument about the party—well, if you could call it an argument. I had to prove that everything was fine. That nothing would go wrong and we'd be laughing tomorrow about what a splendid night we had and just how wrong she'd been about everything. Positive thinking and all that.

Luckily, Clover came around enough to agree to dress in a couple's costume with me. I was giddy just thinking about it. We went for Betty Rubble and Wilma Flintstone. Clover was the perfect Wilma with her red hair and I donned a short black, bobbed wig for the evening that covered my silver hair entirely. It completely changed how I looked and made me feel all mysterious. Like a new person.

The only change we made to the costumes was that we were a super *dead* Betty and Wilma so we covered the dresses and ourselves in fake blood. That cheap stuff you find at party shops that will probably stain our skin and be a bitch to wash off. We both looked super cute but also super sexy—Halloween goal accomplished.

When I caught Clo's eye across our room, I couldn't help thinking about how Leo would react to seeing her dressed like that. She looked like the perfect girl for a caveman like Leo. Even if the two of them were trying to convince everybody that they hated one another, I just couldn't believe it. One day it was going to blow up in everybody's faces and I would happily be the one telling her "I told you so."

Maybe my outfit would spark something between me and Ollie, something more than what had already transpired between us. The kisses and stolen moments we shared had been life-changing. *Okay, a bit dramatic there, Sky.* But they *had* been life-affirming.

Fuck, I'm even making myself *want to vomit.*

CLOVER and I made our way over to the clearing in the woods around eight. We didn't want to get there too early and look desperate, but we also didn't want to arrive too late and have all the premium alcohol be gone. It was always a fine line, or so Clover told me.

'Sky, you still have time to bow out of this, you know. We can go back to our room and nobody will even know we were here,' Clo said as we got closer to the clearing.

'Why would we do that? It's Ollie's birthday, and I won't bail on that.' I shook my head and rolled my eyes at the same time, which was pretty impressive actually if you asked me, but it also probably made me look slightly possessed.

I was a bit bored with Clo's overprotectiveness. I knew she was trying to look out for me, and I totally got why after she told me a little of what happened to her last year, but I couldn't help getting frustrated. Just because you understood something, it didn't mean it couldn't piss you off.

'Plus, it was a direct order from a member of *The Sect*, so not like I can disobey. I don't want to give the dicks here more reason to harass me.'

'And since when have we cared what the other dickheads who go here think?' Clo asked, one eyebrow raised.

'Well...' I didn't want to say anything to upset her, but you know, I also wasn't gonna lie to the girl either. 'Clo, we've always cared. Even if we don't admit it out loud.'

'Bullshit!' she exclaimed, throwing her arms in the air. Catching my eye, we both burst into a fit of giggles. Leaves rustled ahead of us, signalling someone's arrival.

'There you two are!' Griff shouted at us from up ahead. 'I've been waiting for you to get here. Now the party can truly begin.'

He hadn't met us at our room because he'd helped set up with the other members of the "ruling class." He hadn't told us what he was dressing as because according to him, he wanted to *knock our socks off*.

Griff came towards us, dressed as Prince Harry, which made me smile super wide. Of course he was. With his hair, I should have known he would have dressed as Harry. Actually, I was slightly annoyed that I hadn't guessed it.

'Fuck me. You two are looking mighty fine tonight. I must say, my lady luck, that I would love to add to your pearl necklace,' he said with a wink. That cheeky grin was ever present on his face. Sometimes, though I'd never admit it to him—imagine the reaction—there were times I wished it were Griff who I liked. But even though he *was* hiding a buff body, I just didn't fancy him. At. All. There was something so carefree about Griff, and his cheekiness always felt infectious, but I'd sold my heart to a beast, and I didn't think I would get it back anytime soon. Unless he was the one to throw it back in my face.

'Oh, ha-ha,' Clover responded, raising her eyebrows at him, almost daring him to repeat what he'd said. 'You are such a filthy bastard, Griff, I swear.'

I couldn't help my guffaw. His filthy jokes often caught me off guard, but I was tickled more than usual.

'You wound me, kind lady,' Griff said, smirking at Clo. 'Or maybe it's the fact that my *pearls* aren't the ones you want. Ay?'

'Oh, piss off,' Clover said, shoving him on the shoulder, causing him to stumble backwards a little. For a split second, his smile slipped, but it was back within moments. She laughed at him, and I knew that none of Griff's words affected her. 'Are you taking us to the party or what?'

'Follow me, ladies. The night has just begun.'

<hr>

THE PARTY WAS LIVELY by the time we made it deep enough into the woods to where the party was. I spotted Ollie and Leo straight away, both of them with an O girl on each arm. I quickly looked away before Ollie saw me staring. What on earth was he doing with Ophelia of all people hanging on his arm?

Griff didn't leave our side to join them the way I thought he would.

Recently, Griff was choosing us over them a lot, but I didn't want to think about what that may mean. I wanted to believe he was doing it because he liked us both, but there was another part of me that thought he could have been asked to spy on us by Ollie or Leo—or both. Especially after what Clover told me the other night.

Pumpkins, fake cobwebs, and gravestones decorated the wooded area as far as my eye could see, giving the entire place a super creepy feel. There were ghosts and witches hanging from the trees, and the alcohol table over on the right-hand side was covered in skulls and other spooky items. I wasn't sure from where I stood, but it looked as if there were fake eyeballs floating in the large punch bowl placed in the centre of the table. I didn't even want to guess at what was actually in the punch bowl, but it was probably something a lot stronger than all the alcohol I'd had in my life put together. After what happened the last time I came to a party, I was going to make sure I only drank from an unopened bottle. I wanted to remember the night. I didn't want to wake up with no knowledge of what went down.

I looked over at Ollie, who was dressed as Batman. He looked better than any Batman I'd seen before; in actual life and in the movies. The mask fit his face perfectly, really highlighting his blue eyes and full lips. The lanterns lighting the area put everyone into shadows, making the place look sinister and spooky, setting the ultimate Halloween party vibe. A chill shot through me and goosebumps prickled on my entire body, but that could be due to my dress being super short and revealing and the air being super cold.

Leo, dressed as The Joker, stood with Odette by his side, dressed as Harley Quinn. If I didn't hate her, I would totally love their couples costume. It was really well done, and they looked great together. Something I wouldn't mention to Clover.

Shit, I thought as I spotted the large table overflowing with presents, a five-tier cake standing proud beside them. *Fuck*. I didn't get Ollie a present. I had no money, and I wasn't even sure I could get him something he didn't already own. I also wasn't going to be one of those cliché bitches who gave their virginity as a present. I wasn't ready for that, and I hated the whole bullshit idea that virginity was a gift to give in the first place. Gross.

On the edge of the party, Ollie and Leo still stood looking over at us, ignoring the girls at their sides, but not making a move to come over to us.

'What's up with those assholes?' Clover asked, nudging Griff in the side, nodding in the boys' direction.

'Who even knows, girly tots. They've both been acting strange recently,' Griff said, his tone conspiring.

'Strange as in…' I trailed off, waiting for him to pick up the dropped thread.

'Can't explain it.' He shrugged. 'Ollie barely has anything to do with Leo or the girls outside of swimming or classes now. But we're all super tight, so it makes sense that he's talking to him. It's his birthday, after all.'

'Yeah, that's fine, but why the fuck is Ophelia hanging off his arm looking like a tramp?' Clover asked, voicing what was going through my mind. Ophelia, dressed as some kind of slutty nurse, stood next to Ollie, practically pawing at him. Maybe she was a zombie nurse? Honestly, I didn't want to get close enough to find out. I was just happy that she wasn't in a couples costume with Ollie. That wouldn't fly with me.

Even though the two of us weren't a couple or anything, I still felt like there was something brewing between us. Bubbling away in the cauldron, soon to boil over. Something I intended to find out more about later in the evening—if the boy ever came over to talk to me.

Shit, I could go over to him. Be bold. Take the bull by the horns and all those cliché sayings. Walk over to him and demand his attention. And I planned to go...

After a drink.

'Let's get a drink,' I announced to Clo and Griff, turning to face the two of them.

'Or we could wait here,' Griff said.

'Why?'

''Cause your boy's coming over.'

I turned on the spot. Ollie had untangled himself from Ophelia and was walking over to where the three of us stood.

Guess I wasn't getting that drink first.

Nineteen

'HEY, BEAUTIFUL. YOU LOOK KILLER.'

His words covered me, like honey dripped on my head, travelling down to my blood-soaked toes. His blue eyes locked on mine before trailing up and down my body, taking in every inch of me.

Ollie looked as if he wanted to eat me whole.

'I look dead. So less killer, more like I bumped into a killer,' I joked.

'Well, you're definitely the best dead girl I've had the fortune of meeting,' he said.

'Is there any good fortune in meeting a dead girl?'

'Depends on the occasion,' he bantered back. His top lip rose on one side. 'Right now, I'd say it's a great thing.'

He leaned down and kissed my cheek. The kiss promised more, his lips grazing my skin briefly, leaving a tingling heat in their wake.

'You scrub up well too, Clo,' Ollie said through gritted teeth. Probably not all that genuine, but I could tell he was trying for me, which I appreciated.

'Thanks, dickhead. S'pose you don't look too bad,' Clo replied.

'That must have hurt, Clo,' Griff piped up.

'It really, really did. But I thought I'd try and be kind. You know, it being his birthday and all,' she said, a wide smile on her face, turning to look at Ollie. 'Plus, my girl seems to see something in you, so don't fuck it up.'

'Thanks for that.'

'She's not wrong, dude. I'll be pissed if you fuck it up, too. You've got an angel there,' Griff said, wrapping his arm around my shoulders, squeezing me close.

'Griff, you are such a cutie patootie,' I cooed, reaching up and scratching under his chin like you would a child. 'Remind me to give you a shoulder massage the next time we watch films together.'

'Hey!' Ollie interjected. 'Where's my shoulder massage?'

'You never give me any!' I shrugged. 'Plus, Griff is my boy.'

'I see how it is,' Ollie said and tickled me on my side, causing me to laugh and detach myself from Griff's arm. 'I'll be getting you back sometime soon, New Girl.'

'Well, as lovely as this is to watch, I want to get fucked up,' Clover announced, taking Griff's hand and leading him towards the table with the large punch bowl. Ollie had stopped tickling me and moved to look me in the eye, tucking a piece of the wig's hair behind my ear, away from my face.

'Do you want a drink?'

'Only if it's unopened. Don't want a repeat of last time.'

He nodded. 'Trust me, Sky. That won't be happening again.'

'So you know who did it?' I asked, wondering if he'd been keeping a secret from me. Would it not happen again because he'd told the people responsible to knock it off? Or because he thought he was above it all?

'No...' He shook his head. 'But I made it clear that if any harm comes to you, I'll make whoever is responsible pay.'

I knew he wasn't telling the whole truth. His eyes were flitting around, not focusing on one spot, and when he looked back at me, he was fixated on a spot over my shoulder rather than me.

'Okay...'

'Let me go get us some drinks and then we can dance, yeah?'

I agreed and off he went to the table where Clover and Griff were still standing. Ollie shared some words with them, then made his way back to me, holding two bottles; one was beer and the other was some kind of alcopop. Three guesses as to who was having what.

Drinking when dancing, while difficult, was also a lot of fun. We were laughing and joking around with one another in a way we never had before, and a smile was planted firmly on my face. Ollie had loosened up, and the only explanation I could think of was that he was more drunk than I realised. No matter the reason, I enjoyed seeing a side of him I'd never witnessed before. He seemed more like Griff in a sense. Carefree. As if a weight was lifted off him somehow, and I was so happy that I came here tonight. Clover's warning was a distant memory. It almost seemed stupid that I'd been so apprehensive about tonight.

As we danced, I could feel every ridge, every muscle, and I just wanted to lick him all over.

'You are hot as fuck, Sky,' he whispered in my ear, causing tingles to erupt all over my body. 'This outfit is honestly amazing.'

'It w-was my idea,' I said, quite proud of myself. I wanted to pick something that nobody else would choose. Nothing worse than being dressed the same as all the other basic bitches or the O girls. It was my first time attending a fancy dress party, so I wanted the most original outfit I could think of.

'You chose well,' he said, sending a wolfish smile my way. 'You look amazing. I really wish I could peel this dress off of you.'

'Maybe if you play your cards right, mister, you could,' I whispered, a flush filling my cheeks. Flirting with Ollie was fun, especially as I was the one instigating it. He'd said a lot of shit to me in the past that was borderline flirty and a lot that was borderline *not*. It was rare that we spoke so freely in a back and forth with both of us as active participants.

'It really must be my birthday.'

I laughed and hugged him tight to me, leaning up to instigate a kiss between us. One I felt certain was our best yet.

THE ONLY DOWNSIDE to a party in the woods was the complete lack of toilets. I tried my best to hold it in all evening, but I'd hit that point. Hit that peak and I knew I was about to break the seal and potentially ruin the rest of my evening, but I couldn't help myself. I needed to go.

I walked in the direction of the trees, away from the rest of the crowd, wandering off on my own. I told the others where I was heading, and I was pretty sure they heard me. Clo had nodded at me, at least.

Once I could no longer hear the sounds of the party around me, I found a well-hidden tree, away from everything. I quickly peed, then stood still for a moment, not ready to head straight back to the party. I was having such a good time, but I needed a minute or two alone to process it all. Rifling through my bag to find the packet of tissues I put there—I'd learned from the last time—my fingers brushed against a folded piece of paper.

Hm. Don't remember putting that there.

Knowing me, I could have put it in my bag forever ago. It was super rare I cleaned my bag out, and I always wanted to joke about how it reminded me of Mary Poppins's magic bag, but I'd never had any friends to joke about it with. Huh. Must remember to use that line with Clover sometime.

I giggled to myself. *Man, I'm funny.*

Maybe I was more drunk than I realised. Knew I should have eaten more at dinner, but my nerves had got the best of me.

Anyway, the paper.

I pulled it out of my bag and read it, smiling with each line.

> **Little One,**
> **Meet me in the Pool House at Midnight.**
> **I want to ring my birthday in with you.**
> **And only you.**

I looked at my phone. The time was a quarter to midnight, and I was a good ten minutes away from the pool house, so I knew I needed to hurry to meet him on time. There was no guarantee I'd find the piece of paper he dropped in my bag, so I wondered why he never mentioned it to me. Probably wanted to be all mysterious and romantic or some shit. I supposed if I hadn't found the note, he would've just taken me to the pool house himself.

Stumbling my way through the trees, I headed to the pool house with one thing on my mind: to kiss Ollie at midnight.

I made it to the pool house with a minute or two to spare and quickly made my way inside. Unable to see him in the entrance hall, I walked into the pool room itself. Ollie loved swimming and being beside the water, so it would make sense that he would wait for me there. He'd told me once it was a place he felt at peace.

The way the water in the pool moved, and the way the moonlight hit it through the window, made the room look super cool. There were no words to describe it, but the reflection of the water looked so pretty, so mesmerising. In my drunken state, I thought it was one of the most beautiful things I'd ever seen.

I stopped and stared. Taking in the tranquil feel of the water.

Walking around the edge, I got lost in my own thoughts.

I hope Ollie doesn't expect me to sleep with him tonight.

I hoped I hadn't given him the impression that I was ready for that, even if I had joked with him earlier about peeling my dress off. *Fuck.* Had I fuelled the monster? Unleashed a beast that wanted me to the point he wouldn't listen to what I wanted?

No. Course not. *Stop being so fucking stupid, Sky.*

Maybe one day I would be ready to have sex with Ollie, if things continued to progress the way they currently were.

Lost in my thoughts, I jumped when I heard Ollie enter the room. The door slammed behind him, and the noise reverberated around the large room. Each footstep echoed, the water and the large ceiling causing every sound to amplify, but I didn't turn around. It felt intimate. The tension building between us. A midnight tryst was so romantic—and super fucking sexy.

His breath touched my neck and he took off my wig to brush

his fingers through my hair. The touch was hard, as he pressed down into my scalp, putting pressure there. I tingled all over.

His hands rested on my back at the bottom of my spine. It felt familiar and private. Intimate.

His hands pushed forward, and I flew through the air, entering the pool with a loud splash.

The water rushed up around me, entering my ears, my nose, and my mouth. I thrashed around, trying to make my way back up to the surface, but I couldn't. The fight to stop myself from opening my mouth was taking up most of my energy.

A hand gripped the top of my head. Holding me down. Forcing me under.

Fuck. Water filled my mouth. I tried to get away, but there was no escape.

I couldn't breathe. My vision spotted, darkening around the edges, and a sense of déjà vu hit me.

How have I ended up here?

My mind slipped away.

Maybe a little sleep would be okay.

Twenty

'SHIT.'

A faint voice swore above me. I shivered, and I felt even worse than I did after they drugged me at the party in the woods. What was it with me and Hawthorn parties?

All I could think was that I did *not* want to see Clover soon. She'd undoubtedly tell me I told you so.

'Can you hear me, baby?'

I was certain it was Ollie's voice, but confusion filled me because he never called me baby. My ears were clogged, as if still underwater, and I couldn't reach him from under the weight of it.

Ollie! I called in my head. *Ollie!*

'Baby girl, I really need you to answer me,' he pleaded. 'Or just open your eyes for me.'

I'm trying!

My scream was trapped inside my head, yet I wanted so desperately to reach him. To open my eyes and see what was happening around me. Figure out why I felt so cold; so wet. I knew when I opened my eyes, I would be hit with a light so bright, I could see it through my eyelids.

'Ollie, dude, we need to call an ambulance,' Griff said urgently. His worry hit me straight in the heart. I didn't want to cause him to worry. I doubled my efforts, trying even harder to open my eyes and reassure him that I was all right.

'I'm with Griff. Stop being such a massive dick and do the

right thing,' Clover pleaded, causing a sharp pain to stab through my heart. The two of them had grown to mean so much to me in such a brief space of time. If nothing else came from the scholarship, I would still be so glad I took my place here because of them. Shit, oxygen clearly was leaving my brain. I was starting to get sappy.

I needed to knock that off, fast.

Wake. The. Fuck. Up.

'Call an ambulance and everybody will know our shit,' Ollie growled.

'Maybe he's right,' Leo said. For once, he didn't sound bored. Although, he didn't exactly sound worried either. He sounded interested.

'Not you too, Leo,' Ollie snarled, but then his tone softened. 'Baby, it's me, please open your eyes.'

Almost as if a switch turned on in my brain—or, you know, the fact I needed to take a deep breath—I sat bolt upright. Coughing and spluttering up water, gasping in an attempt to take in deep lungfuls of air. I was right in thinking the light was going to be far too bright.

I was beside the pool, surrounded by Ollie, Leo, Griff, and Clover. Clover's makeup was streaking down her face, the black mascara marks showing her despair. Griff had his arm around her shoulders, looking sombre.

Leo looked like hell. I'd never seen him show much expression outside of boredom, but he looked anything but bored when his gaze locked on mine. His hair was wild, as if he'd been running his fingers through it and pulling it in every direction. It tugged at my heart. Maybe he cared a little more about me than he let on.

Ollie was the last of them I focused on.

If I thought Leo looked like hell, then Ollie looked like he'd been living there for the last year. He'd taken off his Batman mask, his face pale and sickly looking, as if the worry had seeped into his pores. He moved as if he was going to hug me, but I darted back out of his reach. Somebody had tried to drown me, and Ollie was the person who wanted to meet me here in the first place. He was the only reason I was there.

I had to be cautious.

'Get away from her,' Clover bit out. Her face transformed from that of somebody upset to that of somebody who was burning up with anger, an accusatory look in her eyes. 'You did this to her.'

'What?' he shouted so loud that I flinched.

'You! I can't figure out how, Oliver, but I know you're the reason for this.'

'Wow. How did you reach that conclusion?' His tone was as cold as ice, filled with derision.

'Don't talk to her like that,' Griff said.

'Lay off her? Dude, she's implying I had something to do with this!'

'Sky must feel similar because she just moved away from you, bro,' Leo said. He moved closer to me. 'I'll take you to the hospital wing.'

I went into his arms and let him pull me to my feet. For some reason, he was the safer option. The guy who barely spoke to me was the one I sought out for comfort.

'Don't walk away, Sky. Or at least let me take you,' Ollie said, almost begging me, but his eyes didn't match his tone as they flashed with anger.

'No, I'll g-go with Leo,' I said, my body breaking out into shivers.

'And how are you going to explain this?' Ollie asked Leo.

'I'm a Hawthorn. I don't exactly *need* to explain this,' Leo replied in his most haughty tone.

'Oh, using Daddy's name once again. That's rich,' Ollie spat.

'Let them go,' Griff said, still holding Clo, as he looked at Ollie, trying to make him back down before turning to Leo. 'Go on, bro. Go make sure our girl's okay.'

Leo nodded before the two of us ambled away, leaving the other three standing beside the edge of the pool. Ollie and Griff were still growling at one another, but I couldn't hear what they were saying. It sounded like Ollie was professing his innocence.

Shame it seemed to be falling on deaf ears. Including mine.

THE HOSPITAL WING looked no different from when I was there last and I let Leo do the talking with the head nurse. She looked rather worried at having a soaking wet dead Betty Rubble and a harried-looking Joker in the room with her.

The nurse checked me over, and I lay down on the bed she assigned me, as she wanted me to stay overnight so they could monitor me. I got comfortable, prepared to be there until morning, and tried not to think too hard about the whole nearly drowning thing.

'Thanks, Leo,' I mumbled and smiled tentatively at him. 'You didn't have to bring me here.'

'Yeah, Sky, I did,' he replied, looking at me. I waited for more, but it never came.

Instead, he got comfy in the seat next to my bed and stayed silent, slumping down, not intending to move soon. I was trying to understand his motivation, but I couldn't figure it out for the life of me. Other than the odd occasion where I bumped into him in empty hallways, I'd spent little time with Leo. Nothing one-on-one.

It made me feel like a child, too scared to talk, not knowing what to say, and too embarrassed that I would mess up somehow.

An hour passed. We must have fallen into a very light sleep as a commotion somewhere else in the wing startled us both awake. Somebody was shouting and throwing items around.

Great. Ollie, Griff, and Clover must have arrived.

'Skylar! Skylar!' Ollie called. My name got louder the closer he got, and when he flew through the curtain surrounding my bed, he looked frantic, like he'd been trying to get away from Griff and Clover for a lot longer than he'd wanted to be. 'Skylar, I promise I didn't do this to you.'

'Calm down, bro,' Leo said. He stood, raising his hands at Ollie to keep him back and away from me. 'The nurse said to stay calm and not distress Sky too much.'

'Since when have you known what's best for Sky?' Ollie asked. His tone was filled with suspicion, like Leo and I were hiding something from him. 'You two don't even talk to each other!'

'Just leave it, Ollie. Say what you've come here to say and then leave so Skylar can rest.' Leo's words were definite and his tone brooked no argument.

'Skylar, believe me. I wouldn't do that to you,' Ollie said. His eyes bored into mine, causing the opposite effect of the calm he was trying to instil. 'What were you even doing at the pool?'

'You asked me to meet you there,' I said. 'You left me a note in my b-bag.'

'No, baby, I didn't. You must have left your bag somewhere and somebody played a mean trick on you,' he said, attempting to placate me or convince me I was wrong. The same way he did with when I was drugged.

I didn't take it off once, I thought, but didn't voice it out loud. I shook my head at him instead. *A mean trick? Bit of an understatement.*

'Then they must have slipped it into your bag when you weren't paying attention,' he tried again to give a plausible solution.

'It's a bum bag, dude. There's no way somebody could have slipped shit in there without her noticing or at least feeling it,' Leo said, sounding bored again, but this time he wasn't directing it at me.

'I swear to you, Oliver, that I would have n-noticed.'

He was making me feel small, and I didn't like it one bit.

'What did the note say, baby?' he asked.

'To meet you at midnight, to ring in your birthday.' I smiled faintly at him. 'Happy birthday, Ollie.'

He smiled in return and took a couple of deep breaths to calm himself down. I reckoned seeing me in the hospital wing, alive and safe, made him feel slightly better.

That was when Clover and Griff burst through the curtain.

'That nurse woman is such a job's worth,' Griff grumbled. 'Wouldn't let us through as you two douche canoes are already here. Tried to tell her that Sky here would prefer us two, but she wasn't listening to a word of it.'

'I'm happy you're here,' I said as Leo allowed them to get close enough to hug me. I felt overwhelmed at the amount of love surrounding me. 'I was just telling Ollie and Leo about the note I got.'

'What note?' Clover asked, her eyebrows furrowed, and she looked just as perplexed as everybody else.

'To meet Ollie at the pool at midnight.'

'Okay...' Clo said, tapering off. 'Why didn't you tell any of us you were going there?'

'I found the note when I was going to the toilet. It seemed pointless to walk back to you when I could head straight to the school.' I shrugged. It had made total sense to me a couple of hours ago. In hindsight, it wasn't the best decision I'd ever made, but I'd made it and there was shit all I could do about it.

'Makes sense.' Clo shrugged, gazing off into the distance.

'How did you know I was there?' I'd been wondering about it ever since Ollie was so adamant it wasn't him, because if he didn't send the note, then the pool wouldn't be the first place to look for me.

'We didn't. We were searching the trees for you for a while, but then Leo came over to us and told us to look at the school. The pool house was the closest building from where we exited the trees,' said Clo, her eyes narrowing when she mentioned Leo's involvement. It made sense they searched there first, as the pool house was closest when I exited the trees, too.

'Which is pretty suspicious, Leo,' Ollie said in an accusing tone, turning his glare on Leo.

'Dude, I heard the girls talking about it. They'd spotted Sky walking off alone and were hoping she'd come to harm,' Leo said with a shrug. Ollie might not, but I believed Leo. He sounded sincere to me.

'So proof that they had something to do with it,' snapped Clo.

'Not really, Clover, but nice try,' Leo said, the words clipped. It was strange to hear Clover's name said so formally. So stiff.

'Got any better ideas, twat?' she asked. Her eyes glinted with challenge.

'No. But I know it wasn't the girls. They wouldn't have the strength,' Leo sneered back.

'Funny that. They definitely had the strength when they were beating on Skylar in the bathrooms a few weeks ago,' Clo said, her voice rising with every word she uttered.

The room went silent. Everybody nodded, seeming to agree that the girls' motives seemed shady. Even if they weren't solely responsible, I felt sure they knew more than they were letting on. But something deep inside of me knew that it wasn't one of them in the pool room. I could tell from the footsteps, from the height of the person standing behind me, that it was a guy. The scent, the strength, there was no way a girl had done this.

'Do you still have the note, Sky?' Griff asked, reaching for my hand and squeezing it tight. I squeezed his back, the warmth filling me, as it travelled up my arm and into my body.

'It's in my bag. Or at least it should be,' I told them. My bag had gone into the water when I did, so I wasn't sure how much the contents had suffered.

Clover grabbed my bag and had a good root through it, finding the note. It wasn't completely untouched by water, but it was still legible. The four of them passed it around, inspecting it thoroughly, trying to figure out where it had come from and who had written it.

The nurse came along, having realised that none of the people who came back here had returned.

'Miss Crescent needs her rest, so you need to be leaving now,' she said, her manner brisk and no-nonsense.

Instantly, Ollie and Leo disputed who was going to stay with me. I stayed quiet because honestly, I wasn't getting in the middle of those two. I also didn't know which one I *wanted* to have with me. It would make sense for me to want Ollie nearby, but there was still a tiny part of me that was cautious of him.

Clover and Griff accepted that they were being kicked out and leaned down to give me an awkward hug simultaneously. It was the most awkward group hug I'd ever been a part of. Actually, it was the *only* group hug I'd ever been a part of.

'See you tomorrow, Sky,' Clo said.

'We'll be here bright and early, New Girl,' whispered Griff.

With a smile, they left together, leaving me with Leo and Ollie.

They both stayed, neither of them accepting defeat. The silence between the three of us was so fucking loud, but nobody broke it.

Eventually, I fell asleep to the sounds of their breathing. Just as I was about to drift off, I heard four words. Quiet, hanging there in the darkness.

'I'm so sorry, Sky.'

But I wasn't sure which one of them said it.

Twenty-One

OLLIE

'WHAT THE FUCK did you just say to her?' My blood boiled. The anger I felt toward him in that moment was ready to be unleashed, a black cloud swarming above us all.

'Nothing important.' Leo leaned back from where he'd been hovering over Sky and looked at me head-on, daring me to ask him to repeat his words. I wanted to wipe that fucking smirk off his face; break his nose and watch the blood gush out.

But I wouldn't do that.

Knowing Leo, he'd enjoy it.

'Want to explain this shit to me?' I gestured between him and where Sky was sleeping, pissed I even had to ask.

'Explain what?' he drawled, looking at me with his disinterested eyes.

In all the years I'd known him, it was rare for excitement to fill his eyes.

'Well, there must be some fucking reason you're still sat here at her side?' My fists clenched, wondering what bullshit he was going to spew in response. The wanker's expression didn't change.

'I care about her,' he said, raising his eyebrow at me.

Care about her my arse, I thought but didn't voice it aloud. Leo didn't care about much. It was one of the reasons we were close and had been since birth—well, that, and the fact we share blood.

'Fuck you,' I spat. 'You've got an agenda here.'

'Good luck trying to get your head around that one, dickhead.' Leo shrugged his shoulders, no longer looking at me but staring intently at Sky in the hospital bed. She appeared so peaceful in sleep, you wouldn't know that her night had gone the way it had.

'Then tell me something. Who did this?' I asked, hoping he'd know more than I did. 'Cause, fuck, I knew nothing here. I hated flying blind. Somebody had attempted to drown Sky, and I didn't have a fucking scooby who had done it.

Hawthorn was *my* school. Nothing happened here without one of us knowing about it. The twats here had no idea just how far our reach truly was, yet we'd heard nothing. Knew nothing about who may have been planning to harm her. *Kill* her.

'No clue, mate,' Leo replied with a half-hearted shrug, still staring at Sky. If I didn't know better, I would think he wanted her, but that couldn't be the case.

There was no scenario where that could ever happen.

She's mine—for now.

'The note, then. Any ideas?' I scratched the underside of my jaw, contemplating who could have given Sky the note. For it to have been slipped into her bag, somebody had to have got close enough to do it, but the question was: who?

At no point had I left her side the whole evening. There had been no opportunity for anybody to get to her. I'd made sure of it.

The Set had it out for her, and I didn't want them getting to her—not at my birthday party, at least.

'God, you're a massive cunt.' Leo's bored drawl took me out of my thoughts.

'Explain that to me,'

'You know how. Don't act like you give a crap about her when we both know that's bullshit.'

'Stop talking,' I demanded. Skylar could wake up at any time, after all, and I didn't need her to hear any of Leo's lies. She'd just started to trust me, and I wanted to keep that trust as long as I could. Already I knew I'd have to grovel for how the evening had gone, and I had fuck all to do with it.

'You afraid?' he growled, his lip curling up at the side.

'Of you?' I scoffed. 'Hardly.'

'Maybe you should be,' he said, his threat clear. I'd never been scared of the fucker in my life and I highly doubted that would change.

'You figure that, how?'

'There's a lot more at work here than we know, clearly. You think the girls did this?'

'I have no fucking clue. Seems too intelligent for them. Especially without a ringleader,' I said, mulling it over. I doubted the girls could pull off a stunt so impressive, definitely not without help.

'Who's saying they don't have one?' he asked, but then laughed. We both knew who called the shots around here, and it wasn't Odette—or any of her cronies.

'Touché.'

Both of us fell silent, our anger dissipating into the air. Neither of us wanted to be mad at the other. *Fuck, in this life there are bigger fish to fry.*

After ten minutes of silence, Leo looked over at me again.

'Do you *like* her?' he asked, nodding his head in Sky's direction.

'Course I like her,' I replied nonchalantly.

'You know what I mean.'

I rubbed my face in frustration. I knew what he meant, but honestly, it wasn't something I'd thought of too hard. Yeah, she was hot as fuck. Yeah, I wanted to rip her to shreds and then put her together again, just to destroy her more. But did I like *her*?

'Fuck knows, mate.'

'I do,' he mumbled.

'Do what?'

'Like her. I know the plans, but she's got spirit.'

'She's got something,' I responded, trying to brush his words off. I didn't need Leo interested in the new girl. Fuck, I didn't need to be interested in the new girl. I wanted nobody interested in her.

'It won't save her,' Leo said ominously.

'Right, *nothing* will save her.'

Glad we both agreed on that point, I slumped further in the hard chair and crossed my arms across my chest, attempting to get comfy enough to sleep. Across the bed, I saw Leo doing the same. Fuck, the chairs were hard as rocks.

'You could leave,' I told him.

'Why would I do that?' he asked, once again raising his eyebrow and tilting his lip up. Fucker.

''Cause you don't need to be here,' I muttered, irritated by his presence.

'Neither do you.'

'She's mine,' I growled.

'For now,' he drawled.

'For now,' I conceded.

Twenty-Two

MY ONE NIGHT in the hospital flew by.

I didn't wake in the night, and by the time I woke, both Ollie and Leo were quiet.

'How are you feeling?' Ollie asked when he saw my eyelids flutter awake, coming closer to my side. 'Do you need anything?'

'I'm okay, thanks,' I whispered, blinking at the harsh lighting.

'I'll be off.' Leo stood from the plastic chair, not looking at either of us, but addressing us both. 'See you later.'

I nodded, and Ollie didn't respond to him, too focused on making sure I was okay. As he fussed around me, trying to call the nurse to get me breakfast and a glass of water, my phone screen lit up on the table next to me.

It was from Leo.

I mean it, Stutter. Call me if you need me.

A smile covered my face, but then a frown came and wiped it away. I was curious about Leo's motives. He always acted so secretive and he clearly didn't want anybody to know that he was texting me. I could understand why he wanted to avoid conflict with Ollie and Clover, but I got the impression they weren't the only reason he wanted to keep our friendship of sorts on the down-low. I hid my phone in my bag so Ollie wouldn't see it over my shoulder.

Once he found the nurse and got me a drink of water, I was more than ready to leave the hospital wing, whether Ollie wanted me to or not. I needed my own bed.

'Can we go?' I jutted out my bottom lip and batted my eyelashes, hoping it would have an effect on him. There were no mirrors in the room, though, and I probably looked like a mess with makeup streaked down my face and my hair clinging to my scalp.

'New Girl, I promise you I didn't do this,' he said. Oddly, I didn't hate it when he called me New Girl anymore. At first, it was a slur of sorts, but ever since he and Griff started to use it affectionately, it felt different.

I tilted my head to look up at him.

'Ollie, please, can we do this later?' I asked, my eyes finding his. 'I'm so tired and I just want to be in my own bed.'

'Let me at least walk you back to your room.'

'Okay.' It was easier to concede to his request than it was to fight him on it. I wasn't lying when I said I didn't have the energy.

Nearly drowning takes a lot out of a girl.

He walked me back to my room, both of us staying silent, and only when we arrived back did he talk. The moment I got the door open, I stepped into my dorm, using my body to cover the entrance so he couldn't slip around me.

'Can I come over later tonight?' he asked, pushing his luck.

Clover, who was hovering by her bed, scoffed at his question, telling me without words she wouldn't stay quiet if he came to our room later on. Not like I had the strength to have the two of them getting into it again, especially when my head felt the way it did. It stabbed like an axe was attempting to split it in two at any moment.

'How about I come over to you tomorrow if I'm feeling better?' I asked, tentative, not wanting to wake the beast I'd glimpsed before.

It was a fair and solid compromise. Plus, it meant we could talk with no distractions, and no Clover talking louder than me, or worse, talking for me.

'Okay,' he conceded reluctantly. His lips brushed against the top of my head and the resulting tingles it gave me travelled down to my toes. A quick moment of pressure, fleeting, and gone just as fast.

'I'll text you. I promise,' I said, closing my dorm door in his face.

I turned around to find Clover standing directly in front of me, blocking the path to my bed. The bed I'd desperately dreamed of all night while trapped in the lumpy and uncomfortable hospital bed. I gritted my teeth as I prepared myself for whatever she felt the compulsion to say next.

'You can't trust him, Skylar,' she blurted out, looking fit to burst.

'Why n-not?'

'Because he sprinted off ahead!' I could tell she'd been holding it in all night, gutted she couldn't get me alone earlier. 'We arrived after he did, by at least five minutes.'

'Okay...' I said, unsure what else to say. I understood where Clo was coming from, and sure, I hadn't realised they didn't all arrive together, but still. We were talking about Ollie. Dark and mysterious Ollie. Didn't mean he was my would-be murderer. 'How long does it take to fall unconscious from drowning?'

'Like I bloody know,' Clo replied, her phone appearing in her hand in an instant. I knew what that meant. Google. Clo loved to Google search everything. For example, the two of us would be watching a film, and I'd innocently ask what other projects an actor starred in, and she'd have a list of their entire filmography in less than one minute flat.

'So?'

'A-ha!' she exclaimed, her eyes shining in triumph. 'Two minutes. It takes two minutes to become unconscious. I *knew* the fucker had the time and the opportunity.'

THE NEXT DAY I was outside Ollie's door, trying to build up enough courage to knock and alert him to my presence. The butterflies in my stomach were causing havoc, and I felt sick. For five minutes I stared at the door with a blank expression, and I could sense the other kids who were passing the hall were staring at me.

On Sundays, students could relax and visit with friends without repercussions from the staff that monitored the halls. Griff had told me that the only reason he and Ollie could visit with us on weeknights was because they were a part of *The Sect*, and therefore above the average school rules. It had its perks, for sure. The pizza delivery being the main one in my eyes.

Man, I love pizza.

I would never understand how people didn't just want to eat it every single day. I would if I could. Easily. Happily.

No more procrastinating, distracting thoughts. Time to lift my hand to the black door in front of me.

I'd never noticed the ominous and foreboding nature of Ollie's door before. Showed how observant I was.

I needed to sum up the courage to hear Ollie out. To listen, and not just assume the worst because all the pieces looked bad. *Really bad.* I didn't feel scared of being alone with him, exactly, but a sense of dread was rising in my gut with every second I put off seeing him. When Ollie lost his temper, he frightened me, enough to create a seed of doubt.

Finally, I knocked on the door in the pattern Clover and I used. If it annoyed him, then tough shit.

I heard him moving around inside of his room straight away, and I barely waited ten seconds before the door opened wide and he pulled me close to him in a tight hug.

'Sky, I was so worried last night,' he said, squeezing me even tighter to him. So tight, I could hear his heart pounding underneath my ear. All around us, I could feel his fear as if it were a tangible thing. 'Please don't do that to me again.'

'I can assure you I don't intend to,' I said, my voice muffled by his taut pecs. I chuckled, as if any of it was my choice in the first place. Oh yes, Ollie, I just loved nearly drowning. *Real highlight of my night.* 'I've had enough happen to me this year to last a lifetime.'

He let me out of his warm embrace but grabbed my hand to pull me further into his room, kicking the door closed behind us. Then, as if he remembered himself, he went back and locked it.

I raised my eyebrows at the action, giving him a stern look. Not sure it translated too well, though, as he was looking at me in the way I imagined the wolf looked at Little Red Riding Hood. Like he couldn't wait to eat her whole.

'Expecting something?'

'Nope,' he said, a genuine smile on his face. 'Just thought you'd like some privacy. Knowing that dickhead Griff, he'd happily burst in here to check on you. The fact that it would irritate me would be a bonus for him.'

I laughed at the thought of it, but I'd give him that one. Griff would totally try and do something like that. However, unlike Ollie, I knew Griff was keeping Clo company. Leo also knew I was with Ollie because I texted him to tell him. He hadn't responded, but the two blue ticks had appeared, so I knew he'd seen my message.

'So...' I trailed off, looking around at my surroundings. Ollie's room always looked barely lived in, unlike my room. Should I sit on the bed? Or was that too presumptuous?

I didn't want him to assume I'd forgiven him and we could just skip straight back to where we were before everything happened. With sure footsteps, I chose to sit on his gaming chair instead. It gave me enough distance from him and I could breathe without his scent overwhelming my senses. Just being in his room was hard enough.

Once I was comfy, and he'd seated himself on the edge of his bed facing me, I demanded, 'Talk.'

'Where shall I start?'

'I've heard the beginning is a good place. You know, usually,' I smarted.

'Well, aren't you a comedienne? I meant more, what do you wanna know?'

'You wanted to talk to *me*, remember?' I said, acting a bit bitchier than usual, but feeling entitled to it.

'I wanted to prove to you it wasn't me,' he said. The way he looked at me, so contrite, made me want to just believe him with no further grovelling. My heart panged at the sincerity in his tone, but my head told me not to be so stupid. I couldn't put my faith in a contrite look. 'I promise you, I didn't give you that note. I had no fucking idea where you'd gone and I was so worried that somebody had hurt you.'

'Somebody did hurt me.'

'I know'—he winced—'and I'm sorry.'

'Why apologise if you had nothing to do with it?'

What did he have to apologise for?

'I'm sorry that I didn't stick by your side the whole time,' he clarified.

I could tell he meant his words. That he really was pissed at himself for not staying with me the entire night.

'If I had, none of this would've happened.'

'You know, Ollie, when you say shit like that, it makes me think you had something to do with it.'

'Right,' he huffed. 'I knew this would happen! You've let Clover get inside your fucking head.'

'What?' I asked, shocked by the change in his tone, by his eyes glinting with cruelty. 'W-what does that even mean?'

'You heard me, Skylar. Clover has been turning you against me, twisting shit like she always does.' His eyes narrowed in disgust.

'No, Oliver, she hasn't. Am I not allowed to form my own opinions?'

'Of course,' he said, brushing away my words as if that wasn't the real problem here. As if he hadn't meant it in the way I heard it. 'It's just suspicious timing. Even you can see that, surely.'

'Can see what?'

'You *know* what,' he said imploringly. 'You've been attacked, and now Clover's turning you against me. How well do you know her, really?'

'Seriously?' I asked, shocked at his implication. 'For starters, Clover has said nothing! Second, I'd like to think I know her pretty well, thank you very much.' I was on a roll. I took a deep breath. 'How well do I know *you*, really?'

'Explain what you mean. Now!'

'I just don't know where I stand with you. Like. Not at all.'

'Where would you like to stand?' he asked, his tone lighter. Amused.

'W-what?' The way he was looking at me caused a shiver to run down my spine. He was still standing, coming a little closer with each second.

'What do you want from me, Sky?'

I ran my fingers through my hair and looked everywhere in the room but at him. Ollie was somebody I couldn't figure out, and as much as I felt attracted to him and wanted to be with him, I also wanted to run far, far away from him.

The way I felt for him made me feel like a young teenager with their first crush. And in a sense, it was true. Ollie was my first crush and I was still a teenager, with little experience to fall back on.

Should I be bold? Tell him what I wanted, for real, and hope he wanted the same thing?

Fuck it. I was going to take a leaf out of a confident person's book and go for it. I wanted so badly to believe him, to give the attraction growing between us a try, that I threw caution to the wind.

'I want you.'

He blinked, looking thrown back that I'd gone for it. Bet he didn't think I had it in me. Or thought I'd stutter my way through something, as a flush grew on my cheeks.

'I want you,' I repeated, louder this time.

Clearly he'd never expected me to be so open and honest with him. To just come out and say what I wanted, damn the conse-quences.

'Shit, Sky. That isn't what I thought you were going to say,' he said, looking flustered, a blush on his pale cheeks.

'So…' Ollie said and slowly made his way towards me. I was frozen. Unable to move, trapped by his gaze. 'How about we make this official?'

'Huh?'

'How do you feel about being my girlfriend?' he asked, standing in front of me, and I looked up at him, falling into his blue gaze. I felt like his prey.

'S-sorry, what?'

'Be my girlfriend.'

It wasn't a question.

Twenty-Three

'BE YOUR GIRLFRIEND?' I sputtered, raising my eyebrow at him.

'Yeah. That's what you want, isn't it?'

'Right…' It was what I wanted, but was it what *he* wanted? I wasn't going to agree to be in a relationship with him if he was only doing it to appease me, to make me happy. 'But do you want to be my boyfriend?'

He cocked his head and reached out to grab my hand in his. I let him take it, but stayed silent, waiting for him to say something.

'Why would I ask if I didn't want it?'

'I don't know,' I said with a defeated shrug. 'And technically, you didn't ask.'

'What did I do then?'

'You demanded.'

Ollie scoffed, rubbing his thumb on my hand, in an effort to soothe me. It wasn't working, though.

'Skylar, please, will you be my girlfriend?'

'Well, seeing as you've asked me so nicely,' I said, poking my tongue out at him.

'Is that a yes?'

'Yep. Now stop digging.' I laughed, and he did the same. It was a lighthearted laugh, and it sounded different from the others he usually gave. It felt like praise. Like he was the sun and I was basking in his rays.

'How shall we spend the rest of the day?' he asked, dragging me from the chair so we could lie on his bed.

'Not like that,' I sputtered. Just because he was my *boyfriend*, it didn't mean I was going to give up the goods just like that!

He laughed, bright and airy. 'No, Sky. I just want to be comfortable. Standing up and looking down at you wasn't much fun.'

'Okay,' I conceded. 'But no funny business, Mr Brandon.'

'Whoa,' he said, letting go of my hand to put his flat palms towards me. 'I promise. I just want to cuddle and watch a film, that's all.'

'That's what they all say,' I joked, narrowing my eyes in faux suspicion.

'Skylar,' he whined. 'Why are you making this so difficult?'

'Got to get my kicks where I can,' I said, finally following him and getting on top of the bed with him. 'Let's just watch a movie and order pizza.'

'Isn't that your solution for everything?'

'Yep.' I nodded. 'And I don't see it ever changing, so you better get used to it.'

He laughed, pulling me close to his side. 'Whatever you say, babe.'

'CHRISTMAS BREAK IS COMING UP.'

'Right...' I trailed off, adjusting my position on the bed to face him. The two of us were in his room on his bed watching a film in the way we spent most evenings together since becoming an official couple.

We may have only been dating for a short time, but spending time with him was the best part of my days. He made me smile. He made me laugh. He also made me question myself and my life and the way I'd just accepted people treating me badly.

'And I was wondering if you had any plans.'

'For Christmas break?' I thought about it for a second and shook my head. 'Nope. Guess I'll spend it home alone while Mum and Andy do their own thing.'

'Well...' He rubbed his finger up and down my arm, giving me chills. 'Would you like to spend it with me?'

'Just you?'

'No,' he said with a small smile. 'Griff, Clo, and Leo are game for coming too.'

'Clo's agreed to come knowing Leo's gonna be there?' I raised my eyebrow in disbelief.

'Not quite.' Ollie winced. 'When Griff asked her, Leo didn't plan on coming with us, so of course Clo agreed.'

'Then what happened?'

'Leo changed his mind when he heard Clo was coming.'

'Of course he did.' I laughed, imagining the joy on Leo's face when he heard he could torment Clo. 'Why would he pass up an opportunity to piss her off?'

'Right,' Ollie agreed, his smile returning to his face. 'So you'll come?'

'Duh! Not like I want to spend time with Mum and Andy. Thanks for inviting me.'

'No problem,' he said, inching closer on the bed, leaning his head down to mine. His breath fanned the skin on my neck, making my nerves thrum underneath my skin and my pulse skyrocket. He pressed a lingering kiss on my neck, and my breath left me in a short burst. Being on his bed with him always felt a little like tempting fate, and when he kissed me like that, it only worsened.

I met his bright blue eyes and could see the longing in his gaze —his want of me. The corner of his mouth tilted up in a teasing, yet lazy smile. His thumb began to softly stroke the skin on my stomach underneath my shirt that had risen up when I moved onto my side. In every spot his thumb touched, my skin burned, and my stomach was filling with more butterflies the lower his thumb travelled.

'That blush on your face is beautiful,' he whispered. Even his tone lowering was enough to send my thoughts into the stratosphere. 'You're beautiful.'

'Thanks,' I hushed out, holding my breath for whatever was to come next.

He placed another kiss on my neck. Then another. And another.

'Is this okay?' He hummed in between kisses and I nodded, unable to speak. He leaned his forehead against mine and the connection felt good, safe, and a rush of feeling flooded my veins.

I tilted my face forward, pressed my lips against his, and really kissed him in the way I loved. All tongues and lips. Sensuous and serious, I lost myself in the kiss, as my body heated with a longing for him. I couldn't believe he was mine to kiss. To touch.

My hands went to his sides, and I grabbed his hips, pulling him closer to me.

He ran his tongue along my lower lip, and his fingers began trailing up and down my abdomen, holding me close, while my hands continued to grip his hips.

Fuck, Ollie knew how to kiss.

He grabbed my leg and lifted it to drape it over his hip, pulling my core even closer to his hard dick, the thin material of my underwear and his trousers the only thing keeping us apart.

A shiver ran through my body.

Every time we made out on Ollie's bed, things began to feel more serious between us, and my mind went to the idea of losing my virginity to him.

And I knew I wanted to.

Just not yet.

I wasn't ready to go so far with him, even though I knew it was going to happen. It was inevitable. A forgone conclusion.

Ollie moved his hands to the buttons of my shirt, undoing each one with quick fingers, and I wondered how many shirts he'd undone before to have such a skill with it. Once my shirt was open, he reached around my back and undid my bra clasp one-handed.

I broke our kiss so I could move back from him and get rid of both my shirt and bra, throwing them onto his bedroom floor with abandon.

When I moved back towards him, Ollie took one of my nipples into his mouth, while he massaged the other. A cry left my lips and I was in heaven. His tongue circled me before he took a tentative bite to test my reaction. He knew I loved it, though, so he bit harder the next time.

It was Ollie who broke our connection next, moving so he could take his shirt off, so that our skin could touch. His eyes locked with mine, a hungry look that captured my soul within them, and I licked my lips in anticipation.

'You're fucking beautiful,' he said in a hoarse whisper. 'I could stare at you for days.'

'Right back at ya,' I said, a smile playing on my lips before I pressed my lips on his once more. Our kisses became more frantic, and my fingers went to the button on his trousers, wanting to get him down to his boxers. My skirt had ridden up, and things were escalating fast.

'Ollie,' I moaned against his lips, stopping my hand from travelling into his trousers. 'We need to stop.'

'Why?' he asked, his hands bunching my skirt up around my waist, leaving my lace underwear available to him.

'We should cool down.'

He let out a small sigh but didn't argue with me. He removed his hands from my skirt and wrapped one around my back to pull me closer. My head buried into his bare chest, and I breathed in his scent. A kiss was placed on my head, and both of us lay there, breathing in small pants, willing our heart rates to calm down.

He grabbed a blanket from behind him and put it over our bodies, covering us from the world.

'Do you want to put your shirt back on?' he asked, and I shook my head.

'We can stay like this,' I said. 'Unless it's too distracting for you?'

'Feeling your skin against mine is one of my favourite things,

New Girl. I think I can keep my hands to myself...' His smile was wolfish. 'Unless you don't want me to.'

I smiled in return, my breathing back to its normal pace.

'Thanks for being cool about this.' Then I felt I needed to clarify what I meant. 'For being cool about the fact that I'm not ready yet to... you know.'

'No rush, Sky. You'll let me know when you're ready. There's no need to thank me.'

I placed one final kiss on his lips and swooned at how much of a gentleman he was being about it all.

'Now, let's watch a film,' I said.

'Your wish is my command.'

Twenty-Four

CHRISTMAS BREAK CAME AROUND SUPER FAST after that, or at least it felt like it did.

Clover believed *The Set* were responsible for both my drugging and drowning, but Griff and Ollie were adamant that they knew the girls had nothing to do with it.

Apparently, the rulers of the school had their own set of rules that us mere plebeians had no knowledge of, and the girls wouldn't have been able to make such enormous steps without two of the boys agreeing. They'd stressed that they would never agree and clarified that Leo didn't have that kind of power alone.

I'd never mentioned Leo giving me his number to any of them. Well, thrusting his number on me by texting me first. It felt like something I should keep a secret. Something for only me to know, and because I knew this, I didn't think Leo would've set the girls on me. No matter how many times Clover tried to convince me otherwise.

Christmas Day itself was Griff's birthday, which I reckoned had some bearing on the fact that he thought he was God's gift to the world.

Honestly, I was pretty sure he'd even joked to me recently that he thought of himself as the second coming of Christ. I'd just rolled my eyes at him and laughed.

The four of us were spending the holidays at Griff's parents' estate as they weren't there and the entire mansion would sit empty otherwise. Griff had never mentioned his parents, so maybe it wasn't that unusual that they weren't here to spend Christmas, or his birthday, with him. They hadn't attended Parents' Day either, and nobody had questioned it. It was like one of those unspoken things between everybody.

To be fair, if my mum had the opportunity to leave me alone for my birthday, she most definitely would. What I did know was that Griff was an only child and that without Leo and Ollie, his childhood would have been extremely lonely. It made me realise that Griff's cheeky, cheery personality probably had something to do with his upbringing. He used humour as a coping mechanism for something darker.

My relationship with Ollie had grown so fast, and it still felt super surreal to me that I could call that gorgeous specimen of a human my boyfriend.

Clover was still trying to make me at least question him about the drugging and the drowning, but I wouldn't bite anymore. He was the one who had been there for me after both instances; who had looked after me and ensured that I was okay. He'd never given me an actual sign that it could have involved him. Okay, he'd acted shady and had been hot and cold with me ever since I'd met him, but Clo was trying to imply that was because his ocean blue eyes and his wide smile blinded me. Which yeah, they definitely did. But that wasn't why I trusted him. Not completely. His actions after the fact just didn't add up to him being the person responsible. The way Clover told it, though, I should believe that Ollie held me under the water one minute and then gave me mouth to mouth the next. *Insert eye roll here.*

We'd arrived at Griff's estate a few days ago and I still couldn't believe I was spending Christmas in such an elegant, yet slightly intimidating house. Mansion. Whatever you wanted to call it—it was huge.

Christmas Eve Eve came, and we were all sitting together in the cinema room and a conversation started about what film we should put on next. There was a huge projector screen at the front, and sofas and reclining forest green chairs dotted the rest of the room. A popcorn machine was in a corner, as was a slushy machine, and the wealth those items alone still made me pause. At home I was lucky we owned a toaster.

Clover, Leo, and Griff were sitting on the corner sofa. Ollie's arms were wrapped around me as we sat separate from the others, together on one of the love seats. His arms were warm around my waist, anchoring me to my surroundings. My anxiety around him had definitely improved since we'd become a couple.

'I want to watch *Polar Express*,' Clover announced to everybody in the room.

'No way! That film's for Christmas Eve itself. How about *The Nightmare Before Christmas*?' Leo asked, his tone bored as per usual, but him speaking at all gave away the fact that he was about to get some entertainment.

'That's a Halloween movie!' Clover's voice rose.

'It isn't,' Leo drawled. 'But fine. Let's watch *Die Hard*.'

'That is *definitely* not a Christmas movie!' Clover said, her cheeks flushing a deep shade of red, her face slowly matching her hair. It always surprised me when she couldn't see that Leo did most things just to rile her up.

It had been like this between them ever since we arrived. Clover and Leo had been at each other's throats the entire time and hadn't been able to agree on anything. Not on snacks, or on the best time was to give presents, or on what to watch. Basically, anything that *could* divide opinion, they disagreed on. I knew it was getting under Clover's skin, but I also knew Leo was getting a major kick out of it if the grin on his face when she wasn't looking was anything to go by.

'It definitely is a Christmas film. The entire film revolves around an office Christmas party. Am I wrong?' Leo asked the room, gesturing at Griff to back him up.

'Sorry, dude, you're on your own for this one.' Griff shrugged his shoulders. 'I'm all for *Santa Clause 2*.'

'I'm with Griff, too,' Ollie piped up, smiling down at me. He knew it was one of my favourites.

'*Polar Express* and *Muppets Christmas Carol* are on tomorrow's agenda. They're definitely Christmas Eve films,' Ollie added, his tone ensuring there would be no argument.

I'd told him this yesterday, so I was glad he'd been listening to me. It made me feel warm and cosy, knowing he hadn't just ignored my ramblings. I *loved* those films, and they were easily my top three. There was just something about the Muppets that made me smile, no matter how down I felt. *I mean, who doesn't find Animal and Miss Piggy hilarious?*

It was nice to feel heard with Ollie. The past Christmases I'd spent with my mum had been pretty dire and we'd never spent time doing what *I* wanted to do. It was always her food, her songs, and her films, which happened to be the awful kind the Christmas Movie Channel showed all season. They were her jam. The ones that were obviously made straight for TV and should have never seen the light of day.

'Sounds like we all agree,' Leo said. Clover looked belligerently at him and he added, 'Well, all of us that matter, anyway.'

I rolled my eyes at their pettiness. I slipped my phone out of my pocket, trying to hide the screen from Ollie's watching gaze. I blind texted Leo.

WILL YOU KNOCK IT OFF?

I was so sick of the shit between them. I'd hoped that spending time together at the estate in such a small group would improve the frostiness between them. But nope, it had just made it one thousand times worse. *Go figure.*

WHO SAID I'M THE ONE THAT NEEDS TO KNOCK SHIT OFF, STUTTER?

Leo could get under my skin too, don't get me wrong, so I understood how Clover was feeling, but I also found Leo's boredom and overall dick-ish behaviour kind of charming—and being fully honest—really fucking hot.

Not that I'd ever tell him—or anybody else—that.

Christmas morning was everything I'd dreamt it would be and more.

I'd told the guys I'd never had a great Christmas experience, and they were all determined to make sure this year would be the best one I'd ever had. There were so many presents placed under the biggest tree I'd ever seen, and we had cheesy music playing the entire morning. Well, most of them were cheesy. Now and then a classic slipped through the cracks, which led to Griff singing 'Good King Wenceslas' at the top of his lungs—and extremely off-key.

It was all a little overwhelming.

I'd opened a fuck ton of cool gifts: multiple designer hand-bags, plenty of books, clothes, and a brand-new phone. All of which seemed excessive. My current phone was relatively new, and I got one from the school when I started, so I was surprised to see the boys had got me the newest model.

Even Leo had gone all out and got me a real diamond necklace with matching earrings. He'd also handed me a tiny gift box, impeccably wrapped in white paper covered in red berries. Inside, there was a tiny glass bottle with an even smaller rolled up scroll of paper trapped inside. A card sat next to the bottle that read: **Merry Christmas …**

'It's a tiny telegram in a bottle,' he whispered to me as I exam-ined it, turning the tiny glass bottle over in my fingers. Ollie had left the room, and Clover and Griff were paying more attention to each other than to us two.

'I love it,' I gushed, surprised by the gift. 'I love tiny things.'

We both laughed.

'Not in all things, Stutter, I'm sure.'

I smiled and said, 'No, not in all things. Thank you, Leo.'

'The note inside is real, but don't open it yet. I'll let you know when.'

Inside, my stomach bubbled with nerves. Not knowing what he wrote on the note would be torture for me, and there was no way of knowing how long he'd make me wait, either. I quickly put it back in the box it came in and placed it inside one of the many bags they'd gifted me.

Ollie reentered the room and dropped down beside me before pulling me to him once again, placing a kiss on my forehead. Warmth filled me at his gesture, but I also felt dirty, as if I was keeping a secret from him.

'I'll be back in a moment.' I excused myself from around the tree and went to the kitchen. I needed a moment to myself to just process what was happening. In the past, I was lucky if my mum was home all day on Christmas day, let alone if she gave me a present.

Griff flew in and saw me standing there, almost hyperventilating. He put his arms around me in a massive bear hug and whispered in my ear, 'It's all gravy, Sky.'

'Yeah, I'm fine. I've said happy birthday, right?' I couldn't remember if I'd said it or not. Damn, having your birthday on Christmas day couldn't be fun. The day's about a dead dude, or presents and shit, and you're lucky if people even remember you.

'Yeah, you're good,' he said. Releasing me, Griff opened the cupboard and pulled out mugs to make drinks, most likely an alcoholic one, even though we were all underage and it wasn't even three in the afternoon, but hey, Christmas usually led to rule breaking.

'You don't need to make those for everyone. Let me help,' I told him, wanting to feel useful and to take my mind off the amount of gifts I'd received.

The two of us made the drinks together—peppermint schnapps hot chocolate—and joined everybody again to watch Christmas day TV together.

It was the best day, and by far the best Christmas of my life.

I finally felt like I belonged, like I was part of a group that mattered, that cared about me. And, fuck, it felt good!

Twenty-Five

CHRISTMAS BEING OVER COULD ONLY MEAN one thing: New Year's Eve was upon us. Which meant the New Year's Gala was also encroaching, and I knew I wasn't ready for it.

Not one bit.

Ever since Ollie invited me, I'd been anxious about it and I'd even tried to get out of it a couple of times, but he was having none of it.

'Are you sure I need to go?' I whined. The two of us were on the sofa on Christmas evening after everybody else had gone to bed, snuggling up with the fire crackling away in the large ornate fireplace, and the Christmas tree covering the room in a warm white glow. 'I won't know anybody there.'

'You'll know me, and Griff, and Leo, and Clover. Plus our parents. Isn't that enough?'

'I suppose...' I trailed off, snuggling closer to his chest so I didn't have to look him in the eye. 'Thank you for the dress.'

'I can't wait to see you in it, New Girl. You're gonna be the most beautiful girl at the gala.'

A flush travelled up my neck, covering my face, and burning my ears.

Ollie had arranged for me and Clover to be chauffeur driven to the nearest expensive boutique and have our dresses designed and created bespoke especially for us. He'd had to pay extra for them to be ready on time, and I didn't even want to consider just how much it had cost him.

'I doubt it,' I whispered. 'I just hope you like what I chose.'

'Babe, you could wear a potato sack and I'd love you in it.'

'You're just saying that!' I laughed, poking him in the ribs with my pointer finger, digging in a little more than necessary. 'But thanks.'

'Trust me,' he said, moving to lift my head so our eyes locked together. 'It's going to be a night you'll always remember.'

He placed a kiss on my forehead and I gulped at his implication, wondering if he meant what I thought he meant.

I shook myself from my thoughts and came back to my senses. We were back at school, as the gala itself was being held in the main hall, and I was with Clover in Ollie's room, getting ready for the guys to come get us at seven. According to Ollie, the gala was for a charity the school always supported and that was why it wasn't held at some posh hotel or stately home.

Ever since we became a couple, I found myself getting lost in Ollie's eyes more often than not, and it meant that a lot of the time I forgot what he told me the moment after he said it. *Yes, I'm aware of how disgustingly lovey-dovey that sounds.*

Shoot me.

I looked at myself in the full-length mirror in front of me, running my hands down the material of the dress, trying to ground myself in the moment.

Our final fittings had been a couple of days ago, and I was excited for Ollie to see me for the first time. For the first time in my life, I believed I looked good in something. *Real fucking good.*

The light blue of the dress suited my pale skin tone perfectly, and it also went with my silver-purple hair. I felt like a mix between a fairy-tale princess and an elven queen in a fantasy novel. The second I'd seen myself in it, I'd fallen in love, as it reminded me of Cinderella's classic dress for the ball.

It was an A-line gown with off-the-shoulder half sleeves. Blue flowers trailed from the bust down to the waist, high-lighting the curves of my body, adding to the look of a real-life princess.

Growing up, my self-confidence was low. Part of me was constantly worried that the reason I didn't have friends was because I was unattractive. Almost like my mind had convinced me I was too ugly to be seen with.

Being with Ollie, even for a short time, had changed how I saw myself.

I no longer looked in a mirror and questioned what I saw. I didn't worry that I was too fat, or too curvy, for people to love me. Even if this thing between us didn't last, I'd always be thankful to him for making me feel cherished in a way I'd never experienced before.

I also hoped the way I looked in the dress would lead to Ollie wanting to rip it off me after ringing in the New Year together and we were alone. The timing felt right, and I knew I wanted to lose my virginity to him. We'd been close enough once or twice, but we'd never gone through with it. I hadn't been ready. It was an enormous step and something you couldn't take back after. I had nothing against the girls who just wanted it gone, and I couldn't say that I was saving it for the person I'd be with forever—I wasn't even saving it per se—I just knew I wanted it to be with somebody who cared about me. Somebody who meant something to me, and somebody *I* meant something to back.

Clover entered the room from the bathroom and stopped dead.

'Fuck me, Sky!' she squealed, her eyes widening. 'You look beautiful.'

'I look beautiful? Pur-lease.' I rolled my eyes at her compliment. 'You look stunning, Clover. Really, honestly, truly beautiful.'

She was wearing a long satin jade green gown with a low V-neck and spaghetti straps. The slit went up to her mid-thigh, and when she moved, you got a quick flash of her leg. It looked amazing with her hair colour too. She had debated wearing red to try and break the stigma, but she hadn't found a material she liked enough.

Our eyes shimmered with unshed tears at the sight of each other looking so good, but we quickly laughed and stopped ourselves, not wanting to ruin the makeup we'd spent the better part of two hours on. I didn't want to have to touch it up before we even left the room.

'Ollie is going to cream his pants when he sees you.'

'Ew, Clo, did you have to lower the tone with the word *cream*?' I fake gagged, but really that word genuinely made me want to gag. There was nothing sexy about that term—like at all.

'Fine.' She laughed. 'Seriously, though, Ollie is going to want to rip that dress off you when he gets here.'

'Well, I won't let him before the gala...' I trailed off, a hint of a smile playing on my lips.

Clover looked at me, her mouth agape.

'Whoa, Sky. You think you're ready for that?'

'Yeah, I do. It just feels right, ya know?'

She nodded in response, scepticism rife on her features.

'Did you just know?' I asked her abruptly. Clo wasn't a virgin, and although she hadn't told me much about her first time, I knew she'd talk to me with honesty.

'Mhm,' she said, a thoughtful expression on her face, almost as if she was envisioning the day she'd said yes to her first. 'But I would take it back now if I could.'

'Thanks for the vote of confidence,' I said, sarcasm thick in my tone. 'Even if this isn't the right thing in the long run, Clo, I know it's the right thing for me *now* and that's all I can go on.'

'True, and for your sake, my beautiful bestie, I hope you're right about him,' she said, stopping her sentence when we heard a knock on the door. Our eyes locked, and all of a sudden all my nerves came rushing to me.

'Shit!' I whisper-yelled to Clo, who gave me an evil smirk in return.

Clover yelled, 'Come in.'

They entered, and the surrounding air turned to ice, leaving me slightly lightheaded.

Griff was the first to see us, his eyebrows rising when he took us in fully.

'Wow, you girls clean up nicely!' He hugged me briefly and

then moved to hug Clover. Her hug lasted a lot longer than mine, but I was too anxious to see Ollie to comment on it.

It was at that moment that Leo entered the room and saw the two of them hugging. For the briefest of moments, Leo looked lost, but he covered it up within a moment, and when Ollie entered the room, I lost interest in what the others were doing. All I could see was *him*.

Ollie looked the hottest I'd ever seen him look. *Ever*. Which trust me, was tough, seeing as even in our school uniform, I was into it. Into him. Of course I liked his personality, but his looks definitely helped, especially on those occasions when he'd acted like I had a disease you could catch simply by breathing the same air.

He was wearing a black tuxedo jacket with black skinny fit suit trousers and honestly, I was in love. I wiped the corner of my mouth with my hand, just in case some drool had escaped.

'This dress is fucking amazing. I want to rip it off you and taste what's hiding underneath. Do we even need to go to this thing?' Ollie asked. His eyes were heated, staring into mine. I could feel the flame and I honestly just wanted to burn in it.

'You're the one who said we have to go to this thing, so we're definitely going,' I scolded him, but it didn't reach my eyes. Or my smile.

'Fine. But tonight you're mine,' he said, his words filled with delicious promise.

I shivered and goosebumps popped up all over my arms. The night held even more potential than it had a few moments before, and you wouldn't find me complaining.

Maybe I'd enjoy the gala after all.

Twenty-Six

WE ENTERED THE HALL, and my breath left me as I took in our surroundings. It had been transformed into a woodland winter wonderland. The colour white was everywhere, mixed with fake tree trunks in the centre of each table that stemmed upwards and covered the table in a canopy of bright white lights.

The gala was filled with older people dressed in their finest suits and expensive gowns, and I felt completely out of my depth. I hadn't grown up in this world. The fanciest event I'd attended was a wedding reception in a barn a few years ago. And believe me, there had been nothing fancy about it. The groom was drunk before midday and the bride's cleavage spilled out over the top of her dress so much that she nip-slipped every five minutes.

Ollie's dad, Henry, was standing over by Lottie and Edward Hawthorn across the room. They looked exactly how I always imagined rich, powerful people would look at an event, dripping in diamonds and clad in designer suits.

'You've got this,' Ollie murmured out of the side of his mouth, squeezing my hand. 'You look amazing.'

I nodded, too nervous to reply, as we made our way over to the parents, and the greetings and handshakes started up instantly.

I knew Ollie wanted me to enjoy the evening but, mainly, he wanted to show me off as his piece of arm candy to his father, and to all of his father's associates. Part of me was thrilled that he thought I could be considered arm candy, and the other part of me found it insulting that I was amounting to nothing more than my looks. Then again, my confidence in myself was so low that whenever I thought about it, I was back to being thrilled all over again. It had become a vicious cycle, playing out in a never-ending loop in my head.

'Skylar, you look enchanting this evening,' Lottie said with a kind smile, and her eyes made me feel at ease. You would never know that she was as old as she was. Standing next to Leo, she looked like she could be his older sister. 'Clover, darling, you look amazing as always.' She leant down and kissed her cheek, and Clover gave her a tentative smile in return.

'Hey, Mum. Dad,' Leo said and gave his mum a kiss on the cheek and hugged her tight. Edward nodded at Leo and looked happy enough to see him, even if the slight grimace on his face said otherwise.

Edward and Ollie had a much frostier response to one another. They barely made eye contact, and sort of nodded towards each other. After seeing the two of them together on Parents' Day, I'd known there were a few issues between them, but I hadn't expected the iciness currently emanating off them.

'Oliver. Skylar,' he greeted us each with a nod, smiling so wide at me his teeth were on show.

Henry Brandon was an imposing man, standing tall at over six feet and in a black suit that looked more expensive than my entire wardrobe—make that my new wardrobe. He was intimidating, and I wasn't the only person who thought that, because everybody else in attendance seemed to be giving them a wide berth. 'Glad you could join us this evening.'

Ollie rolled his eyes in my peripheral. Without putting much thought into the action, I reached out and took his hand in mine, intertwining our fingers tight together. His lips twitched in response, forming a small smile that lasted for all of a second, but I saw it and it made me feel good inside, like I'd done something right.

'Evening, Dad. How was your Christmas?' Ollie asked tersely.

'Fine, thanks, Son. Spent it at the townhouse. You know how it just hasn't been the same for me since your mum died,' Henry said, looking away from us, trying to school his features back into those of somebody indifferent, but it didn't quite work. I could tell he missed his wife. 'I hope you all behaved yourself on the estate.'

'We did.' Ollie was being curt, not giving his dad much of anything to work with.

I took pity on Henry, who was trying, which was more than I could say about Ollie, and piped up instead, 'We had a lovely time, thank you.'

Within seconds, my hand was icy and empty. I'd obviously said or done the wrong thing, as Ollie not only removed his hand from mine, but he also took a visible step away from me. No matter how many times I believed I was getting somewhere with him, growing closer and understanding his inner workings, I was proved wrong. Clearly, I was an idiot who should've known better.

'After dinner, I must introduce you two to some of my colleagues. I've told them how a young, beautiful girl has swept my Oliver off his feet. They said they'll believe it when they see it,' he chortled, as if he'd just told a rather funny joke and not some well-worn remark.

'We look forward to it,' Ollie spoke through gritted teeth and it was obvious to everybody in the circle that he wasn't telling the truth.

'I hope my son got you some wonderful gifts, Skylar.' Henry continued talking as if Ollie wasn't giving him the cold shoulder.

'He did!' I said, smiling at him, making up for the frostiness from my boyfriend. 'I've never been so spoiled in my life.'

'I would say you're extremely lucky, but I can tell it's my son who's extremely lucky to have you.'

The group broke out into awkward laughter, and although my smile stayed on my face, I was unsure how to continue the conversation.

'If you'll excuse me,' Ollie bit out before he turned away from our conversation and walked away at a fast clip without another word, leaving me standing there with Henry, Leo, and his parents. Clover and Griff must have slipped away when the conversation started, and I wished I'd noticed and gone with them.

'He'll be back soon,' Henry said to me in a jovial tone, amused by his son's antics.

Minutes passed in silence. I wanted so badly to be rescued, I didn't even care by who.

'Come with me, Stutter,' Leo said, grabbing my stiff hand in his much larger one. The warmth of his hand surprised me and sent a shockwave of care through my arm.

Leo swept me through the hall, passing people I either recognised as students from school or their parents, out the main doors, and into the next corridor.

Ollie was standing alone further up the hallway, facing away from us, staring at the wall. His hands were clenched beside him in anger.

He turned around and I gasped at the twisted smile on his face.

Stalking towards us, I cowered a little into Leo's side, apprehensive after seeing his expression. When he left the hall, he was pissed off, but I didn't think he was angry at me.

'Come here,' Ollie commanded with a crook of his finger, and like a silly, submissive heroine, I went towards him willingly, and into his arms without question.

He hugged me against him, his tobacco and vanilla scent filling me with joy, the heat of our bodies causing my nipples to harden, and I squirmed at the flood of want rushing through my body.

The whisper in my ear sent my need for him into overdrive. 'Let's go, Little One.'

Ollie led me away with him, gripping my hand in his, stretching my arm as he moved further down the hall until I had no choice but to follow. Nobody was around, and when I looked back at Leo, he was gone, too. The hallway was deserted and, shielded by the dark, we continued until we were in front of a wooden door that he opened with no hesitation.

'In here,' he commanded, placing his palm on the small of my back, giving me a quick but gentle shove inside.

Once inside, he turned me to face him, and I was once again taken by just how fucking hot he was. Even with a livid expression covering his features. His anger was palpable, coming off of him in waves and entering the small space around us. The closet was tiny, with barely enough room for a few shelves and a mop and bucket.

'What the fuck do you think you're doing, Skylar?' he growled, and with every word, spittle left his mouth, and I watched it fall in the small space between us.

'I-I,' I said, stuttering again, trying to voice the thoughts that were scrambling around in my head. Common sense was battling it out with an apology. I didn't get time to say more, though, as Ollie violently captured my lips with his, the kiss hard, with no ounce of love and affection in the action. It was a pure need. Pure emotion driving his actions that was *definitely* not love.

'Don't say anything around my dad,' he bit out. 'You're here to stay quiet and look pretty.'

Sorry? My anger rushed forward, and I tried to take control of the kiss.

Locked in a fight of teeth and tongue, both of us tried to gain the upper hand. His hardness was pressing into me, making me want him even more. Every time we got closer to having sex, all I could think about was doing the deed with him, and I'd already decided I wanted to make it happen after the gala.

He pushed the bodice of my dress down, uncovering me, and took a hard nipple into his mouth with a bite. The sensation was otherworldly, and I knew I could come just from the feel of his tongue and teeth alone.

'Fuck,' I moaned as he sucked my nipple into his mouth hard enough I worried he'd leave marks.

With a pop, he let go and looked up at me, covering his mouth with his finger. 'Shh, Little One, or someone will hear.'

He stood back to his full height, trailing his hands down my body until he reached my skirt. The full skirt of the dress made it impossible for him to get anywhere further no matter what angle he tried.

Ollie groaned, part in frustration and the other in need. His trousers didn't present the same problem for my hand, though. I undid the top button and ventured inside to wrap my hand around his hard dick with no problem. There was nothing quite like the warmth of a cock in your hand, the little twitches of excitement, and the small beads of pre-cum sitting on the tip. He thrust into my hand, the two of us completely caught up in the moment, forgetting we were in a caretaker's cupboard with an entire hall of parents and students nearby.

Lost in the sensations. The emotions.

All of it.

A loud, hard knock came on the door.

'Shit,' I cursed, thrown back into the moment.

'Dinner's about to begin. Get out of there.' Leo's gruff voice made its way through the door, sounding pissed.

'Looks like our fun's over, Little One,' Ollie said with a harsh laugh and gave one last sharp pinch on my nipple to tease me before he begrudgingly helped me pull my dress back into place.

'Later,' he promised, the whispered word like a threat.

It made me shiver... but in excitement, never fear.

THE DINNER WAS awkward and stilted between all parties sitting at our table. I was sitting next to Ollie. Griff and Clover were next to me, followed by Leo and his parents, and Henry finished the circle on Ollie's other side. Every so often, a question would be asked and answered, then the table would return to silence.

Henry's gaze seared me as he was looking in our direction, but whenever I looked at him to catch him in the act, he was looking elsewhere or had started up a conversation with Lottie.

With the torture of dinner finally ended, the announcer

encouraged everybody to congregate in front of the stage to watch the swing band play.

'Come on, everybody! Don't be shy. The band won't play to an empty dance floor!'

My eyes locked with Clo's, the glint in her eye matching the one I was giving her.

'Shall we?' She was already standing, reaching out her hand to me.

'We shall!' I replied, joining her.

Clover took my hand, pulling me towards the dance floor as the band started to play one of our favourite Frank Sinatra songs. It was nice to just let loose and dance and sing along with her; to pretend like we weren't out of our element here, surrounded by people who made more in a month than our families did in an entire year—or five.

Next, a slow song came on, and I felt somebody come up behind me.

'May I have this dance?' a deep voice asked.

I swirled around to find Henry standing behind me, a sly grin on his face. If I thought Clo was going to save me, I was wrong, because she motioned with her hands that she was going to get a drink and got out of the area in rapid time.

Thanks a lot, jelly tot.

'O-of course,' I replied, seeing no other option but to agree.

Our hands came together, and we moved into the traditional slow dance position. Not being much of a dancer, I hoped Henry was well versed and able to help me through without having me fall flat on my arse. I didn't want to humiliate myself, or Ollie for that matter.

'Skylar, I've been wanting to talk to you alone,' Henry said, as the two of us began to move in unison. *So far, so good.*

I spotted Ollie standing over at the side of the dance floor by the bar, with Leo and Griff by his side, all three of them staring at us. Ollie looked wary, Leo seemed bored, and although Griff was smiling at me, his eyes gave away how he was truly feeling, filled with apprehension.

'How come?' I asked, nervous laughter bubbling out of me. People like Henry Brandon could smell fear. They didn't get where they were without having that sense ingrained in them. He must be having a field day assessing me.

'It's rare Oliver leaves you alone, and there are some things I wanted to ask without him around.' His eyes glistened, a lopsided grin taking over the bottom half of his face.

I nodded, still none the wiser as to why he wanted to talk to me alone. Surely there was nothing he needed to say to me without Ollie around?

'Now's your ch-chance,' I joked. Joking around didn't help the nerves, though. If anything, it made the nausea moving around in my stomach worse. It felt as if my entire body was responding to being close to Henry in a negative way.

'After meeting your delightful mother, I felt rather intrigued to learn more about your father.' I looked at his face, unable to read his expression. 'Oliver didn't have an answer when I mentioned it to him.'

Why would Henry want to know about my dad? There was nothing I could tell him, as I knew *nothing* about him.

'I...' I trailed off, not quite sure what to tell him. After a pause, I decided to go with the truth. 'I d-don't know who he is, sir.'

Henry's eyebrows knitted together, assessing me. I expected him to comment more about my dad, but all he said was, 'No need to call me *sir*, dear. Call me Henry.'

'Henry,' I whispered, feeling caught in a trap, a web I didn't know how to untangle myself from. 'I'm sorry I don't know more.'

'No need to apologise. Forgive me for intruding.'

His hands moved lower, slowly, heading from my waist to my hips. All of it felt wrong and bile rose in my throat. He was making me uncomfortable the way Andy had, and all I wanted to do in that moment was take a brush to my skin and scrub off every touch that wasn't Ollie's.

'It's fine,' I told him. I pulled myself away from his touch, trying to keep my disgust out of my expression. 'I must go find

Ollie before he comes and gives you grief for stealing his girl. Thank you for the d-dance.'

'It was my pleasure entirely. I'll see you soon, Skylar,' he said. His tone ominous; his words a threat.

I located Ollie and Leo near the entrance, so I headed towards the two of them. Moments from reaching them, a body barged into my side, knocking me off-balance. I quickly righted myself, turning to see who had bumped into me.

I should've known without looking.

'Watch where you're going, bitch,' Odette said, her tone scathing. 'I nearly spilled my drink because of you.'

'Sorry,' I apologised quietly. It killed me inside to apologise to her, but I really wanted to just make it to Ollie and Leo, and I knew if I didn't say sorry, I could be stuck with them for far longer than I would like to be. 'I didn't see you there.'

'What Ollie sees in you I'll never know,' she said with scorn, but I didn't miss the flash of envy in her wide eyes.

'Well...' Olivia said, about to add her two cents to the conversation, but Odette jutted her elbow out to shut her up. She grunted in pain, but knew her place in the hierarchy and didn't say any more.

'You are nothing but trash. You've never belonged here at Hawthorn, but don't worry, everybody will see that for themselves soon,' Odette warned.

With that, the two of them dispersed, leaving me alone once more. Odette's parting words weren't overly encouraging, but with Henry's threat still ringing in my ears, I focused on that more. After all, the girls had already tried to get me kicked out of Hawthorn. Fuck, they'd also potentially orchestrated my drugging and near drowning, too. *Can't a girl catch a break around here?*

Making it back to Ollie's side, the only place I wanted to be for the rest of the evening, he checked me all over to see if I was all in one piece. His eyes simmered with heat as he took me in, checking me out in other ways. All night I'd been taking him in, mostly because I couldn't believe that somebody as gorgeous as him was *my* boyfriend. Fingers crossed he saw tonight ending the way I did.

In bed. Naked. Wrapped up in one another.

Who was I kidding? He was a guy. That was probably how he wished *every* night between us ended.

'Shit. It's already five to midnight. I've got to go,' Leo announced.

I jumped at the sound of his voice. I'd been so preoccupied with looking at Ollie, and him looking at me, that I'd totally forgotten that Leo was still standing with us.

'Where's he off to?' I asked, but Ollie shrugged, then his arms encapsulated me, pulling me up against his hard body in a tight embrace. Heat filled me.

What a way to start a new year.

The room erupted into a countdown.

'Ten!'

I turned to face Ollie. Looking into the depths of his blue eyes, I saw a few different emotions flicker in his gaze, but none of them stayed for long.

'Five!'

A mixture of caring, lust, and anger all played out on his face in quick succession, warring to be the dominant emotion. He settled on a serene look, or as serene a look as I'd ever seen on him, anyway.

'Happy New Year!' The room burst into cheers and glasses clinking. The smacking of lips and the sound of fireworks outside filling the air.

'Happy New Year,' he whispered.

'Happy New Year,' I said in return, a wide smile hurting my cheeks.

Our midnight kiss was like the one I'd dreamt about receiving ever since I was a young girl, wishing I had a boyfriend like the girls in movies. I'd had nobody to share one with before, and I'd spent a lot of my previous New Year's at home alone while Mum and Andy were at the local pub with their friends.

The passion in the kiss wasn't lost on me, and happiness overtook my insides. *This must be what it's like to feel wanted.*

I'd wanted that feeling forever, the feeling of being desired.

The new year held so much promise and I couldn't wait to see what it had in store for me.

Twenty-Seven

THE MOMENT the door of Ollie's suite closed behind us, a chill ran down my spine. I'd been anticipating this moment for quite some time, and it was finally here. Ollie grabbed my waist from behind, then his lips trailed kisses up and down my neck.

The room was lit by moonlight, adding to the magical atmosphere I'd created in my mind, and every now and then the light caught Ollie's eyes, the spark in them beckoning me forward. His hands roamed while I put mine around his neck, pulling his mouth closer for more kisses.

Feverish kisses. Desperate kisses.

Ollie took a step back and ripped his tie off, looking free of the burden the moment it was gone.

Tearing his jacket off with a growl. His eyes burned as they locked with mine.

'I cannot fucking wait to get you out of that dress. You've been torturing me all night.'

'I've done no such thing—'

He cut me off abruptly, slamming into me as he crushed his mouth to mine, his hunger calling to my own in an instant. His body pushed against mine as he devoured me like a starving man, even biting at my lips. He caught my bottom lip and pulled just enough to make me feel at his mercy for a moment.

'Get naked and lie on the bed,' Ollie demanded, pushing me

onto the bed with a little too much force, and I stumbled, nearly tripping on the skirt of the gown.

'Help me?' I asked, hoping my nerves would calm the fuck down soon.

He grabbed my hands and pulled me back to my feet. Spinning me around, he slowly unzipped my dress, leaving my back bare and exposed to the air.

To him.

'Finally. Just the way I want you.' Gripping the fabric of the ball gown, Ollie yanked it to the floor, leaving me standing before him in nothing but my light blue lace underwear set. He growled appreciatively.

I turned to face him and stepped out of the material at my feet.

With the way Ollie was looking at me, I thought I'd combust from all the sexual energy surrounding us.

My hands shaking, I removed my bra and slowly slid my bottoms down, watching his eyes as they tracked my every movement. I opened my mouth, unsure what I planned to say, but his hand slapped down over my mouth, eyes burning.

'No talking, New Girl. You're mine tonight, no questions asked.'

I'm sure if I actually told him no, he wouldn't force it, but we both knew we'd been aching to go to town on each other for a while. I may not have loved how he was bossing me around, but I also couldn't deny how hot it was.

'Now get your arse on the bed,' he commanded. A slight shiver ran down my back, but I meekly sat on the bed and watched him without a word, waiting to see what he did next. 'And don't move.'

Again, I contemplated not giving him power over me, but with my hunger growing, the hesitation was easily brushed aside.

Once I was settled with my back on the mattress, I watched Ollie as he pulled off his shirt, hunger rising as I took in his muscular frame. Whatever he had planned, I was certain it would be nothing but enjoyable for me.

The anticipation climbed with every piece of clothing he removed. Nerves filled me, my stomach a sea of thrashing waves. We'd never been so far before, never been so bare to one another.

After what felt like forever, he stood before me naked, a smirk playing on his lips.

His dick was big. Really big. Even though I'd touched it before tonight, I'd never considered its size. I knew every teenage virgin seemed to say it, in every film and book, but I really didn't know how he was going to fit.

Ollie kneeled by my feet, looking over my body, a contemplative look on his face. I stared back, feigning more confidence than I really felt. Nerves knotted in my stomach. Knowing Ollie, he wouldn't be very gentle with me. I was excited by the prospect, but also terrified. What if it hurt?

But I couldn't let myself think that way. I wanted this with him. I wanted to feel him so far inside of me, we became one person. One soul.

Anticipation and terror rose when he pulled my legs apart, allowing him access to my pussy. He didn't immediately attack, though, giving me a moment to process everything that was happening. He kissed and nibbled at my legs first, thankfully allowing me to relax a little by the time he got to the lace knickers, and I started to feel a little less fearful of what he'd do to me.

It took a moment, but with a deep breath, I allowed myself to get washed away by the sensation of his mouth moving from my knee to my hip on one leg and then the other. I slowly relaxed and focused on enjoying myself.

Ollie's hot breath caressed me as his mouth hovered just over me, and I let out a pleased sigh. *What a tease,* I thought when his teeth scraped over my hip. One hand slipped under my back while the other grasped the lace band at the top of my knickers.

It seemed effortless when he pulled them free with his teeth and one hand, lifting me just enough with the other to assist.

God, why does he have to be so hot? So good at this?

It was achingly sweet and frustrating at the same time.

'Come on, New Girl,' Ollie said, his face again hovering above my pussy. 'Don't tell me I was the only one fantasising about this all night. Of kissing you... biting you... teasing you until you scream for me to let you cum. Then slamming into you until your brain short-circuits and your pussy clenches me so hard, I combust.' He sighed playfully, sending hot air brushing over my already aching bundle of nerves.

A sharp squeak of surprise and exhilaration left me when his mouth descended at last, softly brushing over my clit. *Ah, shit.* He definitely had all the power over me. He always did.

My back arched hard when his fingers dug into my hips, pulling me even harder against his mouth, each fingertip sending just enough pain into my body to heighten the experience.

I tasted blood when my teeth cut into my lips to hold back a scream, as I felt the pleasure building, racing toward something I knew would be too intense, like I was a rocket flying directly into the sun.

Somehow, when I did hit that point, there was no pain. It wasn't so overwhelming that it hurt like I thought it would. It was nothing but the purest pleasure I'd ever experienced.

It danced along the edge of being too much, but that somehow made it all the better, like the euphoria of just avoiding something that could kill me.

When I finally came back to myself, Ollie was kissing and biting at my hips, waiting for me to recover while still clearly hungry himself.

'Damn,' I murmured once I remembered what words were. 'That was... Wow.'

Words failed me.

Looking up at me, Ollie smirked and moved his position to hover above me. His hand wandered down my body until I felt a long digit enter me, followed soon after by a second and then a third. My wetness eased his movement and I honestly couldn't think of a time I'd been this wet before.

'Are you sure about this, Sky?' he whispered, his words skating across my skin. The moment became more real the second he uttered my name.

Not *New Girl*.

Sky.

I nodded and sighed in pleasure, his thumb lazily circling my clit. 'Please.'

My voice came out as a whimper, my eyes were at half mast, and I shivered just looking at Ollie's full lips. He kissed me hard, removing his fingers to wrap them around my hips and the head of his cock nudged against my entrance.

Fuck, if he didn't put his dick where we both wanted it soon, I was going to take over.

The moment his cock breached my entrance, I winced.

Shit. The initial sting hurt. My eyes watered, but it wasn't long before the pain eased and I whispered, 'You can keep going.'

With delicious slowness, he slipped inside, inch by inch, and I relished in the tight, stretched feeling of him inside me. It was everything I'd imagined, but also, so much more.

We both let out a small moan once he was completely inside.

He started thrusting slowly at first, but then something broke in him and he began to thrust in earnest, creating sensations I didn't even know I could feel.

'Fuck,' I moaned.

Our breathing escalated together, to the point I started feeling lightheaded, all thoughts escaping me as my world became nothing but Ollie's hands gripping me roughly and the thrusting of his cock as it slid in and out, each hit bringing me closer and closer to another orgasm.

His breath was hot in my ear, one hand on my nipple pinching me hard, the other grasping my wrist and pinning it above my head. No way for me to move it. No way to be free from him.

Not that I wanted to be.

My free hand was in his hair, pulling sections every time he hit that spot inside of me that was elusive to most. I'd never felt this close to somebody before and there were tears in my eyes, both from emotion and the passion between us. It was over-whelming.

'Fuck,' Ollie hissed out through his teeth. Just the sound of his moan caused the sensation of butterflies in my stomach.

'Touch me,' I said desperately to Ollie. I needed him to rub my clit. Now.

He understood instantly, and the second he brushed his thumb over the spot, I came.

I moaned, 'Ollie!'

'Fuck!' Ollie ground out, the words the final push for me to fall into another orgasm, my scream melting into the mattress as I felt like my world shattered around me. His cock somehow swelled larger at the same time, filling me in a whole new way that made the orgasm even more satisfying.

My moan seemed to push Ollie over the edge, as after a few more deep strokes, I felt him spill inside of me.

Spent, Ollie collapsed to the bed beside me, both of us panting. I didn't move from my stomach for a while, exhaustion already creeping in, pulling me to delve into sleep. I already ached a little between my legs, but thankfully it was nothing like the pain I dreaded.

Shit.

We didn't use a condom.

Thank fuck for the school's weird rule about health check-ups and contraception.

Ollie got up and went to his en-suite and returned with a wet towel he then used to clean me. It was strange, but that act felt more intimate to me than the whole *losing my virginity thing* that just happened.

After a moment, Ollie moved to lie beside me, and we were silent for a while. The events of the evening were catching up with us both.

'How are you feeling?' he asked, his voice thick.

'I'm good. That was—fuck, Ollie—that was. Wow,' I sputtered out. I was finding words hard. I felt incoherent. Like my entire body and brain were made of mush, and I'd never be able to form complete sentences again. I wondered if every girl felt like this when they first discovered sex. I made a mental note to ask Clover.

'Told you I wanted to find out how your stutter sounded with my dick deep inside of you. Trust me, baby, it did not disappoint.'

I could only describe the sound that left me next as an embarrassed chuckle. I had sex with Ollie. *Like, what?* Yeah, it had been on the agenda for some time now, and I'd known pretty much from day one that I wanted to have sex with him. But wanting something and having it become reality were two very different things; and they came with two very different emotions.

I fell asleep in Ollie's arms as the little spoon, and I felt safe. Protected. And damn did it feel good.

Twenty-Eight

I WOKE up the next morning with a start. On opening my eyes, it took me a second to adjust and remember that I was in Ollie's room, in Ollie's bed, and that he was lying next to me.

To remember that the two of us had sex after returning from the gala, before falling asleep sated and wrapped up in one another's arms.

Still sound asleep, Ollie looked so peaceful. His eyebrows were relaxed and I could honestly say I'd never seen such a serene look on his face. When awake, his mind was constantly working a mile a minute, and he never seemed to switch off and just sit and relax. Seeing him so vulnerable made him seem more human. Like an actual person, with actual emotions—almost.

I got up and went to the toilet, still lost in my thoughts about the night before. I contemplated brushing my hair and sorting out my face, but I decided not to. Ollie had seen me at my worst, meaning there was no need to hide who I really was. It pissed me off that I'd even considered it, because as a rule, I'd never understood that whole concept. If brushing your hair first thing in the morning made a difference to a relationship, you needed to reevaluate.

I got back into bed and Ollie mumbled, 'Morning,' then pulled me back up against his chest and I got comfortable again. I didn't know the time, but the new year already felt promising, even if it had barely begun. We must have fallen back asleep, though, as the next time I opened my eyes, the light coming through the windows made me think it was closer to late afternoon.

Back at home, I didn't have blinds on my windows because my mum had refused to pay for them. Apparently, she and Andy would rather spend the money on something more important— I'd never found out what was more important, but there you go. Because of this, I was pretty good at being able to decipher what time it was just by how the world looked as it came through the windows. Not a helpful skill at all, but a relatively cool one.

'Afternoon,' Ollie mumbled this time before kissing up and down my neck, covering every patch of skin available. 'How are you feeling?'

'I'm good,' I told him. Feeling like I needed to emphasise my words, I wriggled against him. I could feel his dick pressing into my lower back and I smiled. '*Really* good actually.' He pulled back, so I had some space to turn in, and I shuffled myself around to face him.

He was about to say something more when we heard a piercing scream from out in the hall. At first, neither of us moved, but clearly other people who lived in Ollie's wing of the school did, as the commotion outside got louder.

'Skylar,' Griff shouted through the door. I found it a little odd he was calling my name when he was knocking on Ollie's door. Why wouldn't he be calling for him?

Quickly, I threw on one of Ollie's tops and a pair of his tracksuit bottoms that I rolled up at the waist so they didn't instantly fall down. I shuffled my way to the door and opened it to see a frantic-looking Griff, his hair standing up on end as if he'd been pulling at it for hours, staring at me with worry in his eyes.

'What's up?' I asked, keeping my tone light. I looked past him and saw a group of students hovering at the end of the hall, whispering about something with worried expressions. I nudged my head towards the gathering. 'What's going on down there?'

'Come with me,' he said urgently as Ollie came up behind me. 'You too.'

We followed Griff out of the room, but instead of heading into his on the right, he took us into the room on the left. Leo stood in the middle of the room, a bored expression playing on his face, but his foot was tapping in a frustrated rhythm, so maybe he wasn't as bored as he wanted to come across.

'What's going on, dickheads?' Ollie asked, looking at them both with raised brows, sceptical of their motivation.

'Olivia's dead,' Griff said, panicked. He looked sick, like he was one breath away from losing the contents of his stomach entirely.

'Who?' I asked. All three guys swung their gazes to me, and I blushed at the disbelief on their faces. Clearly, I was meant to know who they meant without question.

Olivia. Olivia.

It took me another moment to picture Olivia in my mind.

'Oh!' I gasped, covering my mouth with my hand. 'Olivia.'

The fourth member of *The Set*. To be fair, I'd forgotten she existed for the most part. It was rare I had much to do with her, as it always seemed to be Odette, Ophelia, or Oralie giving me a hard time. Olivia had been a silent companion.

'What?' Ollie barked, his anger a surprise, making me jump beside him. 'How?'

'Somebody killed her,' Leo said, monotone.

'Stabbed,' Griff added. 'She told the girls at the gala she was going back to some guy's house but wouldn't tell them whose house. All she'd say was that they'd be shocked if they knew the truth.'

'How do we know what happened if she went back to some old dude's house?' Ollie asked, sounding bored now that he'd heard more. 'She wasn't even on campus.'

'That's just it, though. They found her on the grounds.' Griff's tone was urgent. 'Her body was lying on the steps of the pool house. They found her first thing, but you know how gossip goes around, so it spread round the school pretty fast.'

Leo stayed silent, standing still in the centre of the room, contemplating everything that was being said. Assessing everyone's reactions. Taking it all in.

'So, why have you got us out of bed?' Ollie asked, pissed. 'You could have told us at dinner.'

'The girl's dead, Oliver!' Griff growled.

'Olivia was holding a lock of Skylar's hair and a piece of her blue dress from last night,' Leo said as he locked his gaze on mine, ignoring the tension building between Ollie and Griff.

'Sorry, w-what?' I sputtered, confused as fuck. Why would she have been holding my hair, or some of my dress? How?

'Yep,' Griff answered me, then looked at Ollie. 'So, that's why we came and got you, wanker.'

'Who found her?' I asked. I had to know. Not that it was okay for whoever found her, but it would be worse if it was a pupil in one of the younger years.

'Ms Hawthorn,' Leo responded in a dull tone.

Wonderful. The woman already acted like she couldn't stand me. Now that I guessed I'd become a suspect, she would hate me even more.

Fuck, would I be considered a suspect?

'Guys,' I said, looking at them all. 'Will the police think *I* did it?'

The responses from the guys in the room with me weren't positive ones. The winces and unfinished sentences gave away the answer.

I understood. A corpse showing up holding your hair—distinctively coloured hair at that—definitely didn't help my cause.

'So, what shall we do about it?' Ollie looked pissed still. Whether he was aiming it at me or them, I didn't know. Either way, it wasn't any of our faults. He had to know that much.

'No clue, man. That's why we wanted you two here, so we could talk it out.' Griff looked exasperated with Ollie, and I totally got why. He was acting like a total dick. I knew he had different plans of how he'd expected this morning to go—so did I, if I was being honest—but it wasn't like we could help it. You'd think he'd be a little more caring that Olivia was dead. He'd known her for years, after all. Plus, his girlfriend was being implicated in her death. Surely he cared about that?

'Doesn't sound like there's much to talk about. Olivia's dead and Sky's being implicated,' he deadpanned.

Let me just take back my last thought.

'God, you are such a frustrating dick, you know that?' Griff asked, his face slowly turning the shade of a tomato. I'd never seen him so angry before. 'Who would do this to Sky?'

'W-what do you mean? Shouldn't we be asking who would do this to Olivia?'

'Not being funny, New Girl, but literally anybody could have done this to Olivia,' Griff said with a shrug. 'No. Somebody planted your hair and dress on purpose and we need to figure out who.' He gave a questioning look to both Leo and Ollie, one I didn't fully understand.

Great.

More secrets.

Twenty-Nine

SCHOOL STARTED BACK up a week after the gala, and things with Ollie were amazing. Ever since that night, we were inseparable. He'd bribed the dorm monitors into letting me stay in his suite every night, and there was no way I was going to turn that down. I didn't even want to think about how much money had exchanged hands for that to happen, because if I did, I'd feel a bit like he was *paying* to spend time with me. *And that's just icky.*

You know how when you read or heard about girls losing their V-card? They always said some crap about how different they felt or how much sex they wanted to have now that the barrier was gone?

I'm now one of those basic heroines.

All I could think about was *him*. Spending time with him, in the biblical sense, but also just watching films together and enjoying one another's company. My thoughts were even boring me, but I couldn't help it. I was truly happy for the first time in a long time.

After Olivia's body had been found, investigators invaded the school and questioned everybody. They summoned every single student individually to Ms Hawthorn's office, and we all had to relay our whereabouts from that evening. Even those who hadn't attended the gala were being questioned, just in case they were the mysterious person she planned to go home with.

I had no clue what strings Ollie pulled, but they allowed him to sit beside me throughout the interview—seeing as we'd spent the evening together anyway, I supposed it made sense to question us at the same time.

'*Miss Crescent. Master Brandon. I'm Detective Saunders and this is my partner Detective Smith. We've asked you here to answer a couple of questions in regards to the death of Olivia. This is an informal chat, just to learn of your whereabouts,*' the tall, slim detective said, sitting down in the chair in front of us, next to his short, round co-worker. '*Where were you between the hours of one and four in the morning?*'

'*We were in bed,*' Ollie replied, bored. '*Where else would we have been?*'

Detective Saunders ignored Ollie and continued his line of questioning.

'*Do you have any idea how Olivia came to hold your dress and hair, Miss Crescent?*'

I gulped, opening and closing my mouth like a fish, unsure how to answer.

'*No, she doesn't.*' Ollie sat up straighter in his chair, his stare focused on the two detectives sitting in front of us. '*Somebody is framing her.*'

'*And why would somebody have a reason to frame you, Miss Crescent?*' Detective Smith's narrow glare turned to me, and once again, I was at a loss for words. If I answered truthfully, that Olivia and her friends were the ones bullying me, it would make me look even more suspicious than I already did.

'*Isn't that your job?*' Ollie snapped back, not letting the detectives intimidate him the way they were me. '*To figure out people's motives?*'

'*We're aware of our job, Master Brandon,*' Detective Saunders said with a brittle smile. '*The two of you are free to go, but we'd like you to remain available for future enquiries.*'

The way he said it made me laugh inside. As if the two of us had anywhere else to go except school. Not like we were about to do a runner out of the country. I didn't even have a passport.

'*It's been a pleasure,*' Ollie said, standing from his chair and reaching his hand down to help me out of mine.

I didn't say another word as we silently left the room. Once outside,

I took the deep breath my lungs needed—one my body had refused to take when sitting in front of two men who believed I was a cold-hearted killer.

After that, things went back to normal. Or, as normal as they could around Hawthorn.

'So, my dick is obviously the biggest,' Griff said at the exact moment I tuned into the conversation going on around me.

I sputtered, causing my drink to spray out of my mouth. Griff raised an eyebrow at me, the smirk on his face giving away the fact that he was trying to shock and was more than pleased that it worked.

'Oh, give over, Griff. Like I'm even going to say anything to boost your ego, or that dickhead's for that matter.' Clover nudged her head towards Leo and Odette, who were sitting at a table across the room with the other members of *The Set*.

'I'm just saying, my little lady luck, that if you *want* to look, you'll be happy with what you find. More than happy, actually. Fucking ecstatic. Maybe you'll even shed a tear.'

Clover hit him hard on the arm, but I could see that she was trying to hold her laughter in. I didn't hold back, though. There was just something so lovable about that stupid boy, even if I knew he was hiding something from me. If I was being honest with myself, I knew most people were. Especially the ones who used humour as a way to hide from those around them; those closest to them.

'Shut up, prick.' Ollie looked amused, but there was an under-lying look of distaste in his expression. I couldn't figure out whether it was aimed at Griff or Clo, though.

'You kill me, Griff,' I said, chuckling. 'Please can we move off the subject of dick size?'

'Miss Skylar, are you sure you don't wanna join in?' he asked, his grin ever present.

I shook my head in response, going back to eating my gourmet meal. 'Join in with what? Not like I can make any comparison notes for you.'

'True, true. But you could just lie and make me feel good, you know, as my best friend,' he said, and I smiled at his words. Having people to call friends made me ecstatic, but at times like this, I wondered why I kept them around.

Oh, who am I kidding?

I tried my hardest not to do anything that would cause them to stop being my friend. I couldn't go back to being a friendless loser—being here had made me fully understand just how empty and miserable my life had been before.

'Pretty sure I'm her best friend, dickweed. Eat your food and shut up,' Clover told him, effectively putting an end to that conversation.

RECENTLY, Ollie had been talking to me about Clover—how he was worried about her. Worried that her words would cause me to question him or his actions sometime in the near future.

'You're being paranoid,' I told him, not even looking up from my textbook. Homework was more important than his worries. I needed to pass everything in order to keep my scholarship. 'Just don't do anything that would make Clo chat shit about you to me, and then we'll be golden.'

'But she might do it anyway.'

'Ollie,' I said, looking up into his wary expression. 'Can we drop it? I get it. You don't trust Clover, and funny enough, she doesn't trust you. So let's just leave it there and move on.'

'But—'

'No buts!' My voice rose as I lost my cool. We were in the library and I knew the librarian liked me, so she'd let me off once, but she wouldn't if I continued shouting. I lowered my voice again. 'I may be quiet, and maybe I don't always stand up for myself the way I should, but I can think for myself. Regardless of how Clover feels towards you, it won't sway my feelings for you.'

'You promise?'

'Yes,' I stressed. 'Now please, talk about literally anything else.'

'I think Leo's gonna ask Odette to be his girlfriend soon.'

'Yeah?' I wondered where that came from, but I did tell him to change the subject to literally anything else. 'I didn't think he actually liked her.'

'What makes you think that?'

'I don't know.' I shrugged. 'I thought he was with her for convenience.'

'Convenience?'

'Sex,' I said, being blunt. Since I'd lost my virginity, I was able to talk about it a lot easier. The word didn't scare me anymore. 'And I always thought it was a way for him to piss Clo off.'

'I've never asked him, to be honest,' Ollie said, frowning. 'But who knows. This is Leo we're talking about.'

'True,' I replied. Leo *was* a mystery. 'Guess we'll never know his motives.'

'Sky...' he trailed off, and I went back to reading the page in front of me. 'Valentine's Day is coming up.'

'Right,' I replied, distracted.

'And I've got a question to ask you.'

'Okay.'

'Sky, will you at least look at me?' His finger prodded under my chin, tilting my head up to look at him again. I smiled, laughing inside at how serious he seemed. 'I want to ask you if you'd like to come to London for the weekend with me?'

'When?'

'Valentine's Day...'

'Oh.' I laughed, nervous. I wanted to go with him, but an entire weekend away from school with Ollie both sounded like a dream and a nightmare. That wasn't what I said, though. Instead, I said, 'I'd love to.'

'Great!' Ollie said, placing a kiss on my forehead. 'This is probably gonna sound a little forward, but I've already booked the hotel and show.'

'Oh,' I said, unease filling my gut. 'You have?'

'It's Valentine's Day weekend,' he said, as if that explained everything, and I supposed it did, if you'd ever had a date or a reason to celebrate that day.

'Will we be allowed to leave school with no issue?'

'Yeah,' he said with a nod. 'We're allowed to leave at the weekend, and we can do overnight stays with permission from our parents. I got my dad to write a letter, and then I was going to falsify one from your mum.'

'Wow. You've got it all worked out, haven't you?'

'I want to spend time with you. Is that a problem?' His tone came out a little stilted, and I knew I'd hit a nerve, whether I'd meant to or not.

'No!' I said, wanting to appease him. 'I'd love to spend time with you away from here, Ollie. I promise.'

'I'm sorry,' he said, blowing out a breath. 'I'm trying to stop acting like a dick, but it's harder than I thought.'

The sheepish smile on his face warmed me. Yeah, he definitely acted like a massive prick a lot of the time, but there was something endearing about it. Maybe I was a stupid bitch who was blinded by first lust, and that was why I let him get away with his behaviour, but I couldn't help myself. The boy looked *good*.

'I forgive you,' I said, gripping his fingers in mine.

Thirty

A COUPLE OF DAYS LATER, Odette and Leo became an official couple, and shit hit the fan.

I'd been given a reprieve from *The Set* and no harm had come to me since Halloween after the whole being held under water situation. But it was a new year. Apparently, I was fair game again.

It made little sense to me that things were getting worse after somebody who supposedly cared about me was dating my bully. Leo had told me multiple times to go to him if I needed help, so I'd thought by him dating Odette for "real" it would have gone the other way and ended the bullying entirely. Clearly that had been wishful thinking on my part.

At the academy, the bathroom toilet walls were covered in graffiti. Apparently, the graffitied walls had existed forever, and no matter how often the school painted over them, they would always just reappear the next day. It was a constant battle between the caretaker and the students.

My name was on every toilet stall wall.

Every time they painted the messages over, they came back worse and more aggressive. The school had given up after the first three repaints and since then, was letting them accumulate.

Skylar Crescent should kill herself.

SC doesn't deserve OB

You have to be a low level of scum to call your daughter Skylar.

There were arrows coming off of the original comments, with more comments underneath. I wanted to be disgusted at how many girls had stooped to this level, but really, I wasn't. It didn't surprise me at all.

Eurgh, she's a skank.

Wish Ophelia would hit her harder.

Whoever attempted to drown her should have done a better job.

Even I could admit that some were funny and so obviously false.

SC has gonorrhoea.

SC is a walking STD.

And my personal favourite:

Sky fingers herself with an electric toothbrush.

Original *and* classy. The best kind of slur.

The messages weren't just all over the bathrooms. Nope. They were all over the Hive too. On every message board and feed. Literally every single place that students had the chance to slag me off, they were doing it. These words were repeated in whispers in every corridor, every class, and at mealtimes. I thought my sort of friendship with Leo meant things would get better, seeing as he was dating the ringleader, but he hadn't stopped jack shit from happening to me. My hair was pulled, my clothes covered in paint from paint balloons they threw at me, and the essays I had sent off electronically were being altered somehow. They came back from the teacher with a poor grade, the wording completely different from what I'd written and sent in. But I had no proof, and when I tried to tell a teacher about it, they pretended not to hear me.

I tried my best not to let any of it affect me. Tried to keep my head held high and stay above it all. Tried to tell myself they were all just jealous or spiteful—or both.

A majority of the girls grumbled about me using a witch's spell to get both Ollie and Griff under my thumb. *How pathetic.* Like I'd just been sitting in my room with Clover saying spells over a cauldron like some *Macbeth* shit. Petty girls really did say and believe anything to help themselves buy into their own delusions. I had to keep reminding myself of that.

The other thing that was getting me down was my relationship with Clover.

Clover had been acting funky ever since Leo and Odette officially got together, to the point where she wouldn't be anywhere near them, barely spent any time with us, and basically became a hermit that stayed in our room. It was odd behaviour, even for her, and I didn't know what to do to make it better. Not like I could ask Ollie for help as he and Clover barely tolerated each other at the best of times.

I just wasn't sure what to do to make things go back to how they were before. Not like I was going to split up with Ollie to appease Clover. But I also didn't want to lose a friendship—my only female friendship—because of a guy. Hoes before bros and all that.

'Want to watch a film tonight?' Clo asked as the two of us were walking back from dinner, hooking her arm through mine.

'Err...' I wasn't sure what to say but decided to go with the truth. 'I was going to hang out with Ollie tonight.' I cringed, worried she was going to start an argument with me or switch from a playful mood into one made of pure bitchiness.

'Oh. Right.' Her tone had soured. So much so, I could taste it.

'But I can cancel,' I said, feeling guilty, and got out my phone straight away to cancel my plans with Ollie. Yeah, he'd probably be a little pissed at me and blame it on Clo, but I hadn't spent time with Clover, just us two, in a while and I could tell she was missing me. I missed her too, and things were so weird between us, it would do us good to spend time alone. Hopefully, if we spent the evening chilling out, things might go back to being a little more normal.

'Only if you're sure?' she asked. She looked happier, though, like she really wanted me to cancel but wouldn't voice it out loud.

'Course I'm sure. You're my girl,' I told her. When I saw the smile beaming on her face, I knew I'd made the correct decision. 'Let's go watch *a* film and eat some popcorn.'

'Sounds good to me.' She pulled me closer to her side, and I knew that eventually we'd be okay.

'Do you think that's how American schools actually are?' Clo asked me out of nowhere, pausing the film we were watching.

'What do you mean?'

'Like, all cliquey and bitchy?'

'Clo, it's like that here,' I said, laughing at her. But now that she mentioned it, I thought a little deeper. I'd always wondered about American schools and whether they were depicted correctly. 'Not like *The Set* are a bundle of laughs, is it?'

'True. Although I've always wondered where the appeal is, ya know? Like, why do so many people want to be one of the popular girls? Why do people care so much about Odette's opinion?' Clo asked, her brows furrowed, and her eyes went blank.

'I have no idea. Only thing I can think of is the fact that people are attracted to power. If a person wields power, they're instantly more appealing.' I shrugged, tasting the theory on my tongue.

'Sort of like how Ollie and Leo are sexier because of the power they hold?'

'Yep. Exactly that,' I replied without much thought. It took me a moment to realise that not only had she brought up Leo's name, but she'd also called him sexy. What the fuck was happening? 'Clo, are you feeling all right?'

'I think so...' Her voice went higher at the end, so it came out sounding more like a question than a statement—the epitome of uncertainty.

'You just used the name Leo and the word sexier in the same sentence.'

'I mean, I may hate him... but damn, he's fine,' Clo said, chuckling.

'Yeah, he totally is,' I agreed, laughing along with her, and I could feel the iciness between us slowly melting away. It felt like it had back at the beginning of term, when we'd just met and the guys hadn't got between us yet. 'They're both sexy and they know it.'

'They definitely know it. I think that's one of the many reasons I detest Leo so much. He flaunts his looks to anybody with eyes, I swear. He's a rich bastard too, and that usually has all the girls fighting for his attention. Look at Odette.'

'Odette's not exactly full of brains, though, is she?' I said. I couldn't be certain as she was in the year above and I didn't share any classes with her, but from the conversations I *had* overhead, the girl wasn't the brightest. Couldn't always be helped, though. Sometimes people struggled at school and that was okay. But I could tell Odette didn't care. She believed that she'd bag a Hawthorn and never have to work again—something I'd *legiterally* heard her say.

Oh, for fuck's sake.

I'd started to think like Griff.

I hoped Leo would see sense soon when it came to Odette. Seeing as he was looking out for me, part of me wanted to look out for him in return.

'It irritates me how she's all over him at all times.'

'Why does it bother you?'

Clover looked at me, her eyes narrowed. I still hadn't told her that Leo and I were in contact via texting. It was almost as if I'd kept the secret too long and, if revealed, it would look worse than it was. She'd think I was hiding it from her—which was exactly the case, but still.

'It doesn't. Just don't want to see him used by her,' I said with an uninterested shrug.

'Believe me, I think he's the one doing the using.' Clo pretended to gag and stuck her finger into her open mouth.

'I've walked across those two too often now,' I said without thinking. 'It's not a sight I need again.'

Clover went quiet, probably imagining the image I'd just put into her head.

'Thanks for the visuals, Sky,' she said. I felt a pain in my shoulder and caught sight of Clover's fist as it moved back from the punch it had just delivered. I grunted.

'Bitch,' I muttered.

Clover just grinned at me like a maniac, teeth and all.

'Whore,' she replied, with her smile still firmly in place. I rolled my eyes, and we went back to watching the movie. The only thing breaking the silence was our popcorn eating. It was nice spending time with her like this.

No boys.

No distractions.

Thirty-One

ON A TUESDAY MORNING, History was the first class of the day and it excited me to sit with Ollie. He had swim practice before school, so I was waiting for him at my locker, lost in my own thoughts, when a wet sensation spread from my head downward.

Liquid covered my head.

Freezing liquid.

All I could think was that I hoped it wasn't pee, but that would surely be warm, not ice-cold. The smell gave it away as some kind of ice slush drink that smelled super sweet and was super sticky.

For fuck's sake. I was wearing my last clean uniform. The others were all in for cleaning and Clover wore a different size uniform to me, so it wasn't even like I could go up to our room and steal hers for the day. I didn't even know where the staff did the uniform cleaning, so not like I could venture there and see if mine was clean already—or if they had any spare.

'Shit, Sky,' Griff said, appearing in an instant.

Whoever had put the drink over my head had long since disappeared. I hadn't even got a glimpse of who had done it, but who was I kidding, it could literally have been any student at the school—of any age.

'Listen up!' Griff called out to the hallway and every student in our vicinity stopped and turned to look at him, some with quizzical expressions, others looking bored but knowing they had no choice but to listen to him. 'If I see anybody picking on Skylar, or throwing shit at her, or tripping her up, then you *will* face the consequences. *The Set* may have told you that this shit is okay, but as a member of *The Sect* I will make your lives here hell. Now, go to class!'

Everybody scattered as quickly as possible, bumping into one another in their hurry to get away from Griff's wrath. I'd never seen him look so mad. I expected it of Ollie, and even Leo to an extent, but not happy-go-lucky, cheeky Griff.

'Are you okay?' he asked, taking my appearance in from head to toe.

'Yeah, I'm okay,' I said and gave a tentative smile, 'but I smell like a blue raspberry.'

'Haven't you always wondered what a blue raspberry is? Like, what? How? They're not even real,' he said. His lip curled up at the side, a laugh fighting to leave him, but he seemed determined to keep a straight face.

I laughed at Griff's obvious attempt to cheer me up. Although he was telling the truth. Who decided what a blue raspberry was or what it tasted and smelled like?

While I was caught up in my laughter, Ophelia and Oralie swanned over to us in silence. The smug look on both of their faces told me that even if they weren't the ones who'd poured the drink on my head, they definitely had okayed it.

'Did you have anything to do with this?' Griff harshly whispered to the two of them, trying not to draw any more attention to the four of us. Bless him for trying, but we'd been the centre of attention before the girls had even come along. The girls entering the scene had just made us more interesting to the onlookers.

'Who, us?' asked Ophelia, using that look that all pretty girls thought would get them off the hook. A bite of the lip. A flutter of eyelashes. She moved her head to survey the entire corridor and everybody watching. Her voice was louder than normal, and I knew she wanted people to hear her.

'Yes, you two. Who else would have planned this?' Griff growled, bored of their shit.

'Pretty sure, *Griffin*, there are many people here who would do this to the New Girl. We don't tolerate trash around here. Hawthorn Academy has always been for the elite,' said Ophelia.

Sadly, I knew there was a lot of truth in Ophelia's words. A large number of students would go out of their way wanting to get on *The Set*'s good side and would achieve it by terrorising me.

'I'll be talking to Leo about this,' Griff threatened them, but I wasn't sure what difference it would make. Wasn't like Leo being 'on my side' had helped me much thus far.

I wanted to think that Leo had my back, at least a tiny bit, even if he wasn't able to come right out and say that we were friends. I wanted to get Leo alone to ask him the questions burning through my brain. To find out why he acted like he cared about me via text but was also happy to sleep with the ringleader of my bullies and let her set the entire school on me. It didn't add up, and it wasn't like I could discuss it with anybody else. Nobody knew that Leo and I were in contact with each other.

'Leo's on our side. He can't stand this piece of shit either,' Oralie piped up, shaking her head at Griff.

Now, I was even more confused than normal, and fuck, I hated feeling confused. It was one of my biggest pet hates in life. Anything that made me feel stupid was something I typically avoided.

'Come on, New Girl, let's go get you another uniform,' Griff said over his shoulder as he walked away from the scene. I followed Griff quickly, getting away from the girls, who looked as if they were out for my blood.

Griff knew everything about Hawthorn. Literally, Griff seemed to know every secret and every staff member.

'How come you know everything there is to know here?' I asked, my voice shaking as I tried to keep my focus ahead of me and not behind where I could still feel the glare of the girls' stares.

'It always makes sense to know as much as you can about a place like this.'

Which I guess made sense, even if it was a little cryptic.

Ever since he was eleven, Griff had been a student at the academy, and I could totally imagine the three boys learning all they could in order to survive. Leo's dad owned the place, so maybe he knew the most, but the other two weren't far behind in knowledge about the inner workings of it all.

You didn't get to rule the school without knowing everything about everyone.

According to Ollie and Griff, they even had dirt on the girls, but they hadn't utilised it yet—or so they said. I couldn't see why they had reason to lie, but a large part of my gut didn't trust them.

They were waiting for the girls to do something really dark, which basically meant they needed to succeed in killing me because they'd already drugged and nearly drowned me, and the boys had done fuck all about it. I didn't *want* to doubt them or be that annoying girl who asked too many questions, but something didn't add up.

Actually, something fucking reeked.

Something besides me and the blue raspberry slush I wore.

***

SOMETHING WAS PLAYING on my mind, and the more I thought about it, the more I couldn't hold it in anymore.

Clover and I were in our room, both studying and getting on with our homework, but I had to tell her the thing sitting on the tip of my tongue.

I still hadn't told her about what happened between Ollie and me after the gala. No matter how much Clo disliked Ollie, I still wanted to share it with her. Best friends didn't always need to like, or agree with, each other's decisions, but they needed to be supportive and understanding, regardless. I just hoped that when I told her, she didn't stab me with her pencil or something drastic.

'Clo,' I called across the room, louder than necessary, but once I knew I was going to tell her, I needed to just spit it out. But when she looked at me, I wanted to pussy out and keep quiet. What if she judged me too hard? My only other option was to talk to Griff about it, and no matter how great he was, I didn't want to talk about sex with him. Maybe Ollie had already told him. After that kiss in the library, Griff knew by the next period, so it would make sense for Griff to know already.

My mind wandered off... Clo harshly called my name to grab my attention.

'Earth to Skylar!'

'Huh?'

'You said my name, then stared off into the distance. You okay?' she asked. I could tell she was worried about my mental state because she'd moved over and sat down next to me on my bed. She knew I wasn't a huge hugger but risked my wrath anyway by entering my personal bubble, wrapping her arm around my shoulder, tucking me closer to her body.

'Right, I did do that,' I mumbled. I took a deep breath, preparing myself to tell her.

The moment she felt me take in the deep breath, something clicked in her mind. I looked at her as her face soured, almost crumbling into itself, and the look of disgust hit me hard in the gut.

'Please,' she begged, shaking her head. She took in a deep breath to match mine. 'Seriously, Sky, please don't tell me you fucked that arsehole?'

'I can safely say I didn't fuck any arsehole.' I went with humour—and deflection. *Sue me.*

'Fuck off, you absolute comedienne.' I could tell she wanted to stay stern, but her face cracked a little. 'You know what I bloody meant.'

'C'mon. I am kinda funny.' I nudged her with my elbow, on purpose digging into her rib a little more than necessary. I was feeling aggressive towards her, so an elbow dig seemed perfectly adequate.

'Yeah, funny-looking for sure,' she said, and I nudged her harder. 'Ow!'

'Stop being a bitch,' I told her.

'Stop trying to tell me shit I don't want to hear then.'

The gigantic sigh I made in response was so loud, I bet everyone on the school grounds heard it.

'Do not sigh at me,' she reprimanded with a wagging finger. 'I'm trying to look out for you, but, girl, you are not making this easy for me.'

'Should I? You've not made getting to know you easy for me.'

'Touché.'

We both started laughing before we lay down on our backs and got comfortable.

'I know I sound like a massive dick ninety-nine percent of the time, Sky, but I promise you that I'm looking out for you. I know what they're capable of.'

'I get that but just try to be a *little* happier for me.'

'I'll try,' she huffed. 'So, spit it out then.'

'Fine.' I took another deep breath. 'I slept with Ollie.'

'Beside him or...'

I could tell by the naughty glint in Clo's eye that she was trying to make me say the words out loud.

'Fine,' I said, covering my face with my hands, thinking that would make it easier to say the next part. 'I had sex with Ollie after the gala.'

'I knew it!' she exclaimed, almost poking me in the eye with her finger. 'I knew you were acting differently. I mean, it was a toss-up between that or, you know, the whole Olivia being found dead thing.'

'Wow, Clo, didn't know you were so sensitive.'

'Piss off. I know you know what I mean,' she said, and I smiled at her.

It was something we said a lot to one another. To the point that in texts with one another we'd shortened it to IKYKWIM, and both saved it as a shortcut on our keyboards. It was that thing we said that solidified our friendship in my mind.

'I get you. But yeah, Olivia definitely threw me for a loop.' Then I registered the rest of her sentence. 'What do you mean I've been acting differently?'

'Honestly, I can't explain it. It felt like you were avoiding me, so subconsciously maybe you were without meaning to.'

'I guess I could've been without knowing it…'

'It's all good,' she said, setting me at east. 'I want all the juicy deets.'

'Do you actually?' I asked, sceptical.

'Of course. I may not like the boy, but you're my best friend. Course I wanna know everything!' Getting comfortable, she crossed her legs and leaned forward a little.

'Well, I'm not sure what to say, actually.' I was at a loss, and I felt a tad bit embarrassed just talking openly about it with her. It had been hard enough to spit out I was no longer a virgin. 'It was good.'

'Just good?' Clo looked at me with one raised eyebrow, pity filling her gaze.

'More than good,' I said with a laugh. 'Finding words is hard.'

'That sentence was shocking! You're meant to be the English student out of us.'

'Meant to be? I *am* the English student out of us,' I said. I picked up the closest pillow and threw it at her, but she dodged it. 'I don't know, Clo. It was really, really good. Like, orgasm on the first try, good.'

'Whoa. Now that *is* good!' She actually looked impressed for a moment. Then remembered it was Ollie we were talking about and caught herself. 'I'm surprised he knew how.'

'Oh, ha-ha. Hilarious.'

'You know I am. Seriously, though. No regrets?'

'No regrets.' I shook my head emphatically. 'At. All.'

'I'm glad then,' she said and leaned over to hug me briefly, and I was happy that she hadn't made me feel shitty about my decision. 'Happy for you, girl.'

'Thanks,' I said, unsure if she meant it fully, but I was happy that she'd said it, even if it was pretend. 'The timing felt right.'

'As long as you're okay with it, then shit, it doesn't matter what anybody else thinks. I've got your back.'

For the rest of the evening, the two of us spent our time

gossiping about students, teachers, and celebrities. The whole time, though, I wished I'd felt comfortable asking her for more in-depth sex knowledge. It wasn't like Clo wouldn't tell me shit and be honest with me; it was more me not wanting to rub in my relationship with Ollie more than necessary. I knew she wasn't jealous of *him*. Actually, most of the time I thought she was plotting his demise. However, I knew she *was* jealous of Odette, no matter how many times she'd said otherwise. When she thought nobody was looking, she'd glance in Leo and Odette's direction, trying to watch them unnoticed. Leo would turn to look back at her, but he'd always find her looking at anything but them. Being an outsider, I could see it all happening. Even if the two of them thought it was secretive.

I'd given up asking at this point. She clearly wouldn't tell me anything, and I wasn't in that place with Leo where I could ask him deeply personal shit.

Oh, well. If they wanted to keep shit to themselves, then I wasn't getting involved.

Even if I wanted to.

Thirty-Two

VALENTINE'S DAY.

The first one in my life where I actually had a boyfriend. Somebody to spend the day with—well, actually the weekend with. I was beyond excited. I tried to keep my full excitement to myself, though, as I knew Clover was feeling a little sore on the subject. Especially now that Leo and Odette were official. Whenever I brought Leo up in conversation, though, all Clo said was, 'Leave it, Sky. I don't care who *it* fucks, but I do hope his dick falls off.'

Nice to know how she really felt.

But before I could celebrate with Ollie, I had to get through the school day first. Putting on my uniform before heading to breakfast, I made an extra effort with my hair and makeup—more than usual, anyway. I'd never been so happy to attend an upper school that had a uniform. I had anxiety just thinking of the anxiety I would have if I had to pick out my outfit every single morning. I struggled enough as it was picking out clothes to wear at the weekend, or after school.

Clover hadn't got out of bed yet. She hadn't even stirred. Come to think of it, her *many* alarms hadn't gone off. I left it as late as I could before trying to wake her.

'Clo,' I called across the room, but when that seemed to make no difference, I approached her bed and leant down to her. I softly shook her shoulder, hoping not to shock her too much.

'Fuck!' she startled and bolted upright—hitting my nose with her head in the process.

'Fuck!' I exclaimed as I tried to stop my vision from seeing multiple Clovers. My nose was gushing blood in an instant, and I ran to the kitchenette to grab some tissue. Of all the days, I did *not* need Ollie to come get me for breakfast and find me looking like the victim of a crime.

'I am so, so sorry, Sky! Shit! I know how much you've been looking forward to today,' she apologised, breathless.

'It's okay, really. It's not like you meant to do it.' I tried to smile, but it was hard to do while holding the tissue against my nose. I only had the one clean school shirt—something that was starting to become an issue of mine.

At that exact moment there came a hard knock on our door, followed by three quick raps. It was a code Griff had made up so we'd always know when it was him at our door, and Ollie had adopted it. I rolled my eyes, knowing we would have to explain the shit that had just transpired. I knew Ollie only put up with Clover's presence because of my friendship with her, and I seriously didn't want to give him any more reason to dislike her.

I opened the door to find Ollie leaning up against the frame, holding a massive share size bag of crisps and an even larger bag of chocolates. On seeing me, he smiled, but his face faltered when he took in the state I was in.

'What the fuck?' he asked as he launched himself into the room, slamming the door behind him.

I knew he'd closed the door so nobody in the corridor could look in and spy, but it made me feel wary nonetheless. Clover didn't hurt me on purpose, but knowing Ollie the way I did, he wouldn't see it that way.

Arms surrounded me again, pulling me into a hug I never wanted to end. My mind was moving a mile a minute, so I hadn't realised that Ollie and Clover had continued talking. Actually, they were *shouting*.

'I didn't mean to do it, *Oliver*. Sky was leaning over me to wake me up and she scared the shit out of me. It was a knee-jerk reaction. Nothing more to it.'

I could tell by the look on Clo's face and the shade of red it was turning that it wasn't the first time she'd told him what happened. I knew I needed to get involved and stick up for Clover. It really had been an accident.

'Oh, so this has nothing to do with the fact that today is Valentine's Day and that you didn't set your alarms because you were hoping to skip this day entirely? Nothing to do with last year or Leo?' Ollie's chest vibrated as he spoke, the sensation causing me to try and loosen the hug so I could look at Clover, but he just tightened his grip on me. His fingertips pressed into my skin hard. I winced, sure he was leaving marks on my skin.

'You think you know everything, don't you? People like you make me fucking sick,' she spat, livid that he'd mentioned the L word.

'You just want Sky all to yourself. You know that you have no fucking chance of making any other friends in your pathetic fucking life, so you want to latch on to my girlfriend,' Ollie said, his anger growing with every word. 'I won't let you take her down with you.'

'Take her down with *me*? God,' she scoffed, rolling her eyes. 'You're actually delusional! Tell me you're hearing this shit, Sky?'

I broke free from Ollie's hold and looked at Clover. Her green eyes were filled with unshed tears and I knew the dam could burst at any moment. I also knew she would hate herself if it happened in front of Ollie.

'Babe, I'll meet you outside in two minutes, okay?' I said to Ollie, knowing I needed to get him gone before Clo broke, whether he got pissed at me or not. I didn't want him to think I was choosing Clover over him, but I also needed to let him know that she was my best friend and I wasn't gonna stop caring about her just because she hurt my nose that wasn't even bleeding anymore. It wasn't like she'd broken it or even caused me to need a change of clothes. Accidents happened—Ollie should know that better than anyone.

'Fine,' he spat, 'but you better not take too long, Sky. I won't be waiting out there like a dick forever.'

I sighed, biting my tongue. He was a prick, and I for sure would make my ire known to him later in the evening, but for the moment, I knew it wasn't worth responding to.

'I'll be two minutes, tops,' I said, standing on my tiptoes to kiss his cheek to placate him. He nodded, and after sending another filthy look Clover's way, he put down the bags of food he was still holding and left the room, letting the door slam behind him. The force of the door slamming closed caused a shock wave of sound to emanate throughout the room.

Clover faced me, a look of pity on her face.

'Do you get it now, Sky? Can you see even slightly where I'm coming from?' she asked, her voice small but her words sure.

'I mean...' I trailed off. I could see Clover's point of view, but I also slightly understood where Ollie was coming from, too. Clo had a lot of internal anger for Leo and, by proxy, Ollie. The two of them weren't ever going to be friends, but I hated that I was being lumped in the middle of their feud. 'I get you. Can you also slightly see where he's coming from, though?'

'Sorry,' she said with scorn. 'But are you asking me if I agree that I'm trying to take you down with me?' Her anger was palpable. It tasted all burnt and bitter. 'Why are you so determined to fuck up our friendship and choose his side?'

'There aren't any sides here, Clo. I just want my best friend and my boyfriend to get along. So please, do me a small favour and just be civil for now. It's Valentine's Day. Please,' I pleaded. I'd never had a best friend or a boyfriend, and I just wanted both of them to get along.

'I'll try for now, but I swear to you, Skylar, if I find out he's playing you in any way, shape, or form, I will do everything I can to make you see the truth.'

I nodded. I didn't think he was hiding shit from me, but I could tell Clo thought he was.

'Go. Enjoy your weekend,' she said and hugged me, then made a shooing motion. I left the room quickly, knowing that Ollie was still waiting on the other side of the door for me. I reckoned he was probably five seconds away from busting through the door with impatience.

After the weekend was over, I was going to sit down and weigh up just what Clover had told me. I wanted to believe that I trusted my own judgement, but honestly, I was so out of my league here.

And that was what unsettled me most.

Thirty-Three

THE DAY MOVED FAST and the next thing I knew, we were in London eating at a fancy restaurant I'd never heard of.

Everybody had left me alone at school. It was a pleasant surprise seeing as I'd totally expected some kind of Valentine's Day prank. *The Sect* issued some kind of warning on the Hive to leave me alone, but I was surprised people had listened. I hadn't actually read the warning as I didn't want to read the hateful comments that would accompany it, but Clover had told me the gist of it the night before. It was the first time there'd been a *Sect* sanctioned pause.

I felt bad all day about what had happened between Ollie and Clover that morning, but if I was being honest with myself, it had been brewing for some time, always lurking underneath the surface. No matter how many times he'd tried to prove himself as worthy, she'd found a reason why he must be false.

And I meant what I said to myself. After the weekend, I would think through everything, not letting either of them cloud my opinion.

My mind came back to the restaurant, and I glanced across at Ollie, who was looking down at the plate in front of him. Every few minutes, I nearly pinched myself, wondering how my life had changed so much in such a short period of time. I didn't know what I'd done in a past life, but clearly something was starting to go right for me.

The two of us had a full, packed schedule for the weekend before returning to school, and it all felt so surreal. We'd checked into the hotel under Leo's name, something to do with the age you had to be to book a room, and I didn't question it. Although I was pretty certain that if they'd thrown enough money around, that wouldn't have mattered at all. One thing I'd learned from these guys and those at the academy was that if you had enough money to waste, people would do literally anything for you. Even if they didn't want to.

I reckoned Ollie actually enjoyed the secretive nature of the arrangement—and really, so did I. It felt sordid, in the very best way.

'Quick question. Why do fancy restaurants have so many pieces of cutlery?' I asked him, staring down at the large plate of food in front of me. I knew that it wasn't a very original question, but seriously, a fork's a fork, right? Like, who really needed that much cutlery for one meal?

'Pretty sure it's another way to make the little people feel little.' Ollie smirked, not realising that he'd lumped me in with the 'little people' he was mocking.

'Right...' I mumbled. I smiled half-heartedly, taking in the surrounding scenery. I was glad I'd been dining in the dining room at Hawthorn for the last few months. Otherwise, I'd have been even more star-struck with how fancy the place looked. Although the restaurant was more sleek and modern—no dark, ornate, wooden panels in sight.

Ollie's cutlery clattered as it landed on his plate. Lips pursed and eyebrows narrowed, I could tell that something had irritated him. Specifically, that *I* had irritated him.

'What's the matter?' he asked, his eyes hard; the spark that had been there a moment ago fading, about to disappear entirely. 'Tell me.'

'N-nothing,' I said, using the universal code girls used to signify that they were not okay but wanted you to try harder to get a real response.

'I'm not doing this shit, Sky. Tell me. Now.' He slammed his hand down on the table, causing me to jump and the plates and glasses to clink. His rage had come out of nowhere.

'I just don't like being considered a *little* person. It's different for you. You grew up with money.' I shook my head at him, not wanting to get into it here. We'd been having such a great time together. It was our first time out of school with nobody else there, and I wanted to enjoy it to the fullest. Not argue over something silly. Christmas had been good, and we'd spent some time alone, but the others were always down the hall, or at least somewhere close by in the house. 'I didn't have a lot growing up. At all. Fuck, before I got the scholarship here, I worked my butt off trying to keep food on the table.'

'Not like you had to do that, Skylar,' he drawled, his cavalier attitude pissing me off. Dismissing what I said without even fully processing it. 'Cora could have got a job.'

A laugh came out of me, so loud that the people sitting at the tables nearby turned their heads to look in our direction. I hated that he was talking about my mum as if he knew her better than I did. As if she would have gone and got a job if I'd simply told her to. *Yeah, right...*

'Cora does nothing she doesn't have to. Trust me on that.'

'Andy should have found work, then. Been the man of the house,' he said with a shrug, choosing to ignore my tone and continuing to pursue the conversation. *Silly boy.*

'Sorry, but did you meet the same people that I know? Can you even hear yourself right now?' I asked, disbelieving. I'd stopped eating too, but, unlike Ollie, I'd put my cutlery down gently. Everything I was hearing out of his mouth right now was honest bullshit.

Pure and utter bullshit.

'You could have refused to work. Forced their hands.'

'What and not eat?' I rolled my eyes at his ignorance. 'K.'

I couldn't with him. If I continued talking to him, I'd get mad, and it'd ruin our weekend before it had even begun. I picked up my cutlery and continued eating, ignoring him. The two of us ate in an awkward silence.

Ten of the most uncomfortable minutes of my life passed. Then finally, Ollie looked up from his empty plate.

'Sorry,' he mumbled, so quiet that I only just caught it. I was going to make him sweat a little, though. No way was I just taking his piss-poor sorry at face value.

'Can you hear somebody talking?' I asked the empty space, acting childish but fully aware of it. 'Or was it the wind?'

'Oh, ha-ha, you twat,' he said. He was smiling at me, though, so I knew he didn't actually mean it. 'I'm sorry, okay? What I said was out of order.' He had a sheepish look on his face, and I knew he was replaying his words in his head and hearing them from my perspective. Or at least that was what I assumed he was doing. I mean, that was what he should have been doing.

'I'm going to accept your apology. I mean, it mostly sounded sincere,' I joked, smiling at him close-mouthed while twisting my hair around my finger. It was an attempt at flirting, but I wasn't sure I was doing an outstanding job of it. Ollie's expression was one of bemusement, as if he wasn't sure whether I was flirting and trying to be sexy, or whether I was just constipated.

I stopped my attempt and then promptly burst into laughter. Fuck me, was there anybody more awkward on their first Valentine's Day date than me? I knew we'd been dating for a while now, but the whole weekend felt serious. Real.

We went back to sitting in silence, but it was a comfortable one. The silence you could enjoy with somebody you shared a bond with.

For dessert, I chose a simple basic bitch option of raspberry sorbet. I'd never really been that into sweet food—chocolate and cake just weren't my thing. When I'd first told Clover, she'd looked at me as if I had three heads. She was incredulous and ever since had forced me to try everything she baked in class in order to convert me. Turned out, there wasn't too much left for me to try and nothing so far had made me fall in love. At one point, she was so offended, I thought it'd come in between our friendship. Even more than my relationship with Ollie had already come between us.

Ollie clearly had no qualms about eating what they called *a proper dessert*. He'd got this real fancy look pie tart thing—at least I *thought* it was a tart. Either way, he seemed to enjoy it.

Good for him.

THE CAR PULLED up at the front of our rather posh hotel and I waited for Ollie to get out first and open my door for me. Every time he did something chivalrous, I swooned inside. He could be a dick, a proper beast, but then he'd melt me by acting like a real prince.

Or maybe I just had *really* low expectations.

I followed him to our room, still high from the show we saw and the evening we'd had. There was something about him that just made me happy whenever I was around him.

Did I question his intentions still?

Sure.

And it may be stupid of me, but I wanted to be his girlfriend, even with the doubts swimming through my mind.

On entering the dark suite, I instantly gravitated towards the large floor-to-ceiling glass windows that looked out onto the London skyline. I loved London at night. Ever since I was young, I'd loved the story of Peter Pan. The boy who never grew up. A story filled with adventure, pirates, mermaids, and fairies. Who the fuck didn't dream of that? I used to fall asleep wondering what it would be like to fly high above London, to look down and see tiny cars the size of ants, people barely a speck, if visible at all. Looking down on it all, rising above the little people—rising above the position life had handed you. *Shit. Now I sound like Ollie.*

He came up behind me on silent feet to wrap his arms around my waist. I transferred my weight back into him, using him as my support, in more ways than one.

'It looks beautiful like this,' I whispered. The darkness surrounding us was in contrast to the brightness of the world outside. I'd never been a city girl. Never wanted to live or work in the city. But damn, I would consider changing my mind if I could look out at such a beautiful view every night. The view was everything to the dreamer inside of me. To the girl who lived with her nose stuck in a book, the Belle of her own story.

'My view's beautiful,' Ollie whispered, leaning down to brush his mouth against my ear. His breath caused shivers to cover me from head to toe with goosebumps.

Heat rushed through me and my stomach filled with jitters at his words.

Was it a line? Of course.

Did it work? *Of fucking course.*

'Have you ever thought of what it would be like to fly over a view like this?' I asked, my words the only noise in the large, minimalistic room.

'What, like on a plane?' Ollie asked, confusion mingling with his sultry voice. 'I know what that's like.'

'I guess,' I replied quietly, feeling stupid for asking the question. Of course he'd seen the city from above on a plane. He'd lived a much different life than the one I'd known. 'I've never been on one.'

'Never been on a plane?' he asked, the surprise in his tone a little insulting.

'Nope. Mum wasn't big on taking trips when I was growing up. Not ones that would cost a fortune outside of the country, anyway. If you couldn't drive there within five hours, then we didn't go, and even that was a push.'

When I was younger, I'd always been so jealous of the girls at school who would come back after the holidays with a tan and braided hair. It seemed so exotic to seven-year-old me. My mum drove us to Calais once, but only because she could get cheaper cigarettes over the French border than she could at home. We were in France for a grand total of six hours, tops.

'Maybe one day I'll get to take you on one,' Ollie murmured, and when I turned in his arms to look at his face, I caught him deep in thought. His light blue eyes glazed over, like he wasn't in the room with me, but was instead somewhere else entirely. He did that often, and at first, it had worried me, wondering where his mind went, but now I let it happen without comment.

He'd come back to me.

He always did.

'Let's go to bed,' Ollie whispered, his eyes glistening with an emotion I couldn't place as he took my small hand in his larger one. We moved towards the largest bed I'd ever seen, the sheets a luxurious cotton that beckoned me in. It was beyond anything I'd experienced before, and as much as I didn't want to, I felt small and unsure.

Gently, Ollie let go of my hand to remove his clothes, one item at a time, as I sat on the edge of the bed, staring up at him in awe. No matter how many times I saw him, I couldn't help looking at him like it was the first time. His broad shoulders, his taut stomach, every single part of him turned me on. Every time I looked at him, I forgot we were the same age because he looked older than me. More experienced and otherworldly.

Excited for his touch, I lay down in anticipation, my dress rising up and resting on my thighs. Before I could get comfortable, Ollie gripped my hand once again and pulled me back to sitting. Naked, he was standing directly in front of me and my eyes rested on his dick. I licked my lips and grazed my bottom lip with my teeth, a small smile curling the corners of my mouth.

I took his hard length in my hand, barely able to wrap it around fully, and it twitched in my grasp. Licking the tip, I tasted his salty pre-cum, instantly wanting more. The moan that left his mouth filled me with warmth, proud I had such an effect on him, as his eyes filled with want when he looked down at me. I opened my mouth, and he slid his cock inside. I felt hesitant at first, but his reactions helped me shed the nerves, a buzzing feeling sitting low in my stomach.

'Fuck,' he said, his voice thick, causing the hairs on my body to stand on end.

I let go completely, his praise spurring me on as I stretched my mouth wider, drawing him in and to the back of my throat, sucking and licking my way up and down his length in a slow, rhythmic motion.

He reached for me, his fingers feathering up my arms until they stopped at my neck. The brush of his thumb on my bottom lip caused a chill to trickle down to my toes and I closed my eyes, the sensations overwhelming me.

'Open your eyes,' Ollie demanded.

I opened them instantly, wanting to see his face. His dark indigo eyes were locked on mine, boring into my soul. My heart beat in an unnatural pattern, getting faster with every inhale. My entire body was growing hotter from his stare.

I need him. Now.

As if he could hear my thoughts, he slid from my mouth with a light popping sound, knocking my confidence, but then he pushed me down onto the bed, holding me there with his strength, his body moulding to mine.

'I need my cum inside you,' he whispered, his tone rasping. He kissed me slow and deep. 'But not here.'

Ollie kissed me again, bruising me as his hand reached between us to travel under my skirt.

My back arched involuntarily off the mattress as his large hand palmed me through my underwear.

'I need to feel you here,' he murmured, giving one last long kiss to my neck as his knuckles ran along my slit. 'So fucking wet.'

I writhed under his touch, whispering, 'P-please,' even though I didn't know what I was asking for.

Without hesitating, Ollie lifted himself off my body, grasped my legs to align himself, then slowly moved my underwear to the side to allow himself the access he needed.

In one slow movement, he filled me to the hilt. Our bodies trembled with desire and his forehead came down to rest on mine. The action was tender, almost *too* tender.

He stayed there, quiet, for the longest time.

The two of us silent, no words between us, our connection saying all that was necessary. The darkness of the room created an intimate vibe. Nobody could see us.

The intimacy overwhelmed me, the silence deafening. I broke it with a whisper. 'I need more.'

I pulled his lips to mine, and I sucked on his bottom lip, a tease of teeth making little bites.

He pushed up on his arms to take me in, to look me in the eye, and I saw apprehension lying underneath the surface of his. I swallowed, my nerves threatening to stop this beautiful moment.

With his lips slightly parted, his hand trailed down the centre of my chest. His smile tugged on the corner of his lips as he bunched up the material of my dress, as if he needed it gone. Needed to see me bare to him; see where the two of us joined as one. No barrier between us.

Ollie took his time, lazily thrusting into me until we were both breathless and fixated on only each other, racing for the release we both chased.

'Shit.' The muscles in his broad chest seemed to coil tight, his chin dropping as his hand grasped my hips, pulling me to him with urgency. They held me in place, tight, desperate, as if scared I'd fly away from his grasp.

A tortured growl vibrated from his throat.

'Come with me,' he demanded.

The pad of his thumb found my clit, teasing it in slow, pressured circles and sending me into a frenzy as my body fought for release.

'Oh my God,' I panted, almost at the peak.

My walls suffocated him, clenching and unclenching, as my body tumbled over the edge, over the precipice, and into the best kind of ecstasy, and he came willingly with me.

Our eyes locked. Ollie's blue stare filled with hunger, yet also with wonder.

I smiled softly at him, the only words on the tip of my tongue ones I wouldn't voice out loud. Couldn't voice out loud.

I think I'm falling for you.

Thirty-Four

MONDAY MORNING CAME, and I was still on a major high from my trip with Ollie. We'd had such a wonderful time, and even though I'd told myself I was going to sit down and weigh up Clover's worries once I got back, the weekend made me not want to. After the wonderful time we'd had together, nothing negative was going to compute in my brain for a while. My brain was basically mush when it came to thoughts of Ollie. It was a heart-shaped pile of squidgy matter, and I was a sucker for letting it happen. Since day one, Clover had warned me against the boys and there I was in a relationship with one of them.

Spending time together over the weekend without the distraction of school and other people was exactly what our relationship needed. Every day, I fell a little more in love with him. I couldn't stop the train even if I tried—and believe me, I'd tried. Not like I was going to tell him how I felt, though. I didn't want to scare him off, and I knew without a doubt he wasn't ready to hear it. Nobody liked the clingy girl who gushed her feelings too fast.

'Ready to get this shit show on the road?' Clover asked me as we left breakfast, Griff and Ollie trailing along behind us. They were in deep discussion about something swim team related— honestly, I tried to keep up with them, but I had no clue about any of it.

The four of us were heading to an entire school mandatory assembly. I had seen little of Ms Hawthorn as of late, and no part of me felt upset by that. Every now and again I'd see her in the hallway up ahead, but when that happened, either Griff or Ollie would purposefully lead us in a different direction. Pretty sure they were avoiding her more than I was.

'Any idea what it could be about?' I asked.

'Probably announcing the annual charity fundraiser. Takes place at the end of the Easter term every year,' Clo answered, matter-of-fact.

'Who decides what the fundraiser is?'

'*The Set*. But everybody in the upper two years has to take part in some capacity. Last year it was a silent auction ball that I could hide away during while working in the cloakroom.'

'Fingers crossed for us that we're able to hide away this year,' I said. We locked our arms together, only breaking apart when we reached the hall.

Ollie dropped into the seat next to me on one side and Griff the other. I'd grown quite fond of being in the middle of an Ollie and Griff sandwich. The jealous stares started the moment we sat down—girls of every age giving me the evil eye. *Petty much.*

As usual, the hall was full of chatter until Ms Hawthorn appeared on the stage and then all talking ceased. Just like that. Her mere presence had an effect on everybody and more than once, I'd wondered how she had the school so under her control. Nobody wanted to get on her bad side.

'Quiet now,' Ms Hawthorn said once she'd reached centre stage, even though you could have heard a pin drop in the auditorium and her words were unnecessary. She had always hit me as somebody who took a thrill out of being in control. 'I have gathered you all here today to discuss the end of term charity effort this year.'

I wondered if Ollie knew what it was going to be. Surely if it was decided by *The Set*, the boys would have some clue of what it was. However, when I'd asked, he'd changed the subject.

'This year, boys and girls, we shall put on a charity fashion show for the school charity.'

The room erupted into noise all at once. Instantly, groaning came from the older years, and the younger years cheered and laughed as if this was one of the best outcomes.

I looked behind me to catch Clover's eye. I found her sitting a couple of rows behind me with Leo and Odette next to her. She looked back at me; her face livid, her brows furrowed in anger, and the straight line of her mouth told me just how pissed off she was.

'Settle down, children. Settle down,' Ms Hawthorn spoke softly, but her words cut through the noise regardless. 'The students of the upper years will be organising and modelling in the show. Odette Aston has the list of assigned roles. The Hive will have a copy of the list too, so make sure you are aware of what we expect of you.'

Her gaze found mine, and I swore her facial expression became even more severe, like her grey eyes were looking into my soul, or maybe attempting to poke around in my grey matter somehow.

'That will be all for today. In rows, you are to depart the auditorium quietly and in single file. Make haste to your first period.'

With that last sentence, Ms Hawthorn took a step away from the microphone and stayed there. As each row slowly left the hall, I saw her assessing everybody. I had a feeling that nothing happened at *her* school without her knowing about it. Meaning she knew about my multiple attacks and hadn't once called me into her office about any of them. Not sure why it was only hitting me as odd now; but fuck me, that was odd. She'd called me in about the video after Parents' Day, but really, that had been a tactic to pacify the parents who had witnessed it and nothing more.

I found myself lost in thought, leaving the room in silence with Griff and Ollie beside me, and it was only when we entered the hallway again and Griff spoke that I came out of my trance.

'Reckon they'll ask me to model underwear?' he joked, wagging his eyebrows comically. 'Everybody needs to see this package, right?'

Ollie and I chuckled at him. *Honestly, this boy.* I could never decide whether he was playing around or if a part of him slightly believed his own hype. He flirted with everybody—and I mean *everybody*. I'd never seen him with anybody outside of our group, either. Even at the parties we'd been to, he'd stuck by Clover's and my sides throughout.

His words settled into my brain, trickling in at a slow pace. I sputtered, 'S-sorry, they could ask us to model underwear?' I could hear the incredulity in my tone, my shock radiating through me in stages. We were sixteen, for fuck's sake. Well, the upper years were aged from sixteen to eighteen, but only people with an early birthday in year thirteen were actually eighteen. Respectable institution, my arse. They constantly sold that vision to the people shedding out the big bucks, but clearly, they were full of shit.

'Potentially. I mean, Odette and her cronies set this up, remember? They'd love to show off their figures in front of a large crowd,' Griff said, turning to face me.

'How large of a crowd?' I asked, swallowing down my anxiety. The cogs started to turn in Griff's head, as he tried to come up with a suitable answer that would placate me.

'A couple of hundred, I guess? It depends. Last year's silent auction ball had a large audience—you know how much rich people love flaunting their wealth. They were all fighting to outdo one another. The year before, though, was boring and barely any parents attended.'

'What was it?' I asked, curious.

'Honestly, it was so shit, I can't even remember. But I will say, the elite love to appear benevolent. Even if they couldn't give any fucks in actuality,' he said, shrugging.

'Right...' My sentence hung in the air, and I felt none the wiser about any of it.

Clover came and joined us, having finally fought her way out of the hall and through the masses of younger years, all congregating together to discuss the news.

'Girl, you are not gonna like this.' Clover fidgeted, rubbing her hands on her thighs, clearly agitated.

Well, shit. That sounded foreboding.

'Stop with the dramatics. Some of us have places to be,' Ollie said, assessing her. His eyes narrowed—the way you'd look at shit on your shoe.

The two of them still weren't on the best of terms, and to be honest, I was over it. If they wanted to act like bloody children, then I wouldn't stop them.

'Go on, Lady Luck, don't keep us in suspense,' Griff said, playing with Clo's hair, wrapping a strand around his fingers and twirling.

'Right. So, I got waylaid by dickface and ogre number one as they just wouldn't leave the row and they weren't letting me pass. Odette had her list of roles, ready to bark at anyone who wanted to listen. I found out what's "expected of us".'

I giggled at her choice of words.

'And...?' I tried my best not to roll my eyes at her, but she was dragging it all out a little longer than she needed to. The suspense clearly gave her a thrill.

'And we've been assigned to model in the show!' She ended her sentence with a big flourish, both arms raised above her head before flopping down; all heavy and full of purpose.

'W-we what?' I screeched, causing everybody near us in the hallway to turn and look in our direction. I always seemed to draw attention, and not always in a good way. 'We have to m-model? Model what?'

I started hyperventilating, feeling the onset of a mini panic attack, and obviously it was at that moment that Odette and Leo finally left the hall and became witnesses to my meltdown. *The Set* had done this shit to me on purpose. The smug look on Odette's face told me as much.

'Whatever the coordinators decide you'll look best in,' Odette said as she gave me a snotty look from head to toe. 'But let's be honest, New Girl, I highly doubt they'll find anything that will look good on your boxy frame.'

Yep. I resemble a box because I'm not stick thin with my ribs show-ing. Nice one, Odette.

I didn't say what I was thinking, though. Nope. All I uttered was, 'Oh.'

Nice one, Sky.

'Let's go,' Leo said as he pulled Odette away from us, walking her down the corridor, his grip firm on her arm as they went. When our group started up their conversation again, I looked down the corridor to see Leo looking back at me. He winked, his lips raised into a smirk before the two of them disappeared into a classroom.

'...you won't even help us. Typical. Don't you think he should, Sky?' Clover asked me and I looked back at the group to see Clover staring at me. Griff was looking over my shoulder to where Leo had just been, his features forming a quizzical look, and Ollie was looking rather proud of himself.

'Huh?' I asked, confused about what Clo wanted me to have an answer to. I'd clearly missed something while Leo held my attention and winked at me.

'Ollie should intervene with *The Set* and put us on cloakroom duty.'

'Err...'

Did I think that? I knew that was what Clover wanted me to think—to agree with her wholeheartedly and hope that we could get out of this shit pile we'd somehow landed in. But I wasn't so sure. The tradition *was* for the girls to organise the charity effort, and I wasn't going to make myself even more hated by trying to mess with tradition.

Rich people took that shit seriously.

Fuck, my mum took tradition seriously, and she lived in a house paid for by benefits—benefits I felt pretty certain they'd swindled, or outright lied, to obtain. Got to love Cora.

Plus, *The Set* wanted me to model for a reason, and I wasn't the kind of person to back down when challenged.

'Oh, for fuck's sake, Skylar. You really are turning into a pathetic, desperate whore, you realise that?' Clover said, derision filling her face. Her features twisted, her whole face contorting in a grotesque manner, and my stomach bottomed out. She'd never looked at me with such scorn in the entire time I'd known her.

She stomped away and all I could do was stand there in shock; frozen in place like an ice statue.

She'd also never spoken to me that way before. Never called me names or made me feel irrelevant. Unimportant.

If I was in a cartoon, my jaw would have dropped to the floor like an anvil, exaggerated and comedic.

But this was real life. And no part of what just happened was comedic.

So, I did what any respectable girl would do in my situation: I cried.

Ollie and Griff both stood still, uncomfortable and unsure of the best action to take. A split moment later, Griff hurried away to catch up with Clover, and Ollie hugged me tight to his hard, warm body.

I instantly felt a little better, but then I remembered that Griff had flounced after Clo, and my stomach sank once more.

'She had no right to say that to you,' Ollie whispered in my ear as he moved us into an alcove so we were away from the foot traffic surrounding us. 'And I don't think that you're pathetic or desperate and you are definitely not a whore.' His eyes hardened on the last word, filled with anger at Clover.

He lifted my chin up, tilting my face so he could see me fully, and I gave him a small, tentative smile. Even though he sort of had to say that, being my boyfriend and all, it still made me happy that he did.

Was I slightly pissed at Griff for ditching me to go after Clo? Yes.

According to her, they'd bullied her last year, and she was here on scholarship too, so it wasn't like she'd been friends with them before I came here.

Okay, so maybe I was more than slightly pissed off. I thought Griff and I were close. Obviously, I'd been blind to the truth.

'Try to forget about her, babe. She's just jealous and bitter and not worth it,' Ollie told me in a calming tone. His hands started rubbing up and down my arms in a soothing, circular motion. It grounded me and although the tears didn't stop, they slowed down. I nodded, mostly to make him feel as if I agreed.

I didn't know if I did, though. I didn't know *how* I was feeling.

'Do you want me to talk to Odette?' he asked, lifting my chin to look into my eyes. 'Because I will if *you* want me to. Clover, of all people, won't force me into it, but I'd do it for you, babe. Believe me, she was trying to save her own arse and not yours like she said.'

I thought about my decision for a minute or two. The two of us were still standing in the alcove, the rest of the hall quiet as pupils moved to their first class of the day.

'Babe, we're going to be late for class,' I told him, but not making any effort to move from his hug. I took a deep, calming breath and said, 'I don't want you to talk to Odette.'

He hugged me tighter, squeezing me to the point that I felt my lungs cry in protest.

'You sure?' he asked as he swept a strand of hair from in front of my face and tucked it behind my ear. Every time he did that, I melted a little more inside.

'Yeah. We don't need to antagonise them more and I can model in the fashion show. How hard can it be?'

Famous last words?

Duh.

Thirty-Five

IT FELT strange not to be on talking terms with Clover. Our room was silent whenever we were both there, and no matter how hard Griff wanted to resolve the issues between us, nothing he'd tried so far had worked.

In my eyes, Clover needed to apologise for what she'd said. It was uncalled for and even if she believed it to be true, I was still fucking insulted she'd put the words out into the universe. She could have continued to think it and I'd have been none the wiser.

'C'mon, Sky, you two need to talk,' Griff implored me as we listened to Mr Sommers drone on about Bentham and Utilitarianism. Okay, I wasn't listening at all. I was in my head thinking about everything and nothing at the same time. My mind stuck in that place where I weighed up my feelings about my friendships and relationships—but also about what pizza toppings I preferred. 'Clo wants to talk to you. I know she does.'

'Not gonna lie to you, Griff, but I'd rather hear that from her. Not once has she tried to talk to me, and we share a fucking room. She's had enough opportunities in the last week.'

I doubted Griff had intended to piss me off, but trust me, he'd succeeded.

The fact she was trying to use Griff as a go between was such a shitty thing to do. It wasn't fair for him to be in the middle, but also, part of me felt like he'd taken her side anyway and had put himself in the centre of it all. Yeah, he was talking to me while in class, but outside of class, he spent every minute with her.

Shit, they weren't even sitting with Ollie and me at dinner or anything.

'She's worried. She knows she fucked up, New Girl. You've just got to give her the chance to say sorry,' Griff said, sounding worried himself.

'I didn't know she needed me to come to her for an apology,' I snapped, irritated that he couldn't see where I was coming from. 'If she's as sorry as you say, then she could have told me already.'

'I've told her that, but she's worried you hate her.'

'Of course I don't hate her. But I do feel like she's been thinking shit about me behind my back for a while. She meant what she said at the time she said it. She called me a whore, Griff.'

'Yeah, at first, I reckon she meant it. But I know she doesn't *actually* think that of you.'

'Oh, has she told you that then during one of your super secret couple's nights?'

Griff blushed, a sheepish expression on his face, as he faltered in his response.

'It's not like that.' His meadow eyes felt as if they were penetrating my soul, reaching deep inside of me, trying to make things right between us. 'She doesn't feel comfortable around Ollie right now. She's worried he's going to retaliate on your behalf.'

'Eurgh, I am sick of her always trying to paint Ollie as the bad guy. He's done nothing to her all year. She believes you've turned over a new fucking leaf, so why can't he have too?' I raised my voice, causing the other students in the class to turn and look at us. The teacher shook his head at us but continued chatting about ethics. Even if he didn't really talk about it, Griff *was* a part of *The Sect* and that gave him sway, even if he never abused that power.

'I did actually say sorry to her,' he mumbled. Maybe he thought being quiet would make me less mad at the fact that he was obviously criticising Ollie, and probably Leo, too. 'Look, Sky, I don't want to fall out with you, but just know that Clover's coming from a good place. A true place. Ollie hasn't always acted this way…' Griff trailed off, not saying any more, which made me even more curious to get to the bottom of what he meant.

'In what sense?' I asked, hoping he'd give me a little more to go on.

But he didn't. He merely said, 'Just be careful, babycakes. You don't have the full picture.'

'Give me the full picture then,' I demanded, frustrated that he was being so cryptic with me.

He shrugged. 'I would, but it's really not my place, babydoll.'

Honestly, his words and attitude disgusted me.

Babycakes? Babydoll? Is he for real?

'You can be a right wanker. You know that?'

'True, but I'm a wanker with your best interests at heart. Remember that,' he said, his whole demeanour condescending.

I continued to ignore him for the rest of the lesson, as I hoped my silence would lead to him revealing something to me.

He didn't.

So when the bell rang, I left the classroom as fast as I could, ignoring him calling my name behind me.

On my way to my next lesson, I stopped in an alcove to root through my schoolbag, willing myself to calm down. Griff had raised my temper and I knew I couldn't go to a lesson with the O girls in a foul mood. Who knew what I'd do?

As I moved my hand through my bag, I felt a note sticking out of the top of my history textbook. I pulled it out to figure out what it was and found a simple, handwritten note in Ollie's distinctive scrawl that read:

Meet me outside after third period.

I read it and wondered when he'd put it in there. Was it a repeat of Halloween and a total trap? Maybe, but that note had been typed to disguise the sender.

Or maybe it was Ollie's idea of romance?

Either way, I'd go stand outside after third to find out, and I could always text him if he didn't show.

Heading into English with a spring in my step, I smiled. How exciting relationship stuff could be.

THE MOMENT my third lesson ended, I rushed outside straight away, barely stopping to take a breath. I wanted to give myself enough time to spot Ollie before lunch. If the note wasn't from today, then I'd know within ten minutes.

'Skylar.' My name sounded like dirt coming out of Odette's mouth. Ever since Olivia had been found with a lock of my hair, I'd worried the girls would escalate, but if anything, they seemed to back off a little. Like they were scared of me, of what I could do to them if they crossed me.

'I'm waiting for Ollie,' I said. Maybe if they knew he was coming soon, they'd bugger off and leave me alone.

'Oh,' Ophelia said, confused, pointing off in the distance. 'I thought I saw him by the tree line a moment ago.'

Right, like I was going to fall for that one. They probably just wanted to get me alone over by the trees. Barely any teachers would be over there, making it a prime spot. They must have been biding their time, waiting for the perfect moment to get me back for harming their friend.

'Thanks. I'll wait for him here,' I said as I got out my phone to text Ollie and find out whether that note was from today. I could also text Leo if shit got out of hand too. I tapped out a quick message while the girls stood and stared at me, their hatred shining on their faces, leaking out into the atmosphere.

HEY, BABY, DID YOU WANT ME TO MEET YOU NOW?

It wasn't long until I got a reply from him.

YEAH, I'LL BE THERE SOON. JUST SETTING UP.

I wondered what he meant by setting up. It being lunch time, maybe he'd sorted some kind of picnic out. That'd be quite cute—sexy and romantic, too. I'd always wanted somebody to care about me and make me cute sandwiches and shit.

'He'll be here in a m-moment,' I told them. Not sure why I felt the need to fill them in, but apparently I wanted to prove something to them. And yeah, I wanted to rub it in a little. Okay. A lot. After all, Ollie had picked *me*. Not one of them, with their over-bleached hair and their obviously enhanced features. But plain old curvy me.

I was frustrated with myself too, though. I'd been doing so well at controlling my stutter and not letting it control me, and then *The Set* came along and fucked it up. My anxiety still lived underneath the surface, lurking in the dark, but I had found it easier to breathe recently.

'Eurgh, I thought you'd got rid of that fucking horrible stutter,' said Oralie, fake shivering. 'You could have been one of us, New Girl, if you weren't such a poor fucking freak.'

I made a big deal of rolling my eyes. Even their insults weren't hitting the mark the way they usually did. Maybe it was my newfound confidence guiding me. Or maybe I'd realised that they were just insecure rich bitches who had no real power over me.

'If you'll excuse me,' I sassed, walking away from them with a sway of the hips, leaving them standing with their mouths wide-open. Pretty sure they were just as shocked as I was.

I'd walked away from them, for maybe the first time, and, damn, did it feel good!

COME MEET ME BY THE TREE LINE.

I followed Ollie's command and went to the edge of the trees to wait for him.

'Hey, beautiful.' Ollie came up behind me and scared the ever-loving shit out of me. I jumped as he grabbed my waist to steady me. 'Fancy a picnic?'

I smiled, turning around so I could see his face. His eyes were the lightest of blues today, like a really clear ocean, or maybe more like a sky on a cloudless day. A super rare sight, but one I welcomed.

'I'd love one. Please tell me you have cheese sandwiches?' I asked, almost whining at him to give me good news. A picnic without cheese sandwiches was a crime.

'Course I do. They're your favourites,' he said simply, like there hadn't been another option for him. My heart thumped an extra beat, my stomach fluttering at his thought and care.

'Let's be honest, they should be *everybody's* favourites. Honestly, there are monsters out there who don't even like cheese. That's some serious effed up shit.'

'But, babe, there are people who like cheese and then there's you.'

Taking my hand, Ollie walked me a little way into the woods to where he'd arranged a picnic blanket and a basket. The blanket was one of those quintessential red check picnic blankets that I swore you saw in every film and TV show and it made me smile. *How cute.*

'Oh, ha-ha. Hilarious,' I said, loving the fact that I felt like I could be myself around him these days. 'I like cheese. Is that a crime?'

'No. But it should be a crime *just* how much you love it.'

'I can't help it if I'm a turophile,' I told him. I'd learned the word for a cheese lover recently, and I thought it sounded like something else entirely, but once learned, a new word must be inserted into every conversation. 'Actually, I found an article the other day about a guy who puts cheese on top of his milk cereal AND on his ice cream.' The look of disgust on Ollie's face was a picture. I wasn't joking—and, of course, the guy was British.

'The day you put cheese on ice cream, babe, is the day I leave you.'

'That's totally fair,' I said with a laugh, accepting his statement as fact.

I got comfortable on the blanket while Ollie sorted out the food and drinks. I couldn't decide what he was hoping to get out of this, but he was winning some definite brownie points, that was for sure.

The food tasted delicious. Alongside cheese sandwiches, Ollie had made the kitchen prepare some of my favourite snacks. It was these sort of things that made me fully realise he must *actually* listen to me. Or notice what foods I loved and always ate more of. I'd never had this level of attention on me and my habits before. If I wasn't already falling in love with him, then I would've after my fourth cheese sandwich triangle.

'Thank you,' I said, finishing my bite with relish. I leaned over to him and gave him a quick kiss on the lips. It was brief but filled with my gratitude. The boy had hit me in the heart.

'It was my pleasure,' he said, a young and wholesome smile on his face. 'I have another surprise for you.'

'You do?' I asked, my lips forming into a matching smile.

'Yep. I'm just gonna go grab it. Don't move from this spot,' he commanded. He stood and left our secluded area at a fast pace. He was out of my eyeline in no time.

I laughed at his retreating back. Where would I even go?

Ten minutes passed, and I worried he wasn't coming back.

A rustle of leaves behind me made me pause.

'Ollie, is that you?' I called out. I hadn't seen anybody else since we entered the woods, and I didn't think it was Ollie as the sound was coming from a totally different direction to the one he'd sprinted off in.

Wonderful.

A dull pain shot through my skull.

What. The. Fuck.

I tried to catch my bearings before the next blow came, but it came too quick. Pain rippled across my shoulder, making its way down my entire right arm.

My cry pierced the air, and bird wings flapped away.

I glimpsed over-bleached blonde hair in my peripheral. Of course it was a member of *The Set* hurting me. Or maybe all three of them. They were watching me when I entered the woods to meet Ollie after all. Purposefully staying close by in case a situation presented itself.

Where the fuck had Ollie gone to?

'Let's teach this little bitch a lesson,' Odette said, then giggling followed from the others.

'Yeah, New Girl,' Ophelia spat. 'This is for Olivia.'

The kicks and punches continued and my vision faded, the pain vibrating through my entire body. *Man, it hurts like a motherfucker.*

Even after the blows ended, all I could feel was pain everywhere.

'Sky? Sky? Are you okay?' a voice called out to me. Footsteps got closer and although I couldn't see him, I knew it was Griff. I couldn't mistake that voice. When I tried to call out to him, no noise came out of me except for a harsh, rasping breath.

His footsteps came closer, then a 'Shit, Sky,' slipped out of his lips, which meant he'd found me.

I wanted to cry in happiness that he was there and that I didn't need to crawl through the woods in my current state.

Although, that wouldn't have happened if Ollie had come back.

Fuck. *None* of it would have happened if Ollie had come back.

The real question was, why didn't he?

Thirty-Six

ONCE AGAIN, I found myself in the hospital wing. I'd spent so much time there since joining Hawthorn, I may as well put my name above a bed and make it permanently mine. Griff sat in the chair beside my bed, cheeks flushed with emotion. After he'd found me and helped me back to the school, he hadn't left my side. He really could be super sweet and caring—the perfect gentleman.

'This is getting fucking ridiculous. I'll be having words with Ollie and Leo later,' he grumbled. He got out his phone and started furiously typing. 'Can't you and Clover beat them up at some point?'

'Erm...' I trailed off, wondering if I could actually throw a punch at Odette.

Don't get me wrong, I'd thought about it. The repercussions didn't seem worth it, though, as we could both lose our scholarships. Plus, Clover was in her last year here and had plans to go to a great university. I couldn't ruin that for her.

Not like we were on talking terms either, so it wasn't like I could ask her.

'Not really,' I said, my tone sure. 'She's not talking to me, anyway.'

'Well, it's not like Ollie and I can. We can make them outcasts, yeah, but we can't physically harm them,' he said. The look on his face told me that fact pissed him off. I also didn't believe they could make them true outcasts, either, otherwise they'd have tried harder already. 'And you and Clo will be fine. I promise.'

I ignored his comment about Clo. Earlier that day he'd been singing a completely different tune, and I didn't want to reignite our argument when I felt so ill.

'I want to hurt her,' I said. 'Believe me, I would love to see Ophelia with a broken nose because I punched her so hard. But I just feel like I'm above that, right?'

'Yes!' Griff said enthusiastically. 'You are above them, New Girl, completely.'

'Thanks, Griff,' I said, smiling at him. He always knew the perfect thing to say that would make me feel better.

'Sky.' Griff's voice got quieter, and he stopped me from grabbing my phone off the counter to text Ollie. 'I need to talk to you.'

'Okay...' I leaned back, getting more comfortable in the bed. 'What about?'

'About my parents,' he whispered, sheepish. Worried, too. 'So, I don't know what you know about them?'

'Not much,' I said with a shrug. 'Nobody will tell me anything.'

'Right.' The chair cushion groaned as he fidgeted. 'So, my mum's name was Eliza Hawthorn and my dad was Damien Cooper. They died when I was five in a car crash. I was in the car too, but I don't remember any of it.'

Shit. He'd completely thrown me off, as I hadn't expected him to tell me that. I'd spent Christmas at his parents' estate and nobody had ever mentioned that they weren't alive. Parents' Day too it was just sort of implied they couldn't be there. Now I felt like a right bitch —I'd grumbled to Griff so many times about my mum and Andy.

'After it happened, I went and lived with Leo. His dad, Edward, is my uncle, 'cause he's my mum's older brother. The other option was to live with my mum's twin, Millie. Ollie's mum.'

Slightly struggling to keep up, I nodded, trying to wrap my head around it all. I knew that the three boys were close and had known each other since they were kids, but I didn't realise they were all related and were cousins with a Hawthorn link.

'So you're related to Ms Hawthorn too?' I asked. Why that was the first question that came to my mind, I had no clue. Maybe it was because I didn't want to say anything else too deep, or say something that would put my foot in it.

'Yep, she's my aunt, but having a different surname means Ollie and I can keep more of a low pro. I forget that you haven't known us all since birth. Most of the kids here have parents that are in the same circle as us, and they all know who we're related to.'

'Wow. Maybe I would've known too if one of you had told me.' How had I known them all as long as I had and not known any of it? I knew the boys were keeping secrets from me, Clover too, but I'd put them to the back of my mind and rationalised that they'd tell me when the time was right.

'Yeah, wow.' He chuckled. He looked lighter, if that were possible. Like finally getting the truth off his chest and letting me in more had made him feel better. 'You okay?'

'Not gonna lie, Griff, I hadn't even registered what your surname was until just now, but honestly, I'm good.' I chuckled too. 'Seriously, though, are you okay?'

'I'm good, New Girl.' The playful smile returned to his face. We were both silent for a moment. 'I really think my mum would have loved you.'

'You reckon?'

'Yeah.' Griff shrugged. 'She was beautiful. Her smile could light up a room.' His eyes were glossed over and I knew his mind had travelled elsewhere. 'You remind me of her.'

'I do?' I asked, surprised.

'Mum was strong. Let nothing faze her. Just like you.'

'I don't think that's entirely true,' I mumbled. 'I definitely let shit faze me.'

'Maybe on the inside, New Girl, but it rarely shows on the outside.'

'Why are you always so nice to me? Even on day one, you weren't horrible to me.'

'Honestly, I'm not sure why I wasn't. They'd instructed me to give you a hard time. New girl in the school, on scholarship, nobody was sure whether you could hack it here.'

'Have I proved that I can hack it now?'

'Girl, you proved you could hack it after that first party in the woods.'

'That feels so long ago. But here I am, still finding myself in here.' I gestured around to the rest of the empty hospital wing.

Griff reached out and took my hand in his, squeezing it tight. The gesture made me feel loved, and as if the two of us shared a secret of sorts. Like I'd made a friend who liked me for me. Not because he wanted in my pants. Not because he had some misguided sense that he needed to protect me. But because he wanted to be my friend and keep me safe. It felt good.

'I'm glad. Not that you're in the hospital wing again, obviously. But the fact that you're here. At Hawthorn still. I worry that one day, you won't want to be friends with me anymore.' His eyes were more green than blue today, and they stared straight into mine. He leaned closer to me and squeezed my hand again. 'Promise me that no matter what else happens this year, we'll still be friends at the end of it?'

I could feel his nerves as he asked. Not sure if the nerves were because he was worried about my answer or just from the fact he'd voiced an insecurity like that out loud. Usually, he came across so carefree. I wondered what was running through his mind and why whatever it was made him feel the need to ask in the first place. And yeah, it was suspicious as fuck.

'I promise,' I answered instantly, no qualms about making the promise, even though I felt unsure of his reasons. I opened my arms wide for a hug and Griff instantly leaned into them. It was one of those tight hugs, where you could hear your ribs groaning in revolt. Believe me, mine were screaming.

I spotted Ollie over Griff's shoulder and I lifted my lips into an unsure smile, slowly leaning out of the hug I'd just started. Griff noticed that my attention was elsewhere and glanced behind him.

'Hey, dude,' Griff said through gritted teeth, anger rippling off of him. 'Wondered when you'd get here to be with your girl.'

'I would have got here faster, but apparently *my girl* and my best friend were too busy getting cosy to let me know where they were.'

Huh? Griff had been writing furious texts the whole time we'd been here, and I'd assumed they'd been to Ollie—but clearly not.

'S-sorry. I thought you knew where we were.' My voice rose at the end, so it came out more like a question. I really thought he knew we were here. Surely he must have known that the girls had got to me again? And if he'd returned to the spot he left me in, surely he could tell from the state of the area that something had happened?

'No. I did not,' he growled. His eyes, like his words, were hard and I could see the anger there. The anger he was directing at me, like any of it was my fault.

I wanted to say, *Oh yeah, Ollie, sorry I didn't tell you where I was while three girls were ganging up on me.*

I rolled my eyes at his shitty attitude.

'Got something to say, sweetheart?' he drawled.

'Oh, I don't know, dickhead. Maybe you should ask her if she's okay?' Griff stood, puffing up his chest, taking a step closer into Ollie's space.

I was pissed. He hadn't asked if I was okay, even after he'd glanced briefly at the bruises forming on my face, but other than that, he hadn't even tried to come closer and touch me.

'Stop it. Both of you,' I shouted loud enough that the two of them stopped sizing one another up and turned to look at me. 'Maybe you should go.'

My eyes were staring intently into Ollie's. As much as I wanted him there to comfort me, it didn't seem like he'd be doing that soon and honestly, *fuck that.* I deserved to have somebody by my side who wanted to be there and cared that I was hurting. Griff had been nothing but nice since he'd found me, and Ollie's presence was ruining the camaraderie we'd established. The cloud of happiness Griff had created had burst.

'You seriously want me to leave and have this fuckwad stay here?' Ollie asked me, one eyebrow raised.

'Y-yes.' I held firm, our eyes boring into one another. 'Go.'

'Fuck this,' Ollie growled.

The curtain around my bed fluttered as he stormed out, the door of the wing slamming not long afterward.

I sighed.

I had wanted him to fight me on it. To grovel, ask to stay. Fuck, even just ask me how I was. But he hadn't. He hadn't fought at all, and it was the worst he'd made me feel in the entire time I'd known him.

I LEFT the hospital wing the next day, and it was Ollie who met me in the morning to take me back to my room.

'Where's Griff?' I asked, having expected him to come get me.

'I asked him if I could come get you,' Ollie said, shifting his weight from leg to leg. 'I need to apologise for how I acted yesterday.'

'You do, yeah,' I said, not letting him off. He'd acted foolish and we both knew it. 'You acted like a right knob.'

'I know. I'm sorry, babe.' He opened his arms and I stepped into them, wrapping mine around his waist, pulling him close. I breathed in his tobacco and vanilla scent, letting it fill my senses and ground me. 'I didn't know how to feel after you got hurt and I lashed out.'

I took a step back so I could see Ollie's face when I asked my next question.

'I've got to ask, Ollie,' I said, doing my best to keep calm and collected. 'Why did you leave me alone?'

'I'd forgotten to bring my gift for you,' he replied instantly, an eyebrow raised, cautious of me and my next sentence. 'So I went to get it.'

'What was it?'

'Your favourite dessert,' he said. It made sense that he'd arranged my favourite dessert for the end of the picnic. My stomach grumbled at the thought of salted caramel cheesecake. 'But when I got back and you weren't there, I may have thrown it in anger.'

'Thanks... I guess?'

'I'll get the kitchen staff to make it for you another day.' He tried to tug me back into his arms, but I resisted. 'What's up?'

'Did you know?' I asked, assessing his gaze, watching his eyes for any flicker of a lie. 'That the girls were going to come hurt me?'

'What?' he roared, snapping his hand back towards him, no longer trying to pull me closer. 'How could you think that of me?'

'I mean...' I was looking for the right words to say—words that wouldn't make him more mad. 'It's a little suspicious, don't you think?'

'What is?'

'That the very moment you left me there, alone, the girls showed up and attacked me.'

'What exactly are you implying, Skylar? Stop beating around the bush and spit it out.' His anger was palpable, and I knew I'd pissed him off, but it didn't matter. I needed to ask. I needed to know the truth—good or bad.

'I'm asking you if you set it up with them. I'm asking whether or not you knew something like that was going to happen.'

'I promise you,' he said, reaching out to grab my hands in his, 'that I didn't know they were going to do that to you. For fuck's sake, Sky. Part of me is irritated that you think that of me, but I know I've not always been the best to you, so I get it, and I'm going to let it go. Life's too short and I like you, you know? I hate seeing you hurt. It kills me to know you're in pain and I can't do anything to stop it.'

The sincerity in his eyes gutted me and made me feel crap for not trusting him. Of course the girls seized the opportunity they saw—literally. They saw me enter the woods, and they must've been close by when Ollie left me alone.

'I'm sorry,' I said, opening his arms up so I could hug his tense body. After I squeezed his ribs, he relented and reciprocated the hug. 'I was just being paranoid.'

'We're good, New Girl.' He placed a kiss on the top of my head, and I sighed with happiness and relief. 'Now let's get out of here.'

'Let's.'

Thirty-Seven

I HAD FELT that ever since Griff had opened up to me, we'd grown even closer. I understood him so much more, and I understood why he covered a lot of his genuine emotions with humour. Yes, he'd annoyed me, but ultimately I knew we'd make up. He was one of my favourite people in this shithole.

One person who wasn't that happy about how close I'd become with Griff was Ollie. Well, 'wasn't that happy' was an enormous understatement.

He was pissed. *Really* pissed.

'If you'd stop spending time with Griff, then maybe we could actually spend some time together?' he grumbled.

'We do spend time together.'

'Yeah, we do, but rarely just the two of us.'

'I don't think you're being fair,' I told him. 'It's not like Clover or Griff crash our time alone often. Fuck, babe, Clo isn't even talking to me still.'

'What did Griff talk to you about?' he asked, accusation thick in his voice.

'When?'

'In the hospital wing. After the woods.'

'Nothing. Nothing of importance to you, anyway. He was telling me about his parents.'

'Sure you're not lying?' He looked so paranoid, and I didn't know why. Something had agitated him. 'Are you keeping shit from me?'

I laughed out loud, literally, in his face. We were sitting next to one another at a table in the library as we shared a free period, both of us trying to work on our English homework. Or at least I was. Ollie had been giving me sex eyes, and I knew he wanted to resolve this tension between us. He didn't seem to understand, though, that he'd caused this tension in the first place. I was matching his energy, not the other way around.

'Why would I lie to you? There's literally nothing to lie about...' Although that wasn't exactly true. I was keeping some of it from him, only because I didn't want to share too much. It was for Griff to talk about, not me. It wasn't my business to talk about *his* business.

'I'm sorry. Just seems like you'd rather spend time with him,' he said, pouting a little, his bottom lip jutting out and looking totally biteable.

'That's not it at all. I want to spend time with both of you and I *do* spend time with both of you.'

'Well, I want to spend time with you alone,' he said. I couldn't be certain, but I thought I glimpsed Ollie's eyes roll in my peripheral.

'Okay? All you have to do is ask or, you know, communicate with me. If I'd known you were feeling insecure, I would have spoken to Griff about it.' I shrugged.

Not having had a boyfriend before, this was all new to me and so stupid. I said nothing about Ollie still spending time with Leo, and I *never* mentioned the fact that he spent time with Odette and Ophelia because of Leo. Those girls were the reason for everything that had happened to me, or so we assumed, yet he acted okay with them when I wasn't around. Come to think of it, that was way worse and even more disrespectful towards me than my friendship with Griff could ever be towards him.

'I'm not insecure,' he spat out, his anger growing, and for the first time, I felt a little scared of him. 'I shouldn't have to beg my girlfriend to spend time with me. You should want to without being asked, Sky.'

'Of course I want to,' I mumbled. I rolled my eyes, probably for the millionth time during the conversation. 'How about tonight we hang out in your room? Just us two.'

I waggled my eyebrows, hoping to make him laugh. Who was I kidding? Ollie rarely laughed out loud. I hoped he'd give me at least a slight smile, though. Fuck, I'd settle for a lip twitch at this rate.

His face didn't move, which made me feel even more stupid. But he did respond with a curt, 'Sure.'

Not overly convincing, but I'd take it. I needed him to be okay with me. I didn't want yet another person I cared about to decide that I wasn't worth knowing. My friendship with Clover being on the rocks had really hurt me. I thought we were closer than that, but she wasn't talking to me still, and when we would both be in our room at the same time, she'd ignore me.

The tension was unbearable.

And I hoped it would be over soon.

OLLIE'S ROOM, ever since New Year's Eve, had become a place I took comfort in. Maybe it was because of the whole losing my V-card thing, but part of it was the fact that I felt closer to Ollie here. Like I could see inside of a tiny portion of his brain and understand him better.

The room was neat and minimalistic. Barely any furniture occupied the room, other than the bed and the sofa. No photos or posters adorned the walls. No personality at all. But really, though, when I thought about it, the room showed his personality perfectly.

The two of us were snuggled together under the duvet in Ollie's massive bed, the credits having just started on one of my favourite action films. Ollie had let me pick the film—he was clearly trying his best to get on my good side.

'Griff told me that Clover wants to apologise,' I blurted out, without thinking about the words themselves. It'd been playing on my mind ever since Griff spoke to me in ethics, but after the attack and our conversation in the hospital wing, it had slipped my mind, but now that it had re-entered, I couldn't think of much else. Ollie groaned the second it left my mouth, moving away from me in the bed slightly to turn and look at me.

'Course she does,' he said sardonically. 'What she did was out of order and she knows it.'

'Right. But should I forgive her?' I asked, unsure whether I even wanted to hear his opinion but needing to know, anyway. Griff was biased whenever I spoke to him about it, and it wasn't like I could ring up Leo and get him to weigh in with his opinion.

'Depends on what she says really, doesn't it?'

'Guess so...'

I reached out to him, hoping to pull him tighter to me again, but he resisted, annoyed at me, but I wasn't sure why. Either he didn't want me to forgive Clover or he was just aggravated that I'd brought it up on our night alone as a couple.

'Look, you clearly want to accept her apology. I can tell that she's been at the front of your mind ever since she said what she said.' Ollie sat up, the cover falling down to his waist, and I got slightly distracted by how good he looked in his bright white school shirt that fit him just right. 'Go running back to her.'

I followed suit and sat up too. 'What's that supposed to mean?'

'It means, little Sky, that you obviously don't give a shit that she was a total cunt to you. You're going to go give her a rim job the second she says sorry. No need to lie and act otherwise.'

'I'm not going to go "give her a rim job" as you've so delicately put it,' I spat, pissed he'd even said that. Having a best friend and wanting them to be happy didn't mean that you were licking their arse. 'But I am going to hear her out. Everyone can say shit in the heat of the moment that they later regret. I'm sure you've done it.'

'Course, but she called you a pathetic, desperate whore. Not exactly something that springs to mind without having thought a little about it first.'

'Rub it in, why don't you,' I said with a wince, the words hurting just as much as they had the first time they were hurled at me.

'I'm just saying. Have some respect for yourself.'

'What did you just say?' My blood boiled in my veins as I fought the urge to hit him. Who did he think he was, telling me I should have respect for myself? What a fucking wanker. I couldn't be near him any longer.

I climbed over him and got out of the bed. Fuck staying here with him. What on earth was happening around here?

'There's no need for you to leave.' Ollie looked at me and I could see the anger on his face, his lip twitching in irritation. 'You're going to let her ruin shit between us? *Again?*'

'Right now, Ollie, you're the one ruining shit between us. I'm gonna go before one of us says something we regret.'

I made my way to the door, opened it with a force I didn't know I possessed, and slammed it behind me. So blinded by my anger, I didn't spot Clover standing in front of me until the very last second. I halted, centimetres away from a full-blown collision.

'Hey,' she mumbled, looking embarrassed I'd caught her standing outside of Ollie's door, her eyes shifting from side to side.

'Hey,' I replied, stopping and taking a deep breath.

'Can we talk?' she asked, shuffling her weight from foot to foot, looking as uncomfortable as I felt inside.

'Sure,' I replied, irritation still in my tone, wanting to get this talk over with. My emotions were all over the place, and I wasn't sure if I trusted my own instincts right now. Fresh from an argument with Ollie probably wasn't the best time to talk to Clo about her hurtful words. 'Let's go back to our room.'

I didn't want to have to talk to her out in the open. Also, I didn't want Ollie to come out of his room and find the two of us standing there together. That would *not* go down well.

We made our way across campus in silence. Neither of us wanted to break the moment, the truce we'd come to while walking.

In no time, thank fuck, we made it back to our room. Clover entered first, and I went in behind her, filled with anxiety. I knew she wanted to apologise, but I also worried that she was planning to give me some "home truths" or some other type of advice that I did not want to hear right now.

'So…' I said as I perched down on the edge of my bed. Across the room, Clover did the same on her bed. Our room was so small, we were still close enough to see each other clearly.

'So…' Clo repeated and I giggled. This was silly. *We* were silly. We were best friends, which meant we were above this shit, or at least we should've been. We shouldn't have let it get to the point where we weren't on speaking terms and were avoiding one another in the halls. 'I am so sorry, Sky. I never should have said what I did, and for the record, I don't think you're a whore. Or desperate or pathetic either. I was mad, and I let my anger out on you.'

Our eyes locked across the room and a tentative smile played on my lips. Her apology was sincere—or so I believed—and really, I just wanted my best friend back. It wasn't fun walking the corridors without somebody to gossip and giggle with.

'Can you forgive me?' she asked, wiping a tear from underneath her eye, looking at me imploringly. 'I've been a right twat.'

I laughed, agreeing with her.

'Guess I could find it in my desperate and pathetic heart to forgive you.'

She laughed at me, and I could tell we were going to be fine. We were like a pot that boiled over and had simmered back down again.

'Promise you forgive me?' Clo pleaded, her eyes watery once again.

'Honestly, Clo, there's not much really for me to forgive. You said something you regret and you've said sorry. Let's just move on and act like it never happened.' I shrugged, not wanting to drag it out too much. And even though I didn't say it out loud, I was still going to be a little wary going forward, just in case it happened again.

'You're the best! I promise I won't let you down,' she said, crossing her legs on the edge of her bed to get comfortable. 'Now, tell me why you stormed out of Ollie's room.'

I rolled my eyes, remembering my argument with Ollie. 'Well...'

And I spent the rest of the evening doing just that. The two of us discussed why boys were such dickheads sometimes and how they didn't even realise it half the time.

It definitely made me feel better.

Thirty-Eight

OLLIE and I still hadn't made up a week later. At first, my anger had blinded me and I hadn't wanted to speak to him at all. He'd texted me a couple of times, but I'd ignored them, too mad to reply. But as time passed, the sadder I got about it all. Every couple had their first fight, but nobody had told me it hurt so bad.

History class was a bit awkward, and Ollie had even moved from the desk next to mine at the back to sit up front next to some girl who looked way too happy about it. Wasn't sure what she was so thrilled about. As far as I was aware, we were still a couple and she had no chance.

As soon as he'd done that, it solidified to me he was being petty and that we should have some space away from each other. Everything had gone super quick after we'd first slept together and taking a step back was probably for the best in the long run. Even if it made my heart physically hurt.

My phone buzzed in my blazer pocket and I removed it and looked when Clover wasn't looking in my direction. She'd taken a rather dim view—putting it politely—of Ollie's actions and was getting annoyed that he was still texting me.

CHECKING IN. YOU OKAY, STUTTER?

I smiled at the text from Leo. Ever since the events of Halloween night, I'd received a similar text once a week, and it made me think about him in a new way. It was super nice of him and totally went against his whole bored vibe. We rarely spoke in person, as he spent all of his time with Odette and *The Set* were still attempting to make my life miserable, but I also didn't feel like he was ignoring me either. The most recent tactic of the students was to put rotting food in my schoolbag and attempt to trip me up in the corridor. Luckily, I always found my balance at the last moment and hadn't gone down face first—yet.

'So, do you think we'll be able to get out of the fashion show?' Clover asked once we sat down for breakfast. 'I mean. Ms Hawthorn's not actually going to penalise us, is she?'

'Honestly, I doubt we can get out of it. I reckon she'd punish us and enjoy doing it,' I replied. The woman had looked like she meant business when she'd announced it during assembly, and the fact it was for charity and to make the school look good meant that we probably had to join in. 'The woman is a bit of a dictator.'

'True. The Hawthorns have always been sketchy mother-fuckers.'

'What do you have against the Hawthorns?' I asked for probably the millionth time.

'Hm?' Clover feigned ignorance. She ate her food, making her mouth so full that she didn't have to respond straight away.

'You know what I mean. You always use every opportunity you can to slate them, but I don't really understand why. Lottie always seems so happy to see you.'

'Hmm. I don't want to talk about it right now, but one day I will.'

'Is that a promise?' I asked, sceptical as all get-out.

'Nope. Just maybe.' We both chuckled, but mine was fake as fuck. It irritated me, or should I say, she was irritating me. I felt like I gave a lot in our friendship and Clo never reciprocated. It didn't help that we'd only recently made up. 'I really don't want to take part in the charity show. I'm worried it'll be like last year.'

'Last year?' I asked, casting my mind back to what she'd told me about it. 'I thought you worked in the cloakroom away from it all?'

'Okay, so don't be mad at me, but I may have lied about what happened at last year's charity thing.'

'Okay…'

'I didn't really work in the cloakroom,' she said. The revelation slightly irritated me, but I kept calm. My face clearly didn't give me away, as she continued without commenting on my sour expression. 'I was one of the girls on stage who announced the winners of the silent auction part of the evening.'

'So what happened?' I asked.

'Well, it was fucking horrible, and they pulled a *Carrie* on me.'

I'd just taken a sip of my coffee and spat it out onto the table in front of me. 'Sorry, what did you just say?'

'They pulled a *Carrie*. When I announced the winner of the weekend getaway to New York, they poured red paint all over my head and they ruined the expensive designer dress I was wearing.'

'You've never mentioned it,' I replied, petulant.

'Course I haven't. It was fucking embarrassing.'

'You could have told me, though. They've done some pretty shitty things to me this year. Would've been nice to know that you understood.' How had she managed to stay silent about it, even when she knew I was going through something similar?

'I know. I knew you'd understand, too,' she said. Her spoon stopped halfway to her mouth. 'I was just ashamed.'

'What's there to be ashamed of?' I asked, baffled at why she'd feel that way around me. We were best friends, and that meant never feeling ashamed around one another.

'I wanted to come across as somebody who had their shit together. You were the one person here who knew nothing of the past. I kind of wanted it to stay that way.'

'What do you mean?'

'Being new here, you knew nothing, and all I wanted was to be your friend.'

'We *are* friends, Clo,' I stressed.

'Yeah, now we are, but I didn't know that to begin with.'

'In the future, you can talk to me about it. If you ever want to.'

'Thanks,' she said with a wide smile, and I hoped she felt

better for telling me the truth. It irked me that nobody had told me about it—not just Clo, but the guys as well.

Clover and I didn't speak for the rest of breakfast, and I couldn't say it was a comfortable silence. We were both lost in our own thoughts, thinking of what we'd said and our feelings about it. I was slightly pissed at her, to be honest. She'd had so many chances to tell me exactly what had happened last year and that she related to what I was experiencing. It made me question our entire friendship and whether it was as solid as I'd believed it to be.

Questioning shit sucks.

WITHOUT OLLIE by my side at all times, I'd been keeping a low profile during school hours. I didn't need somebody to attack me or cover me from head to toe in slush again. The library had recently become a refuge of sorts, and I spent the majority of my free periods there. Mostly because it was easier—and away from the other students. Nobody wanted to be caught dead in the library, after all.

'Sky, I need to talk to you.' Clover came flying towards the table I was occupying, avoiding a trolley of books at the last moment. 'Urgently.'

'Okay...?' Puzzled, I put down my pen and stopped what I was doing.

'In private,' she whispered. I looked around, confused about why Clo had specified privacy when we were the only two people in the back of the library.

'Can we not talk about it here?' I asked with a groan, not wanting to move.

'No. Let's go,' Clover said as she packed up all my things in a hurry, putting them into my bag for me, not giving me a chance to stop her.

Within moments, we were leaving the library, and I found myself speed walking behind her back to our dorm room. She was a woman on a mission.

Rushing inside, Clover almost threw me down onto my bed and took the space beside me. I turned to face her, crossed my legs, and got comfortable. I could sense whatever she wanted to say was gonna be good.

'Sky, there's no simple way for me to say this.'

I rolled my eyes at the dramatics. 'Just tell me. It's obviously important enough to take me away from studying—and from people.'

'Look. I overheard the girls talking and I really think you need to hear what they were saying.'

'Go on.'

'They were talking about what Ollie's got planned.'

'Right...?' I didn't fully understand her point.

'Sky. It's bad shit. Like, he's the reason for everything that's happened to you this year, bad shit.' She made eye contact with me, I could feel her imploring me to believe her. To believe that what she'd been telling me about Ollie all along was true. She'd made her feelings clear about him all year, and for her, what she'd heard was only confirmation that she was right.

'Not trying to be a dick here, but what does that even mean?' I tried to stay calm. Tried to keep my tone casual. Tried not to let my anger show.

'It means that everything that has happened to you this year at the hand of *The Set* or the other students was at Ollie's say so. He's been pulling the strings this whole time.' She grabbed my hand and gave it a tight squeeze.

'A little far-fetched, don't you think?' I asked, laughing, but the look on Clo's face told me she wasn't joking around. She truly believed it all. 'How do you know the girls didn't just say it for your benefit?'

'Sky, they didn't know I could hear them. They thought they were alone.'

'Where were you?' I sounded suspicious, but fuck. I was.

'In the food classroom cupboard getting more supplies. They came in and only checked to see if the classroom was clear, not the cupboard.' Her words were coming out super fast. Soon I'd need subtitles to keep up. 'Odette was telling Ophelia and Oralie how Ollie had come to her during second period to tell her the plan for the fashion show.'

'And pray tell, what exactly is the plan for the fashion show?' Using my best posh British accent, I attempted to make a joke out of the situation.

Clover did *not* appreciate it.

'This isn't a fucking joke, Skylar. I'm trying to save you from being *Carrie*'d too. Not exactly like you can exact your revenge with telekinesis, is it?'

She had a point. They *had* blindsided me on Parents' Day, and we never figured out who took the footage they'd shown, even though my gut told me it was Odette without a doubt.

'No, but think back to Parents' Day and what the girls showed everyone. Ollie didn't film that.'

'One of the girls or Leo must have filmed it for him.' She nodded at me, like it made total sense in her head. 'I was with Griff that whole night, so that rules him out at least.'

I should fucking hope that I can rule Griff out. He really had become one of my closest friends—ever. I didn't want to believe he could have done that to me.

'But we've always known that it was one of the girls. What I mean is, *why* would Ollie orchestrate that? Why would he want that kind of footage made public?' I asked, fine-tuning my question.

'If his end goal is to hurt you, then I'm sure he wouldn't care.'

'Clo. What they showed that day was child pornography! Do you really think he'd risk that just to hurt me?'

Her response was so quiet, I almost didn't hear her words and it was only because I was looking so closely at her face that I saw her lips move. 'I do.'

Wonderful.

'What reason does he even have to hurt me?' I moved on my bed, no longer able to sit still while I listened.

'The girls kept mentioning something about your family and

how you deserve this,' Clo said, leaning forward, her voice a fraction higher than a whisper. She was probably worried somebody was listening through the door, but I didn't want to ask her, because I felt certain I would laugh at her answer.

'My f-family?' I stuttered, unsure what my family would have to do with anybody that attended the academy. My family had never been rich. At all. Then it hit me like a lightning bolt. 'Reckon this has something to do with my dad?'

'Thought you didn't know who he was,' Clo snapped.

'Well, I don't,' I said with a shrug. 'But doesn't mean somebody else doesn't know.'

'Yeah, that's probably it.' She didn't look convinced. 'I don't know, though, Sky, I feel like this year is going to be worse than what happened to me last year. I really wish you'd listen to me. *The Set* plans to reveal the truth about everything at the fashion show, whatever that means.'

If I knew Clover the way I thought I did, she wouldn't drop her suspicions anytime soon. Trust me to get a best friend, and a boyfriend, and have them both hate one another. Of course that was how it was. It would be too easy for them to just get along.

'Well, did you hear anything specific?'

'How much more fucking specific did you want them to get?'

'I don't know. Just seems odd to me they didn't mention any actual part of the plan. Like they *wanted* you to overhear them.' I shrugged. If they'd known Clo was listening, they could have said shit on purpose, knowing she'd run straight to me and repeat what she'd heard. They did talk about it in the cooking classroom, the one place where Clo was always known to be.

'Or they didn't say any part of the plan because they were being cautious, not wanting anybody to learn of their plans.'

Okay, so Clo had a point too. Either scenario could be the correct one, and there was no way to know for sure.

'Just be on your guard, yeah?' Clo asked, raising an eyebrow at me. Her green eyes were shining with worry for me, and I hated that we were still on such awkward footing with each other even after I'd forgiven her. I nodded, and she added, 'You sure you don't want to ask Ollie to see if you can swap roles with some-body else? If their plan revolves around you being on stage, then you can at least make it a little harder for them by working back-stage or something.'

'I'm sure,' I said, my tone hard. 'I'm not exactly on talking terms with Ollie right now, and even if I was, if I asked him to change my role, they'd know I was running scared and I don't want to give those bitches the satisfaction. We're modelling in the show, Clo. Deal with it.'

'Fine. But I don't have to like it.'

Fuck, I didn't like it either, but I meant what I said. I wouldn't bow down in fear. Not to *The Set*. Not to anybody.

Thirty-Nine

Are you free? Can we talk?

THE TEXT from Ollie came through at the end of last period, and I wanted to reply straight away, but at the same time I wanted him to sit and stew for a little longer. I had let him stew for a while, though, and if I was being honest with myself, I wasn't mad with him anymore. Mostly I'd wanted him to realise how silly he was being about my friendship with Griff. He must have realised that Clo and I were friends again, and that I'd accepted her apology for what she did.

Another text came through, and it melted my already thawing heart.

Come to my room, please?

After giving it a moment's thought, I messaged back that I'd meet him at his room after I'd been to my own room to drop my stuff off and get changed out of my uniform. Wearing a stiff blazer and tight skirt all day wasn't the comfiest after a six-hour school day.

I changed into a baggy top and some leggings, not wanting to dress up for Ollie, especially not when he needed to grovel—big time.

Clover came rushing through the door covered in flour, looking harried.

'Where are you off to?' she asked when she saw I'd already changed out of my uniform.

'Going to Ollie's room,' I told her, pulling my jumper over my head so my words came out muffled.

'Oh,' she said. I turned to face her, and she looked confused, like she couldn't understand why I'd be going there. 'You gonna forgive him?'

'I mean, it depends on what he says, but I'm no longer mad at him if that's what you're asking.'

'Honestly, I don't know what I'm asking. Are you going to at least ask him about what I overheard the girls saying?'

'Of course! He's been a dick, and I'm not gonna let him railroad me.' I forced a smile. 'I'm going now, so I'll see you later tonight.'

'I won't wait up,' she said, resigned.

I closed the door on her strained facial expression and tried to put the tension between us to the back of my mind. Something was brewing between us, and I knew that eventually we'd come to blows. Knowing that and accepting it were two completely different things.

OLLIE LIVED in a different building block to us, so I made my way across campus to his as quickly as possible. Walking alone around here always gave me the heebies. You never knew who could be hiding around the corners. Or in plain view.

I knocked on the door, and it opened instantly, warmth surrounding me within seconds. Vanilla and tobacco had recently become my favourite scents. It surrounded me everywhere now, and my brain automatically linked it to Ollie.

Ollie stood on the other side of the door, looking nervous.

'Hey,' he mumbled and moved aside to let me in.

'Hey.' I smiled. Seeing Ollie unsure was unusual, but it was what I needed to see. If I'd arrived and he looked all cocksure, it would've put me off him.

I went and sat on the two-seater sofa he had in his suite and he came and sat beside me. It was different from the last time I came to his room, unsure of myself, not knowing where to sit. I crossed my legs underneath me and turned to face him. For the first time since knowing him, I could see genuine worry in his features. He studied me, scrutinising my face, and I hoped my smile would let him know I wasn't here to fight again.

'Thanks for coming. I wasn't sure you would,' he said. I felt the warmth of his hand on my knee, and as he talked, it moved in a familiar circular motion, creating a swirling pattern.

'That's okay,' I said and continued before he could cut me off. 'But before you say what you want to say, I've got something I want to ask you about first.'

'Okay,' he said, blinking at me. 'What's up?'

'You probably know that I accepted Clo's apology,' I started, and he nodded. 'Well, the other day she overheard something the O girls were talking about that she thought I should know.'

'Okay...'

'They were in the food classroom and they didn't realise Clo was in the cupboard. They were talking about the fashion show, and about *your* plan for it.'

'My plan? For what?'

I shrugged. 'Well, that's just it. Clo didn't overhear any of the actual plan, but they said it had to do with what you wanted them to do to me.'

'I know that Clo won't believe this, but I really hope you do,' he said, imploring me with his eyes. 'I have no plans when it comes to you and the fashion show, other than watching you kill it on the catwalk.'

'So why were the girls talking about that?'

'I've got no clue.' He shrugged. 'Maybe they knew Clo was listening in.'

'That's what I said!' I blurted out, then realised I was meant to be suspicious of him, not agreeing with him. 'So, you promise you've got no clue what they were talking about?'

'I promise, babe.'

My eyes were locked on his, and I couldn't see anything in his gaze that made me distrust him or think he was lying.

'I believe you,' I told him. 'Now go on. Say what you want to say.'

'I'm sorry for being a dick. I should've never snapped at you for your friendship with Griff and I also shouldn't have got annoyed because you wanted to forgive Clo for what she said in anger. I've done things in anger too.' He took a deep breath. 'I'm also sorry for being so petty over the last couple of weeks.

My face must give away my disbelief because as soon as he saw it, he said, 'No need to look so shocked, babe.'

'I-I'm surprised you came straight out and said it, that's all.'

'You are, huh?'

'Yeah, I dunno. Thought you might try to talk circles around me or something,' I said, shrugging. Not like he hadn't done it before.

'Why would I do that?'

'You can be a little forceful,' I told him tentatively.

'Oh yeah?' he said in a calm tone, but his nostrils flared, like he was making an extra effort to come across as composed. 'Forceful how?'

'You sort of railroad me a lot.' I shrugged again, finding it hard to think of exact examples when his eyes were boring into mine the way his were at that moment. And yeah, I'd told Clo earlier that I wouldn't let him railroad me during our conversation, but I'd never said that it hadn't happened before. 'I can't pinpoint an example right now.'

'Well, I'm sorry for that too,' he said, letting out a long exhale. Slowly, his hand moved from my knee to take my hand in his. 'I don't want to be like my dad.'

'Huh?' I asked. Not sure how we'd found ourselves on the topic of Henry, but I'd roll with it.

'My dad has always railroaded everybody around him. He did

it to Millie when I was younger, and he does it to me now. Or at least he tries to.'

'Millie?' I asked.

Ollie surveyed my face, scrutinising me. 'My mother.'

It surprised me to hear him mention his mum. In all the time I'd known him, he'd never actively talked about her.

'Oh.' The shock must have shown on my face as he was still looking at me with questions in his eyes. 'Do you want to talk about her?'

'What about her?'

'Well, you've never mentioned her...' I was tiptoeing around him, worried I'd say something to piss him off and close himself off before we'd even begun. 'What was she like?'

'Obviously she was beautiful. Rich. Full of grace and poise.' He nodded, as if all of this was a given and hadn't really needed voicing out loud. 'She and her twin Eliza were the youngest of the four Hawthorn children and were very close.'

'Eliza was Griff's mum?' I asked, recalling what Griff had told me in the hospital wing.

'Yeah. The two of them were thick as thieves, always keeping secrets from everybody else. It drove their husbands mad, and then when Eliza died, my mum couldn't cope. She went completely off the rails and everybody worried about her.' I lost Ollie to his thoughts, and I could see the torment in his eyes. 'I remember little as I was only five when it happened, but I've heard a lot from the staff that helped raise me and from my dad when he's in a loving mood.'

I stayed silent, not wanting to interrupt his flow with an inane interjection. He didn't need me to speak. He moved our position, so he had his arms around me as I was sitting in between his legs, no longer able to see his face. His voice vibrated through his chest into my back.

'I remember how my dad would treat her, though. He couldn't understand her grief. Wanted her to keep up the impression of a *stiff upper lip*. Henry made her feel small, and I've never wanted to make somebody else feel that way.'

I nodded. Having met Henry Brandon, I could fully believe what he was saying. The man had seemed no-nonsense to me—and creepy as fuck.

'When I was ten, only five years later, Mum decided that she couldn't survive anymore. Didn't want to live in a realm without her twin.' Ollie sniffed behind me, holding back tears. I knew Ollie, and he would never cry in front of me—fuck, I doubted he'd cry in front of anybody. 'She committed suicide. Took a lethal cocktail of pills and alcohol and went to be with her dear Eliza. Left me with *him* without much more than a goodbye.'

I wasn't sure what to say. I knew his mum had died, but I didn't know the circumstances surrounding it were so sad. Unsure what to say next, I paused. I personally hated it when somebody said that they were sorry for your loss. It always seemed so disingenuous to me. Not like they'd known them.

So I said what I would want to hear if I was in that position.

'I bet she's so proud of you, Ollie. I can already tell that you're ten times the man Henry is and fuck, she knows it too.'

'You think so?' he asked, his voice low, and I wondered if anybody had ever told him that before.

'I do. None of it is your fault. Remember that.'

'Right...' he trailed off, distracted.

I could tell by his tone that he didn't believe me, but I knew he wouldn't. I sensed that there was a lot more to it—to him—than what he was showing me on the surface.

I could be patient, show him that I wouldn't be going anywhere, no matter what he thought about himself. Or how much he believed he was like his father.

Forty

MOTHER'S DAY had always been a Sunday that I didn't really care for. Not like I wanted to spend an entire day celebrating my mum, and my nan had died when I was younger. I knew nothing about the guy who helped make me, so I had no clue whether he had a mum alive out there somewhere.

Hawthorn opened up the school grounds on Mother's Day and invited the mums to come and spend the day with their offspring. They set up an Afternoon Tea type thing; the highlight of a proper British afternoon. Meaning Mum would receive an invitation to come here and, after the last time, I knew she was going to come. Free food and booze? Sign her up. She wouldn't turn down that kind of free shit. Especially if the school sent a car for her like last time.

'Clo, is your mum coming today?' I asked, fiddling with the tiny buttons on my floral tea dress as I tried to fasten them.

'God, I hope not,' she responded so fast, I knew she meant it. She'd still never really opened up about her parents, and I knew she hadn't seen them since the beginning of the school year. They were in contact over Christmas via text, but that was the only time she'd mentioned messaging them. Still one more occasion than my mum had texted me, though, so swings and roundabouts and all that.

'Would it be so bad?' I asked.

'Definitely. Lottie Hawthorn's going to be here,' Clover said, as if that explained everything.

'Again, is that a bad thing?' I asked, not really getting it. Leo's mum would be there, so what?

'Yeah,' she muttered. Clo didn't elaborate and I just couldn't be fucked trying to get more out of her. Was her evasion of my questions normal for female friendships? I wished I knew. Not like I could ask Griff because I doubted he'd be able to help much —even if he did love to act like one of the girls.

'Okay... Cool.' I stopped talking to her and continued getting ready. The boys got me some great clothes for Christmas, so my wardrobe had improved so much since I'd first started here. No more stained items with holes in that were obviously cheap or secondhand. I knew beyond doubt that Mum would comment on it, probably out of jealousy. She'd always wished she could afford designer clothing and the newest trends. I didn't even want to think about just what she'd be wearing today. If I knew her as well as I thought I did, there would be animal print on her outfit somewhere.

Great. Can't wait.

Mum wafted into the school in a cloud of knock-off perfume and hairspray. Honestly, I thought she was auditioning for the West End production with the way her blonde hair was coiffed into a rather large bouffant. You couldn't make it up. Of course it was *my* mum looking like she belonged in some bad soap opera from the nineties and not anybody else's.

'Oh, darrrr-ling, don't you look bee-u-tiful,' she said the moment she saw me. Seriously, the woman had no low volume setting. Her voice carried and the entire hall heard her greeting. Shame filled me every time she spoke, and I hated that about myself, but it was an involuntary reaction. 'Your outfit is divine!'

'Thanks, Mum. Happy Mother's Day,' I said, keeping my voice down, not wanting to draw any more attention towards us. Fuck, people already called me a charity case and constantly reminded me that I was there on scholarship. Then Mum came along and made it even more obvious that we were *not* in the same league as the others.

I was also right about her outfit. Mum was wearing a short denim miniskirt, cheap—and very fake—UGG boots and a tight vest top which, you guessed it, was zebra print. But not just a black and white zebra print, nope, it was black and silver glitter zebra print. I shuddered just looking at it. Blatantly a market stall purchase, or maybe it was from one of those shops that sold every item in one size at one price.

'So, what kinda spread they putting on today? I made sure not to eat breakfast, you know, to make the most of being here,' she told me in a conspiratorial manner.

Sometimes you just had to roll your eyes. Especially on those occasions where you were about to either laugh or cry. Really, I should be glad she hadn't shown up drunk. Small mercies and all that.

'Where's that ginger friend of yours?' she asked, her face focused on mine intently.

Ground. Swallow me.

'If you mean Clover, she's back in our room.'

'Shame, I really like her,' said Mum, nodding, clearly remembering the last time she was here. 'She was nice. Glad you've made friends, sweetie. It surprised Andy and me. We didn't think you'd make *any* friends, what with you being so boring and all.'

'Gee, Mum, thanks for that,' I said, thick with sarcasm, but I could tell by the look on her face it didn't register because she believed she was helping me by being honest.

'No problem, darling.' She patted me on the shoulder, nodding at me.

'Afternoon.' A deep voice joined us and before I could turn around, Ollie slung his arm around my shoulders and squeezed me close. I hadn't asked him what he planned to do today, but I thought maybe he'd be spending it with Griff. After all, neither of them was getting a visit today and as much as I grumbled about my mum, at least she could be here. 'Nice to see you again, Cora.'

'Oh, hello, Oliver,' Mum said. I swore she actually tittered at him. 'You are just as handsome as I remember. Still putting up with my moody daughter, I see.'

'Actually, we're in an official relationship now,' he said and smiled at Mum, and as far as I could tell, he wasn't judging her too hard—yet. 'Skylar doesn't act *too* moody with me.'

'Aren't you a lucky one then? I'll let you in on a little secret.' She leaned closer to him, almost putting her lips into his ear. 'Sky's always been difficult. Ever since she was a little girl. Used to write all kinds of things in her diary.'

If I thought shit was embarrassing before, it had nothing on that moment. Her loud arrival and god-awful outfit had clearly been the tip of the iceberg. She'd always had a thing for the Titanic, after all.

'Well, thanks for that, Mum.'

'Oliver should know just who he's dating.' She shrugged, looking around the room, people watching most likely. I loved to watch people too, but my mum was judging everyone. Laughable really, seeing as they were all definitely judging her more. Fuck, *I* was judging her, and we were related.

'I think he knows,' I said. Ollie and I smiled at one another, a stiff smile on his face, his upper lip almost a straight line.

'I'll let you and your mum enjoy the day and I'll see you later, baby.' Ollie gave me a brief kiss on the cheek and I couldn't decide whether I was glad he wouldn't see the shit show that was my mum or if I was mad that he wasn't saving me from being alone with her.

'I'll see you later. I'll text you when Mum goes.'

He nodded, gave my mum a kiss on the cheek too, and then left the two of us alone. The blush on Mum's face from the kiss almost made me laugh. She looked beside herself with joy. Who knew if it was because I had a nice boyfriend or that a handsome young boy had kissed her. I decided to not even ask.

'I honestly don't know how you pulled that one, Sky.' Mum

raised her eyebrows, and her forehead wrinkled, and I knew she didn't know what Ollie saw in me. Whoever said mums were a confidence booster had obviously never met mine. 'He's gorgeous, and you're so drab and plain, honey.'

'Loving this time together, Mum,' I said, my tone dry. 'Let's go get a drink.'

'You know me, Skylar. No need to tell me twice!' she replied, chortling to herself.

There was a bar set up in the main hall again, and the dark-haired bartender visibly winced when he saw us heading in his direction. Nice to see that Cora had made a lasting impression.

'Two gin and lemonades,' Mum said. Using her knuckles, she rapped on the bar, as if that worked in place of a *please*. It didn't. Also, she was ordering both drinks for herself, without a care in the world as to how that looked to other people. Guess she was going to spend the day double parked.

'Diet Coke, please,' I said, beaming at the barman, trying to make my please cover both of our orders.

'Sure thing,' he replied smoothly, no longer wincing. The pitying look in his eyes was worse, and the expression on his face was almost enough to make me wish the ground would devour me whole and spit out my bones. *Fuck, it can keep my bones, too.* I already didn't want to be here with Mum today, but if she got drunk, the day would only decline further.

'Once you've got your drinks, we'll go outside? Think they've set up some stalls out there.' I gestured out the large windows, to where we could see people hovering out by some makeshift stalls. Maybe there'd be a raffle shelling off old body washes and the likes. Mum loved those.

'Ooooh, I would love to see what stalls a fancy-schmancy school like this deems acceptable for a day like today.' Mum got out her mobile and began to pay more attention to that than to me, probably messaging Andy. Back when I lived at home, I'd found her behaviour irritating, but now, I was kind of glad that her focus was off me for a while. 'What time is this Afternoon Tea, then?'

'In a couple of hours, so we've got time,' I said, the *unfortunately* implied but not uttered. No matter how hard things were between me and Mum over the years, I was still too scared to voice them out loud.

'So we can have a few more drinks here first. We're in no rush,' she said, her gaze fixed elsewhere, looking at the stained glass window, the sun shining through and turning the room into various hues of colours.

'The weather's good right now, though, Mum. Never know when rain could strike. We're on top of the hill, remember?' Plus, I didn't want her to have more time to drink.

'A little rain won't hurt us. Well, it might hurt my hair a little,' she guffawed. Loud. Even the people far away on the other side of the room from us looked over with disgusted looks on their botoxed faces. Being honest, it surprised me that any of the mums here could show emotion at all. 'I spent quite some time back combing this beauty.'

Mum started smoothing her hair with her hands, looking too proud of herself. I swore the woman saw something different in the mirror than what everybody else saw.

Hang on. Was I being a snob all because I was wearing a dress more expensive than my mum's rent?

I thought about it for less than a second.

Nope, that had nothing to do with it. Guess I'd always looked down on her for some reason or another. Even when I was standing next to her wearing secondhand clothes, I still looked down on her.

'It looks great, Mum,' I said soothingly. Sometimes it was easier to placate somebody, rather than tell them the truth. 'Top looks good too.' I nearly choked on my lie.

'Do you like it? Leslie got it for me at the market the other weekend,' she said, twirling around with her arms wide, so I could appreciate it from every angle.

Nailed it.

'It's definitely something.'

Forty-One

THREE HOURS later and Mum was three sheets to the wind. I'd known it was going to happen, but I'd hoped it wouldn't anyway. We'd made it outside to look at the stalls, thankfully, and the sun was really shining, which was super rare for a Sunday in March.

'Skylar, darling, is that you?' Lottie Hawthorn seemingly appeared from nowhere and swept me into a big hug. Her Chanel perfume entered my nostrils, warm and deep, and it was exactly how I'd always imagined an older, rich lady would smell. 'You look wonderful!'

'Thank you, Lottie. You remember my mum, Cora?' I asked, sweeping my arm to indicate the woman standing next to me. Not that she needed it. Mum stood out like a sore thumb.

'Yes... Cora, hello.' With a grimace, she nodded daintily at Mum. 'How have you two been? Leo mentioned you had a great Christmas together. I was going to talk to you about it at the gala, but I got distracted.' Lottie swept her arm and motioned Leo over, who had been standing a little distance away.

Coming over to stand beside her, his blond hair glistened extra bright in the sunlight as it shined through the clouds. His blue eyes sparkled at me, like we shared a secret. Which we did. He texted me from time to time checking in, and I'd started to think of him as a friend.

'I'm good, thank you. Leo's telling the truth. Christmas was wonderful,' I replied to Lottie. I smiled at Leo, surprised they'd approached us, especially after seeing my mum wobbling while standing still. A skill mastered by the very best of the drinkers. 'How have you been?'

'I've been well, thank you. So happy I could come here today and see my baby boy.' She rubbed underneath Leo's chin and he blushed, a light pink colour entering his cheeks, looking embarrassed at the affection his mum was showing him. 'Just hoping I don't run into Winifred,' Lottie added in a conspiratorial tone. Seemed mums both rich and poor loved to share confidences—or for a better word, gossip.

Mum and I both looked at each other in confusion. Who the fuck was Winifred? Leo noticed the confusion on both our faces, and he clarified, 'Ms Hawthorn.'

'Ohhhhhh.' Mum and I both said at the same time. I'd honestly never wondered *what* Ms Hawthorn's first name was. Forgot she'd even have one, to be honest.

'How comes?' Mum asked, slurring the end of the sentence.

'Oh, Winifred thinks we should talk because she happens to be my sister-in-law. I've tried to make it clear over the years that just because we're related by law doesn't mean that we're friends,' she said, adding a light laugh at the end to soften the harshness of her words.

'Mum...' Leo said to her in a curt tone. 'You're just likeable. Course she wants to be your friend,' he added, clearly saving himself, because Lottie smiled warmly at him in return.

'Thanks, sweetheart. Would you two like to join us for Afternoon Tea?' Lottie asked, the smile still embedded on her face.

Honestly, I wasn't sure whether we should agree. I thought that, if anything, Leo and Lottie would sit with Odette and her mother, but I realised I hadn't seen either of them. I hadn't seen Leo with Odette in the last week, actually.

'We would love to, wouldn't we, Sky?' Mum answered before I'd even fully formulated my thoughts, emphasising the word *love*.

'Of course,' I said through gritted teeth, not wanting to sound ungrateful but dreading it all nonetheless.

THINGS WERE GOING OKAY.

Well, as okay as they could with Mum ordering Irish coffees instead of going for the traditional English Breakfast tea. The catering staff had filled the platter in the centre of the table with mini sandwich triangles and mini cakes. I'd put a couple on my plate, not wanting to look greedy, but Mum didn't have that worry. She'd instantly piled her plate high, to the point where at least two-thirds of the platter sat on her plate alone.

'So, Skylar, what does your father do?' Lottie asked, attempting to restart the conversation.

'Mum, Skylar's dad isn't around,' Leo said in a hushed tone, giving her a narrowed glare, trying to prevent embarrassment for both me and his mum.

'Oh, I'm so sorry, Skylar, I didn't realise.' Lottie looked flustered, her cheeks the same shade of pink as Leo's had been earlier. I wanted to make it better but had no idea how to. Not like it was her fault. It was an innocent question.

'Don't apologise to her, love. Sky is better off without her father around,' Mum said after a beat. It was probably the most my mum had ever said on the subject of my *father*. She barely mentioned him to me, even when super drunk, and I'd never been able to get much out of anybody who may know more. Her words slowly became more slurred and incoherent. 'You see, Jacob Cooper was a total dick. But damn, he was a hot one.'

'C-cooper?' I only knew one Cooper, Griff, and I thought about how odd it was that my surname could have been the same as his. Instead, I got stuck with Crescent. Sixteen years old and it was the first time I'd ever heard the name of my sperm donor.

'Jacob Cooper?' Lottie and Leo asked simultaneously. Lottie's face was a mixture of confusion and shock. Leo's face was a mix of somebody trying to feign boredom and somebody acting hard to seem as if the news had shocked them, but I could tell it didn't shock him at all. His jaw tightened, the muscles in his cheeks flexing, like he'd known already.

'I said that, didn't I?' Mum asked, laughing at their expressions. 'He was from around here. You know him?'

'Yeah. Or at least I used to know somebody by that name.' Lottie looked like she didn't want to say much more than that. 'Way back when.'

'What a coinky-dink. Well, I've not heard anything from him since Sky was born. He split not long after he found out about her,' Mum said, hitching her thumb in my direction. This was what she'd always told me when I'd asked growing up, so at least that hadn't been a lie.

'Maybe it's for the best, Cora, that you haven't heard from him,' Lottie said, her tone darker than I'd ever heard it. Her words sounded ominous and the closed off look on Lottie's face also made me think there was a whole lot more to the story.

'Oh, I know, Lottie darling, I definitely have found the best in Andy. He's my knight in shining armour,' said Mum, winking at Lottie as she did so. Almost as if the two of them were best friends and in one another's confidence.

And yep. My mum classed the man who kissed me without consent as her knight in shining armour. *Lucky me.*

'He sounds charming,' Leo piped up, trying to take the heat off the subject of my dad. 'Andy seemed like a great guy when you were both here for Parents' Day.' Honestly, if I didn't know Leo, I would have believed his act to be genuine. His eyes were wide with interest and a smile was playing around his mouth. The boy could charm anybody—and I mean anybody. But was he the charmer or the snake?

Mum smiled at Leo's appraisal of Andy, and I could see the cogs forming a sentence. Who knew what would come out of Mum's mouth next.

'Skylar. Why are you with Ollie when you know this perfect specimen?'

Jesus. Could my mum go a day without saying something super cringeworthy? Just one day. Was that too much to ask?

'Mum,' I snapped.

'Ollie's pretty great too, Cora,' Leo said, coming to my rescue by listing a couple of Ollie's great attributes. He finished by saying, 'He really cares about Sky.'

'That's good, of course. But you would also be great for her,' said Mum, the slurring slipping into every other word, and I knew I needed to get Mum out of there before she said anything more.

'Come on, Mum. Andy's probably wanting you to come home soon,' I said, wrapping an arm around her shoulder. I was actually surprised she'd stayed as long as she had without mentioning going home to him. It was super rare that the two of them spent time apart—especially a whole day apart.

'True, darling. It's been so nice to see you two. Lottie, we must do this again.'

I chuckled in my head, slightly confused why my mum was treating it like Lottie herself had invited her here. I nodded along, sure if I agreed with her, then she'd leave quicker. Here's to hoping, anyway.

'I'm sure our paths will cross again.' Lottie smiled, no teeth this time, and nodded at my mum. 'Come on, Leo, let's give these two some space to say goodbye. Can't wait to see you soon, Skylar.'

'Good to see you, Cora. I'll text you, Sky,' Leo said, nodding at me in a secret message of sorts that I didn't understand. I raised an eyebrow at Leo, but he glanced away, ignoring my attempt at eye contact.

We all waved at one another and they left the table. I watched them go, wishing I could talk to Lottie or Leo some more about Jacob Cooper. The thought of my dad had never overly fascinated me—I'd never wanted to learn anything about him, for that matter. Clearly, he ran in classier circles than my mum and I could admit that having a name made me slightly more interested.

I walked Mum outside, and we waited for the car to pull up. I felt more than happy to stand and wait in silence, but apparently she had other ideas.

'Sky, Jacob Cooper is a wanker. You should be glad that I never told you more about him.'

'How did you meet him?' I asked, curious, wondering how much she'd say.

'I was staying at a hotel that had a gala that evening. Bumped into this penguin suit wearing man who had gorgeous blue eyes and black shiny hair.'

'Sounds romantic.'

'It was something,' Mum grumbled under her breath.

The car pulled up and Mum went to get inside. She gave me a brief hug, something she always did, but I'd never hugged her back. Not because it was Mum, but because I didn't like to hug *anybody*.

'See you soon, Mum,' I said, hoping it wouldn't be too soon.

Hey, I'm done with Mum. Where shall I meet you?

I texted Ollie the moment I saw the car meandering down the hill. I was hoping Ollie just wanted to have a chill night in with some pizza or something. I really wasn't feeling up to talking loads or doing much. While staring at my phone, a text came through from Leo that made me smile wider than I had all day.

Thanks for today, Stutter. Somehow, I enjoyed it. We can talk about Jacob Cooper soon. Alone.

I hoped he'd stick to his word and tell me more about him, but Leo and I were never alone. One thing I felt certain about was that the news of my father hadn't surprised him one bit.

Meaning Leo probably knew a lot more than I'd given him credit for.

Fuck.

Forty-Two

CLOVER'S eighteenth birthday came around pretty fast after Mother's Day, and I was super excited for her to see the present I'd arranged for her. It was hard to get her something with no access to money. Ollie had offered to let me use his card, but I didn't want him to think I was with him because he was rich. I'd heard the way the girls at school spoke about the boys as if they were their meal ticket to a better life and it made me sick. I wasn't going to be one of those girls, especially as I didn't come from wealth. I'd look like even more of a gold digger than the one they'd already accused me of being.

It had pained me to do, but I'd messaged my mum, asking her to send me my nan's recipe book. When my nan was alive, she'd loved to bake and had always enlisted me to help her. I'd never really fallen in love with it the way she'd hoped, but she had passed down her recipes to me when she died. I obviously wasn't going to give Clo the original copies as they were in Nan's hand-writing and the only thing of hers I owned, but I was going to give her a scrapbook with copies of them in.

I'd also included pictures of us from the gala, Christmas, and some random fun selfies we'd taken while trying out silly filters. I really hoped she'd like it as I'd been working on it in Ollie's room in secret and it had taken me quite a few hours to put together. It had taken so long because I had made sure, multiple times, I'd copied every recipe and ingredient exactly how my nan had written it. Clo was family to me now, and I wanted to pass on my family's food to her.

We were spending her birthday as just the four of us. Griff had ordered Clo's favourite food, and we were going to watch her favourite films. It was a Thursday night, so our options were pretty limited and we'd all agreed that a gathering in the woods was not the way to go, even if she was hitting a huge milestone.

After classes had ended, I'd rushed back up to our room, trying to get there before her. I wanted to put up some banners and balloons and decorate a bit. I'd never had the chance to do something so grand for somebody before, and I was so excited to see her reaction. Bitch better appreciate all the effort I'd put into making the day a great one for her.

The evening went perfectly, and the four of us had a good time. Ollie even managed to keep his dislike of Clover on the down low, which I was happy about.

Clover had loved her present, and I was so glad I'd thought of it.

'*Sky, this must have taken you forever!*' she gushed, a wide, *beaming smile on her face. 'Thank you so much. I'll cherish this shit, I swear.*'

The guys left around ten, and the moment they did, I jumped into action.

'Right, I'm going for a shower.'

'Ite, babes. Try not to use too much hot water!'

'You're the birthday girl, so you can totally shower first if you want,' I told her, feeling generous today. I hated showers really, so I always needed to psych myself up for them, but I'd let her go first if she wanted to.

'It's cool, just don't take too long.'

It took me ten minutes tops, but when I re-entered our room, Clover was looking at me with a narrowed gaze and her mouth was pursed together into a point.

'Something you want to tell me?' she asked, venom in her voice.

'S-sorry, what?' I asked, confused. I had no idea what could have upset her in such a short timeframe.

'You left your phone out here,' Clo said, her voice so quiet, I had to strain to hear her.

'Right...?'

I usually did when I showered. With a bathroom the size of a toothpick, I worried I'd get it wet and damage it beyond repair. I'd never had a nice phone before and didn't want to fuck it up; it had been a Christmas present from Ollie after all.

'You got a message.' She held my phone out to me.

I froze by my bed, towel still wrapped around me, and wondered what she was going to say next.

'Oh, thanks,' I said as I took my phone from her outreached arm. When I looked down, I saw that it was unlocked and it was opened to my message thread with Leo. Had Clo been going through my texts?

'Is this about my dad?' I asked, remembering the last text from Leo was one where he'd told me we'd talk about Jacob Cooper alone some time soon. 'Mum told me his name on Mother's Day and both Lottie and Leo seemed to recognise the name.'

'Huh?' Her lip curled up at the corner in a sneer. 'When were you with Lottie and Leo?'

Shit, I remembered why I'd "forgotten" to tell her. I hadn't wanted to explain spending time with the Hawthorns. Clover always tried to avoid them whenever we were in the same place.

'Oh, didn't I mention it?' I asked, hoping she'd take the bait, but all she did was look blankly at me, staring through my bullshit. 'They joined us for Afternoon Tea.'

'You definitely didn't mention it. Since when were you and Leo close enough to spend time together?' Clo's incredulous tone irritated me.

'My bad, I thought I did.' I shrugged it off. *God, I am such a liar.* 'Well, Lottie's always been nice to me, and she wanted to join us. Leo didn't exactly get a say.'

'So, your dad?' Clover gazed at me, trying to suss out why I'd failed to mention such big news. 'Who is he?'

'Somebody named Jacob Cooper. You heard of him?'

Clover shook her head. 'I don't think so. It sounds familiar, though.'

'Right? I thought that too, but then I realised it's probably just because Griff's surname is Cooper too.'

'That's probably it,' she said, but her gaze hadn't returned to normal. She was still pissed at me for something. 'But I wasn't going to ask you about your dad.'

'What's up, then?' I asked, glancing down at my phone and looking properly. There was a new message from Leo that I hadn't spotted. When she told me I'd got a message, she didn't say who it was from.

HOPE RED HAS A GOOD BIRTHDAY. HOW IS SHE? LET ME KNOW IF YOU NEED ME, STUTTER.

'Been spying on me for Leo, have you?' she asked, her tone scathing, and I wasn't sure how to respond. I hadn't been spying on her for Leo, but I'd answered questions he had about her. She'd never given me a good enough reason not to, and neither had he.

'It's not like that,' I told her.

'You sure? 'Cause that's exactly what it looks like.'

'Positive. He just checks in every now and again,' I said, not feeling comfortable enough to tell her any more than that. I wasn't exactly in the mood to be kind to her after she'd gone through my phone and broken my privacy. Knowing her, she'd argue it was because she cared about me.

'And you're so stupid, Sky, that you don't even see how shady that is.'

God, I was getting bored with her calling me stupid—or whatever name she'd decided on that day. It may be her birthday, but I wasn't going to let everything slide.

'Shady how? It's the complete opposite of shady.' I took a deep breath, trying to rein my temper in. 'If you know something the boys are hiding, then maybe you should tell me what *you've* been hiding? And don't bullshit me and say nothing!'

Clo's eyes began to fill with tears, and I could see the frustration leaking from her. I'd let her off from answering me so many times.

'It hurts me to talk about it all,' she said, her tone breathy and pained. 'I'm not ready.'

'Fine!' I huffed. 'But the boys have never hidden shit from me the way you have.'

'Oh, continue telling yourself that. The boys are up to something and if you don't want to believe me, then that's on you.' Clover shook her head at me, the sad look on her face sliding away as rage took its place. 'Did you even ask Ollie about what I overheard?'

'I—'

'Actually, don't answer that,' she said. 'Because whatever he said was bullshit. You know what? There's nothing I can do to help you anymore. You're intent on ignoring me and I honestly can't be fucked with it.'

'With it? Or with *me*?' I asked, knowing what she really meant.

'Any of it, Sky. I'm done. I hope they do fuck with you at the fashion show. You deserve it,' she spat spitefully.

With that, she stomped into the bathroom, leaving me standing there in my towel, wet and cold, holding back tears. Unlike the last time she spat shit at me, I knew there wasn't a simple way for us to get back to how we were. She'd pushed me too far. It was different from her snapping at me about being a whore, which was something that still smarted but easy to forgive. Somebody snooping through my phone and severing my trust was different and a lot more serious.

For fuck's sake. Once again, the boys had come between us, causing a chasm that felt too wide for either of us to breach.

Though, I never thought it would be Leo who would cause our rift.

Forty-Three

THE NIGHT of the fashion show arrived, and you could cut the tension with a blunt knife. Everybody had been on edge, but not for the same reasons.

Clover, although barely talking to me, was still adamant that shit was going down tonight. Even though she'd said only a few sentences to me, they'd all had to do with Ollie and what she'd overheard Odette, Oralie, and Ophelia whispering about. I wasn't sure at this point who would be more surprised if shit didn't go down; her or me.

Griff had also been acting distant with me ever since Clo's birthday, choosing once again to side with her. I couldn't find it in me to argue with him, but the entire situation made me sad. I thought we were stronger than that.

Ollie acted on edge, mostly due to the fact that he was worried I actually believed Clover. I'd told him so many times I trusted him and that if what Clover overheard had any truth to it, then he should let me know before it went too far. Not sometime later down the line when I'd found out the truth, but he was adamant that wasn't going to happen.

'Clover's just jealous and bitter, babe,' he said every time I brought it up. And as much as it pained me to say it—or think it —I could see his point. She had been acting a little jealous, but I also needed to weigh up our friendship. We were best friends. Why would she lie? And what would she gain by lying?

Somehow, Ollie had got out of modelling in the show, even though when I thought back on Clo telling me we were going to model, she never explicitly said Ollie would be too. He and Oralie were arranging the music and backgrounds, and I wished I were working alongside him. Instead, I would model six different looks, with five people who weren't my biggest fans: Griff, Clo, Ophelia, Leo, and Odette. It was a crazy world seeing as Leo was the one I felt closest to in that mix. Showed how quickly things could turn to shit in friendships.

An hour until show time and I was in the makeshift dressing room they had given me that was really just one of the French classrooms with a slight makeover. Ollie and I were looking at what they expected me to wear, confused expressions stamped on our features as we flicked through the hangers on the rack.

'You're gonna look great, babe,' he said, giving my arm a quick squeeze to reassure me.

'Thanks for trying to spark my confidence, baby, but I really don't feel like I will. Odette was in charge of who wore what, so I've definitely been given the worst looks out of the six of us. Honestly, the sleepwear makes me look like I'm ready for sleeping... On the streets.'

Odette had not been playing around when she chose my clothes. Even Clover looked a million pounds in her six outfits, and then there was me, wearing clothes from a high street brand while they were all wearing couture. I'd stayed quiet about it, though, because really, it could be a LOT worse. If the clothes were a part of the "messing with me" Clo spoke about, then I could deal. Bad clothes wouldn't be the end of the world.

'Maybe so, but I know you're going to be the hottest one on that stage.' He kissed my cheek softly, then promptly went back to looking at his phone. 'I would.'

A cheeky smile overtook his face, and it made me feel warm inside. We hadn't said it to one another yet or anything like that, but I knew I was in love with him and I hoped he felt the same way, but I hadn't been brave enough to voice it, just in case he didn't. How fucking embarrassing would that be?

'Well, maybe not after you've seen me in the sportswear outfit,' I joked, but part of me wasn't joking. He very well may see me in a different way after he saw the camel toe the leggings gave me. 'What time do you need to head backstage?'

'Guess I should head there now.' He stood, gave me a long kiss on the lips, and gathered his things together. 'Good luck, babe. You'll do great.'

'Th-thanks. Now get out of here before we get distracted.' That kiss had made me want more, made me want his lips to press firmly into mine while his hands roamed south, and mine raked through his dark hair, but it was *not* the time for that to happen.

'I wouldn't mind watching you change into the first outfit,' he said, raising his eyebrows up and down at me in a way that burst the lust bubble. It just didn't do it for me. I laughed and shoved his shoulder in a playful push.

'Get out of here. You'll meet me here as soon as the show is over, yeah?'

'Of course,' he said, then gave me one last lingering kiss before leaving me there alone.

There were six rounds of outfits: swimwear, sleepwear, office wear, sportswear, and formal wear. The one I was most looking forward to was formal wear. A, because my dress was beautiful, and it was the one piece of clothing that didn't look cheap. I think they'd been donated to the school by wealthy benefactors, so Odette hadn't been able to sabotage me. And B, it would mean that the show was over and I'd survived.

I changed into the swimwear and felt sad that I didn't have Clover by my side to get ready with and laugh with to get rid of the nerves. We could have joked about all of it together, united. It annoyed me she was still using Leo's text against me. It wasn't as if I'd asked him to send it, and honestly, the message from Leo wasn't even that exciting. All he'd done was ask how Red's birthday was and if she was okay, which was hardly something to burn him at the stake for.

I felt lonely getting ready, though, especially without Ollie around. Before I started at Hawthorn, feeling lonely was something I was used to, even to an extent something I *enjoyed,* but since the start of the school year I'd stopped feeling alone. I hated that I was back in a space mentally where I was reverting to my old frame of mind.

I just need to get through this show, and then everything will be okay again.

NOBODY HAD EVER MENTIONED to me just how nerve-racking modelling clothes could be. Not that I knew anybody who would have been able to tell me about it, but still, every time I went out on stage, I was close to bricking it. It took everything in me not to trip and fall flat in front of the crowd. One thing that was good was how nice the crowd was—and supportive.

Everywhere I looked while on stage, all I saw were kind eyes staring back at me. There had to be at least five hundred people here, a mix of students and parents, all watching us closely, and it sent my nerves into overdrive.

I'd never felt so scrutinised. It must be how a bug under a microscope felt.

I'd made it through the first five parts of the show with no major mishaps. I'd stayed upright, worn all the clothes the way Odette had told me to, and I hadn't vomited or passed out, so I was counting the night as a win. I'd been the third in the line-up for every look, so at least I wasn't last, and by the time I got to the end of the catwalk, there was somebody else coming down it to steal the attention. My final dress of the show was the most intricate, and it took me some time to get into it and style my hair.

It was a beautiful, yellow satin two-piece. The top was in the Bardot style and was flattering for my cleavage as it had a sweetheart neckline, and because the sleeves were off the shoulders—my signature look—I didn't look as wide as I normally did. The skirt was a flattering A-line skirt with pockets, reaching the floor, and the whole look made me feel like a princess. It reminded me of a modern-day version of Belle's ball gown.

Somehow, I put my hair up in a low, loose chignon, and when I looked in the mirror, I was surprised at the sight of me. The entire look was perfect. I wished Ollie were here to see me, but I knew he'd get a kick out of taking it off me once the show was done.

One of the other students working the show popped their head into the classroom and said, 'Skylar, you're up.'

'Let's get this shit over with,' I said to myself as I followed the guy to the stage. Just one more turn of the catwalk and I was free —not just of the fashion show but of school. It was Easter break and the majority of kids were heading home. Griff had hinted about going to his parents' estate again, but that was before my tiff with him and Clo, so I wasn't sure if the invitation still stood.

The moment I walked up the steps, the air felt different. I couldn't put my finger on what had changed in the brief time it took me to change, but something clearly had.

I looked up to find Odette coming down the steps from the catwalk, and instantly I knew shit was off. The plan had been for Odette to finish the show; to be the last one down the catwalk like she had with every other look.

'Don't trip, New Girl,' she whispered in my ear as she passed, her cool arm brushing up against mine.

Music pumped through the speakers, and I heard my cue. I had no time to change course before a hand on my lower back pushed me up the steps towards the stage.

I tried to keep my head facing forward. Tried not to look at all the heads in the crowd and think about all the eyes glued to me.

I got to the end of the catwalk, and that was when shit changed.

The music cut out abruptly, leaving me standing there not knowing what to do next. A voiceover began to play, and Odette's nasally voice filled the auditorium, reminiscent of the Parents' Day video.

Fuck. Maybe I should have listened to Clover.

I turned to the back of the stage, as a video started to play on the projector screen they'd set up to show background images during the show.

'Hello, everyone,' the voice said, addressing the room. 'I hope you've been enjoying our fashion show this evening and plan to give money to our charity. I know you've all got deep pockets, and the school appreciates your generosity.'

I went to walk back towards the steps, but the voice stopped me.

'Stay right there, Skylar. I think you'll find this next part more interesting.'

That doesn't sound good.

'I'm here to tell you tonight about *our* favourite charity case. Miss Skylar Crescent. Skylar is a scholarship student here at Hawthorn Academy and has had quite the eventful year. I'm sure you all remember Parents' Day.' She laughed, and I saw some heads nodding in the distance, the bright lights stopping me from seeing too much, but I could still see enough to feel the kind eyes turning to judgemental ones. 'Let's have a look at some of her other highlights from the year, shall we?'

The video began to show a reel of everything that had happened to me over the course of the year. Me getting covered in blue raspberry slush in the corridor; me being tripped up and pushed around. Rotting food falling from my locker, how I'd looked after being found beaten in the toilets, and Griff ushering me into the school after finding me at the picnic.

They had literally recorded every single thing that had happened to me and were playing it for everybody to see. And all I could do was stand there and watch it unfold in silence.

'As you can see, Skylar has had a hard time this year. Even her best friends have turned against her.'

The scene changed to footage taken from inside mine and Clover's bedroom. *What the fuck?* How long had there been a camera in there? And who had put it there? My mind instantly went to thinking about what else that camera could have seen, but then the images on the screen once again stole my focus.

The footage playing was of Clover and Griff sitting next to one another on Clo's bed. The date stamped the video as the day she'd called me a whore, so it must be what happened after Griff followed her.

Their heads got closer, the two of them as close as they could be. Then, watching through a dream-like haze, I saw the moment Griff and Clover kissed on the screen.

Betrayal trickled down my body, starting at my head and reaching my fingertips and toes. An ice queen forming, frozen to the spot.

At no point had either of them told me about this. Fuck, they'd never even hinted at it! They'd carried on like nothing much had happened in the time we weren't on talking terms.

I looked around and caught Leo's eye. He was standing by the screen, his expression blank, but I could tell he was unimpressed. The question was whether he was unimpressed with me, or because of the kiss?

'Forgive me,' Odette tittered, sounding unapologetic. 'Let me formally introduce the poor, pathetic case of a human still standing at the end of the stage. Everybody, this here is the daughter of Jacob Cooper, who I believe those amongst this circle knew well.'

Instantaneously, the crowd gasped.

A secret had been outed, and I had no idea why it was such shocking news. I knew that Lottie and Leo had recognised the name, but Leo never had got around to talking to me about it. I'd forgotten to ask him after what had happened with Clover.

The images still flickered on the screen, footage still rolling of every kiss Ollie and I had shared since the start of it all. All the times they'd picked on or harassed me.

The night I'd lost my virginity played next, and although grainy and difficult to decipher, I knew exactly what was being shown on the screen. How dare they? How fucking dare they take that away from me, too?

The only footage that wasn't shown was from the night somebody had tried to drown me. If they had, then we'd know exactly who it was, and I knew the girls didn't want that to become public knowledge if they had something to do with it.

I shivered, the hairs on my arms standing on end. I needed to leave. I couldn't stand here any longer listening to such shit.

'Poor breeding.' Odette's voice filled the room again, and I promised myself there and then, I would make her suffer. I'd been a doormat for too long. I had to stand up for myself and come next term, I was going to become her worst nightmare.

I rushed to the back of the stage, to where the screen was showing footage of my mum and Andy from Parents' Day necking back drinks and acting like the pissheads everybody had already guessed they were.

Shame filled me.

Everybody here knew everything.

Even something I didn't know.

Why did it even fucking matter who my dad was?

Catching Griff's sad and confused look as I climbed down from the stage, I wondered what he was thinking. I could tell he wanted to say something to me, but really, what could he say that would make everything all okay? I felt humiliated once again. *Is everything in my life a lie?*

I should have seen shit coming. Should have listened to Clover when she told me the girls had something planned. But then I remembered how Clo had been lying to me for weeks, too.

I wanted to cry, but I didn't want them to see me crumble. I didn't want to give them the satisfaction of breaking in front of them all. *Fucking rich kids.*

They were all as bad as each other.

So I did the next best thing.

I ran.

Forty-Four

I RAN from the auditorium as fast as I could. I wanted to put as much space between me and those people. I felt cheap. Dirty. Like the charity case they'd constantly told me I was. I kept tripping on the dress I was wearing, the length too long for a quick getaway. Fuck me, no wonder Cinderella lost her shitty glass slipper during her escape.

Heavy footsteps came from behind me, getting closer with every second. For every two steps I took, I swore they were only taking one, which meant they were going to reach me soon. I couldn't let that happen.

I left the main building and ran to the pool house. I definitely wouldn't have headed there if I wasn't in fight-or-flight mode. Not after some unknown person had attempted to drown me there after the Halloween party. But I needed to be alone, and that building was the one place I thought nobody would find me.

After entering the building, I ran up the stairs and made my way to the connecting corridor that led to the hospital wing. I stopped. I heard angry voices coming from that direction, and they were getting louder. I pivoted on the spot and made my way back down the stairs.

I entered the pool room itself and nearly jumped out of my skin when I came face to face with Ollie.

He was standing at the other end of the pool, staring at me

silently. His face hard in anger in a way I'd only seen once or twice.

'Hey. I'm sorry I ran away. I just c-couldn't stay there,' I stuttered my way through my sentence, embarrassed I was finding it hard to talk to him. Which was ridiculous? It was Ollie. The guy I'd lost my virginity to and had had all those meaningful moments and conversations with. Although, when I looked up, it didn't feel as if the same Ollie stood in front of me.

All I wanted was to run to him and fall into his arms, but I stopped myself.

'You deserved what they did.' His tone was ice-cold. I shook my head, his words not making any sense to me. 'You've deserved all of it.'

'S-sorry?'

Where was the Ollie I'd woken up next to that morning? The one who had made Easter break plans with me and kissed me like he would never get enough of me?

'Sky, did you really believe any of this year was real?' he scoffed. 'Every single thing that *The Set* has done to you has been on my command. I asked them to do whatever they could to turn the entire student body against you.'

'But I d-don't understand...' I trailed off. None of it added up. I was so sure that Clover must have misheard everything, that she had just heard the girls' conversation out of context. Ollie had even promised me that he wasn't a part of their plan.

I felt so stupid. I had fallen out with my best friend over Ollie and it turned out that I should have believed her all along. I'd acted like every idiotic heroine I hated.

'That's because you're too stupid to understand anything, Skylar. The fact that you couldn't see the truth right in front of your eyes tells me as much.' Ollie seemed to be enjoying this. I could tell by the smirk on his face. 'The amount of times we've all been laughing at you behind your back and you never even knew.'

Don't cry. I repeated the mantra in my head, knowing if he saw my tears, something would snap between us. Something I wasn't sure we could ever come back from. Maybe I was stupid like he said because nothing made sense. Had I really just been that blind to the truth?

Clover had tried to warn me. Even Griff had made some cryptic comments that I hadn't looked into enough. Things had been going so well with Ollie that I hadn't wanted to rock the boat. Make a nuisance of myself. The only one who had said fuck all was Leo. Nice to know he never meant any of those texts.

I knew things had taken a turn for the worse when I looked into Ollie's eyes and could see the true depth of his hate.

His eyes, normally a startling bright blue, were now a dark indigo filled with anger and loathing. I could see the exact moment the mist descended.

I shivered.

I wasn't sure what else to do, and I didn't know where I could run to.

Trapped.

The worst part was the fact I'd been blind to my situation and had walked willingly to my fate. I was the reason I was there. There was nobody else to blame. I hated myself for it, maybe even more than I hated him at that moment.

I couldn't help but ask, 'W-why are you doing this?'

I had to know. I was certain something must have happened in the last few hours to have caused the change in him. No part of me could accept that it had been coming for longer... the alternative was just too much to think about.

'You don't belong here, Sky.' He smirked at me. 'You never did.'

I crumbled. I could feel the tears pricking my eyes, and I was trying my hardest to stop them from falling.

I should have known better. I should have never fallen for the beast, and I most definitely should have never thought of myself as the beauty in my tale.

I flew out of the room. I couldn't stand to see that look in Ollie's eyes a moment longer. The one that made me feel an inch tall. That made me feel like the charity scholarship case. Since

September, he'd been adamant that he didn't see me that way. More fool me.

I ran around the corner and made my way quickly up the staircase, heading towards the corridor to the hospital wing. Fuck the voices I'd heard.

I made my way along the corridor and turned a corner to head further into the building. It was then that I saw a shadowy, tall figure standing ahead of me in the dark hallway. None of the lights were on as the school was meant to be empty for the holidays. Everybody was over in the auditorium dealing with the fallout from the fashion show. I paused. I needed a moment to try to quiet my breathing—to make myself invisible.

That was when I saw it.

The body lying on the floor at the feet of the figure. I couldn't make out who it was from here, but it definitely looked like a girl. A girl wearing a dress similar to the one Odette had worn as she'd brushed past me.

I tiptoed closer.

The figure still hadn't seen me, too focused on the limp body at their feet to notice me creeping up on them. A body that wasn't moving or making any sound. They were still. My mind tried not to connect the dots as to what a still body meant.

The closer I got, I just knew that the body—the girl—*was* Odette. The dress she had been so smug about earlier torn and covered in dirt. Her face was trapped in a scared expression, her mouth slightly open and her eyes wide—stuck forevermore. Blood covered her stomach, a knife handle visible sticking out in the centre. Bile rose up my throat as I tried to get my breathing under control.

I tried to take a step back, but I somehow caught my footing on the bottom of my skirt, and I gasped at the twist of my ankle. I tried to keep my balance so I wouldn't find myself sprawled at the stranger's feet.

It was the gasp that did it.

The figure turned.

I glimpsed their face, their hair, their eyes—I couldn't breathe. *What the?*

None of what I saw made sense.

It was as if my mind couldn't compute what my eyes were seeing. My vision blurred around the edges and I fought the blackout I knew was coming; the black spots in my vision were already forming, closing in on me. My breathing shallowed, my heart beating so slow, yet so loud, I thought that the person in front of me could hear it as loud as I could.

The figure approached. I tried to turn again, but my legs had turned to jelly, my ankle giving out beneath me. I couldn't move, no matter how much I wanted to. The moonlight coming through the windows caught the glint of a knife.

A knife that was heading in my direction.

A knife getting closer with each step of the figure.

Then pain.

Nothing but pain.

Then nothing at all.

Epilogue

I SMILED as I watched her walk away. Well, more like she ran away.

My plan couldn't have gone better. I'd achieved what I had set out to do.

To ruin her.

To make her feel worthless.

I knew I'd touched a nerve, and I felt pure happiness shoot through me at the thought of her leaving this place and crumbling. I'd wanted to wait until the end of the school year, but things had snowballed of late. The situation started to run away from me and I knew I had to act.

Who knew girls could be such bitches when given free rein?

I didn't feel any guilt, but I knew when to say when. If I'd let it continue, she would have ended up dead. And I didn't want that —not yet, anyway.

I hoped she would never return to Hawthorn Academy. She didn't deserve to be here. With Easter coming up, we had time away from this cursed place and I was hoping she'd make the right decision. The *only* decision. To leave. And never look back.

If she showed her face again, I would make her regret it. It would make the first half of the year feel like a holiday.

After all, things can always get worse.

DISEASE

book two

DISEASE

noun -
a harmful development
something that
is considered very bad in people or society

Prologue

I LOOKED AT HIM, unable to push out the breath I'd held onto since our eyes locked, and wondered how I'd found myself in this position... again.

Something here wasn't right. I just couldn't put my finger on what it was.

He looked back at me with equal distrust in his eyes, and the showdown after the fashion show came to mind.

The image was the same, even if the setting was different. I remembered the dark indigo of his eyes, the way they'd burned in hatred, all aimed towards me; a hatred that had been there long before he'd ever met me.

'Poor little Skylar. How does it feel being the last to know?'

I broke out into all-body shivers, unable to move. Unable to breathe.

We were both standing in the middle of the hall, with nowhere to hide. Nowhere for me to run, either. All eyes were on us—the sideshow that had taken over the New Year's Gala for everybody's entertainment.

One day soon, I hoped there would be a charity function where I wasn't the main attraction.

'It w-was *you*.' My voice left me in a whisper, not wanting to put the thought in my mind out into the universe. Vocalising it would only make it worse.

'It w-was?' he asked, a glint of menace in his eyes.

'You did it.'

'I did what?'

The relaxed posture was at odds with the anger on his face as he mocked me—mocked my stutter. It was something I barely did anymore, yet he was able to bring it out of me as if it had never left in the first place.

I thought back over the previous year, ever since I was stabbed before Easter, and I could only conclude that somehow, it was all my fault. That somehow, I had brought it all upon myself with my actions and decisions.

Was I too trusting, too stupid to see the truth, to see the writing on the wall?

Or had I let my lust guide me like a stupid, naïve girl?

Part One
Revenge

One

OLLIE'S BETRAYAL sat heavy in my stomach.

Heavy in my heart.

At first, I wanted to cry. Well, at first I *did* cry. Have you ever been stabbed and then woke up to the pain of it? That shit hurts! But even after the numbness travelled through me from the copious amount of drugs the hospital gave me, I still cried for me, for him, for us. For everything I'd thought to be true but was clearly a blind bitch about.

For the first week, I couldn't understand where I'd gone so wrong, but as time went on and more memories resurfaced, I realised there were warning signs the entire time I'd known him. Clover had warned me against him from the start, and Leo and Griff—who were his best mates, so really should have been a massive indicator for me—cautioned me multiple times, but I always chose not to listen to any of them. Thinking I knew best. I told myself I *knew* him; I *understood* him. Fat load of shit that was.

It turned out I knew nothing. Nothing about Oliver, but also nothing about Griff or Leo, either, and *nothing* about their true motives. Or the fact that my dad was apparently the cause of all the turmoil. A man I'd never met, nor really wanted to, was somehow fucking me up for reasons unknown to me.

The worst part of it all? I felt stupid. Confused.

And trust me, feeling both stupid and confused were two of my biggest hates in life. Had been ever since I was a kid. I hated feeling like I wasn't in the know, like somebody else knew something I didn't. Or worse, I hated being the last to know.

Yet that was exactly what happened. The fact they were all laughing at me, and my stupidity, all year was enough to make my blood boil in my veins. Oh, how funny it must've been to laugh behind my back at how Skylar Crescent couldn't see through the falsehoods and lies spewed in her direction. Couldn't distinguish the difference between genuine affection and somebody working behind the scenes to ruin their life, ruin their dignity, and their self-worth.

The first indicator things were worse than I realised? Waking up in an actual hospital and not just the hospital wing at the academy. The second indicator? I woke up all alone. There was nobody sitting vigil in the chair by my side and I couldn't recall hearing any visitors during my recent—albeit brief—bouts of consciousness.

Things after the stabbing were all a blur, and the days that followed waking up in a hospital bed weren't much better either. The nurses were nice enough, and the doctor was too when he finally showed up.

I'd been lucky, or so he said. *He*—whoever *he* was—had stabbed me in the abdomen, and the knife hit no major organs, meaning I was going to make a full recovery. Whoever stabbed me had left the weapon in my stomach, which, according to my notes, was what saved my life. The blood loss would've been a lot worse if the knife had been removed and I may not have survived.

Thank you, my attempted murderer, for the consideration.

The police had arrived at the hospital not long after I'd regained full consciousness and told me the weapon had been tested for fingerprints already and that none were present—or so they said. I knew the people I was dealing with were rich mother-fuckers, and there was no way to know just *who* they paid off to live in their back pockets for fun.

The police made it clear, though, that they found it unusual I hadn't tried to remove the knife myself, or at least touch it in my delirious state. It took a lot of restraint to refrain from asking them whether they'd ever been stabbed, and if so, did they remove their own knives?

They'd also asked me whether I had any enemies, anyone who hated me enough to literally *stab me*, but I couldn't think of anybody in particular.

My memory of the entire encounter was lost to me, and they filled in the blanks in a way that implied they thought I was lying about my lack of memory, but I wasn't going to rise to their shit. Not remembering anything that happened was so fucking cliché it hurt, but it didn't change the fact that the last I could recall was fleeing from Ollie after he'd shown his true self.

According to them, Odette Aston was found lying a short distance away from me and had suffered multiple stab wounds from the same knife. Unlike mine, her wounds were fatal. No matter what they said, I couldn't wrap my mind around the fact that Odette was dead. Yeah, she was a total bitch and yeah, she'd made my year so far pretty shit, but even a stone-cold bitch didn't deserve to be killed in a school hallway. Nobody did.

The police left after telling me about Odette and said their detectives would be along within the week to talk to me. *Yay for me.*

With nothing to do but lie in a hospital bed and heal, my thoughts turned to Ollie often and to his entire game. To the way he'd made me believe I meant something to him. Something more than friends. Something that would last a lifetime. Fuck, I'd even lost my virginity to him and fallen out with my best—and only— friend because she had known he was shady and I didn't believe her. Nope, all I did was accuse her of being jealous, which was laughable now that I had time to look back on the first half of this school year and fully dissect it.

I was still trying to grasp the fact that *so much* had happened in such a short period. God, before I started at Hawthorn, the most I had to worry about was my mum or Andy spending all of my earnings on alcohol and tobacco. A worry I'd gladly go back to. Okay, maybe not *gladly,* but still, you get my point.

I'd hoped that *maybe* Clover would come and visit me, but so far I hadn't seen hide nor hair of her. I knew we fought before all the shit happened and that she'd been right all along, but I was so desperate to make amends with her, I wouldn't even care if she came into my room and said, 'I told you so.' At least if she said that to my face, she'd be here. But no, nothing of the sort. Maybe she couldn't forgive me, or maybe we hadn't been true friends after all.

Wouldn't be the first time I was wrong about somebody's true intentions, would it?

AFTER TWO WEEKS, I felt the worst I'd ever felt in my life.

Not physically.

No, physically, I felt great. My wound had healed for the most part, and I felt more clear-headed than ever before.

No, my issue was mental. Mentally, a thick fog surrounded me constantly. A dark, red, forever swirling fog that wouldn't dissipate no matter what I did; no matter what I thought about. I was drowning in my mind and there wasn't much I could do about it.

Fuck. I wasn't even sure I *wanted* to do anything about it.

'Miss Crescent. Are you *sure* there isn't anything more you can tell us?'

I shook my head, bringing myself back into the land of the living, my mind having wandered back to the night of my stabbing. Something that happened with an alarming frequency, yet I still couldn't remember past fleeing from the pool. It was like my mind had blocked out the horror, never to reveal it again.

Detective Smith was standing at the foot of my bed, staring at me in a way that made me think he was trying to scare me and shake me into telling him the truth. If only I knew what the truth was. 'Did Odette Aston have any enemies?'

'Er...' I trailed off. The girl didn't have enemies as much as she had people who detested her and people who feared her. She ruled the school alongside the rest of *The Set* and *Sect*, and it wasn't as if people overly loved them. Not sure how I could explain all that to these two detectives, though, so I went with, 'She was a part of the mean girl group.'

'Yes, we've been told by a'—he looked down at his sheet of paper—'Miss Luck that you were being harassed by Odette and her friends. Lucky for you, your wound erases you from the suspect list.'

'Lucky for me?' I sputtered, mad he'd implied I was *lucky* to have been stabbed.

'That was poor wording,' his colleague, Detective Saunders, piped up. 'What my co-worker means is that the situation means you aren't a suspect.'

Damn straight I'm not a suspect!

'No shit,' I mumbled under my breath. I thought Saunders heard me, but he didn't ask me to clarify or repeat it, so guess I was off the hook. Lucky me.

See. That was what a real *lucky* should sound like.

'Thank you for informing me,' I said, being all extra formal, which I thought might make them suspicious, but neither of their faces changed.

And although I was no longer a suspect in Odette's death, it didn't mean I wasn't still being considered as having had something to do with Olivia's murder. I'd hoped that nearly dying myself would have excluded me, but apparently, I would have had to have been stabbed that night too to be in the clear, and I doubted my guts could've handled that.

As I watched the two detectives in front of me, I had to do my best to hold in the giggles that wanted to burst free. I'd always watched police dramas on TV and thought that certain scenarios must have been exaggerated or invented for the viewers—surely the police weren't that stupid and ridiculous in real life?

But apparently, I was wrong, because my current encounter was only proving they were indeed that ridiculous *and* stupid in real life. Even my alibi the night of the Gala wasn't enough for them not to see me as a suspect in Olivia's death. According to them, I could have snuck out that night with Ollie being none the wiser and returned before he woke. My supposed motive was the bullying I'd suffered at the hand of *The Set*.

In what could only be described as a rehearsed movement, the two of them got up out of their chairs at the same time. It was like the two of them had perfected it to intimidate people they were interrogating or questioning.

'Thank you, Miss Crescent. We'll be in touch if we need to ask you any more questions,' Detective Saunders said, and it solidified what I'd figured out during my time knowing them—he was the nice one.

I waved goodbye, the action limited by the railings of the hospital bed, and my facial expression showed my true feelings towards them, but they didn't turn around to see it.

Joy filled me, knowing they were leaving and I'd have some peace, but then it hit me. Once again, I'd be alone with my own thoughts.

Able to wallow in my self-pity.

Having time alone right now wasn't the best for my mental health. Then again, neither was spending time with Mum and Andy.

Swings and roundabouts and all that jazz.

But after ten minutes of solitude, another knock came at my door. I didn't have the strength to prop myself up on the bed to look. If it was a nurse, they'd come back later if it wasn't urgent, and they'd burst in if it was. That was the way of hospitals.

But then the knock came again—a gentle knock. One so quiet I thought I was making it up at first, but then it repeated, slightly louder, and I fought the heaviness in my neck to lift my head and look in the door's direction.

Clover was standing there, waiting for me to give her permission to enter like it hadn't been over two weeks since we last saw one another, and I almost choked on my shock. The look on her face was one of worry mixed with what could only be described as shame, and I hated to admit even to myself that it gave me a little bit of happiness to know she was feeling so wretched about it all.

'Come in,' I said, loud enough for her to hear me, then I watched as she made her way into my room tentatively, the fear clear in her small steps.

The moment she reached my bed, she burst into tears, sobs wracking her entire body, and the sight made me sad—the happiness inside dissipated as fast as it arrived. The part that worried me, though, was I couldn't tell if I was sad for her or for me. I had every right to be upset at what happened.

My frustration was climbing, and it felt like I had no outlet for it. *Eurgh.* Everything was so fucked!

'Sky,' Clo stuttered out on a sob. 'I am so, so, so very sorry.'

'What are *you* sorry for?' I snapped, a wave of anger hitting me at her apology. What exactly did *she* have to apologise for? Not like she knew what they were doing behind my back.

'For what happened to you,' she whispered, her bottom lip wobbling. 'I knew shit was going down at the show, and I know I warned you, but I should have tried harder to make you see. To get you to listen.'

'No,' I said, and her face crumpled. 'You don't need to apologise for that. I should have listened to you, but I didn't. Plus, not like you could've known that somebody was going to kill Odette and then stab me.'

I tried to smile and pass it all off as one big joke, but I wasn't sure my tone gave enough levity for the situation. Her eyes shifted, darting to look around the room instead of at me. Was that a sign of her guilt? Had she known all along they planned to stab me—whoever *they* were? Or was I just being suspicious? Seeing things in my mind that weren't really there?

The counsellor the hospital assigned me had told me I would find it hard to trust people again. That I'd see shadows and deceit for quite some time before I felt I could open up, and seeing as I'd barely had friends before Hawthorn, and then the first ones I got tried to destroy and potentially end my life, I trusted she was right.

'True.' Clo let out a small giggle but snapped her mouth closed when it registered. 'But I could have followed you once you left the hall, instead of doing what I always do, which is act like a bitch. I just watched you run away without thinking about your safety.' A gasp bubbled up, and she began to sob once more.

I wondered if she was going to mention her kiss with Griff that the girls showed on the video, but I didn't want to push her if she wasn't ready to tell me about it. Which was bullshit really, because I'd never hidden anything from her—especially not something as huge as that.

'Anyway,' she continued with a hiccup, 'I'm sorry for our fight. I should have never stopped being your friend. You needed me to be there for you, unbiased, and I couldn't even do that right. There's so much I need to tell you, but I don't think now's the right time.'

'The police mentioned you spoke to them?'

'Yeah, just routine. You know how it is.' She shrugged her shoulders, and even though the action was cavalier, I had to admit I did in fact know how it was. I'd been questioned after Olivia's death, after all. 'I've got to ask you something, and I'm not sure I'm ready for your answer.'

'You know you can ask me anything,' I said, not a clue what she'd ask but curious nonetheless. What kind of question would put such a deep frown line across her forehead?

'Are you planning to come back to Hawthorn?' Her question was tentative, but her eyes blazed with an emotion I couldn't place. She wanted me to answer one way, that much was obvious, but I wasn't sure what answer would make her happy. I wasn't sure if *any* answer would make her happy.

So I gave her the truth. 'Of course.' To me, it was a no-brainer. There was no way I was letting them all win. 'I'll be back as soon as the hospital lets me leave. I'm already annoyed I'll miss the first couple days back.'

School started again the next day, as the Easter two-week break came to an end, and I was just glad it meant I'd missed no classes or mock exams or anything that would affect my scholarship status. I was determined to complete the year to the best of my ability, even if it killed me.

Something that had somehow become a potential outcome to consider.

'Are you sure that's a good idea?' Clo said, the look on her face telling me she quite possibly thought I'd gone mad. Maybe I had a little, but fuck, why should those rich elitist fuckers decide whether or not I obtained my A-Levels at a fancy establishment like Hawthorn?

'Nope,' I told her, knowing in my gut it was probably one of the worst ideas I'd had in a long time—though trusting Ollie had been *the* worst idea I'd had, and nothing was going to top *that* anytime soon. 'But I'm gonna do it anyway.'

'Then I'll be by your side the whole time.' Clover leaned down, grabbed my hand in hers, and squeezed it tightly. 'That fucker is going to pay for what he's done to you.'

I nodded, glad I had my partner in crime back, but then realised she wasn't going to say anything first, so I decided to be the one to bring up the subject of Griff.

'So, I haven't heard from Griff,' I said, hoping she'd take the bait. She didn't. So I continued, 'Did he know about any of it? All of it?' I had to ask. I had to know who was involved in my torment and who had to pay.

'I think he should be the one to talk to you about it,' she said, as vague an answer as she could get away with. 'I know you must be wondering about that kiss.' She shuffled slightly, her face unsure.

'Of course I am.' It was blunt and to the point, but I didn't want to pussyfoot around with Clover anymore. She was the person I could be the most honest with, the most myself, and I didn't want something like a kiss with Griff to come between us. I added under my breath, 'Not like you've felt comfortable telling me much this year.'

'I was so upset about everything that had happened with you, Sky. It was that day I called you all those horrid names, remember? I just dropped the bomb, then ran off like a total bitch, and Griff followed me to talk me off the ledge. I promise I hadn't expected him to.

'Once we got back to the room, he said some really nice things to me. Things that made me feel better, made me feel important and wanted. It was me who kissed him first. It was my fault.' Her green eyes were staring into mine, wanting me to know how sorry she was about it all, and I wanted to believe her and forgive her straight away, but something was holding me back. 'He wanted to tell you straight away, and I begged him not to.'

'Why?'

'Because I didn't want you to be mad at him or me. I didn't want you to think badly of us. We were lying to you, and I felt like shit about it, because after that first kiss, we realised how much we liked one another and couldn't stop.'

Disgust at myself settled in my gut.

Was I really that much of a judgemental twat? Did she genuinely believe I would've been mad at them or thought badly of them, just because they liked each other?

Why would it matter to me if they kissed, after all? Not like she'd kissed Ollie behind my back.

Yeah, it was a surprise it had been *Griff* she'd kissed and not Leo, but that was all, and the only reason it hurt me at the Fashion Show was because they had blindsided me. Plus, I'd been shocked at the whole *having cameras spying on me in my bedroom* aspect of the situation—something I hadn't forgotten and would need to correct if I was to return to Hawthorn.

'Well, I don't,' I told her, 'and I wouldn't have if you'd told me at the time either.'

'I know that *now*. Can you forgive me?' she asked, widening her green eyes, trying to look as cute as possible so I'd bend.

It totally worked.

'Yeah, of course I can, silly.' Sometimes, it was easier to just leave stuff behind and move on. Forgive but never forget.

'I'm so glad you didn't die, Sky.' A sob left Clo and a twinge of guilt wracked through me. Over the last week, I'd had a lot of terrible thoughts about her and assumed she didn't care about me at all.

Clover leaned down, putting the two of us at eye level, her

eyes glittering with unshed tears. She hugged me to her, and although she was trying to avoid squeezing too tight because of my stab wound, I could sense just how much love she was putting into the hug.

'Let's not fall out again,' Clo said, and I just smiled at her.

I mean, it's all very well her saying it, but like so many things, it's easier said than done.

Two

MY RECOVERY HAD TAKEN SLIGHTLY LONGER than anticipated, and it was pissing me off. The first week of May came and went, and I still hadn't returned to Hawthorn, which made me itch, because I didn't want those fuckers thinking they'd got away with everything. They hadn't run me off, and it annoyed me they thought they'd succeeded in whatever intimidation scheme they came up with.

Classes had returned two weeks ago, and Clover—who had returned to school—told me on one of her visits that the boys had gone back to ruling the school with Ophelia and Oralie at their sides. *The Sect* were back in top form and were acting like the last seven months hadn't happened—like they'd never stopped talking to *The Set* or formed a friendship with a scholarship student.

Odette's funeral had taken place during the break, but Clover had no information about it to tell me except for some snippets she'd heard second-hand. Not like she'd attended that shit show —her words—so all we knew was that the boys went and stayed pretty silent and moody throughout the whole thing.

With Odette gone (in polite terms), Ophelia was the natural leader replacement for their stupid tradition. She'd been as much of a bitch towards me as Odette and had given me my fair share of bruises over the last seven months, so really, she was the perfect fit. *What a bitch.*

'Are you sure you're ready?' Clover asked me, packing my pyjamas into a large duffle bag.

I watched her, trying to determine her feelings from her expression. 'To leave the hospital, or to go back to school?'

'Both, I guess.' Clo was definitely more worried about it all than I was. If anything, I was buzzing with energy at the thought of returning. The revenge boiling in my blood wasn't going to stay dormant for much longer without an explosion.

After *finally* being discharged, I was heading straight back to school. I'd already missed enough classes and fuck, wasn't like I wanted to go back to stay with my mum and Andy for even a day. *I've already suffered enough, thank you very much.*

'For the millionth time, Clo,' I growled. 'I'm more than ready! I want to do this. No, I *need* to do this for my sanity. I can't let them continue to swan around as if they didn't nearly end my life. Until they understand what they've done wrong, I won't be able to move on. Plus, I *need* Ollie to look me in the eye when he tells me everything was a lie.'

'Didn't he kinda already do that?' Clo asked in a tentative tone. I'd told her what had happened with Ollie after the show, both the mean words he'd said and the evil glint in his eye as he'd said them.

I sputtered out, 'W-well, yeah, kind of, but not fully.'

Yes, Ollie had looked me dead in the eyes when he told me I didn't belong at Hawthorn and that I never had, so his feelings on that were pretty clear, but I needed him to look me in the eye and tell me my first time was a lie. That he'd felt no ounce of affection towards me and had taken my virginity simply because he was a cruel bastard who could.

Clo's green eyes shone with sympathy for me, and I could tell she already believed I was doomed.

'If you have to, then I get it, and I'll be here to wipe away your tears.'

'No,' I said, annoyed she'd even suggested I would cry over him anymore. 'I will not shed another tear over that bastard.'

'Big words there, Sky.'

'Maybe, but not like it's a lie.' I shrugged at her, and she nodded in agreement, then continued to help me pick up all of my stuff. No more needed to be said. Not like I'd listen to her, anyway.

I took one last look around the hospital room, then I was ready to go. Clover had somehow convinced Ms Hawthorn to arrange a car for me. Pretty sure she had done it begrudgingly and wasn't too pleased about it, though. Sure, she thought I'd brought too much trouble to her academy as it was.

'Let's do this.' My voice gave off a confidence I wasn't feeling inside.

Fake it until you make it.

HAWTHORN ACADEMY still loomed at the top of the hill—of course it did; not like it had upped and moved—and the ascent towards it still gave me the same anxious feeling in the pit of my stomach as it had that first day back in September. Maybe it was even worse now that I knew the full extent of what could happen to a girl within those walls—or in the surrounding woodland.

Clover sat silently beside me the entire journey, and I knew she was as nervous as me. I could also tell she felt guilty about everything that had happened and knew in the future she'd be there at my side no matter what. She locked her hand in mine, and it was cold to the touch, like sitting next to an ice block, or like when you spent a little too long in the freezer aisle at the local supermarket.

I shivered, and I swore the cold was leaving her body and entering my bones.

'What are you nervous about?' I asked, breaking the frigid silence. 'Something major happen while I've been gone that I should know about?'

'Hm?' Her eyes shifted around the inside of the car, then stopped to take in the leather of the seats in front of us. One of the stitches was loose and I couldn't help but fixate on it while waiting for her to gather a response. 'Nope, nothing major. Why?'

Instantly, my back was up, and I was on my guard. It sounded as if she was keeping something from me, and there was no way I was letting that slide like I had earlier in the year.

'Clo. If you've got shit to say, then say it. I'm not having what happened before starting up again,' I said, nipping her reluctance in the bud straight away.

'Right.' She took a deep breath. 'I was sort of hoping we could wait to talk back at our dorm.' Her eyes flitted to the back of the driver's head. I supposed it made sense she didn't want to say much in front of him. For all we knew, he could be here as a spy for the academy—or worse, *The Sect*.

Wow, paranoid much? Which reminds me...

'Our room had a camera in it... It may even have had a microphone, too. How do we know it's gone?' I had every right to be suspicious. We'd been none the wiser, and for the last few weeks in the hospital, I'd gone over just how many conversations they may have been privy to. There were multiple times where Clo had dragged me out of the library to our room to talk in private, but all along we'd have been better off staying where we were.

'I've had our room gutted from top to bottom. There's no way a camera is hiding in there now. I forced that old witch Hawthorn to have the school pay for a bug jammer too, so if anything is planted in the future, it won't work.'

'How did you pull that off?' I asked, my scepticism rife. The woman had barely acknowledged any of the evil shit *The Set* had pulled on me last term. Fuck, she'd even had the audacity to blame *me* for the majority of what *they* did.

'Let's just say, I twisted her arm,' Clo replied vaguely. Really, did it matter how she'd managed it? Nope. As long as it was in place, I was happy.

The car pulled up to the front of the school, and straight away my body broke out into chills—chills that increased when I spotted Griff standing by the steps of the Academy, tall and imposing. He must be waiting for us.

What. The. Fuck?

'Did you tell him I was coming back today?' I asked Clover,

and from her wince in response, I had my answer. For the last couple of weeks, Clo had made it seem as if she hadn't spoken to any of them since I got hurt out of solidarity.

'No, Sky, I swear I didn't.' Clo's face had gone white, draining itself of colour, and I felt a little stab of guilt for doubting her so fast.

The driver got out of the car and came around to the passenger door to open it for us both. With every step he took closer, my anxiety climbed. There were only a few moments left until I was officially back at Hawthorn Academy, and even though I'd convinced myself it was for the best while lying in my hospital room, it all felt a little different looking up at those ugly gargoyles standing watch over the main entrance, their beady eyes surveying my every move.

Clo exited the car first, but in no time at all, I too was exiting the vehicle and trying my best not to black out or lose my nerves. It was a lot easier to believe in myself and act confident when I wasn't looking into a pair of meadow-green eyes. Eyes that were glinting in the sunlight, trying to gain access to the darker recesses of my mind. Eyes that belonged to Griffin Cooper of all people.

'Hey,' Griff muttered. His hands were wringing together, and I could tell he was worried about my reaction to seeing him there. As he should be. 'How have you been?'

I reckoned it was the first time he hadn't greeted me with his carefree, cheeky grin. Even though I was pissed at him, it was odd. Like something was missing from the picture that made up Griff.

'Fine,' I replied, blunt as fuck. I couldn't look him in the eye, my anger rising simply from being in his vicinity.

He chuckled, anxious. Ever since we'd met, he'd been the confident one, and I'd been the one stuttering my way through life. I doubted he'd ever heard me be so short with him—or with anyone for that matter.

Now, I felt like I was a completely different person. Like I'd been born anew. A phoenix risen from the ashes, brushing off the dirt and debris from the previous terms. Ready to fight again.

'You look well, considering,' Griff said.

Really, Griff? I look well considering? I laughed in his face with derision. 'Considering the fact I've spent the last month in a hospital bed? Or considering the fact I was *stabbed*?'

'Yeah...' he trailed off, not sure what to say. A first for him, I was certain. 'Considering that.'

Clover looked towards him, and I saw red. I wasn't sure what made me snap, but something did. Maybe it was the expression on her face or the fact she looked torn between us both.

'Something you wanna say, Clo?' I turned on the spot to face her, and although she'd changed her expression the moment I swivelled towards her, she hadn't changed it quick enough. I saw the sheepish look she tried to cover.

'Nope,' she replied, hesitant. The two of them were pissing me off more than usual. I needed to talk to Griff alone away from Clover. Otherwise, I'd never get a real answer from him, but I wasn't ready for that yet. I wasn't sure *when* I'd be ready.

'Skylar, can we please talk?' he pleaded, causing me to freeze on the spot. He'd used my name. Not *New Girl*. Not *babycakes* or *babydoll*. But Skylar.

'Not today,' I told him. Even standing outside of the main entrance, those two gargoyles and their buggy eyes looking at me, was a lot harder than I thought it would be. Full disclosure? I thought I would waltz back in, taking names, all while showing them the personal brand of hell only I could deliver.

It would be so easy for my mind to enter a dark space being back and I couldn't allow myself to crumble. Because let's be honest, no matter what I did or how I acted, underneath my façade, I was still that same small, scared, stupid Skylar. The one who'd let a boy deceive her for months and never noticed a thing. Or, should I say, noticed things but chose not to believe them and ignored her best friend over indigo eyes and a chiselled jaw.

'I understand,' Griff said after a moment, his voice pained. 'But you *will* talk to me at some point?'

'Maybe.'

'Let me just say one thing.' Griff took a step closer to us. 'I'm sorry that I've let you down and disappointed you, Sky. I'll do better, I promise. And when you're ready to talk, I'll be waiting, okay?'

I swallowed the emotion that bubbled up inside of me at his words, not wanting to dissect them out in the open.

'Come on, Sky.' Clo grabbed my arm and hooked hers with mine. 'Let's go to our room.' She nodded at Griff in goodbye, all nonchalant. I didn't pull away from her touch, but something inside of me recoiled.

This is Clover, Sky. She didn't stab you. I repeated the words in my head, hoping that if I said it enough, I might start to believe them.

Sure, she'd apologised to me, and I knew she'd meant what she said, but—and it was a big but—I didn't fully trust it.

'We'll see you later,' she told Griff, but her gaze was else-where, taking in everything and anything that wasn't him. Subtle, Clo.

I hadn't actually asked her much about them two, and outside of her brief explanation about their kiss, she hadn't given me much to go on either. Clover was the queen of holding shit back, even from her supposed best friend.

We made our way back to our room, luckily not bumping into anybody on our route—something I'd been scared of—but the fact we saw nobody only led to me feeling even more suspicious. If Griff had known we were coming, then there was no way the rest of them hadn't known. I'd put my very measly bank account on it.

Something wasn't right, and I was going to figure out exactly what it was.

OUR ROOM LOOKED EXACTLY the way I'd left it. Okay, maybe not *exactly* as I left it—my bed was made for once and there weren't any clothes lying around. I had a habit of being a bit of a mess.

Taking full advantage of the made bed, I flopped onto it with a deep sigh, my eyes searching the ceiling for some kind of sign that I was doing the right thing, but I knew there wasn't anything up there for me. There never was.

'Clo, do you believe in fate?' My eyes remained on the ceiling, and I listened as Clo shuffled around the room before she sat down on her bed and settled up against the wall.

'What d'you mean?'

'Pretty simple question, Clo,' I replied with a chuckle, but there wasn't any humour in it. 'Do you believe everything happens for a reason? That everything in life is predetermined and we're just stumbling around on whatever path that's set out for us?'

'Yes and no, I guess, but I think you've got something right with the path thing. I believe everyone is on a path and that every decision is a path. Every path has a fork in the road, and once you decide where to go, you continue on until you reach the next fork. *You* are the deciding factor and *you* decide the fork to take. For me, life is a constant make up of all these different paths and decisions. Does any of that even make sense?' She chuckled, nervous.

I nodded. It made a certain kind of sense to me now that she'd put it out there. I had been given many *forks* since joining Hawthorn, and I'd chosen my path each time, consequences be damned. Like the path where I'd chosen to believe my boyfriend over my best friend.

After a few minutes, I realised I hadn't answered her. 'Yeah, I get you.'

'What about you? What do you believe?'

'Something similar, I suppose. I believe that everything happens for a reason. Because every decision, every move I've made, has led me to now. Led me to this conversation with you.' I took a deep breath, thinking back on the last seven months. On all the small decisions I'd made, both consciously and subconsciously, to get me here. 'Do you realise how many small factors led to this moment?' I asked, really getting into the subject. 'So, so many, Clo.'

'Would you make them all again? If you were given a choice? Knowing what you know now and all that.'

'*Every* decision?' I thought about it for approximately ten seconds. 'Of course I would, Clo. 'Cause I'm here now with you. You're the family I choose for myself.'

Three

WITH EVERY NEW day that passed, I continued to ignore Griff's presence.

If he really meant what he'd said about waiting until I was ready, then he could wait a few more days for me.

A new week began, and I had to return to my classes. I'd only briefly seen Leo across campus once, and I was yet to see Oliver, which wasn't helping my nerves in the slightest. The longer it took, the more my unease grew. Dread sat low in my gut every time I thought about how our first encounter would go. I wasn't sure if it would be worse if he ignored me, or if he attempted to actually talk to me. Both scenarios gave me enough anxiety that I couldn't think of them for too long without getting green around the gills.

'Do you think he'll ask to talk to me?' I'd asked Clo my first night back. 'The way Griff seemed to want to talk to me, I mean.'

Her face was sceptical. 'I doubt it, Sky. The boy's been acting like you don't exist ever since you went to hospital.'

'You think he'll ignore me, then? Leave me alone?'

'For your sake,' she said, raising an eyebrow in my direction, 'I hope so.'

Her words hadn't filled me with much hope, but at least she was being honest with me, which was just as important. Honesty from Clover was a new step for us and I didn't want to do anything to ruin it.

My birthday was coming up soon, and I was worried they were all waiting until then to bring me back down to earth with a bang. I knew my bullies were aware of my birthday and that they'd probably try to give me some kind of treat for it. The kind of treat only they could deliver—if destroying somebody's personal property could ever be classed as a treat.

I woke up early Monday morning, ready for my first day back in class, spending a lot longer than usual in making myself presentable. My hair was curled to perfection, and the flicks of my eyeliner were as symmetrical as I could get them. Not to mention my lips were extra plump from the lip gloss I'd applied. It stung like a bitch, though.

I was making my way across campus for the first time when it happened.

I shit you not, as I reached the front of the main building, the entire atmosphere changed. It was the only way I could explain it. There was barely anybody in my eye line, the quad seemingly deserted, but I knew *he* was nearby. Watching me. I knew it in my blood—no, deep in my soul.

A titter carried itself on the wind and into my ears—an omen, if you want. An irritating laugh that could only belong to one of two people. Well, I suppose these days it could only belong to *one* person—the other one was dead.

Without intending to, my head followed the sound's direction.

And that was when I got my first Oliver sighting. The moment I'd both dreaded and sort of looked forward to in a totally masochistic way.

Standing together by the stairs of the main building were Ophelia, Oralie, and Oliver. A pack; united. A menacing look on each of their faces that cut into me. When I made eye contact with Ollie, a trickle of fear ran up my spine. It was the first time I'd looked at him head-on since shit went down at the end of the fashion show and I still felt just as small as I had then. Just as insignificant.

I hated how he made me feel—which was not as indifferent as

I'd told myself it would be while healing up in a hospital bed. I'd managed to kid myself it would be different, that I'd worked on myself, but there was no way I was going to let my brain fool me again.

I wanted to feel nothing for him. Badly.

But fuck.

The boy looked pretty fucking fine standing there, all while doing nothing at all. And I fucking hated him for it. I fucking hated him for making me feel worthless, and he really did make me feel worthless. A sour taste filled my mouth, or maybe it was bitter, like copper?

Frozen to the spot, unable to move, I stared back at them, wondering what my next move should be. I'd stayed still too long to resume as if nothing had happened, but I also didn't want to let on just how much their appearance was affecting me.

They all made me feel like absolute dogshit. Like I'd stepped out of shit and tried to pass myself off as something else. *I don't know, okay? I'm not great at explaining it.* But you know that feeling in your gut? The one that wouldn't go anywhere. That stayed with you, festered, eating up all the good inside? That was basically how I felt when thinking about them—about *him.*

Finally, the silence was broken.

'Eurgh.' The sound came from the back of Oralie's throat, filled with phlegm. 'This bitch again.' Her grating voice called out in my direction, but all I could do was look at her, a blank expression on my face. I would not rise to it. No matter what shit they tried.

'God, I hoped she'd get the picture,' said Ophelia, joining in, a smug smile playing on her over-glossed lips. 'Didn't you Ollie, baby?'

I almost choked on my spit. Choked on the rancid, over-perfumed air that surrounded me.

Ollie didn't even look over in my direction. He wrapped an arm around Ophelia's shoulder and pulled her close to him, managing to keep his gaze averted.

'C'mon, babe. No need to look at the trash,' he said, his tone flat. It wasn't what I'd expected as his first words, but I'd take it. Calling me trash was a given, right? An easy get out. He squeezed Ophelia's shoulder, and I saw her wince from the strength of it. Nice to know that aspect of his behaviour hadn't changed. Abusive bastard. If I'd started to doubt my resolve, seeing Ophelia wince only solidified my anger towards him.

Tears welled in my eyes, but I knew I couldn't let them fall. Not until I was somewhere private and they couldn't see me. They weren't going to see me cry over them again. But my pillow? Well, that was a different story. I hadn't grown *that* much.

'And she *is* trash,' Oralie piped up again, trying to join in, but even from where I stood I could see the girl had become a third wheel. Where the fuck was Leo and why wasn't he with them? I thought the four of them would be attached at the hip.

'She's worse than that,' Ophelia said with emphasis. 'Skylar Crescent is the biggest twat I've ever met, and honestly, we're worth so much more than her. In every. Single. Way.'

'That's because you've never met yourself.' The words left my lips before I registered them, but I was so glad they had. It was about time I made a stand against their bullshit!

The three of them swept by me, yet Ollie still hadn't caught my eye again. Not since we locked eyes the first moment I spotted them. He'd barely glanced at me after that full stop.

I hope he feels guilty as fuck for everything he's put me through.

I felt superior. If he couldn't look at me, that had to mean something, right? In my eyes, the fact he couldn't look at me meant that maybe he wasn't as unaffected as he wanted me to believe.

And *that*? That made me feel pretty fucking fantastic.

My birthday was a pretty silent affair, which was both a surprise and a blessing.

I mean, I was only turning seventeen, so not exactly that

important of an age, but I'd imagined it going differently back when I was friends with the boys. Back when I had a boyfriend.

Slight touch, though, that everybody at school ignored me, and unlike what I'd suspected, there was no extra harassment during the day. If anything, people were going out of their way to *ignore* me—averting their gazes as I made my way down the hall, or when I sat down in class.

For dinner, Clover and I decided to stay in our room and order pizza, rather than facing the dining hall. I'd risked being in public enough for one birthday. I wasn't sure how Clo had got outside food okayed by Ms Hawthorn, though, and I had my suspicions that maybe she was still in contact with Griff.

'So Ms Hawthorn let us order pizza. No strings attached?' I asked around a bite of my extra cheesy pizza, looking at Clo's face carefully for the slightest reaction.

'Yeah, it's your birthday.' She answered as if that was answer enough, but when it came to Ms Hawthorn, I highly doubted it. First of all, Clo had managed to *have words* with her about the camera in our room, and now pizza for my birthday... I just didn't trust it.

'Did Griff ask her for you?' I asked, trying to keep my suspicions out of my voice.

'Honestly, Sky, I've barely spoken to him, seeing as you haven't spoken to him yet. And I've told you, the thing between me and Griff wasn't that serious. It was a couple of kisses. No biggie.'

'Right, you've said. But if you have feelings for him, then that's okay. I would question you, but I wouldn't be mad.'

'It doesn't matter either way,' she replied, gazing at me intently. 'I'd never do that to you.'

I chose not to tell her that *technically*, she already had. 'Okay.'

We went back to eating in silence, both of us enjoying the food too much to talk about trivial things. My phone lit up from the floor, indicating I'd received a message. Griff had already sent me a birthday text that morning, and Clo was in the room with me, so I wasn't sure who else would be messaging me.

I picked up my phone and the message that greeted me surprised me.

HAPPY BIRTHDAY, STUTTER. ENJOY YOUR PIZZA.

'Are you okay? Your face has gone white.' Clo asked, and I nodded, not wanting to tell her who'd messaged me.

'I'm fine,' I replied, putting my phone down and picking up another slice as if Leo's message hadn't rocked me to the core.

'Have you heard from your mum today?' she asked, changing the subject.

Smooth, Clover.

'Nope.' I took another big bite, ignoring the pang of sadness that disappeared as soon as it arrived.

My mum didn't deserve my sadness. She hadn't even reached out to me, and okay, I hadn't expected gifts or anything, but I had at least expected a text. Just a quick one to say happy birthday, but apparently even that was too fucking hard for her. Shit, her only daughter was stabbed and the woman barely gave a fuck— I'd seen her once since, and only heard from her twice after that.

Not surprising, but hurtful nonetheless.

Four

JUNE CAME AND WITH IT, so did our mock exams. To say that I was shitting it was an understatement. I'd stopped eating because I was so nervous about them.

Not like I didn't have a valid enough reason to be nervous. I'd missed a bit of school while in the hospital and honestly, I hadn't tried to study much since being out of there, either, because whenever I'd attempted it, I got distracted within a minute. Sometimes by something slightly important, but usually just by the colour of the ceiling and the shadows playing there.

It was also kind of hard to keep up with my studies while planning an entire group of people's demises—in my mind— while trying not to focus on the fact somebody hated me enough to stab me. To literally *stab me*. That wasn't something you did when you merely disliked a person. No, that was something you did when you despised them. Thought they were a stain on society. And there were more than enough people at Hawthorn thinking that of me.

Yeah, there was the possibility that they'd targeted me because of what I saw and not due to who I was, but I wasn't ruling anything out. Didn't even really see much of whoever it was anyway.

Okay, okay. I had just forgotten whether I'd recognised them or not.

I was pissed at myself enough as it was and every night I fell asleep hoping I'd remember *something* about the person standing in front of me that night.

But I had absolutely no recollection.

I remembered entering the hallway, gasping, and then everything went black in my mind—fat lot of good that did me.

In my nightmares, the figure in front of me had no face. You know, like how the Grim Reaper or the Ghost of Christmas Future was depicted in every version of *A Christmas Carol*.

So yeah, I could remember fuck all.

Great.

THE INDOOR SPORTS hall was converted into a makeshift exam centre, and I really hated how it felt inside. All cold and impersonal. An echo of breathing, and pens on paper, was making me feel queasy.

There wasn't much hope swimming around my head for the exam, even though it was the last. The others had gone abysmally and that wasn't even me exaggerating.

The air in the hall was hot and stifling, and I couldn't help but break out into a sweat underneath my blazer. Or maybe that was due to my nerves.

I need to keep my scholarship at all costs.

Yes, things at school weren't exactly super, but becoming a student at Hawthorn was still one of the best things to ever happen to me. The chance to study subjects I'd only dreamed of before, plus the fact I had a real chance to attend a decent university, was enough to make me want to stay—stab wounds be damned.

I removed my blazer, hoping there were no dark patches on show. Wiping the sweat off my brow, I looked down at the exam paper in front of me for the gazillionth time.

Henry VIII never seriously abandoned the Catholic faith in the years 1529 to 1547. Discuss.

No matter how many times I stared at the words on the page, they made no more sense than they had the first time I'd read them an hour before. I'd been looking at them for so long they had blurred on the page, each letter all fuzzy around the edges.

Frustrated, I made a small grunting noise, then quickly looked around me to see if anybody had heard. Nobody turned to look at me, so I guess I was in the clear. My shoulders slumped, and instead of looking back at the page, I looked at the clock.

Not that looking at the minute hand moving made me feel any better. I'd been sitting here for an hour and all I'd written was my name, exam number, and an opening statement. Actually, an opening statement might be a slight exaggeration. It was five lines at most.

What the fuck was wrong with me?

I know this shit. The Tudor era was my jam and Henry VIII my absolute fave babe. I knew the answer to the question in my heart, but my head just wasn't delivering anything of use at that moment.

A cough came from my left and I rolled my eyes without meaning to. Because I knew who had coughed, and I could just tell it was on purpose.

I'd done my best the entire exam not to look over at Ollie, and fuck me, it had been *hard*. With his surname starting with B and mine starting with C, he was sitting at the desk parallel to mine in the aisle next to me.

He looked mighty fine—as usual—and as if he had no care in the world. *Nada.* His pen was flying across the page, and I could see from my position that he'd filled one of the sixteen-page answer booklets already. What a prick. There I was, unable to even fully comprehend the question, while he had no issues whatsoever in showing me up.

Ollie's presence at Hawthorn reminded me a little of Henry VIII and his court of friends. Whatever Henry said was law, and with *The Sect* being such a big deal, it was similar, wasn't it?

I turned away from Ollie and my thoughts. Comparing him to a long-dead tyrant wasn't what I needed to be doing, so instead, I watched the invigilators walking around listlessly, up and down the aisles in between the tables, making sure that nobody talked and shared answers.

I'd always wondered whether they played *Chicken* with each other. You know, the game where they both walked down the same aisle until one of them chickened out and turned around. Right now, I hoped they would just to alleviate my boredom—and to take my mind off the fact that I was struggling to remember any of the events that took place between 1529 and 1547.

Stop procrastinating, Sky.

Ollie coughed again, and I saw his smug little smirk out of the corner of my eye. The bastard knew I'd written barely anything and was relishing in it.

Note to self; must talk to Clover about a revenge plan *ASAP*.

THE MOCK EXAM FINALLY FINISHED, and all I wanted to do was get out of the stifling hall as fast as humanly possible, so I could get back to my room, grab a whiteboard, and plot revenge with my best friend. It really was the simple things in life.

I was so focused on where I *wanted* to be that I wasn't anywhere near focused enough on where I actually *was*.

'Will you get out of my way!' a shrill voice pierced my eardrum at the same time a sharp pain shot through my shoulder.

'Fuck.' My voice came out in a low whisper, but I kept my head held high and stayed facing the direction I was heading in—which was the exit to the motherfucking hall. I was so close to making it out of there free. Two steps max.

But nope.

Of course I couldn't just ignore Ophelia's cry without her getting even more mad.

'Will you mind where you're going?' she said, gripping my shoulder where she'd pushed me, to make sure I couldn't keep walking and minding my own business. *Bitch.*

'What?' I growled. 'I can't exactly get out of your way if you're holding me back, can I?'

'You've already got in my way, so you may as well stop and hear what I have to say.' Ophelia's lips curled up into a grin that sent a shiver down my spine. Oralie came up beside her and stood there, blocking my path even more.

I looked around to see if we were holding anybody up, but we were the last to leave the hall. The only others in the room were Ollie and Griff, which, unlike last term when that would've filled me with a sense of safety, now filled my heart with dread.

Clover was back in our room, not having had an exam during that period, and therefore, unable to save me. Not that I needed Clover to save me. I kept reminding myself that I was perfectly capable of rescuing myself, no man or friend needed.

Griff's eye caught mine, and he seemed to sympathise with me if the look in his eyes was an indicator, but he remained silent, watching it all play out. *Coward.* Or maybe it was get back for me ignoring him still?

'And what do you have to say?' I replied, my tone dead. 'Because I can't think of anything you could say that I'd care about.'

'You're an idiot,' Oralie snapped. After the last three hours, I couldn't even deny it in good conscience. I had acted like an idiot throughout the exam, and I was also an idiot when I didn't try harder to get out of the hall before they did. I hadn't even noticed they were behind me, which was unlike me. Usually, I was aware of my surroundings at all times.

'It wasn't me who wanted to talk to you anyway.' She flicked her long hair behind her shoulder and turned away from me. Dismissing me already.

My forehead scrunched up in a frown. 'Then who did?'

'I did.'

My head snapped in Ollie's direction and I sucked in a breath of sheer hatred at his cocky tone.

'You did?' My right foot started tapping on the stone floor as I tried my hardest to keep my cool. There was a reason I'd avoided them all—the main one being I didn't want to be alone with them. I looked over at Griff, who smiled, but unlike in the past, I couldn't find much comfort in it. 'Why?'

He lifted his shoulders in a careless shrug, as if nothing mattered. 'Because.'

'Because, what?' I said through gritted teeth.

'Because I can,' he finished with a wolfish grin. And to him, it really was that simple. 'Why? Did you have somewhere more important to be?'

'Anywhere is more important than wherever you are.'

'I do love it when you show a bit of bite, Skylar.' He took a step closer. 'Makes it all a little more... exciting, don't you think?'

'I don't think about you at all, actually.' I shrugged, hoping I sounded carefree, but knowing I'd probably just made myself seem even more pathetic than they already thought I was. The lie wouldn't hold up in court. That much was for sure.

'Do you enjoy lying to yourself?' He laughed, his bright blue eyes wide and shining with amusement, the movement showing off his chiselled jawline.

'I—'

'Save the bullshit, Skylar. Not like I give a fuck. I just wanted to give you a warning.'

'A warning?' I scoffed, folding my arms across my chest. 'You, of all people, can't exactly warn me about shit.'

'I can do what I want, as you're fully aware.' He took another step closer, and the whiff of his cologne entered my nose, sending a shiver down my spine. Fuck, the boy did smell good. The smell reminded me of the times spent wrapped up in one another— times that were all a lie. 'And I want to warn you not to go home this summer.'

'Why wouldn't I go home?' I laughed, the sound brittle. 'Not like I've got anywhere else to go.'

'Go to Clo's.' His tone brooked no argument, but I couldn't bite my tongue from snapping back at him.

'No can do,' I said, a smile slowly curling my lips up. 'Clo's spending the summer at mine.'

'Skylar.' My name was a warning.

'Oliver.' His name was mocking.

'I mean it.' His hand clenched and unclenched at his side. 'Don't go home.'

'And are you going to tell me *why*? Or am I meant to just take your word for it? Because I can't exactly be safer *here* than at home. Last time I checked, I wasn't stabbed at home.'

'Please,' Griff piped up from his spot beside Ollie. 'I know you don't wanna hear it from him, but I'm asking too. Please don't go home.'

I shook my head, wanting to erase the worry on Griff's face from my mind, turning on the spot to get away from them. 'Whatever.'

'Don't walk away from me,' Ollie growled.

I didn't even dignify his bullshit with an answer. I just kept walking.

Five

LEO CAME for me a couple of days later.

Well, actually, that made it sound a lot more dramatic than it really was.

I was walking down the school hallway, making my way to my next lesson, when an arm snaked out and grabbed me, pulling me into a partially hidden alcove. One of the school's few secret, out-of-the-way spots. Somewhere you could go and make out without the entire school seeing. Something I may or may not have had first-hand experience of.

'Stutter.'

'Leo,' I bit out, knowing who it was without even having to see his face. There was only one person at Hawthorn who called me that. Plus, his scent was super distinctive. 'What do you want?'

He blinked, his lips raised in a pseudo-smile. 'I wanted to talk to you.'

'Let me guess.' I removed his hand from my upper arm and looked him in the eye. 'You don't want me to go home for the summer.'

'What makes you say that?' He put his hand in his pocket, the slight slouch of his body giving off a casual vibe, even though his facial expression was anything but.

'Ollie and Griff have already tried,' I admitted. 'And I'll tell you what I told them—'

'Let me guess,' he mocked, cutting me off. 'You told them you wouldn't.'

'I didn't tell them anything. All I said was I didn't get stabbed at home, which I'd like to point out is a very valid f-fucking point.'

'No, you didn't get stabbed at home.' Leo's tone made me feel stupid. I hated the way he made me feel stupid all the time. It was something I'd noticed last year, and it had only grown since. 'But there's a first for everything. You'd never been stabbed at school before either, and let's be real, Stutter, your old school wasn't exactly classy.'

'Your elitism is showing.' I rolled my eyes at him. 'Hollowdale High may not have been *classy* as you so elegantly put it, but at least I felt like I belonged there. Sure, there may have been some kids walking around with knives in their pockets, but I can tell you I never saw half as much bullshit and bullying there as I've suffered here.'

'Yeah, yeah, cry me a river.' Leo looked behind him, his eyes shifting from side-to-side. Suppose he hadn't told the others he planned to pull me aside and try to talk sense into me.

'Trouble in paradise?' I bit my bottom lip, stopping the smile fighting to break out on my face, as I assessed him.

He turned back to me. 'Paradise?'

'Between you and the boys. Don't want Ollie or Griff to see you talking to me?'

'I couldn't give a fuck if either of those pricks saw me.'

'And I'm meant to believe that when you keep looking over your shoulder?' I laughed. 'Seems to me like you're hiding us in this alcove for a reason and if it isn't to hide from them, then who exactly are we hiding from? Clover?'

'This has fuck all to do with Red,' he growled, grabbing my wrist and pulling me tighter to him so he could whisper the next sentence in my ear. 'This has everything to do with you, and me wanting to make sure you don't fucking die.'

'Leo.' My voice was a whisper, too. 'Why do you even care? We're not exactly friends.'

He inclined his head, a strand of his blond hair falling into his bright blue eye. 'I do care about you.'

'You've had a funny way of showing it.'

'That's just who I am.' He shrugged, not looking repentant in the slightest. 'But it doesn't mean I don't give a shit. Just means I don't want to let you know how I feel. Or anyone, for that matter.'

'And now you're just opening up your heart to me, huh? Bit fishy, don't you think?'

'Sky,' he hushed out, and my stomach bottomed out at his use of my name. 'I need you to tell me you won't go home for the summer. I mean it. It isn't safe.'

'Life isn't safe.'

'Sky,' he groaned. 'You're being a difficult bitch on purpose.'

'Ah, there's the Leo I know and love.'

'You love me?'

'You wish.' I poked him in the side with my free hand, a small giggle escaping. Leo was always so hot and cold, I never knew how to react to him, but for some reason, I also knew when he was playing me. Sort of. 'If I go home, there's not really much you can do about it.'

'Is that a challenge?'

'What kind of challenge would it be?'

'Stutter, I'm a relatively powerful guy. I've got money and my parents own the school. Pretty sure I could ensure you don't go home this summer.'

'And what? Come stay with you at chateau Hawthorn instead? Puh-lease. You want to spend the summer with me as much as I want to spend it with you.'

'So a lot then, yeah?'

'Ha-ha.' I shook my head, looking around us to see that a lot of students had disappeared into their classrooms. 'Neither of us wants to spend the summer together.'

'And I said nothing about spending the summer together.'

'But you said—'

'I said I could ensure you don't go home for the summer. I never said anything about coming to live with me.'

'Whatever.' I sighed. 'So what do you want from me?'

'I want you to find a way not to go home. I don't care how or what you have to do, okay? Just do it. Otherwise, I will.'

'Is that a threat?'

'Stutter, when I threaten you, you're gonna fucking know about it.'

Leo let go of my wrist and brushed himself down, probably wanting to get rid of some imaginary lint or something that would make him look unkempt. People didn't realise it, but Leo cared more about his appearance than Ollie did. Ollie just showed it more to those who didn't know him that well.

'I'll see you around, Stutter.'

He was gone and out of my eyesight so fast I didn't even have the chance to respond.

———

The warnings from Leo, Ollie, and Griff didn't stick around in my brain for long.

I had a lot of other shit on my mind, and those fuckwads weren't going to ruin my day. Or my life.

It was about time that Skylar Crescent stopped being such a walkover and started to think about her revenge.

Because I wanted revenge on them all—I just wasn't sure how the fuck to go about it.

How did one go about revenge? Without it seeming too cliché or stupid?

'Clo?'

'Yeah.' The pen in her mouth muffled the word. Clo was studying the brochure of the university she planned to go to next year and making notes of what she needed. 'What's up?'

'I was just thinking about how to get revenge on the girls and Ollie.' I put my pen down and Clo did the same, lifting her head from the paper to look me over. 'What would you do if you were in my position?'

She laughed, coarse and harsh. 'I wouldn't.'

'What do you mean you wouldn't? Thought you'd be all for it.'

'I've seen a lot since knowing these people, Sky, and I promise you, you will never be on top. They always come out of a situation looking better than you, no matter what, and that's something you need to come to terms with.'

'But why should we have to come to terms with that?' I shuffled in my chair, getting more into our conversation, the textbook open in front of me long forgotten. 'Doesn't that mean we're allowing them to get away with it, and if anything, perpetuating it further?'

'Big words for a Wednesday morning, Skylar.'

'Stop trying to distract me.' The library was super quiet, and there was barely anybody around, so not like there was anyone who could overhear us and pass it along to *The Set* or *The Sect*. 'We could team up and go ham on their arses.'

'We could,' she admitted. 'But I don't want to. Honestly, I don't want to do anything that could jeopardise me getting out of here and leaving all this pomp and bullshit behind. Messing with them would do exactly that. They wouldn't let me get away, and that's all I really, *really* want. You can understand that, right?'

I sighed. Of course I understood, and I couldn't fault her for it either. If I were in her position, I would probably feel the same way.

'I get you. It's just hard, ya know, because I don't want to do it by myself. Fuck, I don't think there's much I could even achieve working alone. I don't know what makes them tick the way you do.'

'Look, if you're really into this whole thing, I'll see what I can do, but I'm not gonna promise anything.'

'Thank you!' I let out an excited squeal. That was surprisingly easier than I'd anticipated. Thought I'd have to wear her down over multiple conversations. 'I promise you'll still get to leave this shithole in a month's time.'

'You can't promise that.'

'Well, no. But there's nothing to hold you here, Clo. You've done your time. Two years of it.'

'Yeah...' She looked up at the ceiling, taking a deep breath. 'You're right. Thanks for understanding, Sky.'

A wide grin covered my face. 'What are best friends for?'

Six

'SKYLAR!' Clover shouted, flying towards me like the devil was on her heels. Maybe he was. 'Have you heard this shit?'

'Heard what?' I asked, wracking my brain to figure out what on earth she could be referring to. As usual, I was sitting in the library at the very back, trying to make myself invisible. I felt a great sense of comfort sitting there and I'd made—sort of but not really—friends with the librarian. She was an older lady who looked like she wouldn't hurt a fly, but she took no crap and didn't let anybody come in and give me grief. I super appreciated her. She was one of my only allies at Hawthorn, and I wouldn't be forgetting that anytime soon.

'Have you heard about my grades?'

'What about them?' I put down my pen and really looked at her. She looked wild, her face bright red—from running, or rage, I couldn't be sure. Her copper hair was flying in all directions, and I knew she had flown across campus to tell me whatever she was biting her tongue to stop herself from blurting out.

'I've failed everything!' she cried, throwing herself down heavily in the seat beside me, her arms flying up in disbelief. She wasn't the only person who didn't believe her. I didn't. There was no way she'd failed *everything*. Sure, she didn't always pay too much attention in class, but she was smart and knuckled down when the time was right. It was her final year at Hawthorn, and unlike me, her exams weren't just mocks. They were the real deal. And the real deal didn't get results for another two months.

'You can't have failed *everything*. There'd be no way to know yet even if you had.'

'No, Skylar,' she said, her face falling into grim truth. 'I've somehow failed every fucking thing. As in, they've given me a "U" in every subject.'

I gasped, and when she shoved her phone with Hive pulled up in front of my face and I saw for myself, I knew she wasn't being overdramatic for once.

'What the actual fuck?' I muttered, staring at the pixels on the screen, thoroughly baffled at the turn of events. 'Results aren't out until August from the exam boards, and it's only July.'

'I was marked absent!' she shrilled. 'Apparently, no Clover Luck attended any of her written exams, so not like I have to wait until August to be told that.'

'For real?' Surely the reach of *The Sect* and *The Set* didn't stretch to being able to have Clo's future ruined. But then Ollie's words after the mock exam a month ago played through my head again, and all of a sudden, I wasn't quite so sure. I'd not told Clover about the exchange as I hadn't wanted her to worry, but maybe I should've done.

'Well, you know who's responsible,' she said, bitterness clear in her tone. Bending over, she hit her head on the table with a thud. 'Ouch! Is anything going to go right for me today?'

'What does this mean, though?' I asked, ignoring her melo-dramatics. 'Surely you can speak to Ms Hawthorn and explain what's happened and they'll rearrange for you to retake them?'

All Clover wanted was to get out of here and attend a banging university—one where nobody knew her or her past, and she could start fresh. She lifted her head and the look of despair on her face gutted me.

'It means,' she said through gritted teeth, 'that I have to return to Hawthorn next year.'

I went to speak, but she continued when she saw me take a breath.

'AND I have to attend *summer school.*' She spat the last two words, and I watched as spittle flew and landed on the table in front of us. I fixated on the spot, deep in thought.

'But why would you have to attend summer school? It doesn't make sense.'

Last time I checked, Hawthorn Academy didn't even run a summer school. Why would they? And if they did, it wouldn't be for free. Every term here cost the parents thousands of pounds, so there was no way they'd give them bed and board during the summer, alongside lessons, for zero funds. Clover, being a scholarship student, relied on the kind hearts of the school's benefactors, and I doubted they were paying extra. The fact she'd failed should be enough for them to kick her out and never offer a scholarship ever again.

A large part of me was thrilled that Clover would attend Hawthorn again next year. It would mean I wasn't alone with all the vultures. That I would have a friend, somebody who could stand by my side while I no doubt withstood more bullying and harassment. Or attempted bullying, at least.

Then it hit me. I hadn't thought to look on Hive for my own grades. To be honest, I'd totally forgotten they were being released. Plus, I was expecting them to be shocking, so I had already sort of written myself off.

I pulled up the app on my phone and navigated to the Results tab under my student profile, my stomach slowly sinking down to my toes.

What I saw didn't surprise me, but it made me sad. I'd been doing so well in my classes, my grades had only suffered when tampered with, and no matter what *The Set* had thrown at me I'd continued fighting. But apparently being stabbed was a completely different ballgame, as I was staring at a page filled with Us too.

Clover leaned over and glanced at my screen. The moment she saw the U's, she winced.

'Shit, I'm sorry, Sky. Do you think it's legit?' Her sympathy for me was radiating from her and it made me feel a tiny bit better to know she cared.

'Honestly, I don't know. I mean, I knew my test results were coming back altered over the last year, and that I'd messed up in the mock exams.' I shrugged. 'Guess I'll be attending summer school right alongside you.' I laughed, sharp and harsh, nudging her with my elbow, trying to cheer us both up.

If I was being one hundred percent honest with myself—and I would never admit to it, even with a gun to my head—I felt relieved. Relieved that I didn't have to go home and spend the summer with my mother and Andy. Relieved that I would eat well and learn more and could finally show the teachers exactly what I was capable of when other pupils didn't sabotage me.

The warning from Ollie came back, clearer than ever.

'Don't go home.'

Would he have done something to make sure I didn't go home? Surely not. The boy didn't give that much of a fuck about me. Otherwise, he'd have tried talking to me again. Or at least wouldn't look at me like shit on his shoe every time we were in the same vicinity.

'Miss Crescent. Miss Luck.' Ms Hawthorn's voice was as no-nonsense as always, like curdled milk or something equally gross. Fuck knows when she'd arrived, or whether she'd overheard any of our conversation, but when I looked up, I found her looming over our table, staring down her nose at us with her eyes pinched tight. 'I expect to see you both in my office on Monday morning, at nine a.m. sharp.'

She walked off straight afterwards, not giving us any time to reply, but what exactly could we say, anyway?

'Guess we're going to find out Monday morning for definite,' Clo said with a resigned sigh.

'I guess so.' I reached out to rub her shoulder. 'At least no matter what happens, Clo, we're together.'

The knock came at ten. *Our* knock. The one Clover and I used to let each other know who was there.

But both Clover and I were in the room, trying to work on our schoolwork, so it wasn't either of us on the other side of our door.

Our puzzled expressions matched when I glanced over at her, and I nodded for her to go open the door. I wasn't risking my safety by opening that thing. My stomach still twinged anytime I felt even slightly unsafe.

Note to self: Get a peephole for the door like they have in hotels. Or even better, a video doorbell.

Then we'd know not to open it if it was somebody wanting to harm us. Especially so late in the evening. Okay, okay. It wasn't late, exactly, but it was pretty close to curfew and we didn't have *The Sect's* protection anymore, so the hall monitors wouldn't turn a blind eye anymore. Their loyalty lay with the others. *Bastards.*

Clo opened the door slowly to reveal Griff standing on the other side, a sheepish look on his face, his meadow-coloured eyes burning into my soul when our gazes locked. Ever since I'd returned to school, I'd avoided him. He'd tried to get me alone once he realised I wasn't coming to him anytime soon, but I wasn't having any of it. In a way, his betrayal had hurt the most. He was the one I'd have put my faith in, and he'd thrown it back in my face.

'Please, can we talk, Sky?' he asked, yet making no move to enter the room, his hands clenching and unclenching at his sides. His stance was timid and so nervous it made me uncomfortable. It was so unlike the Griff I'd grown to know and love.

Clover turned away from Griff to face me, one eyebrow raised in question. I nodded. Fuck it, I may as well listen to what the boy had to say and then send him on his way.

'Go for it,' I replied, my tone more disinterested than my mind.

He shuffled into the room, as if he was trying not to make a big deal about the fact I'd granted him entry. Or maybe he was worried I'd tell him I was kidding or something.

Griff sat down on the floor, obviously deciding that neither of our beds was an option, and it wasn't like we had the space for a sofa, or even an armchair, like the boys had in their suites.

'Skylar Crescent,' he started, looking at me in earnest. 'I am so, so sorry.'

My brain was screaming at me. I knew I should feel something at his words, but all I felt was suspicion because he'd used my full name. He *never* used my full name.

Without thinking it through, words flew out of my mouth. 'What was even real, Griff?'

'All of it, Sky.' His eyes bore into me with a sincerity that travelled into my soul. Then he ruined it by opening his big stupid mouth again. 'Okay, not *all* of it, but I've never lied in my friendship with you. We have a bond, New Girl.'

'Don't call me that,' I spat. The nickname coming from him had never given me a bad vibe. It was always something he called me that filled me with warmth, as opposed to when the girls used it and were clearly trying to make me feel less than. Griff had never made it a slur the way Odette and co. had.

'Okay, okay,' he said, his hands up in a defensive gesture. 'I get it. Lemme think of something else to call you real quick.'

'Can't you just call me Sky?'

'Boring.' He laughed, rubbing his chin with his finger, staring up at the ceiling. 'I've got it! I'll call you Clouds. That cool?'

'Clouds?' There really was no explaining the way that boy's brain worked.

'Yeah,' he said with a cheeky grin, as if the explanation made perfect sense and I was the weird one for questioning it. 'Your name is *Sky*-lar, and that's where clouds live.'

I laughed, caught off guard. 'Okay... we'll go with it.'

He didn't waste a moment. 'Look, Clouds, there's something important I wanted to talk to you about.'

'And what's that?'

'Your dad,' he blurted out. 'I didn't know that was his name until the fashion show. You've got to believe me.'

Well, my dad wasn't where I thought the conversation was going, that was for sure. I'd guessed he was going to get me to forgive him, or to give Ollie another chance, or something like that. My dad hadn't entered my mind in a while—he never really had—and learning his identity hadn't changed that for me.

'Why would I believe you?' I scoffed. 'And why does it matter that you didn't know his name?'

'It matters 'cause *your* dad is *my* uncle,' he replied with emphasis. 'My dad, Damien, was a twin. Sky, this makes us like sisters.'

'No, Griff, this makes us cousins,' I deadpanned. I'd already thought that potentially we could be related after the response from the crowd at the show, but I hadn't dug that hole yet, too scared to learn the truth. Part of me hadn't wanted to believe that yet another person who shared my blood could treat me so poorly. Especially not somebody who'd treated me the way Griff had—like somebody who mattered.

It was going to take a lot for me to decide whether I wanted to let him back in; to trust him that easily. Being family didn't instantly make it all okay.

No, it definitely made it worse.

'Being family doesn't make things between us any better,' I warned, voicing my thoughts.

'I know,' he said with a nod, his cheeky grin disappearing. 'I just want you to know I really am so very sorry and I never wanted to hurt you. Family or not.'

'So, let me get this straight...' I trailed off, slightly overwhelmed by everything, needing to ignore his apology. 'Both of your parents were twins?'

'Weird, right?' he said with a chuckle, his dimples pressed in, teeth all aglow. 'Wonder if I'll have twins.' His head gravitated in Clo's direction, and I smiled inwardly at his obvious feelings for her.

'Well, fuck, there's no hope for them,' Clover quipped.

I laughed along with her. Even the thought of one mini-Griff running around was a worry, let alone two of them born at the same time.

'You want me, Luck. Don't pretend otherwise.' His eyebrows

waggled, and I noticed a faint blush rising on Clo's cheeks. Somebody hadn't been completely truthful when I'd asked if they were still crushing...

'Oh, fuck off,' Clo snapped as she threw a cushion at his head. 'What do you know about us flunking?'

The change in conversation was so abrupt it gave me whiplash.

'Huh?' he asked, confusion evident on his face. His smile vanished in a flash. 'You flunked?'

'Yep,' I replied first, 'but I'm certain mine was real.' I'd had enough time to think about it, and as much as I wanted to put the blame on Ollie and *The Set*, I knew I couldn't.

'And I'm certain that mine *wasn't*,' Clo said. 'So fess up, Griffin Cooper.'

'Babydoll, I have no idea what you're talking about,' Griff said, his tone hesitant. *Huh.* How had I never noticed how poor of a liar the boy was? He shook his head, not wanting to catch my eye. 'What's going on?'

'Ask your best friend, Leo,' Clover spat, causing me to roll my eyes. We had no proof Leo had anything to do with any of it. After my hushed conversation with Leo, my mind had wandered to him more often than it should. What would Leo even gain by flunking us both?

Clo caught me mid eye roll and snapped, 'Sorry, Skylar. Didn't realise he's your best friend now, too?'

I bit my tongue so hard to stop myself from replying to her. She was hurt and fuck, she'd been dealt a blow. The girl wasn't escaping Hawthorn the way she'd dreamt, or as fast as she'd hoped. But that was no reason to take it out on those who cared about her, like me.

'I doubt it's Leo's fault entirely, Clo,' Griff piped up. He moved to sit next to Clo on her bed, and at first I thought she was going to hit him or push him back to the floor. She did neither of those things, though, and kept herself still, not wanting to touch him. 'I'm sure Ollie and the girls have something to do with it, too.'

'How am I meant to know that you aren't bullshitting me right now?'

Griff sighed deeply. 'I've said sorry to Clouds, but maybe I need to say it to you. Clover, I'm sorry for everything, but I promise you, they've excluded me from any serious stuff. They don't tell me shit anymore.' He rubbed his chin with his forefinger, deep in thought. 'Well, turns out they'd never told me shit, anyway.'

'Likely story.' Just by looking over at Clo, I could see that she didn't believe him. Not one bit. But I could also see Griff sitting beside her, attempting to put his arm around her shoulders, and I could see the sincerity in his green eyes.

'Clo, I swear on your life.'

A small gasp left Clo's lips, as she turned to look at him for the first time since the conversation had become between the two of them, excluding me entirely. It was like they'd forgotten I was even there.

'Do you mean that?' she asked, her voice small.

'Of course I do,' he replied straight away, stroking her arm in a loving gesture. 'You know I'd never say that and not mean it.'

Suppose I should let them have some privacy.

Slowly, I stood up and made my way to the door before opening it as quietly as I could and stepping out into the hall to leave them to it.

Did I want the two of them to become a couple? Honestly, no.

But if it sorted shit out and got them both on board with my revenge scheme—that I was yet to tell them about—then I was down with it.

All's fair in love, war, and private school drama.

Seven

ONCE OUTSIDE MY ROOM, I wasn't sure where I could head to feel safe.

Griff and Clo hadn't asked me to leave, so it wasn't that I couldn't stay in my room, but I knew they needed to talk without me there. If there were real feelings between the two of them—whether I liked it or not—it was only fair they got to discuss them without me hanging around like a bad smell.

My feet were moving superfast, in a hurry to make it across campus without being seen, even though I didn't yet have a destination in mind.

I also didn't want to be caught unawares out in the open. The area glowed a deep orange, the sun setting in the distance, and if I didn't know the truth about what really happened at Hawthorn, I'd have thought it looked beautiful and picturesque.

A deep, gravelly voice slithered its way into my ear, and I shivered. I was so immersed in my own world I hadn't spotted anybody near me.

'Fancy seeing you here, Stutter.'

I stalled, nearly tripping over, my feet having stopped before my brain could catch up with the action. And like in a slow-motion movie scene, I looked over my shoulder and locked my gaze with Leo's.

'W-what do you want?' I asked, my stutter returning because of the scare he'd given me. I was much more in control of my stutter these days, but it still crept up when I was nervous or scared. I assumed it always would.

'No need to be like that. I just want to talk.' He'd reached my side and all I could do was stare at him in silence. Hadn't we spoken not that long ago?

What more is there to say?

Leo's hand came up and pushed a piece of my hair that had fallen into my face behind my ear. The touch of his fingers grazing my skin made my cheek warm.

Snap out of it!

'Talk about w-what, exactly?' Trying to keep my anger while looking into his gorgeous blue eyes. His blond hair was wet, and I guessed he'd been at the pool. Leo spent most of his free time at the pool. Rumour had it that he was training for the Olympics, but I wasn't sure how true that was. Another rumour was that he planned to compete at university, which I could believe a little more than the Olympics thing.

'Where are you going?'

'Er...' I looked around us, hoping to see something that'd inspire me.

'Tell me,' he demanded.

Until that moment, I hadn't known where I was headed, but when he pushed me, the word came out. 'Library.'

'Of course you are,' he whispered thoughtfully and nodded at me. 'Off you go then, Stutter. Wouldn't want to bump into somebody while all alone, would you?'

With that, he turned on the spot and walked away. No more words said. Yet I couldn't bring myself to move from the spot he had frozen me to.

Had Leo's arse always looked that good? *...Stop drooling, Sky!*

On reaching the boys' dorm building, he stopped and looked back over his shoulder, eyebrow raised at the look he saw on my face.

He winked at me before heading inside.

What the fuck was going on?

And what had he wanted to talk to me about?

'Little One,' a voice rasped out the moment I entered the library.

Seriously?

I headed further into the library towards the back to my favourite table, ignoring the voice trying to seduce me—and what a seductive voice it was.

Stay in control, Sky.

I quickly grabbed a book from the Classics section and threw myself into a chair, opening the book at a random page and burying my head inside.

'You hate that book,' Ollie said, taking the seat opposite mine. I refused to look up, but it was only then I registered I'd picked up *Wuthering Heights*. It irked me that he knew how much I hated it. He was the bane of my existence. All I could think was: *Don't do it, girl. Don't give in. Don't give him the power.*

I took a deep breath and continued to fake read my least favourite "love story". If I stayed quiet, he'd go away. Wasn't that the saying?

'Are you sad, Skylar?' he asked, his tone condescending. 'Are you going to cry?'

The venom in his tone made me look up and really look at him. Had he always been such a hateful bastard? But once I looked up, and our eyes locked, I couldn't tear my gaze away. Caught in the headlights. Trapped in his stare.

'Fuck you.'

'You'd love to.' He smirked, his eyebrow raised in question.

'N-never again,' I growled.

'Sure, baby girl. Tell yourself that.'

'Why are you t-talking to me?' I asked, trying to avoid his stare, but failing miserably.

'Magnets attract. And you and me'—he pointed between us both—'we're two of the strongest.'

I dropped the book and crossed my arms across my chest, but when I saw Ollie's eyes wander downward, I realised maybe that hadn't been the right choice. Oh, well. Got to stick with it now.

Also, him looking at me said a lot more about who really wanted to fuck who.

'You told me I don't belong here,' I accused, throwing his words from the pool house back at him. Of all the things he'd said to me that night, those were the ones that hit me the hardest.

'You don't.' His tone was factual. The certainty in his words told me he believed they were nothing more than the truth. 'I'm disappointed in you.'

'Disappointed? In me?' I sputtered, livid that I was allowing his words to affect me, but unable to stop myself. 'Why?'

'You returned.'

No bells. No whistles. Just a simple statement. One that caused me to visibly wince.

'I h-had no choice,' I whispered. In my heart, that was how it seemed to me. I hadn't had a choice but to return to Hawthorn. The education. The opportunity. The future. It was all too glittering for me to turn down.

'You had a choice, Little One. Everybody always has a choice. You just made the wrong one.' He laughed. 'Suppose it wouldn't be the first time.'

'What do you w-want?'

'Oh, there are many things I want, Little One. But the one that's running through my head right now? I want you to leave this place and never return. This is your last warning, Skylar. Tomorrow, the wolves will descend.'

The boy needed to make up his mind. Either I needed to leave the school and go home, or I needed to stay away from home for the summer. How could it be both? What a walking contradiction!

I chose to focus on the other part of his statement. 'Wolves?'

'Every fucking person in this school is at my command. Everywhere you turn, there will be somebody there waiting to stab you in the back.'

'Am I meant to be scared?'

'You should be,' he said darkly. His eyes were a deep indigo—soulless and dead. A blank slate, a face of indifference.

I needed to get away from him. Even being in his vicinity was making me question everything. He'd bullied me. He'd been behind everything the girls had done to me. And yet he still had the audacity to demand shit from me.

It didn't help that I'd lost my virginity to him. My brain still found it hard to separate the guy who ruined me at the end of the fashion show from the one I shared heartfelt moments with. Clover was constantly trying to convince me it had all been shady shit, but she was wrong. She chose to only see the dark. The deceit.

Unlike me. I'd seen behind the curtain. I'd seen both the wizard and the showman. And I found it hard to look at it all in such a black-and-white way.

Although, I'd also been sold a lie, so... not like I was the best judge of character when it came to him.

Fuck sticking around to listen to any more of his bullshit. Acting as if the hounds of hell were snapping at my ankles, I made my way out of the library.

Revenge. Revenge. Revenge.

Do not get sidetracked, Skylar!

Pretty eyes and killer smiles can lie and steal the very essence of who you are.

 Eight

THE NEXT DAY, you bet your arse that I was terrified with every step I took. Every class I attended. Every corner I turned.

I knew Ollie hadn't been lying in the library the night before; hadn't been hiding his intent to have the other students here make my day a living nightmare.

I definitely felt as if I'd been lured into a false sense of security ever since returning. For two months I'd been back, had even attended exams, yet other than a few whispers and jeers, nothing much had happened to me.

The other shoe has to drop at some point.

Clo and Griff didn't leave my side all day. After I'd got back to our room the night before, the two of them had made up and were laughing and smiling. The joy between them evident at first glance.

I made sure to wait until Griff had gone before I opened up. Yeah, Griff had apologised to me and it had seemed genuine. Plus, he'd clearly sorted things out with Clo, but I still wasn't going to blindly trust him again. Not straight away. He needed to earn it.

When Griff left, I told Clo the full extent of my run-in with Ollie, making sure to leave out that he'd demanded I not go home for the summer. Didn't need her worrying about that.

'Are the two of you official?' I asked her, wanting to get the gossip. 'You looked pretty cosy when I came in.'

She shrugged. 'I didn't want to put a label on it, so we're just keeping it casual.'

'And was Griff okay with that?'

'Why wouldn't he be?'

'I guess.' I shrugged, not wanting to push her or piss her off. 'As long as you're happy, then so am I.'

For some reason—okay, I knew why—but I'd left out the part where Leo had stopped me. Wasn't opening that can of worms if I didn't have to.

'...right, Sky?' Clo asked, her arm hooked in mine, as we made our way to the cafeteria to grab lunch to take with us to the library.

'Huh?' I shook my head, bringing myself back to my surroundings from where I was still in our room in my mind.

'I knew you weren't listening. Sometimes I wonder why I bother to talk to you. You've always got your head stuck in the clouds, girl.'

'Not always.'

'Sure you don't... I said it's odd we haven't seen Oralie or Ophelia around much.'

'They stick by Ollie's side, I think. Can't Griff answer what they've been up to?'

'Honestly, I don't think Ollie or Leo tell him much anymore. He barely knew shit last year and I think it's only grown worse. They purposefully hid things from him. He never knew who your dad was. Otherwise, he'd never have agreed to any of it.'

I was on the fence about my feelings towards Griff. A large part of me understood it. He hadn't known me at all, and his life-long friends—not to mention cousins—had convinced him to mess with the new girl for fun. He was such a cheeky, fun-loving guy, he would go along with anything if it made him laugh.

But the other part of me thought it was wrong either way, whether he knew about our cousin link or not, it was shitty to bully me. All because I was a scholarship student trying to change my life and better myself. A scholarship student whose father had done something so heinous they bullied me because of it. Something to this day I was still unaware of.

Fuck's sake.

Every time I thought I was feeling better, something hit me and took me back into that headspace again. The headspace of a vulnerable girl who was humiliated by some rich wankers ever since entering Hawthorn's gates.

'Earth to Sky,' Clo called as we stopped outside the hall, waving her hand in front of my face.

'Tonight, make sure Griff comes to our room,' I told her, my tone serious.

'Huh?' she asked, baffled.

'If he wants to help me, and he really is on our side, then get him to come to our room tonight.'

'Okay... Are you sure? Because just the other night you weren't even sure whether you were gonna forgive him or not.'

'Positive. The boy wants to make it up to me? Well, this is a start,' I told her, nodding as if my thought process should be obvious to her without me having to go into too much detail.

'Fine. He'll be there.'

In my best imitation of a movie villain, I replied, 'Excellent.'

I PACED MY ROOM, running my fingers through my hair, going through my plan in my head. The conversation was an important one, and I needed to get it right. The way Griff and Clo responded would dictate the future.

Okay, maybe not the *future*, because that was overly dramatic even for me, but the near future at least. The rest of my time at Hawthorn minimum.

If the two of them got behind me and helped, then we could really have some fun.

Also, I was on edge. Ollie had promised last night in the library that the wolves would descend, but they never did. Nobody even looked at me differently, which made zero sense.

Never before had *The Set* not taken an opportunity to harm me. Same could be said about every other pupil at school, too.

My feet stopped pacing up and down when the door handle jiggled. It opened to reveal Griff and Clo on the other side.

'Yo!' he called as he swanned into the room, his smile wide, with no care in the world. 'You called?'

'If by "called" you mean I asked you to come, then yes, I called.'

'Ah, pleasant lady. How may this knight of the realm be of assistance?' he asked, bending low into one of the deepest bows I'd ever seen. I sputtered a laugh. He could be such a fun goofball at times, it was almost easy to forget his betrayal.

'Knight of the realm?' Clo asked, entering the room behind him, a smile playing on her lips. 'What fucked-up realm is that?'

'This one,' he said, showing all of his teeth. His voice was loud and regal sounding, reminding me of a Shakespearean actor attempting to captivate an audience. 'The Hawthorn realm.'

'Even you saying the name gives me shivers.' Clo shook her body, running her hands up and down her arms.

The two of them went to sit on Clo's bed, and I started my pacing back up, thrown off track since they'd appeared. My entire planned speech left my head when they showed up and my mind was left blank.

'What is it?' Griff asked, his smile falling, sensing my distress. 'What's going on?'

'Right, so... I guess I should start with a question first. Are you on my side?' I asked, scrutinising his face for his gut reaction. Searching for lies and deceit.

'What do you mean?' he asked, his expression unchanged.

'If you had to choose between me and *The Sect,* who would you choose?' My eyes bored into his, wanting him to know just how serious the question—and his answer—would be.

'Are you making me choose?' He raised his eyebrows, his smile completely gone.

'No,' I blurted out because it wasn't an ultimatum. I'd never outright do that to him—to anybody. Maybe subliminally, but never intentionally. 'I'm just trying to decipher where your loyalties lie.' I shrugged.

'Look, I regret last year so much, Clouds. I've got your back,' he said, sincerity shining from his spring-coloured eyes. They were more green today, and they flashed with guilt as he thought of last year. Pretty sure he'd told me he had my back last year, too.

'Well then, buckle up, buttercups,' I said, addressing them both, 'as I've got a plan and I need both of you to help.'

'A plan?' Clo asked, her face blank and tone flat. Griff put his arm around her shoulders and hugged her to him, an intimate gesture they'd never done in front of me before. It was odd to see the two of them cuddling up to one another and acting so coupley.

'A revenge plan,' I replied, emphasising the word revenge. 'A wicked scheme.'

'Revenge?' Clo's tone was pissed. 'I told you I wasn't interested.'

'I remember,' I snapped. 'But I want to get my revenge on Ollie and Leo and definitely on Ophelia and Oralie.' Then I added under my breath, 'Wish I could on Odette.'

'Bit dark, Clouds. Think somebody already got their revenge on Odette, right?' Griff had a point. Somebody *had* stabbed the girl and, unlike me, she didn't survive it.

'Anyway.' I brushed off my callous thoughts. 'I've got some ideas.'

'Plot away,' Griff said, moving his arm back from around Clo to put his hands in a praying position, rippling his fingers like a movie baddie. I chuckled, seeing how similar Griff and I could be, as that was the exact motion I'd made earlier that day when talking to Clo about inviting him to our room. It was the first time I'd considered whether us being family had something to do with our similar actions.

Something for me to unpack later.

'Okay. So. What do Oralie and Ophelia love most?' I asked, even though we all knew the question was rhetorical. 'They love being all-powerful and in charge, right?'

Clover shrugged and Griff's face stayed the same. Questioning my sanity, no doubt.

'Of course they do!' I exclaimed, a little too loud for the small room.

They glanced at one another and then back at me, and I could tell they thought I was suffering mentally. As a rule, I didn't shout with enthusiasm often, so I could understand their concern.

When Clo spoke next, her tone was one I'd expect her to use with a very young child. 'Sky, do you think a revenge plan is healthy?'

'Nope,' I replied, all easy-breezy. 'But it's what I want, so here we are.'

'Okay...'

'Oh, ignore grumpy pants next to me,' Griff said with a smile, leaning back to rest on his hands. 'Continue.'

'They love the power that being a member of *The Set* gives them. They love that the rest of the school cowers when they pass and parts whenever they enter a hallway and so on. I want to stop that. I want to steal their power, and while at it, their hotness.'

'Forgive me if I'm being a little dense,' Clover started, sounding not in the least like she wanted to be forgiven. 'But *how* do you plan to steal their hotness?'

'Well, I can't steal it per se, but there are definitely things we could do to dim their shine.'

'I'm listening,' Griff said with a lopsided grin.

'It depends how petty we want to go, but we could mess with their skin cream, their hair care, their actual hair, and so on.' I'd stopped pacing and was facing them both head-on. Clover's nose wrinkled as her eyes surveyed me. 'Didn't you say when I was in the hospital that you'd be by my side?'

I felt only slightly guilty about using her words against her, but not guilty enough to *not* do it.

'Yes...' she trailed off.

'So be by my side,' I said forcefully. My vengeful heart would do it without her, but it didn't want to do shit alone if it didn't have to.

'I'll help you with the girls.' Griff's tone was full of glee. 'Nobody messes with my cousin and gets away with it.'

'Yay!' I said, choosing not to point out that both he and his best friends messed with me last year more than the girls did. *Pick your battles wisely, Sky.*

'Fine,' Clo huffed out. 'Let me guess, we're going to go for Leo how? Making him ugly too?'

'Not quite, but I thought we could target his relationship with girls.' Then I realised something pretty disconcerting. 'Did Leo even mourn Odette?'

'By mourn...' Griff trailed off, looking around the room. 'You mean?'

'Did he give a shit?' I asked bluntly. When she died, Odette was Leo's girlfriend. Plus, I still wasn't sure who had stabbed her —or me—so I needed to be super careful. What if the guilty party was Leo?

Did I truly believe he could've murdered his girlfriend?

'Of course he didn't,' Clover spat. 'Oh, he pretended well enough at the funeral, but we all know he was only with her to... Well, you get my drift.'

I nodded, and if this had been a text conversation, it would totally be an IKYKWIM moment, which stands for, *I know you know what I mean,* and was something Clo and I used all the time.

'How d'you know that?' Griff scoffed, defensive. 'You didn't even go to the funeral.'

'I just know these things,' Clo said with a shrug.

'You don't think...' I asked, not wanting to complete the thought, even though I'd just asked myself the same thing. Could Leo have been the figure I saw standing over Odette's lifeless body? Did he stab me?

Since returning to school and walking the halls from that night, my nightmares had given me some of my memories back, but not enough for me to see the full picture.

'No.' Griff's abrupt, hard voice made me flinch. 'He was with me during the fashion show. And after it, too.'

'The whole evening?' Clo asked, and as she spoke, I realised

I'd never asked for people's whereabouts since returning. I'd tried my hardest to stay away from them all so bad, I hadn't even thought about it. The only thing I knew was that I'd left Ollie down by the pool, and it couldn't physically be possible for him to be the figure. He would've had to have teleported, and I may be living in a novel, but it wasn't a science fiction one.

It may be stupid of me, but I'd never doubted Griff, and I'd barely considered Leo before the conversation turned to Odette. Clearly, I hadn't been thinking hard enough.

Griff opened his mouth to respond but then shut it comically fast. His voice was a low mumble. 'Well, no. Not the whole evening.'

'When I left the hall, you were alone,' I told him. 'We locked eyes, remember? No Leo in sight.'

'Yeah, and after you ran out, the entire hall went into disarray. The parents were in an uproar, and Ms Hawthorn was trying to save the evening. I spent my time searching for Clo, and Leo was definitely there, too. I saw him more than once.'

'So, there's a period where Leo is unaccounted for?' Clo asked, grabbing his chin so he stopped looking around the room and looked into her mesmerising, yet rather stern, eyes instead.

Griff squirmed in Clo's grasp, not wanting to put the words out into the universe. When his response came, his tone was one of exhaustion.

'Yeah. I guess there is.' He looked so uncomfortable I felt a little sorry for him. Ultimately, Leo was another one of Griff's cousins, and they'd grown up together. Must be shit to think that maybe somebody you love could also potentially be a murderer. Not even just somebody you love, but somebody you share blood with.

'Wonderful,' I deadpanned.

'Back to your plan,' Griff said in an obvious attempt to change the conversation. A bit clumsy, but I could understand his reluctance to continue down that road.

'What about it?' I asked, grabbing the rope he'd thrown out, willing to go down with it. Its very own anchor.

'Oliver. What're you planning to do to ruin him?' Clo let go of Griff's chin, and he turned back to face me, assessing my expression.

'Swimming,' I replied matter-of-factly.

'Swimming,' Griff said, his eyes brightening. 'That could work.'

'I thought so too. He hopes for a scholarship, right?' They both nodded, and I continued, 'I want to destroy any hope he has. I want him to know it was me, and think about me every time he remembers his failures.'

The fact he even wanted to take a scholarship from somebody who needed it pissed me off. The boy was wealthy enough he never needed anything to be paid for him, or handed to him. He was only doing it to prove he could.

'Feisty. Dark.' Griff beamed at me, his dimples pressed in. 'You devious woman. I love it.'

'You do?' I asked. The confirmation felt good, like water being poured onto my head, spreading through me, and the only way I could describe it was a mixture of pure elation and euphoria. It was a long time coming, and the fact Griff didn't reject my ideas gave me a real dopamine boost.

'Yeah!' He stood up abruptly, lurched forward, and wrapped his arms around my waist. Without giving me time to process, he lifted me off the ground and spun us both around, our laughter growing louder with each rotation.

'So you'll help?' I asked him mid-spin. He nodded, still spinning us. I hit his shoulder and shouted, 'Put me down!'

I was still chuckling, but the spinning had started to make me sick. A lot of spinning in quick succession always made me nauseous. Waltzers at the fair were my least favourite ride.

My feet touched the ground, and instantly I felt better. Grounded.

'If this is what you need to heal, then yeah, I'll help,' he said.

I kissed his cheek and beamed at him. 'Thank you!'

'Yeah, yeah. I'm the best, I know,' he joked. Actually, knowing

Griff the way I did, it probably wasn't a joke. He most likely believed it. *Poor, delusional boy.*

'Clo?' I asked, glancing over at her as she hadn't moved from the edge of her bed. My lips formed a pout, pushing out my bottom lip, and I gave her what I hoped were puppy-dog eyes, but were probably just really wide, scary ones.

'Fine. But we need an *actual* plan,' she said begrudgingly.

'Perfect!' I clapped in excitement.

The rest of the evening, the three of us used a whiteboard to map out our plan. I hadn't put too much thought into the actual revenge itself, but more about how to get Clo and Griff to see things my way. With them on board—and pizza—our ideas came thick and fast. Even though some of them were ridiculous and would never work, we finalised a plan of action before midnight.

Would it work? Fuck if I knew.

It would make me feel better either way. I just knew it!

Nine

MONDAY MORNING CAME, and Clover and I made our way at a snail's speed over to Ms Hawthorn's office.

'Wonder what the old bat wants to talk about,' I said to Clo as we walked arm-in-arm.

'Summer school, I suppose,' Clo replied, her tone bored. 'Our official invitation and all that crap.'

'Has the school ever run a summer school before?' Nobody had ever mentioned it, but then again, wasn't like I would've been paying attention if they had. I paid attention to teachers when it came to studies—and not much else.

'Not that I know of.' She shrugged. 'But there's a first for everything.'

'What made you even think you'd have to stick around for it, though? The meeting hasn't happened, yet you seemed pretty certain back when you flunked that you'd be staying. How come?'

Clo averted her gaze, keeping it straight ahead on the hallway in front of us. 'Just a hunch.'

I nodded, not wanting to push her or argue with her. It wasn't worth the breath. It made sense Ms Hawthorn wanted to talk to us about our exams.

Other than us flunking, there hadn't been much happening at school, and the two of us weren't in trouble for anything else.

Oh, wait. There *was* something, actually.

The swim coach's assistant was leaving at the end of the term

to go work somewhere that paid more and guess who was replacing him?

Only Mister Leo "I'm-so-great-at-swimming—no, make that everything" Hawthorn.

Well, okay. Leo had never given me the impression that he thought of himself that way—that was just me being petty—but still, apparently, the boy wanted to stick around Hawthorn, and taking on the swim coach assistant position was the perfect excuse for that. I'd overheard some young sycophants talking about it, and they said Leo had put himself forward for the position rather than being roped into it by his father. So it was something he wanted. If there was one thing I knew about Leo, it was that he wouldn't get strung along by anybody. He only did things if they served him best, not the other way around.

Clo and I reached Ms Hawthorn's office door and knocked, the sound reverberating through the hallway, sending a shiver down my spine. Everything was so ominous all the time in these halls. Guess a big old gothic building had that effect on people.

'Enter,' Ms Hawthorn said from the other side, her tone razor-sharp.

From the moment we stepped over the threshold, something didn't feel right. We weren't the only two students called into the office—Ms Hawthorn had invited Griff, Ollie, and the girls, too.

This has Set/Sect bullshit written all over it.

'Take a seat, girls,' Ms Hawthorn said, gesturing to the empty spots next to Ollie and Griff. I tried to communicate with Griff through our minds, hoping he would look over at me and his face would give away what was happening here, but he didn't get the telepathic messages. Or he did and he was flat out ignoring them. Ignoring me.

We took the available seats and waited, both of us staring straight ahead, ignoring the others in the room with us. My eyes roamed the space opposite me, trying to focus on anything that wasn't Ollie, but all I could find was a chip on the corner of the desk. *Never let them see you falter. Never let them know you're bothered by them.*

'I'm sure you are all aware why you are here,' Ms Hawthorn said, taking a seat in her large, ornate chair behind her desk. It made her look regal; important. An evil queen surveying her subjects. 'All six of you have failed your exams.'

'Really?' Ollie drawled, his tone bored. Taking a quick moment to glance over at him, I saw his laid-back posture in his chair and it instantly made my blood boil. Why was he so casual and unaffected all the time? Did he already know what was happening here? Or was he genuinely not bothered by my presence the way I was with his? I hated to admit to myself that it made my heart hurt knowing I didn't affect him the way he does me.

The overthinking would make me sick if I allowed it to further seep into my psyche.

It made no sense. Well, it made sense that *I'd* failed as I barely wrote a damn word on the answer booklets, but Ollie was definitely in that History exam, and I'd watched him fill in two answer booklets, his hand whizzing across the page for the entire three hours.

Another reason I knew they couldn't have failed?

I'd looked at the boys' grades on Hive myself when they were first posted and both of them had aced every test they took. But somehow, in a mere weekend, their grades were shit, and they had flunked as well?

Yeah. Not buying it for one moment.

'Yes, Master Brandon. Somehow,' she said, her voice rising with scepticism, 'you and Master Cooper have failed everything, including Physical Education. Would you like to explain that to me?'

'Nope,' Griff said, and I knew that if I looked at him, he'd have his signature grin covering his face. You could hear the smile in his voice, and it was pretty infectious. 'Makes perfect sense to me, Ms.'

Failed Physical Education? How? The two of them were the best swimmers in the school underneath Leo, and everybody knew it.

Something shady was going on. Or maybe this was their way to ensure I didn't go home for the summer?

Fuck my life.

Pricks. Absolute pricks! They knew I wouldn't listen to them and were determined to make it happen with or without my agreement. But did they really have to ruin Clo's future to do it? I knew Ollie wasn't her biggest fan, so it made even less sense he'd want to spend another year in her presence. Plus, Griff and Clo were on the precipice of something *more* so I doubted he'd want to fuck up her future.

It just didn't make much sense.

Ophelia and Oralie looked pretty smug at the turn of events, and I wished it were acceptable to go and slap the bitches. Wonder if they were in on it, too?

Either way, I wouldn't let them win. If anything, the fact they were cooping me and Clo up here with them for the entire summer was a good thing! It gave us the perfect chance to enact some revenge while barely anybody else was on campus. Meaning: no witnesses. Nobody would get caught in the crosshairs and that could only be seen as a positive. The only downside was that it would be obvious just *who* was responsible for their misfortune. Not like we could fob it off on some year seven if there weren't any year sevens around.

Oh well. I'd cross that particular bridge when I came to it.

'...the four of you will stay on campus this summer and will attend all the classes we have scheduled for you. There will be eight members of staff on campus, including myself, and I expect you all to be on your best behaviour. This isn't how I wanted to spend my summer, so any misbehaving will be punished accordingly. I'm watching you all.' Ms Hawthorn's grey eyes narrowed, and I swore she could see through me, down to the very depths of my soul. 'Now, get out of my sight.'

'LET ME GUESS,' Clo said once the six of us had piled out of Ms Hawthorn's office. 'You had something to do with this.'

'Who? Me?' Griff asked, sweeping his hand to his heart, open-jawed. 'Would I ever?'

'Yes. Yes, you fucking would.' Clo stomped her foot, and I was lucky I stopped moving closer. Otherwise, she'd have stomped on my toes. Clo always struggled with her temper, but it was even harder for her to control it when she was faced with a cheeky-grinned, bright-eyed Griffin. 'Especially if it meant you got me all alone all summer.'

'We're not going to be alone alone,' Griff pointed out. 'Clouds will be with us. Then there's the issue of the O girls and Ollie. Not to forget Leo.'

'Leo?' I exclaimed, then coughed, hoping to cover up my dramatic reaction. 'Why would Leo be here?'

'He's one of the eight members of staff,' Ollie said, coming to stand beside Griff, as if it was his rightful place. Bastard. Why was he getting under my skin? And why was I letting it happen?

Really, I should have already made the connection myself. There was no way that Ollie and Griff would be here all summer without the pretty, blue-eyed, blond-haired Adonis that most people saw as the true leader of *The Sect*.

'Goody,' Clo deadpanned. 'Beyond thrilled for us all.'

To make matters worse, the guy in question appeared, the expression on his face telling me all I needed to know. He was enjoying every second of Clo's despair. 'No need to be like that, Red.'

'You're getting a real kick out of this, aren't you?' she spat.

'So what if I am?' Leo shrugged, his smirk firmly planted on his face. 'Needs to be some perks to being a teacher.'

'Like staying at school during the summer holidays?' I scoffed. 'Yeah, seems legit.'

'And what would you know about it?' Ollie snapped, raising an eyebrow at me. 'You're the one who failed everything. Maybe you should be grateful for the kindness being shown to you by the staff here.'

'Why is it that I fail to believe any of this is from kindness?'

My laugh was filled with derision. 'I highly doubt you rich wankers have ever done anything out of sheer kindness.'

'You lumping me in with them, Clouds?' Griff faltered.

'If the bank account fits.' I shrugged. 'Look, I'm fed up with this bullshit, so if nobody has anything to say, I'm leaving.'

'And I'm coming with you,' Clo announced, removing herself from Griff's embrace. 'I need to clear my head.'

'But—'

'No,' I cut Griff off. 'Unlike us, Clo's actual future is being messed with. Give her space, and we'll talk to you later.'

'Promise?' The hurt in Griff's eyes wasn't lost on me, but I also couldn't help but feel like he deserved it. I should've told Clo about them asking me not to go home. If I had, then maybe we'd have seen their next move coming and could have helped prevent it somehow instead of both being blindsided.

'Promise. Now piss off.' I shoved his shoulder but gave a small laugh so he knew I wasn't being serious.

On heavy feet, the two of them left with the O girls, leaving me standing with Clover and Leo.

Clo turned to Leo and snapped, 'You can piss off, too.'

'Nice to see your friendly side, Red.'

She jabbed his shoulder with her forefinger. 'I don't have a friendly side when you're involved.'

'Whatever,' he drawled. 'I'll see you later, Stutter.'

'See you later,' I said with a small wave before reaching down to grab Clo's wrist and drag her away. 'Come on, Clo. Let's go back to our room.'

'You not gonna go to class?'

'Fuck class. We've got a whole summer of them, remember?' We began walking at a slow pace back to our room, not paying attention to anything or anyone around.

She groaned. 'Don't remind me! I'm so pissed Leo's sticking around for the summer.'

I nodded with sympathy. Nobody wanted to flaunt their new relationship in their ex's face, even if their ex was somebody as irritating as Leo Hawthorn.

'Those three are joined at the hip. Wonder if they can do anything alone?'

'Well, at least we know they have sex alone,' Clo said off the cuff, and I gasped when her words registered.

'Have you had sex with Griff?' I asked, all thoughts of Leo being here this summer gone.

'Maybe,' she said coyly. I squealed, happy for them if they were happy.

'When did it happen?' I asked, wanting the goss. I knew I was being nosey, but wasn't that what best friends did? Nose into each other's business, no matter whether they wanted to talk about it or not? Right?

'That night he came to apologise to you and you left because the two of us were arguing?' she said, but it came out like a question, as if I would have forgotten already.

Of course I remembered. Leo had accosted me on the quad, and then Ollie had cornered me in the library while the two of them were making up and getting naked. *Wonderful.*

'I remember.'

'It just sort of happened, you know.' She shrugged. 'One moment we were arguing, and then the next, he shut me up with his lips.' She smiled, and I knew she was seeing an X-rated replay of the event in her mind when her eyes glazed over.

'Cute,' I said, and it kind of was. Well, a mixture of cute and odd. The two of them gave off major best friend vibes, but what did I know? I'd lost my virginity to a bellend who was using me and lying the entire time, so not like I could use my experience to judge anybody else's relationship.

Clo's gaze narrowed. 'No need to be a bitch.'

'I actually wasn't.' I laughed, awkward. 'Not on purpose, anyway.' Tension creeped in, and even though the two of us were on uncertain footing right now, I hoped we wouldn't be for much longer. We had been for some time, never knowing the right thing to say to one another.

'Sure. You just come across as one without trying.'

I shrugged and rolled my eyes at her. Couldn't say much in my defence that wouldn't sound false, or wouldn't sound like complete and utter bullshit. Plus, I wasn't rising to the bait. Not anymore.

'Anyway,' she continued, 'I'm happy.'

'That's what matters most.'

And I meant it. That was what mattered most, even if it all seemed rather suspish.

Ten

SCHOOL ENDED, and the students all departed as soon as they could. The end-of-year assembly had been an entire hour of Ms Hawthorn talking about all that the pupils had achieved at Hawthorn over the last school year. All I could think about was what had happened to me in that time. But you know, she and I saw it differently.

There were five days between school ending and summer school starting, and even though I should be filling it with something exciting, I didn't have any money to leave campus and live it up. Griff kept telling me and Clo he'd cover the cost of whatever we wanted to do, but we kept turning him down. Neither of us wanted to feel indebted to him.

Instead, the three of us just stayed in our room and watched films. It was nice to relax together and not have to leave the room or worry about what would happen with anybody else as they all left us alone. Not sure what Griff said to them to make that happen, but whatever it was, I was super thankful.

On the penultimate night, Clo went home to see her family for the evening and didn't invite us, so it was just me and Griff.

I'd known things with Griff were going to take a while to go back to normal, but the moment we were in a room alone together, it became even more apparent. After all the shit that happened last year, the two of us weren't going to just go back to how we were.

I may have forgiven, but I hadn't forgotten. I most likely never would.

He'd hurt me—maybe even more than Ollie had—and definitely more than Leo ever could. The whole thing with Leo was still odd, and I hadn't tried too much to dissect it. I felt like I'd slip down a rabbit hole if I even tried.

Griff had been the one I felt closest to on a friend level. Finding out we were related made it worse, almost. He'd been super emphatic that he hadn't known that our dads were brothers, but just because he didn't know, it didn't mean what he did to me was okay. Not on any level.

Ollie and Leo could have told him at any point throughout the year, but the bastards chose not to. Fuck, they could have told me! They'd hidden so much from both of us; denied us the chance of a family that could love each other. And why did they deny us? In order to play their piss-poor bullying games. And I'd promised myself that from the moment I'd been stabbed, I would no longer be a pawn in those games. I would not let the two of them, alongside *The Set,* walk all over me because of my relation to Jacob Cooper.

Not that I'd got to the bottom of that shit either.

'Griff,' I asked, looking over at him sitting on Clo's bed as if he lived there. 'Can I ask you about Jacob Cooper now?'

'Honestly, Sky. I'm not sure it's my place to tell you,' he said sheepishly, running his hands through his deep auburn hair. I could sense his agitation, but I couldn't place where it stemmed from.

'What do you mean?' I asked, irritated at his reluctance. 'If anyone can talk to me about him, surely it's you! He is my sperm donor after all.'

'Yeah, he is. But what he did was bad, New Girl. Like, Pompeii-bad.'

I ignored his use of the nickname New Girl because I wanted him to keep talking.

'I doubt it was like a volcanic eruption, Griff.'

'In these circles, it may as well have been.' His eyebrows rose, and he was giving me a questioning look. 'You saw the reaction to his name at the fashion show.'

'You rich people are such drama queens.' I laughed. I swear nobody in my old life was that bloody dramatic about their history.

'Yeah, maybe,' he said, shrugging. Then as if a lightning bolt had hit him, he belted out, 'Skylar!'

'What?' I smiled, as bemused by him as ever. He really was a loveable rogue.

'You're rich too!' he shouted, giddy. Infectious.

'Huh?' I asked, my gut response more of a noise than a word. 'How did you work that one out?'

'If we're related, then you're rich, too.'

'I mean, it's a strenuous link, Herc. Doesn't exactly work like that.'

'No, hear me out!' He got more comfortable on Clo's bed, shuffling closer to the edge, like we were two girlfriends sharing confidence. 'My parents left me a fortune. So your dad must have money too and there's no reason why it couldn't go to you.'

'I mean, I guess?' I asked, but it was pretty much a rhetorical question. ' No way to know really. He could've blown every penny he made. Would sort of have to know the guy. I don't even know if he knows I exist, Griff.'

'Would you want to?' he asked me, a serious expression covering his face. No sight of the cheeky grin to put me at ease.

'Want to what? Meet him?' I asked, and actually, it was the first time I'd even thought about it. Even when his name had first been told to me, I'd never considered what it would be like to meet him. Suppose I'd never thought it a possibility.

He blinked. 'Yeah. Why not?'

'Honestly, I've never thought much about it.'

'Makes sense,' he said, his smile returning. 'Not being funny, Clouds, but we'd have to wait for him to pop up, anyway. Nobody has heard from him in a *very long* time.'

'How long?'

'Years.' He scratched his chin and looked to be thinking hard. 'Must have been around the time Millie died.'

'Ollie's mum?' Ollie had told me her name last year when he was pretending to love me.

'Yeah...' he trailed off, and I nodded, mostly because I wasn't sure what else to say. He shook himself out of it in an instant. 'Oh, well. Let's watch a film.'

'You're gonna change the subject? Just like that?'

He nodded. 'Just like that.'

'You're a wanker, you know that?'

'Ah, Clouds. That's just one of the many reasons why you love me.'

I didn't give him the satisfaction of a response, because, honestly? We both knew he was speaking the truth.

GRIFF WAS MORE game than I'd expected him to be about breaking into the girls' rooms and tampering with their toiletries.

'Skylar,' Griff said, holding the key to Ophelia's room high for me to see. 'This is gonna be so much fun!'

'What's the plan?' I'd left the how up to Griff. He knew science stuff, and I definitely did not, so it made sense he chose what we put in what. I wanted to turn their skin a different shade—not burn it off. 'We just gonna break in? How do we even know the girls won't return?'

He brushed my question off. 'Clo's taking care of it.'

'How? They hate her.' I laughed at the thought of Clo trying to keep the O girls occupied. What was she gonna do? Piss them off so much they had to stick around and be so cruel to her she left crying?

'She didn't give me a play-by-play honestly,' Griff said, rubbing his temple in thought. 'We won't be long, though, will we?'

'Doubt it.' I opened the door to Ophelia's room and stepped inside. It looked exactly how I'd imagined. The walls were a pastel pink and all the furniture in the room was pink too. Even the kitchen appliances were pink. 'Whoa! Looks like a pink bomb went off in here.'

'Lia's always loved the colour pink. Says it's her thing.'

'Of course she does, the basic bitch.' I laughed. 'Trust her to have a room so hideous I actually want to leave.'

'Well, we can't leave without doing what we came here to do.' Griff tilted his head in the direction of the bathroom. 'Come on, Clouds. This won't take long.'

Griff disappeared into the en suite, but I didn't follow. 'I should stay out here as a lookout!'

'Whatever you say, mistress,' Griff replied, his voice muffled. I rolled my eyes. It wasn't long until he reappeared, looking triumphant. 'Every lotion and potion I could find has had a little extra *kick* added. It'll be gradual, but damn, it'll be fun to see the look on her face when it works.'

We left Ophelia's room as quick as we'd entered and went next door to Oralie's room.

The layout was the same as the previous one, just flipped, so instead of her bathroom being on the right, it was on the left, and so on. It also wasn't a garish pink colour either, and my eyes were thankful for that fact.

'How did Ophelia and Ollie become a couple?' I asked, knowing I should've kept the thought to myself the moment Griff turned to face me with an accusatory look on his face. He always could see more than I wanted him to.

'What do you mean?'

'Well, one second I was his girlfriend, spending every moment together, then the next, I'm in hospital after being stabbed, and when I return to school four weeks later, he's got another girl hanging all over him as if I never existed.'

'Technically,' Griff said, and I held my breath, knowing whatever came next would hurt. 'He never considered you a real girlfriend...'

'I get that, but—'

'And he knew that if you did come back, he needed to act like you meant nothing to him. Ophelia is the means.'

I could understand that, but it didn't make it easier. 'Do you think he actually likes her?'

'Couldn't tell you.' He shrugged. 'Can't say I'm on speaking terms with the guy right now.'

'You've still not spoken?' I found that hard to believe.

'Nope.' Griff took a step towards the bathroom. Then another. 'I've made it pretty clear which side I'm on and funny enough, Clouds, it isn't Ollie's.'

For the first time, it hit me that Griff had given up his friendships—his family—for me. Ever since I'd accepted his apology, he spent all his time with me or Clover, and nobody else.

'I don't want you to end up resenting me,' I told him, meaning it. I didn't want him to look back on everything and be pissed that he'd stuck by me and disregarded Ollie and Leo because of it. I was his family, but so were they.

'I promise you, I won't.' He sent a cheeky grin my way before heading into the bathroom, calling back to me as he went. 'Keep an eye out for me!'

'I've got your back!' I called back.

Not long after he disappeared, he re-entered the room, smug as fuck with his work. 'I'm so glad I agreed to this.'

'Me too.' I smiled. 'Now let's get out of here before the girls get back. I'm sure Clo's ready to be rescued.'

'I'll text her now to meet us back in your room.'

We left the room and closed it, locking the door behind us the way we'd found it.

On the short walk back to my room, I paused, Griff stopping with me.

'What's up, Clouds?'

'I just wanted to stop and say thank you,' I said, needing Griff to know just how much I appreciated him and his support. 'I'm so glad you're my family.'

He took a step towards me and pulled me into his wide, outstretched arms. 'Give me a hug.'

I stayed still, awkward, enjoying the hug but also hoping it didn't last too long.

'I love you, Clouds. Don't ever forget that.'

My heart was nearly bursting from the happiness in his voice. 'I love you, too, Herc.'

Eleven

HEADING BACK TO MY ROOM, my head in the clouds, my eyes on the floor, I twisted around the corner and abruptly bumped into somebody.

Make that *two* somebodies.

Ollie and Ophelia were making out in the otherwise empty corridor and came apart the moment I knocked into them.

'Watch it, New Girl,' Ophelia screeched, her eyes narrowed on me. 'Are you seriously that fucking stupid that you can't see in front of your own face?'

'S-sorry,' I sputtered, stuttering without thinking. Then, as if my brain caught up with my mouth, I took it back. 'Actually, no. I'm not sorry.'

'What did you just say?' she asked, and the tone of her voice sent a chill down my spine.

Nice one, Sky. Be brave when the girl is within hitting distance.

'I'm not sorry. I didn't see you there.' I took a step back, wanting to get a little further away from them. 'And believe me, I wouldn't want to touch you on purpose. *Either* of you.'

'You expect me to believe that, bitch?' She sneered, flicking her hair over her shoulder with an accusatory glint in her eyes.

'I don't know why you're bothering talking to this nobody, babe. She's scum,' Ollie drawled lazily, not even having the gall to look at me. 'Shame whoever stabbed her didn't aim higher.'

Did he think his words were hurting me? Because they really

fucking weren't. If anything, I was trying my best to stop a laugh from slipping out. It was just all so comedic, like a bad teen movie or something. The boy gave me whiplash with the way he hated me in one breath and wanted to keep me safe in the other.

He didn't know what he wanted. That much was obvious.

'Should have killed her and left Odette,' Ophelia said, venom seeping out of her every pore.

'Well, as n-nice as this is,' I said, about to sidestep around them, but before I could, Ollie stepped into my path.

'Did I say you could leave?' he growled, and I watched as his eyes darkened. 'No, *slut*. You will stay here until I say otherwise.'

'Slut?' I questioned through gritted teeth, even though I should've ignored him and kept walking.

'You heard me'—he took a step closer, his chest touching mine as he leaned down to whisper in my ear—'slut.'

A red mist descended and covered my vision. He made me so angry, my rage coming to the forefront. It was like all of my anger at him from last year had been lying dormant since the library, but the moment he whispered that word into my ear, I remembered exactly why I'd started my revenge plan.

Involuntarily, my hand rose, and I intended to slap him across the face, but before my hand could make contact, his hand gripped my wrist, halting my motion. With every second that passed, the grip got tighter, and I knew I would have a bruise later tonight.

The grasp was threatening, dominant, and a small whimper left my lips.

'You're hurting m-me,' I whispered. Ollie's pupils dilated, and a breath shuddered out of his mouth, breezing across my skin.

'You d-deserve it,' he said. Him mocking my stutter only made me feel more helpless.

'Let her go.' A bored, yet familiar voice entered my ears, and relief travelled from my head down to my toes.

Leo had come up behind me, silently, his face indifferent as always, and I gave him a tentative smile.

He didn't reciprocate.

'This isn't over, New Girl,' Ollie spat, some of it landing on my cheek. Slowly, he let go of my wrist, and I could see his finger marks imprinted there, the entire area red and inflamed. *Bastard.*

'Come on, Ollie. Let's take this back to your room,' Ophelia whined, a smile on her face she probably saw as seductive, but really, I thought it made her look constipated.

The two of them walked away, but only after Ollie barged into me as he went. Leo didn't leave with them, so I looked at him to find his eyes fixated on my wrist.

'I'm not going to thank you,' I snapped, still furious at him for messing me around during our last couple of conversations. I crossed my arms across my chest, hiding my right wrist from his searing gaze.

'Didn't think you would,' he replied, slightly amused at my stance.

'Congratulations on b-becoming a coach,' I said, trying to stay angry but failing miserably. 'I forgot to say it when I saw you the other day.'

Congratulations on becoming a coach? What the *fuck* was wrong with me?

You hate Leo. You want him to suffer. Clearly, I needed to tell myself that a lot more than I had already.

'Cheers, Stutter.' His smile didn't reach his eyes. 'Means a lot coming from you.'

'No p-problem.'

Without waiting for him to say anything else, I stomped away down the hall, no longer looking at the floor but keeping my eyes ahead.

Moments later, I flung open my dorm room door and hurried across the threshold, then slammed the door behind me. Resting my back up against it, I slumped myself down onto the floor, my butt landing on it with a thud. Frustration—at myself, mostly—made me sick to my stomach.

A sour metallic smell hit my nostrils, and I sniffed.

Once.

Twice.

What the fuck is that smell?

It smelled like death. Death and blood.

After actually having smelt a dead body, albeit only momentarily, I worried I was about to have flashbacks. Worried I'd finally remember who had stood over Odette's lifeless body. Even though learning the truth of that night was something I wanted more than anything, I also wasn't ready for it. Not yet. I was scared of what I would see.

I had enough nightmares—I didn't need to have them in my waking hours, too.

Getting to my feet, I slowly made my way around my room, trying to locate where the smell was coming from. I checked everywhere, leaving my bed for last, and having found nothing on my perusal, I worried I was about to find something horrendous.

I pulled back my duvet, not wanting to look but knowing I needed to.

There. In my bed. A large patch of blood covered my duvet, the once cream cover now a dark red.

My nausea rose, and I fought back a gag.

What in the actual fuck is that?

I looked closer. As close as I could get without touching it.

There, in the centre of the bloody patch, lay a gutted rabbit, the innards pulled out of its tiny body, its dead eyes staring up into mine.

A whimper of shock came, and I flew to the bathroom, lifted the toilet lid and dry retched into the bowl. Although nothing came up, I didn't want to move for fear of being sick. Plus, reentering the room would mean looking at the rabbit again.

Who the fuck put it there?

Like ice, a chill trickled through me, travelling through every vein until my entire body was cold. Somebody had been in my room. Somebody had killed a defenceless animal and left its corpse in the place where I slept. A message. But for what purpose?

What were the odds that whoever did this had also stabbed me after the fashion show? Fuck. Pretty high, I would say.

Who could I text?

I grabbed my phone out of my blazer pocket and opened up my messaging app. Without even thinking twice about it, I opened up my thread with *Thorn*.

My room. Now.

Before pressing send, I went back and added a **Please**.

I hoped he would see the text as the plea it truly was and come. That he'd know I had to be really fucking desperate to message him. He'd told me last year I could message whenever I needed—I just hoped he'd meant it, and that the offer still stood.

I didn't even want to think too hard about why I hadn't messaged Clo or Griff first. Sitting by the toilet, I lied to myself, saying that I wanted to protect Clo from it all. That I didn't want to drag Griff down into my shit.

It's official. I've hit an all-time low.

'Skylar!' Leo called, knocking on my dorm door. 'Skylar, I'm coming in!'

The door barged open, and I heard Leo swear. Whether the swearing was because of breaking the door in or him finding the dead rabbit, I couldn't tell.

A figure darkened the bathroom doorway, and the energy it took to lift my head made my vision swim to the point where I saw two of him.

'Stutter,' he said, his tone confused. 'What the fuck is going on?'

I smiled tentatively and said, 'You said to text if I ever needed help.'

Neither of us mentioned that he'd said that back before shit hit the fan. Or that I'd never messaged him when I needed help before, so why was this situation any different.

'What happened?' he asked with a growl, and my stomach tingled in response.

'I don't know,' I whispered, sensing the tears shimmering in my eyes. I must look like a sorry, sore sight, hugging a toilet on the bathroom floor in my school uniform. 'I came here straight from leaving you in the hallway.'

'There's a dead rabbit on your bed,' he said, stating the obvious, a small smile playing on his lips.

'I noticed.' I hiccupped as the tears in my eyes fell. Of course a dead rabbit was the thing that finally made the dam burst. I'd been a vegetarian since I was ten, and animals coming to any harm really hit me deep in my core. A defenceless rabbit had died because of me.

Maybe the person who did it knows that and used it to their advantage to shit me up.

'Is there a note?' he asked, and I started. The thought hadn't even crossed my mind.

'Didn't get close enough to look.' My neck ached looking up at him, but I couldn't bring myself to stand up off the floor. My voice came out in a small whisper. 'Can you go look for me, please?'

His eyes shone with an emotion I couldn't quite place. At first, it looked like pity, but Leo Hawthorn didn't pity anybody. Ever.

He walked off into my room and was back in seconds with a blood-soaked piece of paper dangling from his fingertips. He crouched down, and our eyes met once we were on the same level.

'Can you read it?' Vulnerability emanated off of me, and I did nothing to change it. After the run-in with Ollie and Ophelia, I felt drained.

Leo nodded. 'Sure.'

I watched as he read it in his head first, scrutinising every feature of his face to see if his entire act was one big lie. After all, maybe he'd placed the rabbit there. Maybe he'd known where to find the note, or that there would even be a note, because he had put it there to begin with. But if I didn't trust him even a little, then why did I message him above anyone else?

Leo nudged me with his side. 'Want to know what it says?'

I nodded, too scared to speak. Black spots were creeping in around the edges of my vision, and my breathing speed had increased to the point I was barely keeping it together.

I could really do without another anxiety attack.

'New Girl. Seems you aren't the only one to get caught in the headlights. Run, rabbit, run,' he read aloud.

Even though I knew Leo was just reading the words from the note, I still got a chill from the flat tone he was using.

'Can you g-get rid of it?' I asked, and he tilted his head in response. His blond hair was messy, brushing against his eyelashes, and I had the urge to run my fingers through it.

Where the shit did that thought come from?

'Stutter, are you okay?' He was still crouching down beside me, and his eyes were searching my face for an answer. His large hand reached out and brushed some hair away that had fallen into my eyes the way I'd thought of doing to him.

'Y-yes. Thanks.' We both knew it was a lie, but he didn't call me out on it.

The two of us fell into silence—not an uncomfortable one, but not quite a comfortable one either. I could count on one hand the amount of times Leo and I had been put in such an intimate situation.

He sat down on the bathroom floor proper and pulled me away from the toilet and into his side, the warmth of his body instantly soothing me.

We stayed like that for at least an hour.

Not talking.

Just... existing.

And fuck, it felt good.

Shit, Skylar. Snap out of it!

Twelve

IT WAS the official first day of summer school, so what better day to create a new beginning—create a new Skylar.

My revenge plan was underway, too, which excited me. Griff and I had already added dye to the girls' body lotions and their shampoos and conditioners. It wasn't exactly diabolical, but it would still piss them off. Now, we just had to wait for it to work.

My first lesson of the day was French, meaning I was about to be stuck in a room with Ophelia and Oralie for two whole hours. *Lucky me.*

It was at these times when I wondered if I'd done something wrong in a previous life—or maybe even the life I was living—because clearly somebody had it out for me. I couldn't catch a break.

As if sharing a lesson with them wasn't bad enough, we had a new teacher. Apparently, Mr Pagerson had decided a student being stabbed on campus (and two being murdered) gave him enough reason to go work elsewhere. Honestly, it killed me. Like he thought that working at a state school would be better for his health. *Bless.*

But then I remembered how I'd told Leo his elitist was showing when he'd effectively said the same thing. Shit, was I becoming one of *them* by association?

The new teacher's name was Mr Hawkins, and from what Clover had heard whispered in the dining room before school ended, he was around twenty-five years old and rather handsome. Tall, brooding, with dark hair, the description sounded eerily similar to the one in my mind of Mr Darcy—only one of the hottest literary figures to ever exist. I hadn't seen Mr Hawkins yet to verify the claims, but I guess I'd be finding out within the hour.

After rushing to the cafeteria to grab breakfast, I made my way to the French classroom, noticing for the first time since everybody left just how eerie campus was now. The school was large enough when filled with students, so it only felt even bigger with less than twenty people pottering around. Most of the teachers kept to themselves in the staff quarters, making it even more quiet in the common areas.

The summer heat was blazing down on me, and if I stayed outside much longer, I'd be sweating through my shirt and blazer. *Yep. We still have to wear our uniform, even though it's summer.* Thank fuck I attended a private school with air conditioning. My old school used to be sweltering, the thermometers in the classroom usually showing a disgusting temperature that should have caused the school to close—although it never did—but I digress. Money may not buy class, but it did ensure some perks.

The moment I entered the building, the cool air hit me and I took a deep breath, savouring it. In through the nose, expanding the lungs, and out through the mouth. Or was it supposed to be the other way around? I could never remember. I'd never stayed chill enough to excel at yoga or meditation.

A phlegm-filled scoff came from behind me. *Oralie.* Pretty impressive that I could tell them apart from the sound of their hatred towards me. Useful life skill that.

'You're in our way, bitch.'

'Move!' Ophelia demanded.

Instead of moving out of the way, my feet turned so I was facing the two basic bitches rather than walking away from them.

'Do you feel b-big?' I asked, and aside from the slight stutter, it came out strong. 'Does it make you feel better to make me feel like shit?'

Ophelia gave me a dirty look, her distaste for me radiating in my direction. Oralie's mouth opened in shock, and I knew I'd surprised her. Fuck, I'd surprised *myself*. Neither of them was used to me standing up to them yet; actually opening my mouth and talking back.

To be honest, they didn't scare me half as much without Odette running the show. When Odette was alive, they'd been sheep, mostly, and had instigated none of what happened to me. Just went along for the ride with whatever Odette wanted them to do. They didn't have the brains to work solo.

'You never had Ollie. You were a pity fuck. Get over yourself,' Ophelia spat, and all I could do was laugh at her. Where the fuck had that come from?

Why was she even bringing Ollie up? *Insecure much.*

'Okay?' I chuckled again.

Eventually, after realising I wouldn't be moving anytime soon, they moved around me and headed into the French classroom.

Skylar - 1, Set - 0

I chuckled to myself for a minute longer, but then I spotted the time on the large clock above the exit. *Shit*. I was late to my very first lesson of summer school. Making a bad first impression always sat wrong with me and I avoided it when I could.

I rushed into the room while talking. 'I am so sorry I'm late.'

Looking up, I locked eyes with Mr Hawkins and I instantly saw what all the fuss was about. No wonder he'd sent so many teenagers with hormones going wild into overdrive. His skin was tan, and his hair was a dark brown, and his eyes were the most gorgeous colour, like a light hazelnut. Damn, where did Ms Hawthorn find such a fine specimen? And why was she allowing him around teenagers willingly?

'Take a seat, Miss Crescent,' he said with a smile, dimples and all. I quickly brushed away the sweat forming on my upper lip with the back of my hand.

He gestured to the last free chair in front of him and I took it. He'd rearranged the room so that there were only three desks in front of the board.

As fast as I could, I pulled my pen, notebook, and laptop out of my satchel bag, not wanting to disrupt the lesson any more than I already had. Neither Ophelia nor Oralie said anything, and when I glanced over to look at them, I realised it was because they were too busy drooling over Mr Hawkins to harass me. Maybe having him as our teacher wouldn't be so bad if it meant they'd leave me alone.

'Right, girls, I don't want to be too strict. We're all here when we don't want to be, and I'm sure the four of us can come to some kind of agreement. You listen when I speak and answer when I ask a question, and if you're well-behaved, there will be a reward at the end of each week. Sound good?'

The three of us nodded, caught up in his spell. His voice was like melted honey, all oozing and trickling and—what the fuck?

Had I really just thought that? *If you want to vomit at that, then fair, because even I want to hurt myself for even thinking it.*

I shivered with revulsion at myself. Well, *half* of it was revulsion and the other half was because Mr Hawkins had just caught my eye, and I felt some tingles in places I definitely should not be feeling tingles.

'Sir,' Ophelia said, as Oralie giggled alongside her. 'Can you translate something for me?'

'Sure,' he replied, gracing her with a lopsided grin. I'd never understood why schools hired young, attractive teachers, and then were confused by the students' actions as a result. Not to be confused with me condoning any actions taken by the teacher in those situations. That shit wasn't okay in real life. Fiction life? I'd allow it.

'*Voulez-vous coucher avec moi?*' she purred.

The lack of originality really was something else. I rolled my eyes at her words, noticing how she'd left off the *ce soir* part of her sentence, making it even more suggestive. I expected him to ignore her, or to tell her he wouldn't answer her, but he didn't do either of those things. *Nope.*

'Will you sleep with me?' he drawled, one eyebrow raised.

The two of them burst into fake giggles, and I had to stop

myself from groaning in disgust. Of course they found shit like that funny. The two of them barely had a brain cell to spare.

'Of course,' Ophelia said, batting her eyelashes at him, her eyes wide. Pretty sure the girl believed she looked seductive.

She did not.

To me, her eyelashes looked like spider's legs from the amount of mascara she'd coated onto them and if I were Mr Hawkins, I'd be terrified they were going to just up and walk off her face.

'Nice try, Miss Rogers. Let's start the lesson, shall we?' He winked, and I instantly warmed to him. Okay, he seemed a *little* too taken by the tweedles next to me, but he also had a sense of humour. Guessed you sort of had to when teaching teenagers at only twenty-five. Old Mr Pagerson had barely cracked a smile at anything.

'If you insist, *sir.*'

Good Lord, did the girl have no shame?

'Let's talk about drugs,' Mr Hawkins said, his voice booming throughout the classroom.

I sank into my seat, getting ready for the long haul.

THE END of the lesson didn't come as quick as I would have liked, but it didn't drag either.

Mr Hawkins had set some couple speaking tasks, and he'd picked up on the animosity between the O girls and me, so he had been my speaking partner rather than making us team up as a three.

'Miss Crescent, if you could stay behind, please,' he called out as we were packing our laptops and notebooks away. Mr Hawkins was standing beside his desk—or should I say—leaning against his desk, looking casual. A clear sign of somebody who had no cares in the world. I caught his eye and nodded. Without even looking at them, I knew Ophelia and Oralie were livid that he was asking me to stay behind and not them. Their risk earlier hadn't paid off. How sad.

With a huff, they flounced out of the room and I stood awkwardly by my desk, not wanting to get any closer unless asked.

'Can I call you Sky?' he asked, his eyes assessing my face.

Be a bit awkward to say no. 'S-sure.'

'Cool.' He rubbed his hands together. 'So, Sky, I just wanted to let you know that if anybody harasses you this summer, come and let me know and I'll sort it.'

'Thanks?' I didn't tell him I didn't think he had the power to do shit.

'No problem. Also, I wanted to talk to you about your predicted results from last term.' His brows rose, and he took up a position back in his seat. He grasped his hands together, elbows on his desk. 'Come. Sit.'

Slowly, I moved to the seat and sat down, more uncertain with every step. I couldn't put my finger on it, but there was something screaming at me to get far away. Or to at least leave the classroom. It was okay when Ophelia and Oralie were in the room, too, but once they'd left, it didn't feel quite so good anymore.

'Sky, I want you to know that I'm more than willing to give you extra tutoring sessions this summer, without Ophelia and Oralie around, if you need.'

'Huh?' I blurted.

'Ms Hawthorn has made me aware of the circumstances of last year, and I know those girls bullied you.' His eyes filled with sympathy, and I instantly wanted to wipe his pitying smile off his face. Funny enough, it was the first time anybody had ever used the word "bullied" to describe what happened to me. It seemed too tame for what they'd done.

'Right.' I fidgeted in the chair. 'Well, thank you.' I wanted to get out of there. The longer I sat opposite him, the more uncomfortable I got.

'You're welcome. I'm looking forward to our time together this summer.'

'M-me too.' I bit down the vomit threatening to rise up my throat, with no idea why my gut reaction was that strong. He hadn't moved closer, he hadn't leered at me the way Andy used to, but he gave me the same feeling nonetheless.

'You may leave,' he said with a closed-mouth smile. I grabbed my bag from the floor and moved out of the room at a fast pace. As I reached the doorway, he added, 'Cute stutter, by the way.'

I shuddered and continued out of the room. Not once looking back.

Creepy teacher. *Just what I need.*

Thirteen

THE NEXT DAY, during my free period, I was alone in the library, and instead of warmth filling my gut, my stomach was filled with creeping spiders and wiggling worms.

I hated it. Hated that the library no longer comforted me—no longer filled me with the warm fuzzies like it had before.

Ollie had ruined that for me. Like he had ruined so much else.

And it pissed me the fuck off.

Take my trust. Take my dignity. But fuck anybody who tried to take my love of books.

The anger rippled through me, and if anybody got close enough, they'd burn from the heat emanating from me. I just wanted to be alone with my thoughts. Ollie needed to suffer and I needed to be the one who made it happen. Needed him to feel even an ounce of the pain and humiliation he'd caused me.

He'd taken my heart, blown it up to the size of the moon, and then deflated it, leaving it broken, limp, and lifeless.

There was a major part of me that believed maybe Griff was still full of shit, and that he'd meant nothing of what he said during our heart-to-heart and was still playing me. Still gaining inside information from me and passing it on to Ollie and Leo. Maybe even to Oralie and Ophelia.

Come on, Sky. Stop being such a little paranoid bitch.

I couldn't even trust my mind, and that was never a good sign.

It's said that the mind's the first to go, right?

Getting comfortable at my usual table, I pulled out my trusty paperback copy of *Pride and Prejudice* in an attempt to ignore my raging thoughts.

Jane Austen, take me away.

An hour passed, maybe even two, yet to me, it felt like mere minutes. There was something beautiful about an English literature classic, something that made me fall in love with reading even more, and *Pride and Prejudice* was my ultimate. I'd never thought of myself as much of a romantic, but there was something about this story that transformed everything in my brain.

Other than Ollie, I'd not had much experience with an actual relationship. I laughed scornfully. With Ollie, I didn't even get an experience of a "real relationship".

Really, I was a delusional cow. Or at least I was a reformed one. Knowing the problem was always the first step in resolving the problem.

I'd like to think that since the fashion show I was enlightened. The new and improved Sky. Skylar Crescent 2.0, if you will.

'What the fuck are you doing here?'

Tearing my eyes away from the page reluctantly, I looked up to find the owner of the barked words. Ollie was standing opposite me on the other side of the table, staring me down. His entire expression had my veins turning to ice. His dark indigo eyes narrowed, and his mouth was set into a deep frown.

I opened and then closed my mouth multiple times, resembling a goldfish. A mindless, pointless creature if there ever was one. I'd never wanted a goldfish as a pet because I couldn't understand their purpose.

After what felt like a long time, I stuttered out, 'W-what?'

'You heard me,' he growled, his eyes assessing me. Ollie's hate was evident, even if there was the slight glimmer of lust in his perusal of me. 'But I'll repeat myself. I know your intellect level isn't the highest. What the fuck are you doing here?'

He over enunciated each word, each syllable.

'Here as in the library?' I asked, playing dumb.

'In my eye line.'

My mind had run into a figurative brick wall, and I had no clue how to respond. *Ah, fuck it. What do I have to lose by saying the first thing that enters my mind?*

'*You* walked over to *me*. Clearly, you want me to be in your eye line.'

His face darkened further. A deep growl from his throat shocked us both, and I laughed. You know those laughs where you knew you were in shit, but you hoped that a breathy laugh would get you off the hook? Yep, it was one of those. And from the looks of him, it hadn't had the desired effect.

'Leave,' he demanded, choosing not to retaliate to what I'd said. His lips were turned down, his hand clenching and unclenching at his side, and I knew I'd rattled him. His knuckles turned white, they were clenched so tight. His other hand was in his hair, as he tried to appear nonchalant, but the twitching of his mouth, the glint of anger in his eye, gave his genuine feelings away.

And it made me feel powerful. Big.

'Make me leave,' I said, my tone hard. 'Oh, wait, you've already tried and failed.'

'You should have left this school after the fashion show and never come back.' His eyes narrowed, and his anger was close to burning me. 'I want you to leave this place and never return.'

'So you said,' I smarted, remembering him saying those exact same words in this very spot only a week ago. 'But apparently, you wanted me to stay enough to engineer me being here for the summer.'

I saw him falter a little before the shutters came back down over his disordered expression.

'I will keep telling you to leave until you listen,' he said after he came back to himself.

'You'll be saying it until the cows come home. Or at least until graduation,' I said with a small smile—I couldn't help myself from stooping down to his level.

'You *will* leave, Skylar. You're not safe here.'

If somebody else had said those words, I would have been

more inclined to listen. The thing irking me? He had a valid point. Somebody had it out for me, and I wasn't safe here, but I wasn't safe at home either if he was to be believed. In either scenario, I lost.

'I'm well aware, Oliver.' I hated it when he full-named me, and I knew it pissed him off when I didn't use his nickname in return. Or at least it had, back when we had just met, but maybe that had been a façade too. Another lie. Just one more to add to the long list. 'Not like I'm safe anywhere, is it, dickhead?'

I thought he hadn't heard me until he replied. 'Do you want me to pity you?'

'No,' I uttered, my tone soft. 'But it is the truth.'

'Bullshit,' he barked. He stepped closer to me, having moved from behind the table opposite me to almost standing beside me, his closeness having an effect on my mental capacity.

'What?' I snapped, mad that he was dismissing me, but also pissed at myself that I still let his actions affect me. Still let the actions of a dickhead take up space in my mind rent-free.

His eyebrows raised high on his forehead. 'How on earth are you safer here?'

'Well, at least here I don't have to worry about unwanted advances,' I said. An image of Mr Hawkins popped into my mind and I mumbled, 'Not yet, anyway.'

'Andy?' Ollie asked with a growl, and I nodded, confused why he sounded so angry. I could've sworn I'd told him about the events the day I came to Hawthorn. He scoffed. 'Knew I should've hit the cunt.'

No part of me minded Ollie's anger. If anything, it should have repulsed me, but it didn't. Actually, it sort of excited me a little— no, *a lot*. Watching Ollie punch Andy would be something I welcomed.

Abruptly, I stood up out of my chair and walked away from him. I couldn't be in his bubble any longer. Couldn't just sit still, breathing the same air as him, and not want to reach out and touch his face—his body. Yeah, he was a major prick, but he was a very good-looking prick.

The young adult section of the library beckoned me, the way it always did. The shelves were filled with goodies, and I wanted to grab a book I loved. A comfort read. One of my favourites was pretty old, but because I had had little money growing up, I'd relied a lot on what the local library offered me. To be honest, I was pretty sure that this particular book was old enough that it had been updated recently to change a mention of a fax to a text. *A fax.* That was the age of it. I'd been shooketh when I found it in the library here at Hawthorn; I'd expected all the books here to be dry, boring tomes.

After snatching *Diving In* by Kate Cann off the shelf, I turned and found myself faceplanting into a hard chest.

The shock caused me to drop the book, and I bent down straight away to pick it up.

'Don't move,' Ollie whispered, his voice close. He had crouched down so we were on the same level. His lips touched my ear, causing tingles to travel throughout my body, chilling me to my core. The touch of his breath doing things to my insides I didn't want to admit, even to myself.

He grabbed my arm and yanked it behind my back. I stumbled, trying to keep my balance now that he'd incapacitated me further.

'Straighten up, slowly, and face the shelves,' he growled, low and seductive.

'N-no.' My voice was barely audible above his heavy breathing.

'Do it.'

'You're hurting me,' I whimpered. The pulling on my arm was making my arm rattle in its socket, the sharp pain shooting down from my shoulder making me wince.

'Stand. Up.'

I did as he demanded, straightening and facing the shelves ladened with my favourite books. I focused on their cracked spines, studying every letter, trying to stay in the moment. Something I struggled with at the best of times.

'What are you d-doing?'

I wanted to hit myself for letting a stutter leave my lips. I'd been doing so well recently, keeping my stutter at bay and talking with confidence.

'You make me sick,' he whispered in my ear, unhinged. 'Why did you have to return? Why couldn't you have made everybody happy and stayed gone?'

He pressed up against me, pushing me closer to the shelves, turning my head to the right. My arm was still trapped behind my back, and if he pushed any more, I'd end up with a book spine imprinted on my cheek. His hard dick was pressed up against my lower back, and my nipples hardened in response. My body was betraying my brain. Betraying me.

'I-I—'

'I-I,' he mocked. 'I can see through this act, New Girl.'

'W-what act?' I whimpered again when he tightened the grip on my wrist and used his other hand to pull my other arm to put them together. He was on autopilot, his brain telling him one thing while reality battled to show the truth.

'The one where you act like you hate me.'

'I do hate you,' I whispered, hating him more than ever for putting me in such a vulnerable position. For showing my weakness around him. For not taking no as my answer.

'You only wish you hated me.' His words were poisonous; harsh. And, sadly, so fucking true.

I whimpered, like an injured animal caught by a much larger predator, but it didn't deter him. His teeth bit into my earlobe, a spot he *knew* I found sensitive, and he growled. 'You like this. You want this.'

Is he trying to convince me? Or himself?

One of Ollie's hands gripped my breast, hard, and I flinched. A sharp pain travelled through me from his touch.

His hand travelled further down, leaving a tickling sensation in its wake before breaching the top of my skirt and into my knickers. I squirmed in his hold, thinking that if I made enough movement and sound, somebody would come and find us. The librarian had to be around here somewhere. She knew I was in the back. Maybe she'd notice something was amiss.

'P-please,' I whispered, a tear running down my cheek. I didn't want this. 'No.'

'Shh, Skylar. I've got you.' Maybe he misunderstood my plea? Or maybe he chose not to understand me on purpose? Did I really mean that little to him?

Ollie's long middle finger entered me, my wetness easing the movement.

Another finger entered me, the feeling of fullness more prominent, and both of us moaned. The speed of his fingers increased, and every time he hit that spot inside me, I moaned a little louder. *Fuck.* I didn't want his touch to feel good. I didn't want to enjoy any part of what was happening. Yet I was. And it made me feel so very wrong.

'You are so fucking sexy,' he moaned in my ear, adding a third finger, and the moment he did, I saw stars. *Fuck.*

Ollie and I had been intimate enough times that he knew what to do to turn me on most, so I'd forget my name—forget my no.

I came around his fingers. My heart rate accelerated, pulsing out my orgasm with a loud moan I bit off by gritting my teeth.

'Fuck, New Girl. That was... You're... Fuck.'

'Get off me,' I stammered, wanting his hand gone. Wanting the pressure of him up against me gone. Wanting *him* gone.

When he didn't move fast enough, I shouted.

'Get off me!'

Ollie moved his hand out of my underwear and moved back in an instant. I turned around, tears filling my eyes, threatening to leak out, to look into his. I wanted him to see the despair on my face, the hurt in my heart, and know he was the one who caused it.

'Shit,' he muttered, running his hand through his hair. 'Sky, I—'

He reached for me, but I sidestepped him and continued

walking. I needed to get out of here. Needed to get away from what had just happened.

I couldn't believe I'd let him finger me up against the book stacks without putting up more of a fight. Couldn't believe he hadn't listened to my pleas, listened to *me*.

Before, he had been the first person to truly hear me. To give me the time, and care, to truly listen to me.

Clearly, I was wrong earlier. I'm still *a delusional cow.*

THE DINING ROOM was so empty after everybody left for the summer. The high ceiling meant every voice echoed, and you could hear every clink of cutlery. There were only two tables occupied. One with me, Griff, and Clo. Ollie, Ophelia, Oralie, and Leo occupied the other table.

'So, what do we do first?' Clover asked our table. Ever since I'd rushed out of the library, I'd wanted to keep a low profile. I hadn't wanted Ollie to see me again so soon, but I couldn't come up with an excuse fast enough for Clo and Griff to agree to eat in our room.

The other table was completely silent, not conversing at all, although now and then, a giggle rang out and echoed off the high ceiling. I'd glanced over at Ollie once or twice when he wasn't looking, and from what I could see, he looked fucking miserable. But then again, maybe I was just projecting and seeing what I wanted to see.

'Can't exactly talk about it here,' I said through my teeth. The room was way too quiet to discuss our revenge shit; to discuss anything we didn't want to be overheard.

'I meant this weekend,' she said, looking at me like I had a screw loose.

'This weekend?' I asked, confused about how we'd got here. Had I tuned out a vital part of the conversation?

'We're allowed off campus at the weekends if we want,' Griff said, his face covered in a wide beam. 'It's still our summer, after all.'

'Exactly! So, what do we do first with our freedom?' Clo asked again.

'Hmm.' I hummed, deep in thought. I hadn't really thought about whether we'd be allowed to leave campus or not. It made sense. We were all seventeen or over now. Actually, that reminded me that Leo was turning nineteen at the weekend. 'Is Leo celebrating his birthday?' I blurted louder than I intended, and I heard Leo cough over at the other table, proving my point that there wasn't any privacy in such a large, cavernous room.

'Not like you'd be invited, bitch,' Ophelia spat, calling across to me. I rolled my eyes, not dignifying her with a response. She didn't deserve one.

My phone vibrated in my blazer pocket. Clover had a tendency to peek at my phone over my shoulder, so I had to be all covert ops about reading my messages just in case it was something I didn't want her to see, especially after that time she saw a message to me from Leo. I pulled the phone out and glanced at it under the table.

STUTTER. MEET ME AT OUR PLACE. MY BIRTHDAY. MIDNIGHT.

I glanced over at Leo, to see if he was looking my way, but his gaze was firmly on Ophelia, who was chatting shit about how hot she found Mr Hawkins.

Dismissing the message for now, I looked back at Griff and Clo, who were both giving me a funny, questioning look.

'Have I got something on my face?'

'Just your features,' Griff said with a smile. He went back to eating his food, and I followed suit.

Too lost in thought to even fully taste it.

Fourteen

STUTTER. MEET ME AT OUR PLACE. MY BIRTHDAY. MIDNIGHT.

I READ the message from Leo again and wondered for the umpteenth time what on earth he meant. *Where* on earth he meant?

Ever since the rabbit debacle, we'd barely spoken, choosing to ignore one another in the dining hall or if we saw each other in passing. I hadn't told Clover or Griff about any of it, not wanting to alarm them. Or have them questioning why it was Leo I went running to and not them. Even though technically it was Leo who did the running as I was stunned frozen.

Our place?

For the life of me, I couldn't think of the spot he classed as *our place.*

A list of possibilities ran through my mind. The hallway between the hospital wing and the pool house? The library? I'd never been to his room alone, so it couldn't be there. Plus, he'd moved into the staff quarters since summer started. A no-go area.

As I pondered my dilemma, Clo and Griff entered the room in the middle of a heated debate about some shit I didn't care about. It was happening more frequently since they'd become a couple —or at least a couple with no label. *Insert eye roll here.*

The two of them constantly disagreed about something, even

what to call their relationship. For the most part, I ignored them, but it had started to grate on me.

'I don't understand why you can't just stop talking to them,' Clo said, looking at Griff, her eyebrows twitching.

'Luck, they're my family,' he said, his tone gentle. Placating. Like talking to a child who needed to understand the ways of the world.

'Right, but they're also total cumstains, which I'm pretty sure overrides blood.'

They must be talking about Ollie and Leo. *Again!*

At first, I'd joined in on their conversations about them, throwing in my two cents, but after it didn't go anywhere, I gave up. No use repeating myself on a daily basis to two people who weren't listening anyway.

I chose their distraction to send a quick text to Leo, having ignored his message for an entire week. When he had first sent it, I hadn't allowed myself much longer than three seconds to think about it, but since then, it hadn't left my mind. Kept telling myself I wouldn't stress myself out about whatever he meant—yeah, right.

OUR **SPOT?**

'Bit rich, babe, when you stick by your parents,' Griff snapped back.

'This isn't about my parents,' Clo bit out through gritted teeth. 'This is about Leo and Ollie and the fact that you still act friendly with them when Sky and I aren't around.'

'Is it really, Red?'

'What did you just call me?' Clover seethed, spitting. Her entire face flushed tomato ketchup red, and I wished I were anywhere but in the room with them.

Griff's facial expression sank, his face paler than I'd ever seen it, and I could tell instantly that he knew he'd made a massive mistake. Red was the name Leo used for Clover. It was the name he always used in our texts—back when he was asking after her. He hadn't asked about her in a while, though.

He sputtered, 'I-I... C'mon, Clo, don't be like that.'

'Be like what?' Her entire demeanour was on the defensive, her arms crossed across her chest, her eyebrows raised.

'Like I called you that on purpose to hurt you.' He rolled his eyes, and I winced.

Wrong move, Griff.

'Well, it did,' she spat, the evil eye game strong. Nobody could give the evil eye like Clover. She was a master at it and I was lucky that she'd only directed it at me once or twice in the time I'd known her. Just one look was enough to make you shit yourself, I swear.

I had to butt in—their bullshit was tiring and pretty constant. No matter what they did, I knew the two of them weren't endgame, but they needed to figure that out for themselves. My room was no longer a sanctuary, if it ever was, and I couldn't stay silent any longer.

'Can you two per-lease give it a rest?' My voice was louder than intended, and it stopped the two of them, so they turned to face me for the first time. Griff's face was sincere and apologetic. Clo's eye was still twitching.

'Don't you mean can't *Griffin* give it a rest?' Clo had always acted petty, but she didn't need to turn on me. I wasn't her enemy here. Nobody was.

I rolled my eyes at her childish antics and pretended to think about it for a moment, rubbing my finger on my chin. 'No, I mean both of you.'

'Oh, good lady, you wound me so,' Griff said, sweeping his arm in the air to raise his hand and place it over his heart. 'Thou doth upset me.'

'Oh, hush up!' I laughed, closing the gap between us to nudge him in the ribs.

'Oh, ha, ha. If you two find it so funny, why don't you date!'

'Maybe because that'd be hella wrong?' I laughed because if I didn't laugh I'd get pissed, and she wasn't worth it in the mood she was in. 'Family, remember?'

She turned and stormed away. Well, I say stormed away, but it was more of a flounce. Griff chuckled and then caught himself and covered it with a cough.

'Was it something I said?' he asked me, his dimples pressed in. I shook my head and smiled.

'Honestly, dude, you need to stop messing with her like that. You know Clo doesn't like it.'

He shrugged at me in response, his eyes clear. No emotion telling me either way whether he'd angered her on purpose.

'Listen, Clouds, I like her,' he told me, his expression earnest. 'But I can never decide if I'm just holding the spot, you know?'

'Holding the spot?' It was clear to me he meant Leo, but I wanted to hear it from his mouth, and not just my imagination. Assuming things had already got me into trouble more than once.

'Has Clo ever told you about the past?' he asked, more serious than his usual jolly tone. I shook my head, and he continued, 'One day, you should ask her about it.'

'Right. Like I've never tried to get into that girl's head in the past.' My response was filled with derision, but fuck, I was pissed. At all of it. These two were supposed to be my friends—fuck, they were my *only* friends—but they had secrets I didn't know. A past I couldn't touch.

He inclined his head. 'Don't judge her too harshly.'

'Whatever,' I muttered. 'I'm out.'

Griff nodded and waved at me, letting me know it was cool that I was dashing out on him.

It was only when walking down the hall that I thought to check my phone. With all the theatrics between Clo and Griff, I'd forgotten about messaging Leo.

THE HALLWAY BETWEEN THE HOSPITAL WING AND THE POOL HOUSE. DON'T BE LATE, STUTTER.

Confusion swirled in my brain like a fog. Surely, if he were going to pick one of those corridors, he would have picked the one between the hospital wing and the admin building where he liked to pull me into alcoves? Yet, somehow, *our* hallway was the one where I was stabbed and had found a dead body.

Love that for me.

SUNDAY CAME—LEO's birthday—and after spending the day alone, I went back to my room to find Griff and Clover were both there. They'd made up after their spat the day before, and I wasn't even going to acknowledge it. The two of them were sitting on Clo's bed, cosied up together about to watch something on TV, like nothing ever happened. Like Clo hadn't stormed out last night, acting like a five-year-old.

I nodded at them when I entered and took myself off to the bathroom under the guise of needing a shower. Okay, so I did actually need a shower, but I also just didn't want to be with them if I didn't have to be. Their bullshit was becoming too much to handle.

If I had other friends it wouldn't be such a big deal, but because I didn't, I was stuck.

Once in the bathroom, away from their prying eyes, I pulled out my phone to text Leo. I still wasn't sure whether I was going to meet him later that night, but if I didn't go, it would always plague me. That what-if.

I hated what-ifs.

HAPPY BIRTHDAY! STILL ON FOR MIDNIGHT?

Leo was a mystery to me and he always had been. He was the moody, disinterested one of the three boys, who rarely found amusement in anything—anything that wasn't tormenting Clo, anyway—and for some unknown reason, I wanted to delve deeper and find out what made the boy tick.

The hot water soothed my skin, my soul, as I showered and

washed my hair, taking my time, trying to fill every minute so that I wouldn't anxiously sit around and wait until I had to leave to meet Leo. Because of course I was going to go. I was kidding myself when I told myself I wasn't sure.

My phone was lit up with a new message when I got out, and I snatched it up as fast as I could. The movement unbalanced me, my legs jelly and my feet sliding out from beneath me, and I fell to the floor with a large thudding noise. *Shit, that hurt.*

'Sky?' There was a rustle from the room on the other side of the door, Clover's worried voice coming through it. 'Sky? Are you okay?'

'I'm fine. Don't worry!' I called back, hoping she wouldn't enter the room and find me sprawled out on the floor with my towel barely hanging on. If there was one thing I knew, it was that the position I'd landed in was *not* an attractive one.

Wonder how big the bruise on my arse will be. I'd never had much grace or rhythm, but there was nobody to blame but me. My anxiety over Leo's message was sending me into overdrive.

'You sure?' Clo asked, her voice returned to a lower volume with the panic having receded since my reply.

'Yep,' I called back. 'It's all gravy!'

'Cool beans.'

I listened, waiting to hear her shuffle away from the door before I moved again. The moment I heard her step away, I pulled myself up and rested against the sink cupboard to look at my phone. I had two messages: one from *Thorn*, the other from *Beast*.

What the fuck did he want?

SKYLAR, PLEASE MEET ME TONIGHT AT MIDNIGHT. THERE'S SOMETHING I WISH TO TALK WITH YOU ABOUT. I'LL BE WAITING AT THE TREELINE.

Ollie's text surprised me, but for all the wrong reasons.

The moment I read it, I didn't know what to think. Of course I was fucking suspicious of the fact he wanted to meet at the treeline on the exact same night and time that Leo wanted to meet.

But the boy *had* said please, and that came as the biggest shock of all. He never said please. Maybe he wanted to apologise for what happened in the library…

Leo's message was easier to understand. Simple.

WE'RE STILL ON. EXCITED TO SEE YOU, STUTTER.

Goosebumps appeared all over my body, either from the chill I felt at his message or the water having dried on my skin while I read it.

'Sky, are you sure you're okay? Sounded like you fell,' Griff called through the door and I realised just how long had passed since I'd fallen.

'I'm ite, I promise. I'll be out in a moment.' In a hurry, I changed into my pyjamas. It was a habit of mine to always change out of day clothes into sleepwear as soon as I got back to my room. It was way more comfortable that way, and even though I was planning to meet Leo, I couldn't change my routine. It would alert Griff and Clo that something was up.

Shit, I may even go to meet Leo dressed in my fluffy Cookie Monster pyjamas. Really prove to him that I didn't give a fuck about what he had to say to me.

Least I'd be comfortable.

Does my carelessness sound genuine yet? Does my inner self believe the bullshit it's trying to make me believe?

Nope. I didn't think so, either.

Fifteen

THE CLOCK HIT HALF ELEVEN, and I sat bolt upright in my bed, not having got a wink of sleep. Not that I would've gone to sleep much before midnight on a normal night anyway.

Glancing over at Clo's side of the room, I could see she was fast asleep and snoring away—dead to the world around her. A good sign—and believe me, I was looking for all the signs.

You know how if you tried to creep around, quiet as a mouse, you were more likely to make a loud, crashing noise?

Well, yeah, I knew that if I crept around that would happen to me—I was clumsy as fuck—so I made sure I moved around as I always did at night time. If Clo woke up, I could be all, *Nothing different here* while lying through my teeth. Every night I was up and down anyway, having an overactive bladder, both from anxiety and in general, meaning Clo was used to my heavy foot-steps while she slept.

The door closed with a soft click behind me, and I took a deep breath, excited I'd managed to escape without waking Clover up. Any questions would set me back and make me late. Plus, I just wasn't ready to answer anything she might ask. Not yet.

I made my way across campus, my feet barely touching the ground as I moved faster with each passing second. Even though there was barely anybody on campus, I still found myself looking all around me with every step. Who knew what Ophelia and Oralie got up to at night. My eyes darted into all the dark spots and my paranoia constantly told me that somebody was hiding in the shadows.

The lights in the buildings were dimmed, casting an ominous glow across the grass when I looked out the window to see if my path was clear. There was no way for me to reach the meeting spot without going outside. Maybe that was Leo's game. The dorm buildings weren't attached to any of the others, and the fact I had to go outside, in the pitch-black of night, filled me with dread. Anything could lurk out in the open, or hide in order to pounce out in front of a girl all alone out in the open.

Leo better be about to apologise to me. Otherwise, I wouldn't be impressed. Although I highly doubted he was about to apologise for how he treated me when I first came to school. I wasn't sure what I expected from our talk at all, honestly. Different topics had come and gone from my mind since his first text, but I hadn't settled on anything in particular.

Braving the outside world, knowing I needed to meet Leo for my sanity, I made my way out into the cold air. Something unusual for the time of year, but the weather was always slightly different on top of a hill. The wind was blowing so hard that you could hear it whistling through the trees surrounding the school. A whirling, gushing noise that put me on edge—fuck, everything was putting me on edge. I was living life on the edge, it would seem, and if I were an animal, my ears would be pricked and at attention for sure.

That's it. Compare yourself to a dog, Sky.

The moon shone bright in the sky, and I had to stop myself from halting and staring up at it, getting lost in its beauty. I'd always loved the moon ever since I was a little girl—I'd always felt a connection to it. My name, basically being the phrase moon sky reversed, meant I'd dreamt I was the girl who lived on the moon, who'd come down to earth as punishment, and that was why "they" (whoever "they" were) had given me to Cora. I suppose you could say I'd had an overactive imagination from a super young age and a desire to live a more exciting life than the one I'd landed.

As I came around the front of the main building, I could see the entrance to the treeline where Ollie had asked me to meet him. I thought I'd look over and see the trees and nothing else, but that wasn't the sight that greeted me. If I squinted, I *could* make out a human-shaped outline—although they were too far away for me to determine much about them. My brain assumed Ollie was standing there, but I'd been wrong about things before. Like the idea that Ollie was falling for me...

The decision to meet Leo instead of Ollie was surprisingly easier than I'd thought it would be. Leo had at least tried to talk to me since I was stabbed, and he'd come to my rescue with the rabbit, putting him in my okay books. Ollie had violated my trust and hadn't listened to me enough in the library, and that put him firmly in the not okay books.

And if he wanted to apologise for that, he could do so. Just not at night, in the dark, at the edge of the woods.

With a sigh, I opened the heavy doors of the main building, the groan echoing throughout the empty hall, and all I could think was that I hoped the sound hadn't travelled across to the shadowy figure by the trees.

My heart rate quickened in that way it does when you know you are doing something you shouldn't be. Like the time I'd sprayed myself with my mum's perfume as a kid and had spent the rest of the day terrified she'd find out and tell me off.

Flying up the stairs and around the corner into the hallway, I could see a figure up ahead. *Fuck, that better be Leo.*

'Stutter, you came,' he said, his voice carrying down the hall, smooth and velvety. Seductive. Guess he wasn't worried about anybody hearing us.

'Yep. So, you better talk. Fast.' My tone was clipped, my displeasure radiating off of me. As I got closer to where he stood, Leo's face changed from disinterested to playful, and his lips formed into a smile. Okay, maybe not a smile. But a slight upturn of the right side of his mouth, at least.

'Somebody's testy,' he said, his grin growing wider. 'What's the matter? You in a sulk?'

'I'm not "in a sulk", you twat,' I spat, my anger rising to the surface. 'I just want to know what is so *important* you asked to talk to me in secret at midnight.'

He chuckled at my bunny fingers.

'Could've fooled me,' he drawled. 'I've got a proposition for you, Stutter.'

'Will y-you always call me that?' The fact I'd stuttered when asking my question wasn't lost on me. At first, the name had been a pisstake and a dig, something to rile me up and make me feel small, but after the events of Halloween, it had become an affectionate name of sorts. The kind of name you gave a friend where you were both in on it.

'I thought you liked it?' he asked, his eyebrow rising quizzically. His blue eyes were shining with humour, and I would have sworn that in that moment they sparkled, too.

I shrugged, trying to find the words. 'G-guess it depends on whether it's meant as a dig or not.'

'It's not,' he said, short and to the point. My nerves were still present in the shaking of my hands and the twitch I seemed to have formed in my right eye, but slowly I was easing into Leo's company. I'd have to take him at his word.

'Okay.'

'So... Stutter'—he smiled wolfishly, as I glared at him—'as I said, I've got a proposition for you.'

'And what would that be?' Scepticism was clear in my voice. What could he offer me? After all, I *was* still meant to be working on my revenge plan against *him*.

'I can help with your revenge plan.'

Huh?

'H-how do you know I've got a revenge plan?' *And did I just give away I have a revenge plan with my question?* Shit, had Griff said something to him? Surely he wouldn't betray me like that? Not if he wanted to keep his balls.

'Oh, come off it. It's what happens in those books you read.' He said it so matter-of-fact and delivered it with little thought. A smile came to my lips at the thought of Leo noticing what books I enjoyed reading. *Cute.*

'True. The books do include a lot of revenge.' I pondered his words. 'So, *how* exactly can you h-help? You're included in my revenge plan, you know?' I told him, wanting to clarify that I was just as pissed at him as I was at Ollie. Okay, maybe not as much, but still enough to want to see him pay. 'I want to see you burn too.'

'I'm sure you do, Stutter, but I've only ever had your best interests at heart.'

I coughed. 'Bullshit.'

'I think we should fake being in a relationship,' he said, as if it was the most obvious solution.

'You think we should do what?' I sputtered. *Time to get your ears tested, Skylar.* All those loud songs blasting out of my headphones had clearly affected my hearing, because surely Leo hadn't suggested we pull off a fake relationship. What purpose would it even serve?

'You heard me. I think we should fake a relationship to make Ollie suffer.'

'How does that punish you?'

His smile was bordering on evil. 'Oh, believe me. It'll be punishment enough.'

'You dick.' I shook my head in disbelief, jabbing him in the chest with my fist. 'Not even going to try to sweet talk me?'

He ran his hand through his blond hair, and my eyes travelled to watch his hands. No. I would not let his hands distract me, of all things. *Fuck me—petty, horny Skylar needs to go away, and fast.*

He winked, catching me staring. 'You love it.'

I rolled my eyes at him and said, 'Come on then. Hit me with your master plan.'

'It isn't rocket science, *babe.* We fake date each other and make everybody believe it's real.'

'And what do you g-gain? What do *we* gain?'

'I gain the satisfaction of pissing off your two best friends,' Leo said with a smile. Well, points for the transparency.

I was surprised he had come right out with it. For the entire time I'd known him, Leo had acted as if Clover was shit on his shoe or somebody to tease, and when she and Griff had become somewhat official, he had once again acted completely unaffected. He'd never given the impression that their relationship bothered him, and if he was a good actor in front of them, then I knew he'd be a great actor in our fake couple too.

'And what do I g-gain?'

'You gain the satisfaction of pissing Ollie off. Stutter, you know this will get right under his skin. Fucking up his swimming will hurt him, sure, but seeing you with *me*. That would *kill* him.'

I thought about it, and I couldn't deny that Leo had sound logic. 'I guess.'

'No guessing about it. Tell you what. I'll let you think about it. Weigh up the pros and cons as it were,' he said, his tone one of somebody who believed they were doing you the biggest favour. You know how self-entitled pricks talked down to you, as if you were nothing? Well, it was exactly like that. It was something Leo Hawthorn did a little *too* well.

'And how long do we keep it going for?' I asked, wondering how intent he was on convincing me to go ahead with this. If I was feeling devious, I could use the ploy to my advantage and have it play into my plan of revenge for him. Nobody else would date him, and if I tried hard enough, I may even make him fall a little for me and then rip out his heart.

'You've got one week,' he answered in a low whisper. Shit, Leo could be hot as fuck when he turned on the charm. *Do not fall. Do not fall.* His lips twitched, but he stopped himself from smiling. 'Don't disappoint me, Stutter.'

His threat was slightly dulled in meaning when he reached out to me, tucking a strand of my hair behind my ear. I shivered the moment his skin made contact with mine. Standing with him in an empty, dimly lit hallway at midnight felt illicit. Naughty. And, ultimately, wrong. Yet so very right.

'Happy birthday,' I said, dazed by his proximity, forgetting I'd already wished him a happy birthday earlier in the day.

'Thanks, Stutter,' Leo said as he leaned forward, his lips grazing my ear. His breath touching me made me shiver as it mixed with the cold of the hallway and made goosebumps rise up on my arms. His next sentence was a low whisper. 'We'll talk soon.'

The moment he'd entered my bubble, he left it again, leaving me confused. Confused about why his closeness had affected me so much. Confused about whether I should go through with his crazy scheme or not. Lastly, I was confused why Leo wanted to do it. *Really* wanted to do it, and not the reason he gave me. There had to be a little more to it.

By the time I came to, and by that I meant got my head out of the clouds, Leo was walking away from me in the direction of the pool house stairs. Before turning out of sight, he paused, turned, and winked at me.

Smooth wanker.

Then my irritation at him grew. He could have at least walked me back to my dorm!

Maybe only fake girlfriends got that level of attentiveness.

I crept back across campus, glancing at the treeline when I exited the main building. There was no longer a silhouette at the treeline, and I moved on as quickly as I could.

Clover was still fast asleep when I entered my room, and once I got back in my bed and snuggled under the covers, I lay awake for hours, thinking about my dilemma.

Fuck. What should I do?

At least I had a week to decide, but realistically, it was a case of Sophie's choice.

Sixteen

LEO'S WORDS played on a loop in my mind that entire night, leaving me restless for the week ahead.

Summer school started back up, and nothing out of the ordinary had happened in the last couple of days. The O girls clearly hadn't used the products Griff and I had tampered with yet, so it was a bit of a waiting game. Trust me, we'd know when they had.

Ever since Sunday night, Leo had ignored me in public like he always had, except for sending a wink in my direction anytime he saw me—while nobody else was looking, of course. The world was weird, and I was somehow living in it.

'Skylar,' Ollie growled, coming up behind me in the cafeteria as I grabbed breakfast on Wednesday morning.

I hadn't seen him without my Clo and Griff armour since the library, and honestly, I didn't particularly want to see him yet. No part of me was ready to hash it out, but if he wanted to apologise, I'd be all ears.

'Oliver.' I acknowledged him with a tilt of my head.

I flinched as he grabbed my upper arm to halt me, squeezing slightly to make sure I didn't move away.

'Get off me,' I bit out through gritted teeth, trying to shake my arm out of his grasp. It didn't work, and his grip only tightened more.

'I want to talk to you.'

'We all want a lot of things in life, and sometimes, we just don't get them.' I stopped trying to shake out of his grasp and went completely still. Pretty sure I'd read somewhere that if you went still and played dead, the predator would leave you alone. Not sure the same principle applied to Ollie, but wishful thinking never let me down.

'Talk then,' I demanded, knowing better than to let him take me to a second location. I looked around and other than the one member of kitchen staff still on property, there was nobody else in the room. I knew that Clover and Griff didn't have lessons on a Wednesday morning, so they'd stayed over at his suite last night, giving me a rare night of peace. It was lush.

'Eat dinner with me tonight.'

It wasn't a question, but yet another demand. Ollie had always been good at those. I clenched my jaw, irritated.

'I'd rather not,' I replied. He loosened his grip, and I took the opportunity handed to me, pulled my arm away, and I stepped back.

'I'm not asking,' he drawled, his eyes sparkling. Like the many times I'd looked into his eyes before, I got lost in their depths, trying to find any emotion lying below the surface. Still couldn't find shit, though. Made me wonder if he even had any depths.

I laughed, looking him in the eye. 'And I'm not joking.'

I wanted to give myself a pat on the back at the fact that I'd got that line out without a stutter in sight.

'Last time I checked, New Girl, I'm a member of *The Sect*.'

A gasp fell from my lips at his low blow. Ollie rarely ever mentioned *The Sect*, and he'd never mentioned it when we were in a relationship. He'd barely even acknowledged its existence.

'Okay?' Uncertainty laced my question, but then I realised what he meant. He meant the fucking rules the rest of the school had always adhered to. The rules I'd never taken into consideration.

Rule One: DO NOT approach *The Sect* or *The Set* without being summoned first.

Rule Two: DO NOT look at the above-mentioned groups unless deemed necessary.

Rule Three: DO NOT bring shame upon your family or this fine institution.

Rule Four: NEVER date someone above your class without asking for permission.

Rule Five: NEVER turn down the invitation of somebody from *The Sect* or *The Set*.

We will punish anybody failing to adhere to the above as we see fit.

He was referring to rule five. 'Is that meant to rattle me?'

'You *will* eat dinner with me tonight,' he said with a smirk, ignoring my question. 'No exceptions.'

'We'll see about that,' I replied. Taking the tray with my breakfast, I walked away from him and although I'd planned to go sit at a table, I thought better of it and went to leave the room altogether. I didn't even want to eat the food anymore, so I ditched it before I left the room.

What a waste of a good croissant.

By the time dinner came, I didn't want to sit and eat dinner with Ollie. I'd pretty much decided I wouldn't bow down to him and once I made that choice, I couldn't back down from it.

Who was he to think he could still order me around?

The last ten months, he'd had me riding a rollercoaster of emotions. Every hill, loop, acceleration, and bunny hop had led us here. Plus, I was still none the wiser why he'd done any of it. He hadn't even tried to make up an excuse. Just a, *"You don't belong here, Skylar".*

My blood boiled and defiance ran thick through my veins.

Walking at a fast clip, I headed straight from my last class back to my room, not wanting anybody to spot me. Or more specifically, not wanting Ollie to spot me.

Griff could use his influence to get me a pizza delivered or something. It was summer, so surely outside food was allowed without a reason being given? One thing I knew: I would not eat dinner in the dining hall. No way, no how!

Oliver needed to know that he didn't control me, that he couldn't just say *"jump"* and have me reply with *"how high"* like a little sycophantic follower.

I wasn't Ophelia or Oralie, and I never wanted to be. Even thinking that sentence gave me full-body chills.

Once back at my room, I darted inside just in case Ollie was waiting around a corner to block me in or something drastic.

The moment I entered, my eyes fixated straight on my bed. I didn't want a repeat of the evening I found the rabbit and I never wanted to feel fear alone in my own room. Ever since, I'd tried not to focus on how scared I truly was about it all, because if I gave it too much thought, I would never leave the dorm.

It was almost as if I had replaced my worrying about the unknown person who wanted to harm me by hating Ollie instead. By wanting to make Ophelia and Oralie feel even a fraction as small as they'd made me feel for nearly an entire year now—even if I hadn't done much to exact revenge on them.

'Shit, Sky,' I muttered under my breath, obviously having cracked as I was talking to myself. Ah, fuck it. I was better company than most of the people on campus at that moment.

The dash to my room had distracted me from thinking about too much, but being back in my room, I felt a little lost. I knew I couldn't go to the cafeteria for dinner and that I couldn't give in to Ollie's whims and demands, but it meant that, if Clo or Griff didn't come here tonight, I'd be alone, hungry, and trying to prove a point.

HERC, CAN YOU ORDER ME A PIZZA, PRETTY PLEASE?

I texted Griff, knowing he'd get back to me as soon as he saw it. Griff was one of those people who always replied as fast as they could. He never left a message on read and tried his utmost to be an instant communicator. It pissed Clo off, as she said that it wasn't just my messages he replied to straight away. He found it difficult to ignore somebody, and to be honest, I got it. I'd never needed to text anybody before coming to Hawthorn, having had nobody to text, so once that changed, I tried to be pretty prompt about my replies. Well, as prompt as somebody could be when they kept their phone on silent at all times. The anxiety, plus the sound of the vibration of a phone not on silent, was too much for me.

SURE THING, BABYDOLL. FOUR CHEESE?

YOU KNOW ME SO WELL.

It still surprised me every time Griff showed me he listened to me, showed me he cared about me, and that even though our start had been rocky, things had changed for him. Our relationship meant something to him, and I believed him when he said he hadn't known who I was. Who my dad was.

Jacob Cooper.

The only mention of him came in the conversation with Griff where I'd asked about him, but other than that, nobody had said a peep about him. As if they thought they could drop a bomb at the fashion show, then ignore it when it suited them. The whims of the rich and spoiled.

I'd tried to fish, tried to get Griff to open up a bit, but so far he hadn't taken the bait. Apparently, he could be serious and tight-lipped when he wanted to be. *Go figure.*

A knock came from the door, and I pulled myself out of my thoughts and went to open it a tiny crack. But only a crack wide enough for me to look out and determine whether an axe murderer was waiting for me or not.

Standing on the other side was a confused-looking pizza delivery guy. Bless his soul. Probably thought he was delivering to somebody unhinged, what with the building being empty and it being a school during the summer. I opened the door wider, smiling sheepishly at him.

'Sorry. Didn't know who it was.' For some reason, I felt the need to explain myself, yet the only response I got was a small nod before he thrust the pizza box into my hands, turned around, and walked away without anything else.

Oh, well. Pizza time.

Thank you, Griffin!

Seventeen

I WOKE up feeling refreshed and got ready for the day, then hotfooted it down to my first class. When I realised French with Ophelia and Oralie was my first lesson, my refreshed feeling didn't last too long.

Heading to the French classroom, I once again got lost in my thoughts about Ollie, Leo, and the choice I had to make. I was running out of time and Leo wanted an answer by the end of the week.

'Oi, bitch!' Oralie called from the end of the corridor. My head snapped up to find her storming towards me, Ophelia by her side, sick smiles on their faces.

'Where the fuck were you last night?' Ophelia asked, her bright red lips lifted in a sneer. Since taking a shine to Mr Hawkins, she'd been trying even harder with her makeup and her hair. *Pathetic.*

'In my room,' I said, pausing to look them up and down. 'Why's it matter to you?'

'Ollie told you to have dinner with him last night,' she spat.

Well, I hadn't expected them to say *that.*

In all honesty, I was surprised he'd told them, especially as Ophelia seemed to believe she was in a relationship with Ollie, even if nobody had ever confirmed it. I *had* expected him to show up at my room, though, and when he hadn't, I'd breathed a sigh of relief and gone to sleep feeling pretty smug with myself. Like a winner.

'And *you* didn't show up,' Oralie continued. She'd decided to re-enact a famous music video by putting her blonde hair into pigtail braids with fluffy pom-pom hair ties—it looked extremely classy, as you can imagine—and the uniform she wore completely offset the entire ensemble.

'And there was me thinking you didn't have a brain,' I snarked back, pissed that the two of them were trying to make me feel bad for choosing me over their leader. Why would I choose to have dinner with Oliver?

'Oh, ha-ha, slut. You really should have shown up,' she said, taking a step closer to me. 'If you had, like you were told, we wouldn't have to do this.'

In the blink of an eye, Ophelia launched herself at me, while Oralie did the same and gripped my arm, holding me down. Her grip was tight enough to stop me from running away and from getting free. I winced in pain, struggling in her grasp.

Pain split my face in two. *Shit.*

Ophelia had obviously watched closely last year when Odette punched me on the nose, because she'd just delivered a punch that rivalled it. Maybe even one that had more impact.

Blood trickled onto my top lip, and I licked it off, the taste of copper coating my tongue. My nose throbbed, pain radiating outwards into my cheeks.

'You do not'—hit—'get to'—kick—'disrespect us'—punch —'like that.'

With every word she bit out through gritted teeth, the pain in my face worsened. Punching my stomach, pulling my hair, doing anything in her power to cause me harm.

I struggled in her grip, yet Oralie continued to keep me in place, not letting me move an inch. After more minutes than I could count, the attack still wasn't letting up, and if she wasn't holding me, I would've fallen to the floor. Curled up into the foetal position and whimpered to myself until somebody found me.

But unfortunately for me, I wasn't given the much-needed reprieve.

The hits kept coming. My eyes filled with tears, and it was my sheer willpower that stopped them from leaking out. Black floaters spotted my vision and the outer edges of my vision darkened with a dark circle travelling inwards, making it hard for me to see an inch in front of my face.

'Ms Rogers! Ms Jones!' Mr Hawkins roared. 'I suggest you take a step away from Ms Crescent. Now!'

Treating me as if I weighed the same as a bag of bricks, Oralie let go of my arm, and without her support, I crumpled to the floor, clutching at my bruised ribs.

'Stay where you are!'

I didn't look—couldn't look—but I assumed the girls were trying to flee the scene. Not like they'd get very far on a campus with six students.

'Ms Crescent, stay still and I'll call for help. You two, come with me.'

I didn't respond to him, focusing more on breathing than saying anything. It hurt to breathe—every inhale and exhale rattled through me—and now that I'd been left alone, silent tears fell down my cheeks.

The hallway was empty, and I'd never felt more alone.

After what felt a lot longer than it was, Griff and Clover arrived.

'Shit, Sky. What the fuck happened?' Clo asked, or more like growled. The girl was pissed.

'O girls,' I replied, keeping my sentence short as my breathing was still painful and laboured.

'Bitches,' Griff spat. 'For what reason?'

'Ollie,' I grunted out, wincing as I moved into a seated position now that my help had arrived. 'Dinner.' I looked up at both of them and added, 'Last night.'

'All this 'cause you didn't eat with him?' Clo asked, incredulous. 'To be honest, I'm not surprised. Not after what happened to—'

Griff cut her off with a sharp jab to her ribs. The two of them crouched down, and if I could, I would have laughed at how in sync the two of them had become.

'You're gonna have a nice shiner, Clouds.' With slow movements, Griff reached out and grazed my face with his fingertips. I winced, even the lightest of touches causing a sharp shooting pain through my cheek.

He's right. This is gonna bruise like a bitch.

'Wonderful.' I attempted a smile, but the slight grimace hurt too much. I'd thought I'd known pain after they beat me in the toilets last year, or the time in the woods, but nope. Fuck, getting stabbed was fucking painful, but there was nothing like having your entire body used as a punching bag. The two of them had done worse damage than when there were four. If I wasn't about to spit out blood, I'd probably be impressed with their improvement.

'That fucking cunt,' Clover said, looking at Griff. 'Are you seriously going to let him get away with that?'

'Huh?' Griff asked, his eyebrow quirking up. 'How is this my fault?'

'You're a part of *The Sect*, right?'

'Yes...' he said, trailing off, and I watched as his face clocked the point Clover was about to make. 'But—'

'So, you could have stopped this. A long time ago.' She raised her eyebrow at him, waiting for his answer.

'I-I,' he sputtered. 'It's not that simple, babe.'

'Hm,' she said, turning her nose up at him. 'Seems pretty simple to me.'

'Can we not?' he asked, exasperated. 'This isn't the time. Let's just help our girl here.'

I nodded, not wanting the two of them to fall into an argument. Fucking hell, if they got into it right now, I wouldn't be moving off the hallway floor for at least another hour—and that wasn't gonna fly with me.

Griff stood, brushing his hands on his trousers, and then reached out to grip his hand in mine. Slowly, he pulled me up, and

I stumbled like a baby foal. Eventually, I could stand straight, landing on his arms.

'Ow!' I could feel the full extent of my injuries now that I was upright. 'I want to go back to my room, please.'

'Course. Come on, we'll go now.' Clo linked her arm with mine and we made our way out of the classroom building, our pace slow. Lucky for me, the French classroom was on the ground floor, so we didn't need to go down any stairs. Pretty sure if that were the case, I would have asked Griff to carry me down them like some princess or a bride crossing the threshold.

If I hadn't wanted to hurt Ophelia and Oralie before—and I had—I definitely did as I slowly walked away. I'd acted like a pussy when it came to my revenge plan, but I was no longer going to play ball. I wanted to hurt them in any way I could.

Down with the bitches.

Off with their heads.

HISTORY CLASS during summer school was even fucking worse than it was during normal term time.

Why?

Because it was just me and Ollie in the room.

No other students there to distract or potentially sit with.

It was even worse to share a classroom with only him after the girls had beat me up, all because I wouldn't eat dinner with him. Seriously, how unhinged was that?

An hour had passed, but that hadn't changed the deep anger sitting in my gut. If anything, it had only fuelled it further. I'd spent the last hour in my room icing my eye, but I wasn't going to let them stop me from passing my exams a second time, which meant I had to emerge and head to History even when it was the last thing I wanted.

My eye was in the first stage of the healing process, meaning it was an angry red, but not yet bruised, and my nose still felt tender. I'd definitely looked better, but then after what they did to me last year, I'd definitely looked *worse* too.

I was the first to enter the room, so I took my seat at one of the only tables in the front and began to set up my laptop, ready for the lesson.

A body flopped in the seat beside me, and it took all my power to keep my head facing the board. When he spoke, I had to work twice as hard to stay focused. 'How are you feeling today?'

How am I feeling today? I wanted to scream. Shout in his face. Hit him. Anything to show him how fucking stupid his question was. Of course I wasn't feeling okay!

'Skylar,' he growled, reaching out to tilt my head in his direction. 'I'm talking to you.'

'I gathered that,' I bit out. 'I was ignoring you.'

He rolled his eyes. 'And why are you ignoring me?'

'Are you really that obtuse?' I spat, pissed he was making me talk even after I'd said I didn't want to talk to him. 'Why the fuck would I want to talk to you? You set your dogs on me.'

'I did what?' His eyes widened when he looked at me, as if he was only just noticing the state of my face. 'What the heck happened to you?'

'As if you don't know.'

'Why would I waste my breath asking if I already knew?'

Did I believe him? Not really, but the look on his face was endearing enough that I felt compelled to answer. 'You've wasted your breath a lot in the past. Like all those times you told me you liked me or cared about me.'

Okay, so that wasn't what I'd intended to say, but it had slipped out. And with it out there, a weight lifted from my shoulders. To snap at him, to say how I felt, helped me to feel better.

'Skylar—'

I cut whatever bullshit he was about to spout off. 'No. You don't get to say my name like you give a shit. I'm not having it. The girls beat me up because I didn't have dinner with you. Is that the kind of thing you enjoy? You get off on siccing other girls on me and swooping in afterward to play the hero?'

My anger was rising, the hatred bubbling thick.

'You think I did that?'

'I *know* you did that.' It had never crossed my mind that he hadn't. Of course it was him. How else would Ophelia and Oralie know I didn't eat dinner with him after he'd asked me to? Ophelia was his girlfriend, so the girl must be truly blinded by lust or love or something else to go along with whatever Ollie wanted from her. All of it was so fucked up.

'I didn't,' he said plainly, trying to communicate something through his gaze that I chose not to understand or interpret. If he had something to say, he could use his words. If not, he could go to hell for all I cared. 'I would never.'

'With your track record, Oliver, that's a little hard to believe.'

'Believe what you want, Sky, but I promise you, I never want to hurt you again.'

Our teacher entered the classroom at that moment—thank fuck—and Ollie had to stop paying attention to me. He turned to face the board, as did I, and neither of us spoke for the rest of the hour.

And when he tried to hold me back from leaving once the lesson finished, I pulled out of his grip before he could bruise me further. Walking away without once looking back, my heart broke into even smaller pieces than before. I hadn't even known it was possible for it to split further, but like most things with Ollie, they always surprised me.

Eighteen

THE NEXT MORNING, my entire body ached. My skin had started to bruise, and my eye had acquired a shiner overnight. I should have stayed in bed, but the whole reason I was at school during the summer was because I'd failed my exams and I needed to pass my retakes in September. Otherwise, I'd lose my scholarship—and my chance of a better life.

At the last moment, I made the decision to go through the admin building before my lesson, to grab some breakfast en route, even though it was nearly lunchtime. *Sue me.*

Wandering through the corridor, I minded my business and kept my head down, not wanting to bump into Ophelia or Oralie—or Ollie, for that matter. Griff had offered to walk me everywhere, but I didn't want to look scared of them; didn't want to give them even more power.

I still couldn't believe yesterday had happened. Okay, I *could* believe it had happened, but I found the reasoning behind it bullshit. I didn't eat dinner with a member of their self-appointed royalty. Big fucking deal. They'd never implemented the rules on me before.

'Get in here,' a voice growled in my ear, as hands covered my eyes so I couldn't see anything. Warm palms touched the bottom of my back and pushed me forward, and I stumbled a little at a ridge on the floor. *Shit*, they were taking me to a second location.

It smelled of cleaning supplies and the powerful scent of

bleach irritated my nose, making me lightheaded. Although my nerves were also playing a part in that feeling.

'Stay still,' the recognisable voice demanded.

I didn't dare to move or open my eyes. Even though the hands were no longer on my face, I didn't want to see where I was—or who I was with. Seeing would only make it real. Plus, it still hurt to move into certain positions, and I didn't want to injure myself further.

The hands removed from my eyes and a piece of material covered them, then they moved to cover my mouth as I tried to let out a muffled scream.

'Don't, Little One.'

Fuck. I'd known it was Ollie. The tobacco and vanilla scent he carried with him everywhere surrounded us, reaching through the potent smell of bleach and solvent. Once I knew it was him for certain, I stopped fighting, even though I knew I should make whatever Ollie had planned harder for him. I shouldn't just give in, let him have his way here.

But I knew I would.

What a mess.

'Stay quiet and we won't have an issue here,' he drawled in my ear. As much as I didn't want to feel anything towards him, especially after the events of the day before, his actions turned me on. My nipples were sharp points and I could feel myself getting wetter with each second—Ollie always had that effect on me. Goosebumps erupted all over my arms, and I gasped.

His mouth trailed tender kisses up and down my neck, interspersed with little bites, and I shivered from the excitement overwhelming me. Ollie had been the only person who ever made me feel this way.

Like he knew just what I needed, he pressed himself flush against my back and put his arms around me, cupping my breasts with his large palms, roughly squeezing them, causing a tiny moan to escape my parted lips.

'You like that?' he whispered, taunting me. It was the most

intimate the two of us had been in a long time, yet it didn't feel wrong. Or right.

Shit, I was meant to still be mad at him. *Think of your revenge, Skylar.*

But then Ollie pinched my nipples, hard, and I was a goner. Fuck it. My revenge could wait until after... whatever this was.

Even though he'd blindfolded me, I could sense the room around us; could sense where Ollie was. His hard dick was pressing into my back, and I wanted nothing more than to grab it and place my hand around its warmth. It was like all of my sexual feelings towards him were no longer repressed, and they wanted to come out and play.

I leaned my head back, opening my neck up for him to bite, making it easier for him to kiss, lick, and bite from my shoulder to my earlobe.

'We don't have long, Little One,' he told me, his tone conspiring—the two of us sharing a secret. An illicit meeting.

His hands moved from my front and I heard his zip, the shuffling of his clothing, the heaviness of his breathing.

My mouth opened, my brain telling me to ask what I should do with my skirt, but I stopped myself before I made a sound. He'd told me not to speak and there was something sexy as fuck about not talking. Powerful.

I didn't have to think about it for long, as he pushed my skirt up above my hips in one violent motion, baring me to the cold air. He moved my underwear to the side, and before I could get used to the feeling, he thrust his finger inside me, my wetness acting as a lubricant, making it easy for him to add another digit—then a third. *Fuck.*

One of us should stop whatever was happening, but I really, *really* didn't want to, and I hoped he didn't want to either.

I moaned, loud, and in a flash, his hand was once again covering my mouth.

'Don't ruin this,' he threatened.

Caught up in the moment, I stilled. And even though he hadn't listened to me in the library, something in the air felt different. The whole situation was different. I hadn't said no, because in my heart, I still wanted him.

I nodded—or attempted to, anyway. The position he had trapped me in made it difficult for me to move much. And fuck, was it hot.

His fingers disappeared, and in a moment, his dick replaced them, hard and ready to invade my tight walls. In one violent movement, he fully seated himself inside of me, and I gasped at the sensation. From the position he'd trapped me in, he felt bigger than normal. It had been a while since we'd last had sex and I'd forgotten how amazing he felt.

With a grunt, he began to thrust, his cock filling me slowly and completely. Even after all of the times I'd had sex with him, it was still amazing to feel every inch of him slide into me like this, as if I were being taken for the first time all over again.

Fuck. I'd missed the feeling of him. I could be a big girl and admit that to myself.

I panted, sweat pooling in the centre of my chest, the speed of my breathing increasing with each thrust.

The way he stretched me, the way he moved, was everything I liked about having sex with Ollie. My body writhed beneath his, eager and willing. It was a raw act of possession, and I could feel the passion rising in me, like the hottest fire, clouding my thoughts and causing me to see stars.

The waves of pleasure hit a crescendo, and the two of us went over the edge at the same time, his hot cum filling me as we both groaned.

'Don't say a word, Little One,' he growled in my ear. 'And *don't turn around.*'

I stayed still, doing as he asked, while he righted his clothing. The door opened, and taking the warmth with him, Ollie left the closet, leaving me alone.

Alone, used, and sore, but smiling.

Geez, Sky. Get some self-respect.

THE EVENTS of the day raced through my brain in a constant loop. A snapshot of every moment, of every touch.

Shit. I'd let Ollie fuck me in the caretaker's closet and had put up zero resistance. It was the same place we'd hooked up on the night I lost my virginity and the memories had come rushing back. The feeling I had when I was around him was unlike any I'd experienced around another person, and it was hard to remember he'd played me when my heart was beating in such a fast rhythm around him.

I'd let him touch me, even though just the day before I'd accused him of having the girls attack me. Sure, the girls may have decided to attack me without his consent, but he must have known that by telling them I'd defied him, they would retaliate.

Like a bullet to the gut, ripping me from the inside out, I realised Ollie's game.

He intended to use the rules to make me do his bidding. To make me eat dinner with him, talk with him—spend time with him.

The sadness I experienced at the realisation overwhelmed me. Could I never break free of his hold?

Shit.

I couldn't continue to defy him and then have two basic bitches beat me up as my "punishment", and then sleep with him in a closet! I needed to fight back; I needed to knock them down a peg. Or five.

If I were being honest with myself, something I rarely liked to do but found myself doing anyway, I'd expected to hear from Leo at some point during the day. Had expected him to use such an unfortunate scenario as a way to convince me further to join him in his fake relationship scheme. It probably would've worked, too. I was so mad at myself, at Ollie, at the O girls, that I'd have agreed to anything.

He wanted an answer in twenty-four hours, and it had become pretty obvious what my answer *should* be, but what my answer *would* be was still unknown.

Yeah, yeah. I know. You're a dumb bitch, Skylar.

I felt conflicted. You know when your head and your heart were battling it out, and even though you knew the winner, you still wanted to root for the underdog? Yep. That was basically my mental space.

'Clo,' I called out to her, hoping she hadn't fallen asleep yet. For the last hour, she'd not said a word, so I wasn't sure if she'd answer me.

'Yeah,' she replied, her voice tired and a little muffled.

'What do you do when your head and your heart are telling you two different things?' I blurted out. When I'd called out her name, I wasn't sure what I was actually going to say when she answered, so the words left my lips without much thought behind them.

'Honestly,' she said, a deep sigh accompanying the word, her voice sounding even more tired with the weight of it. 'I'm probably not the best person to ask.'

Her exhausted sounding words echoed in our small room.

'What d'you mean?'

'Well, last time my heart and my head disagreed, I just ran away from it all. It was easier to give it all up than actually make a choice.' She sounded so resigned and fed up, and I knew I should let her come to me when she was ready, but fuck, the girl never gave me anything and I had no idea when I'd get another chance to delve into it.

'Why?' I asked, hoping I didn't sound too eager. Didn't want to scare her off straight away.

'Loyalty, mostly. To my family,' she muttered, and I had to strain to hear her, as she was so quiet.

I wondered if the dilemma she was talking about had anything to do with what happened between her and Leo.

'Makes sense,' I said, even though I was bullshitting. None of it made sense to me, but I'd never felt loyalty to my mum in that way, so I couldn't relate.

'No, it doesn't,' she said with a low, dark chuckle. 'Why are you asking, anyway?'

I rolled over, getting comfortable on my left side so I could face her across the room, and I heard her shuffle to do the same. Our room was too dark to see each other, and Clo resembled a dark, lumpy shadow, but it felt better to be facing one another while we opened up to each other the way I'd always hoped we would.

'Ollie,' was all I said in response. I didn't need to give any more details. A best friend just knew and Clo didn't disappoint.

'Yeah,' she said with a sigh that echoed throughout the dark, and otherwise silent, room.

'I should listen to my head, right?' Did my voice go up at the end like I wasn't sure? Well, if it did, I'd deny it until I was blue in the face.

'That's what I did,' Clo said, distracted and deep in thought. 'Hurts less.'

'I guess.'

I'd agreed with her, but my mind was saying: really, did it? Clo may be happy with Griff, but I found it hard to believe that her shit with Leo hurt less just because she'd run away from it. It wouldn't surprise me if she hadn't come to terms with it. The way she acted around him spoke volumes about her true feelings, and the fact Leo was asking me to be his fake girlfriend to piss her off also said a lot.

'Don't let him get away with his shit, Sky,' Clo said. The rustling of covers told me she'd moved to lie on her back once again, our moment over.

'I won't,' I whispered, the lie loud.

Nineteen

TONIGHT WAS the night Leo wanted my definitive answer, and after I'd sort of but not really come to terms with how I felt about the whole sex in the closet situation with Ollie, I felt pretty sure of the option I was going to pick, but I hadn't fully committed yet.

I was in my room, contemplating my options again, pacing up and down the small floor space as I was prone to do when stressed, when Griff and Clo bustled into the room mid-conversation, making a racket. It was like the two of them could never enter the room without being in the middle of some heated debate of sorts.

'Babe, I can't help it if I'm a stud muffin,' Griff said, an over-large smile planted on his face. Clover, who was looking at him, rolled her eyes affectionately.

'A stud muffin?' We both laughed. It wasn't that Griff couldn't be classed as a stud muffin, because he definitely could, but it sort of defeated the object when you announced it yourself.

'Would you prefer I refer to myself as a major hunk?' he asked, his white teeth beaming.

'No. No, I would not. I'd prefer you not refer to yourself as anything at all,' Clo said, laughing at him in earnest, wrinkles forming around her eyes.

It was conversations like the one I was witnessing that made me think the two of them were sweet together, and they did have some chemistry, but I felt no heat emanating from them. Saw nothing that made me believe there was more than a deep friendship there. It certainly wasn't love. Not real, I'd kill for you, love. But then again, who was I to talk about love? Not like I'd had much experience with the real deal.

I'd been weighing up my pros and cons for agreeing to Leo's scheme, and Clover's strained relationship with Leo was a major con. Top of the list kind of con. I wasn't sure if she'd forgive me if I went through with it, and I knew I *could* just tell her it was all fake, but then I wouldn't be keeping up my end of the bargain with Leo and he'd call it all off.

The real question: did I care more about pissing off Ollie than I did about Clover's feelings?

And why wasn't the answer easy?

Why did it all have to be so complicated?

'What do you have planned tonight, Sky?' Clo asked me once the two of them had settled on her bed and got comfortable. I scoffed—a response in itself. It was rare I had plans in the evening.

'Oh, you know me. Always off out and about gallivanting.' I wondered if I'd layered enough sarcasm into that one sentence... Whoever said sarcasm was the lowest form of wit could fuck off.

'Ha-ha, Clouds,' Griff said with a chuckle. 'Want to watch a film with us?'

'Of course!' I answered enthusiastically—and falsely. The enthusiasm was feigned, and I'd actually hoped that the two of them were planning to spend the evening in Griff's room so I could continue to pace and worry without an audience. I'd told the two of them they didn't need to constantly check on me and keep me company, but they thought I was covering up my genuine feelings. Or that I was too afraid to reach out and ask for help. If anything, it was the opposite. I'd been trying not to hurt *their* feelings.

'Before we watch the film, I wanted to talk to you both about something,' Griff announced, wringing his hands together in his lap, a faint blush blooming into his freckled cheeks.

'Shoot,' I said back, wanting him to get on with it so I could pretend to watch the film while my brain was thinking about anything else.

'How intent are you on this revenge plan of yours?'

'Very intent,' Clo snapped, nudging him in the side like they'd discussed it before between the two of them and had chosen not to speak to me about it.

'What makes you ask?' I asked.

'Well...' he trailed off, looking around the room, becoming very distracted with our photo collage on the wall. The collage was something Clo and I had worked on since the start of rooming together and it was a cluttered mess of pictures—but I loved it. Hadn't loved removing the pictures of me and Ollie that were on there, but you live and you learn. 'I just don't know if it's a good idea.'

'A good idea?' Clo asked, her perfectly shaped eyebrows downturned.

'Come on, Griff. Spit it out,' I said. I wanted Griff to clarify what he meant and not pussyfoot around it. Clo and I had spoken at the same time, meaning that neither of our questions was distinctive.

Clover repeated herself first. 'A good idea how?'

'Well, don't you think they'll have something in place to retaliate? They've left you alone since you returned, Sky. Do you want to risk disrupting the balance?'

I nodded at him, letting him know I'd heard him and had thought the same thing myself. I'd even considered that Leo's plan was really a ruse to have me let my guard down so they could make my life worse.

'So, what? Sky's meant to just act like last year didn't happen?' Clo snapped.

'I don't mean that, babe.' Griff glanced at me, his eyes pleading for some form of backup if things went south. 'I mean that nobody has harassed Sky in at least a couple of days, and we haven't exactly achieved much, anyway.'

'A couple of days! Are you telling me we should back off

because they haven't hurt her in *a couple of days?*' Clo said with derision. 'The past week is nothing compared to the thirty-plus weeks they hurt her.'

'But maybe they've learned their lesson?' Griff was trying, I could see that much, but he also wasn't getting the hint that maybe it wasn't the right time to talk about it—and maybe he should stay silent before Clover bit his head off.

'Are you fucking serious?' Her mouth was moments from foaming.

'What now?' he asked in that way boys did when they didn't realise that the words leaving their mouths were going to get them into a whole world of trouble.

'What'—Clo's eye twitched, and I feared for Griff's well-being —'now?'

'Oh, come off it, babe. You know I didn't mean it like that.'

'Maybe it's best if you leave,' she said, scooting over on her bed and putting distance between them. The moment she moved, Griff's face fell and turned into a mixture of sad and mad.

'Is that what you want?' he asked her.

She huffed and I got the impression that a lot more was resting on her shoulders than Griff questioning our revenge plan and motives.

'Yes,' she said sullenly, her arms crossed in front of her chest.

I gave Griff a sympathetic look from across the room, hoping Clo didn't catch it. Being the third wheel was starting to affect me. The three of us were a unit, but the moment those two started arguing, it disrupted the dynamics. Girl code also dictated that I had to be on Clover's side—she'd been my friend first, after all. Even if she hadn't quite followed the code in the past with me.

'Okay,' he whispered, his bottom lip trembling. 'I'll go then.'

He got to his feet and made his way to the door, and by his slow pace, I knew he was just waiting for Clo to call him back, not thinking he'd ever make it to the door.

'Bye,' she said, choosing to lie down and turn to face the wall so she wasn't looking at him anymore.

So petty.

'See you later, Clouds,' Griff said, his hand hovering above the door handle.

'See you later,' I replied, returning his tentative smile with a slight smile and a wave.

He left, making as little noise as he could, and the moment the door had closed behind him, I threw my pillow at the back of Clo's head.

'Ouch!'

'What the fuck did you do that for?' I pointed towards the door. 'Why are you being so ridiculous about this? That boy would do anything to make you smile, and there you are, kicking him out over something silly.'

'It isn't *silly*, Skylar. He was completely disregarding the way those bastards have treated you. The way he *helped* them treat you!'

'Right, but he was disregarding how they've treated *me*. Why does it upset *you* so much?'

At my words, Clo manoeuvred herself so she was sitting up and looking over at me.

'I don't like it when people walk all over the people I care about,' she replied, looking me in the eye. Tears glistened in hers, the light catching a tear trail as it streaked down her cheek.

'I get you.' My response was simple, and maybe it lacked empathy, but I had no real clue how to answer her. 'And I appreciate you, Clo. Accept that fact fast, 'cause I'm not sure when I'll repeat it.'

'I feel the same about you. I know that sometimes you think I'm just trying to be difficult or make things harder than they need to be, but I am always coming from a place of love.'

'I know. And after last year, I've learnt my lesson.' I exhaled, feeling heavy.

'Thank fuck for that,' she said, relieved.

THE CLOCK STRUCK MIDNIGHT.

And unlike Cinderella, who at that hour was running away from her Prince Charming, I was walking towards—well, not my Prince Charming, that was for sure.

I got to our meeting spot before Leo because maybe I'd rushed to get there before him, but that was neither here nor there, right?

Waiting in the dim hallway for him to show up, I observed my surroundings. Mostly I walked down it, taking nothing in; usually because I had Clover talking my ears off, or we were bumping into Leo with some girl wrapped around him, and that became all I could see, but standing there alone, I noticed how old the building was. Hawthorn was old, and I knew that, but I'd never appreciated it anywhere but the library.

Footsteps echoed down the empty hallway, and I turned to see Leo sauntering towards me, no care in the world. A thought hit my mind, an unbidden one at that, and I knew my cheeks flushed as a result, because all I could think about was how fucking hot he looked walking towards me.

His blond hair was long on top and swept over to the left, and the way he raked his fingers through it should be a crime. So effortless and casual, making him ten times more attractive.

Fuck. It wouldn't do me any good going into our conversation with *those* types of thoughts plaguing my mind.

'Hello, Stutter. Fancy seeing you here,' Leo said with a smirk. 'Nice shiner.'

'Hey...' My words ran off, unsure what else to say. We both knew my eye looked like shit. Self-consciously, I touched it and even though it no longer hurt, last time I'd looked in the mirror, the bruise looked brutal.

I wanted him to just come out with it. To ask me what my answer was so we could be done with it and move on, but like everything with Leo, it wasn't that easy.

'How are the two lovebirds?' he asked, surprising me with the direction of his thoughts.

Must remember, Leo never does the things I think he will.

'Clover and Griff?' I asked to clarify, although it was unlikely he meant anybody else. The only other couple on campus was

Ollie and Ophelia, and I knew that was a load of bullshit as Ollie had seduced me twice already since summer started, so he didn't care much about her if that was how he acted.

'Of course,' he bit out through gritted teeth. Maybe it hurt to admit it. His blue eyes were dark, angry and intense. Very intense. Mesmerised, I couldn't look away.

'They're...' I struggled to think of another word, switching my weight from foot to foot, fidgeting. 'They're okay, I guess.'

'You guess?' he echoed back at me. 'Well, well, well. That won't do.'

'No?' I raised my eyebrows, certain that my forehead had wrinkles from the force of the expression. *I do not need wrinkles before the age of forty.*

'Of course not,' Leo said, ice attaching itself to every syllable. 'So what say you, Skylar Crescent?'

'Promise me something first,' I said, trying to sound strong and in control. Trying to sound like somebody who knew what they wanted.

'And what would that be?' His eyes glinted with menace, and I shuddered.

'I want you to promise me that we end this when I say so.'

'Is that all?' he asked. I could tell he expected me to say more.

'I also don't want to hurt Clo,' I said as Leo nodded at me, deep in thought. 'And lastly, I—'

Leo cut me off before I could finish my sentence; not that I'd had a sentence in mind, anyway. 'How about we keep the rules to a minimum for now? We can always adjust accordingly,' he said, and I giggled. His wording was so unlike him, yet it fit the moment.

'O-okay,' I stuttered out. 'I'll do it.'

'You will?' he asked, shock lacing his voice, which he attempted to cover with a cough.

'I will. I need Ollie to suffer.' I shrugged. 'And you're my best chance of making that happen.'

Leo's smile turned wolfish. Good thing my nickname wasn't "Red". Otherwise, I'd be waiting for him to eat me whole.

His bright blue eyes, no longer anger filled, were taking me in and sweeping over my face, and I felt as if I were under a microscope. His upper lip curled, a demonic smile that made me think of the devil.

'Perfect. Let the games begin.'

Twenty

THE PLAN: I was going to invite Leo to my movie night with Griff and Clo, and the two of us would flirt, or something like that. We hadn't gone into specifics.

Even just thinking about it gave me crazy anxiety, and, unsurprisingly, I was absolutely bricking telling Clo that Leo and I "liked each other" enough that we'd decided to date.

It was the only way I could think to introduce Clover to the idea of it without outright crushing her. Not that I thought it would crush her. Actually, I just thought it would make her pissed as all get-out.

We were in Griff's suite, a much more spacious room than mine and Clo's small place, and we'd ordered takeaway for dinner. The two of them had ordered Chinese, but ever since having a dodgy one back in the day, I didn't touch the stuff anymore. I'd ordered cheesy chips and mozzarella sticks—my favourite treat. Well, alongside pizza, of course.

'What kind of film are we fancying then, lads?' Clo asked, while we waited for our food to arrive. 'Horror?'

'No!' I shouted, my gut reaction showing, but then I backed down. *Oh, wait.* A scary film would be perfect for me to have an excuse to snuggle up with Leo. 'I take it back. Let's watch that one with the creepy doll.'

'*Annabelle*?' Griff asked, a sinister grin on his normally charming face.

'Nope, no way. I mean that one about the creepy ventriloquist dummy,' I told him. I'd seen it online while browsing, and any film about a ventriloquist dummy was bound to be terrifying in my opinion. Those little fuckers had such creepy faces, and ever since I'd read *Goosebumps* as a kid, they shook me the fuck up.

'Okay...' Griff looked at Clo, and the two of them exchanged a look. One of those secret couple looks they'd made more often recently, highlighting how much of a third wheel I truly was.

'I've got something to tell you,' I said, ready to tell them about Leo coming, but then a knock came and Griff jumped up from the bed and I knew I'd lost my chance to give them a heads-up.

Ah, shit. I'd meant for him to arrive after I'd told them he was coming.

'Food. Food. I love food,' Griff sang as he made his way to open the door. When he opened it, though, it wasn't the delivery person, but Leo.

'You all right?' Griff asked, his tone uncertain. I recalled what Griff had said about holding a space, and I realised he'd probably jumped to a different conclusion about Leo's presence. Oops. Definitely should've given them a heads-up! Bad Skylar.

'Yep,' Leo said, his tone bored. Damn, he really could act like the perfect villain. 'My girl said I could join you.'

I rolled my eyes at his statement. Guess the boy wanted to throw our entire plan out of the window and cause havoc while he was at it.

'Your girl?' Griff growled, his cheeks fire extinguisher red.

'*My girl*. Right, Sky?' he asked, looking over Griff's shoulder and locking his gaze with mine. He wiggled his eyebrows in a very un-Leo-like manner and I snorted.

I smiled at him tentatively, hoping to look coy and flirtatious. Inside, I was a bundle of nerves and felt so guilty I doubted I'd be able to go along with the lie for longer than an hour tops.

My reply came out with a tittering laugh that sounded so false I cringed at myself in my mind. 'Always.'

Griff looked at me, his brow raised in question, and I knew

that if I moved my head in Clo's direction, I'd see her glaring at me, sceptical.

'Since when?' Clo bit out, her arms crossed in front of her chest.

'S-since last night?' Shit. Why did my stutter always crop up at the wrong time? It wanted to give my lies away.

'Right,' Leo said, making his way over to sit down on the sofa beside me. He slung an arm around my shoulder and I froze, a statue of my own making. Griff returned to his bed to sit beside Clo and the room was silent for two minutes.

It was Clover who broke the quiet. 'What happened last night?'

I found the courage to look at her, and I could see the accusation in her gaze.

'We...' I started, looking at Leo for help. All he did was wink. Great, thanks for the help, dickhead. 'The two of us bumped into each other in the hallway, and Leo invited me back to his room to watch a film.'

'What time was that? 'Cause I'm pretty sure you spent the evening with me in our room.' Clo had a valid point. She'd gone to sleep around eleven, so of course she wouldn't know about me leaving.

'Well, y-yes. But after you went to sleep, I went out for some fresh air.'

'You cannot be serious, Skylar,' Clo spat.

'What?' I asked, sounding braver than I felt.

'You cannot be about to date this prick?' she asked. 'Surely you learned your lesson last year?'

Ouch, Clo. *Low blow much.*

'Clouds, what about the plan?' Griff asked, his face blank.

Within a moment, it was us versus them. Couple versus couple—each couple as fake as the other—but for two very different reasons.

'The plan you wanted to forgo?' I retorted, feeling bad that I was calling him out, but also I found it funny how quick he'd changed his tune.

'Er, yeah. That one.' He grinned, his dimples appearing, and I laughed back at him. We both shrugged our shoulders, and he called out, 'Cousin jinx.'

I rolled my eyes, the same way I did every time he said it. It was Griff, so of course he said it a lot, but like so many other quirks of his, it was endearing, and every time, it reminded me I had family in the world. Family that wanted me and loved me.

If you listened to Griff, the fact that we both fell asleep to ASMR and loved watching the same films over and over again was because of our shared DNA. Nothing to do with our own personalities, but everything to do with the Cooper blood flowing through our veins.

I hadn't heard from Mum or Andy since before summer school started. Actually, I'd only heard from them once since I returned to Hawthorn, and that was only because they had been short on their rent and hoped I still had my rich boyfriend to help bail them out!

'Is this what you want?' Griff asked, warming up to the idea once it became clear Leo wasn't trying to win over Clover, and that I was okay with the situation.

'Of course,' I replied. Leo's hand squeezed my shoulder in support—or at least I assumed it was in support and not a warning nudge.

'Well, as long as this is what you want, girlfriend, then I'm happy for you.' Griff calling me girlfriend caused me to laugh so hard I couldn't form words. The boy was like a seesaw. One second he was on the ground, miserable and surly, then the next he was sky-high, happy and giddy, totally forgetting about the low he'd experienced mere seconds before. He was exhausting.

'Thanks, man,' Leo said, a smirk playing on his lips, both teasing and playful, happy the plan was working.

Clo's tone made her displeasure clear. 'This is bullshit.'

'Do you want us to leave?' Leo asked the room, yet literally no syllable sounded genuine. There was no way we'd be leaving, even if I wanted to—and, as awkward as it was, I found myself not wanting to.

'Course not,' Griff said with a chuckle. 'Now, let's watch the film.'

'Anything exciting?' Leo asked, placing a kiss on my temple.

'*Dead Silence*,' I told him. 'A scary movie, so you better be ready to hold me.'

Gosh, I'm a fucking fraud.

My aim for flirtatiousness missed the mark and I was pretty sure it came across as cringe instead. Lucky for me, Leo took the bait and smiled, leaning into me and kissing me once more. My cheeks warmed, and I gulped. *Cute, Sky. A guy loves it when you resemble a goldfish. Or any animal, for that matter.*

'Of course, babe,' he responded, getting a kick out of the entire scenario we'd found ourselves in. Or should I say, put ourselves in? Because we were the only reason any of it was happening.

A knock on the door stopped us from talking more. Food time, baby!

Griff rushed to the door, and on opening it, took the takeaway bags from the delivery guy so fast that the guy at the door flinched at the speed.

'Thanks, dude!' Griff told him as he closed the door on the guy's open-mouthed face before he distributed the food. 'Let's dig in.'

'Such a shame we didn't get you anything,' Clo said, looking anything but sad about it—she appeared smug as fuck, and I laughed at the bite in her voice.

'Actually,' Leo said, looking even more smug than Clover— something I didn't know was possible. 'You got me food, right, babe?'

'Yep,' I answered, handing him over the food I'd got for him. I wasn't getting involved in *that*.

'You are perfect!' He kissed me for the third time—THIRD— before getting comfortable with his food.

Inside, I was feeling pretty crappy. When she thought nobody was watching, Clover's face had fallen, her eyes turning so sad that all I wanted to do was reach out—maybe even let her hug me —anything to put a smile back on her face. But then her green eyes locked with mine and narrowed, and I thought maybe it was for the best I was nowhere near her reach.

———

THE MOVIE WASN'T SCARY, more creepy than anything, but I still held on to Leo throughout. His body warmth, pleasant against mine, caused me to feel flushed and halfway through, I removed my jumper. I was sweating balls! Clo's eyes scrutinised me every few minutes, and I was certain that her eyes had been on us more than they'd been on the movie. She hadn't even gasped, squirmed, or flinched at the big reveal and trust me, the movie was fucked and went places I totally hadn't expected it to. The sign of a great plot twist.

'Well, that was summin' else!' Griff said once the credits finished rolling.

The rest of us were all still sitting in silence, unsure of what to say. Summin' else was putting it lightly!

'Now that the movie's over, shall we go back to my room, babe?' Leo squeezed me tight to him, a gesture that took me by surprise, as I hadn't expected him to go full-hog so early into our ruse. I thought he'd ease me into it, but apparently, that wasn't the case. Maybe he was hoping it would look like we'd liked each other for a while but only just got the guts to admit it? Fuck if I knew.

'Y-yeah. Sure,' I replied, hoping I sounded unaffected by the raging thoughts plaguing my mind. Pissing off Ollie was worth it, yeah, but I didn't enjoy lying to Clo and Griff, and so far, Ollie knew nothing about any of what we were doing.

'You two offskies then?' Griff asked, his cheeky grin becoming a whole lot less wholesome.

'Yeah.' I nodded and smiled at him and Clover, who were still sitting together on his bed. I'd glanced over at them once or twice during the film and seen Clo's head resting on his shoulder and their hands entwined.

Yeah, of course they looked cute as fuck together, but once

again, cute did not a relationship make. There was no heat—no spice. No chemistry.

'Will I see you in our room later? Or do you plan to stay out?' Clo asked, her tone clipped. I wished I could say the bitter note in her voice surprised me, but it didn't. I'd known everything about me and Leo would annoy her, yet I'd gone through with it, anyway.

'We started dating last night,' I told the room and said no more. I wouldn't dignify her petty dig with more of an explanation. Fuck that. So what if I stayed out? Not that I planned to, but still. The relationship was new, fake or not, and I hated Clo's assumption.

'C'mon, Stutter. We don't need to be somewhere we're not wanted,' Leo said.

His words amused me because even though he'd said the right thing, I knew he didn't mean any of it. We all knew he wanted to stay right there, unwanted and a nuisance. But slow and steady wins the race and all that good shit.

The two of us left the room hand in hand, but the moment the door closed behind us, I let go and put some distance between us.

'You did good.' His lips twitched, and I thought maybe they'd form a smile, but of course the moment went without a smile happening. *Go figure.*

'I d-did?' I asked, feeling more uncertain than I should, but the guilt and worry was close to eating me alive. I needed my friends to believe it, so I could convince Ollie and *The Set* that it was real. That the two of us were an actual couple that wanted to be with one another and not just a big joke.

'We riled her up, and they believed it. That's good in my book,' he drawled. 'So, are you coming to my room?'

'Do you think I sh-should?' I assumed Clo would stay with Griff for a while longer, but with the mood we'd put her in, she may decide to go back to our room and sulk once she heard us leave the corridor. Meaning I couldn't be there as she'd see through the lie too early.

Guess that answers that.

Leo's voice held a rasp of excitement. 'Stutter?'

I nodded. 'Let's go.'

'Positive?' he asked, as he shuffled his weight from leg to leg. Nervous energy that he needed an outlet for. I was rinsing my hands together as an outlet for mine.

'Yep. Let's go before I change my mind—and before Clo leaves in a huff.'

'Reckon we've ruined their night that much?' he asked, his face hopeful. Leo's bored expression always disappeared the moment he knew he'd got under Clover's skin.

'For sure. I'm going to get an earful the next time I'm alone with her, so may as well make it worth my while!'

'Perfect. If she does, I'll make an even better plan to irritate Ollie. How about that?'

'Yes!' I blurted out, the word leaving my lips on impulse. Irritating Ollie was the only reason I'd agreed to this hare-brained plan in the first place. Yes, I felt guilty pissing off Clo, but not enough to stop the train. It had already left the station and was full steam ahead and every other train metaphor or cliché you could think of.

'Excellent.'

Honestly, from the look on Leo's face and the mischief shining out of his bright, azure blue eyes, if I were Clo or Ollie, I'd be scared.

Shit. I'm scared.

Twenty-One

I STAYED in Leo's suite until midnight.

The two of us chilled and played old-school video games to pass the time, and then like a perfect gentleman he walked me back to my room.

Before I could make it across the threshold, he grabbed my arm, pulled me close to him, and kissed me on the lips as a goodbye—a goodbye that was witnessed by none other than Clover Luck because I'd already opened the door when he grabbed me.

Why else would he do it?

The moment his lips touched mine, I doubted the overall plan a little. Lying and pretending to be a couple was so different from actually kissing, groping, and all the other escalations I could see unfolding in my mind.

'Bye,' I whispered when the kiss ended, a little shell-shocked and unsure how to proceed.

'Bye, Stutter.' The last expression on his face was one of pure amusement. I smiled at him and gave a little wave.

'Did you have fun?' Clo asked once I'd shut the door on Leo's smirking face. Walking the short distance from the door to my bed, I honestly felt as if I were doing the walk of shame, and Clover's disgusted face implied I was.

'I did, thanks,' I answered as politely as I could. I wouldn't be rising to her pettiness. Not yet, anyway.

'I waited up,' she said, and all I could think was, *Do you want a medal?*

'Thanks.' It came out muffled as I changed out of my clothes into my pyjamas. I'd got my top caught on something, and for a little minute, it trapped me inside my clothing. I stumbled around for a bit, but Clo didn't come to my rescue, and after what felt like *way too long*, I found the opening of my top and sorted myself out.

Once I was changed and no longer being held hostage by my fleece jumper, I got under my covers and instantly moved around to get comfy. The duvet was fluffy and warm and I felt safe. Content.

'What did the two of you do?' she asked, and when I glanced over at her face, I realised how much the question pained her to ask. Yet she'd asked it anyway, even not wanting to hear the answer.

'Played *Spyro* and *Crash Bandicoot*,' I told her, a smile, unbidden, playing on my lips. Even though I'd never been alone with Leo in an intimate setting, I'd had a good time. He was nowhere near as uptight and boring as I'd thought he was. He was charming, funny, and surprisingly, a good sport. Also helped that the boy was pleasing to the eye. 'What did you and Griff get up to?'

'I left not long after you did,' she told me, her voice flat.

I knew it.

'Oh, why's that?' I asked, pretending to be genuine even though I was pretty sure I already knew the actual answer. Yes, I realised how much of a shitty human I had become in the short span of one night, but there was something so thrilling in the whole thing that sparked electricity through my veins. A drug of sorts.

'Just wasn't feeling it.' She shrugged. 'Wanted to come chill here, get some homework done.'

I nodded, all while wondering if the girl believed her own shit —my opinion varied depending on the day. Clover was as much of a mystery to me still as she was the first day I met her. She never gave much away and certainly didn't divulge any secrets, to the point where it was hard to know if I meant as much to her as she did to me. Were we only friends because she'd needed an ally, and I happened to be the other scholarship student at the school *and* we shared a room?

My pillow rustled as I plugged my phone into the speaker within it and set up my videos for the night. The pillow had to be hands down one of my favourite possessions because I could listen to ASMR all night long and not have Clo complain about it.

Pulling my eye mask over my eyes to block out the world, the sound of Clo fidgeting, followed by the click of the bedroom light switch, reached my ears. Just as I was about to turn to face the wall and up the volume on my phone, Clo cleared her throat.

'Yes?' I called out, knowing she wanted my attention but was too afraid to outright come out with whatever bullshit question was stirring within her.

She coughed again.

'Sky, do you really like him?' Her voice was so low I almost missed it.

Trapped, a true rabbit in the headlights, I was glad my eye mask was covering my deceit.

Man, I'm a terrible person.

'I don't know if I'd use the word *really*,' I replied, trying to be honest with her. May as well be, seeing as I was lying about everything else. 'But yeah, I do like him.'

Clo stayed silent and her silence gave me a moment to think over my reply. Then it hit me. It wasn't a total lie!

I *did* like him.

Leo was attractive, kind of mysterious, and a total C-bomb most of the time, but also, he intrigued me. Sometimes he made me laugh, and even though he'd known a lot more than he told me last year, he did also message me and check I was okay. It never came across as if he didn't care about me at all.

Note to self: Ask Leo to explain his role in what happened to me last year.

'I thought so,' Clo mumbled. 'I didn't think you'd do this to me otherwise.'

I opened my mouth but closed it again. The guilt gnawed at my insides. My stomach a tornado of emotions.

'If you're happy, then I suppose I can learn to be, too. Night, Sky.'

'Night, Clo.'

And in that exact moment in time, I felt like the worst human being. Scum of the earth.

The plan better be worth it and it better make Ollie mad. Otherwise, I'd lose a friend for no real gain.

Nice one, Skylar. Great life choices, as usual.

THE NEXT MORNING, neither Clo nor I said any more about the fact I was dating Leo. In order to maintain our friendship, that was probably for the best.

Summer school, lucky for me, started later than regular school. The fact there were only a few members of staff on campus meant they also wanted to sleep in, and there were fewer classes to fit into each day. I hated getting up early, and I'd never understood those early birds who liked to watch the sunrise. If I watched a sunrise, it was because I hadn't been to sleep yet, not because I'd just woken up.

'Want to grab lunch together?' Clo asked from her bed, where she was staring up at the ceiling.

'I was going to eat with Leo,' I told her, already feeling crappy about my life choices. The way her eyes narrowed and her lips pursed only made me feel even worse.

'Oh, right,' she mumbled.

'Sorry,' I said, and I meant it, but that didn't stop it from tasting wrong on my tongue. My stomach was a pit of butterflies being eaten by insects and other horrible, creepy things I hated.

'That's okay.' She was putting a brave face on it, and I appreciated it on a deeper level. She may not be happy, but she wasn't going to let me see it. 'Might see if Griff wants to eat in his room together.' She sat bolt upright, a little more pep in her step, and I glimpsed the briefest smile on her face at the mention of her red-haired beau.

I saw my opening, and fuck me, I ran with it. 'How are things going with him?'

'Good.' Her teeth showed with the beaming smile she sent in my direction. 'Really good, actually.'

'Really?' I asked, trying not to sound too sceptical, but c'mon, I couldn't help it.

'No need to sound so surprised,' she grumbled.

'I just…' I went to say more, but then realised I couldn't tell her I thought she was better suited to my new "boyfriend". Mostly for the obvious, but also because I wasn't sure if I genuinely thought that either. If you'd asked me last year, my feelings on the subject would have differed completely, but things were so different then.

'You just what?'

'Nothing,' I muttered, breaking our eye contact by getting up and heading to the bathroom to get ready for the day. Before I closed the door behind me, Clo sighed—one of those deep sighs from the heart—and I halted my action, hand paused on the door, waiting for whatever words she needed to say.

'This won't come between us, right? You and Leo being a thing and me and him being an ex-thing?' she asked, the courage it had taken her to push those words out clear in her overly bright eyes. I didn't want to walk on eggshells around her, and I knew she didn't want to avoid me. After all, it wasn't me she had a problem with.

'Not if we don't let it,' I said with a laugh. 'And can I just point out this is only like the second time you've even hinted that you were an ex-thing?'

'Eurgh,' she said, the sound coming from the back of her throat. 'Don't remind me about it.'

Her green eyes sparkled back at me, and I knew we were going to be okay. She was my girl and, being honest, we'd come a long way since the start of our friendship. She'd forgiven me for not listening to her about Ollie's true intentions, with only a couple of *I told you sos*. Really, I'd expected more, so I'd taken it as a win.

'So we're good?'

'We're good. You're my best friend, Sky. Leo Hawthorn doesn't mean shit compared to that,' she replied, her smile wide.

'Did a bit of vomit just rise in your throat?' I asked, chuckling, feeling like the moment had got *way too emotional* for me. Anything too emotional made me feel uncomfortable. As a kid, I'd thought everybody felt like that, but apparently, nope. That wasn't the norm at all.

'Yeah, a bit,' Clo said, holding her thumb and forefinger out close together in front of her face. 'Maybe we should get ready now.'

'Yep,' I said and entered the bathroom in a flash, leaving Clo chuckling behind me.

Twenty-Two

'SO, you actually prefer goat cheese on pizza to blue cheese?' I asked, feeling a little ill. A *lot* ill.

'I mean, if I had to choose,' Leo said with an amused smile. 'But people don't feel as strongly about pizza as you do.'

'Valid point.' I chuckled and reached out to touch his hair, acting every inch the doting star-struck girlfriend. The two of us were standing in front of the classroom buildings, passing the time by talking about something and nothing. Nothing deep, but if you were to glance at us from a distance, it would look a lot more important than it was. 'Is anybody around?'

If they were, I'd continue acting all touchy-feely, but if nobody was around, I wouldn't lay it on quite as thick. Best to save the good shit for an audience.

'If I'm correct, and I usually am, Ollie and Ophelia are about to leave the admin building and come over here.'

'You sound very sure,' I said, smiling up at him. Even though we were closer now—both physically and personally—the boy was still a big mystery to me. His true motives were unknown, and that made him dangerous. Yeah, he said he wanted to be my fake boyfriend to piss Clo off and I believed that was a large portion of it, but I also believed there had to be something more, something else driving him. Something *big*.

'They do the same shit every day,' he replied, entertained. Recently, he acted less bored, which made a pleasant change.

Especially if I had to act like we were doing a hell of a lot more in private than playing video games.

'Makes sense. They're boring as fuck.'

Leo looked over my head, and his eyes lit up. 'Showtime.'

His tone was darkly gleeful. The two of us moved, so we were standing closer together, his arms draped over my shoulders, his hands grasped behind my neck, as we stood chest to chest. Or, well, make that chest to face. Leo was at least eight inches taller than me and I needed to crane my neck in order to look up at him. He leaned down, putting his lips level with my ear. 'When I finish this whisper, giggle. Give me flirtatious eyes. Anything to make that douche jealous. Anything to make him believe this is real and hate us both.'

I gave him the tiniest nod to tell him I understood, and the moment he straightened up, I giggled on cue. Batting my eyelashes in what I hoped was a coquettish fashion, I gripped his bicep and smiled.

Fuck, I may as well go for it.

I stood on my tiptoes and planted multiple small kisses on his lips. Ones that from afar would make an onlooker believe I couldn't get enough, that I needed one more kiss, one more touch.

'Good girl,' Leo said in a low murmur, and warmth shot straight... *there.* Shit, was I about to uncover some kind of praise kink? Because of Leo Hawthorn? Damn, I'd stooped lower than I'd realised. 'They're coming over here. Ollie's face looks even more pissed off than normal.'

'Score,' I said, speaking with a wide smile I thought might look flirty. Flirting didn't come easy to me—it wasn't in my nature.

Ollie and Ophelia descended the steps, the two of them looking like a picture-perfect couple. It was only when you knew them you saw the true rot on the inside leaking out. Ophelia's long flowing blonde hair was model straight and always styled to perfection, and Ollie's attractive features meant he could be a model too. Plus, I knew what he hid beneath his clothes. I mean, so did everybody else, seeing as he was a part of the school swim team and liked to show off at all opportunities, but still, I'd like to think I was special and had seen a whole lot more than others.

My stomach sank.

Of course you're not special, Sky. He'd had sexual partners before me. I was just the last on a long list. Or maybe not even the last. God, I had to stop thinking. In general. Full stop. Could I survive the summer with shit for brains?

'You look like somebody killed your rabbit,' Leo said, his tone bored. My face must have shown my shock at his reference as he backtracked. 'Figure of speech, Stutter.'

'Pretty sure that's a dog or cat, dickweed.'

He smirked, but it disappeared when my hand squeezed his bicep extra hard, hoping to hurt him even the tiniest fraction.

'What the fuck do you two think you're doing?' Ollie growled. They stopped next to us, and Leo and I made a big deal out of having to break apart, shifty eyeballs and all, to stand side by side.

Leo, holding my hand in his, lifted it like a trophy of sorts. 'Kissing my girl.'

'*Your* girl?' Ollie spat, taking a step towards Leo. His eye twitched, and his top lip formed a snarl. Watching the colour form in his cheeks brought me joy. Literal joy. I bit my cheek, so I didn't look too happy about it.

'Last time I checked,' Leo said with a shrug, tugging at my hand so he could manoeuvre us into a different position. He put his arm around my back and rested his hand on my bum, tucking me closer to his body.

Ollie's eyes darted between the two of us.

'Since when?' he roared, his anger growing with every second. Ophelia, still standing beside him, all but forgotten.

'Since my birthday,' Leo lied. 'Well, that was the night I told her how I felt, and lucky for me, Sky felt the same way back.'

I smiled, loving how he'd twisted the truth to fit our purpose. Technically, it was only a little white lie. We *had* discussed his plan on the night of his birthday.

'Is that why you didn't meet me that night?' Ollie asked, looking at me for the first time since they'd come over to us.

'Yep,' I said, popping my P to irritate him further. I shrugged. 'Meeting Leo was more important.'

Ollie's fists clenched tightly at his sides. Every action, every sign of how pissed off he was, only fuelled me more. It made the fire inside of me burst into actual flames. Ones that wanted to continue burning for a long time.

Fuck him. And not that kind of fuck. No, I wanted him to suffer the way I had when he crushed my heart in his palm.

I needed to stay strong. Stay focused.

Determination is key.

'I find that hard to believe,' Ophelia said with a titter. 'Everybody knows Leo isn't interested in anybody but—'

Leo cut her off, ensuring she didn't finish her sentence. 'I'm interested in Stutter. No need to twist shit.'

To further sell the lie, Leo kissed the top of my head, and I smiled wide enough for the two arseholes in front of us to notice the shit-eating grin covering my face.

'No need to justify it to these dicks,' I said aloud, and even though I was looking at Leo, everybody knew I meant my words for them. Standing next to Leo, a unified front, I felt invincible. Or at least like I could speak to Ollie and Ophelia without any hint of a stutter.

'Come on, babe. Let's go back to my room,' Leo said, using his bored tone once again, our purpose achieved.

'Let's. Sorry we can't stick around and chat,' I said to Ollie and Ophelia, feeling smug as fuck.

The two of us didn't wait for either of them to respond and walked away with our arms still awkwardly around each other's waists. 'Do you think they believed it?' I whispered, not wanting my voice to somehow carry back to them on the wind. Not like that actually happened outside of fiction and animated movies, but you could never be too careful.

'For now,' Leo murmured back, 'but that was only the beginning. We've got a long way to go, Stutter.'

'We've got this,' I said, slightly louder when we reached the building that housed the staff rooms.

'You better hope so.'

I rolled my eyes. *Ominous much?*

LATER THAT SAME DAY, I was leaving my room when I bumped into none other than a furious Ollie.

He pushed me back into my room, closing the door behind him, and pressed his back up against the door to block my way around him. I stepped back so there was a safe distance between us.

Clover had classes all day, so she wasn't around. It wouldn't surprise me if he'd known Clo's schedule and that was why he'd chosen now to strike.

'What d-do you want?' I asked, all my bravado from earlier having disappeared once I no longer had Leo standing at my side. He'd needed to go do something, so we'd split up and planned to meet up again for dinner.

'Just wanted to talk,' he said, one eyebrow raised. 'Are you scared of me?'

I could tell by the dark expression on his face that he got a kick out of that thought. A short, sharp thrill at the thought of intimidating me.

'N-no.' Pretty sure neither of us bought it.

'Want to tell me what's going on?' he asked, taking a tiny step towards me. I took the same tiny-sized step back, keeping the distance between us the same.

'What d-do you mean?' I took another step back, knowing there wasn't much more space behind me to move into. My room was only so big, and soon, I'd be landing arse first on my bed.

'I m-mean, how come you and Leo are suddenly an item?'

'An item?' I asked with a scoff to throw him off by mocking his word choice, while trying to ignore him mocking my stutter. 'Maybe because we like each other.'

'Likely story.'

'Sorry?' I brushed my hair behind my ear, feigning ignorance.

'You expect me to believe you?' He looked me up and down. 'Sure it isn't just a way to get back at me?'

'Why would it be?' I clenched my hands into a tight fist, and I knew I was going to have moon-shaped indents in my palms later. *Do not punch him. Do not punch him.* 'The world doesn't revolve around you, Oliver.'

'Because you still want me. We both know it.'

Do not punch him!

'We do?' Clearly, there were two delusional people in the room living in denial. 'I do?'

'Yes. You do,' he bit out through gritted teeth, almost like he wanted me to believe it as much as he wanted to. 'You don't want Leo.'

'You sure about that?' I raised my eyebrows and crossed my arms across my chest, realising too late that my action was bound to catch his eye and draw his eyes to my boobs.

His eyes did exactly that. *Predictable bastard.*

'I am.' His salacious grin chilled me. 'You felt something towards me in the library.'

'You're delusional,' I blurted out, too surprised for my stutter to rear its irritating head.

'Oh, I am, am I?' he asked, taking another step towards me. His eyes held a sinister glint, and he had pushed me into a corner. Or, more like, pushed me to the edge of my bed. 'Swear on my life that you're not doing this to get at me.'

I faltered. Why the fuck did he have to bring out the *swear on my life* card?

I'd mentioned to him once that to me, it was a very serious thing. That I wouldn't swear on his life if I didn't mean my words. Initially, I'd introduced it to establish trust in our relationship.

Turns out, he'd never taken it seriously, because he'd never taken our relationship seriously.

His words had trapped me.

Of course, I could swear on his life and be a liar and annihilate my own principles in the process, or I could *not*, and have him know the truth. I went for an in-between reply.

'I swear,' I whispered. 'Genuinely, I like Leo.'

It felt like a dirty secret. But the thing was, I wasn't lying when I'd told Clover and I wasn't lying to Ollie, either. I *did* like Leo.

'Well, he could never like you,' he spat, maliciousness clear to me in each syllable. 'You don't belong with him. He'll never see you as anything more than a pawn in his game with Clover.'

'Then who do I belong with?' I asked, wondering how he was going to respond. The fact he believed I belonged with anyone made me laugh—internally, anyway.

Ollie opened his mouth and then shut it again.

Did I want him to say it was him I belonged with?

And how would I react if he did?

Not like it fucking mattered.

I looked deep into his bright blue eyes, hoping to see something lying beneath the surface. 'That's what I thought.'

A small laugh left my lips and it triggered something in Ollie. His lips turned up at the edges—not quite a smile, but no longer angry either. Once again, he stepped closer to me, but this time I didn't feel threatened. His anger had dissipated, and I couldn't quite figure out the emotion left in its place.

'Sky,' he said and reached out to touch my cheek. I shivered at his touch, the warmth of his fingers warming my insides even though I didn't want them to. 'One day you'll see.'

'See what?' I asked, wondering what on earth he could mean.

'The truth,' he said, his tone low. 'But just know this, Skylar. Not everything between us was a lie, and one day, I'll get to prove that to you. I'll see myself out.'

And with that, he was gone, and I was left feeling alone and confused.

Twenty-Three

SUMMER WAS MOVING FASTER than I'd expected.

We were already over halfway through the break, and yet nothing much of note had happened since Ollie cornered me in my bedroom. Nope. He'd gone straight back to ignoring my existence—well, as much as he could—and pretending me and Leo weren't a thing.

So much for proving shit.

Leo and I were spending every spare moment with each other, except for when I was in class, and it shocked me, but we hadn't argued or become bored of one another yet. It turned out the two of us were good at being friends and getting along, and on the odd occasion, kissing and hugging.

Trust me, I'm as surprised as you are.

Clover and Griff were still making whatever the thing between them was work, and I for one wasn't going to tell them my true opinions without provocation.

Ophelia was still simping over Ollie, and Oralie was the third wheel at all times.

When I learned I'd be stuck at Hawthorn for the summer holidays, I would've never imagined things to be so boring and routine. Other than their one attempt, the girls hadn't even tried to punch me or anything. Seemed like a wasted chance to me.

Then there was the learning itself.

Mr Hawkins hadn't been joking when he told me we were to

embark on private French lessons. The schedule had changed, and I was expected to stay longer than Ophelia and Oralie to continue learning French one-on-one. Ever since that first lesson, the man gave off a creepy vibe, but I couldn't place my finger on the reason. It wasn't like he'd made a move on me or said anything else to make me wary.

When I told Leo about the ick he gave me, he was surprisingly caring about it.

'If he keeps making you feel weird, let me know, Stutter. No teacher should give you the creeps. Especially not in a place like this that kids pay a fuck ton to attend. My words from last year still stand.'

When he'd finished talking, I nodded and gave him a quick peck on the cheek to show my gratitude. If we weren't in a fake relationship to piss others off, I'd worry a little about my heart.

The heart that thawed a little more with every hour we spent together.

I arrived at my French class in a rush, having just left Leo's suite minutes before.

'Ms Crescent,' Mr Hawkins said when I entered the classroom, brushing my hands through my hair to make it more presentable. 'For a change, you're the first one to arrive.'

'I am?' I looked around the room, confused. The O girls always showed before I did in hopes some of their flirting was going to rub off on Mr Hawkins. Ever since summer started, the two of them flirted with Mr Hawkins like it was their job. They were hoping he'd bite, eventually, but so far they'd got nowhere. 'How unusual.'

He was looking at me, his stare never leaving my face, and I shuffled on the spot, wanting to go to my seat but also not wanting to get any closer to him.

'*En français*,' he said with a smile, and I glanced at the door, hoping the girls would fly through it and derail our conversation. The man gave me the creeps. It was as simple as that.

Dreams did come true, as at that moment, Ophelia flew through the door, nearly taking me out as she did so.

'YOU BITCH!' The anger in Ophelia's voice took me by surprise, and the moment I took in her appearance as she stood in front of the board, I burst into laughter. Real stomach-hurting chortles. The girl looked crazed: her skin a dark shade of purple and her ice-blonde hair no longer ice-blonde, but the brightest orange.

Ah, so she'd used the products Griff and I had tampered with. *Finally!*

Oralie appeared behind her, her skin a similar hue, but her hair was a bright green, and I lost it with laughter once again. There was no way I could take either of them seriously looking like *that*.

'You did this to us!' Oralie shouted, throwing herself in my direction, gearing her arm back, and I expected her fist to make contact with my face, but Mr Hawkins stood in between us and took her punch in his stomach instead.

'Girls,' he said, placating, breathing normally, like he hadn't just been punched. 'Calm down. There's no way of knowing whether Ms Crescent did this to you.'

'Yes, there is!' Ophelia spat. 'There's nobody else on campus who would want to embarrass us and make us ugly!'

'And are you hurt?' he asked, looking them both over from top to toe.

'Well, n-no,' sputtered Oralie. 'But she *wanted* to hurt us.'

'Yes, Ms Jones, but if I recall, you planned to punch Ms Crescent just now?'

Oralie stayed silent.

'Plus, I found the two of you punching Ms Crescent a week ago, so if she had something to do with this, then I can't blame her.'

Ophelia and Oralie dropped their jaws in disbelief.

'Our parents will hear about this!' Ophelia shrieked and Oralie nodded profusely behind her.

'I'm sure they will. I'm also sure Ms Hawthorn will hear about this, too. Now sit down. We've got a lesson to get to.'

I still hadn't stopped laughing, and seeing the shock on their faces just made me laugh more. As revenge plans go, it had been a little simplistic and childish, but man, what fun!

Ophelia leaned over in her chair and whispered, 'Sleep with one eye open, bitch.'

THE EVENING after the girls had showed up looking... different... Ollie had sat down in the chair next to me at the dining table while I waited for Leo, Griff, and Clo to show up.

'Excuse me?' I said the moment he sat down. 'Can I help you?'

'Knock it off, will you?' His mouth took on an unpleasant twist.

'Knock what off?' I pretended I had no idea what he was talking about, but it made sense he was talking about Ophelia and Oralie.

'I've seen what you did to the girls and it isn't on.'

'Isn't on? Ha! Are you having me on right now?' I laughed. 'There's no way to prove it was me, anyway.'

'I don't have to prove anything. You're the only person on campus who would bother with something so petty.'

'You have to admit it was pretty amusing.'

His face didn't even twitch.

'Even if it was me, which I'm not saying it was, why would I stop? Not like they've ever stopped their crap with me.'

'They will from now on. After they hurt you for not having dinner with me, I made it clear if they touched you again, they'd regret it.'

'And you think you wield that much power over them?' I rolled my eyes at his optimism. He may think he ruled the school —and the O girls—but I knew better. They did what they wanted, when they wanted. Their whole lives, they'd been told they could do anything and their money and power would mean they never suffered because of it. 'Those girls would drop you if it suited them.'

'Ophelia's my girlfriend, so I highly doubt that.' His words shocked me. I hadn't expected him to come out and say it. 'And Lee and I have known each other since we were two. She wouldn't turn on me. Neither of them would.'

'Whatever you say.' I looked towards the dining room door, hoping to see Leo walk through, or even Griff and Clo, but it was empty. Trust me to come to dinner early and alone. 'I don't really care either way.'

'You can lie to yourself all you want, Skylar, but you can't lie to me. I see right through you and always have. I see *you*.' He leaned forward, putting himself in my bubble. 'I don't want us to fight anymore.'

'I didn't realise we were fighting,' I said with a pout. 'I thought you'd decided I was scum of the earth and I'd decided you weren't worth my time. Or something to that effect anyway. Ollie, get up and go bother somebody else.'

'There's nobody in here but you to bother.'

'Then leave the room for all I care.' I huffed, getting bored with him being near me. At first I was having fun with it, but he'd overstayed his welcome by at least five minutes. 'I'm waiting for my boyfriend.'

'Want to remind me how the two of you became a thing?'

'Not particularly.' And not just because I didn't actually know the version of events we were meant to stick to...

'If you'd met me that night, maybe things would be different.' Ollie's eyes bored into mine, and I had to look away from the intensity in them. '*We* would be different.'

I shrugged. 'Maybe, but I guess we'll never know.'

'I could tell you now,' he said, and I frowned. He could tell me what? My blank stare clued him in to my confusion. 'What I wanted to say to you that night.'

'How about you tell both of us,' Leo said, taking his rightful place in the other seat next to me. He pulled me in, placed a kiss on my head, and held me close while staring Ollie down. There was something awfully sexy about a territorial Leo. 'I'm sure we'd both love to hear it.'

'I'd rather tell only Skylar,' Ollie said, not missing a beat. 'If you ever want to talk, Sky, you know where to find me. Or you can text me. I assume you still have my number.'

Of course I still had his number, but it didn't mean I'd use it.

'I'm okay. Thanks,' I said, leaning back into Leo's embrace. The epitome of a happy couple. The happiest. 'It wouldn't have changed anything.'

'Sure it wouldn't,' Ollie drawled. 'I'll leave you two to your evening.'

'Don't fancy joining us, mate?' Leo laughed, not meaning a word, and I worried Ollie knew that and would jump on the invitation. Lucky for me, Ollie shook his head, his eyes dark.

'I've got a girlfriend to go see.'

Leo shrugged. 'Suit yourself.'

Ollie finally stood from the chair and left the room, leaving me and Leo alone together. 'Thanks for the rescue.'

'You didn't need rescuing, Stutter. Not this time.' I turned to face him and was blinded by the rare wide smile covering the bottom half of his face. 'I heard you when I came in. You were holding your own.'

'He doesn't hold the power over me anymore.'

'Good.' Leo squeezed my hand, then turned to read the menu on the table. 'I'm proud of you and how far you've come.'

'Thanks.' I opened the menu and glanced at it, but I wasn't seeing the words written on the page, my mind filled with happiness from Leo's praise. 'You're not so bad yourself.'

Leo's eyes really were beautiful when they shone like that. Carefree. Happy. So different from the eyes I looked into last year and only saw boredom in. But which one was the façade? The bored guy who gave a shit about nothing, or the one with open eyes who gave a shit about me?

'...having pizza tonight.'

'Huh?' I shook my head, looking at his lips as if the first half of his sentence would appear there.

'There's stonebaked margherita on the menu tonight.' He pointed at my menu on the table in front of me. 'Guess we both know what you're having.'

I laughed. 'Yep. You know me so well.'

'Anyone who's seen your eating habits would know what meal you'd pick.'

'True,' I agreed. 'And let me guess'—I perused the menu, trying to correctly guess Leo's choice—'you'll be having the steak, rare.'

'Looks like you know me just as well,' he said with a wolfish smile. 'Aren't we the lucky ones?'

'Aren't we just!' I tried not to dwell on the unsaid part of my sentence. *Wonder when it'll end?*

Twenty-Four

LEO

AT SOME POINT in the last month, I'd fucked up.

Everything had seemed so simple at first. Ask Stutter to be my fake girlfriend, make Clover jealous, and piss Ollie off all in one fell swoop with zero effort on my part. Stutter was a pretty girl, and I liked her as a person when she wasn't miserable about the way Ollie treated her, so it seemed like a win-win to me. It was a brilliant plan.

It was also something I'd done without being told to.

I'd gone rogue, so to speak.

'You think we can complete this tonight?' Stutter asked, pausing the game and moving her gaze from the TV to face me. The two of us were in my room, sitting on the bed playing *Spyro*, after another day of faking everything in front of those fuckers I called my friends.

Actually, I was watching her play while I did fuck all but admire her. She was trying her hardest to make that little purple fucker fly the wrong way. She'd seen a hack online, or something like that, and she was adamant she could crack the game faster if she could just fly through the cliff.

'Don't see why not?' I replied, blinking at her. 'If you can figure out how to do it.'

'Hm, true,' she said with a smile, then turned back to the game, even more determined than before to make it work. That was something I'd noticed about Skylar—she loved to win and had quite the competitive streak. If you doubted her, she'd do her best to prove you wrong, no matter how long it took.

Her lips always looked best when smiling. All full, plump, and they made me think of things I shouldn't be thinking of—like what it would be like to bite her lip as I thrust inside her. Or how her glossy lips would look wrapped around my cock.

I had to adjust myself, hoping she was as unobservant as she'd always been around us all.

Stutter had the tendency to be oblivious.

Somehow she'd believed Ollie last year, when it was pretty obvious to everybody else that he was playing her. Even Red fucking noticed, and she wasn't always the sharpest tool. She also happened to be a backstabbing fucking bitch and the whole reason I was sitting here hard for her best friend in the first place.

'Leo?'

'Yeah,' I replied, the thought of Red causing my dick to die down. She was an instant libido killer.

'Has Ollie said anything to you?' she asked, her tone uncertain, telling me she didn't want to know the answer but had asked, regardless. Sky was a curious thing and she couldn't leave questions unasked, even if the answer was going to make her day worse.

'About?' I drawled, wanting her to work for it.

'About us? About me?'

'Not gonna lie, Stutter, not like I talk to the boy much these days. Not since my birthday, at least. Wonder why that is.' I laughed, but it held little humour in it.

And I wasn't lying. I barely spoke to him outside of the times we were all together, or when I needed to for *Sect* stuff. The prick deserved to be excluded from what I was doing. He didn't get to call the shots around here and not have any repercussions for his shitty actions.

'You don't?' she asked, pausing the game once again and putting the controller down to give me her full attention. It was nice to have her attention, her bright eyes taking in every part of my face as she tried to figure something out. I hadn't yet figured out what it was she was searching for.

The two of us were lying on top of the duvet, and she moved onto her side to face me. I stayed where I was, not wanting to make the situation even more intimate. I didn't need more on my plate.

'When do I have the time?' I shrugged. 'I'm mostly with you.'

'Yeah, true.' She blinked, her eyes a blue I wanted to look at longer. 'What about during swim practice?'

I chuckled, once again reminded how little Stutter knew about the swim team and what happened at practice. The girl was totally oblivious—Stutter never noticed things unless they were in front of her face and sometimes even then they went over her head.

'He swims,' I replied.

She nudged me in the side. 'Hey! You make me sound stupid.'

'Do I?' I asked, raising my eyebrow at her. 'Or do you do that all by yourself?'

'I am not stupid!' she said and then laughed. 'No, I totally can be stupid.'

'Glad you realise it.'

I turned and looked at her, once again feeling my dick twitch when she turned her full beam smile in my direction. No wonder Ollie became whipped—even if the prick couldn't admit it to himself. He'd rather dig himself a hole with Ophelia than admit he fucked up and lost a good thing.

'I wonder what Griff and Clo are up to right now.'

'No, you don't,' I said, knowing that *I* definitely didn't want to know, but not for the reason I usually didn't want to know. To be honest, I'd reached a point where I just didn't give a shit about them. Or about anybody that wasn't in the room.

Shit.

Things were definitely getting twisted.

I'd started to actually *like* Stutter. And not just in that friend-ship way we'd had before. Or in a protective way I'd felt last year when... well, when shit went down.

'Kiss me,' I blurted, no thought behind the statement, and once it had made its way into the atmosphere, I'd look like a right wanker trying to take it back. I tried to stay casual and act cava-lier, as if I was in full control of my faculties.

'Huh?' she asked as her eyes looked at my face, taking in every part, until her eyes locked with mine.

'Kiss. Me.'

'W-why?' she stuttered, and my dick responded. Damn, that stutter really did something to me. Like Ollie last year, *I* was wondering what it sounded like with *my* dick deep inside her.

'Don't you want to?' I asked, turning it around on her. If she said no, I'd leave it at that, no harm done. The ball, as always, was in Stutter's court.

'I...' She took a deep breath. 'Is that what you want?'

Neither a yes nor a no. Helpful. 'We should probably practise, right? Make sure that when we kiss in public, it looks natural. Like we do it in private.'

'To keep up the lie?'

I nodded. If my agreement was what she needed to hear to believe it—to justify it in her head—then I'd agree.

'Okay,' she whispered.

I turned onto my side, so our foreheads touched, and our lips inched closer together. Gently putting her chin in my hold, I tilted her head so I could look into the depth of colour swimming in her irises and the doubt that lingered under the surface.

'Are you s-sure?'

Responding with words seemed cheap, and even though she was a scholarship student, Skylar was anything but cheap. My lips touched hers, urgent and exploratory. Stutter gasped slightly and parted her lips. My tongue explored, and then, like a switch turning on, she ripped herself out of my hold.

'That's enough practice for now,' she said in a hushed voice, her eyes wide.

I nodded and lay back to face the ceiling again, breathing deep to stop myself from claiming her. We both needed to cool down. 'Sure, Stutter. Don't want you to like kissing me *too* much, do we?'

My question was meant to sound casual and offhand, but it came out strained.

Fuck.

Maybe it wasn't just my dick that wanted a piece of Stutter.

THE REST of summer passed the way the first month did—odd spurts of excitement, mixed with long, tedious bouts of boredom.

Ollie was barely talking to me. Griff spoke to me but only if Stutter was present.

'What's the plan?' I leaned forward and murmured in Sky's ear, the two of us standing close together, chests touching while we waited in an alcove outside the hall for Griff and Clo to join us for lunch. I'd arranged for us to go off campus and get lunch at her favourite café down the hill in town, and although Stutter didn't know about it yet, I knew she'd love it.

'Tonight?' she asked, tilting her head up to look into my eyes. I nodded. 'Same as usual, I guess.'

Hawthorn Academy was a place I hated and loved in equal measure. For most of my life, I'd spent all my summer and winter breaks on campus at the family estate, and when it wasn't school time, the place was peaceful and somewhere I could be and think without having to put on an act.

I never thought I'd be ready for other students to arrive, but fuck, I was. Having only six students on campus meant there wasn't enough going on, and my plan with Stutter didn't have as much clout as it would when the rest of the student body was watching it unfold. The real revenge was having Ollie seen as less than by the Hawthorn population, and even though he was my cousin and therefore family, I still wanted to knock the wanker down a bit.

'I had an idea of what we could do Friday night,' I said. Sky raised her eyebrow, waiting for me to continue.

'Yeah?' she asked when I didn't say anything.

'Yeah,' I said with a nod. 'But it's a surprise.'

'You know I hate surprises.'

'You'll probably hate this one, too,' I said, a dark smile playing on my lips. *Probably* was an understatement. She'd *definitely* hate it. Maybe not as much as she'd hate me if she knew the truth about everything I was doing...

'Great. I'm thrilled,' she deadpanned, and I gave a low chuckle.

I lifted one hand from where it was resting on Sky's arse to tuck her hair behind my ear. 'Promise, Stutter, it'll be fun. I wouldn't drag you into something you'd hate.'

'I find that hard to believe,' she whispered. The kiss I gave her in reply was involuntary. She was making me feel things I knew I shouldn't feel, yet I couldn't help myself. I was enjoying our deception too much. I was enjoying her company just as much. Why shouldn't I get something out of it? Something as fun as pissing off Clover.

And pissing off Clover was a fuck ton of fun. Every time she was around us, she pretended not to care, but when she thought we weren't looking, her eyes didn't leave the area where Sky's and my bodies touched.

'Ready for lunch, bitches?' Griff's voice brought me back to the moment, the thought of Clover forgotten, even though she was heading towards us from the end of the hall. Sky laughed, stepping back from my embrace to face them.

'Ready for what, exactly?' Clover asked. 'Crappy school food?'

'No way! We're leaving campus. The car's waiting outside.' Griff beamed at us, and for the tiniest second, a twinge of guilt ran through me. I wanted Clo to hurt, sure, but Griff was my cousin. Family. I hated that he was getting caught in every crosshair, but there was nothing to be done about it. I had to let the chips fall and pick up the pieces after the fact.

'Come on, Stutter. Let's get the fuck out of dodge.'

Sky instantly moved into my outstretched arm, and I pulled her close once more before standing beside her and holding her hand. Her responding squeeze made me smile.

Sky's enthusiasm was one of the many endearing things about her. 'Let's do this shit!'

Twenty-Five

EVERY SLASHER HORROR movie included an end of summer camp out, right?

Yep, that's what I thought.

But apparently, I wanted to be the new dead girl in a remake of *Friday the 13th* because here I was, getting ready to go camp out in the woods with the boys. From what Leo had told me, Ollie and *The Set* were going to be there, but all I had to do was make Ollie jealous and ignore them otherwise.

Easier said than done.

'You wearing that?' Leo asked, looking me up and down, his eyes appraising.

I looked down to remind myself of my outfit, wondering why Leo was asking. Did he mean it in a good way, or like *you're wearing garbage, Sky, go change?*

My black dress showed major cleavage, and the skirt flowed out at my waist, showing off my hourglass curves. The dress itself was pretty plain, but we were camping out, not going to the Ritz.

'I was going to?'

'You look hot,' he said. My lips twitched upwards, an involuntary movement, and my insides warmed. Leo could deliver the simplest of lines but make me feel fantastic about myself. Things between us were heating up and I wasn't sure if it was all a game to him.

'Thanks. You look pretty good, too.'

The smile Leo graced me with could only be described as wolfish and seductive. Spending more time with him had changed my perception of him—for the better—and a small part of me wished we were spending the night together without the others.

'So, we're sharing a tent?' he asked, his eyebrow raised. I took back my praise of him. He could be such a prick. He knew the answer already, but he just wanted to embarrass me and make me say it out loud.

'Y-yes.' My cheeks flushed, and my chest turned a dark shade of red with nerves.

'How far are you willing to go to sell this, Stutter?'

'I...' *Shit, how far was I willing to go?* 'I don't know,' I replied. 'Why?'

'We're all going to be in close proximity. And any light inside a tent shows what is going on inside. Plus, our tent is small.'

'How small is small?' My eyebrows furrowed, praying he wasn't about to tell me it was one of those two-man pop-up things. The boy had enough money to at least upgrade our tent to a four-man, surely!

'Think we've got ourselves a pop-up,' he replied with a grin, almost as if he knew the thoughts going through my head. He was getting a kick out of all of it and fair play to him. He knew what would grate on Clo the most, and the two of us being in a two-man tent with barely any space to move? Yeah, that'd send her over the edge.

'Yay,' I cheered.

'It'll be fine, Stutter. We won't do anything you don't want to do.' His blue eyes looked earnest, and the sincerity shone out at me. I released a breath, knowing Leo meant his words. He wasn't Ollie, who still hadn't apologised—or even mentioned—the closet since.

'I mean, we can kiss.' He nodded, and I added, 'And hug, act touchy-feely. Stuff we've already done.'

'Define touchy-feely?'

'I don't know… ' My cheeks warmed. You'd have thought a virgin was standing before him, but really, it was just little, old, inexperienced me.

His words were playing on a loop in my mind. *How far are you willing to go to sell this?*

'Sky, what do you mean?' he asked, and the fact that he used my name set my racing heart at ease. 'I don't want you to be uncomfortable.'

'You can grope my bum?' I asked, then burst out into laughter. He'd already done that before, so it wasn't like I was saying something we hadn't already agreed to. 'Touch me up, I guess?' His eyes locked with mine. 'Stop looking at me like that! The fact you're making me say shit is causing me to break out into a rash.'

'Calm down, Stutter. I can make it work,' he said, and the look in his eye made me move closer to him. Close enough that I could wrap my arms around him and grope *his* bum. His large hands warmed my waist as he rested them there, and the intimacy for once didn't feel forced. Trying to get my mind away from that avenue, I searched for something else to wonder about. God forbid my mind be blank without thought for once.

A thought hit me and I muttered, 'Poor Oralie. She'll be seventh wheeling it tonight.'

How awkward. If I were her, I wouldn't show up, but there was no way in hell that girl would do that. The FOMO was real. If I were her, I'd rather stay in my room alone, watching films or reading an excellent book, than go spend a creepy night in the woods with three couples.

Fuck, I'd rather do that and I was a part of one of the "couples". Honestly, all three pairings were as fake as the next, just for different reasons.

'That's the goal, right? Making the O girls suffer alongside Ollie?' he asked. 'Feeling sympathy for the twat, Stutter?'

I scoffed, trying to cover up the fact that my heart was feeling bad for the girl who'd tormented me last year with no remorse. *Get your head in the game.*

'Eurgh, I sort of hate myself.' I chuckled.

'Why?'

'I should want her to feel awkward, should want her to suffer, and trust me, this will definitely cause her ego to suffer. She believes she should be your girlfriend.'

'Probably.' He shrugged, and my body moved with his motion. 'But she's not.'

'True. I am, 'cause we're both dickheads.'

He laughed at that, and I joined him. We broke apart, and I continued getting ready for an evening I already knew I wouldn't enjoy.

'Come on, grumps. I'll make sure you have a good time,' he said.

I wasn't even going to question how he knew my mind. 'Promise?'

'Promise. And if not, we can just get trashed.'

'Sounds like a plan, Batman.'

I took a deep breath, gearing myself up to put a jacket on and leave Leo's suite with him.

'Breathe, Stutter. We've got this,' he drawled and took my hand in his. His hand heated my own, and he squeezed to reassure me.

Camp Hawthorn, here we come.

So, this had to be the worst camp out I'd ever attended in my life.

I mean, it was the *only* camp out I'd ever attended in my life, but semantics.

In the middle of the clearing, a large fire raged, and around it there were camp chairs in a semicircle. The flames were the only light in the area and caused everything to have an orange, sinister glow. Clover and Griff were sitting next to each other, heads close together, talking animatedly about something. In their own bubble, ignoring the rest of us.

Ophelia and Ollie were standing together, swaying along to some ballad Oralie was playing out of the Bluetooth speaker she'd hooked up to her phone. The entire view made me cringe. Knowing what I knew of my fake relationship, it had become glaringly obvious to me over the last couple of weeks just how much Ollie was lying with Ophelia. No bone in his body wanted to be near her. I'd even witnessed him flinching when she sank her talons into his arm to grab his attention.

Then there was Leo and me, hands gripped together, standing off to the side, talking in hushed tones about our plan of action. To the outside looking in, I felt certain we looked like a genuine couple talking about private matters.

'Right, we need to liven up this shit,' he whispered, his breath skating across my face and causing me to shiver.

'What do you suggest?' I pressed up onto my tiptoes to whisper into his ear. My skin tingled as if it could sense Ollie's boring stare in our direction, and I knew how intimate this would look to him. 'I'm coming up blank.'

'We need to get everyone to play a game.'

'All right, Jigsaw.' I lowered my feet, knowing that my intention had hit its mark. Leo followed my lead and leant down to whisper in my ear. His lips brushed my ear, and I giggled at the tickling sensation.

'Oh, ha-ha. Help me think of a game.'

'I have never?' I asked, but then thought better of it. 'Truth or dare?'

'Of course,' he said and then warned me. 'Be careful. Those girls will be out for blood.'

'I could say the same to you, but it isn't the girls who would like to see you bleed.'

He chuckled, sending chills down my spine, and kissed my cheek, making a big show of the action, and moved to stand beside me. It burned where his lips had been, and I knew I had turned the colour of a tomato. To me, in that moment, it felt like we were two outsiders looking over the kingdom they intended to overthrow. *Listen to me.* I'd been watching one too many television programmes about the Tudor court.

Swinging his arm around my shoulder, I leaned into him. I hoped we looked as real as we were selling it to be.

'Let's play a game,' I called out. An ominous statement if ever there was one. Instantly, five pairs of eyes were on us and every single pair was sceptical.

'What game are you thinking, Clouds?' Griff called back, his cheeky grin plastered on his face. If there was anybody I trusted and could always rely on, it was him.

'Truth or dare,' Leo said at his normal level. One thing that impressed me about Leo was that no matter what, he made it clear he was above all the petty bullshit. Not going to lie, it made me the slightest bit turned on when he was so himself. He never acted in a way that didn't feel genuine to him, if that made sense? His self-assuredness was extremely hot to me; super appealing.

'I'm down,' Griff said, and as soon as he agreed, the spell was cast over the other people in the clearing.

'Sounds fun,' Ollie drawled, his eyes that dark indigo they turned when he was acting his most devious. *Side note: must not take a dare from Oliver.*

'We're in,' Oralie and Ophelia said in unison. *Creepy.*

'Looks like we're doing this,' Clo said in a sour tone. Couldn't blame her. If the game hadn't been my idea, I would have been running for the edge of the hill the school sat upon.

The seven of us all took our seats around the campfire, the flames flickering on everybody's faces causing every facial expression to alter to something darker. I trusted nobody. My hand was still gripped in Leo's—I was using him as an anchor of sorts. Something tangible and real that would keep me sane; keep me grounded. Somebody there to ensure I didn't throw caution to the wind and forget about my revenge plot.

'Who wants to start?' I asked, and surprise, surprise, nobody jumped up to go first. I looked at Griff sitting opposite me and tried to use our cousin's telepathy to get him to pipe up. The boy loved to hear his own voice every day of the week, so I could do with his gung-ho attitude.

Lucky for me, the communication waves must have opened between us as he smiled and nodded.

'I'll go,' he said. Shit you not, his dimples looked even cuter in the dim fire lighting.

'Truth or dare?' I asked, not knowing what I would do for either of his responses. I was full-blown winging it.

'Dare, of course,' Griff replied as if it were a given. And I suppose it was.

'Err... I dare you to...' I looked around, hoping for inspiration. 'I dare you to climb that tree.' I pointed over to a large hawthorn tree that looked like it could take his weight. He may be tall, but his body was made up of pure muscle, his broad shoulders made even more powerful through the many hours of swim training he put himself through.

'Easy-peasy,' he said, so cocksure that a small part of me hoped he'd fail. That would at least make him think twice before being so confident all the time.

Griff stood and sauntered over to the tree. Sizing it up, I could see his brain working a mile a minute, trying to figure out how to tackle the task. A second later, the boy was off, climbing the tree as if it were nothing at all. He didn't even pause to take a deep breath or to think of his next move.

'No fair!' I realised the boy had some kind of rock climbing skill I hadn't been privy to.

Griff got to the highest branch he could, then laughed and shouted something corny that I couldn't quite make out. Although if I *had* to guess, I'd say he quoted Jack from *Titanic*. Yes, *that* scene. The boy was nothing if not predictable.

He climbed back down as quick as he'd scaled up and jumped the last couple of feet with triumph blazing in his eyes. 'Nice one, Clouds. That's a point for me.'

'There aren't points in truth or dare, Griff,' Clo said with a roll of her eyes, although I could tell she found him amusing all the same.

'There should be,' he grumbled.

'Then there will be,' Ollie piped up. 'The team to reach ten points first, wins. And for every point you forfeit, you drink.'

Everybody met his words with an agreement. Everybody but me. Leo nudged me in the side. A reminder. So I did what was expected of me and said, 'Deal.'

Let the games begin.

HONESTLY, who the fuck would ever believe that a stupid, simple game of truth or dare could go on for three hours?

Apparently, with seven players, each round took an age to complete. Plus, at first there had been a lot of arguing about whether we could give points to answers given to a 'Truth' as there was no way of proving the person was in fact telling the truth.

Fuck me. This had actually seemed like a fun idea when I suggested it. *Oh, how naïve young Skylar of three hours ago was.*

'Truth or dare?' Ophelia slurred, and she wasn't the only one slurring, repeating the words Leo had just said to Clover.

'Truth,' Clo responded lightning fast. The alcohol had made her brave. For the past few rounds, she'd opted for a dare and had failed miserably, so was now rather drunk on the energy drink and vodka she was consuming like it would run out. I'd been trying to drink as little as I could in order to keep my faculties intact, but it seemed nobody else in the circle was doing the same.

Leo chuckled next to me, the glimmer of the flames matching the glint of evil in his eyes. 'Are you jealous of Stutter?'

Clover bristled, her dislike of Leo clear to everybody. Griff's face darkened too.

'Nope,' she replied, scoffing. 'If anything, I feel sorry for her.'

I flinched at her venom. *Gee, Clo, ta muchly.*

'Sorry for her?' Leo asked sardonically. 'Expect us to believe that, Red?'

'Expect you to believe the truth? Yes.' Her statement came out pretty clear, except for the slight slur at the end that changed the meaning.

'You need to drink!' Oralie called out, giddy, watching the events unfold like a tennis match. Her ice-blonde hair had got stuck to her lip gloss, and it had taken a lot of willpower not to stand up and yank it off for her. It was irritating me so much, but I wasn't going to save her from the embarrassment. Both she and Ophelia had blatantly decided the only way they could get through the evening was by getting wasted. *Fair.*

Alongside Leo and me, Ollie was the only other person who hadn't touched their drink much, or at least I hadn't seen him drink loads. Not that I was watching him—often. Of course he wouldn't be drinking. He needed control at all times. Power was more effective when sober.

'Why?' Clo snapped. 'I didn't lie.'

Oralie hiccupped and said in a snooty tone, '*Duh.* I meant Leo needs to drink.'

'Oh.' Clover looked thoroughly schooled and I couldn't help but laugh. The entire scenario I'd found myself in killed me a little inside. What even was life?

'Truth or dare?' Clo asked me, her eyes narrowed. Her venom wasn't unfounded, but I couldn't be arsed to deal with it.

'Truth,' I replied, feeling pretty confident that Clo wouldn't come for me too hard. Although I had just laughed at her, maybe I shouldn't be quite so cocky.

'How do you really feel about Leo?' she asked, triumphant. In my peripheral, I saw Ollie sit up a little straighter, interested in my answer. The whole circle was interested in my answer, including the guy in question sitting next to me, rubbing his hand along my leg. I didn't even have to think twice about it.

'I like him,' I said with a shrug. Everybody knew that to pass a lie detector you had to answer as close to the truth as you could. 'And let's be honest, the boy's fucking hot.'

I'd meant for my last sentence to be kept in the dark, in the back recesses of my brain, but clearly, I had drunk just enough for it to be let loose.

'Tell us how you *really* feel,' Griff said with a chuckle, breaking the tension in that way only he could.

'You think I'm hot, Stutter?' Leo's voice rumbled in his chest and vibrated down my back. His front was pressed up against my back and I was sitting on his lap, the epitome of a couple that couldn't stay away from one another. His arms were wrapped around me, engulfing me and making me feel small, yet warm and somewhat safe.

'You know you are,' I murmured. 'Truth or dare?' My question was aimed in Ollie's direction, wanting to ignore Leo's amused chuckle from behind me. What better way to do that than to ask my ex a question I didn't want an answer to.

'Truth,' he replied, his blue eyes drawing me in, daring me. Ah shit, I hadn't been expecting that! Whenever it had been his turn, he'd gone for a dare.

'Right,' I said, adjusting in Leo's lap so I could nudge him somehow to help me. His breath tickled my ear as he whispered a question I could ask and I squirmed at the way it made me feel. His dick hardened, and we both ignored it, choosing not to blur the line, especially as everyone's eyes were on us. 'Why d-did you lie to me last year?' My stutter reared its ugly head, as it always did when I felt nervous. Man, I'd really begun to hate that part of myself.

'When?' he asked, his eyebrow raised with amusement. The smirk covering his lips made my skin crawl. Who the fuck did this twat think he was? ''Cause there are a few instances you could be referring to.'

Wanker. I racked my brain for a specific time to ask about. A lot of our time together played on my mind in a constant loop, especially when I'd been stuck in my hospital bed, but recently I'd sort of tried to fixate less. An unhealthy fixation wasn't good for my mental state. Plus, Leo was a damn good distraction.

Finally, a memory flashed in my mind. 'Valentine's Day. When you made me believe.'

I couldn't take my eyes away from his face, waiting to spot any changes, any flicker of emotion or remorse he might try to hide deep down, but all I saw was confusion he quickly masked with distaste.

'Made you believe what, New Girl?' He sneered and took a large swig of his drink. 'That I could actually like you?'

Leo's arms squeezed me, giving me the support I needed not to stand up and go deck him. I'd love to rearrange his face with my fists. Okay, maybe I wouldn't. He may be a bastard, but damn, his face was pretty.

'Doesn't answer my q-question.'

'Why did I lie?' he asked, getting a thrill from repeating the words. 'Because you were so fucking gullible. The whole time, we were *all* laughing at you. Including your boy Griff and your *boyfriend* Leo. Everybody was in on it but you. How does it feel to learn you're the butt of a joke and you're the only one oblivious to the punchline?'

Tears filled my eyes, threatening to spill out, but I couldn't let them. Fuck him! Fuck him for trying to make me feel small and worthless, *again*. He'd succeeded after the charity fashion show, but I wouldn't take it any longer. Three months had passed and in that time, my confidence had grown. My self-worth and dignity alongside it.

'Fuck you,' I spat, the only response I could muster up the energy for. He didn't deserve anything more. Leo pulled me closer and kissed me on the head, giving me strength. And if you were to ask me why I said my next sentence, I'd say it was because Leo's kiss had given me the idea. 'Shall we call it a night and go to our tent?'

I turned around and spontaneously gave Leo a lingering kiss full on the lips. The small amount of alcohol running through my system had bolstered me to act with more confidence than usual and I was revelling in it.

'Thought you'd never ask. I'd love to, baby,' Leo replied in a tone low enough to pretend it was for my ears only, but loud enough that everybody heard it.

The fire had died down earlier on in the game and the only sound remaining was a low crackling.

'Let's go then.' I stood, reaching out my hand so that Leo could put his in mine. He didn't disappoint.

Once he was standing too, he pulled me along behind him towards our tent, while I giggled like a giddy girl in lust.

Sometimes, it surprised me how good of an actress I could be.

And the award goes to...

Twenty-Six

MY HANGOVER, luckily for me, was basically non-existent. Probably due to the fact that I'd consumed little alcohol, knowing that a sloppy Skylar would not have been good for the revenge plan. The revenge plan that was starting to seem a little redundant.

The opposite of non-existent? The feelings that were stirring in my stomach for Leo, but maybe that had to do with the fact he was pressed up against my back, having slept with his arm draped over my stomach, holding me close like I'd disappear if he didn't.

The summer heat blazed outside, and the tent lining was covered in tiny drops of condensation that were clinging to the material. I'd never been more glad that I slept wearing an eye mask, as the way the sun shone through the bright green tent was making me feel ill already. The inside of a tent looked so different in the light of day.

In the middle of the night, Leo had shed his T-shirt, and I'd had to remove my leggings. Our body heat, alongside the sleeping bag, had been overwhelming. The air was stuffy, and even after removing my leggings, a slight sheen of sweat still covered me when I awoke.

'Morning, babe,' Leo muttered, his voice thick with sleep. His eyes were still closed, and as much as I wanted to see his bright blues, his long eyelashes looked so pretty when his eyes were closed. Peaceful.

'Morning,' I whispered back, awkward for the first time since we'd started this thing. 'Do you think we did good last night?'

'I think Ollie and Clo both went to their tents miserable as fuck because of us,' he said with a low chuckle. '*You* did good.' His emphasis made my heart flutter. I swear, praise was like a drug to me.

'Thanks.' I blushed, glancing away from him so that he wouldn't notice me staring if he opened his eyes. 'Those noises last night...' I started but didn't want to complete the sentence. Poor Oralie. Grunts and groans could be heard for at least an hour after we went to our tent, and it reminded me of those scenes in films where couples competed to be the loudest. *Which, yeah, how fucked is that?*

'Ha,' Leo scoffed. 'None of that was real.'

'It wasn't?' I asked, unsure. Sure sounded real to me.

'Nope. None of them sound like that when they're fucking— or at least not when they're enjoying it.'

The casual way he said it caught me so off guard I choked on my own spit. I sat bolt upright, my hand flailing around on the floor, trying to locate a bottle of water.

Once my coughing died down, I gasped. 'What do you even mean?' I grabbed the water and gulped it down, trying to soothe my throat.

'Well, I'm telling the truth.' He opened his eyes, a glimmer of mischief shining from them.

'And you know that how?'

'Don't be so dense, Stutter.' To soften the blow of his words, he sat up and kissed my cheek. Already the lines between us were blurred. We spent so much time together it was hard not to fall into the roles we were playacting. He looked me dead in the eye, his face bored once again. 'Remember, if anybody asks, our night went well.'

I nodded, knowing what he wanted me to imply, and I had

already thought of a couple of coy sentences I could feed Clo to make it believable.

'Make him suffer,' he whispered. 'And I doubt he did what you're thinking he did.'

'What? Fuck Ophelia?'

'That,' he replied. 'He's pissed at himself, at you. At a lot of things. But I know him and even if he believes himself capable, he isn't.'

'Are you sticking up for him?'

'Nope, just giving you some background.'

'Okay. Well, maybe keep his background in the background for the time being.' My brows rose, causing my forehead to wrinkle, as I waited for Leo to nod. He did, and I rewarded him with an open-mouthed smile—a rare occurrence.

'As you wish, Stutter.'

'Oh, come on, dickhead'—I chucked my pillow at his head, which he ducked away from fast—'let's get this shit over with.'

THE GROUP PACKED up the tents in silence—well, everybody but Griff. The entire morning, the boy had been singing at the top of his lungs. I'd been attempting to tune him out, but the last time I listened, he had moved on to singing Adele. Or rather, butchering Adele.

Clover's eyes were bloodshot, and the dark circles under her eyes looked pretty rough. Her hangover had hit her hard, I'd say. Energy drinks and vodka were not for the weak.

Ophelia and Oralie had emerged from their tents wearing large circular sunglasses that covered not just their eyes but the majority of their faces too. A major improvement if you asked me.

Ollie had been glaring at me the entire morning and was using any opportunity he could to enter my personal bubble to make me shiver. Then if Leo was already in my bubble, and he couldn't get close enough, he went to Ophelia and attempted to make me uncomfortable that way. It was all a bit predictable, but a pain in the arse regardless.

The difference between Sky of last year and the Sky of this year: she could see through his bullshit. Knowing how fake Leo and I were at our core, I was no longer blind to just how fake Ollie and Ophelia acted together. Well, how fake Ollie acted. Pretty sure Ophelia believed it was real—bless her heart.

'I'm hungry,' Ophelia whined, stomping her foot for good measure. I looked at Leo and rolled my eyes at her antics. His lip twitched in response, which I took as a win.

'Me too,' Oralie whined even louder. Fuck, it wasn't a competition.

'Come eat with us, Skylar.' Ophelia turned to me, and even though I couldn't see her eyes through her dark lenses, I knew they weren't full of human kindness. Nope. They probably had daggers in them.

'I...' I looked around for anybody to save me, but Clo clearly still harboured ill will toward me, and Griff was so busy trying to keep her happy that he wasn't about to come to my aid. Ollie's wolfish grin told me that shit had been his idea. Leo just shrugged, his hands in his pockets, the epitome of casual. *Wonderful.*

'Girls have to eat, right?' Oralie joined in, in cahoots with her best friend—her only friend—totally ignoring the fact they weren't inviting Clover, who was also a girl. Whatever. 'And we totally forgive you for the whole hair thing.'

Ophelia nodded in agreement. 'Yep. Totally forgotten.' She barked a brittle laugh. 'And I've totally forgiven you for dying my skin, too.'

'Totally,' Oralie said. 'Even if we had to scrub our skin for hours.'

Their words were only making me more suspicious of their true intentions, but nobody was saving me, and fuck it, I could look after myself.

'Right.' I looked at Leo, hoping for a knight in shining armour, but all I saw was a knight in shit-covered armour, a bemused expression on his face. Through gritted teeth, I asked, 'Do you mind?'

'Nope,' he replied, popping the P in a way that he knew irritated me. Oh, he was going to pay for that.

'Super!' Ophelia cooed, clapping her hands together while Oralie shimmied her body next to her. What the actual fuck?

'Super,' I deadpanned, still waiting for somebody to announce it was all a big joke.

They didn't.

The three of us walked through the trees in a line, heading back towards the school, the only sound the birds calling to one another. Glad they could keep up a conversation when all I wanted was for the ground to swallow me whole.

'So, New Girl,' Ophelia piped up after we'd been walking for ten very long, very quiet, minutes. 'How did you and Leo become a thing?'

Her question caught me off guard. She wanted the gossip, apparently. Girls baffled me. I'd never understood how you could beat somebody up one moment, then try to befriend them the next.

'Errr...' I took in a deep breath, stalling for time, trying to think of something I could say that sounded genuine. Not like I could say, *Oh well, you know. He texted me for a midnight rendezvous where we plotted like Burke and Hare.* I mean, I could say that, as I was pretty sure that my historical reference would fly over the top of their bleached blonde heads.

'Tell us,' Oralie tittered. 'I've always had a bit of a soft spot for Leo, but I never thought I had a chance. Not until Cl—'

Ophelia elbowed her in the ribs, cutting her off, and from the grunt she let out, it must have been a hard jab.

Eurgh, if you can't beat them, join them.

'I guess I've always had a soft spot for him too,' I told them, throwing in a giggle, trying to convince them I was letting them in on a big secret. That we were in one another's confidence. I needed to know what they wanted from me, and the only way I could think of going about that was by lulling them into a false sense of security.

We would never be friends, and I would never forget what they'd done to me, but I could definitely ride the conversation out and see where they were taking me.

'And you pulled him, you lucky bitch.' Ophelia's eyes were alight with humour, and Oralie giggled. Fuck me, her laugh was the furthest thing from pleasant. It grated, and if I had to listen to it for much longer, my ears would probably start to leak blood.

Finally, the three of us walked out of the trees and made our way to the grand entrance of the school. Those beady-eyed gargoyles watching our approach in silence, and I knew if we were in a cartoon, they'd be gossiping about the worrying sight before them.

Ascending the stairs and entering the large dark wood doors, the three of us must have looked as mismatched as anything. I didn't fit. The two of them were wearing pink, short, skimpy pyjamas and there was me, wearing one of Leo's T-shirts and some old, colour-faded leggings.

Outside of the hall, the two of them stopped, and I did too, worried I'd been taken here just so the two of them could beat me up again. Fool me twice and all that crap.

'Skylar,' Oralie started, and hearing her say my name in such a sickly sweet tone set my teeth on edge. 'We have something we want to say.'

'Yeah, we do,' Ophelia said, her tone equally sickening. 'This may come as a complete shock to you, but the two of us just wanted to tell you how sorry we are for everything.'

'What?' I blurted out, fully having expected bullshit to come out of their mouth, but not *that* kind of bullshit.

'We're sorry, Skylar. Truly,' Ophelia said, while Oralie nodded like a nodding-head dog toy behind her.

'You are?' I hated the uncertainty in my tone, but of course I was sceptical. They'd beat me up a month ago and now wanted me to believe they were sorry for that. Yeah, something didn't add up.

If it looked like shit.

Sounded like shit.

It probably was, in fact, shit.

'We are. Honestly, we don't know what came over us.' The two of them lifted up their sunglasses and rested them on top of their heads, and underneath they were both giving me a wide-eyed, extremely bloodshot stare, their huge eyes caked in last night's dried makeup.

'On what occasion?' I blurted, knowing I shouldn't needle them, to just take it all at face value like they clearly wanted me to, but that wasn't very *me*.

'Don't be like that,' Ophelia snapped, her eyes narrowed, the hint of the mean girl surfacing. 'We mean it.'

Oralie, who was definitely the more subservient of the two, just nodded to agree with her leader.

'Fine,' I said in what I hoped was a placating tone. Shit, I didn't need another black eye. 'Thanks.'

'No problem, New Girl. So, tell us some real tea! Have you fucked Leo?' Ophelia sounded like a gossipy friend. Even the way she'd said New Girl was ten times friendlier than I'd ever heard it before.

What's the catch?

'Wouldn't you like to know?' Was all I said, knowing that my refusal to answer outright would only excite them more. Would have the two of them speculating for days to come.

Both of them broke out into a chorus of, 'Oohh.'

Breakfast was going to be a lot longer than usual.

But it was a start.

Part Two
Progress

Twenty-Seven

THE FIRST WEEK of September finally arrived and along with it came a lot of students and school starting back up—for real and not just summer stuff.

I'd never believed I would be excited for school to start again, but I was more than ready for it. Maybe spending an entire six weeks on campus more than expected had something to do with it?

Summer school had been nowhere near as bad as it could have been, but shitting hell, I needed to be around more people. A wider selection of arseholes, y'know. Variety was the spice of life.

The first day of term, I could sense the tension in the air. Everywhere I went, students either stared or pointed and laughed. Whispering amongst themselves. Waiting for a showdown that wasn't going to come. They'd missed it by leaving.

It became obvious after the first period that a lot of the whispers were about me, about what they'd heard during the summer and speculation about what had happened on campus while they were all at home. However, the whispers that weren't about me were the ones I was more interested in, because they all revolved around *The Set* and how the position was most likely cursed. Nobody wanted to become the third and fourth members, even though every other year, people were vying for the chance. Or at least that was what Griff had whispered to me when we overheard some year eights talking about it.

Even if the two of them hadn't died, both Odette and Olivia would have graduated anyway, so technically the two positions up for grabs would've existed with or without murder. In previous years, *The Sect* and *The Set* got to choose their new members, but Leo had already told me that Griff and Ollie were refusing to add anyone else. Plus, the fact Leo was still on campus meant he could be a member if he wanted.

A thought flashed into my mind and I needed to get it out pronto. 'Leo?'

'Stutter?'

'Do we need to keep our relationship on the DL once school starts back up?' I moved onto my side to face him, and he did the same. 'Now that you're a member of staff and that?'

'Haven't really thought about it,' he said with a half-arsed shrug. 'Not like I'd listen even if Winifred did tell me to stop.'

'What about the parents of the kids who go here? Could they not intervene?'

'Why would they? They pay a lot of money for their kids to be looked after here, sure, but they also pay a lot of money so they're not bothered by the petty stuff. We're pretty much the same age, and you don't swim. Stop worrying.'

'Okay,' I said but knew I wouldn't stop worrying just because Leo told me to. Believe it or not, that wasn't how anxiety worked. Otherwise, we'd all just tell ourselves to get the fuck over it. 'Are you leaving The Sect?'

'Yet another thing I haven't thought about,' he said with a laugh, reaching out to brush my hair from in front of my eyes. 'You do the thinking for us.'

I laughed, but there was a tense edge to it. 'Doesn't it go against tradition? You not leaving, I mean.'

'Probably, but fuck it.' His eyes burned with an intensity that was new to me. 'I'm a Hawthorn. People won't say shit.'

From the talk I'd heard all day, Leo was right, people wouldn't say shit against him on either count.

Breathe. Only eight more months and I'd be free. Hopefully, with a great university to go to. That was the dream—the whole reason I'd returned.

Making my way to my second lesson of the day, I braced myself for the next two hours.

You guessed it, the next lesson was History with Oliver—my favourite—and yeah, okay, we'd no longer be the only two in the classroom like we were in summer, thank fuck, but I was pretty certain he'd still try and sit near me. If he hated me as much as he tried to let on, or wanted me to leave the school, you'd think he'd be on me at all times, make me miserable enough to quit, but he wasn't doing that. He was leaving me to do my thing.

Taking a seat at the back of the classroom, I ignored the attention from the other students. Back before summer, most of the other kids left me alone for the most part. Getting stabbed caused people to give you a wide berth. It seemed in their eyes, I'd had sufficient time to get the fuck over it, and the harassment could once again begin.

'Did you hear?' one girl whispered to her friend, loud enough for me to hear. 'That *trash* is with Leo now.'

'What an upgrade!' the friend replied, fanning herself with her hand. 'Leo has that whole mysterious vibe going on. So much hotter than Ollie.'

'Really? I've always preferred Ollie. He's got that whole chiselled jaw thing going on.' Both girls nodded at one another before turning their piercing gazes in my direction.

I rolled my eyes at them and they quickly snapped their heads back to the front of the room. They stopped talking when Ollie entered, and they weren't the only ones. The whole classroom fell into a silence so quiet you could've heard a pin drop.

I smothered a groan, watching as if in slow motion as he sauntered into the room without a care in the world. *Dickhead.*

As expected, he pulled out the seat at the desk next to me and casually sat down. He knew all eyes were on him, and *I* knew he loved every second of it, even if his face tried to say otherwise. His expression was a mask of stone.

'New Girl,' he said in greeting, as if the entire summer hadn't happened. Like he hadn't ignored my arse since the camp out.

My gaze stayed on the board up ahead.

'No need to be like that,' he said with deceptive calm. I bit my tongue, refraining from stooping to his level. Honestly, the boy acted like he had two personalities and I had to just go along with whatever he did, but it was hard, never knowing what side of him would present itself. 'I'm sure your boyfriend won't mind you talking to me.'

The classroom broke out into titters.

'And I'm sure your girlfriend *will*,' I snapped. As far as I was aware, he was still in a relationship—of sorts—with Ophelia. Sure, the girl had apologised to me, but I wasn't taking that at face value. I wondered how long he'd keep up the charade with Ophelia with school back in session. The students would bow down to her and *The Set* even more than before with Ollie's backing.

Thank fuck I have Leo in my corner.

Ever since the girls' apology, I'd stayed wary of them.

With the school year started, the two of them had avoided my gaze whenever I saw them, but they also hadn't done anything to make me think they still had it out for me. That couldn't be said for the two new members of *The Set*, though.

Celia and Cordelia.

Even their names made me want to barf. Once again, we had two girls with names beginning with the same letter and ending in *ia*. It made me wonder whether their parents had got together and planned it. It wouldn't surprise me—rich people did weird things. Celia and Cordelia were both brunettes, so at least they didn't all *look* the same.

They acted the way the O girls had when I first started at Hawthorn. They had the brattiness of youth—well, the brattiness of a wealthy youth—and the cocksuredness of people who were never penalised for their actions.

'Do you think that now that you've bagged another member of Hawthorn royalty you're something, bitch?' Celia sneered in the hallway one morning as she passed with Cordelia on her heels. Ignoring them, I pulled my French textbook out of my locker, hoping if I said nothing, they'd continue on their merry way.

Wishful thinking and all that shit.

Nope.

'Did you not hear what she just said?' Cordelia called, barging into my shoulder from the side. 'Don't disrespect us, slut.'

'Oh, I heard her,' I replied, 'but I didn't give a shit. Not sure if you've noticed, but I'm no longer a target.'

'Do not fucking speak to me like that,' Cordelia said, shoving me into the lockers with a hard push. The lockers at Hawthorn were made of solid wood, so being pushed into them was like being shoved into a door. *Ouch.*

My head took the full force of the impact, and my vision swam, blurred and spotty.

Oh no, they fucking didn't.

The pain—and the shock—took my breath away, but I wasn't going to let them get away with it. I was going to fight back and show these little pricks a lesson.

Skylar Crescent wasn't going down again without a fight.

I'd never noticed these little bitches last year. Clearly, they were insignificant before joining *The Set* and were making up for it.

Righting myself, I swung for Cordelia's face, landing a back-hander on her cheek with a smack. 'Do not touch me ever again!'

'Skylar!' a voice boomed down the hall. I turned to see Leo storming towards us, a face full of thunder, his eyes blazing with fire, and if I were the girls, I'd be terrified. My punch would mean shit compared to the dressing-down Leo Hawthorn could give them in such a public setting.

Leo's anger had caused a tingling sensation to sit low in my stomach, and my heart jolted. Him going all caveman was super attractive.

'What's up, Leo?' Celia said, her tone simpering. She either couldn't read the look on his face, or maybe she hadn't heard how serious our relationship was these days.

'That's Mr Hawthorn to you,' he growled, not returning her smile. 'And I just saw you provoke Skylar here.'

Cordelia was rubbing her face where my hand had slapped her and I couldn't hide the smile from my face. It felt good to stand up for myself, and I wished I'd done it earlier.

Another person joined our small group.

'Celia. Cordelia.' Ollie accompanied each name with a tilt of the head. 'Skylar, are you okay?'

'I'm fine,' I replied, still smiling wide. 'But maybe Cordelia needs to have her cheek looked at.'

'Why?' Ollie raised an eyebrow, suspicious of the joy on my face, no doubt. It was rare I looked so happy in any of the girls' presence. 'What's happening here?'

'Skylar hit me—' Cordelia started.

'Because you shoved me into a locker!' I cut her off. Leo pulled me close, and I leaned into his warmth. 'Twice!'

'Let me get one thing clear,' Ollie said, looking at the girls, his nostrils flaring. 'Touch Skylar again and Skylar hitting you will be the last thing you have to worry about. Skylar is off-limits. Touch her again and you die.' A group of students had stopped to pay attention when Celia and Cordelia first came over to me, and the group had only got bigger the longer we all stood there. Ollie raised his voice, addressing the entire hallway. 'And that goes for all of you! Skylar is protected by *The Sect* and anybody who goes against that will pay!'

Whispers broke out across the hall.

'But—' Celia stuttered.

'Shut up,' Ollie growled, 'and get out of my sight.'

They didn't need to be told twice. Within seconds, the two of them were a blur in the distance, having moved faster than I knew possible. Maybe they truly were witches.

'Thanks for that,' I said, looking into Ollie's eyes. 'I appreciate it.'

'No need to thank me, Skylar,' he said, his eyes turning away as he rubbed his jaw. Something I knew he did when deep in thought. 'It's because of me they think they can do it in the first place.' He shrugged. 'I'll see you both later.'

'What was that about?' I whispered, turning my head in Leo's direction.

He shook his head, his eyes following Ollie's back. 'Guilt, Stutter. He feels bad.'

'So he should.' And even though it was me who said the words, I wasn't sure I believed them anymore. Well, not entirely. Of course the boy should feel bad for the shit he put me through, but all he needed to do was apologise. Although making it clear to the school I was off-limits was a step in the right direction, and I couldn't overlook that. I gathered my things and shut my locker door. Leo wrapped his arm around my shoulder, and we walked away from the group of kids still hanging around, waiting for whatever happened next.

'If you were having a problem with them, you should've told me,' he chided me, and I felt like a scolded child. The graze of his fingertips on the back of my neck caught me off guard but also instantly calmed me.

'Literally, that's the first time they've spoken to me,' I told him, telling the truth, leaning into his oh-so-welcome touch. 'Think they just wanted to assert their power, make it clear they're big fish here.'

'Well, they're not and like with most people, the power is in their mind only.' On reaching an alcove, he pulled me close, hiding us away from the onlookers in the hallway. It was odd to be standing here with him, in a position I'd been in with Ollie more than once last school year. 'What lesson have you got next?'

'I have a free now, but French after that.' Looking at Leo, I realised how attractive I found him. Okay, that was bullshit. I already knew how devilishly handsome he was, but with him no longer in uniform, he seemed even more alluring.

As the assistant swim coach, he wore casual clothes; grey joggers and a white fitted T-shirt. No idea why, but I fucking adored a guy in grey. Especially *this* guy. His muscles rippled underneath as he reached out to stroke my arms, and my pulse quickened.

'You're free now?' A cheeky glint flashed in his electric blue eyes. 'How should we spend it?'

I blinked, a thrill running through me at the seduction in his tone. 'You don't need to be anywhere?'

'Only wherever you are.'

I blushed, not knowing whether he was acting up for the students still filtering through the hallway, or whether he genuinely meant it.

'Oh, shut up!' I scoffed, and a small chuckle escaped my lips. I beamed at him, happy in that moment, the two of us holding one another close. 'Let's go to your room.'

'That's one of the best ideas you've had, Stutter.'

If I could have paused the moment, I would have.

But sadly, we rarely get what we wish for in life.

Twenty-Eight

MR HAWKINS.

There was something terribly fucking off about that man.

Attractive? Yes.

Creepy? *Fuck yes.*

Ever since the end of summer, I'd hoped he wouldn't want to continue our private tutoring sessions. Hoped his schedule would make him too busy, or that I'd improved enough to not need them, but he'd told me we should wait until after my next mock exam to know for definite. If he were anybody else, I'd agree. It made sense for the lessons to continue—didn't mean I had to like it.

I watched as he prowled in front of the board, answering a question from some girl in the front row who hadn't stopped batting her eyelashes at him since he entered. It was sickening to watch, but I couldn't draw my eyes away from it.

When the lesson came to an end, and the rest of the students were filing out of the classroom, making loads of noise as they did, I threw my notebook into my bag, hoping to get out as quickly as I could. Then I heard him. 'Ms Crescent, I'd like you to stay behind to discuss our tutoring schedule.'

I looked over to where he was standing, and his eyes were alight with an emotion I couldn't place. My stomach dropped, and I inhaled a deep breath before responding. 'Sure.'

He waited until everybody else had vacated the classroom before he spoke again.

'Sky,' he said, dropping my surname the moment everyone was out of earshot. 'I've arranged a schedule for us to work on your français.' He gave a small chortle, as if he'd told a funny joke.

He hadn't.

'Cool beans,' I said, itching to get out of here and head to lunch, shuffling from foot to foot, wondering if he was going to say any more. After a pause, one in which he'd said nothing, I went to walk away, but a movement in my peripheral stopped me.

Mr Hawkins had moved around his desk, so he was standing on my side of it—the pungent scent of his cologne entered my nostrils, a spicy, overwhelming smell, but expensive. It burned.

'I thought we could have a session now,' he asked, and with every word, he took a small step closer to the door. 'You're free, yeah?'

'It's lunchtime,' I told him. My stomach rumbled to make a point, and all I wanted was to go meet Clo. We'd agreed that because it was the first day back, we'd eat lunch together, just us two, no Griff or Leo allowed.

'It is,' he said, unbothered. 'But you need to pass your exam, don't you?'

The bolt of the door being pushed across brought me out of the funk I'd slipped into. His light brown eyes were no longer light, but the deepest black. His entire face twisted into an expression that struck fear in me. Gone was the nice guy. The handsome teacher all the girls wanted the attention of.

'We both know you want to pass. So, let's practise now.' His tone was ominous, his demeanour twisted, and the enormity of the situation registered in my brain.

Without even making a conscious decision, I moved a step back even though I had nowhere to go. I was a big enough girl to admit I was scared.

Terrified, actually.

He may be tall and thin, but that didn't mean he wasn't

strong. He could overpower me if he wanted to, and if the gleam in his eyes was any indication, he wanted to. The bulge in his slacks told me all I needed to know. The power he wielded excited him and trapping me gave him a sick thrill.

I wondered how long he'd been planning to get me alone, or whether he had seen the opportunity and run with it. All summer we were alone in the room, just us two, yet he'd made no move. Now the campus was crawling with people, so why would he choose a time when he could get caught?

Stumbling back, the backs of my legs hit the edge of his desk and my mind reverted back to my bedroom at home on the day I first came to Hawthorn. Like Andy, Mr Hawkins had given me the creeps for some time, but I'd never thought either of them would act upon their sick fantasies.

Glancing around the room, I looked for anything I could use as a shield or a weapon of sorts. With my focus elsewhere, Mr Hawkins bounded across the short distance between us and pushed me up against the desk, leaving me with no room to get free.

His hardness pressed into my stomach and disgust filled me.

'Scared, Skylar?' His face transformed from his sneer, and it was so close to mine, I could see the stubble on his chin. Before, I'd found that sort of unkempt look exciting, attractive, but I knew from that moment on it would forever repulse me. *He* repulsed me.

'N-no,' I said, attempting to sound strong.

My thoughts kept repeating the same thing: *please, please don't do this.*

The door handle rattled, and my wishful thinking went into overdrive. Please let whoever it was on the other side of the door be Leo or Griff, or fuck, I'd even accept it being Ollie. I hoped Clo had raised the alarm when I wasn't waiting for her in the dining hall.

His large hand slowly pushed my chest down until I was lying flat out on the desk. I dug my fingers into his forearms, hoping I could hurt him enough to stop his movement, stop his strength from pushing me down, but it was useless. *I* was useless. I'd never been very strong, and my nails barely left a dent.

'Ever since I laid eyes on you, I knew I had to have you. Had to get you alone. And I tried so hard to fight the urge, but I can't fight it anymore. I want you underneath me, squirming under my touch.' His foul breath covered my face, and it felt like a mask, like clay blocking my skin. 'You are perfect.'

'Somebody will f-find out,' I whispered, showing my fear. I knew I shouldn't, knew it would only arouse him further, but my fear won out.

'You won't say a word,' he growled, pressing me further into the table. 'Not like anybody will believe you.'

'Leo will.' The second the words left my mouth, I doubted them. I hated the way Mr Hawkins was making me doubt Leo of all people. Hated how he'd spouted his poison into my ear and was changing the way I thought.

'Will he really?' he asked, then chuckled sardonically, raising one dark, bushy eyebrow.

'Y-yes.'

He stood up and looked down at me, perusing me from head to toe. With his weight lifted off me, I wondered if I could fight him. Would I have enough strength to beat him?

I moved my hands to my side, to support my weight as I lifted myself up.

'Oh no, you don't,' he said, pushing me back down with one palm with little effort, then undid his tie, opening his top button.

My body wasn't cooperating. My limbs were heavy, like stone blocks weighing me down. There was no way I could try to get free again without him overpowering me. He'd already done it once with ease.

The sound of his zipper echoed in the otherwise silent classroom, and I gulped. Mr Hawkins took advantage of my brief second gasp and shoved his balled-up tie inside my mouth.

'Be quiet, bitch,' he hissed, repositioning himself.

The ripping of my tights disturbed me, and then my fight or

flight kicked in. Fuck him. Fuck the power he was trying to exert over me!

No man, no teacher, nobody in a position of power, should get away with something so heinous. So wrong. So fucking wrong. He wasn't going to get away with it. I wouldn't let him.

Tears filled my eyes as I struggled to breathe through the gag in my mouth. I thrashed around, but I was struggling under his domineering grip. I'd always found it hard to breathe through my nose, and I was fighting to keep my gag reflex under control, the rolled-up fabric filling my mouth completely.

I needed to feel in control of some small fragment of my life.

Breathe in. Breathe out. I stopped fighting and attempted to calm down. A level head may help, may help me see a way out that I hadn't found yet, and I had to try.

'That's it. Stop fighting this. It's inevitable,' he said, his soft voice entering my ear and trickling through me like syrup. Thick, sickly sweet syrup that wouldn't come away no matter how hard I tried to mentally scrub it gone.

With dark intention, he moved my underwear to the side. Air touched my bare skin. A large, thick finger entered me, and I had to swallow to prevent the scream threatening to tear from my throat.

The lack of lubrication meant that his finger was met with obstruction. Not that he cared. My lack of lubrication was only making him want me more. His eyes were wide, bloodshot, and slightly crazed.

'That's it, pretty baby. Open for me.'

I gagged.

Another finger entered me, stretching me too far, and I cried out in pain from behind the tie. The tears still not leaving my eyes, stubborn and strong, blurring my vision.

A thudding noise came from the door, and all I wanted was for somebody to enter and get him away from me. Get his vile fingers out of me.

Please. I'll do anything.

Did I somehow deserve it? Was it somehow my fault? Had I

given him the wrong impression? Laughed too loud at any of his jokes? Smiled too much?

My mind was spiralling.

He was still moving, but I could no longer feel it.

Numb.

Empty.

Alone.

The door burst open, almost flying off its hinges, and I looked towards it, hoping to see somebody who cared about me. Somebody who would rescue me, no questions asked.

'Sky!' Ollie called, flying through the door. I didn't know how he'd got in. All I knew was how thankful I was that he had. Nothing else mattered.

Ollie grabbed Mr Hawkins by the shoulders and pulled him off of me, turned him around, and punched him so hard his face swung out to the side from the power. Ollie's face had turned red, and I knew he was lost to me. He kept punching, even after Mr Hawkins had hit the ground and had fallen unconscious.

Punch. Punch. Punch.

'Ollie!' I screamed, scared of the rage on his face. Scared he was going to kill him. 'Stop!'

He looked at me, blood spattered on his face, his electric blues now darker than ever before. Black, to the point you couldn't tell the pupil from the iris.

'Come back,' I whispered, my tears leaving my eyes and slowly travelling down my cheeks. His eyes softened and creased at the sides. Moving towards me tentatively, so I wouldn't flinch or move away.

'Are you okay?' he asked, glancing back at the unconscious man on the floor when he let out a groan.

'I.' I faltered. 'I d-don't know.'

He wrapped me into a hug, being careful to treat me as if I were a porcelain doll. 'Let me take you to my suite.' He pulled back to look me in the eyes. 'I promise no funny business. I just want to make sure you're okay.'

More tears leaked out at his words. Ollie and I had a

chequered past, but in that moment, I knew he meant every word —he wouldn't cause me harm, and he cared enough about me to want to make sure I was okay. No strings attached.

'What will happen to him?' I asked, my voice wobbling. I tried not to let my gaze go to where *he* was lying, but it was very hard not to look. So instead, I looked down at myself. My uniform was disrupted and ripped, and it made me feel so fucking dirty.

'I'll make a call,' was all Ollie said.

Ollie wrapped a supportive arm around my shoulders, and slowly the two of us made our way out of the classroom, neither of us looking back.

Twenty-Nine

OLLIE

THE MOMENT we made it back to my room, Sky ran to the bathroom without a word and hurled up the contents of her stomach. In an instant, I was at her side, rubbing her back, trying to soothe her with one hand and keep her hair from her face with the other.

The tears were flowing and I crouched there feeling lost. What was I meant to do? I wasn't equipped to help her. I shouldn't be the one helping her. That job fell to Leo these days, and I was fighting the bitterness within. Sky's relationship status wasn't important.

Helping and caring for her was.

After a time, Sky stopped vomiting, flushed the toilet, and propped herself up against it, staring ahead but not seeing anything.

Knowing she wasn't about to bolt or vomit again, I pulled my phone out and messaged Leo.

I'm with Sky. I found her in Hawkins' classroom, his filthy hands all over her. He needs to go. Meet me tomorrow.

I didn't check my phone again to see if he replied, instead putting all of my focus on Sky once more. I wanted her to know I was there for her, even if things between us weren't good—that I cared and hated seeing her so miserable and lost.

'Come on, bub,' I said, crouching down to put us at eye level. 'Want to come get comfortable and watch a film?'

She nodded, wiping her tears with the back of her hands. 'O-okay.'

I helped her to stand, and the two of us hobbled over to my bed. It wasn't lost on me that I'd never expected to see Skylar on my bed again—or in my room. The hatred I'd burned with towards her for too long had thawed, but something was holding me back from talking to her and telling her the truth about why we did what we did. She'd forgiven Griff and Leo, yet was still giving me the cold shoulder.

Not like it mattered at that moment. Even if she was happy with Leo, I would support her whenever she needed.

Sky lay down on the bed, and I scooted in behind her, acting as her big spoon and pulling her close. Was I crossing a line? The last time we'd spoken was in History and I'd acted like a prick to give the other kids a show. *The Sect* needed to show dominance, and I couldn't let anybody know I was bummed about Skylar choosing Leo, or that I cared about her when I'd made it clear the year before she was shit on my shoe.

After an hour of lying together, breathing in her scent, I broke the silence.

Tentatively, I whispered, 'Baby, I think you should have a bath.' Sky was still in the foetal position and my arms were covering her to keep her safe. I didn't want to startle her.

When she didn't respond, I tried again, giving her a gentle squeeze to coax her to open up. To tell me to shut up. Anything. As long as she was talking to me.

'I can help,' I added, hating myself for the words as they left my lips. It wasn't right for me to help. Yes, I'd seen her naked, but under completely different circumstances. She had every right to hate me. To ask me to take her to Leo and tell me to fuck off. Scream at me. Shout. Whisper how she felt. It didn't matter. I just wanted to hear her say *something*.

'Not yet,' she whispered, a crack in her voice.

'Whatever you need,' I assured her. Then I had an idea I thought she might go for. 'Want me to put on *Pride and Prejudice?*'

It was her favourite, and she never turned down the chance to watch Mr Darcy's hand flex.

'Please,' she said, wiping away new tears from underneath her eyes. I couldn't tell what had set her off, but I didn't pry. She'd tell me if she wanted to.

I went about setting up the TV and putting the film on, as Sky chuckled darkly from the bed.

'Everything okay?' I tried not to sound worried, but it was hard. The laugh was like one of those evil villains in a cartoon and it sounded out of place coming from Sky's lips. The springs in the mattress bounced as I got back on the bed, wrapping my arms around her once more.

She shuffled and turned in my arms, putting the two of us chest to chest. She inhaled deeply, looking into my eyes. 'I don't want to cry anymore.'

'What do you want?'

'I don't know,' she murmured, her small button nose wrinkling as she thought about it. My hand reached out to her, to stroke her face, to touch her cute nose. The flinch she gave when my finger made contact with her skin set my blood on fire. The beating I'd given that wanker wasn't enough damage. Touching Skylar was a big mistake.

I caught a tear as it ran down her cheek and all I wanted was to distract her.

'I've watched this film a lot recently,' I confessed.

'You have?' She looked up at me, her nose wrinkling even more than before, and I smiled softly at her. She was so damn beautiful.

'Yeah.' My hand gravitated towards her hip, and I drew patterns there, taking pleasure when she shivered from my touch.

'Why?' Her eyes searched mine, seeking an answer I was reluctant to give, even though I'd started the line of conversation in the first place. My confession, although small, was a big deal for multiple reasons. It could change the vibe, and the tenderness of the last hours could shatter.

'Reminds me of you,' I whispered, glancing at the screen as the opening montage began. Eliza Bennet appeared on screen, and I smiled, for some reason always reminded of my mum and her sister. Guess it was because of Aunt Eliza sharing the name rather than any attributes or actions, but still. Although it felt silly to admit it, the film comforted me in more ways than one.

'In a good way?' she asked, more interested in me than the screen.

I laughed under my breath and admitted, 'Depends.'

'On?'

'On what day it is.'

Her bright blue eyes were staring into mine, searching for a soul I was only just beginning to notice myself. Growing up, I always thought I was soulless. My mum dying only confirmed it. Of course I was. My mother wouldn't have chosen to leave me if I had a soul worth saving.

'Oh well, that explains it,' she joked, showing a hint of the Sky I knew. 'Feel like I know exactly what you mean now.'

'On whether I've spent time around you, or you and Leo, that day,' I admitted, squirming at my truth, but with the start out in the open, it made sense to follow it through. 'On those days, I put this on to remind myself of how much I hate you.'

And that I hate my mum for leaving me the way she did.

'Not gonna lie, but that's pretty fucked up,' she said, chuckling.

'You're telling me,' I said, blunt but soft.

'So, you do hate me?' She bit her bottom lip, and I wished I could bite it. But she wasn't mine. I couldn't do that to her. My hand gripped her hip, pushing in my fingers, feeling her solid beneath me. 'That isn't something you made up to piss me off?'

'I want to hate you,' I admitted. And I meant every word. I wanted to hate her so fucking bad. And for so long I *did* hate her, but that was back before I knew her. Before I heard her laugh, saw her smile, felt her lips pressed against mine. Everything had got so twisted so fast, and I'd had no choice but to continue with the plan even when my mind was battling my heart.

'I wish I hated you, too,' she admitted. 'Would make things a hell of a lot easier.'

Our eyes locked. I gravitated towards her at the same time she gravitated towards me. Like a magnet was pulling our bodies together without our say so, our lips clashed in a mix of lips and tongues, a different kind of passion. It was real. A kiss we both wanted. That wasn't a part of a scheme or some kind of humiliation plot.

A kiss with genuine affection.

Sky moaned into my mouth, and I hardened in my trousers, wanting so badly to do all the things to her I fantasised about at night. She pushed her body closer, hooking her leg over my hip, placing her heat where I wanted her most.

'We should stop,' I whispered in between kisses. 'You're with Leo.'

'No,' she said, trying with all her strength—which wasn't a lot —to pull my head back down to hers to place my lips on hers again.

'Yes,' I growled, using my strength to resist her. I knew it was wrong, but I also knew I wouldn't stop if she told me not to. After the day Sky had, I was letting her lead it wherever she wanted it to go. Never again would I ignore her, or assume she wanted something just because of our past. I'd learned my lesson after the library, and it didn't sit well with me that not too long ago, I'd done a similar thing to what happened in that classroom with Mr Hawkins.

With mental clarity, I moved her leg away and moved back a little to create some space—both mentally and physically —between us.

'Why?' she whispered. Her bottom lip wobbled as tears filled her eyes. *Shit.* I didn't want her to think I was rejecting her. Far from it. I just wanted to make sure she wasn't going to regret any decision she made.

'Because of what happened earlier,' I said, making it clear that was the main reason for my hesitation, but I also didn't want to lie and pretend the library never took place. 'And what happened in the library between us. I was a prick and I didn't listen to you.'

'Please don't remind me,' she pleaded, covering her ears with her hands when she saw me open my mouth to say more. Blocking it out wouldn't work in the long run, but I couldn't bring myself to bring up that blackness again. 'And you're not listening to me now either.'

'Sky...'

'No, Oliver,' she growled, baring her teeth, but then her face softened, and her large blue eyes blinked at me. Wiping the tears away. 'Make me forget.'

'What?'

'You heard me.' She blinked again, her eyes clear and bright and sure. 'Make me forget what happened.'

'Sky...' I repeated. Fuck, I wanted to. I really did, but I also didn't want her to hate me for anything afterwards. Not when we were so at odds all the time. Every thought about her clouded my head. My time with Sky was a rollercoaster—due to my own actions—and now we were parked in the station, deciding whether to have another ride or get out of the vehicle and leave.

'Please.'

'What about Leo?' I asked, hoping I didn't sound bitter. Not like I'd done anything to show I deserved her or to be her boyfriend. Fuck, she probably didn't even know I'd want that. Or maybe she thought Ophelia and I were real.

'He never has to know,' she whispered, closing the gap between us.

Shit. She was going to make saying no hard for me—not that she hadn't already. But my actions would change everything if I let her go through with it.

Fuck it.

You only live once, right? And Skylar Crescent was destined to be mine, Leo be damned. She just didn't see it yet.

With no more thought, my hand grabbed her hip and pulled her close to me, closing the distance.

I swore and captured her lips with mine. Sky's moans ensured all bets were off. She moved on top of me, and I let her. Gave over that control she was so desperately seeking.

Sky moved against me, bucking her hips so that her centre rubbed up against my hard dick, causing the most delicious friction. Roaming her body, my hands explored until they settled on her hips to help guide her, increasing the motion.

We weren't naked, but there was something just as intimate about what was happening between us. Just as fucking powerful and meaningful. Our foreheads pressed together to the point of pain, and the air around us was as intense as the emotions within us. Her blue eyes locked with mine, and I had to blink away the strong wave of lust and love that hit me in the face.

With a grunt, I came in my boxers like a horny virgin teenage boy, and Sky came too, her face exquisite as the pleasure hit her. The strong, overwhelming sense of possessiveness came full force and knocked the breath from my body.

'Fuck, Skylar,' I whispered, my lips grazing the side of her face softly. 'You're it for me. Endgame.'

And I was fucking screwed.

Thirty

I LEFT Ollie asleep in his bed.

I didn't leave a note, and I didn't say goodbye.

Already, I was questioning my actions. Doubting myself and whether I'd done the right thing. Oh, who the fuck was I kidding? Of course I hadn't done the right thing.

Ollie had acted like a completely different person—all sweet and caring—and it had melted the ice wall I erected around myself anytime I was in his presence. He'd learned from the library, too, and had asked me multiple times whether I truly wanted him. Had asked about Leo, even. And then there I was, acting like the biggest piece of trash on the planet, telling him Leo didn't have to know.

Of course the whole thing with Leo was fake, Leo and I both knew it, but recently things were twisting and it hadn't seemed quite so false.

I hung my head in shame, creeping towards Leo's room, hoping not to alert anybody in the building to my presence. The events of the day washed over me, covering me from head to toe, and I wanted to scrub my skin with a sponge until I was left red and raw.

Leo deserved to know all of it, and I intended to leave nothing out.

Not because I owed him shit, but because I *wanted* to. I

wanted to talk to him; felt a compelling need to be honest with him.

The knock on his door echoed in the empty, dark hallway and I shivered, the cold air of the evening seeping its way into my bones.

Leo opened the door, and the minute I saw his face, saw his azure eyes looking at me, I burst into tears. All the emotions and feelings of the day were catching up with me, and I was drained.

'Come in, Stutter.' Leo pulled the door open and moved aside so I could enter. The moment he closed the door behind him, I threw myself into his arms, not giving him a moment to second-guess his reaction. 'Who do I need to beat up?'

'Mr H-Hawkins,' I managed to say through my sobs. 'He a-attacked me. Then Ollie c-came in. And then I... I went to his room and...'

I knew I wasn't making much sense, my tears overwhelming me, my words running into one another.

'Come on,' he said, slowly manoeuvring me to the edge of his bed. We sat down, our hands gripped tightly together—you'd have had to break my fingers to get my hand out of his. I needed his warmth. His safety. 'Take a deep breath, Stutter.'

'I'm so sorry,' I said in a whisper. What kind of shit human came and laid their crap at somebody else's door? Me, that was who. Maybe I was as low as the O girls always told me I was.

'What for?' he asked, frowning. 'Skylar, you've got nothing to apologise for.'

Hearing him use my name had me cracking further. 'Mr Hawkins cornered me in his classroom after the lesson. He tried to'—I swallowed, knowing I couldn't say the word without vomit rising up from my stomach—'you know.'

My voice was barely audible. I worried Leo would make me repeat myself, but he didn't. He just pulled me to him, awkward as fuck with my hands still trapped in his.

I'd always wondered if your heart could fall for two people at the same time. Was it possible to love two people, but in two completely different ways?

My heart fluttered when one of his hands unlatched from mine, and he reached out to touch my cheek to wipe my tears away, a soft smile making his features look kind and approachable and as if he cared. Maybe he did a little? With Leo, it was so hard to know for definite what he was thinking.

'He's gone, Skylar. Nobody touches you and gets away with it.' His calm response was so at odds with Ollie's, but it meant the same to me. A quiet calm could be just as deadly as a raging storm.

'You promise?' I asked. Even though Ollie had said the same thing, I didn't know if he held the power to make it happen. If either of them did. But then I remembered Leo's dad owned the school, so I suppose they had more sway than others.

'Of course,' he said, his words reassuring. He rested his hand on my shoulder, and I shivered. 'How dare he touch you? The fucker's lucky if we leave him alive.'

I smiled for the first time in hours.

Leo had that effect on me.

'There's something else I need to tell you,' I whispered, not wanting the words out in the universe but knowing I couldn't rest until they were out.

'What's up?'

I just needed to blurt it out. 'I made out with Ollie.' I swallowed, my face flushing. 'Actually, I think I sort of—no, not sort of but actually—dry humped him.'

Leo's top lip twitched, and if he started laughing at me, I swear I'd break out into tears again. He could judge me for it, sure, but if he laughed at me, I wasn't sure I'd live it down.

'Stutter,' Leo said, a smile on his lips for real. 'I'm not going to judge you. You had a horrible day and he showed a side he rarely shows anybody. I get it.'

'You don't think I'm a stupid cow?'

'Do you think you're a stupid cow?' His voice was low and smooth and I wanted to drown in it.

'Maybe.' I shrugged. 'I'm meant to be getting revenge on Ollie, not kissing him and making him come.'

'That's enough on the info there, Stutter,' Leo said, but his smile remained, so I knew he wasn't mad at me. 'Emotions can be a bitch, and I don't know a lot in this life, but one thing I do know? You're not a stupid cow. You're the furthest from it.'

'Promise?'

'I promise.' He leaned forward and placed a kiss on my temple. 'Are you staying? Or do you want me to walk you back to your room?'

'Can I stay? I'd rather not face Clover or Griff right now.'

'Oh, so it has nothing to do with my winning company?' he teased.

'Well, I couldn't be so blatant,' I replied with a laugh. 'Can't have you knowing, can I?'

His resulting chuckle sent shockwaves through me. 'There's a spare key for my suite I want you to have. You can come here whenever you need rescuing.'

'Thanks,' I said, surprised and overwhelmed by the gesture.

And for the rest of the evening, he took my mind off of everything. Well, mostly everything. But by the end of the night, I'd forgotten what happened with Ollie, what happened with Mr Hawkins, and most importantly, he made me realise none of it was my fault.

The only thing he couldn't take my mind off was how I felt towards him. How I felt towards Ollie. About Ollie calling us endgame.

And those thoughts were the loudest.

Even as I lay in bed next to Leo, sleeping next to him for the first time since the tent, and the first time in an actual bed, my mind was caught between him and Ollie.

'Sleep, Stutter. Turn your brain off,' he whispered in my ear, squeezing my waist and pulling me closer. 'Sure we can worry more when we wake.'

I smiled to myself, the way I always did when Leo let on just how well he knew me.

Really knew me.

Thirty-One

'HOW ARE THINGS GOING WITH LEO?' Clo asked, looking at me, her gaze intense, the question out of the blue.

Recently, the two of us had had little time to shoot the shit together. Most of the time, Clo was with Griff, even spending most nights with him, and if she was spending the night with him, I spent the night with Leo to keep up the charade. What better way to seem like a real couple than to be joined at the hip?

At first, he had slept in my bed and I'd slept in Clo's, but since the night in his room, we'd become more comfortable around one another and began to share a bed. Snuggles were nice, and I enjoyed being the big spoon. Not that I'd ever tell anybody that. Reckon even if I did, people wouldn't believe that Leo loved being the little spoon.

'Honest?' I asked, and she nodded. 'They're going pretty bloody fantastic.'

It hit me: I was telling the truth. Things *were* great. We got along; we didn't fight much as shit wasn't real. Really, we had all the perks of a real relationship—except the sexual aspect, of course. The thought of a friends-with-benefits arrangement had entered my mind once or twice, but it would complicate and confuse things that were already confused. Also, a small part of me worried it was all in my head and he'd reject me if I even suggested it.

'I'm glad,' she said, while her face looked anything but. Her beautiful green eyes didn't have any sparkle to them, and her lips had turned down at the edges.

'How are things going with Griff?' I asked, wanting to know. Not being funny, but my thoughts on their relationship hadn't changed. It still rang false to me.

'Yeah,' she said, the features of her face unwavering. No joy visible. 'They're okay.'

'Just okay?'

Look, I didn't want to rub it in—not completely—*but* I wanted her to be honest with me. We were best friends. Ride or die. And I hated how she felt like she couldn't open up to me anymore because of Leo. Or at least I assumed it was due to me being with Leo, but maybe the fact I shared blood with Griff didn't help my cause either.

'Yeah, I mean...' She looked around the room, no longer staring at me. 'We're fine.'

'You can tell me anything. You know that, right?'

She barked out a sharp laugh. 'No, Skylar, I don't know that.'

'Clo, if you're not happy, only you can change it,' I said, trying a different tactic. 'You don't have to be with him if you don't want to, you know?'

'I know that. Thank you, Captain Obvious,' she spat, sarcasm thick.

'Okay,' I said, attempting to placate her, my hands up in a *whoa* kind of gesture.

'No need to act like I'm going to bite your head off,' she grumbled, her gaze once again on me. I shuffled around my bed and perched my bum on the edge. Maybe if I sat down, I wouldn't look as threatening.

'I wasn't. I just want you to be happy.' I shrugged, at a loss to know what she wanted to hear. 'And, I don't know, I guess I've always wondered whether you're truly happy. That butterflies overtaking your stomach, can't eat or sleep kind of love.'

'What even is love?' she asked, frustrated.

It was my turn to bark out a laugh. 'Not like I'm the person to know, but I get it. Either way, I want you to have that kind of love.

I want it for Griff, too.' I took a deep breath. 'And I don't think the two of you have that together.'

'You telling me you have that kind of love with Leo?' she spat, her eyebrows rising so high, they were about to disappear into her hairline.

'No,' I replied, taken off guard. I should have realised she'd turn the tables on me. It was one of Clo's defence mechanisms, after all. To fight fire with fire. When feeling threatened, she went out of her way to make others feel worse, to take the heat off herself, with no thought of how the other person felt.

'That's what I thought,' she said with an eye roll.

'I just don't want either you or Griff to get hurt,' I added, knowing I should have just shut my mouth and left it the hell alone. *Dig that hole, Skylar.*

'Thanks for your concern, Sky, but I think you should evaluate your own life first, don't you?'

'Right.' My cheeks warmed, and it was taking a lot for me to keep my anger in check. I knew she was hitting low on purpose, and fuck, it was working.

'Everybody knows you're with Leo out of desperation.'

'Sorry,' I sputtered, 'but what the *fuck* does that even mean?'

'I—' she faltered, the regret swimming in her eyes. But for once, I wasn't going to let her off easily.

'Maybe, Clover, evaluate your life before you judge me about mine. Me and my desperate arse are out of here.' I turned around, grabbed my phone and bag, and without thinking it through, walked to the door and left, slamming it behind me.

Shit, me leaving my room after an argument was becoming a bit of a pattern. It wouldn't surprise me if cracks appeared in the ceiling from the amount of times someone had slammed our door.

I took a deep breath, blinking away the frustrated tears blurring my vision. I had to remember I'd been lying to Clo for quite a while, and there was stuff she didn't know.

There *were* genuine times between Leo and me. Like that time he sat with me in silence and disposed of a dead rabbit for me. I'd never told her about it, because I hadn't wanted her to feel unsafe in our room because of me—again.

One day, Clover and I would go an entire month without disagreeing about stupid shit.

Right?

I looked down the empty corridor, kind of at a loss for where to head. Leo was at the pool with the team, and I didn't want to be around all three of them. I hadn't spoken to Ollie since that day after... after everything, and not like I could seek out Griff for comfort as I was certain Clo would've already messaged him about our spat.

Then I remembered the conversation I'd had with Leo the other night.

There's a spare key for my suite I want you to have. You can come here whenever you need rescuing.

When he'd walked me back to my dorm the morning after, he'd slipped the key into my back pocket during our goodbye hug. Grabbing my bag, I riffled through its contents, trying to locate it.

My fingers found it in moments and I pulled it out in triumph, thankful I hadn't put it elsewhere in my room. How embarrassing would that have been? Having to go back and tell Clo I was getting the key to Leo's suite. No, thank you.

At the fastest pace known to man—okay, the fastest pace known to *me*—I made my way to the staff building. Since becoming the assistant swim coach, Leo had moved out of the boys' dorm building and had been upgraded to the biggest suite of them all.

Leo wasn't due back for at least another hour, so I knew I'd have time to work on my homework without interruption.

The moment I got comfortable on his bed, I sent him a quick text with a selfie. Even though he'd made it clear I could come to his room whenever I needed, I still wanted him to know I was there just in case.

HEY YOU. I'M IN YOUR ROOM. HAD A FIGHT WITH CLO. SEE YOU LATER, TATER.

Within seconds, my phone lit up with his response. I smiled at my screen, hoping he wouldn't be mad because I'd used the key he'd given me. That would be embarrassing. The lines of our fake relationship had blurred and I wasn't sure how to act. I'd expected it to finish once school started back up, but Leo hadn't even hinted at it.

HEY YOURSELF. DON'T GET TOO LONELY WITHOUT ME. IN A WHILE, CROCODILE.

I squealed at his cute response and then stopped myself.

Shit, bollocks, balls. I wasn't meant to be getting giddy about a text from Leo Hawthorn of all people, especially one that referenced a silly kids' nursery rhyme, right?

While I pondered my newfound dilemma, a knock reverberated throughout the suite and I froze. Did I answer it? Or just ignore it and hope whoever was on the other side would leave? Not like it was my place to open the door.

It could be a teacher.

At least I didn't have to worry about Mr Hawkins anymore. Leo was true to his word, and the very next day he was off the premises, escorted by police—something to do with drugs being found in his suite. I assumed Leo and Ollie had framed him, as they'd known I wouldn't have wanted to press charges and regurgitate what happened. I'd not asked for any more details, not wanting to have to think of that repulsive man more than my nightmares already did.

My breathing sped up, my anxiety climbing. The room spotted black, swirling in at the edges, creeping into the centre.

Another knock. *Shit.*

'Little One, it's me,' Ollie's voice called, reaching me and causing the black in my vision to recede as quickly as it had appeared. Instantly, my heart sped up for a different reason. Shouldn't he be at practise with Leo?

'Are you going to open up? Or do I have to force it?' he asked through the door, and even though there was a dark, wooden slab between us, I knew he had a smirking smile on his face.

'O-okay,' I called back, my feet moving of their own accord.

Ollie came into my view, and I couldn't help but form a small smile. His hair was wet, and his blue eyes were sparkling with mischief. He looked fucking delicious, the bastard.

'W-what are you doing here?'

'Leo said I'd find you here,' he drawled, amused. 'You going to let me in?'

'He did?' I stepped back, creating a small gap for him to enter through. He took it, brushing against me as he made his way past, and I shivered at the electricity that travelled between us. I'd said it before, and I'd say it again, but I would have sworn our bodies were drawn to one another. Our magnetism was as strong as ever, never fading.

Clearly, while I'd been in Leo's room thinking of him like a lovesick twat, he'd been telling my enemy where to find me. Okay, enemy was a strong word. We weren't enemies anymore. We'd become people who kissed sometimes and never spoke about it afterwards. Which, yeah? I *was* aware of how fucked up that was.

'How have you been?' he asked, standing in front of me, his heat entering my bubble. All I could do in response was make a noise that I thought may have been a *huh* but could also have just been nonsense. 'We don't talk enough.'

I scoffed at that. *No, Oliver, we don't talk a lot. We just kiss and avoid any feelings that aren't taking place in our underwear.*

I gave him a quizzical look. Or that was my intention, anyway. Pretty sure that instead of looking quizzical, I just looked like somebody with constipation. *Smooth.*

'And I wonder why that is,' I snapped. My anger simmered to the surface, and honestly, before that moment, I hadn't even realised the anger I was still harbouring against him. I'd tried to act cool. Act like I didn't mind that he gave me orgasms in closets and then ignored me afterwards. Act like it didn't bother me that he fingered me in the library, but then made sure I saw his make-out session with Ophelia the very next day. Act like he hadn't walked in and saved me from that fucker and made me feel better afterwards.

'Whoa.' He gestured with his hands, palms forward, as if worried I was a bomb about to explode. Maybe I was. The glint in his eyes caught my glare, and I melted a little. Damn. Ollie's eyes were one of his best features. The chiselled jaw was hot, and his full lips were pretty great to kiss, but those eyes made me see stars.

'What?' I muttered, irritated that his eyes had such an effect on me and my anger.

'You look crazy fucking beautiful when you're mad. Have I told you that?'

'Yeah, once or twice,' I grumbled.

'Interesting.'

I rolled my eyes. 'Seriously, Ollie. Why are you here?'

'I wanted to see you. Talk to you. Apologise to you,' he said, as if that were the most obvious answer. Like I should have known all along he had sought me out to apologise. You know, because he was such an apologetic person.

'I thought you were at swim practise?' I brushed my hair behind my ear, trying to keep my hands—and my mind—busy.

'I left early. I told Leo I wanted to talk to you.' He shrugged.

'I told Leo about what happened between us,' I said, wanting to make it clear I hadn't hidden it from him. Ollie didn't know my relationship wasn't real, and I wanted it to stay that way. I didn't need a repeat. 'After...'

He nodded, his eyes swimming with anger. 'Oh.'

My patience with him breathing the same air as me was wearing thin. 'You want to talk, Oliver, then talk.'

'We're back to Oliver, are we?' He was amused at my frustration. My cheeks were flushed, and I could sense a rash forming on my chest. I hated when that happened, but it always seemed to happen in times of stress or aggravation. An ugly, angry, blotchy rash. Eurgh. 'I thought we were over that.'

'We're not friends,' I told him.

'What are we then?' He laughed at me, a low, deep chuckle that caused the hairs on my arms to stand on end.

'We're nothing,' I said with a sigh, my shoulders rising and dropping as if the weight of the world weighed them down. 'Just people who never really knew one another.'

'What makes you think you never knew me?'

'Are you fucking serious?' How could he even stand there and ask me that question with a straight face? Seriously, how did this boy sleep easy at night?

'Come off it, Sky. Not everything between us was fake.'

'Explain,' I demanded, my throat scratchy at how low those words had been uttered. 'Then maybe I'll believe you.'

'All in good time,' he whispered, leaning down to talk into my ear. 'I see you shiver in... anticipation.'

My resulting smile was involuntary. I loved that movie, but—huh? Odd. Last time I'd begged to watch it, back when we were "dating", Ollie had refused. Said it was *too confusing* and *too camp*.

Of course it's camp!

'I thought you hated *Rocky Horror*?'

'Yep,' he drawled, 'but you don't.'

He was right. I didn't hate it. I pulled my head back to look into his eyes, to search them, see if there was any falsehood there. Any lies simmering under the surface. But I couldn't see any. Not that I'd ever known what to look for.

'Right,' I muttered, a bit pissed he knew me better than I knew him. But it made sense. *I've never lied about who I am.*

'Little One, you do know me. The *real* me.'

'P-please, just go.' I shoved him towards the door, wanting him out of my space. Breathing the same air as him was torture most of the time, but in Leo's room, it was too intimate. Too much.

'Fine,' he murmured, 'but I promise we *will* sort this out.' He kissed my cheek, the slightest graze of lips that reached me deep down in my soul—well, there and somewhere else. 'Oh, and before I go. There's a party in the woods Friday night.'

I nodded at him. Of course there was. It was the beginning of school, after all, and the party in the woods I'd attended last year was where the whole *Ollie fingered me up against a tree while the girls filmed it situation* happened. How could I forget such a night?

'See you there,' he said, his tone ominous, and then he opened the door and left me standing there alone, unsure what to do next.

Thirty-Two

NOT LONG AFTER OLLIE LEFT, Leo returned, yet I couldn't get excited. It felt like he'd thrown me to the big bad wolf without a heads-up. Ollie's ominous departing words played in my head in a loop and I wondered whether I should avoid the party on Friday at all costs.

'You okay?' Leo asked, hugging me tight to him.

'You told Ollie I was here?' I asked, not answering him. I hoped hugging me was like hugging a sack of potatoes—or a corpse—cold and unmoving, no part of me reciprocating the tightness of Leo's strong, muscled arms around me. 'Why would you do that?'

One thing I'd learned in all the time I spent with Leo was that the boy could hide his genuine feelings in the bat of an eye. Sometimes, I caught him off guard and saw a glimpse of the real Leo hiding behind the boredom, but it was rare. The moment my question left my lips, his face shuttered over, the darkness creeping in, but not before he looked guilty for the tiniest moment. A blink-and-you'd-miss-it moment in time.

'Did he bother you?' he asked darkly, not denying the fact he'd told him where to find me.

'Not exactly,' I said evasively, taking in a deep breath, preparing myself to ask a hard question, but before I could bring myself to ask it, Leo spoke.

'He told me he wanted to apologise.' He let me out of our hug, and the two of us moved to sit on the edge of his bed. 'Sorry if I fucked up.'

Leo rested his hand on my knee, moving his finger in a repetitive circular motion, causing me to shiver.

'He didn't,' I blurted out. Then to clarify, added, 'Apologise, I mean.'

'Pity,' Leo drawled. 'The boy clearly hasn't learned from his mistakes.'

'What are we doing?' I sputtered. The question plagued me anytime it entered my mind, and my reaction to his message earlier solidified that I needed to clear things up with him. The fact I'd sought solace in his room spoke volumes to me, but I wanted to know where Leo stood before I blurted anything out.

His dark eyebrows slanted into a frown. 'What do you mean?'

'I mean, what are we doing? We've been in this fake relationship for a couple of months, and we've hurt the people we intended to hurt.' I shrugged, unsure of myself. 'Or disgruntled them, at least.'

'You saying you want out?' he asked, his hand coming up to grip the bottom of my chin and move my head so we were nose to nose. His breath touched my face, our lips close enough for my mind to go elsewhere.

Stay focused, Skylar.

The two of us had kissed, yes. Multiple times. Usually, it was for show in front of other people and didn't mean much more. There were a couple of occasions where we'd kissed in private, and I always brushed those off in my mind as the two of us getting caught up in our fake moment. We spent so much time together, it was only natural to explore the chemistry that thrummed between us.

But things felt different. More real.

'N-no,' I whispered. 'Unless you do?'

'I don't,' he whispered back. Our eyes locked, his blues meeting mine, and I realised I'd never seen Leo looking so vulnerable in the entire time I'd known him.

Intimacy crept in, blurring the edges of everything we were meant to be. Of our intentions.

'W-why?' My voice was barely audible, but Leo heard me. His eyes sparkled, intense, but I saw a glimpse of uncertainty he couldn't mask.

'Because, Stutter'—he sighed—'we're not finished yet.'

I let out the breath I'd been holding. 'We're not?'

'No.' He shook his head, his gaze never leaving mine. 'Not in our plan, and not with us.' His words hit me deep in my gut. I hadn't wanted to think too much about how my feelings for him were changing—and they *definitely* were. I no longer saw the bored dickhead I'd thought he was when I looked at him. We'd spent so much time together solo, without having to hide our true selves, I knew his bored demeanour was a front. A coping mechanism of sorts he used to stop anybody getting too close.

'Okay,' I whispered.

His lips touched mine, soft at first, but then like a cable snapping, something changed. The very air around us had heated; had become stifling. The resulting kiss differed from any other we'd shared. It wasn't a passionate kiss to make Clover jealous, or to piss Ollie off; it wasn't a gentle kiss goodnight, or something we'd stumbled upon while watching a romantic film.

No. It was a kiss filled with electricity. Lightning. *Deadly.*

Fuck. I moaned, at the same time Leo moved us so I was lying on my back, with him pressed up against me. My mind was racing. *Abort. Abort.*

But I couldn't bring myself to stop. Or to ask him to stop.

Our tongues were tangled together, neither of us stopping when our teeth clashed. His dick was pressing into me and I shuddered at the forbidden thoughts racing through my head. Leo growled and took my bottom lip between his teeth and bit down so hard I tasted metal.

The fucker had drawn blood.

I should be disgusted, but after that time in the closet with Ollie, I'd been a lot more open to the darker side of life. I'd gone from a timid virgin to some kind of vixen—or at least that was how I felt—and it felt fucking awesome.

One thing I knew about my fake relationship with Leo? That it had helped me grow in confidence. My anxiety still lived in me. I doubted it would ever disappear, but it rarely showed anymore. I couldn't even remember my last anxiety attack—ignoring the moment earlier in the evening when Ollie knocked. And I was totally ignoring it.

'Stutter,' Leo moaned, somehow making the nickname sound like a seductive caress, as opposed to the slur it had started out as. 'Get out of your head.'

'How'd you know I was in there?'

'Because I know you,' he replied in between placing kisses on my neck.

'Leo,' I moaned back, the weight of him causing my lungs to strain a little. Fuck, why was it so hot to hear somebody tell you they knew you? And to actually believe them only made it that much hotter.

He eased off, breaking the kiss to look at me, his eyes searching for an answer to a question he hadn't voiced out loud, but one I could hear just as loud as if he had. *Are you sure? Is this okay?*

Without putting any thought into it, I nodded, encouraging him to continue. He needed little persuading, and instantly his lips were back on mine, his right hand cupping my breast, squeezing me roughly above my uniform.

I gasped and tightened my grip on his hips.

Leo moved and lifted himself off me, but before I could start to protest his absence, he slowly peeled my skirt and underwear down my legs in a slow, seductive way that had me clenching my thighs together.

Shit. Once I was bared to him, he paused in his perusal to kiss me, and instinctively my body arched towards his, wanting to be as close as possible. He broke our kiss and moved down my body, and all I could do was close my eyes to stop myself from feeling too self-conscious.

Leo's tongue touched my folds, and I clenched my thighs, trapping his head between them in an involuntary action. He chuckled. The moment he licked my centre, I lost all sense of what was happening and writhed under his touch.

He stopped to murmur, 'Look at me, Stutter.'

His words caused the hairs on my arms to stand on end, and I opened my eyes to look down at his. It was illicit and private; and so very intimate. A thrill of excitement shot through my veins, as Leo's tongue returned to my core, and he inserted a finger to beckon at that most inner part of me.

A knot formed in my throat, and I bit my lip to stifle my outcry of ecstasy when everything reached its peak.

'Fuck,' Leo said, his voice thick, moving to gaze up at me, and I shivered at the glimmer of possession in his eyes.

No longer able to stop myself, I lifted myself up and grabbed his hair, bringing his head to my level, gripped the back of his neck and pulled his mouth down to mine. He growled and bit my lip again, unleashing a feral side of me. A side I never knew I possessed. I grabbed his waist and fumbled with the button on his trousers, needing to hold his dick in my hand; needing to feel his warmth and how turned on he was. A compulsion of sorts.

'Are you sure?' he asked, using his finger to tilt my chin up; to look me in the eye and see my confirmation.

'P-positive,' I said, breathless. My heart thudded away in my chest as I watched his lips turn up into a satisfied smile. 'Are you?'

'Lie down,' he commanded, and I did as he said, the obedience coming from somewhere deep within. He undid the button of his trousers and took them off, revealing his enormous dick to me. 'Are you a good girl, Stutter?'

Why was it so fucking sexy to be called a good girl? What a fucking rush. I nodded. 'I'm always a good girl.'

'Do you trust me?' he asked, and I nodded once more. I trusted him, and the fact we were about to fuck meant I'd let him in a lot more than I first realised.

His touch set my skin on fire. He grabbed my legs and hooked them over his shoulders. Slowly, he pushed inside me, letting me adjust to every inch. My walls adjusted around him, and I could feel myself clenching and unclenching the further he pushed. *Fuck.*

Once fully seated inside of me, Leo thrust, holding my hips in a tight grip so that we would stay joined together. The emotions swirling in the air spurred us on, and with each thrust, the intensity increased. Our eyes locked; neither one of us wanting to look away. I couldn't believe I was in such an intimate position with Leo. It didn't compute.

I tried to turn my brain off. To swim in the sensation of his touch. But it was hard.

I was an overthinker by nature.

'Come with me,' he whispered, coaxing me. The pad of his thumb found my clit, teasing it in slow, pressured circles and sending me into a frenzy as my body fought for release.

'Oh, fuck,' I panted, almost there.

'Now,' he bit out, and the sound of his voice, the look on his face, pushed me over the edge.

Leo increased his speed, and I knew he was as ready to finish as me. His hot cum filled me, and the sensation overwhelmed me. I groaned in pleasure and went lightheaded.

Fuck.

That was definitely *not* a part of the plan.

Thirty-Three

THE START of the school year party in the woods.

Believe it or not, I wasn't looking forward to it. I didn't have an impressive track record with school parties in the woods—or just the woods in general—and I'd hoped Leo would want to avoid it too.

'Do we have to?' I whined to nobody in particular. I got a resounding response of yes from the other occupants in the room.

Clover, Griff, Leo, and I had all crowded into Clo's and my tiny room. Still couldn't put my finger on why that was, seeing as you could fit our room in Griff's or Leo's at least twice over, but here we were.

'It'll be fun, jelly tot,' Griff said, an enormous grin on his face. He donned a tight-fitted shirt and jeans, and from the appreciative glances Clover kept throwing at him, the boy was going to have some fun tonight.

Since our argument, Clo and I hadn't talked about her relationship with Griff, or mine with Leo. It seemed easier that way. Avoidance may not be healthy, but it meant we didn't argue every time we opened our mouths, so that was a win in my books.

'Yeah, yeah,' I said. Leo came up behind me and wrapped his arms around my waist. I leaned into him and smiled. Ever since the other night in his room, the two of us were more comfortable around one another. More natural.

The line was no longer blurred. It had disappeared entirely.

'You've got this,' he whispered in my ear and I sighed. He knew I was a sucker for ASMR, and he'd been going out of his way to give me tingles. To me, it was like an egg being cracked on the top of my head, travelling down and leaving goo in its wake.

'Shall we pre-drink?' Clo asked, irritation at the two of us obvious if her scowl was any indication. It was a pretty scowl, but a scowl nonetheless.

'I'm game,' I said with a shrug. Not like I was in any rush to head into the woods. I wasn't in any damn musical.

'Fine,' Leo agreed, sounding bored, or at least that was the impression he was trying to give off. I hadn't asked him how he felt about Clo anymore. If I were being honest with myself, I didn't *want* to know the truth, even though I needed to. Maybe I'd ask him once the alcohol hit my system and I was feeling the effects of liquid courage.

'Let's get this show on the road, bitches,' Griff called, pulling a bottle of vodka out of nowhere.

'Dude, you can't call us bitches,' Clo said, chuckling.

'If I can't call us bitches, you can't call me dude,' he replied, a smug grin on his face. The boy loved having a comeback at hand, even if it wasn't his best work.

I rolled my eyes at the two of them and sat on the floor cross-legged. Leo followed suit, arranging himself behind me, never breaking our touch. Clo and Griff sat down too, keeping a bit of distance between their bodies, and Griff placed a deck of cards on the floor in a circle around an empty cup. My groan was involuntary.

'When you said pre-drink, I didn't think you meant *Ring of Fire*.' *Man, I hate this game.* I was never good at the waterfall part, and there was no way in fucking hell that I would drink a dirty cup if I selected the fourth King. No way, no how.

'Yes!' Griff enthusiastically arranged the cards just so. 'It's this or *Bullshit Taxi*.'

I groaned again. It was an amalgamation of *Taxi* and *Bullshit* and one of Griff's favourite games to play. He loved handing out shots to people but rarely got to, as his face gave him away. If there was one thing for certain in life, it was that Griffin Cooper should never sit down at a table and play poker.

'Fine, *Ring of Fire* it is!' I said, faking cheer, pouring myself a vodka lemonade before making Leo a strong whiskey and Coke.

'Thanks, baby,' he said when I handed him the drink.

Clo's eyes narrowed and then I watched—in shock or awe, I couldn't decide—as she grabbed Griff's face and pulled it to hers for a big, sloppy kiss. Griff looked delighted. I sighed, but Leo didn't react. Maybe his face had, and I just couldn't see it, so I turned around and found him distracted, staring at my head, twirling my hair around his finger. I smiled at him, and when his gaze moved to mine, we shared a moment without words.

'You go first,' I said, facing the others once more, feeling only the tiniest bit smug at the look on both Clo's and Griff's faces.

The game started, and with each card turned over, we played the corresponding mini game. The longer we played, the more drunk we got.

Time passed fast, and when I looked at my phone, I saw we'd been pre-drinking for two hours and knew we needed to head to the party soon. My mood soured.

'We need to leave,' I announced to the very drunk people in the room with me. All of us were way past tipsy. 'There's a party going on.'

'You don't even want to go!' Clo pointed at me.

I laughed. 'You're not wrong there.'

'Stutter's right, though. We should go.' Leo squeezed me tight, placing a kiss on my head, sending my hormones into overdrive. The more I'd had to drink, the more I wanted a repeat of our night together. 'Do you think you'll be able to walk there?'

'Sure!' I nodded with every ounce of enthusiasm I could muster. 'I'm Superwoman.'

'Okay.' Leo gave out a low chuckle. 'Let's see your walking superpower.'

So maybe I wasn't Superwoman.

Clo and I stumbled the entire journey, falling over branches and debris, but also our own feet. Every stumble and loss of balance caused us to break out into a giggling fit.

'Stop it!' she whisper-yelled at me through laughter tears, which just made me laugh more. 'I'm going to wet myself.'

'Classy,' Griff said from in front of us. He and Leo were ahead, probably because they weren't falling all over the show.

Ha-ha. What a funny saying. All over the show.

Neither of the boys acted like they'd drunk anywhere near as much as I knew they had. Not once had they stumbled or even swayed in the breeze.

Isn't language funny? As if anybody could actually sway in the breeze.

'Oh, hush.' Clo hooked her arm tighter through mine, using me for support. 'I suppose it wouldn't be very classy of me to suck your dick later either, right?'

Her words caused me to erupt into another round of giggles. My stomach hurt just from how much I was laughing. Out of the corner of my eye, I saw Clo's face blushing a dark red. When I focused back on the treacherous path we were treading, I watched Leo elbowing Griff in that way lads do. It was always a surprise to see the guys getting on, acting the way guys their age should. At times, they seemed older and serious, but then they joked around and reminded me they were the same as everyone else.

Leo's action made me happier than I had been in some time. Would he have done that a year ago? Would he have been happy to hear that *Red* planned to suck another guy's dick? I doubted it.

Was I maybe looking too much into it? Maybe, but fucking sue me.

'Did I just say that super loud?' Clo asked, covering her face with her hands.

'Oh yeah, girl, you did.' I laughed at her expense, happy to not be the butt of the joke.

'Ground eat me whole and let the worms feast on my innards.'

'Oh, stop it. I thought it was funny.'

'You would!' she said but laughed again too, so I knew she was also seeing the funny side of it all. 'I suppose I *am* funny as fuck.'

Her tone was so serious and sure, I couldn't keep my gut reaction in.

'You *are* delusional.'

'You know it,' she muttered under her breath.

We continued walking, close to the party spot now. It had taken us *ages* because we were pissed and I was struggling to see clearly.

A shriek pierced through the air, causing goosebumps to rise on my arms in an instant.

'What the fuck was that?' Griff called out, but before any of us could answer, another ear-splitting yell reached us.

The four of us broke out into a run—*okay, I'm bullshitting*—the boys broke out into a run, and Clover and I sort of jogged behind them. Or walked at a fast pace.

The cold September air whipped at our faces, biting at us, and the two of us were too far from sober, meaning we felt sick pretty fast. We could no longer see the boys, and I couldn't get my bearings. I just hoped we hadn't run astray. Fuck knew who could be out here.

'Shit!' Griff blurted from somewhere further into the trees. Heading towards his shout, we moved as fast as we could. Whatever it was sounded serious.

Stumbling into the clearing, we found Griff and Leo standing over a very badly beaten Ophelia.

'Shit,' Clo hissed beside me.

Ophelia's lips were split, and her eyes were both bruising and swelling up. Blood covered her, and, although I couldn't see much in the darkness, it looked as if it had come from her nose, which sat oddly on her face.

Clover, looking at Ophelia more closely, moved further away and was sick up against a tree. The powerful stench of stomach acid and vodka hit my nose, and I had to hold myself together. I'd always struggled to keep my gag reflex from reacting when somebody else was sick.

'Fuck,' Leo groaned out. 'Sky, help Clo. We're going to take Lia to the hospital wing.'

I nodded, knowing they needed to help her, but also I was shit scared that whoever had hurt her was still lurking nearby. She was in no condition to talk to anybody to let them know what happened. She was trying to stay conscious, but her eyes were rolling back into her skull.

I knew I should feel avenged. Should feel happy that somebody had harmed her the way she'd helped to harm me multiple times.

But I didn't.

I'd made up a shit revenge scheme, sure. One that was pretty moot. But at no point had I wanted anybody to get hurt. I'd just wanted to knock them down a peg.

Something I didn't really care about anymore. I was happy— truly happy—with how my life was going, and holding onto the anger and resentment just seemed stupid. The girls had apologised and Ollie wasn't acting anywhere near as self-important or arsehole-ish.

I felt sick to my stomach, and it wasn't just the cheap vodka swirling around in there causing it.

Somebody had taken everything too far, and I had a gut feeling that whoever had hurt Ophelia had also tried to drown me. There was an unhinged person on campus, and we needed to figure out *who*.

Soon.

But then another emotion hit me—hard.

Disgust.

Disgust aimed at Ollie. He'd instructed *The Set* to hurt me last year. He had been the one who sent them to beat me up in the toilets, and the woods after our picnic, and all those other times he'd orchestrated my torture.

How could he look me in the eye after finding me beaten on the toilet floor?

How could he look at my bruises and my pain and still pretend to care about me? Still kiss me and court me and make me fall in love with him?

Just the sight of Ophelia had my heart twinging with sympathy for her—and I didn't even particularly like the girl!

Over the last month, I'd lost my anger towards him. Lost my fuel and my drive for revenge. And I was okay with that. I'd even let him in, let him worm his way into my heart, in a small capacity. Especially after he'd found me that day, and we'd had a conversation that wasn't filled with venom.

But I wasn't angry.

I was just sad. And, really, that was the lowest he'd ever made me feel.

Thirty-Four

OPHELIA HAD BEEN in the hospital wing for the last couple of days.

'Can I go visit her?' I asked Leo on her third day. 'I'd really like to talk to her.'

'If you want,' he said with a shrug. 'Doubt she'll tell you anything more than what she's said to us.'

'I know,' I agreed. 'But I'd like to talk to her anyway.'

After my lessons ended for the day, Leo escorted me up to the hospital wing, straight to Ophelia's bed. She looked awful, her bruising a dark purple, and her hair was scraped up into a bun high on her head. It was the least put together I'd ever seen her.

When she saw Leo, she began to brush some wisps of her hair that had escaped the bun away from her face. Then she spotted me and rolled her eyes so far back in her head she looked possessed. Nice to know that getting beat up hadn't changed her.

'What is she doing here?' she hissed.

'I promise you I come in peace,' I said, not even letting Leo give some bullshit answer on my behalf. 'I just wanted to talk.'

'So talk.'

'I was kinda hoping we could talk alone? Without Leo here.'

Ophelia's gaze narrowed, and I could tell she was suspicious of me, but I could also see she was curious enough to know what I wanted to let me stay. Which was exactly what I thought would happen.

'I'll leave you girls to it. I'll be outside, Stutter.' He left the room, leaving the two of us alone together. The moment he was out of earshot, Ophelia began talking.

'Hurry up and get on with what you want to say. I'm on some pretty good drugs right about now, so I'd use that to your advantage if I were you.'

'First off,' I started, trying to collect my thoughts and order them so they made sense. 'I wanted to apologise for my petty shit during the summer.' Ophelia opened her mouth and I kept going, not letting her butt in. 'Yes, you deserved it. Actually, you deserved a hell of a lot worse than any of the stupid shit I did to you. But still, I want to put it behind us.'

'Okay...' The suspicious look hadn't wavered. 'Thanks, I guess?'

'Second, I wanted to talk to you about the attack.'

'I've already told the guys I can't remember anything.'

'Yeah, I know.' I nodded. 'But I wasn't sure if there was something missing. Maybe something you hadn't wanted to tell the guys, or a note that had shown up? Anything like that.'

She shook her head, but her eyes were clouded. 'No, I don't think so. I was out in the woods to meet Ollie, and then the next thing I remember is waking up in here with everyone looking at me.'

Her words surprised me. 'You were meeting Ollie?'

'Yeah, he'd sent me a text to meet there rather than at the party itself.' She shrugged, her bony shoulders pointing through her thin gown. 'But I highly doubt it was him who hurt me.'

I wasn't as sure as her, but I also didn't see Ollie doing it either.

'Just frustrating that we don't know who did this to you. Do you reckon it was the same person who stabbed me? Killed Odette and Olivia?'

'Shit,' Ophelia cursed, her eyes widened in alarm. 'I hadn't even connected it, honestly. Been a bit too busy worrying whether any of this will scar or permanently damage my good looks.'

'I'm sure with your money and contacts you could always pay

a surgeon to change anything you're not happy with.' The words were out of my mouth before I thought it through, and I felt like a piece of shit for just assuming that because she had money, she'd go down that route. 'But I doubt it will scar. Nothing you've done to me is visible.'

Once again I'd somehow put my foot in it, but I didn't want to take it back. I may have forgiven her and Oralie, but I would never forget the shit they put me through.

'I know I've said it before, but I really am sorry, New Girl.' She reached out and grabbed my hand in hers. 'We were bitches and honestly, there's nothing I can say to really explain it away. We got a kick out of it. It's really that simple.'

'I get it, and we're good. As long as you never touch me again. Might want to mention that to Celia and Cordelia, too, just in case they didn't get the message from Ollie and Leo last time.'

'Just in case who didn't get the message?' Ollie asked, appearing around the corner like a ghost, holding a bunch of flowers.

'Nothing, babe,' Ophelia replied, fluffing her pillow to sit a little straighter in her bed, her smile wide. 'Sky and I were just having a nice chat.'

'Really?' He raised an eyebrow and I laughed.

'Really,' I affirmed. 'Thanks for agreeing to talk to me. I hope you feel better soon!'

'Thanks.' Ophelia smiled and for once, it was genuine. It wasn't hiding knives or a lie. It was a real smile, and it was actually quite pretty when she wasn't trying so hard.

'I'll leave you two to it.' I gave a small wave before backing away from the bed. The door beckoned and I made it there as quickly as I could, no longer wanting to watch Ollie's faux-mance with Ophelia. Or maybe it wasn't a faux-mance anymore. He'd brought her flowers, after all.

'Skylar, wait up!' Ollie's voice called and I groaned. I'd hoped not to bump into him. Ever since I'd found Ophelia hurt, I couldn't get over the idea that Ollie had aided them in doing that to me. Whenever I thought about it or tried to rationalise it, sadness overwhelmed me.

'What do *you* want?' I couldn't hold in my bite.

'I just wanted to talk to—'

'Well, I don't want to talk to you,' I said, being honest, hoping it'd end the conversation faster.

It didn't.

'What's going on?'

'Ollie'—I sighed and turned to face him—'I just can't be arsed with this right now, okay? I need time.'

He looked at me with confusion. 'Time from what?'

'From being around you!' My eyes filled with tears and I looked away at the ceiling. The stone pillars calmed me, grounded me enough to remind me to keep my cool. 'Actually, I've got a question for you.'

'Okay...'

I crossed my arms across my chest, a fighting stance, and looked at him. *Really* looked at him. Took in the chiselled jaw, the defined cheekbones, and the bright blue of his wary eyes.

'There's something I've not been able to get my head around and I need you to clear it up for me.'

His tone was honest. 'Whatever you want, Sky.'

'How could you instruct people, the girls, to beat me up and then still look at me like you cared about me?' I asked, nearly choking on my words. It was hard to be so open, so vulnerable, in front of Ollie. 'Looking at Ophelia in the woods made me feel sick. Seeing the terror in her eyes, the sadness, the confusion, was like looking at myself on the bathroom floor the day *you* set your minions on me. Did you get off on my pain? Enjoy laughing about it when my back was turned?'

'Skylar,' he said, his eyes pained. 'I never told the girls to hurt you.'

My disbelief manifested itself in a loud scoff. 'Why do I find that so hard to believe?'

'I know it sounds like I'm bullshitting you, but I'm not. I would never have asked them to beat you the way they did. They went too far and believe me when I say I didn't let them get away with it in private.'

'Whatever.' I sighed. 'I can't be around you right now. I'll see you later, okay?'

'Sky, let's talk this out.' His arm reached out for me and I took a step back, not wanting his proximity to make me do something I'd no doubt regret. 'We can go back in and ask Lia. She'll tell you.'

'Tell me what? That she did what Odette told her to do?' I shrugged. 'There's nothing more for me to say right now. Can you at least respect that?'

Ollie went quiet, his protests dying on his lips.

'Thank you,' I said, surprised he'd listened to me without putting up more of a fight. Maybe he truly was listening to me more these days. 'I'll see you around.'

I didn't turn back to look at him as I walked away.

Yay for progress.

Thirty-Five

PARENTS' Day.

The bane of the required school calendar—or at least it was in my eyes. After the events of the last one, I was in no rush to have a repeat, but at least I was the one who invited Mum and Andy this time so I wouldn't be blindsided like before. If the two of them were going to show up in all of their glory, then I wanted to be aware and prepared. I hadn't seen the two of them since, well, a long time ago. I had received a text from my mum after Mr Hawkins was charged for possession, but only because she'd seen a post about it on her social feed.

From the moment I woke up in the morning, dread sat low in my stomach.

'How are you feeling?' Clo called from her bed, still lying and staring up at the ceiling. ''Cause I feel bad and I'm not the one going.'

'Gee, thanks a bunch.' My pillow somehow found its way soaring across the room, hitting Clo on the side of her face. 'Honestly? I feel uneasy as fuck. I've been worrying all night about how today is going to go. I barely slept a wink.'

'I'm aware,' she said. 'You went to the toilet at least ten times.'

'Soz,' I said. 'Didn't mean to keep you up.'

'No big,' she replied as she sat up. 'It was my fault for not staying in Griff's room.'

'Very true. You do seem to spend a lot of time there these days.'

She thought about it for a second. 'Much better company. Not to forget he's gorgeous.'

'And I'm not?'

'You're beautiful, Skylar.' She laughed. 'But you look like you could use a wash.'

'Thanks again!' I joked but got out of bed and went to the bathroom for a quick shower anyway.

When I returned to the room, Clo was already dressed in a cute floral jumpsuit and had curled her hair. She looked bubbly and adorable and not like herself at all.

'Are you feeling okay?' I asked, watching her face.

'Yep.' She looked at me just as intently. 'Why'd you ask?'

'Well, your outfit is very... cutesy.' I'd tried for tact, but who knew if I'd hit the mark. These days, Clo got offended pretty easily, and I felt a bit like I was walking on eggshells.

'You like it?' she asked, giving me a twirl so I could see all angles.

'I do! Didn't think you would, though?'

'Maybe I'm feeling better in myself.' She shrugged, and if a visible weight had been on her shoulders, it would have dropped to the ground with a thud. 'And ready to show my true self.'

'If that's the case, I'm happy about it,' I told her, meaning it. Even if I doubted it.

'Thanks.' She smiled at me. 'So, you reckon you'll spend the day with Leo and his rents?'

'I think so, and if Mum and Andy weren't coming, I'd be totally fine with it. Lottie's always been nice to me, and I don't know enough about Edward to have an opinion,' I said, my thoughts running away with my mouth, forgetting the person I was talking to. Clover didn't have many agreeable things to say about the Hawthorns. I changed the subject. 'You and Griff are coming, right?'

'I mean, we don't have a choice, but at least we're both going to be without parents together.'

'So yours definitely aren't coming?' I asked for maybe the twentieth time. It was like I had word diarrhoea. I just couldn't help it!

'Nope,' she said, glancing away. 'They wouldn't come even if I asked them.'

'That's a shame.' I gave her a tentative smile, but she just rolled her eyes in response.

'No, it's not.'

'Well then. Yay, I guess,' I said with a small chuckle, trying to ease the tension lurking. Clover's parents were still as mysterious to me as they were when I first met her over a year ago, and in all that time, I'd learned nothing new.

'Indeed.' She gave me a taut smile, her lips a thin line. 'Let's get this show on the road.'

'Let's,' I said, gearing myself up for a train wreck of a day.

I MET Leo outside the main entrance, having decided it was best to meet my mum and Andy before they could enter the school. Didn't need a repeat of Mum calling across the hall to me, did I? An entire year had passed and I still wasn't past the embarrassment of that moment. A blush started at my hairline just thinking about it.

From the moment I spotted the black car making its way up the hill, the feeling in my gut just got worse and worse. My hand and Leo's larger one were entwined, and he gave me a quick, reassuring squeeze, as he knew how apprehensive I was about the day.

I'd wondered how everything would be seeing as Odette had outed my father's name in front of everybody at the fashion show. It helped me put Henry Brandon's questions during last year's New Year's Gala into perspective. The way he'd asked meant he'd known the truth or at least had an inkling of my parentage.

'Just breathe, Stutter,' Leo reminded me, his tone low as the car stopped at the bottom of the academy steps. 'We get through dinner and we ditch. I'll even let you choose the movie we watch.'

I nodded, my tongue lying heavy in my mouth, making words too hard to muster. Slowly, I took a breath in through my nose and pushed it out of my mouth. I'd used Google to determine the right order after the last time I'd questioned myself.

The car door opened, and in the exact way I'd assumed she would, my mum stepped out with a big flourish of her arms. The moment our eyes locked, her face became one of pure joy and I knew once she opened her mouth, shit would fall out of it.

'Oh, my darling daughter Skylar. Oh, let Mummy hold you!'

Yep. Pure and utter dog shit.

She flew at me, her arms wide, and the speed of her ascent up the stairs startled me. The heels she wore were so high I worried she'd trip and break her ankle. I gripped Leo's hand harder than before, so that even when she threw her arms around me, he was still anchoring me.

'My beautiful baby girl, I've been so worried about you. That mean man should never have touched one of mine.'

God, I nearly vommed on the spot. *She always knows how to lay it on thick when other people are present.*

'I'm fine, Mum,' I told her, trying to get myself out from in between her arms. Was the mean man the guy who stabbed me? Couldn't be her husband, could it, because that would mean she wasn't completely obtuse about the world around her.

Today, her outfit had to be one of the worst things she owned —maybe. I mean, the woman owned a *lot* of shit, loud clothing. Her top was made from a flimsy, chiffon-esque material and I hoped she wasn't planning on standing under any bright lights today. Otherwise, everybody here would see the underwear she was sporting underneath. The top's print was a snake one in grey —you know, the colour you see on real snakes all the time—and it buttoned up in the front, with god-awful ruffles hiding the buttons. Ruffles that went downward, resembling a certain part of a woman's anatomy. *Urgh.*

She'd teamed the top with white denim jeans and black

stiletto heels. Honestly, if I hadn't been in her bedroom—or her house—I would think there were no mirrors to be found.

While Mum embraced me, my face squished up against her bosom, Andy joined us. He looked his usual ratty self, grey track-suit bottoms matched with a black leather jacket, and his hair unbrushed, reaching his shoulders. *What a delight.*

'Skylar,' he slurred, his arms outstretched. He leaned in, and I dodged him, dragging Leo with me. Leo's face was one of pure horror and if I wasn't trying so hard to get away from the situation, I'd have pissed myself laughing.

'Oh, we are so glad to see you,' Mum said, but instead of looking at me, her eyes were glued to Leo. She looked him up and down, assessing him, and I realised the last time Mum was here, Ollie had been my boyfriend. 'What are you doing on my baby's arm?'

'Leo's my boyfriend now, Mum,' I said, hoping to ward off any tension or awkwardness by coming out with it.

'I'm impressed,' she said, pride shining in her eyes. 'I told you last year this boy is a fine specimen.'

'So you did,' I replied, stifling a laugh.

'Ditched that other one then, did ya?' Andy asked, all while chewing gum and smacking it.

'And so she should have!' Mum's voice was loud as ever, and luckily we were still outside the school building, so nobody inside could hear her—yet. 'That boy has some nerve.'

I rolled my eyes at her theatrics. If a complete stranger were to overhear her, they'd see a caring mother, but I knew better. So did Leo, who just gave my hand a quick squeeze to show he under-stood. Or maybe to calm me down so I didn't lose my cool and punch her. One or the other.

'Mum, he wasn't the one who stabbed me.' I'd told her this more than once, but it never seemed to make its way through all the hairspray vapours into her ears. Today, her brassy blonde hair was shorter than the last time I saw her, and it was as wide and high as it was long.

'You can't remember who stabbed you. That's what the police

officers told me,' she said, nodding vigorously. I tried to focus on her words, but all I could focus on was the fact that her hair didn't move *at all*.

'It wasn't Ollie, Cora,' Leo said, his tone reassuring. He took his hand out of mine and moved his arms to point towards the large doors. 'Shall we head inside?'

'Let's! Oh, I hope they've put on a decent spread again.' Mum came closer to me, looping her arm into mine so that we could walk into the school together. 'One of the true perks of you coming here is the freebies!'

'Mum, it's a sit-down meal, remember?' I asked, already exasperated, and the woman hadn't even been here for a whole ten minutes!

'Yes, yes,' she said, patting my hand with the arm not looped in mine. 'Suppose we may as well head to the bar while we wait.'

'I thought we could meet up with Clover and Griff,' I told her, and then added, 'Lottie will arrive soon, too.'

Pretty certain my mum believed she and Lottie were besties. I was also certain Lottie was a lovely woman who was simply humouring Mum. She wouldn't be the first—or the last.

'Wonderful! Clover's a darling, isn't she?' Mum elongated the word darling, and I cringed internally. Part of me hated how strongly I felt about Mum and how badly she embarrassed me. I hated how strongly I wanted to pretend my mother was more like Lottie Hawthorn.

'That she is,' I said, trying to steer Mum towards the subject tables set out and not the bar at the far end of the room.

Andy had roped poor Leo into a conversation behind me. I'd briefly heard the words *tyres* and *paint job* and honestly, I didn't want to know what the fuck he was boring him about. Cars, I assumed.

Clover and Griff were standing together in the hall, and Mum waved wildly the moment they spotted her. 'Hello!' she called, dropping my arm like a hot potato and continuing to wave, using both arms like one of those car dealership balloon men. 'Cooey!'

The two of them looked at her, amusement lacing both of

their features at Cora's lack of, well, everything. Griff's cheeky chappy grin covered his face as he waved back to her, and Clo was trying hard to disguise a grimace but was doing a pretty shit job of it. Couldn't blame her.

'Wonderful to see you again, Cora,' Griff said, sucking up and acting like a charming, flattering bastard. 'You look fabulous today!'

'Oh, you are such a darling,' Mum tittered, fanning her face with her hand. She moved her gaze to Clo. 'You're a very lucky girlie snagging this one!'

'Something like that,' Clo said, her smile fake as fuck. 'Lovely to see you, Cora.'

'You remember Andy, of course,' Mum said, sweeping her hand out to gesture at her husband. Somehow, the smiles on both Griff's and Clo's faces became even more false with each passing second.

'Of course. Nice to see you,' Clo said through gritted teeth that were still in a smile. Quite impressive if you asked me.

'You look beautiful, you stunner,' Andy said, his eyes leering at Clo, taking her in from top to toe. His pupils dilated when they travelled across her breasts. *Gross.*

'Thanks.' Clo turned to Griff, disgust clear in her features. 'Shall we go get a drink, babe?'

'How wonderful! That's where I want to head. Come with me, dear!' Mum grabbed Clo's arm, hooking it in with hers and almost dragging her away.

Too mortified to laugh, I stayed silent.

Apparently, Griff didn't feel the same way. Well, not until Andy wrapped his arm around his shoulders and said, 'Let's go join our sexy women, shall we?'

Like Clover before him, Griff was dragged in the direction of the bar.

'What the fuck just happened?' I asked Leo, who had stayed by my side silent throughout the whole encounter.

'Honestly, baby, I have no clue.' He chuckled, and I swear the sound of it made my nipples harden.

Down, Skylar. Calm down.

I'D CONCLUDED that the powers that be hated me.

The formal dinner portion of the day finally arrived, and once again, we were placed at a table with the Hawthorns and Henry Brandon, meaning Ollie was sitting with us, too. *You couldn't make this shit up, could you?*

So far, Mum had said nothing, but I knew she was gagging at the bit to talk to Ollie, or rather tell him off, for whatever slight she thought he'd made towards me. On the other side of the table, I could sense that Henry wanted to talk about the elephant in the room—my biological father.

The meal had barely begun, and I was certain that over the six-course meal, somebody would open their big mouth. The question was: who would bite first?

'Well, Oliver,' Mum spat out over the starters. 'I hope you're happy with yourself.'

Here we go.

Ollie sank a little in his seat, not making eye contact with anybody at the table. If I was feeling kinder, I would tell him that nothing would stop Mum once she'd started, so he may as well grin and bear it, but I wasn't feeling overly generous towards him since finding Ophelia in the woods and our conversation afterward.

Griff opened his mouth to join the fray, but a booming voice stopped him. 'Cora, don't you think we should let boys be boys?' The smarmy look on Henry's face made me sick. That statement was one of the many things wrong with the world—a tiny thing in comparison, but still.

'And what exactly do you mean by that, Henry?' Lottie piped up after taking a dainty sip of her cocktail.

'Oh, you know...' he trailed off, and Lottie raised her thin eyebrow, waiting for him to continue.

'No, we *don't* know. Anything to say, young man?' Mum

looked surprisingly fierce—and slightly like a circus clown. Her bright blue eyeshadow reached her too-black filled-in eyebrows, and her coral shade of lipstick caused her lips to blend into her rouged cheeks. Basically, my mum looked a right state.

Ollie coughed, realising he was trapped, and said, 'I'm sorry, Cora.' His expression was uncertain; unsure whether he should apologise to Mum or to me. He made the right choice when he turned to me and said, 'I'm sorry, Skylar.'

'Sorry for what?' Mum slurred, pointing the stem of her wineglass in his direction. Under the table, Leo squeezed my thigh in support and I shuddered. The warmth from his hand travelled through me, and I smiled, glad to have him by my side.

'For everything,' Ollie said, and his tone sounded earnest. I'd taken a sip of my drink at the wrong time and choked, surprised as fuck that he sounded sincere. He'd had so many chances to apologise to me, yet he'd chosen a time when we were in public and I couldn't reply honestly without seeming like a bitch. The only reason he'd said anything was because a drunk woman had pushed him to!

'Although,' Mum continued. 'I heard you saved my baby from that awful, perverted man and for that I thank you.' Mum sounded sincere, and it was the first time in a very long time that my heart felt a bit of love towards her.

The table fell silent at the mention of Mr Hawkins. I hadn't even known Mum knew about what happened. I turned an accusing gaze to each of the boys, wanting to see a crack in their armour, wanting to figure out which one had told her. None of them looked me in the eyes.

The silence was only broken when the servers arrived and placed dishes in front of us that smelled divine. One thing I could agree with Cora on was the fact that Hawthorn definitely knew how to put on a spread in style. I caught Mum's eye, and we shared a conspiratorial look. It was the first time, in a *very* long time, where I felt like the two of us were on the same wavelength. *Minor miracles.*

The meal passed, and after the last of the plates were cleared away, Ms Hawthorn took to the stage, microphone in hand.

'Welcome, parents and students.' Standing in the centre of the stage, she looked as important as she probably believed she was. The stage—the school—was her domain; her forte. Where she felt most at home and in her element. 'Once again, we welcome you to our fine establishment.'

She surveyed the room, her grey eyes narrowed and filled with judgement when they landed on Mum and Andy.

'After the events of last year,' she said pointedly, looking at the table where Ophelia and Oralie were sitting with their parents, 'we do not have an informational video to show you, but we have a band instead. So enjoy the music, and I will be at the back of the hall to answer any and all of your questions.'

As quick as she started talking, she left the stage. I watched her walk off, her gait slightly unbalanced because of a small limp I hadn't noticed when she stepped onto the stage.

'Short and sweet, thank fuck,' Andy blurted out, rubbing his bulbous nose that was red from drink. He disgusted me, and I was thankful summer school had meant I didn't have to return home and be cornered by him again, even if I disagreed with how the boys had made that possible. 'That woman is a witch.'

I coughed as Leo chuckled beside me.

'That *witch* is my sister,' Edward said, a twitch in his eye, as Lottie patted his arm in a soothing gesture. I caught Lottie's eye, and she winked at me in a conspiratorial manner.

'Doesn't make her any less of a witch, mate.' Andy looked at each person sitting at the table, hoping somebody would pipe up and agree with him. Nobody did. The only noise was Edward's grunts of displeasure.

'Well, as fun as this has been,' Griff announced. 'Clover and I have plans to speak with her parents on video call.'

'How come your parents couldn't make it, dear?' Lottie asked, a smile on her face. If Lottie hated Clo's parents, then why did she always seem so genuine when they were brought up in conversation? None of it added up.

'Business,' Clo mumbled, avoiding Lottie's eyeline. 'Lovely to see you all, as always.'

'Let your mum know I'd love to hear from her,' Lottie said.

'Sure,' Clo replied, but I knew she wouldn't. Her face told me as much.

'Bye, darling,' Mum said, her bloodshot eyes struggling to focus on Clo and Griff as they stood to leave. 'Make sure you keep this one happy! He's a keeper.'

Griff winked at Mum, then the two of them left, and I glanced at Leo, who was watching them with a smirk on his face. One day, I expected him to tell me what the fuck had happened between them all.

'It's probably time I head out too, Son,' Henry announced. I'd forgotten that Henry Brandon and Ollie were still with us, my mind having been occupied by Mum, Andy, and the Hawthorn drama.

'Are you not staying over at the house for the swim meet tomorrow?' he asked, looking like a lost little boy seeking their parents' approval. 'I thought you'd want to stick around and watch.'

'No can do. Places to go, people to see, and all that. You understand, don't you, Son?' Henry asked, not really wanting an answer. He'd already made it clear he was getting out of dodge at the earliest opportunity.

'Sure.' Ollie's face darkened. 'If you'll excuse me.'

With that, he stood and walked out of the hall, not looking back once. A pang of sympathy went through me. I hated it when something happened to make me see him as a proper person. One with actual feelings and emotions.

'He's always so touchy.' Henry chortled. To give my mum and Andy credit, they stayed silent.

I was pulled out of my thoughts by my mum clapping her hands together to get everybody's attention. 'So, who's for another round of drinks then?'

Thirty-Six

THE FIRST SWIM meet of the season—and the first since Leo had been assisting with coaching the team—was upon us, and everybody had high hopes for the results.

Griff had been pumped up all morning, telling Clo and me that he was ready to *slay the competition* and I hoped he was going to live up to his own hype. I didn't want to be around him later if he didn't. A surly Griff didn't happen often, but when it did, you hid and waited for him to snap out of his funk.

'You ready to head over to the pool?' Clo asked, grabbing her bag and phone as she prepared to leave our room.

'Yep,' I said, checking that I had everything I needed on me. 'You not pumped up?'

'Pumped up? Who the fuck are you?'

I laughed and shook my head at myself. Pretty certain I'd never used that phrase before in my entire life. 'Honestly, Clo, I don't know where that came from. I think Griff's rubbing off on me.'

'You sounded like an idiot.'

'I'd have to be an idiot to be friends with you,' I replied, laughing harder. She giggled too, and then it became infectious, even though it wasn't that funny. The two of us started laughing to the point of tears. Full-blown, stomach-hurting laughter. I wrapped my arms around myself and clutched my hands on my ribs, bent over to stop the hurt. Clo was doing the same thing, and

I watched as a streak of mascara travelled down her cheek. Infectious laughter soothed the soul as much as it hurt the stomach.

'Fuck sake, Sky.' She tried to give me an evil look, but that just made me laugh more. It was a vicious cycle. 'I'm gonna have to touch up my makeup now!'

Eventually, the two of us got ourselves under control and, after touching up our makeup, we were ready to leave.

'Shit, we're gonna be late,' I said, looking at the time on my phone. We'd been laughing for longer than I thought.

'I'm sure they won't even notice,' Clo said, although her pace picked up.

'Leo will,' I said under my breath. 'He always does.'

'Of course he does. You're his girl, remember?' She sounded both jealous and bothered, and a dagger buried between my ribs. I shouldn't be shocked. The reason Leo wanted to be with me in the first place was to hurt Clover, but things had changed enough that I'd forgotten that was the original goal in his eyes. I wondered if it still was.

'And you're Griff's,' I said, emphasising his name—and my point. Griff was my family, and even though Clo was my best friend, I wouldn't let her ruin him.

'Right,' she muttered, the laughter of a few minutes ago gone, leaving only tension in its wake.

When did shit get so complicated?

WE MOVED FAST ENOUGH that we didn't reach the pool house too late. We'd also done ourselves a favour. We'd missed the earlier races of the younger years and only had to wait a little while for Griff to compete. *Small mercies.*

We sat down, and the second Griff spotted us, he waved enthusiastically. He looked so funny standing in his skimpy speedos with a swim cap on, waving and smiling widely.

Clo sighed and said, 'He is such a massive dork, isn't he?'

'Yeah, he really is. But an endearing one, y'know?'

'Most of the time...' she trailed off. 'Sometimes I wonder if I feel as much for him as he does for me.'

I didn't say I'd thought about it for a while myself. 'And did you come up with an answer?'

'Most of the time I think I feel the same, but then that tiny doubt creeps in. Do you get what I mean?'

'I do,' I replied absentmindedly, looking over at Ollie, who was preparing for his race, and then over at Leo, who smiled when our gazes locked. I smiled back and gave him a tiny wave. *Fuck, now I'm the dork.* 'Boys are confusing.'

'Proper.'

'You think they find us just as baffling?' I asked, curious.

'Oh, yeah, for sure. Griff looks at me sometimes and it's like I can see the cogs turning.'

I laughed at that, imagining the *exact* face she was referring to.

I wished I could give a blow-by-blow account of what happened next. How the races went. How the boys looked—other than fit as fuck—but I couldn't. The events were a blur. All I knew was that Griff and Ollie won their respective races.

Seconds after they awarded the last medal, a shout rang throughout the room, echoing off of the high ceiling. Another loud shout, followed by somebody barging into the room, caused a commotion and every eye was drawn to them.

'Help! Help!' A large, burly-looking man entered, hollering to anybody who could hear him. 'It's Ms Hawthorn. Somebody's attacked her!'

Gasps and whispers started up across the room, and I looked at Clo in shock. I didn't know what to do. I was frozen to the spot, and I sought out Leo across the room. His face was pale, and he looked worried—unnaturally so. Ollie and Griff looked perplexed, and then in sync, the three of them headed in the direction the man had come from.

A few rows in front of us, Edward's head came into my eye line as he stood up and hurried after the boys. It had surprised me the night before when Edward and Lottie announced they were staying, seeing as Leo wasn't competing anymore, but it also highlighted how different they were as parents compared to Henry. No matter what Clo's issues with them were, you couldn't deny that they were supportive parents who loved their only child.

'What the eff is going on here at Hawthorn?' Clo asked, her voice as shocked as I felt. Ms Hawthorn always seemed so untouchable, and the thought of somebody hurting her in her own domain seemed so surreal.

'Who would attack her?' I asked back, having no answers yet plenty of questions. 'Reckon it was the same person who attacked Ophelia? Or me?'

'No way to know for sure,' Clo said, uncertain. 'But I suppose it'd make sense.'

'None of this makes sense.' My brain was drawing a blank. 'It rules out the boys, though.' The three of them had been in our eyesight the whole time, meaning they couldn't have done it.

'Always seeing a bright side, aren't you?' she said with a slight smile.

'I mean,' I replied with a shrug. 'Kind of got to at this school.'

'Should we go follow them or...?' Clo asked, as the two of us watched the other spectators follow Edward and *The Sect*.

'Honestly, it's probably not our place?' Even as I said it, I knew we wouldn't be staying where we were. Too many people had left, and fuck it, we may as well join them. Sort of looked suspicious if we didn't go see—like we had something to hide.

'You're totally right...' Clo said, and then added, 'Let's go.'

The two of us hotfooted it down the stairs, trying to avoid colliding with everybody who was doing the same. Eventually, we got to the door and barged our way through the forming crowd. Breaking free, we stumbled upon Leo, Ollie, and Edward hovering over Ms Hawthorn on the floor. I couldn't see Griff anywhere, and that boy's height meant he could rarely hide. Maybe he'd gone for some help.

Ms Hawthorn was cowering on the floor, holding her limp wrist with her other hand. Her sallow face had already bruised, one of her eyes swollen shut, and it looked to me that there were unshed tears in her open eye.

Leo surveyed the area, and when his eyes landed on me, he beckoned me forward with his hand. I tiptoed forward, making my way to him in silence, not wanting to draw much attention to myself even though everybody was staring at us.

'I don't want you going anywhere alone,' he whispered in my ear, as he pulled me into a hug when I got close enough. 'Stay close to me at all times.'

I tilted my head up to meet his eyes, and after seeing the worry and fear in them, I bobbed my head in agreement. Knowing he wanted to keep me safe was enough for me to agree. Leo's face regained its colour the moment I nodded, but the worry surrounded him like a dark cloud.

'I need you to say it, Stutter.' He placed a kiss on my cheek and then a soft one on my lips. 'I just want you safe.'

'I promise,' I mumbled, wanting to reassure him and not be the person who added to his problems. To lighten the mood between us, I added, 'Not like I'm going to complain about having you at my side at all times.'

'At your beck and call?' he joked.

'Of course,' I replied with a chuckle, but then I remembered what was happening around us, and I sobered. 'What happened to her?'

'Same thing that happened to Ophelia. An unknown person attacked her from behind and she didn't see who it was. Or at least she won't say even if she did. Ol' Aunt Winnie doesn't like to be seen as weak.'

I believed that. The woman gave off those vibes, and I could understand why. She was a female running an elite establishment, ruling in circles that were traditionally male-dominated.

'Where's Griff?' I asked. Clo was still standing at the edge of the crowd, looking lost and alone.

'Gone with Mum to the hospital wing to get the place prepared. That's if Dad can convince Winnie to go there. She's too tough for her own good.'

'Makes sense. She's not the type to allow others to wait on her.' I stepped out of Leo's embrace and gestured over at Clo, feeling she should be a part of this conversation. She and Ollie both came to stand by us at the same time.

'We need to talk,' he whispered. 'Come to my room tonight at seven, all of you.'

'Why should we trust you?' Clover harshly whispered back, but at the same time Leo spoke, overriding Clover's question.

'Sure,' Leo replied, bored. 'We'll be there.'

Curiosity got the better of me—a habit of mine I needed to break, or at least evaluate—but we move.

I gave him my sweetest smile.

'We'll be there.'

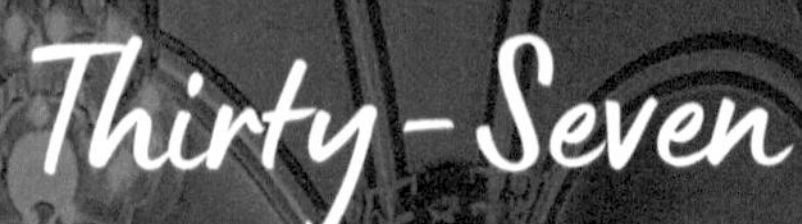

LATER THAT EVENING, the four of us headed to Ollie's suite together deciding there was safety in numbers. Plus, Leo had asked me so nicely not to leave his side, it made me want to be even closer to him at all times. My hormones were working hard, and every little thing Leo did was only making me want him more.

After Edward begged her, Ms Hawthorn had finally agreed to be taken to the hospital wing, and once she'd left, there was no reason for everybody to stick around, so ever since, Leo and I had chilled out in my room with Clo and Griff, just waiting until the time Ollie said to meet.

'Wonder what he wants to tell us,' Clo said, looking back over her shoulder at me and Leo. She and Griff were a few paces in front, swinging their joined hands between them like two kids on a school playground. It was cute.

'No clue,' I said, perplexed. The thought had plagued me all afternoon, and I was still none the wiser about what he wanted from us. It had nothing to do with our relationship or what happened between us, because he'd invited the others too. I looked at Leo, who had been pretty silent all day. 'Any ideas?'

'None,' he said, blunt. *Don't take his mood personally,* I told myself. All day he'd acted odd and until we were alone, I wouldn't find out why. Twice, I'd caught him deep in thought, and I'd had to repeat myself before he heard me. Something had hit him, *hard.*

Ollie's black door beckoned at the end of the hall, calling to me, and I picked up my speed. I tried to tell myself it was because I wanted to know what Ollie wanted—and only that—but I wasn't fooling myself.

Griff pounded on the door with both fists and I wouldn't have been shocked if Ollie opened it and decked him square in the face. Griff's grin was wide. He was doing it to be an annoying bastard on purpose. I laughed a little at his antics and I watched as Clo rolled her eyes at him, her expression amused.

The door creaked open to reveal Ollie on the other side, an eyebrow raised in annoyance. I knew that arsehole's facial expressions, and *he* wasn't amused. 'Get in here, dickhead,' he growled, his lips slightly upturned, showing he wasn't *that* irritated at his cousin.

He stepped back, creating enough room for us to enter, and when I moved past him, his fingers grazed my arm, like he wanted to stop me but had chosen at the last second not to.

From behind me, Leo's hand gripped my arm in the same spot Ollie's fingers had grazed, and I shivered. Being around the two of them at the same time was going to be harder than I'd like. It was the first time with them both in the same place at the same time since my kiss with Ollie and my night with Leo.

Griff and Clo had taken a seat on the sofa, so Leo and I went and joined them. It was a little snug, but it was that or the floor, and even though I was one of those strange people who enjoyed lying on the floor, it didn't feel right in Ollie's room. *I promise you, some of the best thinking takes place on the floor.*

Once we'd settled, and I was leaning into Leo's side, Ollie started pacing in front of us all. We all watched him, staying silent as he did so, waiting for him to get to the point of why he asked us all to his room.

Leo's scent filled my nose, and I checked out a little. Where Ollie smelled of tobacco and vanilla, Leo was a mix of leather and ginger—a real aphrodisiac.

I shook my head, focusing my eyes back on Ollie, who had

finally stopped pacing and was staring at the part of my body touching Leo's. He shook his head, his eyes hooded.

'I found this,' he announced, holding out a crumpled piece of paper.

'Where?' Griff asked.

'On the floor besides Winifred.' Ollie held it out to Leo, who leaned forwards to take it out of his hand.

'What is it?' Clo asked.

'A note,' Leo said, and the two of us read it in silence.

We have warned you.
Breaking the sacred bonds of *The Sanctum* results in death.
Audentes fortuna iuvat. Dulce periculum.

If I thought I was confused earlier, the note only made it ten times worse. The only part that made sense to me was the school motto. *Fortune favours the bold. Danger is sweet.* Underneath, there was a name and signature I didn't recognise, but then again, I'd grown up poor and in a different world to them, so of course I didn't recognise the name. Had the note been intended for Ms Hawthorn?

I took it from Leo and passed it to Clover on my right.

'What the hell is *The Sanctum*?' Griff asked, handing the paper back to Ollie. Griff sounded as befuddled as I felt, and when I looked around the room, I could see that everybody was feeling the same way. Confused.

'I've never heard of them,' Ollie said, pacing once more. It was something I had in common with him. 'But it's linked to the school. The note says as much.'

We all made noises, agreeing with him—all of us except for Leo.

'Should we look into it?' I asked, not knowing what else to say. 'Where would we even start?'

'Do you mean should we research the school's history?' Ollie asked, and I nodded. 'We could, and the best place to start is the library.'

'Sounds like a plan!' Griff piped up, fidgeting in his spot on the sofa. 'Library time, Skylar, your favourite.'

'That is very true,' I said, pondering the situation. Before I agreed, I wanted Leo's opinion. 'What do you think, babe?'

'If you want,' he said, his eyes dark. His mood hadn't improved, so I chose to ignore it for the time being. No point arguing and giving Clover fuel. Or Ollie. Pretty sure he still believed our relationship was fake deep down but doubted himself.

'I'm in,' Clo said.

'I *am* interested in history...' I pretended to think for a moment longer, but I wasn't fooling anybody. 'I'm in.'

'Excellent,' Ollie drawled.

My arms were covered in goosebumps, and a chill crept in. Not because I found Ollie attractive. Nope. Not one bit.

Yeah, I don't believe myself either.

At the earliest opportunity, I went to the library to start my research.

My love of the library served me well when it came to delving into the school's history and trying to find any old yearbooks or articles that would tell us more about what had happened in the school's past.

The librarian, an older kind lady who was hard of hearing, wanted to aid me in any way she could. I thanked her but said I was okay for the time being, that I'd ask for help if I needed it.

We didn't need anybody knowing what we were doing. Especially not somebody on the payroll.

I found it hard to believe that the boys had never looked into the past, or *The Sect* or *The Set* in general. Apparently, it was just something they knew.

I turned to Griff, who was sitting beside me at our usual table at the back of the library. 'Tell me again how you found out about *The Sect?*'

'Uncle Edward told us stories when we were younger, and it was just always a given we would one day rule the school. None of us questioned it.'

'You just accepted it as fact?' I asked to clarify.

'Yeah. He always told us how our parents were members, and so were their parents before them, and so on.' He shrugged, his eyes looking a little lost. 'I never thought to question it, to be honest, Clouds.'

It made sense. The boys had wealth and power—they had all their lives—and they didn't know any different. Didn't know just how fucking weird the whole concept was.

I assumed Ophelia and Oralie had also grown up being told the same thing, and knowing that you could punish anybody that stepped a toe out of line with no repercussions must be pretty heady.

It also made sense to me why Ms Hawthorn had never looked into any of the attacks on me. Had never included the authorities in anything that happened at the school, and had been pissed when the police had briefly investigated the murders of Odette and Olivia.

Because that was what they were. *Murders.*

I'd asked Leo about the investigations when we started our fake relationship, wondering if the police were any closer to finding out who'd stabbed me.

'So did the police find out anything new?'

'Not that I know,' he said, taking a glance at me before returning to the video game we were playing. 'A lot of money changed hands to make them go away fast.'

'Who paid?'

'Dad, I assume.' He shrugged. 'Maybe Winnie. Either way, Stutter, it's best for you that they're no longer digging around. From the last update we got, you were their biggest suspect for what happened to Olivia.'

'But what about Odette? And the person who stabbed me?'

'They've got no idea. Told them to keep us updated.'

'And if you hear anything, you'll let me know. Right?' I asked, knowing he would but wanting that reassurance anyway.

'Of course.' He paused the game to turn and give me a smile. 'I've got your back.'

I pulled myself back to my conversation with Griff. 'So your parents were both members?'

'Yep,' he said with a nod. 'Your dad was a member, too.'

'My d-dad?' I stopped looking through the yearbook in front of me and looked at Griff's face.

'Yeah, course,' he said, still looking down at the documents in front of him, not having noticed the shock his words had put me in. 'They all went to school here. I thought you knew.'

He looked up at me, his smile firm, but then he spotted my expression, and his face fell.

'I'm sorry,' he said, his eyes sympathetic. 'I need to think more before I speak.'

'It's fine,' I said as I looked back down to avoid his pity. *Fuck that.* 'I don't even know the dickhead.'

'Right,' he said, his tone uneasy. 'You're better off, anyway.'

'That's what my mum said.'

'And, as much as it pains me to say this, Clouds, I'm with Cora on this one.' He fake shivered and made me giggle. 'The man's a douche.'

He may be a douche, but Griff was my only link to him, and as much as it pained me to admit it, I wanted to know about him. 'Do you remember him?'

'Not much.' He shrugged. 'He went off the grid when we were pretty young. Before my parents died, otherwise I'd have gone to live with him when they died.'

'I know these are shit words, but I'm sorry they died.' I reached out and squeezed his shoulder. 'I'd have loved to meet your parents.'

'They'd have loved you, and they would never have let you have such a shit upbringing knowing you were their niece. But it's okay. I know they can see us.' His smile was wide, causing me to break out into a wide grin back at him. 'Pretty sure they're ghosts.'

The way he said it was so casual I couldn't help but laugh, spitting out the drink I'd just taken a small sip of. I put my bottle down and tried to calm the nervous giggles threatening to take over. Whenever I thought I knew what he was going to say next, he surprised me and said something left field. Being around him was never boring, that was for damn sure.

'Ghosts?' I questioned, my eyebrow raised.

'Yep,' he answered, not seeming to hear my scepticism. 'They're definitely spirits.'

'You kill me,' I said with a small laugh, picking up my bottle of water again, hoping I'd be able to take a sip again soon without spitting it out. 'I'm sure they're kind spirits.'

'Oh yeah. None of that poltergeist maliciousness.'

'That's good, I guess.' I pointed at the stack of papers Griff had been shifting through. 'Found anything in those documents?'

'Nothing we didn't already know. Just a list of past members,' he grumbled, frustrated he didn't have any better news to tell me. 'And the years they attended.'

'Eurgh,' I said, just as frustrated. 'Maybe I should search the old school newspaper?'

'The school had a newspaper?'

'Yeah, it ran from 1955 to 2000.' A thought hit me. 'Hey, what year were our parents in charge?'

Griff shuffled through the papers, finding the one he wanted. 'Well, our rents graduated in 2000.' Griff nodded, reaching the same conclusion as me. 'So, the year they left school is the year the newspaper ended?'

'Right!' I shouted enthusiastically—maybe a little too much— but fuck, it could be the break we'd been looking for. 'I wonder what the explanation is... Hey, what year did old Winnie become a faculty member?'

'She joined as an assistant the year she graduated, so'—he shuffled the paper again, and I got the impression he was enjoying it, probably thinking it made him look scholarly—'1990.'

'Bet she knows what went on.' I nodded, my thoughts running away with me. I had a suspicion, but no real clue of what or why. 'Could you grab me the yearbook from 2000?'

'You gonna dive into that rabbit hole?' he asked, but the glint in his eye told me he already knew the answer.

'You bet your arse I am,' I said, a grin on my face. Determined once again to uncover whatever it was we needed to know. Before somebody else ended up dead.

Thirty-Eight

HALLOWEEN CAME, which meant another fucking party in the woods, and not just any party.

Oliver's 18th Birthday Bash.

Or at least that was how Griff referred to it and the rest of the school whenever it was spoken about in the halls.

I was attending the party as Leo's date, and we'd come up with a pretty cool outfit idea. I couldn't wait to see how hot he looked wearing it. My outfit last year had been awesome too, so I needed to go one further.

'What do you think?' he asked, entering his room from the bathroom, dressed as a super dead, super suave, Bugsy Siegel. He was wearing a houndstooth patterned suit jacket, white shirt and tie, and grey slacks. Even his shoes were era specific black brogues. He'd even blackened his blond hair and gelled it back.

'Damn!' I whistled. 'Do you think this getup suits me?'

His eyes perused my body and lit up with lust, his tongue peeking out to slowly lick his bottom lip. My black dress was tight with a pencil skirt, and I had teamed it with a long faux fur coat and some black pumps. Virginia Hill in all her fashionable glory.

'You look good, Stutter. Real fucking good.' He grabbed my waist and pulled me to him, then placed a bruising kiss on my temple. I shivered, goosebumps covering my arms in seconds. 'The perfect mobster's girl.'

'You look pretty hot yourself,' I said as I wrapped my arms

around his waist to keep him close. The line between fake and real no longer existed between us and we were both caught in the middle. It was difficult acting so couple-y in public and then switching it off in private—to the point where we were turning it off less and less even when alone.

'You sure we have to go? We could stay here...' he said, the implication behind his words clear. My lips formed a smile on their own, but I pinched his side, anyway, even if I wanted to stay in his room and explore.

'Yep,' I replied, ignoring his suggestion. 'Course we do. Have to show off our love.'

I laughed, and his lips rose into an almost-smile. 'Very true. Got anything in mind to show off tonight or are we winging it?'

'Winging it.' My response was breezy, but my thoughts were anything but. 'I'm sure the perfect opportunity will present itself to show how obsessed with each other we are.'

'I'm sure you're right. You usually are.'

I hit him, but it didn't have much of an impact seeing as we were still standing close together, chests touching. He squeezed his arms around my shoulders in a brief hug and then took a step back.

'For once, Stutter, I wasn't taking the piss,' he drawled with a wink. 'Let's get out of dodge.'

My cheeks warmed. Hopefully, the makeup and all the fake blood would cover it from him.

He reached for my hand, and I entwined my fingers with his. The moment we left the suite, we had to be switched on. What with the campus once again crawling with teachers and students, the act needed to be even more believable at all times.

And the entire time, I had to remind myself that none of it was real.

It could *never* be real.

THE PARTY WAS in full swing by the time we walked into the clearing, the bass of the music thumping all around, and a large crowd of people dancing in the centre.

Like the last Halloween party, witches, ghouls, and ghosts hung from the trees, and the punch bowl had fake eyeballs floating in it. I guessed they'd reused the decorations, which surprised me. I thought rich fuckers enjoyed flaunting their wealth and always used it to buy new things, even when they didn't need to.

Myth busted. Well, for teenage students throwing a Halloween party in the woods at their expensive private school at least.

'Ello, ello, ello,' called Griff, as he sauntered over with Clover on his arm. The two of them were dressed as Hercules and Megara and the effect the two of them had on those around them was clear. They looked great together and happy. Genuinely happy. Leo elbowed me in the ribs, but for once our telepathy was dried up and I had no clue why he'd elbowed me.

'Hello yourself,' I replied, smiling at Griff. Just being in the boy's presence made me feel content. 'You two look great!'

'Thanks,' Clo said, beaming at me. Then she looked at Leo standing at my side and at our clasped hands, frowning. 'You look great too, Sky. Shame about the dead weight.'

She looked Leo up-and-down with disgust.

'He is a super dead mobster and I guess that's pretty weighty,' I said, laughing off her negative vibes. We weren't going to let Clover bring us down. Fuck that.

'Oh, don't listen to old sourpuss here,' Griff said, nudging her in the ribcage. 'Both of you look beautiful.' He batted his eyelashes at us both, causing me to giggle at him.

'So, where's the booze?' I asked, taking my hand away from Leo's and grabbing Clo's arm. The two of us made our way over to the table, laden with alcohol, leaving the boys standing together.

As soon as we were out of earshot, I hissed, 'Where is he?'

'Not here yet,' she replied, knowing without his name who I was referring to. 'He'll be here. It's his birthday party after all.'

'I know. Just thought he'd be here already.' The two of us had reached the table, and I stood surveying the area while Clo went hunting. 'I haven't spoken to him alone since... well, I can't even remember.'

'He's not yours to care about anymore, remember?' Clo said, emphasis on the end of her sentence. 'You're with Leo, and happy, so get the fuck over it.'

She was right, but something still sat unwelcome in the pit of my stomach. Hopefully, it was just gas.

'I'm sure he just wants to make an entrance,' Clo added with a shrug and I nodded, even though I thought that was bullshit. Ollie may be a dick, and he may have the shithole we called a school believing he ruled it, but I knew the truth. He hated the attention and he didn't have his crap together. If he were anybody else, I may even feel sorry for him a little. But it was Ollie, and all I felt was slight dislike—and potentially some lust.

'Here comes the birthday boy!' a voice hollered, breaking up the party.

I stand corrected. But then, when I glimpsed at who was attached to Ollie's body like a python, I knew whose idea it had been to make a late attention-seeking entrance, and it definitely wasn't Ollie.

Ophelia had come dressed as Britney, circa 2001 VMAs. You know, the performance with a snake, pre-head shave? I hated to admit it, but the girl looked fucking stunning. Her bruises had faded and she looked as if she'd never been beaten in the very woods she stood in. I scoffed, keeping up pretences, then looked at Oralie, who was standing next to the couple.

Oralie had taken the sexy memo even further and had come dressed as Britney's rival, 2002 *Dirrty* era Christina. Chaps and all. Jeez, the two of them had really pulled out all the stops to be the most talked about girls in the school.

Ollie clearly hadn't got the early 2000s mandate, as he was dressed like a vampire. I couldn't decide if he was meant to be Edward Cullen or maybe Stefan or Damon. Either way, he looked hot. Surprised they hadn't tried to convince him to double denim it up and come as JT.

Celia and Cordelia were traipsing behind them, in what I could only describe as an oversized scarf that barely covered anything. Maybe they were Romans? They must be freezing—and if they weren't, they would be in an hour or two. October on a hill in England did not make for good partying conditions at the best of times. My faux fur coat was thick and I was still shivering!

'Fucking hell,' Clover said, handing me a drink. I took a sip and spat it out again. Man, that tasted bad! Maybe I should worry that the eyeballs in the bowl were real?

'Is there anything else?' I asked. ''Cause this is vile.'

'Think there are some alcopops,' Clover said, rooting through the ice bucket by her feet. 'Oh wait.'

She straightened, and in her hand was a bottle of vanilla vodka.

'You've hit the motherload,' I replied and in a fit of excitement, kissed her on the cheek.

'Sure you haven't been hitting the hard stuff to pre-game?' she asked, her eyebrow raised in question.

'Nope.' I laughed, knowing she didn't believe me. 'Swear. We're both sober as.'

'Hm.' She mumbled under her breath something I couldn't make out while pouring us some diet cola and vanilla vodkas.

'Thanks,' I said as she handed me my fresh drink. I took a sip and sighed in relief. 'Much better.'

'I'm glad.' She looked around, and her next words were spoken out of the side of her mouth. 'Ollie incoming.'

'Wonderful,' I muttered. I'd been expecting him to seek me out, but I had hoped I'd have Leo by my side when it happened. A buffer of sorts.

'Clover,' he greeted when he was close enough to the two of us. 'Skylar.'

Neither of us spoke back. We just sort of nodded. The barest hint of an acknowledgement we could get away with without being seen as rude.

'Can I talk to you?' he asked, reaching out to touch my wrist.

The moment his fingers grazed my bare skin, I felt electricity run from the spot he touched to every single inch of my body.

'S-sure,' I replied, as Clo asked me with her eyes if I was sure. I tilted my head, thinking it over for a moment, then gave a brief nod. 'I'll see you in a bit, Clo.'

Clo walked off, back over to where Griff and Leo were still standing, without even a 'see you later'. I watched her go, knowing that if I looked at Ollie, I'd probably drool a little. No matter how hard I tried, I wasn't immune to his charms.

'You look fucking perfect,' he said, causing a blush to rise on my cheeks and on my chest, too.

'Leo mentioned, yeah,' I said, knowing it would rile him up but unable to stop my tongue. The small sip of alcohol I'd had was already making me bold.

'Bet he didn't mention you look good enough to eat.'

'I'd rather you didn't,' I said without giving it any thought. It felt nice not to lose my head in his presence. Okay, there was still a chance I would put my foot in my mouth, but fuck, couldn't a girl be happy to get out one sentence without stumbling over every word?

'Shame. I think we'd both enjoy it.' His voice oozed sex appeal, and if I had been alone, I'd have been fanning myself to cool down. 'You always did in the past.'

'I think you're delusional.'

His lips formed a small smile, and I found my gaze focused on his full lips. Knowing what it felt like to kiss those lips, have those lips exploring my body, my mind started wandering somewhere else.

'Your boyfriend is watching us,' he spat, and if I didn't know better, I'd think he was jealous. 'He can't take his eyes off you.'

'Of course,' I said. 'I am his girl, after all.'

I still wasn't the best at flirting or acting seductive, but I hoped my words were having the desired effect.

'His girl? Still?' he growled, taking a step closer to me. Automatically, I took a step back, trying to keep the distance between us. 'Tell me how the fuck that works, Sky.'

'Exactly how you expect it to, Oliver,' I spat out, anger simmering. 'We fuck. We're together.'

I tried to maintain eye contact with his indigo blues, hoping he couldn't hear—or see—the lie I'd just put out into the universe. I'd made it sound like we were at it like rabbits.

'You've fucked him?' Once again, he stepped closer, his tone even lower, the growl darker.

I looked at Leo standing across the clearing. He looked as if he was about to come over and intervene. I shook my head, trying to convey with my eyes I was okay and that I didn't need him—yet.

'Yes,' I said, clear and unwavering. 'Often.'

A low growl left his throat. An actual growl. Like a beast. 'Tell me this. Has Leo heard your stutter with his dick deep inside you?'

I tried to keep my face from heating as I thought of the memory. 'Of course.'

'When?' he bit out, his face pained.

'We've been together since summer, so it's happened more than once.'

'Before?' he asked, his voice small.

'Before?' I repeated, not sure I understood.

'Before we...' He looked uncomfortable and brushed his hand through his hair. 'Before the last time?'

I saw a fork in the path before me. One of those decisions I'd spoken to Clover about back when I first returned to Hawthorn. How you always had forks in the path, each one leading to a different future. On one hand, I could lie to him and say I slept with Leo before the last time we hooked up, even though I hadn't. *Or* I could tell the truth. What did I actually gain by lying? But the truth probably wasn't going to go down well, either. Was it worse to have slept with Leo before I hooked up with Ollie last, or to have hooked up with Ollie and then fallen into Leo's arms?

I went with the truth.

'No,' I replied. 'Not before.'

'Right,' he said in a whisper. He coughed and seemed to knock off whatever thought ran through his mind. 'Can we go somewhere more private to talk?'

'You want to leave your birthday party to talk to me?' I asked, then added, 'Happy birthday, Ollie.'

'Thanks.' His eyes wrinkled at the edges, a smile covering the bottom of his face. 'Can't believe I'm eighteen.'

'You're getting old,' I joked. 'You don't look it, though, so that's a good thing, right?'

He shook his head, his eyes once again glinting with malice. 'Let's go further into the trees.'

'I never said we could leave this spot.'

'You didn't have to.' He turned away from me and started walking, so cocksure I would trail behind.

'I don't want to,' I grumbled but followed him regardless. A large part of me was curious, and unlike the cat, I wasn't dead yet.

With one last glance of assurance to Leo, I followed Ollie at a fast enough pace to keep up with him, not wanting to lose sight of him.

He stopped, far enough away we could only hear the music from the party as a low hum. The bass thumped in the background, but the music itself was indecipherable.

'Sky, there is so much you don't understand.' Our gazes locked, and I wished I could see behind the façade. See the truth. *His* truth. 'So much you need to know.'

'So explain.'

'I can't,' he said, reaching out to touch my arm, lazily running his fingers up and down. 'Not right now. But I want to. Badly.'

'You wanted to talk to me,' I said, irritated that he'd taken me away from the party and my friends just to tell me pointless shit I'd already heard. 'Why ask me to talk if you're not gonna actually talk?'

'And I do. Want to, I mean. I just *can't*.'

'You can't?' My foot began tapping on the woodland floor. Patience wasn't my strong suit. 'Why?'

'If I told you that, I'd have to kill you,' he said with a sad smile. It felt strangely human for somebody so inhuman at times.

'Oh, ha-ha.'

'We can't talk here. Can you meet me tomorrow?' he asked,

his other hand reaching out to me, until both of his hands were on me, my arms clammy through the faux fur from his warmth.

'Where?' I asked him, wondering what he wanted. My interest piqued. I should've flat out denied him, but one thing I'd learned about myself during my time at Hawthorn was that I struggled to deny Ollie anything.

'My room?' he asked, and I shook my head violently.

'Not happening,' I growled. 'Somewhere else.'

'Fine,' he bit out. 'The library?'

'Fine.' I smiled but turned it into a frown as soon as it registered. 'Can I go now?'

'You could stay,' he said wistfully. 'We could enjoy the party together.'

'No, I really couldn't,' I said with a sad smile and a shrug of my shoulders. I walked away before he could say any more. Before he could convince me to stay.

And I knew myself well enough to know that if he'd kissed me, all bets were off.

Welcome back, petty, horny, bitch Skylar.

Thirty-Nine

'DRINK!' I shouted, gesturing at Griff's almost empty cup.

The four of us had decided that the only way to get through the evening, without hurting anybody or starting any arguments, was to get drunk. *Really* fucking drunk.

And what better way to get drunk than to play *Ring of Fire*, followed by *Bullshit Taxi* and then to top it off, the pièce de résistance, *I Have Never*.

Yeah, I was questioning my life choices, too.

'I have never had sex with somebody playing this game,' uttered a random girl from year ten dressed as a nurse. The girls she'd joined the group with all broke out into titters, excited in the way girls got whenever something juicy was about to be said.

I took a drink, as did Leo, Griff, and Clo. I hoped Clo didn't look at me because Ollie wasn't playing, and it was obvious then who I was drinking for. But when I looked over at her, she was staring at Leo, a blush on her cheeks.

Guess that was confirmation enough that he and Clover had fucked in the past. I'd guessed at it, but having the evidence in front of me was nauseating—more than the copious amounts of alcohol swishing around in my stomach.

Drunk Skylar was crude, clearly. And thought of herself in the third person. I giggled but then remembered what I was thinking about.

Without meaning to, I got mad and a little jealous. All she

needed to do now was fuck Ollie, and she'd have hit a *Sect* trifecta. I scoffed.

'You okay, Stutter?' Leo leaned in to whisper in my ear, and I shivered. He kissed my cheek, gentle and sweet. 'You've gone quiet.'

'Yep,' I replied, trying not to sound like a miserable bitch, but most likely failing miserably. Maybe I could blame it on the alcohol?

'Really?' he asked, his tone filled with teasing. 'Sure, it has nothing to do with what you just had confirmed?'

I nodded, gulping. He could see right through me—it hit me that he always had. 'Nothing at all.'

'Sky,' he whispered, and my skin set aflame. 'That was a long time ago. A time I rarely even think about.'

I took another sip of my drink to avoid talking more. I couldn't trust my tongue. Leo leaned back with a small sigh, but not before kissing my cheek again.

Still caught up in my swirling thoughts, I wasn't paying much attention to the game when a commotion came from the left-hand side of the clearing. People were shouting something unintelligible from where we were and a girl screeched. 'Has anybody seen Ollie?'

Ophelia.

She was stumbling through the clearing, but at least she was stumbling because of her inebriation, not because she'd been hurt. When nobody replied, she screeched her question again.

'Nope,' Griff called out, chuckling when she tripped over a branch. Maybe she shouldn't have been wearing such high heels on the woodland floor. 'When'd you last see him?'

'At least half an hour ago,' she spat out as Oralie helped her stand. It was like watching a baby deer flailing around, trying to find their legs. *Cute.*

'Did he not say anything before he went?' Leo asked, a crease between his eyebrows. I wanted to reach out and smooth it out but refrained. The moment seemed too serious for affection somehow. 'Or tell you where he was headed?'

'Just that he had somewhere he needed to be,' she said with a shrug of her shivering shoulders—I knew her outfit would give her frostbite—having now drawn the attention of everybody here.

Somebody cut the music and an eerie hush descended across the area. The couples who had been dirty dancing on the makeshift dance floor looked dazed and confused, like they'd just woken up from a trance.

'Odd,' Griff said but didn't sound overly worried. Nobody else knew what to say. Ollie was an eighteen-year-old boy, who had left his own party for unknown reasons sure, but it didn't mean anything nefarious was going on. Shitting hell, for all we knew he could have just headed back to his room, wanting to be away from it all.

I wouldn't blame him.

My mind recalled the look on his face when he'd asked me to meet him tomorrow. I'd tried to pass it off in my head as sinister or insincere, but when I wasn't breathing in his scent, I could see it for what it was. He'd been unsure to ask me—uncertain, for maybe the first time in the year I'd known him.

Something was wrong. I could sense it. Maybe it was the ghost of Halloween past, but I knew we needed to find him. My gut was sending me warning signs.

I leaned over to Leo and whispered in his ear, 'You don't think?'

I'd told him everything Ollie had said to me. Had asked him whether he thought I should meet with him or not, and Leo had convinced me to go and hear Ollie out.

'Don't think what?' he muttered.

'That he may be hurt?' I looked around the clearing. 'Or maybe hurt himself?'

'Why would you ask that?' Leo questioned, catching my eye. 'Do you know something?'

I shook my head. 'But I don't know... Something feels off about this whole thing. One year ago to the day somebody tried to drown me. Maybe it isn't a coincidence?' I'd tried not to think about it all night—tried not to replay the events of last year—but once I had thought of it, I could think of nothing else. No matter how many times Clover implicated Ollie, I just knew it wasn't him. Even knowing about his scheme to make my life hell still didn't have me believing he'd tried to murder me. 'We should at least look for him. If we find him unharmed, then whatever, at least we checked, you know?'

'Okay. You're right.' Leo's smile stopped the guilt swirling around inside me. 'Shall we go check his room?'

I nodded and mumbled, 'Please.'

Leo stood up, brushed the dirt off his trousers, and reached down his hand for me so he could help me stand. Ever the perfect gentleman these days.

'Come on then,' he said, a twinkle in his eye, and I couldn't help but swoon a little at him. 'Let's go find the prick.'

I reached into my pocket for my phone, thinking maybe Ollie had sent me a text or something. Instead of my phone, my fingers found a wrinkled piece of paper. Déjà vu hit me like a fucking truck. It had last year written all over it. I pulled it out of my pocket and it read:

Sky,
Meet me in the pool house at midnight.
I want to ring in my birthday with you. And only you.

Lost for words and breath, I handed the piece of paper to Leo. The moment he read it, he swore under his breath. He saw what I did. It was the same wording as the note I received last Halloween. The one that led me to the pool house to be nearly drowned. The note Ollie had sworn he had nothing to do with.

'What time is it?' I whispered, my fingers not listening to my brain as I fumbled around in my pocket to grab my phone.

'Quarter past,' Leo replied, bleak. 'Guess we know where to look.'

The two of us trudged back towards the school, avoiding the sloppy drunk people who were stumbling around everywhere. My drink buzz was wearing off, and the cold had crept in slowly, even through my massive coat. Leo's hand firmly in mine was the only warmth.

Eventually, we came upon the school, and in the darkness it loomed in all its gothic glory. Even after so much time, the architecture of the school took my breath away any time I looked at it. It reminded me of the European gothic cathedrals. All towers and spikes. The gargoyles' beady eyes followed us as we moved at a fast pace to the pool house—all-seeing and all-knowing. It had taken us at least fifteen minutes to get to the school, and the note had said to meet thirty minutes ago. Maybe he left after ten minutes, thinking I'd rejected the invitation, and we were worrying about nothing. I hoped we were worrying about nothing.

He must have put the note in my pocket when we spoke away from the party. *If* he gave me the note and it wasn't another fake like last time.

The person who stabbed me still hadn't been revealed and, although I didn't mention it much because I didn't want to dwell on the negative, it plagued me every night. The face of the culprit was still unknown to me. My memories were still lost in the deep recesses of my brain.

Silence greeted us the moment we entered the pool building, and if we were in a movie, crickets would be chirping.

The pool room itself was silent, too, the gentle lapping of water the only noise. The room was dimly lit, the waves reflecting on the ceiling the exact same way they had last Halloween, with the moonlight shining through the window highlighting the pool in all its glory.

'Shit!' Leo shouted, letting go of my hand and rushing toward the edge of the pool. His terror filled me, settling in my gut, and my gaze followed his path.

There. Lying face down in the pool. *A body.*

A body dressed in a tight black T-shirt and jeans.

'Help me!' Leo shouted, wading into the pool until he reached Ollie. He gripped Ollie's collar and with excruciating slowness, he dragged him over to the edge. My legs had locked in place, and I wasn't sure I had the strength to help Leo get Ollie out of the water.

'Is he breathing?' I asked, my voice shrill and panicked in my ears.

'Just,' Leo whispered. He pushed as I pulled and with a lot of effort, we got Ollie out of the water. 'Call Griff,' he demanded, starting to administer CPR.

Being the assistant swim coach, I knew Leo had undergone real training, and I had faith in his ability.

With shaking hands, I dialled Griff, who answered on the first ring.

'Yo, Clouds. Where are you?'

'Come q-quick,' I blurted. 'It's Ollie.'

'Where are you?' he repeated, his tone urgent, picking up on my panic.

'In the pool house.'

'We'll be there in two,' he said, hanging up without a goodbye.

'Is there anything I c-can do?'

Leo didn't waste any time in responding to me, and the only thing I could do was stand there feeling like a spare part, watching as he tried to save Ollie's life. Dread sat low in my stomach. Not only did I know how Ollie was feeling, but I also knew how he must have felt when it was me lying unconscious on the tiled floor last year.

Because no matter what he did to me last year, I knew in my heart he hadn't been the one to hold me under that water. It was a gut feeling, and I had no proof, but I just knew.

Wish I knew who had held me under.

A laboured gasp left Ollie's throat, and Leo let out a nervous laugh. Ollie started to retch and I looked away when the trapped water from his lungs came up. It brought back the memories of how wretched it felt, how hard it was to take a breath, and the impaired vision. My breathing sped up.

No, Skylar. I told myself. *This isn't the time for a panic attack!*

To take my mind away from my panic, I moved to sit down beside Ollie and Leo, not caring that I'd get wet. The heavy door opened, and the sound of the hinges reverberated throughout the room.

'Fuck!' Griff called out. 'What happened?'

'He was in the water facedown when we got here,' I replied, letting Griff hug me when he got down on the floor beside me. Clover stood awkwardly behind the group, her face pale and eyes glazed over. Maybe she was having déjà vu, too.

I rubbed my cheek, surprised to find it wet. I'd started to cry without realising it, but as soon as I knew I was crying, the tears came thick and fast.

'Sky,' Ollie groaned, and I threw myself onto him, draping myself across his chest before realising he'd just been struggling to breathe and maybe it wasn't the best idea I'd had. *Shit*.

Like he was infectious, I pulled myself back at once, chuckled, and stammered out, 'You scared the f-fuck out of us.'

A faint smile graced his lips that was more of a grimace.

'We need to get you to the hospital wing, dude,' Griff said. 'Check that you're okay.'

'No,' Ollie whispered, his breathing strained still. A faint rattle with every breath.

'P-please,' I begged, grasping his hand tightly in mine. His were cold and, for once, not giving me any comfort. 'I'll go with you.'

Leo looked at me, and I saw his slight nod. Whatever I decided to do, he'd have my back.

'No'—Ollie squeezed my hand, and I tore my gaze away from Leo's, settling back onto Ollie's face—'let's go to my room.'

'You should go to the hospital wing,' I said, but then I remembered last year it had been Leo wanting me to go there, not Ollie. Ollie hadn't wanted me to go there either but was outvoted.

'My room,' he repeated. No room for argument.

'We'll come with you,' Leo said and the two of us worked together to help Ollie into a sitting position. After he'd caught his breath a bit, we helped him to stand.

I knew the attention had to be killing him—that he hated being seen as weak. He despised having others look at him as anything less than all-powerful.

Griff took over my position, putting his arm around Ollie for support, and the three of them began to make their way out of the room, Ollie leaning on them both.

Clover and I stayed rooted to the spot, watching the three members of *The Sect* walk away in silence. I sighed and reached out to grab her hand. She startled, shocked I'd initiated contact. Fuck, I barely let the girl hug me without putting up a fight. I just wasn't the touchy-feely type.

'We should follow them,' I whispered, worried that if I raised my voice, the moment would become even more real.

'Let's,' Clo replied, giving my hand a reassuring squeeze. 'It'll be okay, Sky.'

My head hurt; my heart hurt.

One thing I knew for certain.

Halloween is cursed.

Forty

WHEN I OPENED MY EYES, it took a moment for my vision to adjust to my surroundings. The room was dark and unfamiliar at first, then the events of the previous evening hit me.

Halloween. Ollie's birthday party. The pool house. Finding Ollie facedown, lifeless.

I was in Ollie's room.

A heavy arm rested across my chest. An arm that was also attached to the hard body pressed up against my back. A constant gentle snoring in my ear. I looked around the room, making sure I didn't move enough to wake Leo—the snoring culprit.

After we'd taken Ollie back to his room, he'd instantly got into bed and fallen asleep before telling any of us anything. As a group, we decided he shouldn't be left alone, so Leo and I had volunteered to stay just in case and that was how we'd found ourselves sharing Ollie's sofa.

Not gonna lie. It was surprisingly comfy and spacious. Leo wasn't a small guy, after all, what with all those swimmer's muscles he hid under his clothes.

He looked so peaceful in sleep. Serene. I had to stop the urge to run my fingers through his hair—something he rarely allowed me to do when he was awake—and leave him undisturbed.

Slowly, I peeled his arm from around me so I could go to the toilet. He didn't stir, so I hotfooted it to the bathroom, hoping he'd stay in the comfy position I'd left him in and that my space would still be free when I returned.

On my return from the bathroom, I heard a grumble.

'Still going to the toilet five-plus times a night?' Ollie asked. His words made me jump, and I swore under my breath.

'You know me well,' I replied, pausing in my path. For some reason, I hadn't expected him to be awake and knowing he was made going back to Leo's arms feel wrong somehow.

'How about we have that talk now?'

'I...' I tried to come up with a reason why it wasn't the best idea, but honestly, I couldn't think of an excuse that sounded plausible enough. Plus, I doubted I'd be able to fall asleep again knowing he was lying awake so close. 'Yeah, sure.'

I tiptoed to his bed and found him already sitting up, waiting for me, his back resting against the headboard. Sitting on the edge seemed like the best bet, but of course he had to ruin it.

'Get in with me,' he demanded, his voice low but firm as he lifted the duvet and shifted over to make space. 'I won't bite.'

My head swivelled to where Leo was asleep on the sofa, then nodded. After the night Ollie had, I couldn't deny him anything. Even if I knew I should.

Once I was under the cover, I positioned myself up against the headboard, making sure the two of us weren't touching.

We had too many memories together in his bed—too many instances I looked back on and doubted. Every memory was shaded with the deeds that came after. All the good, now rotten.

'Do you like him?' he asked, and without saying his name, I knew he meant Leo. Of course he did. Wasn't like I was flaunting my relationship with anybody else right in front of his face.

'You already asked that at the end of summer, remember? And I told you I did.'

'And that was a couple of months ago. I'm asking whether you like him *now*.'

'I do,' I whispered back, hoping that the dark lighting in the room meant he couldn't see the flush on my face. 'More than when you last asked.'

'Right.' In an instant, he gripped my chin between his thumb and forefinger so we were looking into one another's eyes. 'Look me in the eye and tell me you enjoy fucking him.'

'Y-yes,' I stammered, hoping he couldn't see the swirl of emotions in my eyes. I'd only slept with Leo the one time, but Ollie believed it happened often, and I didn't want him to know I'd lied, but I also didn't want to kick him while he was already down.

'Yes?' he whispered, his breath fanning my face. 'That all you have to say about it?'

'If I didn't enjoy f-fucking him, I wouldn't be with him,' I replied quietly, meaning it, but feeling bad that I did for multiple reasons. It made me sound like good sex was all I cared about in a relationship, which wasn't true, but it also wasn't completely false either. Not that I had much experience. The two guys I'd slept with both happened to be in the room.

Ollie let go of my chin, and I rubbed the spot where his fingers had been. The only bruise being the one on my mind.

He growled low in his throat, and sitting in his bed beside him in the dark the way we were, I'd be lying if I didn't admit the situation flustered me. His growl did a thing to my insides, turning them into a big pile of jelly.

I needed to change the subject away from sex. 'W-what happened tonight?' I whispered, feeling braver once we weren't staring at each other. The darkness hid a lot.

'I went to wait for you,' he said, taking the bait. Or allowing me to change the subject, knowing it was my intention. Didn't care which.

'You gave me that note?' My nerves were climbing, and I was wringing my hands together, mostly to take my focus off him and the emotions swirling in me.

He tilted his neck to look up at the ceiling. 'Yeah. I hoped you'd see it in time and went there to wait just in case.'

'Did you get a sick thrill out of the wording?' There was an edge to my tone. Sharp as a blade. Cutting.

'I thought you'd appreciate the play on words,' he said. 'Or at least would recognise them and be curious enough to come find out what I wanted.'

'You replicated the note from last year on purpose?' I stopped fidgeting and turned to face him. 'Knowing what happened to me that night?'

'Yeah,' he said, a bite of regret lingering in that one word. 'Sounds shitty, I know, but I didn't realise just how fucked up it was until I almost drowned myself tonight.'

'Well, I didn't see the note at all until after midnight. Ophelia came screeching into the clearing, announcing you'd gone missing.'

'Having too much fun with *Leo* to notice my absence?' he spat.

'Jealousy isn't a good look on you.' I took a deep breath. Fuck being treated like shit all because Ollie had a case of the green-eyed monster. I didn't need to stay and have him snap at me. 'Griff and Clo could have stayed tonight, you know? Leo and I could have gone back to his suite and ended the night the way we'd intended to.'

Okay. I'll admit it's a low blow, but he deserves it.

'So, why did you then?' He shuffled an inch closer. 'Stay, I mean.'

'Honestly?' I looked at him, and he nodded slightly, urging me to go on. 'I couldn't leave you even if I wanted to. You never left me last year, and neither did Leo, so it only made sense we both stayed for you this time. Let's not have a repeat where we watch over Leo, ay?'

I tried to ignore the overwhelming sense of shame I felt at being so open and honest with him. I didn't owe him honesty; I didn't owe him shit.

He owed *me*. But in the dark of the night, things were different. Things you'd never say in the light come out to play.

'Let's not,' he whispered, inching closer once again. The tiny hint of light coming in through the window glinted in his eyes, shining with vulnerability. 'Why couldn't you leave?'

'You nearly died, Ollie,' I said softly. 'No matter what happens, I'll never want you dead.'

'Somebody clearly does.'

'You're not alone there,' I said. 'Somebody wants me dead, too.'

He smiled. 'Feels like I should reiterate that whoever it is, it isn't me.'

'Thanks. I'd already come to that conclusion myself, but I'm glad.' I wanted to get the conversation back on track. Back to the events of the night, so we could get to the talk he wanted us to have, and then I could go back to the sofa and fall asleep in another guy's arms. *Classy, Skylar.* Just gut the boy, why don't you? Would be quicker. 'So, you were waiting there for me?'

'Yeah.' Our gazes locked. 'I heard the door open, but I didn't look, worried I'd scare you away if I was too full-on the moment you arrived. Or maybe I was worried I'd turn to see you and Leo enter together, even though I'd asked you to come alone.'

'Go on,' I said in a breathy tone. The only other noise in my ears was my fast beating heart, and though I felt certain he could hear it, I knew he couldn't.

'Next thing I knew, somebody strong had come up behind me and dragged me over to the water. Pushed me in and held my head under.' He blinked, the memory still so fresh.

Tears formed in my eyes, unbidden. The story sounded so familiar—*too* familiar.

He continued, 'I tried to fight them off, to get out of their grip, but I couldn't. They were too strong and had a better angle than me.'

'I know what that feels like.'

'Eerily similar, right?' he asked, and I nodded, not knowing what else to say.

Wiping a tear away from under my eye, Ollie gave me a small, tentative smile.

'I hate you,' I whispered, tasting the lie the second the words formed.

'No, you don't.'

'No, I don't.' I sighed, tired of the bullshit and also just so goddamn tired of everything. Things had shifted between us after he'd saved me from Mr Hawkins' unwanted advances, and it didn't mean I forgave him for everything that came before it. Of course not. Yet having an open conversation with him made me see the times in our relationship last year that were real—or at least I thought they were. Without asking him, I could only guess.

He sighed. 'I don't hate you.'

I started. Those four words weren't what I had expected to hear. 'You d-don't?'

'No.' His light blue eyes were full of an emotion I couldn't place. 'I just wish I did.'

'Why, though?' I asked, ready for whatever answer he gave. He'd wanted to talk to me, and he had the perfect opportunity to tell me everything. Only he could decide whether he was going to take it. 'I've never done anything to you. Fuck, Ollie, you didn't even *know* me when I first started here.'

'It's complicated. What's Griff told you?'

'Griff?' My nose wrinkled, and I frowned. 'Is he meant to have told me something?'

'Has he mentioned your dad?' he asked, and it was as if a lightbulb went off inside my brain. Finally, some answers. Real answers and not just some half-arsed crap.

'Not much. Our dads were brothers, but my dad went off the grid when Griff was young,' I replied. 'That's why he didn't go live with him when his parents died.'

'Going off the grid is one way of putting it,' he said with a low chuckle that held no humour.

'Well, how would you put it, then?' I asked, trying not to let him know how much I wanted to know. How much of a burning desire I had deep down. If he knew how desperate I was for him to keep talking, he may keep it locked away, knowing I'd talk to him again to find out what he knew.

My head hit the pillow with a dull thunk, and some time during our conversation, the two of us had slid down the head-board and repositioned ourselves so we were lying side by side, facing one another. I could move back to a safer position, or I could stay put and hear whatever Ollie had to say. So I chose to get comfy, plumping the pillow, making it easier to rest on.

'Your dad stole a lot of Hawthorn money,' he said, not beating around the bush. Calm and factual. 'Then left town, never to be seen again.'

'How?' I asked, confused. 'Why?'

'Nobody knows. Just that he did and then disappeared into thin air.'

I scoffed and told him, 'Nobody can disappear into thin air. And surely somebody knows how he stole the money or at least where from.'

'True,' Ollie agreed. 'Somebody helped him.'

'Right...'

'That's not the worst of it, though. Your dad'—he paused, at a loss for words—'your dad, he'—he took a deep breath—'he had an affair with my mum.'

I squirmed under his intense gaze. *Griff definitely didn't mention that.*

'When?' I said, barely audible. 'How do you know?'

'When I was young, aged five to nine. It finished just before my mum ended her life. I only remember a little of it, but I remember the arguments between my mum and dad. Shit got bad.'

I stayed silent, hoping he'd continue if I said nothing. It was like the time he'd first spoken to me about his mum, where I could see on his face he wanted to get something off his chest but had spent so long bottling it up, he didn't know how to spit the words out.

'Dad was controlling, like I told you before, and I guess your dad was giving her something mine wasn't?' He glanced away. 'I've never asked my dad about it. Once Mum died, it became a taboo subject.'

'That makes sense,' I mumbled. I'd never even met the guy everybody was talking about. I'd only known of his existence for the last seven months, and really, he was still a figment to me. I'd never even seen a picture. 'Do you remember him?'

'Who?' His eyebrows knitted, deep in thought. 'Your dad?'

'Yeah,' I fidgeted, plumping my pillow again and trying to snuggle further under the cover. 'What was he like?'

'I don't know. In my mind, he just sort of blurs with Uncle Damien.'

'They were identical?' I asked, wracking my brain to remember if Griff had told me.

'No, but as a child, they seemed very similar. Not like Mum and Aunt Eliza.'

Without even thinking my next sentence through, I blurted out, 'Bit weird that Damien and Jacob were banging twins, right?'

When my words registered, I winced. That was our parents I was talking about. *Gross.*

Ollie's face transformed in an instant, his jaw clenched and his eyes glared a hole in my soul. Instantly, I knew I needed to take back my words to get us back to the calm, open conversation we'd been having. *Trust me to put my foot in it.*

'I'm so sorry. I have literally no idea where that came from.' I put my face into the pillow, wanting it to swallow me up. 'I didn't even think about it before I said it.'

'It's okay,' he said, reaching out to force me to face him again. Looking into his eyes, I didn't believe him—he'd closed off from me. Shut down. *Idiot me.*

'What are we doing?' I blurted out, reminding myself Leo was still in the room, asleep on the sofa. He'd been silent, except for the odd snore.

'Sky, you know we could be good together.' His blue eyes were looking deep into mine, trying to look beyond the surface—to look into my soul. 'Deep down, you know we're meant to be together.'

'I do?' I asked, but he was sort of right. We *could* be good together. If y'know, he'd acted like less of a trash human.

'I know I've made your time here hard, and I was a total dick last year.'

I laughed. 'Last year? You were a dick last month!'

'I deserve that,' he admitted. The two of us had moved even

closer together, only a couple of inches separating our bodies, and the heat emanating from him was drawing me in. 'But you can feel this.'

I could. I could feel the heat, the chemistry, and *fuck*, I wanted him.

But I also wanted the other boy in the room, the one who was sleeping through it all. Or, knowing Leo the way I did, the boy was lying awake listening but staying quiet.

'Yeah,' I whispered, 'but that doesn't always change things.'

'I know,' he whispered and gave me a light kiss on the forehead. 'I wish it did.'

'Wishing doesn't change anything,' I whispered. 'I need to get back to sleep. I'm shattered.'

'Go.' He looked at me wistfully. 'I wish I could fall asleep with you once more.'

'Well, maybe if you'd meant everything the first time around, you still would be.' With that, I slunk out of the bed and padded as silently as I could back to the sofa. Sliding under the cover, I got in while Leo made a great show of grumbling about the cold, but I could see through his phoney act.

Kissing him on the lips shut him up.

'Come here,' he said, his voice soft and alluring. He opened his arms, and I moved in between them, settling in a comfortable place, and the weight of them made me feel safe.

A small pressure on the top of my head made me smile.

'Night, baby,' he said.

'G'night, bub,' I replied, snuggling down in his arms.

'Night, Ollie,' Leo called, purposely baiting him out. I jabbed him sharply with my elbow, and he chuckled low in my ear. 'You love it.'

Shit. Maybe I do?

One thing was certain.

I was monumentally screwed.

Forty-One

A COUPLE of days after Halloween, I was in the library, working through the yearbooks from 1993 to 2000.

Flo, the librarian, had hooked me up. When I'd asked for her help, I was worried she'd tell Ms Hawthorn I was looking into the school's history, but I'd not been called into her office, so I was in the clear.

I started with the book from 1993 first, when the parents were age eleven and twelve, bright-eyed and bushy-tailed. Eager.

Flicking through to find their class photo, a chill ran down my spine, as the scent of tobacco and vanilla entered my nose.

Of course Ollie had shown up at the exact moment I was about to look at pictures of our parents.

'What you got there?' he asked, slotting himself into the seat opposite me.

'Yearbook,' I grunted, not even looking up at him. I'd found the class photo and searched the names first, so I would know where to find the parents.

My heart skipped a beat.

Shit, I was about to see a picture of my dad. The man who gave me life and then left Cora in the cold. I'd seen a picture of Griff's dad, so I had an idea of what he could look like, but I still felt nervous. It was different.

'Are you okay?' Ollie asked, and I looked up at him. Mostly to prevent myself from looking for Jacob on the page.

I took a deep breath, gearing myself up to speak to him. 'Honestly? I don't know.'

I looked back down at the book, but my eyes weren't seeing anything. The entire page had become a bottle green blur. Funny how the uniform hadn't changed much in thirty years.

His hand reached out and covered mine on the page. 'I'm here.'

Wanting to put off looking at the page a second longer, I looked up and got trapped in Ollie's stare. He had beautiful blue eyes at the best of times, but at that moment, they looked even better. Maybe that had something to do with there not being lies between us anymore.

Reverse that.

Maybe it had something to do with there not being *as many* lies between us anymore.

He took his hand off mine and leaned forward across the desk. 'Who's that?'

'The year seven class of '93,' I told him, removing my hand so he could look at the page with me. 'Your mum and dad are in the picture.'

'I guessed they would be.' He squinted, leaning closer. His hair brushed my forehead, and I giggled at the tickling sensation. 'There's Mum.'

He pointed to a girl sitting in the front row, her smile wide and her hair in two braids. I could see the resemblance between her and Ollie; they had the same startling blue eyes.

He gave a dark chuckle and shook his head.

'Of course she's sitting next to Eliza.' He pointed again, but even if he hadn't, I would have known who he was talking about. Millie and Eliza were identical in every way. The two of them were even holding hands like some kind of shining twin shit.

'Were they always together?' I asked, partially because I was curious, but also partially because I was avoiding finding Damien and Jacob Cooper in the line-up.

'Inseparable,' he muttered. 'Or so people always say when

they talk about them. I don't have too many memories of them both alive.'

My heart panged, and sympathy moved through me in waves. I'd never had a great relationship with Cora, but at least I'd *had* Cora. She may not be mum of the year, or fuck, even the decade, but at least she was still around, and it made me feel shitty that I didn't appreciate her more.

'It's shit,' I said, summing up all that I could in those two words. Like when he'd first told me about his mum, I didn't want to apologise. A sorry wouldn't help or bring his mum back.

'It is,' he whispered and coughed to hide his discomfort. 'So, guess your old man is in this picture somewhere?'

'Yep,' I said, popping the P, mostly to irritate myself. 'Assume yours is too.'

'Yep,' he said, copying me, but not in the mean way he'd mocked my stutter in the past. He pointed at the page again. 'There's Uncle Edward.'

'Where's Lottie?' I asked, not seeing her name listed.

'She's younger than the others. She'll crop up in the later books.'

That explained why she looked younger than the others, but she was the only female surviving parent, so I hadn't been sure. Also, I could never put my finger on whether she'd had a little filler to help her keep her youthful looks.

'There they are.' Ollie pointed to the back row, where two men were standing side by side, similar enough in appearance, but also, you could tell they weren't identical twins. They both had dark red hair, and when I leaned down and squinted, I could see the freckles on their noses. I could tell which one was Griff's dad. Their cheeky grins were the same, and the dimples, too, but there was something so Griff-like in Damien's features it was obvious who was who. Then I looked at *my* dad, who was a stranger to me. I guessed I could see some resemblances, maybe? Our eyes were a similar shape, and maybe we shared the same nose? I didn't feel a connection, though. I just felt sort of numb.

Ollie had noticed my despondency and chosen not to comment on it. 'Let's keep looking.'

'You joining me?' I didn't think he'd want to stick around, dredging up the past.

'I've got a spare hour to kill,' was his reply.

Over the course of the next hour, the two of us searched through the other books we had and looked for any mention of our parents, *The Sect*, and *The Set*, plus anything else we thought could be relevant.

We weren't having much luck.

In the penultimate book, Ollie stopped dead on a page that contained a collage of pictures, of students of different ages around the school grounds. 'Shit, look at this.'

I took my eyes off the sheet I was reading and looked at what he was pointing at. What the...?

'Is that my dad and your mum?' I asked, knowing that it was but wanting the confirmation.

The two of them were standing in front of one of the trees on the outskirts of the school grounds, with my dad's arm wrapped tightly around Millie. The entire picture looked intimate, and their smiles were secretive, yet happy. 'Guess I just thought your mum was with your dad during their school years.'

Ollie shrugged and pointed to the tree behind them. 'Look there.'

I'd been too focused on the people in the picture to look at the tree, but when I did, I saw their initials JC + MH marked on the bark, in the centre of a carved out heart.

'I thought you said they had an affair when you were younger?' I asked, tracing the heart underneath my fingertip.

'They did, but maybe they were together while at school, too. Dad rarely talks about their time at the academy.' Ollie's voice was low, and I could tell he was mulling the new information over.

'Yeah, maybe...' I wondered what else we didn't know about the past. Probably quite a lot. Fuck, I hadn't even known anything about Hawthorn a year ago other than the fact it was the private school up on the hill, and back then I hadn't known the name of my sperm donor, either.

Suddenly, I had a major urge to seek out the tree from the image. If I found it, then it was real, and it actually happened. *Silly logic, I know.* Especially as that tree was carved years ago and probably didn't even exist anymore.

I got out my phone to send a message, attempting to be discreet about it.

I'M HEADING INTO THE WOODS TO SEARCH FOR A TREE. IF YOU DON'T HEAR FROM ME IN TWO HOURS, PLEASE COME LOOKING FOR ME.

Texting Leo seemed to be the safe thing to do. He was busy all day with swim team stuff, so I knew not to ask him to join me. I'd run into too many issues in the woods in the past and I wanted somebody to know where I was who could rescue me if I needed it. Yeah, I could have messaged Clo or Griff, but I didn't want to involve them until I had a bit more background.

I'VE ALWAYS GOT YOUR BACK, STUTTER.

The message warmed me. The two of us had come so far and I never wanted to lose our newfound relationship, but things were getting real, and I knew I needed to talk about it with him soon. I'd just been putting it off.

I shook myself mentally.

Snap out of it and sort yourself the fuck out.

Yep. Like it was just *that* simple.

FOR SOME FUCKING REASON, I'd allowed Ollie to convince me to let him come into the trees with me.

'I'm going into the woods to find the tree,' I told him after I'd texted Leo.

'Then I'm coming with you,' Ollie announced like it was a given. *'It involves my mum too.'*

'It could take hours.'

'Gives us more time to talk.' He sent a broad smile my way. *'Plus, they call me the tree whisperer.'*

After we'd been searching for an hour, I began to get restless.

'Ollie, don't you think we should head back?' I called. He was up ahead of me, searching every tree he passed.

'No, Sky. We will find it,' he growled out, sounding harsh, but the fact he'd used my actual name told me otherwise. He was frustrated.

'O-kay,' I said, drawing out the start of the word. It was clear to us both I was just humouring him.

'While we search, you want to tell me about what's happening with you and Leo?'

'Not really much to tell,' I grumbled. 'Nothing's changed since we last spoke about it.'

'You going to tell me anyway?' he asked, but I doubted he'd meant it as one. He wanted me to tell him the truth—well, "the truth" he believed to be real because I'd been lying to everybody for so long now I wasn't even sure what was true anymore.

Oh, who am I kidding? I'm still lying.

My thoughts may be snarky, but they were talking straight facts.

'What do you wanna know?' I asked, resigned that he'd be getting his way, but also not doing anything to stop it from happening. I was a sucker. 'There's really not much to tell.'

He looked back at me, choosing his first question carefully. 'How did you get together?'

'It's like we said. On his birthday, we met up and told one another how we felt.' I continued walking, searching the trees. 'Decided to give it a try and see how it went.'

'And how is it going?' he drawled, stopping his search for the tree to look at me.

'Truthfully'—I took a deep breath, gearing myself up to spit it out—'it's going a damn lot better than I expected. We get each other, you know? He knows me.'

His face darkened, his eyebrows furrowed, and his eyes were boring a hole into my head. I felt like I was on trial for a crime I'd never intended to commit.

'I'd be lying if I said I liked it.' He took a step closer as I took a step back. I stumbled on a twig and nearly lost my balance. 'I never thought Leo would be happy with anybody that wasn't Clover.'

I shrugged, not sure how to answer. 'Things have definitely gone differently than I expected.'

My cheeks warmed at the mention of Leo being happy with Clover. I really needed to talk to Leo.

'And you're truly happy?'

'Is that s-so hard to believe?'

'You do know he could never love you?' he asked, but for once, it didn't sound mean or like he wanted to make me miserable. It almost seemed like he hadn't wanted to say it.

'I don't know that, and neither do you. Besides, there's no way to know for sure without me asking him, and funny enough, I wasn't planning to do that anytime soon.'

Ollie started walking again, and I hoped that would be the end of our Leo conversation. Or maybe of any conversation. My wish was answered for roughly two minutes, but then he spoke once more. 'Sky, you know I really am sorry, don't you?'

'Truth?' I asked, and he tilted his head in what I assumed was a nod. 'No, I don't.'

He looked perplexed, and the pure baffled look on his face made me scoff. 'Oh.'

'Well, you've never actually apologised to me, have you?'

'I—' he started, but I cut him off.

'Not that bullshit fake-ass apology you gave at Parents' Day, but a genuine apology. One that was because you meant it and not because people expected you to. Or because Cora basically forced you into it.'

'Your mum can be very persuasive,' he said with a smile. He

strode towards me, grabbing my hands in his when he was close enough and locked his gaze with mine.

'Skylar, I am so sorry.' He brushed my hair behind my ear. 'I was a complete dick to you, and I let my hatred for your dad skew my feelings for you. I'd decided before I met you I would hate you no matter what and that I would make you suffer. But when I met you, you weren't what I expected and shit got muddled.'

'What did you expect me to be like?'

He laughed. 'Honestly, Sky, I expected you to be a little money-grabbing whore. Somebody trashy who knew who her dad was and would act entitled now that she was finally at the school she should have always attended.' His whole demeanour was grave, and I could feel his seriousness and practically taste his sorrow in the air. 'As we both know, I was very, very wrong in my assumptions.'

Emotion overwhelmed me, and I had to look away. Glancing down at my feet, I watched as I shuffled them about and disrupted some debris. Anything to take my gaze off of his bright ocean-blue eyes that wanted to drown me with their newfound sweetness and sincerity.

'You get why I'm struggling to believe you?' I said, still facing the floor, so the wind carried away my voice.

'Yeah,' he mumbled but persevered, 'but I'm telling the truth this time.'

'*This time.*'

I wanted to give him a hard time. Wanted to make him squirm. But it seemed at odds with the kind of person I was. Because the fact of the matter was, he'd hurt me. No, not physically—although he most likely instructed the girls to—but mentally, and emotionally, he had.

Ollie's fingers clamped on my chin, pulling my face up to look at him. 'Skylar, I swear on your life that I am sorry and that I'm telling the truth.'

'You hurt me,' I said, going with honesty. 'More than once.'

'I know, and all I can say is that I'm a total dick.' He stepped closer to kiss me on the forehead. A loving gesture rather than a crappy, sarcastic one. 'Forgive me.'

'You can't just demand that I forgive you,' I said with a scoff. 'But I'll think about it. Let's keep searching for this tree.'

Ollie's face lit up, but when he spotted me looking, he covered it up with a scowl just as fast.

We headed off again, searching each tree for the markings, and after what felt like a very long time, Ollie called out from up ahead. 'Over here!'

I ran to where he had shouted from, being careful not to trip on the uneven ground.

'How did you find it?' I called but stopped dead when I saw Ollie—and the dead carcass at his feet. 'What the fuck is that?'

'A goat,' he said, his brows raised in a question of sorts. 'A rather dead one. There was a note attached to the tree.'

Ollie stretched out his arm, a piece of paper in his fingertips.

New Girl. The saying is like a deer caught in the headlights.
I couldn't find a deer, so this sacrificial goat is the next best thing.
After all, somebody here is the scapegoat.

Instantly, I knew the note was from the same person who'd left the dead rabbit in my dorm room back at the start of summer.

Somebody was the scapegoat? I had no clue who that could refer to. Or why. *Bloody riddles.*

'Is that *the* tree?' I asked Ollie, not wanting to talk about the note or why it was addressed to me. His pale face told me he had no clue what the fuck was going on and he definitely didn't know about the rabbit. There was also no way he knew he was about to stumble across a dead animal.

From the smell, it hadn't been here long. It was a fresh kill, although the displaced leaves and trail of blood told me it hadn't died at the spot we'd found it. *Which, duh, Skylar?* Even I knew there were no goats living in these woods.

'I assume so.' He took the note back. 'But it looks like somebody else got here first. Something was on this tree, but it's been carved out.' He moved out of the way, so I could see what he was talking about. And sure enough, there was a gap in the trunk where somebody had taken a knife and carved off the outer layer.

'Why?' I sputtered, wondering what anybody outside of us two would want with it. We couldn't even be sure they'd carved out what we were looking for. 'Who even knew this was here?'

'Did you tell anybody we were coming out here?' he asked, raising a questioning brow at me. I shook my head violently, but then unease settled in my gut. 'Or what we were looking for?'

I took out my phone to take a picture of the tree. I needed proof of what I was seeing. Plus, I wanted to compare it to the tree in the picture in the yearbook.

Looking at my home screen, I saw that I'd received a message while we'd been searching.

Everything going okay, Stutter?

Shit. I'd forgotten to text Leo after two hours to let him know I was okay. Ollie's words repeated in my head. *Did you tell anybody?*

I had told nobody about the tree, but I *had* told Leo where I was heading. He wouldn't have had the time to do all of that, though, right?

Sure it took longer than two hours to carve out a tree and drag a dead goat. Plus, where would you even find a goat to slaughter on such short notice?

The feeling in my stomach told me I wasn't quite as sure about the answer to those questions as I'd like to be.

Forty-Two

'STUTTER!' Leo's voice called from somewhere nearby. 'Skylar!'

'Leo?' I called back. 'We're—' I paused, unsure where we were. 'Somewhere near if you can hear me.'

'I thought you said you didn't tell anybody we were out here?' Ollie said in an accusing tone.

Leo came into view up ahead and I waved, ignoring Ollie's question. 'Hey! What are you doing out here?'

'You told me to stage a rescue if I didn't hear from you in two hours.' Leo came closer and Ollie growled. 'When you didn't reply to my text, I thought I better head out here and see what was going on. I wouldn't have been so worried if I knew you were with Ollie.'

'It's cool,' I said, waving his worry off. 'We were about to head back, anyway.'

'Were we?' Ollie asked, still giving Leo an irritated glare. 'Because we just found a dead goat and a note addressed to you.'

'Want to go into a little more detail?' Leo asked Ollie, coming to stand beside me, pulling me into his body with an outstretched hand. 'What did the note say?'

Ollie thrust the note into Leo's other hand. 'Read it yourself.'

Leo read the note in silence, then looked at us both with a shuttered off expression. 'What the fuck does it even mean?'

'No clue,' I said. 'Was sort of hoping maybe you'd have a little more insight?'

'Sorry to disappoint you, Stutter, but I've not got a clue.' Leo handed the note back to me and I put it in my inside blazer pocket, so I could add it to the others when I got back to my room. I was amassing quite a collection! Lucky me.

'That's cool because neither do we,' I said with a forced smile. Not that I'd expected Leo to understand the note, but it was irritating to know he couldn't help and that we were no better off than before. 'Shall we head back? It's getting a little chilly out here and there's not much we can do. Plus, that goat *stinks*.'

'What brought you two out here, anyway?' Leo asked, looking around the patch of trees we'd stopped in. 'Seems an odd place to go in search of.'

'Just something we found in an old yearbook,' I told him. 'Means we're on the right track, though, doesn't it?'

'If you say so, Stutter.' Leo laughed at me, but I knew it wasn't meant in a nasty way. He just found it amusing how serious I was taking researching the school's history—he'd told me multiple times how cute he found it. 'Ready to head to dinner?'

'Duh!' I glanced at Ollie and the brittle smile he was faking, and saw a chance to make things a little right in the world. 'Want to join us?'

'Me?' Ollie asked, looking around as if he'd find somebody standing behind him. In the middle of the woods. Nobody around for miles. I rolled my eyes but kept my smile in his direction.

'Yes, you. Who else would I be asking? The goat?'

Ollie chuckled. 'Are you sure?'

'Yeah! The more, the merrier.' I looked over at Leo. 'Right, babe?'

Leo shrugged and gave me an assessing look. 'Right. It'll be good to have you back, mate.'

'Only if you're sure?' Ollie didn't look convinced. 'Won't Griff and Clover mind?'

'Course not,' I said, not knowing whether they would or not

but also not really caring either way. 'It's always good to have a buffer from Griff's bullshit anyway.'

The three of us laughed and I could feel the ice melting, just a little.

'That's very true!' Ollie laughed. 'The boy does talk a lot of crap.'

'Proper,' Leo agreed. 'So you coming with us?'

'Yeah, I think I will. Thanks.' Ollie shook Leo's hand and all of a sudden they were mates again, no questions asked.

Boys are weird.

'No problem. Now let's get a hurry on because I'm starving!'

We headed back to school as a unit, the three of us having a stilted conversation about something and nothing, and I smiled inwardly. It felt good, ya know? Like something was once again the way it should be.

And I once again realised how far I'd come in such a short time.

'How's the research going?' Leo looked at me with care shining from his gaze and my heart about melted right there on his bedroom floor. 'Find anything else out since the woods?'

'Not yet.' I grimaced. 'But we will. I've asked Flo to help.'

The incident in the woods had happened a week ago, and yet I was no further in my mission to find out what the fuck happened and why somebody had killed a goat and left me a note.

Hey, that rhymes! I'm a poetic genius. Maybe spending all my time in the library *was* paying off.

'The ancient librarian?' He chuckled. 'Trust you to ask the oldest person here to help you.'

'Flo's a sweetheart! Plus, if she's the oldest person here, then maybe she was here when our parents were and can tell us a lot of what we don't know.'

'You're always the optimist, aren't you, Stutter?'

'Yep.' I nodded, ignoring his laugh. 'I really think Flo wants to help us.'

'Remember, she's employed by my aunt. She won't tell you more than she's allowed.'

I paused in my pacing, once again forgetting that Ms Hawthorn was his aunt. The woman was so hard and poison-faced, it was easy to forget she had a family. A family that cared, even if they acted otherwise a lot of the time. The way they'd all reacted to her being attacked on the day of the swim meet entered my mind. Their worry had been palpable and clearly they cared a little more than they let on.

'True, but a girl can hope, right?'

He nodded, and I went to sit beside him.

'Somebody left her that note,' I said, resting my hand on his thigh. 'And I want to know who.'

'Somebody or some group of people we're not meant to know about.' He lifted my hand and placed a gentle kiss on the back of it, his lips soft. Sometimes he could be so fucking endearing.

'Right,' I agreed. 'But it doesn't stop me wanting to know.'

'You are a nosey one,' he said, and I knew he meant it. I was nosey, and he'd mentioned it before, usually when I tried to earwig at the conversation taking place next to us during dinner.

'True.' I chuckled. 'But you love that about me.'

I'd been joking, but when the words left my lips, the room went quiet. I couldn't keep my hands still, waiting for Leo to speak; to break the quiet that had descended over us. He didn't need to say anything profound or even exciting. Just words to break the tension.

'I think I do,' he admitted, his voice so soft I had to strain to hear him. I stopped my pacing and went to sit beside him on the bed, the shock stopping me from being able to do anything else.

My heart was beating at an alarming rate—so fast I thought it would be visible to him, like a silly cartoon heart stretching my chest. His words, and their meaning, were something we'd been tiptoeing around, neither of us brave enough to voice the truth, and now that he'd put it out there, the full extent of my feelings came rushing to the forefront of my mind.

Shit.

'You do?' I whispered, gulping away my nerves. I'd known the moment would come—that the conversation would come—but I still wasn't ready for it, or the repercussions that may come from it.

'Honestly, Stutter, I don't know.' Leo looked at me, a mixture of love and grief on his face. 'I think I do.'

'I thought we were just...' I looked away, unable to keep his stare. 'We started this as a revenge plot.'

'We did.'

'Didn't enact a lot of revenge, did we?' I chuckled. 'Pissed off some people, though.'

'Oh, we definitely pissed them off. Rattled some cages. But that's not what we're talking about right now.' His fingers gripped my chin. 'Look at me, Stutter.'

'I'm afraid of what I'll say,' I admitted but turned to look at him anyway. 'This may have started out as a plot and a means to an end, but it's become one of the most real things to ever happen to me.'

'It feels weird to say it, but I feel the same way,' Leo said, his tone cracking. 'What do we do?'

'You're asking me?' I laughed at the absurdity of it all. 'I was kinda hoping you'd tell me what you thought we should do.'

'If you want the truth,' he said, and I nodded. 'Then I don't want us to do anything different. I want to keep seeing where this thing is going between us.'

'Right...' My mind was turning over all the questions I wanted to ask him, wondering which one I should ask first. 'I just want to make sure we're on the same page.'

'Stutter,' he moaned. 'Do I need to talk about my feelings with you?'

'Maybe,' I said with a laugh. 'But only if you want to.'

'I wouldn't even know where to start, but there's one thing I will tell you.'

'And what's that?'

'I like you, Stutter. I more than like you. At least a little.' Leo locked eyes with me and my heart fluttered. When he turned his attention to me, it made me feel like the only girl that mattered. The only one he saw. 'And I hope you feel the same way, at least a little.'

'I'd be lying if I said I didn't,' I admitted, telling him the truth. 'But what about Clover?'

'What about her?'

'Don't be obtuse on purpose!' I punched his shoulder, with no real force behind it. 'I asked a valid question.'

'And I'll turn it back on you,' he replied. 'What about Ollie?'

'What about him?' I joked, my grin wide. 'No, but seriously'— I took a deep breath—'I'm not thinking about him right now. Or the past. Just us.'

'And that's how I feel about Clover.' Leo brushed his fingertips against my cheek. 'In the beginning, you know I was doing this all to piss her off. But then I stopped thinking about her when I was with you, alone, and as time went on, I stopped thinking about her even when she was around.'

'We're nightmares, aren't we?' Leo cracked a smile at my poor attempt at humour. Deep down, I knew it was my fault. Hadn't every film or book taught us that a fake relationship scheme *never* went the way you intended it to? Everybody always ended up falling.

And that was what was happening between me and Leo.

We were falling. *Really* falling.

To top it all off? I wasn't sure I wanted to stop.

Forty - Three

'DO you think if I were a superhero, I'd be a good one?' Griff asked the table, his tone serious.

It was another meal, and another one of Griff's incessant questions where nothing truly mattered—the question or the answer—but we were all expected to answer as seriously as we could. A game of sorts. A way to pass the time.

'What?' I sputtered, accidentally spitting out some of my soda.

'If I were a superhero,' Griff stated slowly, as if *I* was the one who was acting oddly. 'Would I be a good one?'

'How do we define good?' Ollie asked, rubbing his chin with his forefinger, taking the question a lot more seriously than Clover or me. Clo rolled her eyes behind Griff's head, when he turned to look at Ollie.

'You know, like Superman or Batman.' Griff nodded, getting into the topic, glad one of us was humouring him.

'Is Batman good?' Ollie asked, his eyes alight with interest. 'Or is he just a wealthy dickhead with a complex?'

'Hm, good point.' Griff smiled wide. 'We've met a few of them.'

'Wealthy dickheads?' Leo asked, picking up his glass to take a sip of his water. His other hand was beneath the table, resting firmly on my thigh as he played with the hem of my skirt. 'Or specifically wealthy dickheads with a complex?'

'I mean, you're sitting next to one,' Griff said with a chuckle, and Ollie reached across the table and flicked him on the forehead.

'And you're a prick,' Ollie said.

Clo and I laughed at the three of them, and it felt like before. Actually, it felt better than before because Leo was around. The girls sat at their own table, holding court for all the kids who wanted to get close to them in the hopes they'd get special treatment.

The rest of the meal went well—surprisingly well—seeing as it was only the third time all five of us had eaten together.

'Can I walk you back to your room?' Leo asked, and I quirked my eyebrow, wondering why he had to ask. It was a given.

'Yeah...' I gave him an assessing look. 'Any particular reason?'

He laughed and leaned in to whisper in my ear, 'I just didn't want to give Ollie a chance to ask you.'

'I doubt he would've,' I replied, turning to whisper in his ear. The three others at the table gave us quizzical looks.

'Don't underestimate him, Stutter. He's apologised for real and he's realised how bad he fucked things up with you.'

'Whatever you say.'

'Me and Stutter are getting out of here,' he announced to the table. 'Enjoy the rest of your evening.'

Everybody murmured their goodbyes, then the two of us made our way back to my room.

'That dinner wasn't awful, was it?' I asked, swinging our arms in between us. 'I'd say it was a success.'

'Indeed.'

'You okay? You seem a little down.'

'I'm good, Stutter,' he said, squeezing my hand. 'Just thinking.'

'Well, don't hurt yourself.' I laughed, but he stayed quiet.

My bedroom door came into view. There was a note attached to the door by a knife. A big, sharp motherfucker with a large black grip handle.

'Don't touch that!' Leo said, reaching to stop my outstretched hand from touching the note or the knife.

A chill crept down my spine, and my mind went back to the night I'd found the dead rabbit on my bed. Every time the image entered my thoughts, nausea rose in my gut. We still didn't know who placed it there and, as much as I tried to put it to the back of my mind, it still sat there uninvited.

Not forgetting that I was stabbed with a knife. *Shit.* My hand clenched my stomach, hoping I could keep down the bile threatening to rise. 'Leo,' I whispered, my voice breaking. 'You don't think...?'

'No,' he said, knowing what I meant. 'The police have the knife that stabbed you.'

My breathing became easier. 'That's good then.'

'Let me get the note,' Leo said and I nodded, letting him snatch the note from behind the knife. Then on second thought, he took the knife, too. 'Maybe this will come in handy.'

We entered my room, moving to my bed and sitting on the edge of the mattress. Leo handed the note over and I made quick work of unfolding the piece of paper. Scrawled unfamiliar handwriting greeted me and I had to squint to understand the message.

> Skylar, there is so much I wish I could tell you.
> Don't trust anyone.
> Take this knife for protection.
> Hope to see you at the New Year's gala.

There was no name attached. No signature sign-off.

'Who do you think this is from?' I asked Leo, handing the note to him so he could read it better. 'Clearly, whoever it is, plans to go to the gala.'

Leo turned the note over, then refolded it with meticulous care. 'I've got no idea, but I don't think they're friendly.'

'What makes you think that?' I glanced at the knife in his hand. 'They've literally given me a massive knife for protection.'

'I just get a bad vibe,' he said, turning the knife around in his hand, studying it. 'There are two weeks until the gala. I'll keep an eye out for anybody and see if any of the guys know anything.' I nodded. 'It'll be okay, Stutter.'

'You promise?' It was an unfair question—he couldn't promise me that everything would be okay, but I didn't take the question back.

'I promise,' he replied, placing a kiss on my forehead. 'I'll always have your back.'

Shit, when did he become so fucking cute?

STANDING in an alcove in the admin building, Leo and I were holding on to one another tight, minding our own business in between classes, when a cough came up behind us.

'What's going on here?' Ollie walked over to where the two of us were standing, a sly smile on his face. 'The two of you seem suspicious.'

'We're literally just standing here,' I said, and even though I knew I didn't need to, I took a step back from Leo. Ever since Ollie's apology, things between us were at least civil, and I didn't want to do anything to disrupt the truce we'd found ourselves in.

'Is there a reason why you've bothered us?' Leo drawled, not even bothering to look in Ollie's direction. 'We were having such a good time before you showed up.'

'Really?' Ollie laughed. ''Cause Sky was looking pretty bored when I walked over here.'

Before I could say something to refute Ollie's bullshit, Ms Hawthorn's voice cut across the noise in the hall.

'Son, I'll see you in my office,' she said sharply, addressing Ollie as she walked past. Her face was sour, as per usual, and her grey hair resembled a dish scrubbing brush stuck to the top of her head.

'Did you just call me son?' Ollie demanded, heat emanating off of him, and it was like standing too close to burning flames. He turned to face Ms Hawthorn, who'd halted her stride when Ollie had spoken back.

'Did you just question me?' Ms Hawthorn's glare was piercing.

I stood, frozen. Leo quirked an eyebrow but seemed otherwise unbothered. The whole scenario reeked of *odd*. She'd never called him son before. Why would she? She was his mother's sister, yeah, but that didn't mean she could call him a name he'd reserved in his mind for Millie's memory.

'I did, you bitch,' he snarled, his teeth bared.

'My apologies, Master Brandon,' she said through gritted teeth, the apology paining her. I felt certain she would rather have eaten live bees than grovel to Ollie.

Ollie faced me, his eyes boring into mine. 'Who the fuck does she think she is?'

I didn't know how to respond. I reckoned it was a slip of the tongue and Ollie felt overly sensitive about it because of the reminders that word gave him. Also, whenever his dad called him Son, it was usually followed by something demeaning or shitty.

'Sure she meant nothing by it,' Leo said, bored of the interruption. 'She's probably losing her marbles, mate.'

'Unlike you to stick up for Winnie,' Ollie said, assessing Leo.

'Does she have children?' I asked, knowing the answer, but mostly wanting to stop the guys from arguing. The two of them hadn't acted the same around one another since Halloween, and I was too much of a coward to ask either one of them why.

'Nope,' Ollie said, his eyes hard. 'The miserable bitch found nobody that loved her enough to want to go on a date with her, let alone fuck her.'

'Oh,' I said and fell silent once more. It was clear to me that Ollie didn't think much of his aunt, but the way he'd said it was filled with so much venom I wondered if there was a history between them I hadn't heard. Leo gripped my arms, pulling me tighter to him again, no longer willing to wait for Ollie to piss off.

'No, guess I wouldn't,' I responded matter-of-factly, too tired to argue with him. And I knew how he'd meant it. I didn't understand money things—not really.

'Let's go to lunch,' Leo said, smiling at me with that tilted lip I loved the most, ignoring Ollie completely. 'You hungry?'

'Am I hungry? Pfft! It's like you don't even know me,' I said with a chuckle. I could always eat—especially if the meal contained cheese or carbs.

'I'll join you,' Ollie said, ready to follow us wherever we headed. 'Where are Griff and Clover at?'

'No idea,' Leo bit out. 'Come on then.'

The three of us headed towards the hall, Leo with his arm wrapped around my waist and Ollie walking on my other side. It was odd to spend time with both of them again, especially as it was Leo wrapped around me and not Ollie, but it also felt right. I couldn't explain it even if I wanted to.

No matter what, there was a tiny part of me still waiting for the other shoe to drop.

Forty-Four

TIME FLEW, and in no time we were all together for Christmas break at Griff's parents' estate.

Ever since Leo and I had found the note—and the knife—we'd theorised who could be behind it, but nobody we thought of made sense.

Ollie would have spoken to me about it in person. Handed the knife into my palm. After his note on Halloween went wrong, I doubted the boy would ever let a note do the talking for him ever again.

Griff also would've handed it over in person, but I also didn't believe Griff thought me to be in enough danger to even think I needed a knife for protection in the first place.

Same went for Clover.

None of it made much sense, so Leo and I had decided we'd wait until the gala and assess the situation from there.

So there we were, the five of us, sitting in the cinema room on Christmas Eve, overloading on sugar and chocolate, *The Muppets Christmas Carol* playing in the background, and Leo's arms hugging me tight to his muscled chest.

'Don't eat too much chocolate,' Clover said, looking in my direction from her position wrapped up in a blanket, sitting on Griff's lap. 'We've got our final fittings for our dresses on the 27th.'

'Clo, I've had one hot chocolate and I'm about to have some seashells. Think I'll be okay.'

Clo shrugged, her face still uncertain. 'Well, I'm just saying.'

'And I'm saying Stutter looks good no matter what and she can eat the damn chocolates if she wants, dress be damned.' Leo's voice rumbled in my ear and a smile instantly lit up my face. 'We're paying the shop enough that if it doesn't fit, they'll fix it in time.'

Leo always knew the right words to say.

It was because of him that Clover and I even had something to wear to the upcoming gala—it wasn't like I had money lying around to go and buy an expensive dress to wear only once—and it made sense to ask for it as my Christmas present.

Leo had wanted to go all out, but I made it clear that wasn't what the holiday was about for me. Sure, gifts were great and I'd be a liar if I said I'd turn them down, but I'd much rather spend time with him.

What do you get the boy who has access to everything he wants?

Right. There wasn't an answer to that question.

So, I went with the next best thing—I got Leo nothing. Well, that was a small lie. I baked some goodies for him with the help of Clover. Okay, that was an even smaller lie. Clover made most of them and I weighed out the ingredients. Basically, I helped the way I used to help my nan. Meaning, I didn't help whatsoever.

Leo had been so thankful, bless him, and had even tried to compliment my icing of the words, *Merry Christmas.*

'Thanks, babe,' I said, turning around and placing a kiss on his stubbled cheek. 'Appreciate you sticking up for me.'

'How many times do I have to tell you I've got your back, Stutter?'

I laughed. 'Maybe I'll start believing it sometime soon.'

'Probably best if you do.'

THE CHRISTMAS TREE in the living room was the biggest one I'd seen in a home.

It was beautiful.

The white lights glittered and shone off the silver baubles. The white and red candy canes dotted around made me smile, and I couldn't take my eyes off of it all. It was a masterpiece.

It was yet another sign of what money could get you.

Back at home, Mum had bought a fake tree back in the nineties and was still bringing it out year after year, never having been able to afford a real one, or even a larger pre-lit one from the supermarket—even with my discount back when I worked there.

'Hey,' Ollie said from somewhere behind me.

'Hey,' I replied, looking at the silver-glittered star tree topper. 'You okay? Having a good Christmas so far?'

'Yeah, I'm good, thanks. It's been fun, surprisingly.' He came closer. 'I'm glad y'all invited me.'

'Didn't think it would be?'

'Spending time with you and Leo? I wasn't sure if I could cope with seeing it so close without any buffers.' He chuckled, coming up behind me. I looked over my shoulder at him, but he pushed my chin back so I was facing the tree. 'I'd rather talk to your back if you don't mind.'

'If you must,' I said, respecting his wants. 'I'm all ears.'

'Sky, I know I've said sorry already, but I feel like I need to say it again at least another hundred times. You never deserved what I did to you—what I asked others to do to you. I expected you to be so different from how you are, which is a breath of fresh air compared to the girls I'm so used to being around.'

My eyes stayed on the star. 'I don't know what to say.'

'Don't say anything,' Ollie said, taking another step closer. 'I got you a present, but I wasn't sure whether to give it to you in front of everyone.'

'Why? It isn't a dick pic, is it?' I joked, my laughter getting stuck in my throat. *Why make a joke about that, Sky?* We were still trying to navigate the new, tentative friendship we'd somehow stumbled into after his apology.

Ollie moved his hands, swept my hair off from the back of my neck, and placed a cold, thin-chained necklace on me. 'I hope you like it.'

I turned around to look at him. 'Thank you.'

Our eyes locked, and an emotion that felt a lot like love surged through me. Or maybe it was lust? Once again the thought of loving two people at once ran through my head. Leo and Ollie were such different people, but they both made me feel deeply.

'You haven't even seen it yet,' he said, his lips curling up into a smile. 'You're welcome, though.'

'Well, let's go find a mirror,' I told him, heading to the bathroom without waiting to see if he was following me. The bathroom I gravitated towards was fucking massive, the kind that belonged in a wealthy person's house. All marble, with a clawfoot tub in the centre, and it was my dream bathroom.

One wall was a floor-to-ceiling mirror, and I walked straight up to it to admire the necklace.

Fuck. It was beautiful.

It had a silver chain, with a North Star pendant hanging from the centre—a North Star made up of genuine diamonds—and shitting hell, it was the most lavish and expensive gift I'd ever received.

'I saw it and it reminded me of you and that night at the hotel in London,' Ollie said. He must have entered the room while I was observing and admiring the necklace in the mirror.

'Valentine's Day?' I asked, as I remembered that night and all the emotions that came with it. 'By the window?'

'Yeah,' he muttered, uncertain whether he should even talk about that night. 'That night...' He paused, gathering his thoughts. I was looking at him in the mirror, so it didn't feel as intimate, but it felt important. 'That was the night I doubted myself the most.'

'Doubted what?'

'Doubted my plan.' He shrugged, his eyes boring into mine. 'It was that night I realised I was falling for you, too.'

'Too?' Yeah, okay, I hadn't been subtle about how I'd felt back then, but I'd only thought I was falling at that point, and we'd never spoken about it afterward.

'I knew how you felt,' he said, low, guilt lacing his tone. 'It was the reason we knew the plan would work.'

'We?' My heart dropped, and even though I knew who he was about to mention, it didn't make it hurt less. It hurt more having it all confirmed. Things with Griff and Leo were so far away from how they were when they'd planned to make my life hell, but it didn't stop it from hurting.

'*The Sect* and *The Set*.' The way he said the group's official names told me he was trying to shirk the full responsibility—or soften the blow a little.

'Right,' I said.

'Sky, at first I wanted so bad to hurt you. To make you hate the place so much you'd leave Hawthorn and never return, but then something shifted. I got to know you, and I knew what I was doing was twisted, but I couldn't stop it. Stop myself. Plus, by then the train had left the station.'

'I get it, sort of.' I shrugged. 'But what I will never get is how you could instruct the girls to beat me up.'

'I didn't,' he replied, adamant. His eyes were blazing, and his words were clear. 'I've told you so many times that wasn't me.'

'You d-didn't?' I asked, wanting so badly to believe.

'No. Never. I told them to intimidate you, that's all.'

I turned around to face him, touching the star around my neck. 'Swear?'

'Skylar, I swear on your life. Things just got out of hand.' He lowered his eyes and shuffled, moving his weight from leg to leg, which was one of *my* nervous habits, but I guessed there was a first time for everything.

'Super out of hand,' I said with a small laugh, trying to ease the tension that had seeped into the room and surrounded us.

'Totally,' he said in a fake, exaggerated accent and I laughed more.

'I forgive you, you know,' I whispered, wanting him to know that I no longer held a grudge towards him. If I was honest, I hadn't for a while. Everything in my life had righted itself, and I was no longer the same girl who joined Hawthorn with no friends and no confidence.

'I'd understand if you didn't, but I'm so fucking glad you do.' He smiled. 'So we're friends, yeah? For real this time, no tricks or plots or schemes?'

'Sure,' I replied. 'As long as you're always honest with me. Even if my outfit is awful and my hair looks like a bee's nest. Got it?'

He chuckled. 'Got it.'

Forty-Five

THE NEW YEAR'S GALA.

Fuck, had it been an entire year since the last one?

So much had happened in the past year, and honestly, some-times I thought about pinching myself to check I was living in the real world. And sometimes I pinched myself, just to double-check I wasn't making the same mistakes as last year but with a different guy.

Leo and I were attending as a couple, and I was more than ready to make our official debut as a couple. A *real* couple, and not just a fake one like we'd been during Parents' Day. It was hard to pinpoint the moment it'd become real to me, but I was beyond glad it had.

'Hey, babe, you ready for this?' Clo asked, dressed in a stun-ning, short satin red dress that suited her skin tone perfectly. Even with her hair, she looked killer. The front gave off a conservative vibe, but when she turned around, it was entirely backless until you came to a bow resting just above her bum cheeks. The skirt was a full swing skirt, making the dress fun and flirty. She looked a million dollars.

'You look banging!' I told her. 'The shop did such a good job, didn't they?'

'They've really taken it in at the right place, haven't they? I never even knew I had curves to accentuate.' Clo stood in front of our full-length mirror, assessing herself from head to toe, constantly smoothing her hands on the skirt. 'Do you think I need to thank Leo?'

'Probably best to.' My reply was muffled, a hairpin trapped between my lips. Clover had put my hair into curls, pinning the right-hand side flat to my head, reminding me of old Hollywood starlets. 'He did pay for it all.'

Leo had been super generous, paying for both Clo's and my dresses, plus any alterations we wanted. It was his Christmas gift to me, and it was so bloody thoughtful, I couldn't stop thanking him—in more ways than just with words.

I had followed my self-imposed theme of wearing princess-type dresses. I'd tried Cinderella and Belle, so for the gala I was channelling my inner Tiana. My dress was a dark emerald green, stopping at just above my knees, and it sparkled every time I moved.

I looked over at Clo and smiled. 'Right. I'm ready as I'll ever be.'

'Let's do this shit,' she said, coming forward to loop her arm in mine.

The two of us had chosen to get ready in our tiny closet room away from the boys. It wasn't that we didn't want them around, but we'd just spent the entire Christmas break with them, and it was nice to have time with Clo just the two of us—it didn't happen often these days. Most of the time I was with Leo while she was with Griff, or we were hanging around as a group of five.

Over the past year, the two of us had grown, both as people and as best friends. Yeah, we didn't have the conveniences of Leo's or Griff's enormous bathroom or the space their rooms would have given us, but I kinda liked it. Whether we liked it or not, we were the scholarship kids, and our room was a part of that journey. We didn't need a massive room with pink appliances and furniture to be happy.

We were meeting the boys in front of the hall, and as usual, I felt self-conscious walking across campus with my arm linked in Clo's. Even though I'd attended a couple of Hawthorn events, it still didn't feel natural to me yet to wear such expensive clothes, but the guys had promised me that one day soon it would.

Ollie had said, *'One day, Sky, you'll feel just at home in a formal gown as you do a summer dress.'*

I smiled at the memory. We'd been talking about how I genuinely believed I'd never fit in with the lifestyle they were all accustomed to. Since finding out I was half-Cooper, apparently, I needed to come to terms with wealth—and fast.

'Hello! Earth to Skylar!' Clo called as she waved a hand in front of my face to grab my attention. 'Where did you just go?'

'Err...' I trailed off. 'Just thinking about money, really.'

She shrugged, obviously having hoped for something a little more exciting. 'Fair enough.'

We made it to the entrance of the large auditorium and halted. Leo and Griff were standing outside the hall, waiting for us, and fuck me, Leo looked *fine*. The sight of him made me drool a little, and I attempted to subtly wipe it away without notice. Pretty certain Clo saw me in her peripheral, but she said nothing. Probably because her reaction to Griff wasn't much different.

He may be my relative, but I could accept that he also looked good! He was wearing a dark tartan suit, subtle yet loud, almost. It always amazed me how Griff could stand out and be the centre of attention while still somehow staying under a lot of peoples' radars. There was an effortlessness to him. A quality that was often overlooked.

'You two look amazing,' Griff enthused, taking me in from top to toe and then moving his gaze over to Clo. 'Babe, you are beautiful.'

A flush covered Clo's face, her cheeks going a deep red, a small smile playing on her thin lips. I had to admit, against my better judgement, that the two of them had grown on me as a couple. They seemed genuinely happy, and as long as they were happy, so was I.

It also made me happy that Leo didn't seem to care about how happy they were.

I took my eyes away from them and found myself locking

onto Leo's gaze. His eyes had darkened, the way they did during sex—something we'd done more than once after we made our feelings for each other known—or when he was at his most turned on.

'You are fucking perfection,' he growled, leaning down to my ear. Pulling me close, I sighed with happiness and his warmth enveloped me. *Fuck*, falling had never felt so good.

'You scrub up pretty well,' I told him, my voice low. 'But I think I'd prefer it on the floor.'

'Well, isn't that brazen of you, Stutter.' His eyes lit up. 'I like the way you think.'

I wrapped my arms around the back of his neck, pulling his face down so it came level with mine. In my heels, the gap wasn't as big between us and I felt more in my element, more in control.

Our lips crashed together, and we shared a brief, but passionate, kiss before Clo and Griff cleared their throats. 'There'll be time for that later, lovebirds,' Griff said, waggling his eyebrows comically. We chuckled at him and broke apart.

'Oh, leave them alone, dickhead,' Clo piped up, and I cheered in response with a laugh.

'Where's Ollie?' I asked, realising he wasn't with them. 'I thought he was meeting us here.'

'So did we,' Leo said with a shrug. 'But neither of us has heard from him.'

'Strange.' I looked around at the crowd of people entering the school, hoping to spot his brown hair above the throng, but I couldn't see him anywhere. 'Maybe he's already in there?'

'Maybe,' Griff said. 'Only one way to find out. My lady.' He reached out his arm for Clo to put hers through, and Leo did the same for me.

Entering the gala on Leo's arm was a dream. One I didn't want to wake up from.

The four of us headed into the hall, all eyes turning to look as we entered. I spotted Lottie and Edward Hawthorn on the far side, meaning we had to pass everybody else to reach them. They were standing with Henry Brandon and... Ollie?

Why would he be with his dad, without us all for a buffer, if he didn't have to?

Without a word, we made our way over, and we ignored all the glares we were getting.

'Son,' Edward said, pride in his voice, reaching out to take Leo into a bear hug. 'You've scrubbed up nice as always. Skylar, dear, you look beautiful.'

'Thank you!' I reached forward and kissed both his cheeks, while Lottie was hugging Leo with even more force than Edward had. Once she let go of Leo, I kissed Lottie's cheeks, happy to be in her presence. Leo really did have great parents. 'You look stunning!'

'In this old thing?' Lottie laughed, giving me a twirl. 'Hello, Griffin. Clover.'

They murmured their greetings, and I turned to face Ollie and Henry. Ollie's eyes locked with mine and I quirked an eyebrow in his direction as if to say, *Are you feeling okay? Do you need rescuing?*

He looked away, either not understanding my telepathic question, or ignoring it completely.

I caught Griff's eye, and his face mirrored my thoughts; baffled, but keeping quiet.

'Skylar,' Henry said, noticing our presence, as his gaze travelled from my eyes down to my feet, and then travelled back up and rested on my chest. The guys coughed, and Henry once again looked at my face. 'You look absolutely stunning, as per usual. Leo is very lucky to have you.'

'Thank you,' I replied, my gut swirling, feeling uncomfortable. I gritted my teeth, making sure my smile was firm on my face. 'You're too kind.'

'Modest, too,' he said with a chortle. I glimpsed Lottie's and Edward's faces, and the two of them were wearing fake smiles too.

Guess I'm not the only person here lying.

Ollie smiled at me. 'He's not lying, Little One. You look amazing.'

A sharp intake of breath came from my side. 'Can I speak with you in private?' Leo asked Ollie through gritted teeth.

I took a step away from Leo's side to find him glaring at Ollie, super angry.

'Is it important? I'm having an *enlightening* talk with my dad.' The emphasis wasn't lost on anyone. None of it made sense.

Leo didn't let it bother him, though, and insisted, 'Come on, mate. The quicker we leave, the faster we return.'

'I've been summoned.' Ollie laughed. 'We'll be back soon.'

'Don't be too long, you two,' Lottie said. 'The meal starts soon.'

They nodded in acknowledgement and walked out of the hall, already deep in conversation. Even from across the hall, I could tell it was a heated discussion.

What the fuck is going on?

WHEN THE TWO of them came back, you wouldn't have known there had been any tension between them earlier. They were laughing and joking and seemed fine. Okay, maybe not laughing and joking, but they *were* half smiling, which was basically the same thing when it came to Leo and Ollie.

They joined us at the table and, although things were a little awkward at first, the conversation flowed once we'd eaten our starters. So many topics were covered it was hard to keep up. The food was so good I became more interested in that than whatever was being said.

So what? I love food, all right?

After the meal, the band started playing on the stage and I grabbed Clo's hand and pulled her up.

'Come fly with me,' I said with a giggle, dragging her over to the area they'd cleared for dancing.

'Only if you don't tread on my toes,' she replied, laughing.

'No promises. You know how clumsy I can be!' I smiled, so glad to be sharing the moment with her. It really felt as if Clo and I had come full circle since last New Year's. We were stronger and were entering the new year as the best of friends. *Real* friends. Somebody I'd actively choose to spend time with outside of Hawthorn and not just because we were both roped into sharing a bedroom.

We were the first two on the floor, and as soon as people saw us, they migrated our way, no longer afraid to get up and dance. The two of us were dancing away, singing along to all the songs, and just in general, thoroughly enjoying ourselves.

The music changed and became smoother. Slower.

A tall figure came up behind me, causing a shadow, and leaned down to whisper in my ear, 'Shall we dance, Stutter?'

'Didn't think slow dancing was your thing,' I replied, looking up into Leo's blue eyes.

'It's not,' he admitted. 'But I couldn't leave you looking so stunning out here without a partner. Some other guy would've snapped you up.'

'I doubt that.' I laughed. 'But thanks for the ego boost.'

'Sky'—he looked around the room, swaying from side to side —'every guy in here is jealous of me tonight, and it isn't solely because I'm the Hawthorn heir.'

'Oof, I love it when you're conceited,' I joked, looking around to see where his gaze was focused. My eyes landed on Ollie standing off to the side of the dance floor, a wide, shit-eating grin on his face. 'What did you need to talk to Ollie about earlier?'

'Nothing important.' He shrugged my words off and didn't elaborate.

'Important enough you needed to go somewhere private.' My eyes narrowed with suspicion. 'So must've been a little important.'

He let out a deep sigh. 'If you really must know.'

I waited.

'Skylar, there's something I need to tell you.' His voice was distant; his eyes shifty.

'Can I cut in?' Ollie asked, his eyes aglint with some unknown emotion. 'Please?'

'Actually—' I started, but Ollie cut me off.

'Leo won't mind, will you, mate?'

Leo's face said he minded a lot, but for some reason, instead of telling Ollie that, he said, 'Sure. But not for too long.'

Leo stepped out of my embrace, and within an instant, Ollie's body replaced him. He looked just as good as Leo in his suit, and when I'd spotted him across the hall when we arrived, I'd had to hide my natural reaction to just how good he looked. His hands came up to rest on my waist, and I locked my hands together around his neck.

We slow-danced in silence for a little while.

'Did you think this time last year we'd be here?' I asked, saying the thought that had been playing on my mind all evening. The end of a year always made people remember the past, and I couldn't help but compare everything to last year. A year ago, we'd slept together for the first time, and even though I knew it hadn't been real on his part, it still was real for me. 'So much has happened.'

He smiled. 'Who'd have thought Griff and Clover would be a legit couple at this point?'

'Not me!' I chuckled, happy the two of us were getting along without any awkward tension. 'And did you think I'd be with Leo? 'Cause I sure as hell didn't!'

Ollie stopped dancing abruptly, taking his hands off of my waist, and stepped back from me. Instantly, I was cold without his touch.

'Once again, Little One, you've been deceived.' His voice was raised, and the people nearest us stopped to look and listen.

Deceived?

'W-what?' I asked, stuttering in my confusion. I'd been doing so well, barely a stutter in weeks, yet one line from him derailed my progress completely.

I looked at him. *Really* looked at him. There was something off in his eyes. I couldn't place it and I thought I'd seen most of Ollie's emotions.

He looked back at me with equal distrust in his eyes, and the showdown after the fashion show came to mind.

The image was the same, even if the setting was different. I remembered the dark indigo of his eyes, the way they'd burned in hatred, all aimed towards me; a hatred that had been there for long before he'd ever met me.

The way they'd burned in hatred while staring at me while standing over Odette's dead body.

Fuck. What?

Was that an actual memory or my mind playing tricks on me?

I'd had wine with dinner, but I'd eaten enough that I didn't think it would've made much of an impact on me.

'Poor little Skylar. How does it feel being the last to know?'

I broke out into all-body shivers, unable to move. Unable to breathe. My whole body turned clammy at the unearthed memory. 'Being the last to know w-what?'

Surely I wasn't remembering it right? There was no way Ollie was able to get from the pool room to above Odette's dead body without some kind of teleportation.

We were both standing in the middle of the hall with nowhere to hide. Nowhere for me to run, either. All eyes were on us—the sideshow that had taken over the New Year's Gala for everybody's entertainment. I wanted to flee. Wanted to run away from the hate and the stares.

One day soon, I hoped there would be a charity function I wasn't the main attraction at.

'It w-was *you*.' My voice left me in a whisper, not wanting to put the thought in my mind out into the universe. Vocalising it would only make it worse. 'Wasn't it?'

'It w-was?' he stuttered, a glint of menace in his eyes, the smile he'd had all night disappearing.

'You d-did it. It was you.'

'I d-did what?' His relaxed posture was at odds with the anger on his face as he mocked me—mocked my stutter. It was something I barely did anymore, yet he was able to bring it out of me as if it had never left in the first place.

My thoughts were running away from me. There was no way Ollie had drowned himself on Halloween, and there was no way he could have attacked Ms Hawthorn during the swim team meet. There was no way he had the time to leave the pool room and stab Odette upstairs in the hallway. Something didn't add up.

'You stabbed me?' I shouted, but it came out as a question because of how unsure I was. If people weren't paying attention before, they definitely were after my voice echoes throughout the hall. The band stopped playing and everything seemed to come to a halt.

'Leo can answer that question,' Ollie drawled.

'What's Leo got to do with any of this?' I looked around, hoping to find Leo in the crowd, but I couldn't see him.

Ollie opened his mouth, to explain further, determined to shatter me with his words with a sparkle in his eye.

'Get out of my way!' a deep voice shouted over the whispers, drawing everybody's gaze. 'Move!'

A figure hurtled forward, breaking through the crowd, and everybody, including me, gasped.

What on earth is going on here?

Forty-Six

MY EYES COULDN'T MAKE sense of what they were seeing.

In front of me, hatred still shining in his eyes, was Ollie. The Ollie we'd been with the entire evening, but unlike the events of the fashion show, he was no longer aiming the hatred in his eyes at me.

He aimed it at the newcomer who'd burst into the hall.

The newcomer who was the spitting image of him—another Ollie. His eyes were wild, his hair unbrushed and wayward.

What. In. The. Actual. Fuck?

'Skylar,' the unkept Ollie said, his eyes pleading with me to understand. 'I promise this isn't what it looks like! This imposter took me last night. Locked me in a room tied to a bed. I've only just been able to break free.'

'Skylar,' the Ollie who'd been at the gala all night said. His eyes, so similar to the clone standing next to him, were dark and cold. 'This guy's the imposter!'

'But who the f-fuck is he?' I asked, not knowing who to believe.

Ollie had a twin? How had I not known Ollie had a twin? Nobody had ever said anything about it to me. Even when I'd made my jokes about my dad and Griff's dad, who were twins, banging Ollie's mum and her sister, also twins.

Because Ollie being a twin *was* the only logical explanation. The only thing in the hall at that moment that made sense. Right?

The crowd had hushed. Barely a whisper could be heard, the only noise coming from glasses being refilled and drinks being slurped. Everybody was watching the drama unfold. If I wasn't living in the centre of it, I'd have done the same.

I looked frantically around the room, trying to find Leo or Griff and Clover, but the only person who stood out from the crowd to me was Henry Brandon, who looked as shocked as I was. His face had paled, and there was a mixture of shock and fear in his eyes.

It made no sense. How had the news shocked him? Surely if anyone knew, it was him.

'I have no idea,' Ollie on the right shouted, running his hands through his hair. A gesture I always associated with a frustrated Ollie. 'Who the fuck are you?'

'I'm Ollie,' he said with a smirk, enjoying himself. 'Aren't I?'

He locked eyes with me, the question aimed at me, and I wished somebody would rescue me from the situation I'd somehow found myself in.

My eyes kept flicking between the two of them, watching a game of fucked up tennis.

Shit, was this a case of an *actual* impostor? I'd seen a movie like that once—a horror film, of course—where somebody came along and tried to steal someone else's entire life. A chill ran down my spine. Who was the real Ollie?

'I-I...' I trailed off, blindsided. 'Tell me the truth.'

'Just tell them, Son,' a voice called from the crowd, but it wasn't Henry's. The voice came from a female and everybody in the crowd gasped, turning around to find the culprit.

I could tell *whoever he was* didn't want to tell. That he was getting a kick out of this—a sick thrill—and wanted to keep up the charade for as long as possible.

Ms Hawthorn stepped into the area, breaking free of the circle of onlookers.

'Orlando, tell them,' she demanded, her voice scratchy. She'd worn an evening gown, but all I could see was a modern-day Ms Havisham of sorts. Dressed in a musty dress—decaying. Bitter.

Orlando?

What in the actual fucking fuckity fuck is happening right now?

I watched *Orlando* squirm before covering it up with a swagger. 'Fine,' he called out, addressing everybody in the room, a wide smile on his face. 'The game is up. The name's Orlando Hawthorn. Pleased to meet you.'

The room erupted. The sound of people moving and gossiping, rising, but all I could focus on were the two boys standing before me.

Leo appeared at my side, grabbing my hand tightly, an urgent whisper on his lips. 'We need to get out of here, Stutter. I don't trust this one bit.'

'Wait up!' Orlando called to us, his eyes locked on the spot where our hands met with great curiosity. 'You not gonna tell her?'

Leo shifted beside me, ready to turn and leave without giving Orlando an answer, but I was also curious and didn't want to leave without knowing.

'Tell me what?'

'Leo's been keeping secrets from you, Little One.' Orlando's smile was pure evil. 'More than a few.'

My stomach dropped, a thought entering my mind unbidden and unwelcome. Did I need to revisit every memory I had with Oliver? Did I need to doubt every interaction and worry that I'd been with Orlando instead?

Leo tugged my hand again. 'I can explain everything, just not here.'

Did Leo already know about Orlando? My heart splintered at the thought. Orlando had said while we were dancing I'd once again been deceived, and once he revealed himself, it made sense he was talking about himself. But what if he wasn't talking about himself at all?

'We can't leave without Ollie,' I said, looking across at the boy with an equally shattered heart. He was so shocked he still hadn't moved. Lost in his own head, unable to hear Griff and Clo, who were trying to get him to move, talking to him, urging him to leave with them.

'Nobody's going anywhere until we get to the bottom of this!' Edward stepped forward, brandishing a gun.

What in the actual fuck? Since when did tight-laced Edward Hawthorn own a *gun*?

'Dad?' Leo's voice wobbled, and his grip on my arm tightened. A bruise would form within hours. 'What are you doing?'

'Stay where you are!' Edward shouted, using a tone I'd never heard from him. Serious, powerful, and in charge.

I'd never seen a real-life gun before. Even growing up in a poorer area, I'd never witnessed something like this or been in close proximity to unhinged people holding deadly weapons.

The knife strapped against my leg was useless—the saying never bring a knife to a gun fight reverberating through my skull.

'Oh, *Uncle Eddy*,' Orlando mocked, moving his hand to his jacket pocket. 'I wouldn't do that if I were you.' Orlando pulled out a gun and aimed it at Edward, the two in a life-or-death stand-off.

Nobody knew what to do. Everyone was frozen in time; in disbelief.

'Don't do it,' Leo shouted, but he was no longer facing his dad. He was looking at Orlando, a plea in his gaze. 'This wasn't a part of our deal!'

My heart fully shattered, pieces scattered all over the floor, the pain indescribable. Worse than being stabbed by your ex-boyfriend's secret twin brother.

'Your d-deal?' I sputtered. 'You knew about him? About this?'

A single tear trickled down my cheek, the only indication of my broken soul. How had I put myself in the same situation twice? Did all the boys at Hawthorn lie and deceive to reach their goals? Or was that the case for every boy everywhere?

Leo glanced at me, a brief look, before he turned back to the stand-off a short distance away. 'Stutter, I can explain when there's not a gun pointed at my dad's head.'

Orlando had pointed his gun at Edward and all hell broke loose. People tried to flee, but they only ended up running into one another. A few made it to the doors, but they were closed, heavy, and nobody was thinking straight.

I was so distracted by those fleeing, I forgot the terror unfolding in front of my face.

A gunshot rang out.

A scream.

Then, silence.

Epilogue

TONIGHT WENT EXACTLY how I wanted it to. With a few minor glitches, true, but who could have guessed that he would ruin everything we had worked so hard for. I thought I'd taught him better than that.

You'd think everybody involved at Hawthorn would know they weren't going to be getting a *happily ever after*. That nonsense only ever happened in fairy tales and films.

They didn't deserve their happily ever after. Not after everything they'd done.

They disgusted me.

Every single one of them.

The boy shouldn't have ruined the plan like that. He too needed to be taught a lesson.

In the future, I couldn't trust anybody but me to enact my plans. They say if you want a job done, it's always best to do it yourself.

I wouldn't be forgetting that again.

It was a shame about the Cooper boy. I'd been quite fond of his father, after all. Shame his bitch of a mother didn't do what was right. She was a selfish cunt who deserved everything that happened to her. I only wished she'd suffered more.

It really had been a shame about her husband's death.

Now I guess you truly could say like father, like son.

Yes.
The New Year was starting exactly how I'd wanted it to.
With a bang.

DISTURBED

book three

DISTURBED

adjective -
emotionally or psychologically troubled

Prologue

MY HEART POUNDED in my chest, threatening to leave it.

Numb. Lost. *Whole*.

I was all of those things and more. Bile sat in my stomach.

'Skylar!' Ollie's voice sounded as if it was coming from behind a door. Or a wall. One I couldn't penetrate. 'Skylar!'

His face appeared in front of mine.

I watched his mouth move, but the words were still foggy.

'We've got to go!'

One

GRIFF'S FACE looked the same, if a little bruised, and I smiled, thrilled to be in his presence even if we were in the dank hospital.

'How are you feeling today?' I asked.

The first time I'd visited him, he looked so small in the bed—the bright white sheets had swallowed him as he lay sleeping—and even though a week had passed since the shooting, I still wanted to shield him from the world.

'You look better!'

'Cheers, Clouds. You don't look so bad yourself.'

'I look like shit, Griff. No need to butter me up,' I replied, sending a small smile his way. Being around him made me happy. Yes, he may be my family, but he was also one of my best friends.

'Nah,' he dragged out. 'You look a tad tired, 'tis all.'

The aftermath of New Year's was a blur, and I still hadn't come to terms with any of it. The one thing I remembered vividly: the gunshot that had rung out throughout the hall and disrupted the peace. A second gunshot came after the first.

The one that shattered everything.

The first shot had hit Griff. The second, Clover.

'I am tired,' I replied, rubbing my face. 'I'm not sleeping well.'

'I bet.' He nodded. 'Not much better in this place. There's someone on the ward who constantly shouts about not wanting to be attacked by the soldiers, poor guy. I'm hoping I get to leave soon.'

The paramedics had grazed Griff's shoulder, and the paramedics had rushed him to the hospital, where he had made a pretty speedy recovery. In typical Griff fashion, he acted like a cheeky patient with every nurse assigned to his care, and flirted his way to an extra pudding every evening.

'I doubt they'll keep you here much longer.' My words sounded hollow—I had no clue how long they planned to keep him there—but Griff appreciated them, regardless.

Clo hadn't been as lucky.

They were both staying in the hospital I'd stayed in after my stabbing. A *private* hospital I'd since found out and cost a fuck ton of money. Goes to show how little attention I paid while in residence, as I'd stayed three weeks and hadn't realised somebody was paying for my stay there—in a room all to myself no less.

'Have you heard the latest from Ollie?' Griff asked, and I shook my head. Things were weird between all of us and since the gala, even though he'd barely left my side, Ollie existed in his own spiral of hurt, trying to figure out how his family had lied to him his entire life. And who had lied to him, and what they'd lied about.

It would be some time until he rooted out where the deceit started. To know how long the family had let it fester.

'I've not spoken to him today,' I said. 'Why? What's going on?'

Ollie was staying with his father at the house on the Hawthorn grounds, and I was staying in my dorm at Hawthorn alone. Leo was staying in his suite in the staff quarters. The same Leo who had told me not so long ago he was falling for me, yet could no longer make eye contact for more than a second.

I needed to get him alone, needed to corner him somehow and find out what he knew, because after everything Orlando said at the gala, it was apparent Leo knew a lot more than the rest of us.

Then there was the issue of Orlando himself.

' ... out on bail.' Griff's lips turned down, and I shook my head to clear the cobwebs.

'Sorry?'

He took a deep breath and repeated himself. 'Orlando's out on bail.'

Of course he fucking is.

Back at the academy, after the ambulance took away Griff and Clo, Detectives Smith and Saunders arrived at the scene full of questions. My dislike of them grew with each passing month, and the way they swanned onto the scene and inserted themselves into the aftermath pissed me off even more.

They questioned me—the two of them still believed I murdered a girl, after all—but I didn't say a word about any of it. Fuck them and fuck their opinions of me.

For Orlando to be out on bail, major money had to have changed hands.

Back before I started my scholarship at Hawthorn Academy, I used to think that having money, significant money, would change my life for the better, but after spending so much time around the truly wealthy, I wasn't so sure how true that opinion was anymore.

Money had hurt the Hawthorns more than it had saved them.

'Does that mean he'll be on Hawthorn grounds?' I asked, worried I'd have to look him in the eye for the foreseeable future, wondering what he knew about me, what he'd seen.

The constant thought of Orlando swirled through my brain on repeat, never ceasing. When alone, and trying to sleep, questions rushed to the forefront of my mind and I had no answers for any of them.

Questions like: What memories had I shared with Orlando? Or: What if the moments I loved with Ollie weren't Ollie at all?

So far, Ollie and I hadn't sat down and discussed it, but we would soon. Everything had got so twisted so fast it was hard to see a way out of it all without something imploding or exploding —that something being me.

'Not sure.' Griff shrugged. 'Ollie said he'd made bail, and he'd tell me more when he comes to visit tomorrow.'

'Fair enough. Has Leo come to see you at all?' I asked, deciding to stop pussyfooting around the question I wanted the answer to most. I wanted to know if he'd visited Griff, and maybe more importantly, I wanted to know if he'd seen Clover.

'Erm ...' Griff turned away to face out the window, the sheepish expression covering his face clear even from his side profile. 'Not today.'

'Yesterday?' I asked. I'd badger him until he gave me a straight answer. I didn't give a shit anymore. 'Day before that?'

'No and no,' Griff said, looking me in the eye. 'He's been busy.'

'Oh, he has, has he? Cause I've seen him around campus, and let me tell you, the boy didn't seem busy at all. Nope. If anything, I'd say he was avoiding moi.'

Griff coughed, then said in a low whisper, 'He's busy with Orlando stuff, but he's told me not to say anything.'

'Why would he tell you not to tell me?'

Griff rubbed his chin, a distant stare in his eyes. 'He wants to speak to you about it himself.'

'How generous of him,' I said in a droll tone. 'To talk to me, he'd have to look at me, wouldn't he?' I sounded like a whining teenager and all I'd need to do was stamp my foot to fit the bill. I truly believed we'd shared something special and were on the cusp of something ... more.

'I'm sure he will soon, Clouds. He's a little messed in the head right now.'

'Aren't we all? Clover's barely conscious, and you're trapped in here because you were both shot! Then Ollie's having to deal with the fallout of having a SECRET twin he knew nothing about!' I ended in a frustrated scream. Sure, Leo was having a hard time, but fuck, he wasn't the only one.

'I get it, Sky. Give him time.'

'Fine,' I huffed out, crossing my arms across my chest. Talking about Leo made me angry and sad in equal measure. 'No more talking about arseholes. How are you?'

'I'm okay, I promise.' He smiled at me, his dimples showing. 'I can't wait to get out of here.'

'Surely you're not champing at the bit to get back to school?' I laughed. Nobody was rushing back to the academy, surely? Multiple students had died since I started and they still hadn't brought the murderer to justice.

Even though we all had a pretty good idea of who the murderer was now. Or at least I was certain I did.

'I am a little. I feel so useless here. I want to help you figure out all this Sanctum stuff, and I can't do shit from here.'

I nodded. The boy had a point. So much was still unknown about the goings on at Hawthorn, *The Sanctum* being one of the biggest mysteries.

'I get you, but I also want you better.'

'I want to go see Clo,' he whispered. Since they were both admitted, the hospital staff hadn't allowed Griff to see her much, as they didn't like too many people entering the ward she was in. They'd wheeled him down to see her a couple of times, but not enough. Not like she'd known, anyway, seeing as she hadn't stopped sleeping since being admitted. Not that I'd say that part out loud.

'You'll be able to soon, I promise. I'll make sure it happens. Or, maybe more like, I'll convince Ollie to pay somebody.'

He smiled slightly, the shadow of his former self staring back at me. I'd become so accustomed to seeing Griff with his usual cheeky grin, I didn't know how to behave without him cracking jokes. He reminded me of a lost child; vulnerable and afraid.

'I'll hold you to that,' he said. I moved closer to his bed and pulled him into a tight hug. The fact I'd nearly lost him pinched my gut, and I'd barely had him in my life long enough. He was the only family I had besides Cora, and I didn't want him to disappear. The boy got me. We were scarily similar for two people who had experienced entirely different upbringings.

He squeezed back, surprisingly hard for somebody laid up in a hospital bed, but then again, he was a skilled swimmer with super muscles hiding underneath those clothes.

'Sky.' Griff pulled himself back from my hold, forcing me to look him in the eyes. 'I'm so glad you're my family. You know I love you, right?'

His eyes were uncertain, his watery gaze causing emotion to rise inside of me. We'd never been so open with one another. Never been so honest. Not in a serious way, at least.

'Yeah. I do,' I told him. 'And you know I love you right back, yeah?'

'Course I do,' he said, his tone once again lighthearted, as if he wasn't sad and choked up two seconds prior. 'I mean, how could you not?'

We both laughed and hugged again before we settled down to watch a film. The rest of the time spent together was in a comfortable silence, neither of us needing to talk to fill the space.

One thing I knew for certain in this life?

Griffin Cooper was one of the best.

Simple as.

Two

SCHOOL STARTING BACK UP WAS both a blessing and a curse.

I wanted to get back to normal. Wanted to learn enough, study enough, ace my exams and get the hell out of dodge when the year ended, leaving Hawthorn and all of its shit behind me.

But being back at school wasn't the same.

Not without Clover. Not without Griff.

Not to mention the fact I'd still not spoken to Leo—and not from a lack of trying. At my lowest point I'd even messaged him asking to meet, and the bastard had left me on read.

It also wasn't the same because I spent a lot of time pondering what times I had shared with Ollie and those I had shared with Orlando, if any. In the week since the Orlando revelation, it had become obvious from a couple of things I'd said to Ollie and his responses that some of our moments together hadn't happened the way I thought they had.

Clover should be beside me. Living with me. Studying with me so we'd both get to escape at the end of the year. To leave the grasp of Hawthorn Academy and the gargoyles and ghouls that lived among the debris and decay.

Okay, okay. They lived above the entrance.

Everything was tainted now, and I didn't know how to come to terms with it on my own.

The entire school was required to attend an assembly on the

first morning back, so I made my way there on dragging feet, not wanting to hear anything Ms Hawthorn had to say.

I took a spot in the last row of the rack seating, and Ollie took the empty spot next to me. It was as if a silent agreement existed between the two of us to watch out for the other while everything remained so up in the air.

Ollie leaned down and murmured in my ear, 'Wonder what the old bat has to say.'

'No idea,' I murmured back. 'Reckon she'll mention the events of the gala? Some students were lucky and weren't there to witness the fuckery.'

'Maybe she's going to pretend it never happened,' Ollie said in a dark tone. He had a point. Only a handful of students were witness to it, so maybe she wouldn't mention it at all. The local newspaper, The Beurre Banner, hadn't even posted an article about the shooting or Orlando's appearance. Just a small piece about the gala itself and the wealthy people who had attended.

I shrugged, not having the words to reassure either of us, as we waited for Ms Hawthorn to make her way across the stage to the microphone stand in the centre.

A hush fell over the room when she made her appearance. And what shocked me the most? Orlando by her side, walking in step with her. The pure smugness on his face set my blood boiling, and I knew whatever news Winifred had to impart wouldn't be good for us—for me.

The students who hadn't yet heard about the existence of Orlando all gasped and fell into whispers. Heads turned in unison to where we were sitting.

Ms Hawthorn got to the microphone and made a small cough into it. All heads snapped back in her direction.

'Students,' she said, her voice at its normal level, assessing the room with her piercing gaze. 'I have an announcement.'

The room stilled.

'My son, Orlando,' she said, waving an arm in his direction, 'will now attend Hawthorn Academy as a student in the thirteenth year, and I hope you will all make him welcome here. He will be my eyes and ears at the academy.'

'Wonderful,' I said to Ollie out of the side of my mouth. He bristled next to me, his knee moving up and down, the agitation needing an outlet.

'Do not let him near you,' he warned. 'You'd think Leo would've at least given us a heads up about our new classmate.'

Our eyes went over to where the staff were sitting on the stage. Leo sat on the far right, his face as attractive as the last time I kissed it ten days ago.

Had it truly only been ten days since I last kissed him? Ten days since I called him mine—at least in my head—even though we'd never truly defined our relationship.

His eyes locked with mine, and he averted his gaze, turning to face Ms Hawthorn and Orlando. Orlando's mouth moved, but whatever words he spoke weren't computing in my brain.

' ... wait to study here.' Orlando smiled, showing off his straight white teeth, and a chill ran down my spine.

Ms Hawthorn must have paid off a lot of parents and law enforcement higher ups to make it happen. Or maybe she'd paid for an excellent lawyer.

Orlando should have been in prison awaiting his trial for attempting to kill Clover rather than at some private school his mother owned. He should continue to hide away, the way he had his whole life. Joining the students and studying here like he had done nothing wrong didn't sit right, surely?

Like he hadn't shot a pupil.

Like he hadn't drugged me at the party in the woods.

Like he hadn't nearly drowned his twin brother.

Like he hadn't nearly drowned me.

Because deep down, my gut told me Orlando was responsible for it all, even if I had no proof—yet.

I needed an hour alone with him. An hour to interrogate him and get him to spill all. But nobody—meaning Ollie—would let me be alone with him to find out for definite. He did his best to stay with me at all times, probably to keep me away from Orlando, and maybe from Leo, too.

Everything was so up in the air, and although I knew Ollie meant well, it still stifled me. Even though he'd apologised to me back before the gala, things still weren't back to normal between us. Not that they ever were. The guy had used me in a revenge plot, after all. We'd never had a normal.

No matter what happened next, I would speak to Orlando.

Alone.

And no fucker was going to stop me.

Three

OLLIE and I were sitting at dinner on the last day of the week when holding back became utterly impossible.

'I'm going to talk to Orlando alone.'

'Don't you think you should talk to Leo first?' he asked, his fork paused halfway to his mouth. 'We know nothing about Orlando or what he wants. What if he wants to get you alone so he can hurt you? We've got no way of knowing anything about his mental state.'

'He won't,' I replied, trying to sound confident, but not sure I achieved the desired effect. My gut told me Orlando wouldn't hurt me—at least not in the physical sense. He never had before. Or maybe he had. How the fuck was I to know without asking him?

'How can you be so sure?'

'I can't. But I've been alone with him before and nothing bad happened.' I shrugged and returned to my food. The dining hall always served good food, but since Orlando became a student, the food had got even fancier. As if Ms Hawthorn was attempting to make up for lost time and giving her son the best of the best.

'Yes, and look what happened then!' Ollie shouted, his face flushing a deep red. 'He's hurt you every time.'

'We have no way of knowing,' I whispered, knowing my words were true, but not sure what I meant. For all I knew, the times I'd seen him were when he'd harmed me.

I had no proof otherwise.

'No, Skylar. I'm putting my foot down.'

'You're putting your foot down?' Was he for fucking real right now? Who did he think he was to dictate my actions? We weren't even a couple.

'Yes,' he bit out, his anger growing. 'You will not see him alone and that's final.'

We finished our meal in silence and once I'd emptied my plate, I excused myself and went back to my room. My head killed, like somebody had taken a brick and pounded at it.

In the same spot.

Repeatedly.

I went to my bathroom, opened the cabinet above the sink, and grabbed some ibuprofen and threw them in my mouth, swallowing the tablets dry. When I closed the cabinet door, I caught sight of myself in the mirror and didn't like what greeted me.

Limp hair and the purple bruised hollows under my eyes that let anybody who glanced my way know I lacked sleep lately.

Once back in my room, I paced, unable to stop myself, livid at Ollie. How dare he think he had anything to do with my actions? The bastard had done as many bad things to me in my time at Hawthorn as anybody else—maybe even more.

Mid-pace, something sitting on the shelf above my bed caught my eye, and I stepped closer to get a better look.

Oh, yeah! The tiny message in a bottle Leo had given me for my first Christmas at Griff's parents' estate. Back before shit hit the fan.

What did Leo say when he handed it to me? That he'd let me know when I could open it?

Huh. At no point during our relationship had he mentioned it. Maybe he'd forgotten about it like I had, seeing as it was a relatively unimportant thing in the grand scheme of life here at Hawthorn.

Maybe whatever it said inside the bottle would convince him to talk to me.

Yes, I wanted to talk to Orlando, but talking to Leo should be higher on my priority list.

CAN I OPEN THE MESSAGE IN A BOTTLE NOW?

It didn't take long for him to reply, which surprised me, seeing as he'd avoided every other message I'd sent him since the gala.

SURE, STUTTER. AND I'M SORRY IN ADVANCE.

Leo Hawthorn would never give out an apology without having thought it through first. Whatever was written on the paper inside the bottle, Leo considered it apology-worthy, and that made my stomach drop. Ever since Orlando had shown up at the gala and said what he had about Leo, every moment between us had become shaded and I didn't know how to come to terms with it all.

I grabbed the bottle off my shelf, being careful with it. Be just my luck if I broke it or smashed it at the pivotal moment.

I'd propped up the card—the one from the box the bottle came in—and I hadn't glanced at it since the day I got it.

It read:

Merry Christmas ...

I placed it down and picked up the bottle.

Gently, I uncorked the stopper and realised I wouldn't be able to get the paper out without some tweezers.

Back into the bathroom I went to locate my make-up bag and once I found it, I rooted through until I found the only pair of tweezers I owned, with a pug face at the top. A distant cousin gifted them to me for Christmas one year. You know the type of gift—one from somebody who knows fuck all about you but is needed to give you *something* so they show up with a beauty set. *What a stellar gift.*

I took them back to my bed, sat down, and held the bottle as close to my face as I could without seeing double. The thin and tiny piece of paper inside wouldn't be an easy grab.

Good thing I loved the game Operation. It was one of those fun games anybody could take part in even if they had little skill, but the real highlight? It only needed one player. And growing up, those were the games I liked best.

Channelling my inner love of the game, I got the tiny piece of paper out of the stupid glass bottle and placed it in my hand. It was the same size as the paper on the inside of a fortune cookie and it took a lot of careful manoeuvring to open the darn thing.

My fingers trembled, unfurling the piece of paper in stages, the sweat from my hands making everything harder. Even holding it made me nervous. What on earth could be on there to make Leo so shit up?

The note made my blood boil.

I can't wait to finally meet you, Little One.

I stayed frozen to the spot, my mind whirling. Of course Orlando had chosen this note, no doubt about it.

What had Leo said when he handed it to me?

'The note inside is real, but don't open it yet. I'll let you know when.'

Well, the bastard never had. He'd never mentioned it again, allowing it to collect dust on my shelf. Every time he'd visited, did his eyes go to it? Did his deceit ever bother him, or did he think of me as something to play with? Make the new girl fall for a lie and laugh at it behind her back. Again.

My phone was in my hand before I even registered that I'd thrown the bottle onto my bed with the stupid little note next to it and picked it up. Fuck him for avoiding me. Fuck him trying to stop the conversation from happening. Things were going to happen on my time and not anybody else's.

My room. Now.

A knock sounded on the door, small and timid, like the coward standing behind it.

'Let me in, Stutter.'

Either the boy had teleported outside my door the moment he'd received my text, or he'd already made his way to my room the moment I'd asked if I could read the bottle. Probably the smartest thing he'd done in weeks.

I opened the door, not wanting to catch his eye, and turned my back to let him into the room. I couldn't even glimpse at him without fury filling me. The red mist returned—and I didn't know how to get it to leave without exploding.

'Skylar.'

My name broke me. He only ever used it if he wanted me to listen, truly listen, to what he had to say.

Until the gala, I saw myself in a relationship with Leo in the future. I could envision it. See it in my mind and feel good about what the next steps held.

All I could muster out was, 'You knew about him.'

He didn't deny it.

'You knew about him and at no point did you think to tell me? At no point during whatever we had did you think it'd be kind to fucking tell me the truth? What the fuck, Leo? I thought we—' I stopped myself. 'It hurts.'

I looked into his eyes for the first time, and the pain I saw there gutted me further. I'd be picking up my innards for the foreseeable future if he kept assessing me like that. The pain. The sadness. All of it. It was like a vice around my heart—around my very soul—and I couldn't glance at it for longer than a mere moment. My eyes went to his hands, limp and lost at his sides, then to the muscled chest I knew lurked under his shirt, then away to the walls. If I wanted to stay sane, watching him wouldn't help.

'I wish I had something to say that wouldn't hurt more,' Leo whispered, barely loud enough for me to hear over the loud thrumming of my heart. My ears pounded with the rhythm and I wanted to scream.

'So, Orlando gave you this to give to me on Christmas Day?'

'Yeah,' he replied, his tone relieved, and he seemed glad I'd broken the awkward silence. 'He wanted you to have a gift from him you couldn't trace back to him yet. You know how he is with his mind games.'

'No,' I bit out. 'I don't. Because I didn't fucking know he existed! I want the truth, Leo. Even if it's shit and makes me hate you forever. I deserve it.'

He nodded. 'You do, but I don't even know where to start. There are some things I can't tell you, no matter how much I want to. How much I've always wanted to.'

'Start with something easy,' I replied, not wanting to give him an inch. 'How did you get wrapped up in Orlando's shit?'

He took a deep breath, and I expected him to fob me off again, but he went and surprised me by speaking.

'During the summer, we stay at the house on the grounds here. Have done for as long as I can remember. But the summer before you started here, Ollie and Griff went abroad with Henry and left me here with my parents and Winifred. And then my parents went away for their anniversary and for the first time it was me and my aunt alone.'

I nodded, following his words, not wanting to interrupt his flow.

'With my parents gone, Winnie sat me down at dinner and told me about a select group of people called *The Sanctum*. After dinner finished, she took me out into the woods to meet them. They were all there waiting for me. Them, and Orlando.'

Okay, I wasn't expecting that.

'*The Sanctum*?' My brain pounded in my skull. 'You know who they are?'

He shook his head. 'No. They all wore hoods and hid their faces, but I could take a guess.'

'And Winifred is what? In charge?'

'She was ...' he trailed off, a thoughtful expression on his face. 'But after her getting beat at the swim meeting, I'd say it's changed.'

'Then what happened?'

'They told me they were inducting me into *The Sanctum* as the newest Hawthorn member and I didn't have a choice, and as the newest member, I needed to do certain ... tasks for them.'

'And those tasks included being Orlando's bitch boy?' I snapped, my anger simmering over.

Leo winced. 'Something like that, yeah.'

'Why didn't you tell me? Or Ollie? He had a right to know, yet you kept it from him, from all of us. Why?'

'They threatened the people I care about. My parents. Ollie. Griff. Red. You.' He sighed. 'I couldn't risk not helping them.'

'You could've told us something. Anything! We were all blind-sided at the gala. He took Ollie captive for fuck's sake and you knew! You made me love you, knowing the truth.'

His hand reached out and grabbed mine.

'I am so sorry, Stutter. I know my words don't cut it, but I'm going to make shit up to you. I promise.'

'Quite a big promise to make,' I muttered, removing my hand from his grasp. 'I need you to leave.'

'I'll leave,' he said. 'I just want you to know nothing between us was fake, not in the end. I meant everything I said.'

My heart beat an unnatural rhythm, half of it wanting him to keep saying such sweet words, the other half ready to batter him.

'Stutter, I had to help them. Help him. You can see that, can't you?'

'What I can see is a coward. A liar. You had so many chances to tell me. To hint at something not being quite right. Everything you did caused me pain, and I'm not sure how long it'll take me to get over it. If I can get over it.'

I walked to the door, ready to open it and shove him through it, when a knock came.

Four

'SKYLAR!' Ollie's voice called through the door, interrupting the moment.

I flicked my gaze between the door and Leo, trying to decide what to do for the best, even though neither option was stellar.

'Skylar!' Ollie called again. 'Can we talk, please?'

Leo tilted his head, his eyes burning into my skin, and I shook my head. Not sure what I was saying no to, but it was something. I opened the door, narrowly avoiding Ollie's raised fist as he went to knock again. The relief on his face when he saw me woke up the butterflies in my stomach—it was rare to see such a genuine reaction on his face—but his relief soured when he spotted Leo standing behind me.

'I can see you've already got company.'

'Leo's leaving,' I said. 'Aren't you?'

'Apparently so,' Leo murmured, his eyes remaining on me. 'Let me know when we can talk again, Stutter.'

I nodded and said, 'I'll message you.'

He opened and closed his mouth, wanting to say more, but wouldn't with Ollie standing there. Things still needed to be said, and they were too intimate to have a witness.

Leo walked to the door, and with one last longing glance my way, he left the room, throwing a 'See you two later,' over his shoulder.

'Are you okay?' Ollie asked, closing the door behind him and stepping into my room. I gave a terse nod, letting out the breath I'd held in while waiting for Leo to leave. 'What did he want?'

'I asked him here,' I said, my eyes going back to the tiny bottle and note discarded on my bed. 'I needed to ask him a couple of questions about ... everything.'

'Did you get the answers you wanted?'

'Sort of.' I shrugged, deflated. The heaviness of the last hour hit me and I slumped down on my bed. 'What did you want to talk about?'

Ollie's eyes darted around the room. Maybe I'd caught him off guard. 'Huh?'

'You came here wanting to talk to me,' I pointed out. 'So, talk. The floor is yours. '

'I came to apologise. I acted like a prick at dinner and you don't deserve it. I've been all out of sorts since ... well, everything. I know it's not an excuse, but it's all I have.'

'It isn't all you have.'

His left eyebrow turned down as his right quirked up. Did I need to spell everything out for him?

'You came to apologise,' I said and sigh. 'But none of your sentences contained an apology.'

He had the decency to appear sheepish. 'Right. I should prob- ably try again.'

I chuckled at the uncertainty on his face. 'Maybe.'

Not sure what it said about me, but I sort of loved it when Ollie acted out of sorts. All confused and uncertain and cute. It was one thing that made him seem human—more real—and those times weren't often enough, so I always grabbed them and held on with both hands.

'I'm sorry, Sky, for being such a dick about it all. If you need to talk to Orlando, then I'll have to sit down and accept it. It's hard for me, you know?'

'I know,' I hushed out, patting the empty spot on the bed next to me in invitation. 'I don't think there's a guidebook on what to do when you find out you've got a secret twin. Or what to do when your second boyfriend betrays you in the space of a year.'

'I should probably say sorry for that too, huh?'

'Pretty sure you already did.' I smiled at him. 'But you can again if you want. Can never hear the word sorry leave your lips too often.'

Ollie smiled too, and my eyes drifted to his lips. No, Skylar.

'I don't think I'll ever say it enough,' he admitted. 'I am sorry, though. For everything I did. It was shitty of me and even though I knew it, I just couldn't see it. Does that make sense?'

'Not at all, actually.'

We both laughed, and I lay back and examined the ceiling so I could talk without having to watch his reaction to my words. He followed me, lying beside me, our arms grazing each other, and the warmth settling in my arm from his was surprisingly nice.

'This whole Orlando thing has messed me up, Sky.' His whispered words were pained. 'I've always hated my dad and put my mum on such a pedestal, and to find out she lied to him about something so serious, I don't know how to handle everything. How to come to terms with it. And the worst part? I can't even ask her why she did what she did because she's dead. Because she chose not to be here anymore. And that hurts. Like really fucking hurts.'

In my chest, my heart split in two for him. My relationship with my mum wasn't great or anything, but she'd never done something so ... shitty. Sure, she'd spent all my money and had married an absolute douche-canoe of a man, but she'd never hidden a secret sibling from me. Well, we'll ignore the whole keeping me in the dark about my father thing for the time being. Easier that way.

Ollie's fingertips lightly gripped mine, sending a tingle down my arm, and I let him. If he wanted to use me as his anchor, I'd allow it. Fuck, I'd allow him to do a whole lot more—which said a lot about me and my mindset. None of it good.

'Why do you think she did it?'

'What part?'

'Hid Orlando from everybody,' I clarified. 'Told nobody about him and gave him to her sister, of all people.'

'I don't know.' His voice broke. 'My dad left today, but I've asked him to come back next month so I can talk to him about it. Get to the truth. See if he really knew nothing or if he's a talented actor.'

'Do you think he would have acted so in the dark? Because when I saw him at the gala, the man looked crushed.'

Ollie went quiet before a rush of breath left him. 'I don't know. He'd never let Winifred, of all people, raise one of his kids, which is how I know Mum kept him in the dark. Especially not a son. An heir.'

'From what I know of your dad, it sounds unlikely. I always got the vibe that he hated her.'

'He *does* hate her. He's never been able to stand her and nobody has ever said why. Griff and I have tried to figure it out, but we've come up blank every time. I'd ask Leo about it but ...'

'But you're not talking to him right now,' I finished for him.

'Right. If the bastard could hide such important stuff from us, then he's not worthy of our conversation.'

'Don't judge him too harshly.'

Ollie turned to face me, but I stayed put, scanning the ceiling so I couldn't see the questioning look I'd no doubt find on his face. My words sounded suspiciously like I was sticking up for Leo Hawthorn, and after everything, I shouldn't be doing that. But I couldn't let Ollie fall out with one of his closest friends without hearing him out first.

'That's how it is, is it? One conversation with him and he's wrapped you around his finger again.' Ollie sat up abruptly. 'I'm out of here. Let me know when you're not kissing Leo's arse.'

I sat up too, watching him storm to the door, grasping the handle and flinging it open.

'You're being ridiculous.'

'I don't want to hear it.' The sound of the door slamming against the frame reverberated throughout my small room, lingering. Stupid of me to talk positively about Leo to Ollie really, especially after he'd found us in here together.

My insides jumbled. My thoughts thoroughly scrambled.

What was I meant to do? Nothing I could do, really. They'd have to mend the rift between them in their own time, and I needed to stay well out of it. And while I did that, I also needed to figure out my feelings towards them both. You know, simple stuff.

Ha!

They'd both lied to me. Betrayed me. Dragged me down to the lowest of the low.

Yet I cared about them still.

Well, fuck me.

Five

GRIFF'S RETURN to school came at exactly the right time.

With Ollie not talking to me and me not talking to Leo, chilling out in my room, or in the library, alone became super appealing. Not much else to do, really.

I spent the weekend thinking everything over: my feelings, the events of the past, and most importantly, what I could do to move forward. I'd drawn no conclusions as yet, but I was trying. Which was the most important thing, right?

Bouncing on my toes, I waited at the bottom of the steps outside the school's main entrance, waiting for the car with Griff inside to make its way up the hill and to my feet.

We texted daily, and I knew the boy was more than ready to get back to school and away from somewhere so boring and clinical, as he called it.

The wind whipped my violet hair in front of my face and I swatted it away, ready to get back inside to the comforting warmth—well, to a degree.

After an eternity but was probably in actuality ten minutes, a car crept its way up the hill, moving so slowly I could run the distance and back by the time it made its way to me, and I couldn't run for shit.

And then it pulled up in front of me, an ecstatic Griffin peeping at me through the open window. 'Clouds!'

'Hey, Griff,' I said, fighting back the tears swarming my vision.

His entire aura had dimmed, but his wide smile was still affixed to his face like he hadn't just spent time in the hospital after being literally shot. 'Fancy seeing you here.'

'You missed me?' he asked, before opening the door with a flourish and slowly stepping out, tentative movements marring his usual buoyancy. Even with slower steps, his urgent energy bubbled up in the air. Infectious.

'Of course,' I said with ease. 'It's been no fun around here without you.'

'*Obviously.*' He nodded, and then together we rushed forward and launched into a big hug, melting my insides and making them mush. There was a warmth about Griff. Something innate nobody could steal, no matter how much they tried. 'The boys still giving you a hard time?'

'More like I've been giving them a hard time.' I laughed, locking my arm with his so the two of us could make our way to the dorms together. 'Things are ... tense.'

'Have you spoken to them? Properly?'

The hallway is empty, our footsteps echoing around us, as the rest of the school is busy with classes.

'Define properly.' Griff turned and narrowed his eyes. 'Okay, okay. I've spoken to Leo a little, and Ollie and I are getting there. I've not said two words to Orlando, and believe me, I want to, but I've not yet worked up the courage.'

'Want me to be there when you do?'

'Thanks for the offer, but I think it's something I need to do alone.'

Griff nodded, deep in thought, and I didn't interrupt. Sometimes it was nice to stay silent with those you love and care about.

Once the two of us made it back to my room, he broke the silence.

'Odd being in here without her, isn't it?'

Of course, he wanted to talk about Clover; her being his girlfriend and all. Or was she? The last time I'd asked Clo, they weren't putting a label on things, but things could've changed. It seemed insensitive to ask Griff, so I didn't.

'I keep expecting her to barge through the door, her face filled with thunder,' I admitted. 'Or blabbering away about something. Usually something to do with my actions and poor decisions.'

'She has a lot of opinions, doesn't she?' Griff's warm tone told me he missed her. We both did. 'She'll be back soon.'

'Did they let you go see her before you left?'

He nodded. 'Yep. She was asleep, so I spoke at her rather than to her, but the nurses told me she'd most likely be out within a week or so.'

'That's good news.' Mental note: message Clover. It wouldn't surprise me if she actively chose to 'be asleep' whenever Griff visited, because I'd had a few messages from her over the week-end, so I knew she was awake for a lot of the time. I'd planned to go visit her, but she'd told me not to bother—no point in both of us missing out on school work.

'Once she's back, things will be back to normal.'

'Not quite. We still need to figure out what Orlando's doing, who *The Sanctum* are, and what Leo's involvement in all this is.'

'What did he tell you?' Griff sat on the edge of Clo's bed facing me, the sun shining through the window onto his red hair, turning it almost a burnt auburn colour.

'He knew about Orlando all along. He's met *The Sanctum*.' I counted each thing he'd told me off on my fingers. 'Oh, and they've initiated him, or plan to.'

The interested expression on Griff's face remained, but he said nothing, waiting for me to get my bearings and continue. Every time I remembered what Leo had told me, his face swam into my mind, and I couldn't focus on anything except for the fact everything between us had been a big fat lie.

'It makes no sense. Why wouldn't he have told me and Ollie?'

'Maybe he couldn't?' I'd been thinking about it all ever since Leo told me about *The Sanctum*'s initiation and how they expected him to go along with what they wanted. 'He said they threatened all our lives.'

'Nice to know he cares so much about us all.'

'Of course he does,' I said, without even having to think about it. 'The boy may be an arsehole ninety-nine per cent of the time, but the remaining one per cent gives a shit and you can bet it's the part of him that cares about us.'

'I'm sorry things with him haven't gone the way you thought they would.'

I shrugged, running my fingertips along the duvet, not wanting to focus on Griff's words, or in the sympathy I could hear lacing every word.

Ah, time for a subject change. 'Want to grab a pizza for dinner?'

Griff nodded his head like an enthusiastic pet. 'You bet!'

Six

WITH GRIFF BACK, school fell into a routine.

Either Ollie or Griff were never far away from my side, or worse, they sandwiched me between them both. In their eyes, Orlando posed a threat, as did Leo, and neither of them wanted me to get even more hurt than I already had been. Yes, it irritated me to have two shadows, but it also warmed my heart that they cared enough to do it at all.

But then an opportunity arose to be alone, and I jumped on it.

'Are you sure you'll be okay?' Ollie asked, pausing at the entrance to the changing rooms.

'Ollie,' I said, as if I hadn't already said it thirty times before. 'I'm gonna be sitting up in the stands watching you guys train while working on some homework. You'll be able to see me the whole time.'

'I know, but—'

'But nothing.' I put my foot down … metaphorically. 'If anything happens—which it won't—then you'll be able to hear me scream for your assistance.'

He took a step closer to me, and my breathing hitched involuntarily. 'You taking the piss out of my worrying?'

'N-no.'

'Your stutter gives you away, Skylar.'

I made a pfft noise. 'When doesn't it?'

'You'll still be sitting there when I finish, yeah?'

'Yep.'

'Then we can talk later?' The hope in his words made my head hurt. 'Really talk?'

'Sure. You go swim, then we can talk, but only if you do the whole practice and don't skip out early to make sure I'm okay!'

'If you're sure.'

'Oliver, if you don't fuck off in the next two seconds, I swear to you, I'm gonna beat your arse!'

He moved away from me and I laughed as the changing room door closed behind him before I made my way to the seating overlooking the swimming pool. I got comfortable—as comfortable as you could get in those plastic shitty chairs—and pulled out my History textbook and my notebook.

I'd planned to write an essay about Stalinist Russia, but I wrote a different heading across the top of my blank page. One that had nothing to do with education.

Ollie vs Orlando

The rhythmic tapping of my pen echoed, and my mind entered a trance. There were things I needed the answers to, and until I wrote them down, I wouldn't remember them. Any time they'd popped into my head over the last few weeks, I'd batted them away as quick as they'd arrived, worried they'd do me damage if I examined them. But I couldn't ignore shit. Not anymore.

My hand flew across the page, writing everything I could think of.

- First time we spoke in the Hospital Wing (surely Ollie … right?)

- Closet make-out session during the first New Year's Gala (Ollie?)

- Who drugged me at the first ever party in the woods (Orlando?)

- Too many times in the library to count (must think of individual instances)

- Who set The Set on me? (Ollie?)

- Who killed Odette and Olivia? (Orlando?)

Once I'd finished the list, I ripped the page out of my note-book and folded it into fours before placing it in the zipped pocket of my schoolbag. There were loads more times to add, but I could add them as they came to mind.

My eyes couldn't help being drawn to the boys in the pool, and a smile came to my lips. Fuck me, Ollie was hot.

Ollie always looked fucking hot whenever he swam.

The way his muscles rippled under the water's surface. The way his body glided through the water like a powerful machine making waves.

Since school had started back up, he had been swimming a lot. Apparently, having your secret twin brother nearly drown you in the exact pool you trained in didn't put you off something you truly loved. If anything, it made you work and train even harder.

Go figure.

I pulled out my phone, the thought of writing about Stalin out the window, and pulled up Hive. The moment the screen loaded, pictures of Ophelia and Oralie on either side of a smirking Orlando assaulted my eyes. I scoffed. Idiots.

Since the camp out, and everything that happened after it, I'd not had any issues with the girls at all. No, the three of us would never be friends, but we were acquaintances now, which was enough. Yet if they continued to hang out with Orlando, I might question their sanity more than I already had ...

'Hey, Little One,' a voice said from behind me.

I jumped, my bum physically leaving the seat, startled. It landed back down with a thud.

Three guesses to who.

'H-hello,' I replied. I'd always turned into a stuttering mess around Orlando and I doubted that would change just because I now knew who he really was.

'What are you doing sitting here all alone? Watching my brother make a tit out of himself?' he said, a soft smile dancing on his lips.

I'd kissed those lips, hadn't I?

'Something like that.' I kept my gaze ahead to where Ollie and Griff were swimming laps. Leo's gaze locked with mine from where he stood next to the pool, and he raised his right eyebrow in question. I gave him a small shake of my head in response. 'I wondered when you'd seek me out.'

'You gonna pretend I haven't tried to get you alone already?' Orlando's eyes lit up. The bright blue of them shining even brighter in the pool house lighting. Like a picture-perfect model. Obviously. He was Ollie's identical twin, after all.

'No.' I shrugged. 'But I did wonder how long it'd take for you to make it happen regardless of the guys sticking by my side all the time,' I said in a hushed voice, not wanting it to carry down to the pool.

Ollie hadn't yet registered Orlando's arrival, and I wanted it to stay that way. He was too involved in his swimming to take notice of his surroundings, something he'd learned so he could win races and never get distracted by the competition. It also meant he blocked out a lot. He'd glanced up maybe once since we'd arrived.

Orlando laughed, but it lacked any joy. 'Those boys have you on a tight leash, don't they?'

'Those boys,' I emphasised, 'don't have me on any leash. I'm a grown girl and I can make my own decisions.'

'Sure, Little One. If it's so easy to break away from them and come talk to me, then why haven't you?'

'Could it be the fact you're a massive fucking liar? Or maybe because you're an imposter who's pretended to be his twin brother on more than one occasion?'

'Hm.' Orlando stared at Ollie, his eyes narrowed on the face disappearing and reappearing from under the waves. Ollie's forehead wrinkled and his eyebrows furrowed low, deep in concentration. 'Want to get out of here?'

'No!' It was a knee jerk reaction—one I hadn't fully thought through. I scanned around me and then down to Ollie to check he hadn't heard my shout. When he didn't call out, or stop swimming, I clocked the opportunity handed to me and came to my senses. 'Where would we even go?'

'The caretaker's closet?' He wagged his eyebrows, then chuckled after spotting my face, and said, 'I'm kidding. I thought we could go to the library.'

I mentally crossed off the line on my folded piece of paper that read, Closet make-out session during the first New Year's Gala (Ollie?) and then reversed it. I needed to be certain before crossing anything out. When I could, I'd alter it to say, Closet make-out session during the first New Year's Gala (Orlando?).

'The library?' I asked, sceptical.

He shrugged like it was a no-brainer. 'You feel most comfortable there. And you'll feel better knowing Flo is around and she takes no shit.'

'I have to warn you,' I said, smiling. 'I'm sort of her favourite. Flo won't let you mess me around.'

I smiled and then stopped myself. Was it fucked that my insides were warm and fuzzy because Orlando knew something like that about me because he'd paid enough attention to me while pretending to be his brother? He knew I loved the library above all else.

I didn't want to answer.

'I don't know ...' I trailed off. 'The guys may notice me missing.'

'Hate to break it to you, Little One, but they won't. There's another hour of practice, minimum.'

'You ask your little bitch Leo to make that the case, huh?'

He didn't dignify my sniping with a reply.

I weighed up my two options. Either I could sit and pretend to not write about Stalin for another hour, or I could go with

Orlando and learn some truths. An opportunity like this to talk to Orlando with no witnesses wouldn't come around again.

'Fine. But I leave when I want to. No exceptions.'

'Of course,' he said, reaching out his hand for me to take a hold of. 'I'd never want to make you uncomfortable.'

I found *that* hard to believe.

Seven

BEING ALONE with Orlando didn't feel as wrong as I thought it would. If anything, it was comfortable—easy. Like we'd known each other for a long time. And I supposed we had, sort of.

Shit got harder to wrap my head around daily.

'So …' I trailed off.

'So,' he replied, a wolfish grin melting me. 'How are you doing, Little One?'

'Honestly? I have no proper answer.' I chuckled. 'Things are fucked.'

'They are,' he agreed. 'And I suppose you've got a couple of questions for me.'

'You've supposed right.' I glanced around, making sure our conversation remained private. 'I'm not sure where to start.'

'How about I start the conversation for you? Hey, my name's Orlando. Skylar, right?' He held out his hand for me to shake, but I stared at him, keeping my hand to myself. 'I've waited a long time to introduce myself to you.'

'Is that so?' My eyebrows climbed on my forehead. 'Because you've had plenty of opportunities to introduce yourself, and funny enough, you've chosen not to every time.'

'I couldn't.'

'Of course you could. Don't lie. You *chose* not to.' I crossed my arms across my chest, staring him down, hoping to make him as uncomfortable as I could. 'Leo told me you recruited him into your shitty sanctum.'

'He did, huh?' Orlando's pointer finger rubbed at his jaw and a little shiver ran through me. He looked so much like his brother. It was uncanny. 'Did he tell you anything else?'

'You threatened my life if he didn't play ball.'

He stopped rubbing his jaw and narrowed his eyes into slits. 'Interesting.'

'Not how it happened?'

'It doesn't matter how it happened.' He waved his hand, brushing me off. 'What matters is you've been ignoring me, and now I've got you here alone, I don't want to waste our time together talking about that wanker. Somebody will come and break us up sooner rather than later.'

I didn't contradict him, because he was probably right. I doubted Ollie or Griff—or even Leo—were going to let me disappear with their sworn enemy for long without interfering. My fingers picked at a thread on my bottle green blazer, keeping busy, but my eyes locked on the imposter in front of me. There was something so familiar about him it hurt.

'So, what do you want to talk about if not your little lapdog?'

'I thought it was time we talked, Little One. I'm here to answer your questions, if I can. No ulterior motives.'

'Okay.' I nodded, mind made up. 'I've got a question for you, and if you don't answer, then I'm walking away right now and you won't get time alone with me like this again.'

'I'm sure I could convince you otherwise.'

I ignored his cocksure expression. Wanker.

'Before you arrived at the pool, I was writing a list.' Orlando remained quiet, waiting for me to continue. 'One weighing up what events were actually you and not your brother.'

'And did you come to any conclusions?'

'You killed Odette and Olivia.' As the words tumbled from my lips, I watched his face for any reaction, but he'd had a lot of practice at hiding his emotions to give me anything I could analyse. 'You drugged me at the first party in the woods.' His left eyelid twitched. 'You stabbed me after the fashion show.' His top lip quirked. I took a deep breath and finished with the one I thought would drag the strongest reaction from him. 'You pulled me into the caretaker's closet and fucked me.'

'A memory I replay in my head every night.'

My stomach twinged at the confirmation, but ever since I'd seen Orlando at the gala and realised who he was, I'd known that moment was all his. Ollie would never have risked showing his true feelings towards me, especially not as I flaunted a relationship with his best friend, and he pretended to be into an O girl.

'Of course you do, you sick bastard,' I spat, but it didn't hold anywhere near as much venom behind it as there should've been. The fucker had violated me, pretended to be somebody else, yet rage still didn't fill me the way everybody expected it to.

'But as for your other points ... I didn't kill Olivia,' he told me, staring into my eyes.

An icy shiver fell over me, and I didn't believe a word he'd said.

'Trust me, Little One.'

'Trust you?' I scoffed. 'You expect me to trust you after you've admitted to something so heinous?'

'You trust Ollie, Griff, and Leo after everything they've done to you. How's it any different?'

'Because they've said sorry! They've never hurt me or tried to kill me, for starters. You know it isn't anywhere near the same.'

'Did those fuckers ever tell you how you ended up at Hawthorn? About how they made sure you were here to bully and destroy?'

'We've never spoken about it,' I said. What was his angle?

'They introduced the scholarship so you would come here and so Clover could return. Everything they've done is to hurt you both.'

So Clover could return? But she'd never been to Hawthorn before ...

'That makes no sense,' I said. 'Clo never came here before the scholarship. She knew the Hawthorns from childhood. Something to do with her parents.'

It made sense the boys had introduced the scholarship to get us to the school. They'd hated us both in equal measure and you couldn't enact a revenge scheme on somebody without them being in front of you. Not an effective one, at least.

'You've always thought Clover was hiding something from you and knew a lot more about the school and the people here than she let on. Why's it hard to believe she came here before?'

'I—' I rattled my brain to remember something she'd told me. Anything to put an explanation in place, so I didn't have to believe Orlando's accusations. But he'd made a valid point. It had crossed my mind that maybe Clover held a few things back from me.

The moment her health improved, I'd have to ask her.

Orlando raised his eyebrows. 'I've got no reason to lie to you, Little One. Not anymore.'

'Okay, if you've not got anything to hide from me, then you'll answer a couple of questions I have.'

'I'll answer anything I can.'

'Right ...' I flicked through the filing cabinet of my brain, trying to find the correct thing to ask first. If I went in too hard, he may bolt. 'Why are *The Sanctum* after us?'

He raised an eyebrow, but I stood my ground. It needed answering, and I wouldn't let his quirked eyebrows stop me from asking.

'Isn't it obvious?' He shuffled in his seat. 'They want your dad to return.'

'Okay ...' I shuffled in my seat, getting a little closer to him. 'Then what's the reason for going after Ollie?'

'Oh.' Orlando laughed. 'I wanted to make my brother suffer for everything wrong. That fucker became the chosen one. The one our mother wanted to keep. The one she didn't cast away to her bitch of a sister.'

'But why did Millie give you away in the first place? And why did your dad not know about you before the gala?'

'That's a lot to answer in one brief conversation.' The smirk on his face wasn't as unaffected as usual. 'You know, Little One, I've often wondered why she gave me up. Did I seem evil from birth? Did I cry, and he didn't?' He shook his head, his anger snapping once more into place. 'I guess we'll never know.'

'I'm sorry,' I whispered, even though I had nothing to apologise for and as a rule, I hated it when people apologised for something they had no control over. 'People are pretty crappy.'

'Trust nobody. Not Leo. Not Griff and especially not Ollie. Not even me.'

I nodded, wanting to agree with him, but knowing my heart would find it hard to disregard my trust of Griff and Ollie—heck, even Leo I sort of trusted, and he'd betrayed me as of late. Bastard.

'Promise me.' His tone became urgent as his hand darted out to grip mine, a sharp shooting pain running up my arm from the tight squeeze he gave me. 'Promise you'll put yourself first, no matter what happens with all this.'

'I p-promise,' I stuttered, caught off guard by the intensity in his blue gaze.

His responding nod was firm. 'Good.'

Eight

OLLIE'S WRATH when he banged on my dorm door wasn't a surprise.

I should've returned to his practice at the pool, but when I left Orlando in the library, I couldn't bring myself to head back to the pool. I'd needed time to think about what he'd told me before I faced Ollie—or any of the boys.

'Skylar, open up!'

'I'm not opening this door until you calm the fuck down,' I called back. Sure, be pissed at me for putting myself in danger, but I wouldn't allow him to railroad me anymore. If he wanted to talk about it, then we could talk like calm, rational adults. Not petty children throwing their toys out of the pram.

'If I promise to calm down, will you let me in?'

I thought about it for a moment, knowing it'd make the boy on the other side of the door stew for a little longer. Riling Ollie up could be really fun sometimes.

I nodded, then remembered he couldn't see me through the door, so said, 'Sure.'

'You've sort of got to open the door for me to come in.'

'Oh, yeah.' I opened the door, and he came straight in, his agitation still there, but I could tell he was doing his best to keep it in. 'So ...'

Ollie didn't wait long before he exploded.

'How dare you speak to him alone!'

'How dare you think you can talk to me like that! I let you in because you said you'd calm down. Not sounding too calm to me.' I shouted back. 'You were busy and the two of us went to the library and were in view of Flo the whole time.'

'Skylar, if he ever did anything to hurt you, I—'

'You'd what?' I growled. 'Because the last time I checked, you fucking hurt me worse than he ever has!'

'He tried to drown you.'

'You turned the entire school against me, made me believe you loved me, and then left me heartbroken.'

'He stabbed you!'

Okay, Ollie had a point there, but I wouldn't let him walk all over me. Not anymore. 'You may as well have done from the pain you caused.' I took a deep breath. 'Ollie, I don't want to fight about this. I spoke to him. It's already done. So please, can we talk about what he told me and figure out a way to stop more shit from going down?'

He nodded, reluctant to concede, but I knew he'd do it, anyway.

'He said little, but it's clear to me we need to be worried about *The Sanctum* and what they're capable of. They want my dad.'

'They do?'

'Yeah. Orlando told me.' I shrugged. 'He also said you made up the scholarship to get me here. By any chance, did it have something to do with my dad, too?'

'It's complicated.'

'I know.' My heart twinged in sympathy for the lost-looking boy in front of me. 'But for us to move forward, we need to clear the air.'

'Can we take a rain check? I need to get it all untangled in my mind, and the moment I do, I promise I'll explain everything.'

'Fine.'

His blue eyes locked with mine, a raging storm within them, and he pushed his hair back.

'I'm sorry for going off on you earlier. The thought of you getting hurt again drives me so angry mad. Skylar, I know with everything that's happened you won't believe me, but I love you and I want what's best for you, and if that means saying nothing when you decide something I'm unhappy with, then I need to accept that.'

My mind stuttered, his sentence disappearing in my brain after the three words I thought I'd never hear from him.

'Th-thank you.' I got more comfortable on top of my bed. 'You wanna hear a bit more about what I spoke to Orlando about?'

'If you want to tell me, sure.' He smiled. 'I'll always listen to you.'

I smiled back—I couldn't help myself when he said such cute things. 'I talked to Orlando about a list I've written. I want to figure out what events were actually him and not you.'

'Sky,' he whispered, rubbing his finger across mine. 'I want to figure shit out, too. Together.'

'Then you need to stop being so overprotective of me.'

'I worry about you.'

'I know.' I let out a small chuckle. 'And I'm not telling you to stop, because I kinda like it. But I need you to let me do my own thing.'

'Okay, I can try. So, what's on this list of yours?'

'Orlando answered one of my main ones.'

'What was it?'

'Turns out,' I said, trying for a joking tone, but not sure if it delivered. 'A couple of times I thought I hooked up with you … weren't you.'

The change in Ollie's face was instantaneous. 'I'll fucking kill him!'

'Ollie—'

'No, Sky!' He cut me off. 'The bastard raped you, and you expect me to ignore that?'

'No, but—'

'There's nothing you can say to justify it! You can't seriously be about to defend him?'

'Of course not. I don't even know how I feel about it all except violated. Mad. Confused. Do you know how hard it is to look upon memories I liked and see the reflection distorted? All shined with vomit or something and now I've got to clean it away to get to the bottom.'

'Such an imaginative way of putting it.'

I brushed Ollie off. 'Don't you dare be mad at me for not feeling or acting the way you expect me to, okay? Not when I don't even know how I feel.'

Ollie's face turned sombre. 'I'm here for you, Sky. Just know you can talk to me about any of this whenever you want and I'll try my best to keep a cool head. It's hard, though.'

'Yeah ...' I trailed off, before laying back on my bed, facing up to the ceiling instead of at his perfect face. My stomach dipped around him and being alone in my room, talking about such vulnerable things, didn't help matters. 'All of this is hard, but we'll get through it. We've weathered worse storms, right?'

'I suppose.'

'Ollie,' I whispered, not wanting to startle him, but putting enough weight into his name, he knew whatever came next was serious. 'I've forgiven you for everything you've done and I'm laying here trying to stop myself from kissing you. If we can get past, well ... the past, then we can get through all of this shit, too.'

'You're thinking about kissing me?' His whisper mixed with laughter. The bed beneath me jostled as he turned onto his side to face me. 'Of course, I've hoped ...' he trailed off. I felt compelled to face him and turned onto my side so I could see the indecision flitting across his features. It always took me by surprise how attractive he was. How much I wanted him simply from looking at him; from seeing the little frown on his brow and knowing he was thinking deeply about something.

'You've hoped?'

'Hoped you'd reciprocate the feelings I have for you and one day you'd want me the way I've always wanted you.'

I scoffed. 'You haven't always wanted me.'

'Yes, I have. Even when I wanted to hate you, I couldn't help but want to get to know you better, to want to be in your company, and to want to be with you.'

I moved an inch.

Ollie moved an inch.

Until our noses were touching and his breath skated across my face.

'Is it okay if I kiss you?'

The butterflies in my stomach flew around in a frenzy, the question sending me over the edge. Had he ever asked before? I couldn't recall—doubted I could even remember my name—but the fact he had … Well, there was only one answer.

'Yes.' The word left me in a hushed breath. 'Kiss me, Ollie.'

Our lips clashed together in a passionate embrace, the instant spark of heat from our touching lips filling me with warmth, and I wanted him above all else. His hand came and grabbed the back of my neck, pulling me closer, and I moaned at the sensation of it all.

Fuck. The boy could kiss.

Hands wandered and our moaning increased, the two of us lost in the moment of finally giving in to our desires. Things were heating up—fast—and I knew things needed to slow down a little before the train went off the tracks.

After fuck knew how long, we broke apart, both needing to cool down. He pulled back and the smile he gave me made me want to pounce on him straight away, but I knew I shouldn't.

Our heavy breathing slowed, and the intensity in our locked gaze was almost too much for me to handle.

Once the atmosphere in my room had returned to normal, I took a deep breath and faced Ollie. 'So, what's our first plan of action?'

'We can discuss tomorrow,' he murmured, rubbing his thumb against my face. 'Is it okay if I stay here tonight? I'll sleep in Clo's bed. I need to be close to you, you know, just in case.'

My heart filled with an emotion I didn't want to inspect too closely, especially after our make-out session.

So, I said, 'Sure. You can stay in my bed though, if you'd like?'

Nine

WAKING up in Ollie's arms was like coming home.

And this time around? It felt real.

Things were so different from the last time we'd shared a bed together, and not only because I'd had a relationship with Leo in the in-between. Or maybe it was. Who the fuck knew?

Maybe I was a terrible human.

'Morning,' Ollie mumbled in my ear, pulling me from my darker thoughts. 'You sleep well?'

'Mmm.' I moved in the bed and turned to face him, so his hard dick no longer pressed into my back. Temptation like that before ten in the morning—unnecessarily cruel. Especially after the kissing session we'd had the night before.

Baby steps, Skylar.

He placed a kiss on my forehead, a gentle brush of the lips, and it once again awakened my body.

'I slept the best I've slept in a *long* time.' He blinked, a soft smile playing on his lips. 'I've missed falling asleep with you wrapped safe in my arms.'

'Mmm,' I repeated, noncommittal.

'Play it coy, Sky, but I know you well enough to see the light in your eyes and the smile you're trying to hide.'

My stomach tingled as he touched it, threatening to tickle me, but stopping before he did any damage. I always appreciated a teasing, playful Ollie, because I rarely witnessed it.

'Are we going to make a plan today?' I asked, wanting to change the subject away from anything banter-filled, so I didn't cave and launch myself on him.

'If that's what you want,' he said, his amusement laced in his tone. 'Suppose you want to get Griff in on it, too?'

I nodded. 'Well, yeah. Not gonna leave the boy out, am I? Oh! You've reminded me. Have you heard anything from the hospital about Clover?'

'No, but I can call them in a bit once we're up. Do you mind if I grab a shower?'

'Your room's close and has a much bigger bathroom,' I pointed out. 'You just want a reason to get semi-naked in front of me.'

'Maybe.' He smiled. 'But I'd rather see you semi-naked in front of me. Or naked. I'd never say no to that.'

A laugh left me. 'Of course you wouldn't.'

His face went serious.

'Sky, I'd never do anything you didn't want. If you never want to repeat last night, I'll understand. But also, if you do ever want more with me, then I'll be all over it with bells on.'

I chuckled.

Ollie reached his hand out and cupped my face. His blue eyes seared into mine.

'I want to be in your life, in any way you'll have me.'

Tears rushed to my eyes, but I blinked them away. Something about the moment seemed serious. Real. And if it was real, then my response mattered more than it ever had.

'I know.' I leaned forward and placed a soft kiss on his lips. 'And I don't want you to think I don't want you in my life, either. I'm just…'

'Confused?'

'Sort of, yeah. I loved you, back before I knew the truth about everything, and it's hard for me to forget the betrayal, even if I have forgiven you for everything.'

'You've truly forgiven me. You mean it?'

'I've got no reason to lie to you,' I said. 'I forgave you a while ago. Truly.'

The blinding smile Ollie gave me in return made the vulnerability of telling the truth worth it. Because sure, I would never forget what he did to me, or the lies he told, but I also could forgive them. Since all those things happened, worse things had taken their place in my mind.

Ollie's betrayal was no longer the bigger fish.

I slipped out of bed and went to the bathroom to go to the toilet and brush my teeth. By the time I returned, Ollie sat upright in the bed, his phone in his hand as he scrolled mindlessly.

'There's an announcement on *The Hive*.' His eyes remained on his phone. 'Seems Orlando's decided as a Hawthorn legacy he's an automatic member of *The Sect*.'

'Seems like a bit of a reach, but go off.'

I made my way back to the bed and got under the covers once more, propping my back up against the headboard before resting my head against Ollie's shoulder.

'If he's going to be a member, then I won't be. I'll speak to the others, but if he wants some stupid fucking legacy, then he can have it. I want no part in it.'

'Are you sure?' I asked, needing to play devil's advocate even though I didn't give a shit. If you asked me, both *The Set* and *The Sect* could fuck right off.

'Yeah. It's a stupid tradition started no doubt about it by a grade-A arsehole.' Ollie put his phone down. 'You've helped me see the bullshit for what it really is.'

'Glad I could help.' My lips went to his shoulder without thinking. His warm and soft bare skin under my mouth had me wanting to continue trailing kisses down ...

'You okay there?' He teased

'I'm good.' I sat back again, pretending some kind of lust demon hadn't taken over my senses. 'And very proud of you.'

'I could get used to you being proud of me if it means you touch me like that.'

LATER IN THE DAY, I found myself in Ollie's room with Griff and Ollie, and the three of us were discussing what we were all gonna do next.

The two of them were talking while I assessed them both, wondering when this had become my new normal. A family of sorts—one I'd found—making every day a little easier to exist in.

I wished Leo and Clover were with us, but it also made sense in a way they weren't. I had no idea how to proceed with Leo in the future, and Clover and Griff had their own stuff to sort out. As long as Clo got better and returned to school, I'd be happy.

' ... then maybe we can find out what this bloody *Sanctum* wants with us and Leo.' Griff rubbed his hand through his auburn hair, pacing in front of the sofa where Ollie lounged. 'They've turned him against us, and there's no way there isn't a valid reason.'

'I agree,' Ollie said.

'Well, he told me they threatened all our lives,' I piped up, not wanting them to hate their cousin or doubt his loyalty. 'Surely a valid enough reason?'

'But he didn't know you.' Ollie leaned forward, his elbows going to his knees, deep in thought. 'And we were all pretty sure he hated you as much as we did back then.'

I shrugged. 'Maybe. He said he cared about Clo at first and I became more important later on.'

'Either way,' Griff said, 'I can understand it. I'd do the same if you or Clo were at risk. It's the reason I don't want to beat the dickhead for his actions.'

Ollie nodded. 'We've all made crappy choices over the last year.'

'Some more than others.' I laughed. It still felt odd to laugh all the pain and terror off, but I'd got to a point where I couldn't dwell on it any longer. 'But it's what we all choose to do now that matters.'

'And what do you think we should choose to do, Clouds?'

I'd been thinking about it and the best way to get closer to everything flashed in my mind like an obvious solution—one I hadn't wanted to touch but knew I had to.

I took a deep breath. My next sentence would go down as well as … okay, I got nothing. It wouldn't go down well, basically.

'I think I need to get closer to Orlando,' I said.

'You'll do no such thing!' Ollie shouted.

'But it makes sense!' I shouted back. 'And you know I'm right. You don't want me hurt, and yes, I'm not thrilled either, BUT if it means we can get to the bottom of this crap before somebody else dies, then that's what needs to happen.'

'What are you saying?' Griff stopped his pacing.

'I'm saying I want to get a confession from him. Make sure he gets locked up forever. He's out on bail for shooting you, right? But we need to pile more charges on him if we want any of them to stick. He's got money to make this go away.'

'And what makes you think he'd confess to killing somebody to you?'

'He denied killing Olivia when I accused him, but he and I both know he stabbed me—and therefore stabbed and killed Odette. Maybe if I changed my statement with the police and told them I'd remembered the truth when he revealed himself at the gala?'

'They'll wonder why it's taken you so long to come forward. Assume you're doing it for an angle.' Ollie rubbed his jaw. 'But if you want to talk to them, I'll go with you.'

'I'd rather have a confession to take them than my hazy memories.' The boys nodded. 'And I think he'll talk to me, open up to me, if I give him the chance.'

'Ollie.' Griff started pacing again, his nervous energy needing an outlet. 'I think Clouds is right. We should at least give it a go. We can't rule it out.'

'There has to be something else we can do.'

'There probably is, sure.' I walked over to Ollie and sat down next to him, gripping his hand tight in mine. 'But I don't think it'll be anywhere near as effective, and I think we need to talk to Leo and let him know our plan. Maybe he can help us.'

'Send him a text.'

No need to tell me twice. I pulled out my phone and pulled up my conversation thread with Leo and tapped out a quick message.

Is there any way the three of us can meet with you?

Ollie glanced down at my phone, saw my message, then turned my chin to face him.

'While we wait for Leo to pull his head out of his arse, let's think about this, Sky. Really think about this. Do you think it's safe for you to be around my brother?'

'I know you don't want me to say yes, but I don't think he'll hurt me. Especially now he doesn't have to hide who he is from me. I kind of got the impression when I spoke to him he wanted me to get to know him and not the person he's been pretending to be.' And no, Orlando hadn't said those exact words to me or anything, but I'd got the sense he wanted to talk to me about something secretive but had held himself back.

My phone lit up in my hand.

LET'S MEET IN ACTUAL PRIVATE. TONIGHT. MIDNIGHT.

In actual private? What the fuck does that mean?

Ollie, once again eyeing my phone over my shoulder like a nosey bastard, said, 'I know where he means. Looks like you're being let in on one of our many family secrets.'

'I can't wait.'

Ten

AT TEN MINUTES TO MIDNIGHT, the three of us made our way from Ollie's room to the mysterious secret meeting place.

'So where are we heading?' I asked in a hushed whisper.

'The tunnels,' Ollie replied, his hand squeezing mine. 'When we were younger, it was how we referred to them in front of our parents and whoever else who might lurk and listen in on our conversations. "Actual private" became our code. Welcome to the club.'

I smiled, loving being included—like they were inviting me to join something exclusive.

Something the boys had shared between themselves and were now allowing me to be a part of.

'Do you think Leo will tell us anything important?' Griff asked the valid question, something we'd all wondered, I bet.

'I hope so, but I didn't give him any details about what we wanted to talk about.'

We stopped in the hospital wing and the boys ushered us over to a panel in the wall disguising a hidden door.

The panel blended in and looked no different from the others on either side of it—no wonder I'd passed it multiple times since coming to Hawthorn without thinking of anything suspicious.

There was nobody around us, the corridor empty except for us three, but then again, we were in the hospital wing at midnight, so the quiet, eerie atmosphere made sense.

Bit suspicious the school needed an entire wing for a hospital, right?

'Why does this place have an entire wing for injured people?'

'They used it as a hospital during the war, Clouds. For once, the Hawthorns were useful for something other than lining their own pockets.'

Huh. Made sense.

I nodded, absorbing the information and drinking it in like a true history nerd. It was pretty fucking cool, actually.

Ollie, bored with waiting for me and Griff to stop talking, opened the door a fraction, wide enough for us to fit through. Griff went first, then me second, and I found myself in a dimly lit second hallway.

I voiced my thoughts out loud. 'This is so fucking weird.'

'You get used to it,' Ollie said, joining us in the hall and closing the door gently behind him. In the dimmer light, he looked even more handsome than usual. All dark, tall, and brooding. His face half hidden by shadows. 'We'll meet him just up ahead at the intersection. Now, we've got to be quiet while we're here.'

Ollie walked on, with me and Griff trailing along behind, actively trying to make as little noise as possible. The hall could lead anywhere, but I had faith the guys weren't leading me to my slaughter. There was no way to know whether somebody lurked on the other side of the wall, who could hear us, so walking on tiptoe and speaking in hushed tones couldn't be avoided.

I lived for the spy-movie-meets-secret-academy-novels vibes of it all.

On the outside, I tried to keep a cool head about me and hoped none of my excitement showed on my face.

'Hey,' Leo said from up ahead. 'You made it.'

'We asked to meet you, remember?' Ollie said, with no malice attached. A statement of facts.

'You're late,' Leo replied.

'We're like two minutes late. Calm your tits.' Griff laughed, before giving Leo a fist bump. Seeing a genuine smile on Griff's face aimed in Leo's direction of all people, well, it warmed me from head to toe.

'We don't have long. Orlando will wonder where I am in an hour's time.'

'How does it feel to be his little bitch?' Ollie taunted, a creep of malice reaching his tone now the initial pleasantries were out of the way. Other than at swim practice, the two of them didn't speak to each other much and if they had, I had no idea what they'd spoken about. 'Can't even disappear for longer than an hour before being checked up on.'

'Whatever,' Leo drawled. 'We've got more important things to be talking about and we don't have long. You gonna continue to waste the short time we have with shitty statements?'

'No.' Ollie's surly response meant I had to dampen the twitch in my lip, threatening to turn into a full-blown smile. *You can do it, Skylar.*

Leo nodded. 'Good. Shut your mouth and listen to me.'

Griff and I nodded, too. We all wanted to get the most out of this conversation. I squeezed Ollie's waist from where I stood slightly behind him to get across my point. *Shut up and listen, Oliver.*

The boy struggled with that, but now wasn't the time for him to be his typical cantankerous self. Nobody had the time for that shit.

Leo rolled his eyes and ran his hand through his hair, the agitation dripping off him in waves—or maybe I noticed it because of how close we'd got not too long ago.

'Where do you want me to start?' Leo asked, looking at me for the first time since we'd arrived.

'What's Orlando's game?' Ollie asked, taking the lead.

'In what sense?' Leo replied, being difficult and awkward because he could.

'Well, he's decided he's a part of *The Sect* for starters,' I said, needing to guide the conversation somewhere. 'Is there an ulterior motive we should know about?'

'I don't know—'

'Plus,' I cut Leo off, 'he still needs you to do things for him, otherwise he wouldn't be watching you like a hawk.'

'To be honest.' Leo shuffled his weight from his left side to his right. 'I think he wants to cause havoc, Stutter.'

I let the words sink into my head and I could understand his point. Orlando had already caused enough havoc since revealing himself and becoming a student, and he didn't plan to stop. But he'd also caused enough havoc while hiding behind Ollie's persona, so what had made him reveal his identity?

Yes, now he could control the school, as himself, but he didn't seem to take the opportunity the way I'd expected him to.

'Okay ...' I took a step out from behind Ollie and moved to stand beside him instead. 'But that's his personal agenda. What's his part with *The Sanctum*?'

'Isn't it obvious, Stutter? They're still hoping your dad will show up.'

'My dad? Anybody going to explain what he's got to do with their shit?'

'They think if you're in danger, he'll come here after all these years.'

I shook my head, not believing for a second we'd learned their true motive. 'I've been hurt plenty since coming here and he hasn't arrived so far, so it looks like they're tough out of luck.'

'*The Sanctum* doesn't tell me and Orlando everything, or anywhere near as much as I'd like. They're keeping their cards close to their chest.' Leo shrugged.

'So, Orlando's a piece on the chessboard the same as you?' Ollie asked, rubbing his jaw.

'A more important one, but yes,' Leo agreed.

'We can use it to our advantage,' Ollie said, and I hummed in agreement. He had a valid point. Not that I had any idea about what we could do, or how we could use it to our advantage.

'What does Orlando want with me?' I whispered, my gut

churning. Orlando wanted me to play into his plot like putty, and I needed to make sure I didn't let that happen.

Ollie moved to stand behind me and rested his chin on my head, wrapping his arms around my waist.

Safe. Comfortable.

'At first, he wanted to hurt you. We all did. So, there's nothing new there. But now I think he wants you. As his girl.'

I coughed, almost choking on my breath, Ollie's squeeze on my hips keeping me grounded.

'He's hoping I'll be his girlfriend?' I said, thinking out loud. 'Do you think he's got so used to emulating his brother's life he wants to steal it?'

Nobody mentioned the fact Ollie and I were no longer together, but Leo shuffled his feet and turned his gaze to Ollie's hands placed on my hips.

The thought had struck me like lightning, and the moment it did, I understood. His endgame! He wanted his brother's life.

Maybe he fully believed Millie's choice took away his true childhood.

He'd said to me, "I've wondered why she gave me up. Did I seem evil from birth? Did I cry, and he didn't?"

Orlando felt wronged, and he thought by taking everything away from his brother, leaving him with nothing, he'd feel better about his lot in life.

I needed to convince him otherwise. He wouldn't feel better about it, and stealing shit from Ollie wouldn't be the solution he hoped it would be. If emptiness filled him now, it still would later down the road if he didn't come to terms with the why. Without forgiving those who had done him dirty, he'd remain in his miserable pit.

'I think so,' Leo said. 'And he won't listen to anybody telling him it won't work out the way he thinks it will.'

'Why would he listen to anybody?' Griff piped up. 'His mum gave him up and never mentioned him again to anybody. Can understand why the dick's sour.'

The four of us went silent. Griff had a fair point.

'I need to talk to him,' I said. 'Maybe I can help.'

Griff and Ollie stayed silent. I'd expected them to talk me out of it a little. Instead, they were learning to accept they wouldn't deter me with their protests.

'I'll set it up and message you.' Leo gave me a faint smile. 'Good luck, Stutter. You'll need it.'

Eleven

IT TOOK Leo a while to arrange for me to meet Orlando. Any time I messaged and asked about the holdup, he fobbed me off with some lame excuse.

Finally, something got sorted and Orlando agreed to meet me the next day and even though I shouldn't want to be alone with him, shouldn't smile at the thought of getting to see him in private, I couldn't help it.

Everything about my life was complicated, and my love life? Well, that was even more fucking complicated.

I'd loved Ollie, and he'd betrayed me.

I'd fallen for Leo, and he betrayed me too ...

Orlando had betrayed me too by lying about everything, and yes, I was aware how fucked up it all was, because not only had he assaulted me, but he also sure as hell put a knife into my stomach. Who knew what else he'd done in his pursuit of stealing his brother's life?

'Are you sure about this, Clouds?' Griff's gentle and kind face held no judgement. 'I can come along if you'd like, as moral support.'

'I don't think he'll talk to me with you there.' I gave him a half smile. 'And I promise you, no matter what he tells me, I'll pass it along to you straight after.'

'I know you're right.' His fingers played mindlessly with his pen. 'It sucks we have to do all this on his terms, you know? I get he's had a hard life, but fuck, Clouds, haven't we all?'

I nodded; my tongue weighed down in my mouth. We all had things happen we'd rather forget. Griff's parents had died when he was young. Ollie's mum had ended her own life. Clover, well, I didn't know what happened to her, but the way she and Leo acted around one another, something had definitely taken place to scar them both.

'He feels like he lost out on family. On a life. No matter how much we understand, and have similar skeletons in our closets, he will still see himself as the victim. He will never see it any other way.'

'What makes you so certain?'

'I don't know.' My mind swam with the words Orlando had already spoken to me on the subject. 'I know him somehow. Understand his thinking.'

'If you say so.' Griff stopped playing with his pen and glimpsed up at the board, some ethical problem plastered on it. 'Is it weird I hate the bastard, but also want to forgive him and see if we can sort it out? He resembles Ollie so much it's a mindfuck.'

'And he's your family, too,' I pointed out. 'It makes sense you want to help him, the way you've helped me.'

'I've not really done much for you, Clouds.' He wrote whatever we needed to know down, thank fuck, because I hadn't paid attention to any words leaving our teacher's mouth. 'I wish I could do more. Give you your own money. Help pay your way through university. Make it so you don't have to rely on anybody ever again.'

'I don't expect you to do that.' I batted his shoulder with the palm of my hand, my heart happy to hear his love for me. 'And besides, I'm happy with making my way in this world by myself. Not like I even know my dad. Would seem wrong to use his name and status to get ahead.'

'I suppose.' Griff didn't sound sure. 'Just sucks how the uncle I remember doesn't match up with the one who's screwed you over.'

'I forget you remember my dad, even a little.'

Even though I'd come to terms with the fact Griff and I were cousins, it still didn't compute he knew somebody I shared blood and DNA with better than I did.

'My memory is a little fuzzy.' He winced. 'And a lot of the memories I have of him include my parents, so they're from a long time ago.'

'Anything stick out in your mind?' I asked, starved for even the slightest mention of something to show me my dad wasn't a complete waste of space.

A smile came to Griff's face. 'Uncle Jacob helped me when I got stung by a bee one time. I was outside in the garden alone, playing on the red slide set I had out there, and I got stung on my arm by a very large, super angry bee.' He laughed, lost in the past. 'I was terrified, and it hurt so bad, and I screamed, unable to see anybody who could help me. But then Uncle Jacob arrived in a flash. He helped me down from the slide and rushed me into the house, put cream on it, and made me laugh so I'd forget the stinging pain.'

I smiled at his cute story. But it hurt me as much as it warmed me. Not that I'd had a red slide in my garden, or a bee sting as a kid, but it still bothered me knowing I would never have those memories with my dad the way Griff had.

'Sounds like he cared about you,' I said, trying to blink away my depressing thoughts.

'He'd care about you too if he was here.'

'We don't know for definite, Griff.' It didn't help to think about it. Not if I wanted to stay sane.

'How do we know he knows about you?' Griff nudged my ribs. 'He might not even know you exist!'

'You think Cora kept her gigantic trap shut about my existence?' I laughed at the thought. My mum would've run her mouth the moment she found out about me. No way would she have ignored the potential payout me having a rich father would bring her. 'That woman can't even keep her mouth shut about the fact she thinks both Leo and Ollie are attractive. Plus, *The Sanctum* assumes he knows about me, otherwise their plan wouldn't be to hurt me to get to him.'

'Cora does like the sound of her own voice,' Griff agreed. 'But without asking her, we don't know.'

'I'll add it to my list of things I need to find out about.' A list growing longer by the day.

'We'll get to the bottom of all this, Clouds. I promise you.'

I MET Orlando at the time he'd chosen, in the spot he'd picked, and found him already there, pacing, waiting for me.

He stopped when he saw me walking towards him, and his eyebrows relaxed.

'You came.'

'Of course I came.' I shrugged, confused by his surprise. 'I wanted this arranged.'

'I thought it might be a trick.' He came to stand in front of me. 'When Leo told me you wanted to meet me, I thought maybe my bigheaded brother would come instead.'

'Well, it isn't a trick.' I swung my arms around. 'Here I am.'

'Where did you want to go?' he asked, reaching out his hand for mine. 'To the library?'

I placed my hand in his. 'No. I thought we could go back to my room? Nobody will overhear us there.'

'Your room?' He faltered, missing a step, but correcting it before I could comment. 'I've never been in your room.'

'There's a first time for everything.' I walked away from him and he followed, our hands still locked together. 'If we stay out in public, then anybody could listen in.'

'And my brother knows about this?' Orlando's tone was sceptical, and rightfully so.

'He does.' I nodded.

Sort of.

'Okay then. Let's go to your room.'

The two of us walked in silence, drawing the eye of every

student and teacher we passed on our way. People were staring at me walking down the hallways hand in hand with my ex-boyfriend's biggest enemy—not to forget the guy who stabbed me.

Thankfully, we arrived at my door sharpish.

'I'm surprised Ollie or Griff aren't standing outside acting as your bodyguards.'

'I'm my own person,' I said in a tone more sullen than I'd have liked. His words had hit a nerve. 'I don't need a bodyguard.'

'But they hover around you, anyway.'

'Because they care about me.'

'I care about you.'

'It's not the same.' I opened my door, unable to look at him. He may believe he cares about me, but he doesn't. Not really. 'Welcome to my humble abode.'

'It's about the same size as mine.' He laughed, entering the room behind me and closing the door.

He'd handed me the perfect opportunity to ask something I'd been thinking about ever since he revealed himself.

'I've been wondering, actually ... Where do you live? Where's your room?'

He laughed, bitter. 'In the house on the grounds with my mum.' He spat the word. 'Hidden and locked away in the attic like a proper British ghost.'

'Ah, yes. Rich British families are very adept at hiding their secrets away in a place rarely seen by society.'

Orlando grunted and took a step closer to the bed before pausing. 'Er, do you mind if I sit on the edge of the bed?'

I blinked, surprised he'd asked, and nodded my head.

He sat down and continued, 'My mum always told me she'd announce my existence one day, but that she had to wait for the right time, and at seven, I believed her. But then more and more time passed, and I remained hidden away, unable to socialise or make friends. Unable to create a bond with my brother and cousins.'

'Sounds shit. I'm sorry.'

'Nothing for you to be sorry about.' He shrugged. 'Not like you told the witch Hawthorn to lock me away with the bats.'

'There were bats up there with you?'

Orlando's grim nod told me all I needed. 'The entire room reeked of misery. When I turned fourteen, Mum announced I was going to join *The Sanctum*.'

'Rather young, isn't it?' I went and sat on the edge of Clover's bed so I could look across at him. Catch every expression on his face. Analyse every movement. Every tick.

'They made an exception for me and thank fuck they did. They were the people who knew about me, and it was nice to be included and be a part of something bigger. I'm sure you can understand? Being an only child and friendless before coming here and all.'

'Nice to know you've worked on your tact,' I teased. Orlando grimaced, and I couldn't help but laugh at him. 'I'm joking with you.' I crossed my legs underneath my body and got comfortable. 'And you're right, I can understand that. Before I came to Hawthorn and made friends with Griff and Clo, I'd been an outsider back at my old school—at least in my perception—and it seemed to me like I didn't belong. And now I've got a proper family. One who has my back and supports me through everything.'

'Nice for some.'

'You could have one, too,' I pointed out, not accepting even one ounce of his surliness. If the boy wanted to behave like a child, then so be it, but coddling him wouldn't solve anything. 'You know, if you hadn't chosen a life of crime and murder.'

'I didn't choose it. It chose me. Literally. When *The Sanctum* decides you're one of them, there's not much you can do. You either join up or someone you love dies.'

'What if you don't have anybody you love?'

'Everybody loves something or someone, Little One.'

Twelve

'I DIDN'T LEARN MUCH,' I said, finishing my story.

My words were the only sound in the quiet hospital room alongside Clover's soft snoring.

I studied my best friend and sighed. When I'd arrived, she was bright-eyed and ready to hear about everything she'd missed out on, but after an hour, her eyelids fluttered shut and I didn't want to wake her.

Anytime Griff came to visit, she pretended to be asleep, and I wouldn't let that shit fly much longer. It was getting pretty ridiculous. If she didn't want to be with Griff, then she needed to have an honest conversation with him and tell the truth. Let the chips fall where they may.

The doctor had said Clo could return to school in two weeks' time and we were all more than ready to have her back. Visiting her in the hospital couldn't compete with having her beside me in our tiny box of a room all the time.

Clo's sheets rustled, and her eyes opened. 'Sky?'

'I'm still here,' I replied.

'Sorry I fell asleep.' She brushed the tiny glob of spit from her bottom lip. 'I've been finding it so hard to stay awake with the medication they keep plying me with.'

She'd given me the perfect opening.

'Ah ... So, is that why Griff keeps reporting you as asleep every time he returns?'

The blush travelled from her forehead down to her chin.

'Got anything to say?' I shuffled my chair closer to the side of her bed. 'Because I'm struggling to keep a straight face whenever he asks me if you've been awake when I've visited.'

'It's complicated.'

'Well, make it less complicated.' I snapped. 'Because if you don't want to be with him, then you need to tell him. He'll be upset, sure, but isn't stringing him along so much worse?'

'I don't know if I want to dump him.'

'Thought you hadn't put a label on things?'

She made a throwaway gesture with her hand. 'We haven't. I don't know how I feel, okay? Not like anything around here has been easy for any of us the last couple of years.'

'Talking about the last couple of years ...' I trailed off, unsure how to breach the subject of Clo's history at Hawthorn. Orlando had told me of her attending the school before, but it hadn't come up in conversation with the boys yet, and I guess a large part of me was putting it off, because if true, it was yet another lie they'd all kept from me.

'Yes?'

'Orlando mentioned something interesting a couple of weeks back.'

'He did?' Clover pushed herself higher, rearranging her pillows. 'What?'

'He told me you were a student at Hawthorn, and they used the scholarship to bring you back.' I watched to see if her expression changed. 'Anything you want to tell me?'

She swallowed hard. 'Sky, I promise I've wanted to tell you for the longest time, but I haven't known how to.'

That didn't sound good, but I bit my tongue from retorting too quickly.

'Yeah, I started Hawthorn in year seven and left before the end of year nine. The Hawthorns covered my costs here for those years, but not as a scholarship or anything. My parents worked for the Hawthorns and our family lived in the house at the back of their estate since I was like three or something stupid. I can't remember a time before the Hawthorns.' Clo's hands rinsed together in her lap, her gaze studying the movement, unable to make eye contact. 'But when we were in year nine, everything changed.'

She went silent, lost in the past.

After a moment, I shattered the silence. 'What happened?'

'Things went missing around the estate. Small things at first, you know, like the odd vase here and the odd plate there. But then bigger pieces disappeared overnight. And Edward or Lottie weren't the ones getting rid of these items. Some of them were family heirlooms and had been in the home for generations.

'After three months of this happening, Edward accused my parents of stealing the items from them to sell and turn a profit. And from there, everything turned sour real fucking fast.'

The story surprised me. Yes, I'd expected something of the sort, but the way Edward and Charlotte treated Clo at school events told me they didn't hold a grudge towards her.

'Edward and Lottie stopped paying for your schooling?'

Clo shook her head. 'I turned them down.'

A conversation I'd overheard between Clo and Griff floated into my mind.

"Bit rich, babe, when you stick by your parents."

'I remember Griff saying you sided with your parents,' I said, wanting the conversation to continue flowing. 'Is that what made you leave Hawthorn?'

Clo gulped some water from the cup on her bedside table. It seemed silly to point out it had been sitting there since before I'd arrived. 'Yeah, among other things. I suppose you've guessed the history between me and Leo?'

I fake gasped. 'You and Leo have a history?'

'Oh, shut up!' Clo leaned over and smacked the part of my body she could reach. 'Okay, so maybe I've been nowhere near as subtle as I thought.'

'Neither of you is subtle around the other.'

That got a deep laugh out of Clo. 'No, I suppose you're right. I can't explain it, Sky. Leo Hawthorn brings out the worst in me. It's like I see him, and hear him, and want to stab the bastard in the eye.'

I laughed, ignoring the twinge in my stomach. With Leo, I struggled to analyse anything. Everything seemed too fresh to go over.

'Anyway, Leo and I fractured big time once I took my parents' side and moved with them out of the area.'

'What made you return when the scholarship letter arrived?'

She fidgeted in her bed. 'Truth?'

I nodded.

'I missed them all. I thought everything would be okay and when I returned, the four of us would pick up the way we had been before. We both know that's not what happened.

'And then when you joined, I knew they planned to make your life hell the way they had mine. I didn't tell you the truth, because yes, I felt embarrassed. And it really was nice to have one person not know what went down. But also, I wanted you to listen to my fears about their actions without thinking I had an ulterior motive, all because I hated them for what they did to me.'

'I get it, I do.' I shook my head, letting the information settle in my membrane. 'Even if I wish you'd told me it all a lot sooner.'

'Can you forgive me?'

'Don't ask such a stupid question.' I flicked her hand. 'You're my best friend. And sure, I'm pissed at you hiding things, but you almost dying sort of puts it all into perspective for me, ya know?'

'Well, now you know how it feels!' Clo laughed. 'Between you being stabbed and drowned and drugged, I've barely been able to keep myself sane.'

'I apologise if someone's attempted murders have inconvenienced you.'

'You mean Orlando's attempted murders, right?'

'We don't have confirmation,' I said, tasting the lie as it left my lips. Did I need confirmation when my own memories told me the truth?

'Okay, Skylar. Live in denial alongside me a little longer.'

'How was she?' Griff asked the moment my foot left the car and touched the grounds of Hawthorn Academy.

'Fine,' I said, brushing down my skirt. 'They reckon she'll be back within the month.'

'Good.' He nodded, then stepped forward to place his arm in mine. 'It's not right being here without her.'

'No, it isn't.' I agreed. 'She told me about her parents.'

'She did?'

'Yeah. Orlando mentioned she was a student here back in the day and she said something that gave me the perfect opportunity to ask her about it.'

'I'm glad she told you. It sucked keeping it to myself.'

'I get you were honouring her wishes, but it makes me sad, ya know? I get it wasn't your place to say anything, the same way it wasn't hers to tell me about your parents.'

'Right.'

The two of us made our way into the quiet main building. I'd come back during dinner time so barely anybody floated about, all of them occupied with eating or something else mundane.

'Where's Ollie?' I asked.

'In the dining room. I said we'd meet him there the moment you got back.'

'Wonderful! I'm starved. The hospital may cost a few bob, but the options for visitors aren't stellar.'

The two of us found Ollie sitting at our usual table alone, his face dark, his gaze locked on Orlando sitting at a table with *The Set*. Orlando was in the middle of telling a story the girls found hilarious if their laughter and red faces were any indication. Ophelia threw her head back, her mouth so wide it resembled a black hole.

'How dare he sit over there like none of this is fucked up?' Ollie grumbled the moment we took our seats beside him. No greeting needed. There were already plates for me and Griff—

Ollie must have ordered for us—and at the sight of the pizza, my mouth watered.

'I think he's aware it's fucked up, mate,' Griff said around a large bite of his steak. 'Has to act like it doesn't bother him, though, right?'

'What do you mean?' I asked. Neither me nor Ollie acknowledged the moment he placed his hand on my thigh under the table.

'Well, he has to act like none of this has bothered him. It wouldn't look good for him to appear from the shadows and crumble. It would show up his mum, *The Sanctum*, among others. But honestly, it wouldn't surprise me if he thought this was even more fucked up than you do, Ollie.'

'What's that supposed to mean?' Ollie snapped, turning his pissed off face in Griff's direction. It irked him—rightfully so— whenever anybody said something even remotely positive about his twin. 'The guy's a dick, and a murderer, Griff. He shouldn't be here.'

'Never said he should. Just saying I'm sure he knows how fucked up this all is, that's all.' Griff shrugged and went back to cutting up his dinner.

'And nobody has proved he murdered anybody,' I whispered. 'All we have are my memories and I didn't see him stab Odette or anything.'

'No,' Ollie agreed. 'But he did stab you, so if he can do that, then stabbing Odette isn't outside of his wheelhouse, is it?'

'Why don't you ask him?'

'I don't want to talk to the prick. Ever.'

'He's your twin. You don't have to like it, but you have to accept it.' Reasoning with him, or at least attempting to. 'Aren't you even a little intrigued?'

Ollie's hand on my thigh tightened, squeezing me to the point of pain.

'No,' he bit out. 'I don't want to have anything to do with him until I speak to my dad.'

'Understandable, mate,' Griff said, and I nodded in agreement.

'Is he still coming this weekend?' I asked, trying to visualise the calendar in my head and failing miserably. Who even knew the fucking day of the week anymore? Not me.

'Clouds, it is the weekend.' Griff reached over and put his hand on my forehead.

'Right.' I'd have hit my head with the palm of my hand if it didn't mean hitting Griff. 'Duh! Silly me.'

'He's said we can discuss it all tomorrow. Winifred and Orlando are going off grounds for the day and we'll have the house all to ourselves.'

'Want me to be there for support?' I didn't particularly want to be there, but if Ollie said yes, then I would.

'Thanks, Sky.' The palm on my leg loosened. 'But this is something I need to do alone.'

Thirteen

'I'LL BE LEAVING AGAIN TOMORROW.' Dad shuffled in his dark green wing back armchair. 'I can't take any more time off from the company, and I'm not gaining much by staying here.'

I nodded in understanding, even if I didn't understand a bit.

Yes, I could grasp the fact my dad needed to get back to work. Couldn't stop making the Brandon millions even after learning you've had a son you didn't know shit about for eighteen years.

But that was Henry Brandon for you. The man didn't care about much aside from himself.

The table between us had empty glasses and a bottle of whiskey on, yet neither of us had reached to touch them. The conversation we were about to embark on needed to be done completely sober.

'And I guess I need to address the elephant in the room,' Dad continued, examining the lit fireplace, the flames dancing on his face. 'It would seem your mother hid something important from us both.'

Fuck having this conversation sober.

The decanter was in my hand; the stopper pulled out, and the whiskey poured into the glasses within seconds. I handed one to my dad, who took it with a nod of thanks, then sat back and took a large sip of mine.

The liquid burned on its way down my throat.

'So, you didn't know?'

'No,' Dad whispered. 'I didn't. I thought he died.'

'How?'

No matter how many times I tried to wrap my head around it, I couldn't come to a place where it made sense my dad hadn't known.

If I didn't look exactly like Orlando, I'd question whether we were related, or whether it was all a ploy of Winifred's so she could gain the upper hand and take control of the Hawthorn and Brandon fortunes.

She wanted nothing more than all the money under her command. We all knew it.

But Orlando had my face; had my DNA running through his veins and I couldn't deny it, no matter how much we all may have wanted to.

Dad shook his head. 'I'd known your mum was pregnant with twins, but I wasn't in the delivery room when you came along. I'd been working up north and came as soon as I heard she'd gone into labour.'

He took a long draw of his whiskey, his eyes lost in the past.

'By the time I arrived, you were here. Blue-eyed and strong-jawed. You were everything we'd dreamed of. Then I asked after your brother ...' He rubbed his stubbled jaw. 'They told me he didn't make it because of a complication.'

'And you never thought to tell me?' Everything in my mind jumbled together. Scrambled and shitty. If my dad was telling the truth—and I couldn't see a good enough reason for him to lie—then why hadn't anybody told me I had a twin, even one who hadn't survived?

'Your mum and I decided not to. We thought it for the best, Oliver.' Tears welled in his eyes. 'We didn't want you to live with the burden of the truth.'

'Learning I'm a twin wouldn't have been a burden.'

'No, you're right.' Dad nodded. 'But learning you were the reason your twin didn't live would have been.'

'She told you I killed him?' I blinked, this new reality of mine blurring before me. 'How?'

'He became tangled in your umbilical cord.' Dad laughed, the sound sour. 'Well, we both know it for the lie it is now, but at the time, keeping you in the dark benefitted us.'

I stayed silent, letting his words enter my bloodstream and sit there. My mum lied to us both. She knew the whole time Orlando was alive and breathing and living with her sister, of all people. The sister she hated. The sister she'd hated her whole life.

'Have you spoken to him?'

'Who? Orlando?' I shook my head. 'I'd rather not, thanks.'

'Your aunt won't let me see him.' The tears in Dad's eyes became thicker and fuck me. I couldn't handle it if the man started crying. I'd probably break out into a run and leave the house pronto. 'Says he doesn't want to talk to me. That I should respect his wishes.'

At a loss, I shrugged.

Dad sensed I didn't want to talk about Orlando anymore. Or maybe he had no words left, either.

'Oliver, there's something I need to tell you and I know it'll be hard for you to hear. But the last year, before your mum died ...' He trailed off, his eyes still fixed on the glow from the flames. 'The last year was hell.'

He turned his gaze to me, his eyes boring into mine, and I could see the red veins in his eyes. Could see how exhausted and messed up the big revelation had made him.

An anger burned in them, too.

'Hell?' I sputtered, my memory not lining up with the use of that word. 'For Mum, you mean.'

'Yes.' Dad's tone sent a chill up my spine. 'Your mother lived in a state of hell, Oliver. The world always seemed too much for her. There were times your mother could be vindictive, mean, and downright nasty.'

I couldn't let him speak badly about her. Not without butting in. 'That's not—'

'Oliver.' He cut me off. 'You were too young to see the truth of the situation. We both tried to keep the other side of her from you.'

I scoffed. Deep down, I'd known he would discredit my mother's memory. He'd always found any opportunity he could to do so ever since I could remember.

'I was ten!' I slammed the now-empty glass down. 'Ten isn't too young to see how you acted. How you treated her.'

'You're remembering the past wearing rose-coloured glasses, Oliver,' Dad growled, his anger rising to match mine. 'Your mother was unwell. She searched for every escape she could find. Wanted a different life for herself but knew it to be impossible.'

'It was impossible because you wouldn't set her free!'

Dad slammed his empty tumbler down, matching my ire. 'I did no such thing. All I ever did was try to save her from herself. Both when we were younger, right until her passing.'

'Even if any of that bullshit's true, the last year of her life being hell doesn't explain why she'd hide a second son from you or why she'd let Winifred raise him.'

'I wish I knew the answer. But your mum ... she did what she wanted. No matter who got hurt in the crossfire.'

'What does that even mean?' I shouted, so close to jumping out of my chair and punching my father square in the jaw.

'As you know, when you were five, your aunt Eliza died.'

I nodded, biting my tongue. The taste of copper filled my mouth, and I laughed darkly, keeping my mouth closed so the blood wouldn't leak down my chin.

'Well, Aunt Eliza and Uncle Damien didn't die unprovoked.'

I opened my blood-filled mouth to ask a question, but another shout got there before I could.

'What do you mean?' Griff roared from the doorway. Leo close on his heels.

Dad grimaced at Griff's appearance and shuffled in his chair, straightening up.

The two of them came to stand beside the fireplace. 'Tell me. What do you mean?' Griff repeated.

'I can't tell you. Nothing concrete, anyway.' Dad shook his head, troubled. 'But what I can tell you is your mother didn't handle it well at all, Oliver. She went off with Jacob Cooper and started an affair. Disregarded her commitments to you. To me.'

Leo and Griff took the remaining empty seats in silence.

'Her health declined more each year, and throughout every battle she fought, I stayed by her side. Ready to pick up the pieces. Yet every time she ran back to him.'

He took a deep breath.

'Son. You have no idea what I have done for you. What I continue to do for you.'

I stayed silent, still biting my tongue, but for a different reason. If I opened my mouth, I would spit out all the hatred sitting on my heart—but not hatred aimed at my dad. Oh, no. Hatred aimed at Jacob fucking Cooper.

'Your precious Millie,' Dad said, his face contorted as he stood from his chair, 'was a bitch. She did everything in her power to get out of this life. To get out of being here for you, and for me. She'd never wanted to marry me, but I thought we'd make each other happy, arranged marriage or not. I've never been more wrong in my life.'

Maybe I spoke too soon. Seemed I could still find a lot of hatred for my dad, too.

My entire childhood, I'd seen how Henry treated Millie. Had seen how he railroaded her. Had made her feel small, as if she weren't any better than shit on his shoe. No wonder she'd run into Jacob Cooper's arms.

I'd never blamed her for seeking the attention she deserved from elsewhere.

No.

I blamed Jacob Cooper.

I blamed him for leaving her and causing her to see no other way but to do what she did.

His actions had led us all here. And, yes, I may slowly be

coming to terms with the fact he was the father of the girl I love, but I couldn't deny that bringing Skylar into this world was the one good thing the fucker had done in his rotten life.

I could no longer bite my tongue—both metaphorically and physically.

'You made her miserable,' I spat, looking up at my father. 'You caused her to seek out Jacob Cooper, and you're the reason she's dead. You're the reason she can't be here right now and defend her actions.'

'Now, look here, son,' Dad said, and I leapt out of my chair so the two of us were standing chest to chest.

Leo jumped up, too, ready to step in if anything turned physical. I'd deal with that prick later.

'You look here,' I said, my voice raised louder so my dad couldn't interrupt me. 'There's a reason she never told you about Orlando. There's a reason she chose to leave this earth rather than spend another day with you. I hope you're happy with yourself.'

I took one last glance at my dad and left the room. It wasn't safe for me to be around any of them any longer. Listening to my father's vile lies had pushed me to the edge.

Millie may have been a lot of things, sure, but a bitch? No, I couldn't accept that bullshit, and I planned to do everything in my power to prove it.

I needed to find Sky. Seek solace in the one person at this school who had never lied to me.

She would understand my need to know more about Mum's past, and she'd help me find it. The girl loved a challenge, and learning all she could about Hawthorn shit was already high on her to-do list.

'Ollie, wait up!'

A growl left my throat unbidden at my cousin's shout.

I'd wait all right.

I waited until Leo got close enough, pulled my hand into a fist, and then I landed a punch dead centre of his face.

Fourteen

VALENTINE'S DAY.

How the fuck were we already living through another Valentine's Day?

From the moment I woke up, everything seemed different to last year, for many reasons, and I didn't know how to spend my day. I hoped the couples of the school didn't walk around shoving their love in everybody's faces. Nobody liked a PDA: public display of affection.

Why did the day feel so different?

For starters, I didn't wake up Clover and get punched in the face. A nicer start, but I'd have preferred a bloody nose if it meant she'd woken up in the bed parallel to mine.

Secondly, I didn't have a boyfriend this year—and yes, I classed Ollie as an ex-boyfriend. It may not have been real for him, but it was for me, which mattered most. Full stop. End of story.

And lastly, a mere month and a half ago, I'd envisioned this day with a different guy by my side.

A guy who still did nothing more than glance at me across campus and frown when he caught me glimpsing back.

'Little One.'

The hairs on my arms stood on end at the smooth, sultry tone of Orlando. He sounded the same as his brother, and every single time, it disconcerted me.

'Orlando,' I replied, turning on the spot to face him. 'What do I owe the pleasure?'

'No need to be like that. I thought after our little talk in your room, you'd be more open to being seen with me.'

'I have no issue being seen with you. Most people will assume you're Ollie, the way they always have.'

'Low blow, Little One, but factual, so I'll let you off.'

I sighed, weary in my bones. 'What do you want? Your brother's gonna show up in a moment and I can't be arsed to watch you clones fight one another.'

'Why do you assume we'd fight?'

'Because I know your brother. He's got a lot of pent-up anger towards you, towards the world, and he'd love an outlet for it. Don't walk into his fists for no reason.'

'I have no intention of walking into Oliver's fists. Besides, Leo's already done that, and I don't want a pretty shiner like he's got. It'd ruin this gorgeous face.' Orlando stopped moving from side to side and waved his hand in front of his—admittedly gorgeous—face. It didn't help that he had the same face as Oliver, and at a glance, they blurred into one person.

Leo had run into Ollie's fists? News to me.

When I talked to Ollie last night after his talk with his dad, he hadn't mentioned Leo being there, or really much of what they all said. He told me he'd fill me in once he wrapped his head around it and I didn't want to push him before he was ready, so I'd left it.

Orlando's talking made my mind centre back into the here and now. 'I hoped maybe we could meet later.'

'Where?'

He ignored my question. 'I've got a gift I want to give you.'

'A gift?'

'It is Valentine's Day, Little One. Or have you forgotten?'

'How could I forget?' I asked, gesturing towards the younger years over by the treeline passing around large red heart cards to one another. 'I don't understand why you'd give me a gift.'

'It's the first time I can give you one without hiding behind somebody else. I'm gonna jump on the chance.'

'And what makes you think I want a gift from you?'

'Trust me, Little One. You'll want this one.'

'You can't meet him alone, Sky.'

I rolled my eyes to the heavens and bit down the angry retort sitting on my tongue.

'Oliver, you're a little overbearing, did you know?'

'I'd rather you think I'm overbearing than have you wind up dead on the pool house steps.'

'Orlando won't kill me if I meet up with him. Is there any reason you don't want me to go aside from the fact you think I'm weak and can't fight for myself?'

'Now you're putting words into my mouth.' Ollie shook his head. 'If you must know, I hoped we could grab dinner together tonight.'

A lot of hoping coming my way from the Brandon twins today.

'We always grab dinner together.'

He let out an exasperated sigh. 'I mean *together* together.'

'Oliver Brandon,' I said, a smile playing on my lips. 'Is this your neanderthal way of asking me out on a date?'

'Maybe.' It came out mumbled.

I waited, stifling the laugh I purposefully held in. It was yet another one of those instances where Ollie looked cute, all out of sorts. He needed to stop doing that, otherwise I might get some stupid idea in my head and think he likes me for real.

He took a deep breath. 'Skylar, would you like to have dinner tonight? As a date.'

The laugh I'd held back came out. 'Well ...'

Ollie shifted his weight and raised an eyebrow in my direction. 'Are you going to make a man beg, Sky?'

'If I thought you'd actually beg then, yeah, I'd totally be game to see that.' I laughed. Ollie wouldn't beg me for anything, even if hell froze over.

But to my surprise, and shock, and also kind of embarrassment, Ollie got down in front of me on his knees, his hands gripped together in front of his chest.

'Skylar Crescent. Please, I beg of you, have dinner with me tonight, as a date. I promise I won't fuck it up. Fuck, I won't even complain when you meet Orlando alone afterwards.'

My cheeks burned. Jeez, who knew having somebody beg in front of you in public was so discomforting?

'Get up, you stupid bastard.' I nudged his shoulder with my hand, but he didn't move an inch. 'Ollie, seriously, get up.' He still didn't move, a glint of menace shining in his blue eyes. 'Yes! Yes, I'll have a dinner date with you tonight if you please, please, get up off the grass right this instant.'

The smirk on his face as he stood up filled me with violence. Violence I would never act upon, but he had a face you wanted to hit now and then.

'Trust you to act like an idiot,' I said, breaking the tension. 'I'm sure you're all smug now you got what you wanted.'

'Sky, haven't you figured it out yet?' He placed his hands around my lower arms, the most earnest expression in his eyes when our gazes locked. 'Spending time with you is all I want. Everything else is a bonus.'

***

'Tell me the truth,' Ollie said, grabbing my hand so our arms would swing between us as we walked. 'You're thrilled you said yes.'

I laughed, not wanting to confirm or deny.

I'd spent a lot longer than usual getting myself ready for dinner and let's be honest, I knew what it meant deep down even if I didn't want to analyse it.

Ollie showed up to my room looking absolutely bloody gorgeous in a grey suit and I struggled hard to step out into the hall and close the door behind me, rather than staying put and asking him to join me inside.

What was it about the boy that made me melt?

Like he could make me do anything he wanted, from a mere touch or glimpse or sentence or ... well, anything.

'Did I mention you look amazing?' The words covered me from top to toe in a glow. Compliments were always welcome, but ones from Ollie were the icing on top of the cake.

Get a grip, girl.

'Thank you,' I said. 'I'd be a liar if I said you looked anything but amazing yourself.'

'Sky, I ...' The tone of his voice alarmed me. Okay, maybe not that dramatic, but it settled in my stomach in a way that made me think he may be about to get gushy, or say something to ruin the peace between us.

'If the next thing out of your mouth is gonna be deep, wait until we've got some food in front of us, okay?' At least then I could move food around my plate with my fork and not look at him as I did so.

'Ay, ay, captain.'

'Seriously?' I laughed. 'You're such a dork, Oliver.'

'Coming from the girl who spends most of her days reading or learning about events which took place absolute donkeys ago.'

'Hmm.'

The two of us kept walking, but before we came upon the dining room, Ollie diverted us to the left, away from both the school exit and the dining hall.

'Where are we eating?' Nobody else seemed to be around and I didn't recognise where we headed. 'Where else on campus is there?'

He smiled, the corners of his lips curling up in the way they did when something highly amused him. 'You'll see.'

'Okay ...' I trailed off, letting him guide me in whichever way he chose by our grasped hands. 'Did I tell you Orlando said he had a gift for me?'

Ollie hummed noncommittally.

'Well, do you think I should find out what it is?'

'You should do whatever you think is best,' Ollie said, and his diplomatic act surprised me. Then he opened his mouth and dashed it all away. 'I think you'd be stupid to encourage him further, but what do I know?'

'How to be a dick,' I muttered, but his face didn't change, so who knew if he heard me or not.

Ollie stopped in front of a door I'd never needed to enter before, hidden off to the side. 'Here we are.'

'And here is ...'

'The private dining room, mainly used for visitors to the school or small meetings when parents come.'

He opened the door, a grand gesture of sorts, and waited for me to walk inside first.

At first glance, the room appeared the same as the main dining hall, but a fraction of the size.

A table was set up for the two of us in the centre of the room, but before I headed to my seat, something caught my eye on the wall opposite the entrance.

What the?

I screamed.

My eyes, my brain, unable to comprehend the view.

Because there, dangling from a wooden beam running down from the ceiling like some sick marionette puppet, hung the rotting, decaying corpse of Mr Hawkins.

Fifteen

'GUESS WE DON'T NEED to ask Orlando about the gift anymore,' Ollie said, his tone deadpan.

But me? The shockwaves running through my body prevented me from speaking.

Of course, Ollie could joke at a time like this.

The moment I'd realised the sight before me, I'd turned away. I didn't need the vision of him haunting my dreams more than he already managed to, and I stayed back, not wanting to get a closer look.

One thing that didn't surprise me? The fact Orlando gave me a dead body and believed it to be a reasonable Valentine's day present. What says love more than a rotting corpse of the man who assaulted you not so long ago? Wait … Why did my stomach drop in a nervous yet excited way at the thought?

Fuck, Sky.

Do not go getting a thrill at the fact Orlando took matters into his own hands and delivered the only proper punishment he could.

A waiter entered, saw the body, paled, and turned to walk straight out again.

'Oh no you don't,' Ollie said, stopping the man mid-step.

'What can I do for you, Master Brandon?' the waiter asked, timid as fuck.

'You can call the police for a start. Then I suggest you go get my good-for-nothing aunt and tell her about this mess.' He waved his hand toward Mr Hawkins, encompassing the *mess* he wanted sorted. 'Then you can find us somewhere else to eat where the stench of death isn't lingering over the table.'

'Y-yes, S-sir.'

The waiter rushed off, and I swallowed down a giggle threatening to burst out of me. 'Wow. Nice to know you can reduce others into a stuttering fool.'

'Nice to know you haven't lost your sense of humour,' he said. I took two steps towards him and he reached me in the middle, holding the lower part of my arms in place, grounding me. 'Are you okay?'

I let out a gust of air. 'I'm not sure.'

The steadiness and warmth of his hands on my skin soothed me. Things may be awkward and unsure with Ollie, but with each day, he proved he cared about me.

'That's understandable. Shit, Sky. I hated the man, and wanted to see him dead, so can't imagine how you feel, but this? It's grotesque.'

Grotesque. Twisted. Monstrous. *Disturbed.*

It was all of those and more.

Yet …

The two of us remained in our bubble, silent, while we waited for the masses to arrive, because of course they would. There were no secrets at Hawthorn—no way to hide what went on behind closed doors, no matter how much you may want to.

Students hovered outside the door, seemingly too afraid to cross the threshold. The buzz of their whispers, the hushed excitement, all of it created a symphony of sorts.

I leaned in closer to Ollie, placing my lips against his ear. To onlookers, we'd appear to be in a close embrace. 'This doesn't look good for either of us.'

'You don't say?' he joked, but then his face turned serious. 'It looks worse for me. Nobody's gonna think you're capable of murdering a man, let alone having the strength to truss him up like a dead pig in a butcher's window.'

'The police already hate me and think I killed Olivia.' My frustration at the police's stupidity had me shaking my head. Those wankers. Detectives Smith and Saunders would have a bloody field day with this. 'Maybe they'll think I put you up to this or something.'

'You'd have no reason to stage it like this. Me? I arranged the room, the dinner ... God, Sky, everybody saw me on my knees on the grounds earlier today *begging* you to come on this date.' His eyes glazed over, seeing something I couldn't see. 'This must be his game.'

'Who? Orlando?'

Ollie nodded, his dark hair brushing against the side of my face. 'Leo said he wants to take over my life. Steal it. Well, what better way than to have me locked up forever more?'

'We won't let it happen.'

'I'm not sure we're gonna have much say in it.'

With such an ominous statement out there, Ollie turned quiet again. We said nothing more, not even after the police arrived and questioned us both about why we were there and who'd known about it and so on.

We still hadn't said another word to each other when the police asked—albeit in a way evident to all it wasn't a request and more of a demand—Ollie to return to the station with them so they could talk to him further.

Our eyes locked as he followed the detectives out of the room.

His said: *Fuck.*

Mine said: *I think I love you.*

But lucky for me, he couldn't understand eyes.

I PACED my room for hours.

After Ollie followed the police, I'd spoken to Ms Hawthorn, who seemed uninterested in the whole thing.

Of course she did the bitch. She knew the truth of it all. I could see it plain on her face the moment she surveyed the room and saw Orlando's handiwork.

Suppose having a murderous son didn't shock her too much, seeing as he'd already killed before and most likely would kill again.

The thought sobered me.

Ollie's text came at a quarter to twelve.

I'M BACK. SHALL I HEAD TO YOU, OR WOULD YOU PREFER TO COME TO ME?

I didn't even need to think about it.

I'M ON MY WAY.

Within moments, I grabbed my phone, dorm key, and slipped on some shoes.

I made it to his room in record time.

'Hey,' he said when he opened the door. The redness under his eyes and the upright status of his hair told me he'd rubbed his tired eyes and pulled his hand through his hair more times than he could count. I hated to see him so dishevelled.

Ollie and dishevelled were two words I would never expect to see together.

'Hey.' I moved into his room, kicking off my slippers as I did so, before pulling him into the biggest, hardest hug. 'Are you okay?'

'I'm fine.' His arms squeezed me, relaxing once the hug had gone on a little too long to stay platonic. 'Those wankers think I did it.'

'It makes me wonder if the two of them ever solve any crimes or if they bumble around in life hoping for the best.'

Ollie laughed. 'Well, this time around, they have a couple of things to fuel their fire.'

'Like?'

'Like the fact Orlando and I share literal DNA.' He ran his hand through his hair, walking over to sit on the edge of his bed. I, like a well-trained puppy, followed him and did the same. 'And I'm not even being facetious. The one thing setting us apart is our fingerprints.'

'And I assume Orlando would never be stupid enough to leave prints anywhere.'

'Wouldn't surprise me if he'd left hair, or saliva, or something on the body so they could point it at me, too. They said they'll be questioning him later on, but I'm sure Winifred will make it hard for them.'

'He's already on bail, though,' I said, fiddling with the hem of my pyjama top for something to do. 'Surely they'll investigate him more in depth because of it.'

'Money talks, Sky. It always has and it always will.'

Shitting hell, what a depressing thought.

Yet one I couldn't deny.

'So, what do we do about it?'

'Hope the bastard left his prints on the guy. Or that the police see this for what it is.'

'And if neither of those come to pass?'

'Fuck, I don't know. Guess we could always run away.'

I laughed. 'Be serious.'

'I'm trying.' He flopped down onto the bed, pulling me down with him. 'I wonder when this will all end, you know? We've got demons at every exit.'

'Not just when, but also how,' I said. 'I don't see Orlando giving up.'

'Me either.'

'But he is on bail for a serious crime, and as much as I've seen the corrupt way they deal with things here, I'm still a little hopeful. Only a tad, sure, but enough. I came to Hawthorn to get good grades and go to a good university and live a good life and fuck, I'm gonna do those things.'

The words rushed from my lips

Bottled up, now bubbled over.

Ollie turned to his side to face me. 'I believe in you, Skylar.' His fingers grazed the side of my face, his gaze one of awe. 'What I can't believe is that you're here, with me, letting me touch you, be near you.' His breath fluttered my eyelashes. 'You're beautiful, funny, kind, understanding, and all the things I'm not.'

'Not true,' I said, a playful smile on my lips. 'You are pretty funny.'

His chuckle reverberated through the room.

'Thanks,' he said. 'We need to get the gang together, don't we? Make a plan of action.'

'I thought we'd decided I was gonna get closer to Orlando?'

He sat, abrupt. 'You still wanna go through with it?'

'Why wouldn't I?'

'Skylar.' He said my name as if I were a child to be scolded. 'His idea of a gift today has got me in a lot of shit. He killed a man for you, and wants you to know it.'

I shrugged, staring up at Ollie. 'Even more reason to get close to him, no? He's trying to grab my attention, and fucking hell, he's got it.'

'I don't want you to get hurt.'

'And I appreciate you for that.' His warm skin under my fingers made me shiver. 'But we need to be smart about this. Maybe he'll slip up.'

'Maybe,' Ollie agreed. 'Or maybe he'll get bored and murder you, too.'

Sixteen

CLOVER'S RETURN came at the best time.

A couple of weeks had passed since the whole dead body in the dining room thing and no matter how hard I tried to pin him down, Orlando avoided me like the plague. The bastard.

He knew my game; what I wanted.

And he was playing one right back.

Ollie had gone into the police station a second time to answer more questions, but they had nothing and he returned the same day.

Weirdly, life went on.

Lessons took place, food got eaten, and I spent time with all the boys except Leo.

And absolutely nothing built any momentum.

'I am so happy you're back! I don't even think you *know* how much I've missed you.'

'Ditto.' Clo laughed. She'd returned an hour ago and started reorganising her clothes the moment she got into our room. It calmed her, or so she said. I thought she needed something to do with her hands while we spoke—something to do to prevent her from having to face my direction and see my disapproval about her not having ended things with Griff yet. 'I never thought I'd say this, but I'd much rather be here at Hawthorn than at the hospital another minute.'

'Wow, Clover Luck admitting she'd rather be at Hawthorn? I've heard everything now.'

'Oh, shut up. You've stayed there. You know the tedium.'

I nodded, able to sympathise. My time in the hospital after getting stabbed was the worst. Well, aside from getting stabbed. That really sucked.

'I also know I've got a lot to fill you in on, but also somehow nothing to tell.'

I'd texted most of it to her, and we'd face timed too so I didn't have too much to add. The joys of technology, making conversations in person pointless ninety-nine per cent of the time.

Jesus, when did I get so old?

Clo nodded sagely. 'Feel that.'

'It's all fucked, isn't it?' I watched her as she methodically took out all her tops from the top drawer of the chest of drawers, placed them on her bed, and then folded them one by one, before placing them back in the drawer. Quite soothing, actually. The monotony of it.

'Tis ...' She paused in her folding, her tension-filled stiff back facing me. 'Have you heard from Leo?'

'Nope.' I laughed. 'Since we met him in the walls, he's stayed silent, to us at least. He talks to Orlando instead.'

'How are you doing, really?' Clo turned to me reluctantly. 'I know I've been a bit of a cow about him and you and blah blah.' She waved her hand to encapsulate everything, and I understood the unspoken words. 'But I know his betrayal did a number on you.'

Understatement of the century.

'Yeah ...' It was my turn to turn away from her. 'I wouldn't say I'm over it or anything, but it's not in the front of my mind.'

'Really?' Pretty sure if I were to glance at her I'd see a cocked head and a raised brow, but out of principle, I kept my gaze averted. So who knew?

'Really.' *Good, it sounded convincing.* 'There's more important shit to face. And yeah, okay, I'd like an actual explanation from him or an apology or *something*, but I can wait. It'll come in time.'

'You think he's gonna say sorry?'

Suppose I needed to stop averting my gaze. I turned toward her, and sure enough, her cocked head and raised brow greeted me.

'I think so, yeah. I know you and him ...' I trailed off, not wanting to get into it again. 'But we were real, and it meant something, and even though he made some poor decisions, he's not bad or evil at the heart of it all. More like a messed up rich kid who got dragged into a secret society who threatened to murder all those he loves.'

'So normal every day shit?'

'Around here, yeah.' We laughed, the sound freeing. 'Imagine if we were at a normal school? Life would be so boring.'

'Boring, yet safe.'

'True.'

Clover went back to her folding, and I went back to staring at her back. 'What's our plan?'

'I've been thinking about searching Hawthorn House,' I said. The idea had come to me a week ago, but I'd waited for her to return before putting it into action. I liked having the boys around, but you couldn't beat spending time plotting and scheming with your best friend. 'Wanna join me?'

'Assume the boys will join us?'

I nodded. 'I haven't asked them yet, but Ollie and Griff, yeah. No Leo. He'd tell Orlando which we don't need.'

'I'm in. When you thinking?'

'Not sure yet. Got to wait for Orlando and Winifred to disappear for long enough to do it without their eyes on us the whole time.'

'Do they ever leave?'

I thought about it for a moment. 'Eurgh, maybe I do have to include Leo.'

'Why?'

'Because he'll know when they're off to a *Sanctum* meeting and can give us the heads up.'

A growl came from low in Clo's throat. 'I do hate it when the bastard has a use.'

'It is mighty frustrating, but at this stage, I think it's unavoidable.' Leo always seemed to know everything and if he knew we were searching the house, he may even keep them out longer, so we're not discovered.

Clover's grave nod made me smile. 'Like Leo himself. Every time I think I'm free of him, there he is.'

'I'll message the guys. Are you ready to see Griff?' A thought hit. 'He knows you're back today, right?'

'He does.' She let out a deep sigh. 'I should talk to him, shouldn't I?'

'About?' I asked, but she didn't need to answer. I'd put the question out into the universe to feign ignorance. Or maybe so I didn't have to say something rude like, *you think?*

'About how I'm feeling.'

'And how are you feeling?' I sat up a little straighter, resting my back against the cold wall.

'I still haven't decided whether I want to end it,' Clo said, sitting down on her bed so she could look over at me opposite her. 'But he should know I'm not certain about us. He deserves to.'

'He does,' I agreed. 'Remember, if he responds poorly, to stand your ground. I love Griff like a brother, but he has a tendency to be a little too happy-go-lucky about everything. To live in a certain level of denial.'

'I'll ask to go back to his place with him tonight after we've spoken about Hawthorn House.' The glint in Clover's green eyes showed her resolve. 'Talk to him then and see how it goes.'

'Sounds like a plan,' I said. I messaged the guys in our group chat. 'Knowing them, they'll be here within five minutes.'

Clover laughed. 'They are pretty desperate.'

'Quite endearing though.' I laughed. 'Let's hope they'll be agreeable to the plan without too much coaxing.'

Clover replied in an ominous tone. 'Let's hope we don't find any more secret Hawthorns lurking in the walls.'

———

' ... he'll keep them occupied, I'm sure of it,' I concluded.

Ollie and Griff were sitting on my bed, and Clo sat on hers. It created a much-needed divide between us all.

My heart almost broke at seeing the relief on Griff's face when he spotted Clo looking well and restored. *Hm.* How many messages and calls of his had she missed or ignored while feigning illness or sleep? I probably should have dug a little deeper when he came up in our earlier conversation, but I didn't want to push her. Clover didn't do well when pushed—she lashed out and made you hurt as much as she hurt. Not one of her better qualities, and I couldn't say I liked that side of her, but I doubted she took pride in it.

'What if Leo doesn't uphold his end of the deal and caves and Orlando about it?'

'Then we say you were searching for something for your dad,' I said, having thought it all through. 'He stayed there after the gala for a while, right?'

'He did,' Ollie said, assessing me. 'How long have you been cooking this up?'

I laughed. 'A week or so. If the parents left anything behind, it'd be there.'

'It'd also be the first place she'd put things if Winifred had anything of our parents' she wanted to hide.' Griff rubbed his jaw. 'I'd love to find something of my mum or dad's. I know I have the estate and everything in it, but something from their time here would be pretty cool. It's like they'd wiped their time at the academy from their life after they left.'

'It's odd,' I said. 'What happened for them to all ... disintegrate?'

'We'll figure it out,' Ollie said, a certainty to his tone I found rather attractive. 'We always do.'

'Here, here!' Griff raised his non-existent glass in the air.

The four of us back together, laughing and joking around, made me happy in a way not much else did. Without being able to see the future, I had no way of knowing whether these times would last past Hawthorn—or even the next few months—but I did know at that moment I loved them all and wanted them to be in my life forever.

Here's to hoping I survived long enough for it to happen.

Seventeen

LEO HAD DELIVERED the goods with little prompting.

Orlando and Ms Hawthorn were off campus doing *Sanctum* business and we were snooping around Hawthorn House and had at least three hours until they returned.

Happy days all around!

'Do you think we'll find something?' Griff asked, a cloth of fabric pinched in between his fingers held at least three inches away from his unusually disgusted face. 'This place has always given me the heebies.'

'Oh yeah?' The boys had spent all their holidays here over the years and I expected them to at least *like* being here. Guess none of those holidays were their choices, though.

Does anybody truly like doing something they're forced into?

'It's always been so ...' Griff waved his hand, the red fabric fluttering. 'Lifeless.'

I looked around the room, trying to see it through his eyes, but the bare walls were all I could take in. 'I get what you mean. Like for you guys, this place was temporary, but for Winifred, this is home.'

'Right!' Griff put down the fabric and went to inspect a cabinet next to the enormous four poster bed in the centre of the room. 'This is her home—Orlando's home too, come to think of it —and it's as if nobody ever enters.'

'Orlando never got to have one of these rooms,' I said, fingers grazing along the spines of the books living on a shelf. I noted none of them seemed like appealing reads. Understandable, I supposed, if they were all merely for show. 'He told me he stayed up in the attic, or at least I think he did. Between me and you, I find it hard to take in what he says.'

Griff paused his perusing. 'Why?'

'For starters, he looks so much like Ollie. It fucks with my head a little.' Griff nodded. 'And then there's the whole *I've kissed him and more while thinking he was somebody else* thing. Probably the thing putting a spanner in the works the most.'

'Makes sense,' Griff said.

'Yeah, but that doesn't mean I like it. Everything's so fucked and every time I move forward or come to terms with what happened to me ...' I shook my head, struggling to articulate what I meant in a way Griff would understand. 'I don't know. It's all so hard.'

'It'll get easier, Clouds.' Griff moved across the room and brought me into the biggest bear hug. His lips placed a gentle kiss on my head, and I leaned into his warmth. 'We'll get to the bottom of who wants you dead and why, and then we can be free of this shithole.'

I nodded against his chest, my words muffled. 'If you say so.'

'I do say so, and I know all.'

We moved apart. 'Ah, Griffin Cooper, the omniscient.' I bowed low. 'I am blessed to be in your presence.'

He barked a laugh. 'Good one.'

The two of us went back to searching the room, neither of us knowing what to look out for, when somebody else entered the room with a heavy tread. I turned, expecting to see Ollie in the doorway, but my heart jolted at the sight of Leo there instead.

'Hey,' he said.

'Hey.' I turned my head to Griff, who had turned to stare at Leo, suspicion in his gaze. 'What are you doing here?'

'I thought I could come help,' Leo said. It always knocked me off guard to see him so ... awkward. Uncomfortable in his own skin. It didn't fit my idea of him, of the Leo I think about a lot more than I probably should. Scratch that. There's no probably about it.

'Err ... sure,' I said, sending a tentative smile his way. 'We're nearly done in here, but you can help with the next room if you want?'

Griff shuffled towards the door. 'I'll go find Clover and help her.'

Coward.

Neither me nor Leo stopped him from leaving. If Ollie caught wind about me and Leo being alone together, he'd appear, so anything the two of us needed or wanted to say to each other had to happen pronto.

Once Griff got far enough away he wouldn't hear, I said, 'What are you doing here?'

'No ulterior motive, Stutter. I'm here to help.'

My gaze narrowed on his too-perfect features, trying to find a fault and only getting salty when finding none, and assessed him.

'Okay, well ...' I looked around the room. We'd already searched most places. 'How about you help me go through these books and then we can move on?'

Leo came over to the bookcase and started on the top row while I crouched down to begin at the bottom.

'Sky,' he said after a few minutes, jolting me from my thoughts. It unnerved me any time he used my name.

'Yes?'

'I'm sorry.'

Should I stand up and let him tell me to my face? Staying put and remaining at knee height seemed the best plan of action.

No.

Don't be so silly, Skylar.

I stood up, tilting my head to look him in the eye. 'What for now?'

He sighed, running his hand through his hair. 'I don't think the word "everything" suffices, but it's all I can think of.'

'Everything is a cop-out.' I scoffed. 'Maybe get a little more specific.'

His lips lifted at the corners by a fraction.

'I can do that.'

I waited. If he had something to say to me, then he needed no more prompting.

'Skylar, I am so sorry for betraying you and not telling you about him. Everything got so out of hand and I acted like a total prick towards you. At first, when I suggested we fake date I wanted to spite everyone. Except maybe Griff.

'But then I realised how much I loved hanging out with you and enjoyed your company, and I wanted to spend more and more time with you. The line got blurred pretty fucking fast and every time I opened my mouth to tell you the truth, something stopped me or something more important happened and stole our focus.'

'Why didn't you give me a heads up before the gala? You let him steal me away in a dance and reveal it all and did nothing to tell me or to stop it. You knew he'd taken Ollie's place. Fuck, you helped him to take Ollie's place multiple times. You helped him *fool* me. Knowing all he did and his true identity.'

'I know, and I accept if you can't ever forgive me. I can barely forgive myself.'

I made a noise, a *pshh,* 'I find that hard to believe. You're Leo Hawthorn. You'll get over it soon enough and go back to your surly, slightly amused ways.'

'You don't think much of me, do you?'

'Leo,' I said, blinking at the beautiful yet ugly sight of him before me, wanting to make sense of my emotions but not having the time or the strength to do so right then. 'I try not to think of you at all.'

I LEFT Leo to search the next room alone and headed up to the attic by myself so I could get some peace. Or attempt to, at least.

My mind whirled.

Apologies. Betrayals. Murder attempts. Heartbreak.

Just another day at Hawthorn Academy.

One room took up the entire attic, and the moment I entered, I knew I stood in Orlando's room. His lair. The place he withered and hid and plotted and schemed.

Really, the place looked fucking miserable. All dank and dark and barely lived in, yet at the same time, you could tell he'd tried to make it cosy. A collage of pictures adorned the walls; ones taken from a distance he'd spied to get, ones with me or Winifred or of him alone, taken by somebody else.

A half-life. Lived by somebody unable to act freely.

Do not feel sorry for the bastard. I chastised myself. *Don't go getting all sentimental.*

Easier said than done. Not with the truth of his existence laid out before me in such disrepair and decay.

The room had a single bed placed in the left-hand corner. All thin metal railings and a thread-bare mattress which had seen better days.

Against my will, my heart hurt for the little boy subjected to this, and to the teenager that boy had become.

Seeing pictures of myself staring down at me from the walls unsettled me in a way I couldn't explain. Some of them were ones I'd posed for with him, and were actually of Orlando, but others ... they were of me from afar. Taken through gaps in a door, or maybe even from inside those secret tunnels. Who the fuck knew except Orlando? Asking him for clarification didn't make the top of my to-do list funny enough.

Oh, by the way, I stumbled across your room and ever since, I've wondered where and how you took those candid shots of me. Do tell.

Yeah, not happening.

A box in the right-hand corner of the room drew my eye. Most likely because there was fuck-all else for me to peek at, excluding a bedside cabinet and a chest of drawers and wardrobe combo.

A large, ornate, old trunk chest.

And my hand twitched to open it and delve into all its secrets. So I did.

Books and newspapers filled the chest to the brim and what at first glance appeared to be junk, but I reckoned had a purpose if Orlando had deigned to keep it. Especially as it seemed he kept little else.

I picked up the sheet of paper from the top, sat down on the dusty wooden floor cross-legged, and read.

———

The truth about Hawthorn Academy and what really goes on behind closed doors at the elite establishment.

Whistleblowers have caused a great deal of upset for those who run Hawthorn Academy in the past few weeks. The story is still unfolding, but we secured the latest scoop.

Both former and current students of the elite establishment Hawthorn Academy, located in Beurre, have started a petition and investigation into the goings on and malpractices of both faculty and students.

Hazing is rife at boarding schools, and it would seem Hawthorn Academy is no different when it comes to this age-old tradition.

Insiders, who wish to remain anonymous, have told all to our reporters, including a previously unknown story of a girl dying during an initiation ...

Story continues on page 12

SANDY PARKS DEAD, FOUND IN SCHOOL BATHROOM

The students who found her are staying quiet, but we know the truth.

On Friday 2nd February, Sandy Parks entered the girls' bathroom on the second floor of the English building ... and never walked out.

Her death has been deemed an apparent suicide by the police, but we all know they can be bought, don't we?

What The Set and The Sect don't want you to know:

The Set (most importantly Millie and Eliza Hawthorn), and *The Sect* (Damien and Jacob Cooper, Edward Hawthorn and Henry Brandon) were all present either before or after Sandy entered said bathroom, lurking around. What are they hiding? Well, wouldn't you like to know?

And don't worry, because we've got you.

Everybody knows the two groups have rules which students must adhere to at all times, and if you knew anything about Sandy Parks, you'd know she didn't abide by those rules.

She was an outlier.

An anomaly.

And the Hawthorn twins did *not* like that!

And they wanted her to pay for her crimes.

Are they capable of murder? Only they know the answer, but us students here at the Hawthorn Herald believe they're capable and more ...

My dearest, Jacob,

How I long to see you, be near you, touch you.

I understand why these things cannot yet come to pass, but I want you to know I miss you and wish you were here by my side every single day of my life.

Baby Oliver is doing well, even if he cries a lot for a toddler. At times, I wonder if he's crying because he senses the truth, but then I remember it's most likely wind and my day continues.

As for your daughter, Cora named her Skylar Crescent, which tells you everything you need to know about the upbringing she's about to receive. Maybe one day you'll get to meet her.

I'd love to hold her, but I can't be seen visiting anybody on the other side of The Divide. I hope you understand and won't judge me too harshly for it.

You never were one to judge me for my life's decisions, as poor as they may be.

Sometimes, I wish we were still at Hawthorn together, happy, and unburdened by the events of the past. Yet I know it's a dream. One I wake up from every morning and put into my mind at the start of every night.

Your brother and my sister are still sickeningly happy and are in love in every way. Being around them, I see what we could've been, if circumstances had allowed.

Their boy, Griffin, is the spitting image of you as a child. To look at him is hard, as I see how a child of ours would be, and it hurts.

Please come back to Beurre one day and take me away from this sorrow, this misery I call life.

Love you with all my heart,

Millie

P.S. I know you are already aware of this, but I feel the need to reiterate it. Henry can never learn the truth of what we did. If he does and I die, know his blood-soaked hands are the culprit, and seek my justice.

COOPER COUPLE KILLED IN CAR CRASH, FIVE-YEAR-OLD SON SURVIVES

Eighteen

ONCE I FINISHED READING, I called the guys up to me so they could see it all for themselves.

I took pictures while I waited so we could view them later, away from the darkness of the place.

The letter from Millie to my father proved he knew of my existence, but then again, the letter had never been sent, otherwise Orlando wouldn't have an original copy of it.

Did Winifred stop the correspondence between them? Infiltrate the system somewhere along the way and ensure it never reached its destination?

The day had brought up as many questions as it had answers, and I was so, so very tired of it all.

The four of us had returned to Ollie's room, sans Leo, and were sitting around on the floor, uneaten pizza going cold on the coffee table in front of us. Which, if you know anything about me and/or our group, you'd know that was fucking unusual.

Ollie's hand rested on my knee like it belonged there.

Maybe it was time to stop fooling myself and accept it did … belong there, I mean.

'So,' Clover said, breaking the fraught silence. 'What do we do?'

'What do we do?' I repeated, broken. Little we could do at present. 'What do you mean?'

'Well.' Her tentative tone matched the tentative look in her jade-green eyes. 'We set out to find something, and we did, even if we found something completely different from what we expected.'

'Right...'

Griff and Ollie remained quiet. Griff wringing his hands together in his lap while Ollie drew circles on my knee, attempting to distract himself. One of his more loveable quirks, by far. Whenever he got lost in thought, happy or sad, he circled patterns on my body.

'So,' Clo continued, 'we've got something to work with now. We can flick through the yearbooks and see if there are any mentions of Sandy Parks. We can talk to Leo and ask him when *The Sanctum* meets next and see if there's a way for us to spy, which will prove to us once and for all whether he's on our side. Plus, Mother's Day is coming up.'

'Nobody else has a mother coming,' I pointed out. I'd already accepted Cora would show her brash self even if I didn't invite her, so once again, I'd sent her an invitation to get ahead of the curve. Lottie, Leo's mum, had even been kind enough to offer Cora a lift, so they'd arrive and leave together.

Lottie truly was my idea of a modern-day saint.

Yes, she'd offered when Leo and I were still together, but she hadn't redacted it even after everything went down at the start of the year.

'Not true. Leo will be with you.'

'Yeah, I suppose.' I placed my hand on top of Ollie's, silently supporting him and to imply my feelings about spending the day working with Leo, all without saying a word. I hoped he got my meaning, but maybe I needed to speak to him about it later, once Griff and Clo left. 'I'll talk to him.'

Clover nodded, accepting it without saying something stupid like *I can talk to him.*

'Maybe Cora will tell me more about my dad,' I said. 'I don't like to encourage her drinking, but it seems this situation might call for it.'

'Not gonna lie, Clouds. Your mum is pretty hilarious after a couple of drinks.'

I bit my tongue. My snap response didn't seem appropriate.

There was a reason Orlando had a printout of the heading of the article talking about Griff's parents' accident. One none of us wanted to talk about.

'You wanna come sit with her, then?' I said instead. Griff's cheeky grin, not seen on his face as often recently, sprung to his face.

'As tempting as that is … no.'

The three of us laughed. Ollie didn't. It was as if he wasn't in the room with us, so lost in his own demons.

I couldn't draw him out of his head with these two here.

'Why don't we call it a night? We can sleep on all we've learned and talk about it tomorrow. I'll message Leo and get the ball rolling about talking to Lottie and Cora together on Mother's Day,' I said.

Griff and Clover mumbled their agreement.

'You're the best, Clouds.'

***

Hawthorn Academy always fell still in the middle of the night.

Barely any noise, barely any movement, or at least not any I could hear from Ollie's room at the end of the hall.

He feigned sleep beside me, his back to my chest being the little spoon.

I hadn't yet called him out on it, as I'd tried to fall asleep myself and leave him to his thoughts, but how much longer I could leave it for was up in the air.

'I know you're awake,' he murmured. 'I'm sorry for shutting you out.'

'That's okay.' My arm was slung across his side, my hand resting on his hip. There was something so intimate about being with him in his most unguarded moments I hadn't got used to yet. Skylar of old would squeal at her current reality. How close the two of us had become, an intimacy built from sharing secrets and thoughts and our minds.

Even I'm sick of how sick I sound.

But I couldn't help it. Ollie made me feel all the things all at once.

'Seeing her handwriting shit me up.'

'I get it. You don't have to explain yourself to me.'

He turned to face me, my arm remaining draped across his body. 'I don't have to, no, but I want to. I like talking to you.'

'I like talking to you, too,' I whispered, my breath causing his eyelashes to flutter. 'But it can wait. We don't have to do this tonight.'

'If I don't talk it over, I'm never gonna get any sleep.'

I brushed my lips against his in the barest hint of a kiss. 'Okay. Talk away.'

He inhaled through his nose, exhaled through his mouth.

My eyes transfixed on his lips, watched and waited.

Fuck, he's beautiful.

'It was so weird to see her writing, see her basically admit to doing what she did, and show no remorse for it. Or maybe she had remorse. I don't know. And that's what fucking sucks the most and will forever suck. I will never know what went through her head because she left me and never shared her secrets.

'And the fact your dad could show up, as much as I've always hated him and wanted him dead, fills me with a sense of excitement I can't explain even if I tried. Because maybe, just maybe, he'll have some knowledge we don't have. Can answer the questions burning the back of my brain.'

His words washed over me. It was my turn to draw circles on his skin.

'Every time I have a moment to myself, a moment of peace, my mind wanders to her, to him, to my aunt, to you and your dad, and I'm struggling to keep it together.'

Heart officially broken. The pain in his voice gutted me the way not much could. If I hadn't forgiven him for all the crap he put me through, I would now.

Ollie had changed so much in the past year, and he most definitely wasn't the same person I met on my first day at the academy.

My eyes met his, and the tears lingering at the corners of his eyes caught me off guard.

Ollie upset or Ollie in tears—well, it was never easy to see.

'All of this is a mess,' I whispered. 'And I know you feel you have to keep it together in front of everybody else, but you never have to with me. I'm here for you, O.'

'I'm so thankful you've forgiven me, Sky. I don't know what I'd do without you.'

'You'd survive the way you always have.'

'Yeah, maybe,' he said. 'But I'm glad I don't have to.'

Our conversation got derailed by kisses. Man, kissing Ollie again had the butterflies living in my stomach in overdrive. They didn't know what to do with themselves.

A little—okay, a long—time later, we paused the kisses and gazed at each other.

'I wonder what Lottie and Cora will say,' Ollie said, his lips resting on my forehead, grounding me.

'Guess we're going to have to wait until Mother's Day,' I replied.

My favourite day of the year. *Not.*

Nineteen

'LITTLE ONE, WAIT UP!'

Orlando's voice travelled down the empty corridor and my feet stopped of their own volition.

'Oh, I'm good enough to talk to now, am I?' I scoffed, tapping my right foot on the floor—my frustration towards him in physical form.

His top lip curved up. 'Upset I've ignored you?'

A sound came from the back of my throat. 'Not upset.'

'What then?'

'Pissed. Livid. Fuming. Take your pick.' I continued walking, and the boy followed, his steps matching mine. 'Only you would think it okay to leave me a dead body as a gift, then refuse to talk to me afterwards.'

He laughed. 'So you didn't like your present?'

My stomach roiled, the image of Mr Hawkins's body strung up flashing in my mind. It featured frequently in my nightmares, but I tried to never think of it while awake.

'You're sick,' I said. 'I know shit's happened to you, but fucking hell, you're twisted, Orlando.'

'And you'd rather me be vanilla and boring like my brother?'

'Least your brother understands right from wrong.'

'Does he? Because if I remember right, he bullied you and convinced the entire school to do the same.'

'Bullying and group coercion are a tad different to *murder*.'

The library came into view and I let out a deep breath. *My happy place.*

'You make it sound so black and white, Little One.'

'Because it is.'

My blood boiled. He always acted so arrogant, so important, so *right*. To the point where it made me question myself and my values. My beliefs.

'It isn't.' He shook his head and his disappointment bothered me. How bloody ridiculous of me! Why should I care how he feels?

'Whatever. What do you want, anyway?'

'To see you,' he said. The answer, so simple, it should've been obvious. 'We've not spent time together recently.'

'Once again, because you've *avoided* me.'

'Well, I'm here now. Can I sit with you?' He gestured to the back toward my usual table, and I nodded without enthusiasm.

The two of us sat down, and I ignored him, getting my things out of my bag and setting them up on the table, ready to tackle my homework.

Orlando, who I could see in my peripheral vision, seemed amused at my attempt to ignore him. *Bastard.*

'So ...' He prodded my elbow. 'Did you enjoy poking around?'

I raised my eyebrows his way. 'Huh?'

Orlando laughed. 'Oh, come on, Little One. I'm well aware you and the rest of the Scooby Gang played detective on the weekend.'

What would be best? To hold my tongue or find out who told him?

'I don't know what you're talking about.'

'Lying doesn't suit you. And no, before you ask, nobody told me anything. Not even Leo the arse-kisser.'

'Then what makes you so sure we were there?' I raised my eyebrows. He always seemed so cocky. So sure of himself. It made me burn inside, the way he went through life acting as if his past more than made up for him being an arsehole in the present.

It didn't.

Not entirely, anyway.

'You think I don't have cameras set up?' He scoffed. 'I thought you knew me better, Little One.'

It was my turn to scoff. 'I barely know you.'

'Not true.'

'Orlando.' I hoped my use of his first name had him realising my seriousness. 'All I know of you is you lied to me while masquerading as your brother, and you assaulted me, stabbed me, and attempted to drown me. None of those put you in a favourable light.'

'My brother isn't a saint.'

'He's never pretended to be.'

'Oh, which makes him better than me, does it?' Orlando spat.

'Why are you picking a fight with me?' I asked, putting down my pen and giving him my full attention. 'I'm not the one you're angry with.'

'Not like I can take it out on *her*.' He rubbed his jaw, and I watched the path his finger made, afraid to find anger or anguish in his eyes. 'She's not around.'

'She gave you away before she died, though.' It seemed silly to point it out and add to his ire, but I couldn't help myself. *Keep poking the bear, Skylar.*

'And what do you mean?'

'So, there was an overlap in time where she could have made an effort to see you, or spend time with you.' Maybe I should think through what I wanted to say before saying it, but it seemed my mouth liked to run away from me before I could catch up. 'Did you ever spend any time with her?'

'Once. For a grand total of two hours.'

'I want to say sorry, but that's bullshit because I've got nothing to be sorry for. Millie's the one who should be sorry. Maybe she had a reason to do what she did?'

'No reason would be enough for me. A reason is an excuse, no matter which way you turn it.'

I didn't agree. Not fully. Sometimes a reason is just that—a reasonable explanation—and not an excuse.

Orlando had made up his mind, though. All his life he'd

thought about it and come to his conclusion, probably a long time ago.

'I suppose,' I mumbled. Blinked.

How long would it take for me to not see Ollie when I looked at him? The mind fuck of it all kept fucking me up more, the two of them blurring into one.

Orlando's fingers grazed the back of my hand. 'Penny for your thoughts?'

'It'd cost you more than a penny,' I joked. 'Half the time I've got no bloody clue what's going on up there.' I pointed to my head. 'It's a minefield.'

'I'm sure mine could give yours a run for its money.'

'I'm not gonna fight you. Rarely do I enter into battles, knowing I won't win.'

'Can't say I've seen you enter many battles,' he said, taking my words seriously. 'And no, your run-ins with *The Set* don't count.'

'How are you finding hanging out with them? Is being a member, or should I say the *only* member, of *The Sect* everything you thought it'd be?'

'You think I'm silly for caring.'

'I never said that.'

His lips turned up at the corners. 'You didn't have to. Your face gives you away.'

'Talk to me then. Explain.' I placed my hand on his where it rested on top of the table. I'd told the boys I could get close to Orlando and use it to my advantage, but in reality, I'd been doing a pretty piss-poor job of it. 'I want to understand.'

'All my life I didn't fit in,' Orlando said. His bottom lip wobbled from keeping his emotions under wraps. 'Wasn't given the same opportunities as my brother or my cousins.' His bright blue eyes accosted mine, trapping me. 'And now I can have those things. They're mine for the taking.'

'By brute force, you mean,' I said, unable to bite my tongue.

'Nothing brute about it. I declared myself to be a member of *The Sect,* sure, but there was no violence involved. Oliver and the others stood down and left me to it.'

'You can't blame them.'

'I blame them for a lot of things.'

'Them and everyone else, yeah.' I squeezed his fingers to seem kind or approachable or who the fuck knew what, really. Orlando may be fucked up, and he may be a violent prick who deserved to rot behind bars for the rest of his life, but I couldn't bring myself to act too harshly toward him. It would be like kicking a puppy or knocking a vulnerable person over. Unnecessary and mean.

'Wouldn't you?' He bit out. 'You have as much reason as I do to hate them all, Sky, yet you don't. You've let them worm their way into your brain.'

'Maybe so. Or maybe I'm my own person and I've realised shit on my own. You seem to think I'm incapable of thinking for myself.'

I snatched my hand back.

He blew out a breath through gritted teeth. 'I don't think you're incapable of thinking for yourself.'

'Then what do you think?'

'You're being manipulated and you can't even see it.'

God, that made me laugh! '*Someone* is trying to manipulate me, yes, but I don't think it's Oliver.'

'That's how it is, then. You think so poorly of me?'

'Orlando, you've not given me much else to go on. You're lucky I'm even sitting here talking to you!'

'Little One, I—'

I cut him off. 'No. No excuses. Own your shit or I'm leaving.'

'Own my shit?'

I nodded. 'Think it's time, don't you?'

'Can we go somewhere more private?'

'Where's more private than an empty library hidden at the back?' I asked, darting my gaze around to find nobody else within earshot. Orlando opened his mouth to answer. 'The question was rhetorical.'

'Fine.' He bit out. 'I'm sorry for everything.'

'And by everything you mean ...'

The contempt on his face would've made me laugh in any

other circumstance, but I made sure my face stayed unmoved. Why was I even giving him a chance to fess up and tell the truth? Not like he'd taken the opportunity in the past whenever it presented itself.

'Fine!' he snapped when I remained quiet. 'So, you asked me about a list back when I joined, remember?'

I nodded. I remembered the list. I reached into the inside pocket of my blazer and pulled out the well-worn piece of paper I carried around at all times.

Ollie v Orlando

- First time we spoke in the Hospital Wing (surely Ollie ... right?)

- Closet make-out session during the first New Year's Gala (Orlando?) Orlando

- Who drugged me at the first ever party in the woods (Orlando?) Orlando

- Too many times in the library to count (must think of individual instances)

- Who set The Set on me? (Ollie?)

- Who killed Odette and Olivia? (Orlando?) Orlando

- Odette

'Can I see?' Orlando asked, his hand open, waiting for me to hand it over. I gave a slight nod of my head and handed it over. 'If I answer these, does that count toward owning my shit?'

'Yeah, I'd say it does.'

'Okay. The top one, about the hospital wing? Me.'

I failed to hide the incredulousness from my tone. '*You?*'

'Yep.' He popped the p, no doubt to irritate me. 'The real Ollie knocked on your door, but you'd passed out, so after he helped Leo get you to the hospital wing, he bolted. Decided it would be best to introduce himself to you at assembly the next morning.'

'And you know this because ...'

'Because Leo messaged me the moment Ollie left and told me to get my arse down to the hospital wing pronto if I wanted to meet you face-to-face. So I did.'

The first conversation between me and Ollie, wait, between me and *Orlando,* was hard to recall. Everything about my first evening at Hawthorn was fuzzy. Passing out does that to a girl.

'And then you called me beautiful,' Orlando continued, unable to see the turmoil in my eyes. His words sparked something in my brain.

'Right, and then you told me you were glad I noticed you.'

Another snippet of his words came back to me from our first meeting.

'Maybe you should remember that fear is good. Being scared can ensure you live. That you don't make life-threatening mistakes. Ever considered that, Little One?'

I blinked at Orlando in front of me. 'You called me Little One.'

'I did. I wanted a name for you nobody else would use. So when you learned the truth, you'd know things that were me and those that weren't.'

I felt like a fool. A big fucking fool who couldn't see the world correctly. How had I missed so much? It never even entered my mind to question the times Ollie used a nickname for me and those he didn't.

Was anything on my list even Ollie?

I repeated the thought to Orlando.

'Technically, he set *The Set* on you. Kind of. It's complicated.'

'Uncomplicate it,' I said through gritted teeth, having thoroughly lost my patience. 'Explain what you mean.'

'Back when Ollie first came up with his bullying plot, he had the O girls wrapped around his little finger. He could do no wrong in their eyes and they'd do everything he asked of them. But once you came here, and he met you, well, he had doubts about how far his conscience would allow him to go.'

'Right ...'

'He told the girls to back off a bit; to not go as far as before.

The day they beat you up in the toilets, he was livid.' A sick and twisted smile came to Orlando's lips. 'But what my dear brother didn't realise? Any time he told the girls to cool down, I went behind his back and met with them and contradicted him.'

My heart stuttered. 'You're the reason they escalated?'

He shrugged, as if his answer wouldn't cut me in two. 'Partially. I can't take any credit for the charity fashion show, even if I'd like to.'

'Thanks for telling me,' I said, my thanks feeling dirty and like a betrayal to myself. 'I've got some homework to do now.'

He put his hands up in a placating gesture. 'I'll leave you to it.'

The chair dragged along the wooden floor when he pushed back and the noise of it went straight through me. I hated those types of noises. You know, like nails on a chalkboard or the scrape of a knife and fork when they clashed? *Eurgh.* I shivered just thinking about it.

Orlando's finger pressed against my chin. He turned my head, and I blinked, finding his across from mine within touching distance. 'I am sorry, Little One. Even if you never believe me.'

Before I could put a stop to it, Orlando's lips touched mine. A soft, gentle kiss. A goodbye kiss, of sorts.

And for a split second, my lips moved with his. I joined the kiss as an active participant for a moment.

Fuck.

Twenty

MOTHER'S DAY CAME AROUND, and even though we'd all been building it up in our minds for the last two weeks, it came without much fanfare.

Unlike my mother.

Who arrived with fanfare and so much more.

'Skylar, my darling, how I've missed you!' Mum flew at me, wrapping me up in her bony arms, a hug for the ages. 'You are so beautiful. Truly stunnin!'

'Thanks Mum,' I mumbled. I took her in from head to toe and cringed, per usual. Today's ensemble was, well, it was a *look*, that was for sure.

A bright dress, in a pattern yet to be determined, and leggings underneath. Strappy stiletto heels on her feet, her tattoo of a rosary necklace on show. She'd got said tattoo because she'd seen it on a celebrity and loved it, so wanted to get it herself and not because the woman had a religious bone in her body.

The trend, not the meaning, mattered most to her.

'Skylar, dear, you do look rather wonderful,' Lottie said. Her bright smile lit up every room she entered, and it instantly made me happier. If you got close enough, you could see the tension lines forming at the creases of her eyes. Trust a short car ride sitting next to my mum to break somebody's Botox.

'Thank you, Lottie. You look amazing yourself, as always.'

She waved me off. 'In this old thing?' She laughed. 'Now where is my son?'

'He's on his way.' I stood on tiptoes, trying to spot Leo's head above the crowd.

'Unlike him to be late,' Lottie said.

'He had something he couldn't get out of,' I replied, not mentioning how the *something* was acting as an errand boy for Orlando. When I first asked Leo to confront the mums with me, he seemed uncertain, but a couple of days later he texted to say he'd do it.

I hated how we were no longer on talking terms in the way we used to be. I wished he'd open up to me so we could talk it all over, but until I forgave him or at the least accepted his apology, it seemed like a far-off day.

Huh. Sounds like a me problem, actually.

'Thank you both for coming,' I said, filling the time until Leo arrived. 'Been up to anything exciting since I saw you last?'

'Oh, you know me!' Mum said, knocking my shoulder with her thin, veiny hand. 'Bit o'this and a bit o'that.'

I nodded, because yes, her response made sense to me. What else did her life consist of other than visiting the market, lounging around beside her shitty husband, and gossiping away with Leslie?

'Sounds lovely,' Lottie said, her smile saying the opposite. 'Can't say I've got anything to report. Edward's been busy with ...' she trailed off, unsure how to finish. 'Everything.'

Maybe that was her way of referring to the fact Edward held a literal gun at Orlando during the shit show of a gala.

Pretty sure he never fired it ...

'I'm so sorry I'm late.' Leo's voice came from behind me. He placed a kiss on his mother's cheek before doing the same on Cora's. Smooth bastard.

No lingering glint in his eyes told me he felt awkward about being there with me and our mums. Nothing to hint at how he felt about the events of the past year.

Last Mother's Day, the four of us spent it together, but Leo and I were barely friends back then.

It also was the day Jacob Cooper, my father, first got mentioned. And I still knew as little now as I did then.

'That's alright, darling!' Mum's lipstick covered teeth beamed at him. In her eyes, Leo could do no wrong. 'You're looking rather dashing today, young man. I hope you're treating my Skylar well.'

'Mum,' I mumbled, not wanting to draw attention to us more than her loud, booming voice already did. 'Me and Leo aren't together anymore.'

'A mother can dream for that to change, can't she?' She nudged Lottie's arm. 'We'd both love to see you two happy.'

'Thank you, Cora,' Leo said, his tone one he often used with my mum. Placating and friendly, mixed alongside a twinge of distaste. My favourite. 'But Skylar's done the right thing. You should be proud of the daughter you've raised.' *Pfft*, like she had much to do with how I turned out. 'I don't deserve her.'

'Poppycock! You're doing the thing all men do, downplaying your many, many wonderful qualities.'

I rolled my eyes, unable to stop myself any longer. The woman, alongside being rather delusional, didn't know when to quit. Or maybe she did, and she ignored the red flashing lights in her head on purpose.

'I assure you,' I said tersely, 'he isn't.' I put my arm through Mum's, ready to sweep her away if she didn't shut her mouth. 'Shall we head through into the hall?'

'We must stop at the bar on the way! I'm absolutely parched!'

'Leave the bottle!' Mum told the waiter. 'No need for you to keep coming over and topping us up.'

God, was it possible for the woman to make me cringe more?

Mum burped. 'Oof! Soz about that everybody. Wine on an empty stomach makes a mess of the best of us.'

Ah, as always, the answer was a big fat resounding yes.

The ground could open and swallow me and it still wouldn't be enough.

Nothing could save me from my reality, no matter how many times I'd wished for a different mum—a different family.

'Mum,' Leo said, after the waiters took away the first course. 'Sky and I have got a few questions for you about the past.' He sat back in his chair. 'You too, Cora.'

Leo, ever the cool, calm, and collected one of the two of us. *Bastard.*

'I can't say I didn't see this day coming.' Lottie sighed, indicating a whole weight lived on her shoulders. 'But remember you two, I don't know as much as Edward or Henry.'

'Of course,' I said, fiddling with the fork next to my main plate. When I first joined Hawthorn, the cutlery of a fancy meal scared the shit out of me, like knowing what to use and when, but now? Now I was a pro.

A lot could change in eighteen months.

'What happened back when you all went here?' Leo asked, his hand touching Lottie's on top of the table. I'd always loved their relationship, how sweet and genuine it seemed, and my heart panged.

'A lot happened, Leo,' Lottie chuckled. 'You'll have to get a little more specific.'

'A girl died, Mum,' Leo said, getting to the point. 'And a lot seems to imply Dad and his friends had something to do with it.'

'How'd you find out? All the records are sealed and a lot of money was thrown at the problem to make it go away.' Lottie took her hand from Leo's and fiddled with the napkin on her lap. 'Winnie did a lot to help them all back then. Maybe you should talk to her.'

'Talk to the woman who hid a kid from the entire family for years?' Leo raised a sardonic eyebrow towards his mum. 'Funny enough, Mum, I don't think she'd tell us much.'

'I can't tell you much either,' Lottie said. 'I'm a few years younger and didn't know any of them then. I know what your dad's told me since, and the whispers I heard at the time.'

'Anything would help us, Lottie,' I said. 'Please.'

'All I know is the girl's family accepted payment and the matter never went any further. Winifred hushed a lot up as she'd joined the faculty the same year, so was in a better position to make it all go away. No matter how much the Hawthorns seemed to dislike one another, they always had each other's backs, no matter what. Millie and Eliza made a mistake, and Edward and Winifred did all they could to make sure nobody ever learned of it.'

'So, the girl died because of Millie and Eliza?' I asked, frowning.

'I never said that.' Lottie pursed her lips. 'But I have my suspicions, yes.'

'Thank you,' I said. I could tell from the sad expression on her face she wished she had more to tell us. If Lottie knew more, then we'd know it too. 'We appreciate you telling us.'

Leo nodded, assessing his mum. 'And Cora,' he said, turning to my mum, who had stayed quiet. No doubt drinking the bottle of wine she'd made the waiter leave. 'I know you may not want to talk about this, but we have to ask.'

'And if you know nothing, that's cool, too,' I added. I didn't want her to think we were putting her under an inquisition or anything. Mum didn't handle getting called out well.

Mum glanced between the three of us, a shrewd expression on her face, the fog of alcohol lingering but not as thick as a moment ago. 'If this is about your dad, Skylar, then no fear.' Mum's words slurred, so it sounded more like *iz-zis-bout-dad-sssskylar-n-fear*.

Lottie squinted in her direction, and I shrank down in my chair a fraction. Every time she spoke, my embarrassment levels climbed a notch, but for the first time it hit me that maybe that was a part of the problem?

Mum, even if a total mess, never acted ashamed of her actions or like she regretted the fact she wasn't the best human. If anything, she embraced it in a way I could only dream of embracing my own issues. Maybe a lesson lurked in there some-where. Something about being unabashed and unashamed to be yourself. Maybe …

' … coming here.'

Leo and Lottie's gasps at whatever Mum said while my mind disappeared into itself forced me to pay attention.

'You've done what?' Lottie asked, her shock palpable.

'So the last time we all got together,' Mum said, as if we'd all decided to hang out because we liked each other, 'got me thinking about Jacob.

'Which had my mind going back to a letter I got from him a while back now. It told me what to do if I ever needed to contact him for whatever reason. So, I thought, well why not reach out and fill him in on the goings on here? Tell him his daughter faced potential assault and murder at every corner and see what he had to say for himself. And like I knew he would, he said he'd come back.'

My stomach filled with nerves, and sickness swirled.

'You … reached out to my dad?' I couldn't believe it. At no point in my life had she thought to reach out to him, yet all of sudden, she had. Why?

My eyes narrowed on her bloodshot ones.

'Mum, is everything okay?' I asked. 'You've always told me we're better off without him.'

'And we are.' She gave a decisive nod. 'But we both know I'm not the best mum at the best of times, Skylar, and I wanted to help you. He is rather rich, you know?'

Ah, and there it is.

If my dad appeared and gave me money, then by proxy, Cora would come into money—or so she assumed.

'It's exciting, isn't it?' Cora laughed, raising her glass to cheer us, oblivious to the tension at the table. 'Let's drink to me, for solving all our problems!'

Twenty-One

THE REST of the day passed so fucking slowly I almost gauged my eyes out with the dessert spoon, waiting for it all to be over.

Leo seemed to be suffering as much as me.

A lingered look and a shared smile spoke volumes.

'Oh, darling, hasn't today been the most marvellous!' The powerful stench of Mum's perfume itched my nostrils. How on earth did it still smell so strong after so many hours? Cause I could guarantee it was a cheap knock-off found at the local market. 'I do love seeing you here, making friends in all the right places.'

Translation: *wealthy places.*

'Thanks, Mum,' I said, returning her hug half-heartedly. 'Get home safe.'

'I'll make sure she does,' Lottie said, her smile tight. 'It's so lovely to see you again, Skylar. Wish Clover a happy birthday tomorrow for me, please?'

I nodded. 'Of course.'

Lottie remembering Clo's birthday after everything between the two families went through showed her sweet and genuine nature.

Leo and Lottie said their goodbyes, but I didn't listen in. No, instead I watched as Cora stumbled to the top of the steps outside the main entrance. Bless her. Maybe I needed to cut her more

"

slack. She tried her best ... even if her best had never been good enough by my standards.

I watched as Lottie took Mum's arm and placed it into the crook of her elbow and guided her down to the car safely.

Leo and I remained at the top and waited for them to depart, waving as they did so.

'So ...' Leo said once the car disappeared from sight. 'Didn't learn much, did we?'

'Nope,' I said, then laughed. 'Except for the fact my dad's about to arrive and give *The Sanctum* everything they've wanted this whole time. Not to mention piss Ollie off.'

'God, Cora's a hoot. As if she's had this in her back pocket the whole time.'

I shook my head. 'I've stopped trying to understand her. I've never managed to in the past and it ends up giving me a headache.'

'That's fair, Stutter.' He turned to face me, and I couldn't place his expression, which was odd because I thought I knew all his facial movements. 'Orlando won't hear about the impending arrival from me.'

'In theory then, he shouldn't hear about it at all, because I sure as fuck ain't gonna tell him.'

I rubbed my arms to keep warm, the chill of the March air settling in. It'd make sense to go back inside, but inside meant telling Ollie—and Clo and Griff—what we'd learned and I wanted to put it off for a little longer.

'He has his ways,' Leo said. 'Hopefully nobody at the next table listened in, or one of the wait staff.'

'They all seemed pretty occupied. Didn't you see the incident between Celia and Cordelia's parents? Think most eyes and ears saw and heard the display, lucky for us.'

Leo nodded, his lips pursed, and somehow became the spitting image of his mum. I blinked.

'You know the worst part of all this?' I asked, hugging myself. 'Mum doesn't even realise she's done something wrong. Or at least something that could fuck up a lot of people's lives, including mine. Probably thinking about the potential payout she could get out of him.'

'You don't think highly of her, do you?' He sounded both bemused and a little critical.

I frowned at him. He'd spent enough time with her, and me, and us together to know the answer. Why did his tone bother me?

Leo's opinion should mean shit to me. Not like he was the walking epitome of a person walking the straight and narrow.

'I just ...' I said, reluctant to put my thoughts out into the universe. 'I can't explain it. It's like I can't overlook her faults, no matter how hard I try. She's flawed, aren't we all? But hers flash at me anytime I'm around her, or converse with her, or even think about her.'

A stone sunk to the bottom of my stomach. Acknowledging my flaws was hard.

'Surprised you don't feel strongly about my flaws,' Leo said. His lips curved into a small smile. 'Because there's a lot of them.'

'Understatement of the century.' Others were flooding the stairs and the school grounds, saying goodbye to their mums or meeting up with friends. We were no longer alone, but neither of us moved. 'I've had a lot of years to think about Cora. Give me another ten years and then maybe your issues will be as bright.'

'Sky—' he started, but I cut him off.

'If you're about to apologise again, I might hit you.'

He chuckled. 'I mean it, though.'

'I know.'

'So GLAD YOU didn't have to be there,' I said, blinking at Ollie's face, having a hard time coming to terms with the fact the two of us had fallen into a pattern of sorts without defining what *this* was.

Then my sentence repeated in my head. *Fuck.*

'I didn't mean it like that,' I blurted out. 'I wish you could be there because your mum was there.' I figuratively hit my forehead with the palm of my hand. 'I meant …'

Ollie smirked, running his fingers down my bare shoulder to my elbow. 'Sky, it's fine. I get what you mean. Don't have a conniption about it, okay?'

'Okay,' I whispered.

The TV lit up his face, whatever was playing on the screen playing out across his features in a light show, and a sense of calm covered me.

'Ollie, how the fuck am I meant to deal with my dad arriving?'

'What d'you mean?'

'That'—I shuffled up his bed, putting my arm under the pillow and pulling it towards me—'it's all a bit fucking weird. He isn't real to me. Never has been. But since learning I'm actually going to meet him? It's all a bit much.'

'I'll be there by your side the whole time.'

'But we don't even know when he's showing up!' I rubbed my eye, pressing in, wanting it to alleviate the pressure building there. 'What if you're not there?'

'Then you message me straight away and I'll come running. Sky, we're in this together.'

'Are you sure? Because I don't want you to see him if it's gonna bring everything up for you. He's not worth it.'

'You mean more to me than my hatred towards him ever could.'

'Promise?'

'Sky,' he whispered, softly touching my cheek, 'I don't think you get how much I feel for you.'

My chest hurt, both good and bad fighting one another in equal measure. Getting my hopes up, or jumping to conclusions, hadn't done me much good in the past. Best not start again now.

'I …'

He stopped me. 'You don't have to say anything.'

'I know, but I want to.' I took a deep breath. 'I guess I'm waiting for the other shoe to drop, as they say. Things are so different between us now, sure, but there's still a little nagging voice in the back of my brain who tells me you can't possibly like me for real and I'm being fooled again.'

'It's my fault the doubt's there. Fuck, I put it there.'

I couldn't deny it. Leo had added to it, but Ollie was the instigator of the original betrayal.

'And I don't know if a promise will even hold the weight it should because of all my previous bullshit, but I promise you, this isn't anything like the past.'

I nodded, tongue too tied to speak.

Ollie leaned forward to graze his lips across mine in a gentle, soothing kiss.

Our eyes locked when he leaned back to look me over.

'You mean more to me than anything, and I'm going to spend every day of my life proving it to you.'

Twenty-Two

THE FOUR OF us were on the campus grounds, taking in the warmer weather.

Orlando and *The Set* were nearby, laughing and joking and acting like twats to grab my attention, no doubt. It hurt, but I needed to ignore him. To get close to him, he needed to come to me next time. I'd done enough chasing.

He'd see through me if I acted too desperate and forgiving.

The five of them had reinforced the rules listed on *The Hive* app and had added some new ones as well. We seemed to be immune to them, but the other students weren't so lucky.

Ophelia acted like the Queen, fully in her element, alongside Orlando as her King.

Pathetic.

'Look at them over there,' Ollie said, his eyes drawn to the same spot as mine. 'How have we ended up in such a fucked up parallel universe?'

'Beats me,' Griff said. 'I don't know how everybody else here isn't in an uproar.'

I scoffed. 'Why would they be? The new rules mean they'll get beaten up or bullied for saying anything against Orlando or the girls. I'm surprised the parents haven't stepped in, but who knows what Winnie has on them all? She seems the type to keep information against everyone for blackmail purposes.'

'You've sussed our aunt out well, Clouds.' Griff's gaze moved away from the group. 'I, for one, am glad we don't have to pretend about any of the bullshit anymore.'

'You mean *The Sect*?' I asked. Griff rarely spoke about any of that kind of thing with me, so I didn't realise how much he didn't care about it all.

He nodded. 'I never did care.' He shrugged. 'I went along with Ollie and Leo because it was easier for everyone.'

Ollie narrowed his eyes at Griff, but stayed quiet. He had his thinking stance in place, and I'd learned to leave him to it when he got into that head space.

'God, you're so full of shit.' Clover said it so scornfully it nearly knocked me back. She stared at Griff as if seeing him for the first time. 'You bloody loved it. You always have loved attention and being a part of the tradition gave you what you needed and some. Don't downplay it because you've realised how pathetic you were from observing and judging Orlando.'

Griff opened his mouth. Closed it again. The wind ruffled his red hair, the colour brighter in the soft sunlight.

'Sorry?' he sputtered.

'You heard me.' Clo crossed her arms over her chest, her stance one of a woman willing to fight. *Oh, great.* She should have spoken to him back when she returned from the hospital, but nope, she'd wanted to live in denial for a little longer. Now it was all about to spill up and over in the middle of campus. Ollie and I were a part of the collateral damage by standing close to them. 'You act like you're so smooth, so casual, so cool ... We all know the real you.'

'Clo,' he said, taking a step toward her, an outstretched hand she avoided by stepping back herself. 'Let's go back to your room and we can talk about whatever this is, yeah?'

'No.' She shook her head. 'I don't want to, okay? I ...' She blew out some breath. 'If we go somewhere alone, then this won't go the way I want it to. The way it *needs* to.'

'Okay,' Griff said, his tone placating her. God, my heart broke for him, but I froze in place, unable to do anything to stop the implosion happening before my eyes.

'I'm sorry,' Clo said. 'For a lot of things, really. Griff, you mean a lot to me.' She took his hand in hers. 'But this isn't working and I think it's best if we end it here.'

'Clo, if you'll give me ... us ... the time to talk in private,' Griff said, but she cut him off.

'I can't. I'm sorry. Maybe it's best we have some time apart.'

Ollie and I stood shocked at everything unfolding in front of us, knowing not to get involved but also unable to walk away from the display. Devastation played out on Griff's face.

Griff's bottom lip wobbled. 'B-but—'

'Please don't make this harder.' Clo let his hand go and took a step back. 'I'm gonna go back to my room. I'll see you all later, okay?'

I nodded. Ollie shrugged his shoulders and Griff stared at her, shell-shocked.

Clover sent a half-smile in my direction, then left in the direction of our room. As if she hadn't dropped a bomb. As if the shockwaves of her words weren't still reverberating through our small group.

I moved from my spot beside Ollie to Griff's side, pulling him into an embrace. 'Wanna ditch Ethics?'

He nodded against my shoulder. 'Please.'

'We'll go to your room.' I looked over at Ollie. 'You coming?'

In the evening, I left Griff and Ollie and went back to my room, unsure what mood I'd find Clover in.

She hadn't come to dinner, and I hadn't seen her in the halls on her way to and from classes, so chances were she stayed up in our room all day, wallowing in her misery.

I gave a timid knock on the door before letting myself in. 'Clo, it's me.'

She sniffled, her body buried under the duvet.

'Do you want me to leave?'

Another sniffle. Some movement. A muffled, 'No.'

I took it as an invitation to stay. Doubt I'd get much more out of her until she was ready.

It sounded odd, but I needed reassurance from her that now she and Griff were over, things wouldn't change between us. That I wouldn't get put in the middle of the two of them if everything remained tense.

I got comfortable on top of my bed. Who knew how long it'd be before Clover uttered a word to me? Either way, I would be there when she did.

My mind wandered, as minds were known to do.

Everything had turned to shit at a faster pace than usual.

My anxiety spiked at a ridiculous rate, my relationships unravelling before me, an empty spool beside tangled threads, all mixed up and knotted.

Mum's words, said so casually on Mother's Day, kept coming back to me. *'Like I knew he would, he said he'd come back.'*

But when would he come back? In a few days, a week, or a month? Or worse, longer?

The unknown killed me. The fact he could arrive, disrupt my life, and make himself a target for *The Sanctum*, was enough to have me praying he wouldn't show his face—and believe me, I never prayed for shit. It seemed wrong to pray to a being I didn't believe in, but on the off chance it worked as some sort of manifestation, I couldn't pass up the opportunity.

Jacob Cooper, the ever elusive father of mine, would become a lot more real if he came to Hawthorn, and I was unprepared.

His impending arrival had the ability to make things a fuck ton worse.

There was also a slight chance things could improve.

Wouldn't mind a future-telling crystal ball right about now.

'Sky,' Clo said, her voice clearer. Her head popped out from under the duvet, while the rest of her body stayed hidden. She resembled a slug with a human head. Or a caterpillar wrapping itself into its chrysalis. Or some kind of monster from an episode of *Doctor Who*. One of the three, at least.

'Yeah?'

'Do you think I did the right thing?'

I pondered her question. 'Well, I guess it depends what you're asking. You did the right thing in ending it, but did you do the right thing by dumping him in front of me and Ollie in the middle of campus? Er, maybe not.'

She sighed. 'It was shitty, but I meant what I said. If I didn't do it right then and there, I'd have made excuses *again* and let it go on for even longer.'

'I get it. Whatever you did would have upset him.'

'I know.' She sniffled, wiping a stray tear under her right eye. 'I'm such a cow.'

'You're not,' I said. A gut reaction of sorts. You know how the expected answer comes out unbidden before you could think it through? Well, it happened to the best of us.

Because Clover acted like a cow at times. *Fuck, doesn't everybody?*

'He'll forgive me, won't he?'

'He will. This is Griff we're talking about. I reckon it'll take time, but he's the best person out of all of us.'

'Not hard that, is it?' Clover laughed. 'We've all got our faults.'

'Wouldn't be human without them.' I went over to her bed and sat down on the edge. 'Want a hug?'

'Skylar Crescent is offering me a hug?'

'Oh, shut up. You make me sound like an ice queen.'

'You're not, Sky.' Her tone was earnest. 'If Griff is the best of us, then you're a close runner-up.'

'I find that hard to believe.'

'Well, you are. You're the one who wants to give Orlando a chance to prove who he is. The rest of us would leave him to the rats if the opportunity arose.'

'His life hasn't been easy,' I said, hearing the excuse clear as day.

'Neither has yours, but don't see you killing anybody and stringing them up like a set of Christmas lights.'

The image of Mr Hawkins's body flashed in my head, the same way it had in my nightmares ever since I saw it.

I'd yet to speak to Orlando about it. I may be the one willing to get close to him and see if he had anything worth saving lurking deep down, but it didn't mean I wanted to get *too* close and get blinded by him. The way he resembled Ollie confused me a lot more than it should.

'We're not talking about me right now.' I shuffled back on the bed to rest my back against the wall, stretching my arm out for Clo to hug me if she wanted. 'I'm proud of you, by the way.'

'You are? What for?'

'For doing the hard thing.'

Twenty-Three

GRIFFIN NEEDED CHEERING UP.

The split a week ago had thrown him off a lot more than I thought possible. Yes, I expected him to get sad and morose, to be down in the dumps for a little minute, but this was worse than even that. His actions were that of a completely different person. One who didn't smile; didn't laugh or joke.

I hated every single second of it, and determined to do something about it, I got permission to take him off campus for the day to the cafe we all loved in town. A change of scenery would do him good.

'Clouds, you don't have to waste your weekend spending time with me,' Griff said when he opened the door to my smiling face. 'I'll make you miserable, and it won't do to have us both sad.'

'You could never make me sad, Griff.'

'I did last year,' he pointed out, a glimmer of his smile appearing before leaving as fast as it arrived. 'You know how sorry I am, right?'

I shoved his shoulder lightly. 'We're well past whatever it is you're referring to, so stop making excuses and come into town with me.'

'I suppose I could eat some cheesy chips.'

I nodded. 'Of course you could. Now let's go, we're wasting daylight.'

THE BOTTLE of ketchup made a noise as I squeezed it, making both me and Griff laugh like the children we were at heart.

'Thanks for this, Clouds.'

'No need to thank me. You'd do the same for me. Shit, you have done the same for me two times over already.'

He winced. 'You spoken to Leo?'

'Yeah, we've talked. He apologised a bit, and I think I'm gonna accept it pretty soon. I'll never forget what he did, or the way he toyed with me to begin with, but ... I don't know. The whole reason we "got together" in the first place was to piss off Ollie and Clover. Not like I can hold too much against him.'

'You can hold the whole knowing about Orlando's existence thing against him, though.'

'Well, yeah.' I took a bite of my chips, so I didn't have to say anything more yet. My anger at Leo had left me. As had—most—of my feelings towards him.

'I don't judge you for any of it,' Griff said, swallowing his own mouthful of chips. 'And I won't judge you for anything you do in the future, either.'

I took a swig of my water. 'The same goes for you, of course.'

'Of course.' Griff smiled across the table. 'We're Griff and Sky, and together, we're unstoppable.'

'I brought you here to cheer you up,' I said. 'Not so you'd work your magic on me and make me smile.'

'I love you, Sky.'

'I love you, Griff. Forever and always.'

'Do you think you'd rather be a bear with a human head, or a human with a bear's head?'

I thought through my answer carefully.

'If I'm a human with a bear's head, is the head proportionate to my body, or is it abnormally large?'

Griff rubbed his chin, taking it as serious as I hoped he would.

'I guess it would have to be proportionate, wouldn't it? Otherwise, your neck wouldn't be able to hold it up. You'd end up in hospital, or worse.'

'Okay, well, as long as my bear's head isn't too large, I'll choose that one,' I said, happy with my decision. 'What about you?'

'We can be a pair of bear headed humans together. Right pair we'd make at family gatherings.'

'Not like our family gatherings would have anybody but us two.'

'Oh, yeah,' Griff said. 'Suppose so. Unless your dad shows.'

'Don't remind me.' I placed my arm into the crook of Griff's elbow, ready to walk up the stairs into the main building. 'Do you reckon he'll show?'

'Jacob? Cora seemed certain he would.'

'Cora's always certain she'll win the lottery, but that's never happened either.'

'Your mum is something else.' Griff chuckled. 'She's a force, like you.'

'Are you comparing me to my mum?' I couldn't decide if his words were what mattered most or if it was offensive that he thought even a little of me was like her.

'I guess,' he said, not sensing the danger. 'I know you don't get along, and she's treated you poorly all your life, but well, it doesn't mean you aren't similar in some ways.'

'Tread carefully, Griffin Cooper.'

'Full-naming me?' He chuckled harder. 'Okay, I'll leave it out. We going in?'

'Yeah, I need to stop by the office to sign us back in.' I smiled up at the gargoyles. When did Hawthorn become more like home than my mum's place? 'You wanna watch a film together or shall I leave you alone?'

'You can come to my room. I've been saving a TV series for us to watch together. Some kind of musical thing.'

'Sounds right up my alley.' I pushed open the heavy door at

the entrance using my shoulder, putting my full weight into it. The doors may very well be beautiful and ornate, but shitting hell, they weren't easy to open.

I stumbled inside, Griff's laughter ringing through the large entrance hall. My arse landed on the floor, the thud audible to all. 'Shit.'

Griff stopped laughing. He stopped everything.

I took in his shocked expression, his jaw hanging wide open.

'D-dad?' he stuttered, blinking fast.

Dad?

Once I got myself up, I turned to face whatever had shocked Griff so much.

A man stood in the hall, tall, with light brown hair, and an expensive suit on.

I put it together rather fast. It wasn't Griff's dad standing at the entrance of Hawthorn Academy like he owned the place.

No.

It was mine.

Twenty-Four

'I CAN'T BELIEVE Jacob's here.'

'And what? He was waiting in the main building alone?' Ollie brushed a strand of hair back, which had wriggled loose from my ponytail behind my ear.

'Yeah. Griff thought he'd seen his dad at first. His face went sheet-white, and I expected him to keel over.'

'What happened next?'

'I froze, then when I realised, I bolted out of there as fast as my legs would carry me. I want to talk to him, but not until I'm ready.'

'According to Leo, he's staying over at Hawthorn House.'

'When did he tell you?' I asked, narrowing my eyes at him. 'I didn't think you and Leo were on talking terms.'

'We're not.' I waited. It didn't take long for Ollie to cave. 'He texts me from time to time.'

'Kept that quiet, haven't you?'

'I haven't kept it from you on purpose,' he said. 'More like I haven't found the right time to bring it up. Wasn't sure where you stood with him right now.'

'He's apologised,' I said.

'Have you forgiven him?'

'Don't think I'll ever forgive him, but maybe one day we can be friends again.'

No matter what went down with Leo, I missed him. Even

before things became ... difficult ... between us, we'd found a sort of friendship together—a kinship of sorts.

'How do you feel about it all?'

'We'll never go back to the ways things were,' Ollie said, 'but I don't want to ice him out my whole life.'

'He has helped us recently.'

'He has, but he also caused a lot of the problems so ...'

My fingers trailed up his arm, loving the smoothness of his bare skin underneath my fingertips.

'Enough about Leo,' Ollie said. 'Let's talk about your birthday.'

I groaned. 'Do we have to?'

'What you got against your birthday?'

I gave him the evil eye. 'Nothing. I don't wanna celebrate it.'

'But you're gonna be eighteen! We can't ignore it because a few knob heads are trying to ruin our fun.'

'Trying to ruin our fun? Ollie, they're trying to kill me.' I scoffed. Talk about an understatement.

He laughed. 'Either way, it's your birthday and we're gonna do something.'

'What you got in mind?'

'A party in the woods for everyone.'

'I'm pretty sure it's like the worst idea ever.'

'Maybe, but I miss letting loose with no worries.'

'We've never been able to.' I pointed out.

'Believe it or not, a time existed where parties at this place weren't a total disaster.'

'I find that rather hard to believe.'

'Okay, so maybe not a *total* disaster and a mere *minor* disaster instead.'

We cracked up, laughing at what we both knew to be true. No party at Hawthorn went well.

'Fine, but if the party goes tits up, then don't come complaining to me, you hear?'

Ollie laughed and kissed my cheek. 'I hear.'

I still hadn't told him about the kiss Orlando planted on me. It meant nothing to me. A blip in time, where I acted poorly, but not one I wanted to repeat.

Things were weird between Ollie and me. We weren't a couple, as far as I knew, but we spent every waking moment together. Either we slept in my room or his, and we ate all meals together. Recently he'd been more free with his physical touch and affection too, giving gentle touches and placing soft kisses on my cheek or my forehead or hand.

If he was showing me he could be a gentleman, it was working.

'While on the topic of your birthday, I've got something I want to ask you.'

'Go for it,' I said. God, I could fall into his bright blue eyes and swim around for days and never get bored.

'Sky, would you like to come away with me this weekend?'

Come away? I blinked at him, repeating his words in my head to decipher them. 'Away? Like to a hotel or s-something?'

'Yeah.' He gulped, his nerves on show for me to see. 'In London.'

I wanted to, but the memory from the last time we stayed in a hotel together still smarted. Back then, he was using my heart as a tennis ball while denying his own in the process.

Maybe he wanted a re-do.

Maybe I also wanted a re-do.

'Okay,' I whispered. 'I'd like that.'

'Yeah?' The relief on his face made me smile. Seeing Ollie unsettled would never get old. It reminded me of his humanity.

'Yeah. Thank you.'

WE RARELY ATE dinner together in the dining room these days. With Griff and Clo having entered a stalemate of sorts, when we were all in the same place, things were still a little awkward.

'Are you sure you're up to it?' I asked Clo in our room before we went down to meet the boys for dinner. 'We don't have to if you don't wanna.'

'I want me and Griff to remain friends and splitting the group up isn't the answer to making it happen.'

'No, I agree.' But how to put it delicately? 'The split might have hurt Griff more than you, though.'

Not sure if my sentence held the tact I aimed for.

'Has he said something to you about it?' Clover frowned, fiddling with the hem of her skirt. 'Should I stay up here and you go alone?'

'Don't be silly! I didn't mean that.' I shook my head, tongue-tied. In my head, what I wanted to get across made sense, but the words weren't coming out right. 'Ignore me.'

'If it gets awkward at any point, I'll come back up here and you can sneak me up a plate of chips. How's that sound?'

'It's a deal.' I smiled. 'Now come on. I'm starving!'

We went down to the hall without talking, both of us lost in our own heads.

Ollie waited outside the dining room, Griff at his side, shuffling his feet, his eyes locked on the ground. Griff always acted so confidently. I never knew how to approach him when he acted so differently than usual.

'Hey guys,' I said on arrival. 'What's going on?'

'Not much. Been waiting for you,' Ollie said. He placed a kiss on my cheek and I smiled. Recently, he'd become a lot more touchy-feely, taking pleasure in touching me freely or placing kisses on my cheek or head. When we slept beside one another each night, other than spooning me or grazing his fingertips along my arm, he kept to himself. A perfect gentleman.

A large part of me wanted him to shake off the persona of being a gentleman and act on the inevitable.

Because at this point, I could accept we were inevitable.

Both my heart and my head told me we were, which was good enough for me. I hoped Ollie felt the same way, but time would tell. He'd spent his whole life covering up his true feelings, and it was a mechanism of sorts he hid behind when necessary.

'Shall we get in there?' Clover asked, rubbing her stomach. 'I'm starved.'

I narrowed my eyes her way. 'Starved?' I laughed. 'You baked a dozen brownies today.'

'Your point?' She tapped her foot on the ground and crossed her arms across her chest, which made me laugh harder.

'And you ate half!' I said.

'I did.' A decisive nod of her head drove her point home. 'But it doesn't mean I'm not hungry now. Girl's gotta eat to survive, Skylar.'

'Then let's go eat and shut you up.' I headed into the hall, the three of them following in step behind me, and a gasp rang out through the room. I turned my head to look back at the others and whispered out of the side of my mouth, 'Is it me, or is everyone staring our way?'

'They're looking at us alright,' Griff whispered back, his eyes locked ahead to where *The Set* were sitting with Orlando. 'Wonder what dick features said to them all?'

'What makes you think it's him?' I asked, ignoring the stares as I took a seat at our regular circular table.

'The smug, smirking smile on his face, for starters,' Griff said, sitting in the seat next to me. 'He's basically the cat who got everything he ever wanted.'

Clover sat down next to Ollie, who had already taken his spot next to me, and the four of us continued small talk, all while pretending we were oblivious to the tension in the air. If we ignored it, maybe it'd go away.

Yeah right.

Things never went away at Hawthorn. They stayed in the background, or under the surface, biding their time until you least expected it.

What was worse? Waiting for something bad to happen, or having it happen straight away? Either way, you remained on edge.

The waiter came to our table and took our order, disappearing as silent as he arrived.

Griff, who hadn't stopped fidgeting in his seat since we sat, leaned in to whisper in my ear. 'Orlando's standing up. Think he's heading over here.'

'Wonderful,' I mumbled. 'Just what we need.'

My eyes found Orlando as he moved through the room, stepping out of waiters' way and avoiding collisions with any students leaving towards us.

Ollie's hand gripped my knee under the table, either to send support to me or to keep himself in check. I welcomed his touch, no matter the reason.

'Well, well, well.' Orlando's voice trickled through me like honey. *Smooth bastard.* It bloody irked me the way he sent my emotions on such a rollercoaster. 'If it isn't the person I've been waiting to see.'

He meant me, right?

'Oliver.' Orlando turned to him. 'You've been avoiding me.'

Okay ... maybe he didn't mean me. My heart stuttered at the insult, the wrongness of that not lost on me, but stutter away it did.

Ollie, rather unimpressed his brother had come over in the first place, let alone had the audacity to talk to him, didn't respond.

'Okay, I can play your game. Little One, you okay?'

I rolled my eyes at his obvious attempt to piss off Ollie. Sadly, it worked.

'Don't you dare talk to her,' Ollie growled and sat up straighter in his chair. 'You've got my attention. Now, what do you want?'

'Oh, nothing in particular.' Orlando's smirk grew. 'Did Skylar tell you about our talk?'

'What talk?' Ollie voiced the same question I had, because as far as I could remember, we hadn't spoken alone in a while. Not since before Mother's Day ...

Shit.

He meant the kiss.

I squirmed in my chair, hoping nobody could see my face as

the realisation hit of what Orlando intended to do. If I was being honest with myself, I had myself to blame. Telling Ollie should've been at the top of my priority list, even if it meant nothing and we weren't technically a couple.

Orlando rubbed his chin, pretending he had to think about it, when the bastard already knew *exactly* the talk he referred to. 'Must've been a while back, come to think of it. In the library.'

Ollie and Griff both swung their heads in my direction, while Clo's gaze narrowed on my face from opposite me.

'It can't have been important, because Sky's never mentioned anything about it,' Ollie said. Oh, how I admired his confidence.

Griff and Clo glanced at each other and shared a tentative smile. If this was the thing to make them comfortable being together again, then fuck, I had to run with it and allow it to play out in whatever way Orlando wanted. He'd orchestrated us all into this scenario, after all.

'Or maybe it was *too* important, and that's why she never mentioned a thing about it to you.' Orlando took the empty seat between Clo and Griff, and banged his palms down on the table. 'Assuming she never told you about our kiss, either.'

Orlando took the pin out of the grenade he held and threw it down.

The resulting explosion went the way you'd expect it to.

Ollie removed his hand from my leg, his chair screeching as he pushed it away from the table—from me—and stood up. 'What did you say?'

'I thought you and Sky were closer now.' Orlando shook his head. 'Sorry if I dropped a bomb.'

Nobody believed his insincere words.

Ollie turned to face me, not giving his brother the satisfaction. 'Is this true?'

'He kissed me, yeah.' No point in denying it. 'And it's slipped my mind ever since because it meant *nothing*.'

'Oh, don't be like that, Little One. No need to hide from me.'

'I'm not.' I shrugged. 'I'm being honest.'

'You're lying because Ollie's staring at you!' Orlando stood from his chair. My laugh came out awkward and barking, but I couldn't help it. The two of them were twins when angry—which, yeah, duh—and even their actions were mirrored. Both of them were rubbing their jaws and staring daggers at me. Kinda nice to have something unite them—even if it was through their displeasure at me.

'I think you should leave, Orlando,' Clover said, finding her voice in the chaos. 'I'm sure Skylar will seek you out if she wishes.'

Orlando hadn't taken his eyes from me. The black of his pupil overtook his eye. Evil through and through.

'You'll pay for this, Little One.'

Twenty-Five

RETURNING to the hotel in London with Ollie had apprehension running through me.

A crime scene from Skylar past. It held a lot of memories—tainted ones from a time where Ollie lied to me as often as he breathed. Glad to know he'd worked on that.

'I thought I'd leave the evening up to you,' he said once we made it up to the room. From the moment we entered, my body gravitated towards the ceiling to floor window. Viewing the city in this way always filled me with such warmth. 'Didn't want you to think I didn't care about you.'

'Thanks,' I mumbled. The only word I could think of to describe my emotional state: overwhelmed. I always found it odd whenever Ollie tried to show me how much he'd changed. Like if I believed him, he'd pull the rug out from under me, and everything would twist and once more I'd be the punchline of a joke. 'Do we have to go out?'

'Not if you don't want to.' He stood in the centre of the room, surveying everything around him. 'We could spend the night watching the sun go down over the skyline if you like?'

I smiled. He knew how much I loved this view of London.

'The view from here is beautiful,' I said.

'My view's always beautiful when I'm looking at you.'

'Smooth.' I laughed to hide my uneasiness.

His eyes locked with mine, but he stayed still. 'I mean it.'

I waved him away, afraid to fall too heavy for his suave words, but knowing in my heart I'd fallen already. Something about him sang to my heart. A chemistry existed between us that I couldn't deny.

'Sky,' Ollie said, taking a step towards where I stood frozen by the window. Whenever he moved, I sensed it deep in my bones. 'I wanted to take this time to talk to you, and I planned to wait until dinner, but honestly, I think I'll explode if I don't come out with it now.'

'Okay ...'

What did he want to talk about? Did he want to end things between us even though technically there wasn't even an "us" to end? *No, don't be so fucking silly, Skylar.* Why would he have bothered to arrange a weekend stay away? He wouldn't have. Not if he planned to tell me he wanted nothing to do with me anymore.

After Orlando had crashed dinner to reveal our kiss, I thought things would get even more tense between us, but nothing changed. Ollie asked for my version of events once we were back in his room, and after I'd told him, he was more than happy to forget it ever happened.

"My brother orchestrated it so he had something to hold over you, babe, and unlucky for him, it didn't work."

We hadn't spoken of it since, but now, in an empty hotel room watching Ollie pace in front of me, my mind couldn't help but jump to conclusions. All of them horrible.

' ... forward.' Ollie stopped talking, his right eyebrow raised in question. 'Everything alright?'

'Yeah, yeah. Sorry about that. Got lost in my head for a second there. What were you saying?'

His entire body moved from the force of the breath he exhaled. 'I've forgotten what I said.' He laughed, rubbing his jaw. 'Okay, let's try this again.' He took a step closer. 'Skylar, I know a lot of shit's happened and I'm at fault for most of it, but I feel like we're in a better place again. After everything I did, I don't deserve your forgiveness, but I'm so glad you gave it, and now I've got it, I never want to do anything to make it go.'

I tried to process his sentences to make sense of where his mental path headed, but I also didn't want to get my hopes up in case he threw me a curve ball.

'Skylar, it would make the happiest person alive if I could once again call you my girlfriend.'

'G-girlfriend?' I stuttered, my nerves on show, but not at the idea of being his girlfriend. It hadn't occurred to me how much I wanted to be a couple again until he said the words. No, my nerves were for something else entirely. My worry stemmed from the thought of Orlando's reaction. He wanted to steal Ollie's life, and if I became his girlfriend, would he become even more determined to make me his?

'Sky?' Ollie said after I remained silent for a fraction too long. 'There's no pressure here, I promise. I'm sorry. I shouldn't have assumed because you agreed to come stay away—'

I found his rambling pretty fucking adorable, and it made me smile, all teeth and gums, so I cut him off. 'Stop talking for a second.' My laugh softened the harshness of the words. 'I'd love to be your girlfriend.'

'You would?' The shock on his face made me laugh harder. Gosh, he was so dang cute.

'Of course I would!' I closed the distance between us and wrapped my arms around his shoulder, clasping my hands together at the nape of his neck. 'Lately we've acted like a couple, but without the label.'

'True. So you're good with this?'

'Ollie, I'm *more* than good with this.'

Our lips gravitated together, the magnet strong at work once more, and what started as a gentle kiss became something a little less so.

We kissed for hours, and every moment, I fell further.

'Baby, come to bed.'

My voice carried across the room.

Ollie sat in the armchair, his black jogging bottoms sitting low on his waist, staring out of the hotel window made of floor to ceiling glass.

Ollie had carried his issues and worries to London, and it killed me to see him so out of sorts.

'In a moment,' he said. 'Go to sleep, Skylar.'

I got out of bed and wrapped a sheet around myself to keep my dignity. We were on a high enough floor and nobody could see in, but I still didn't want to walk around in the nude. I went and joined him, draping myself and the sheet over him. He opened his arms, and I straddled him, as I wrapped my arms around his neck and linked them so he couldn't move me.

'Come sleep with me,' I whispered in his ear. 'We have to go back to school tomorrow, and I want to make the most of our time away from the Hawthorn bullshit.'

'I don't want to make you feel shitty,' he mumbled, gripping me tighter. 'And I'm too in my head.'

'You know you can talk to me.'

'I don't know if I can,' he said, sounding vulnerable. 'It's so hard to form the words. My mind is clouded, Sky. I'm so fucked up about all of this.'

'I know, baby.' I kissed his cheek and moved one of my hands to ruffle his hair. These intimate moments, when the world was silent, were some of the best. It helped me forget we were two teenagers trying to survive adult bullshit we hadn't asked for. 'Are you thinking about Millie again?'

He nodded slightly.

I struggled to connect with him about it all in a meaningful way, and not just a way that came across false. I didn't have a great relationship with mine, and even though she hadn't been too bad during the Mother's Day festivities, Cora and I still had a long way to go until we were in a good place. The actual test in my eyes would be my birthday. If she texted me, I'd maybe be able to forgive her a little.

Ollie didn't have the option.

He had secrets, lies, and pain. Not to mention a secret twin.

In my quiet moments, when I watched him struggle, I disliked Millie more and more. Maybe it was shitty of me to feel so strongly about a woman I would never meet, but I couldn't help it. My heart connected with Ollie's in a way I couldn't describe, and knowing the pain she caused him meant she'd pained me, too.

'What's going through your tortured mind?' I asked, trying to get him to open up. Wanting to climb inside of his head and swim around in his brain matter.

Bit fucking dark, Skylar.

'Why would she give him up?' The tone of his voice made my heart melt and caused tears to well in my eyes, glad I'd buried my head in his chest so he couldn't see them.

Ollie was proud, and not the kind of person to confront his issues head on.

He also sounded sad about Orlando for the first time. I often wondered if he wished he could get to know his brother, but his pride and anger were both getting in the way.

'Why would she abandon me?'

It took me a moment to follow his change of subject. 'I wish I could answer, O.' His inner child lurked in his eyes, sad and hopeful at the same time. 'But your mum's illness ruled her.'

'That's no excuse!' he spat. 'She could have tried harder. Tried to get better, for me.' His voice cracked, and I kissed his cheek again, hoping my love for him would show in the action.

'Maybe.' I sighed. The moonlight and city lights left him half in the shadows. 'We can't rewrite the past.'

'I know,' Ollie said, his eyes haunted. 'But it doesn't mean I can't be angry about her choices, because I am Sky. I'm pissed. I've always looked up to Mum and wished she was still around. I always thought of her as everything good and pure in this world; somebody who got hurt by life and circumstance.'

I continued to run my fingers through his hair to soothe him. I stayed silent, knowing he didn't need my words right now.

'They killed her sister,' he whispered. 'Whoever they are. They did this to her. If Eliza hadn't died, Mum may have made a different decision. Things wouldn't be the way they are.'

'And I wouldn't be here,' I murmured, an involuntary slip of the tongue. If the past didn't unfold the way it had, then the present wouldn't be how it is, and I firmly believed that. Everything happened the way it did, for good or bad.

I placed my cheek up against his chest. The thrumming of his heart kept me grounded, stopping me from focusing on the slither of anger inside.

'Right,' he said. 'But I'd still have my mum.'

The hurt at his sentence pierced my heart, like a harpoon making a clear wound, entering and exiting in one swift motion.

I wanted to move off him, go back to bed and curl up in the foetal position and breathe.

'Right,' I agreed through gritted teeth.

'I'm a dick,' he said after a beat. I nodded against his chest, not wanting to raise my head and make eye contact. He sounded so defeated. So knocked down by life and I couldn't help. Couldn't reach him.

And the idea scared me.

'Maybe it would've been better if she'd given me up,' he said, resigned.

I moved so fast it surprised me I didn't give myself whiplash. Listening to him talk crap about himself made me mad, and I wouldn't listen in silence anymore.

'Don't say that.' I gripped his chin in between my thumb and forefinger, locking him in place so we were staring into one another's eyes. My baby blues met his equally blue ones.

God, imagine the blue eyes of our children.

Wait. Woah. Where the fuck had that thought come from?

I shook it off and focused back on the beautiful, broken boy.

'You do not get to think of yourself that way.' My tone brooked no argument. If he wanted to talk shit about himself, he wouldn't get to do it without repercussions from me. 'Only I get to think shit about you, you understand me?'

He chuckled darkly, but I saw his eyes lighten a little.

'You must have thought a lot of shit in the last eighteen months.' He gave a small smile.

'Oh, you bet your arse I have,' I agreed. No way would I beat around the bush. I respected him more than that. 'But, I've also thought a lot of good thoughts, too. Mainly ones about your chest, your face … your dick.'

His whole body shook with his laughter, and I smiled. I'd shocked him.

'You like my dick, Miss Crescent?' he asked, one eyebrow raised. His grin turned devilish, full of dark thoughts and some not so dark thoughts.

'I do, Mr Brandon,' I said, 'but I'd like you without it.'

'Is that a promise?' He moved me so I straddled him, my knees on either side of his thighs. His hardness underneath me pressed against the spot I wanted it most.

'Hmm,' I mused. 'Now I'm not so sure.'

Ollie squeezed my ribs, and I let out a little laugh. I wasn't ticklish per se, but I also got a little squeamish when somebody tried. Bastard knew it, too.

His dick twitched underneath me, and I smiled.

'Let's go to bed,' I whispered in his ear.

'Or,' he whispered back, 'we could stay right here.'

'Oh, yeah?'

'Yep,' he said, squeezing my waist now tighter than before. 'We're in the perfect spot in front of the city. Live a little.'

'If you insist.'

Twenty-Six

MY EIGHTEENTH BIRTHDAY, one I was lucky enough to be alive to see, arrived and celebrating it fell very far down on the priority list.

Not now Jacob Cooper had shown his face.

When Griff and I had found him in the school hall, waiting for us to get back, something overtook me and I legged it out of there as fast as my legs would carry me.

Hadn't seen or spoken to the man since.

Griff told me Winifred had invited him to stay at Hawthorn House as her guest, and as much as I felt sorry for the man's predicament, I didn't plan to storm over there and demand answers from him without thinking it through.

No. He could sit and stew for a bit longer.

I'd go to him when ready and not a moment before.

' ... this top?'

I blinked over at Clo, standing in front of the wardrobe, hands on her hips, an expectant expression searing through me.

'Sorry?'

'Have you listened to a word I've said?' Clo's tone told me she was getting bored with me tuning her out and living in my head.

'Clo,' I said, ignoring her question. 'Do you think a party tonight is a good idea?'

Griff and Ollie had arranged a party, and it had to be the worst idea they'd had in a long time. Yet because they were doing it for me, I couldn't get mad.

The other students at school would benefit more than me, but in a way, it meant I was doing my bit by giving everyone something fun to make them forget people were being assaulted and/or murdered.

Even five months later, it sounded ridiculous to me.

Orlando still being a student here was laughable.

'What do you mean?' she asked.

'I mean what I said. Do you think a party in the woods tonight is a good idea?'

'When are they ever a good idea?' Clo laughed, pulling a top off its hanger and putting it on. 'I can't say this one is more ill-advised than any of the others.'

'Now, see, usually I'd agree with you, but this time I'm not so sure. My dad's here, which means *The Sanctum* is gonna make a move on him soon, right?'

Clo shrugged. 'One more night before you talk to him won't make much difference.'

'I suppose.' I couldn't explain why, but my stomach told me I didn't like any of this. 'I've got a bad feeling, tis all.'

'You've always got a bad feeling,' Clo said, but not unkindly. More a statement of fact than a mean observation.

'It's been warranted in the past.'

'Except for the times it would've saved you from nearly dying.'

Okay, the girl has a point there.

'Whatever,' I said. 'Maybe I should forget my worries for the night.'

'Sensible of you.' Clo nudged her head to the two plastic cups filled to the brim with vodka and coke. 'Now drink up, otherwise you'll worry more.'

'Oh, ha, ha.'

'Sky, come on. Let's forget everything for the night and enjoy ourselves. We don't have long left here together.'

'We've got three months,' I deadpanned.

'Which is nothing in the grand scheme of life.' She pointed at me. 'Get dressed. Now.'

Hiding from the party became more and more appealing with each passing second.

I understood why Ollie and Griff had wanted to make this happen, had wanted to make me forget all the other birthdays in life my mum or others had forgotten or ignored on purpose, but I'd have much preferred to stay in with the people who mattered most to me.

'You okay, baby?' Ollie asked, handing me a glass of violet gin and lemonade that glowed under the twinkle lights placed on the trees.

'I'm good.' I took a large gulp of the liquid.

'Are you sure?' he asked, pulling me closer to him and turning me around to place my back up against his front, his muscled arms gripping me in place.

'Yeah, just thinking.' I pushed myself further back into his arms, the safety of them filling me with an emotion I wanted to bottle up and take out on rainy days.

Ollie kissed the top of my head, and I squirmed a little—in a good way.

We may not be a couple again, but standing under these trees, the connection between us thrummed loud. A genuine connection. One that thrummed underneath every interaction, every bad time and every good time.

'Sky, I want to make you happy no matter what. You know that, right?' he asked, his gaze seared into mine.

'Sometimes,' I whispered. 'But sometimes I have no clue.'

'Well, I need to do a better job then, don't I?' he whispered back. The moment was intimate, and like all intimate moments between me and Ollie, it came to an abrupt end.

A hard body jostled into me, knocking me to the side as they went by, not stopping to glance back at who they'd accosted.

'Fuck,' I said, my dress now covered in the sickly sweet smell of violet. 'Wanker!'

I stepped out of Ollie's embrace and brushed off the liquid, but as per usual, my actions did nothing to aid the mess.

'Who was it?' he asked, his tone low.

'Nobody important,' I said. I grabbed his arm to stop him from heading off like a bull in a china shop and pulled him back to face me.

'Are you hurt?'

'Nope, just wet,' I said, then laughed. Wet, but not the birthday wet I wanted to be, that was for damn sure.

How much alcohol have I had?

The thought of having sex with Ollie occupied my thoughts often, especially after the events of last weekend.

Instead of spending the evening with wankstains I disliked, Ollie and I could have been enjoying our own private celebration —alone.

And I know we did last weekend at the hotel, but I'd happily do it all over again.

'Why are we around people again?' I asked.

'Huh?' he growled, distracted, still fixated on whether they hurt me.

'Why aren't we celebrating alone?' I waggled my eyebrows.

'We can do *that* anytime.'

So, yeah, true, we could have sex whenever we wanted now we were an official couple, for real this time, and spent every night together, but I also hated the way he said it. The implication of it.

Like I was a sure thing. *Easy.*

I peeled myself out of his grip.

'Skylar!' Griff hollered from somewhere nearby and I turned around, searching all over to see if I could find his shock of red hair hiding amongst the other people.

'Yeah?' I called back, unable to see him. I moved away from Ollie and searched the surrounding crowd.

'Clouds!' Griff called again.

'Oof!' I said as air left my lungs in a rush, our bodies colliding. He barrelled into the side of me, causing the two of us to fall flat on the floor. 'What did you do that for?' I snapped.

Griff laughed, a cheeky chuckle in my ear, getting a kick out of this. It was nice to hear him giggle, so I couldn't be too mad.

'Ah, come off it, Clouds. It didn't hurt.' He moved back off of me and assessed me from head to toe.

'How d'you know?' I asked, raising my eyebrow. I mean, I wasn't hurt, but not like he could tell from briefly glimpsing at me.

'Can just tell.' He shrugged. 'I know you, Clouds. I've seen you hurt more than enough times now.'

His last words were darker, his tone hushed, and a tug came on my heart strings for him. I never stopped to consider how my constant beatings were affecting him. Griff always came across so happy-go-lucky I assumed those instances had run off of him like water down a duck's back.

'Griff,' I whispered, reaching out to grasp his hands in mine. 'I'm sorry.'

'What are you sorry for?' he asked, squeezing my hands. 'Sky, you have nothing to apologise for. You can't help that people wanna hurt you.'

'I feel bad. Like everything these past eighteen months or whatever is my fault.'

'That's bullshit, and you know it. There was no way you could've known coming here would go the way it did. I mean, fuck, Clouds, you didn't know about your father before you came here. How could you know they'd rigged the scholarship all along?'

'I-I—' I stuttered, unsure of what to say.

'Sky, none of this is your fault, so don't you ever apologise to me again unless it's for some shit you did do like eating the last slice of pizza without asking the room if they wanted it,' he said, the accusatory look on his face making me smile.

'That was one time! *And*,' I stressed, 'I thought the pizza was mine. So why would I have needed to ask?'

'Yeah, yeah. Tell it to the judge,' he said, beating his fist into his chest.

My hand made contact with his shoulder, and I pushed him further onto the dirty ground. 'You kill me, kid.'

I moved and pushed myself up from the floor, so I sat upright once again. Griff reached out his hand so I could pull him up. I had to use all my strength. Fuck, the boy had muscles.

'Are you enjoying yourself?' he asked.

I took in the hoards of students milling around us, dotted around the clearing.

'I ...' My eyes met his.. 'Honestly, Griff, I don't know.'

'Me and Ollie meant well.'

'I know,' I said and hauled myself back to standing. I put my hand out for him to grasp, then pulled him up, too. Griff smiled at me.

'I love you, Sky.' His eyes met mine, the green and blue ocean hue of them glowing in the dark of the woods.

'I love you, too.'

***

'LITTLE ONE,' a growl in my ear stopped me in my movement.

I'd headed away from the party, wanting to get away. The loud music hurt my head, and I wanted to think without being the centre of attention.

Before coming to Hawthorn, barely anybody knew my name, let alone looked at me and cared about what I did or who I spent time with.

'Orlando,' I said, knowing it was him without having to turn. Who else would call me Little One?

'What's the birthday girl doing out here all alone?' he drawled, and a chill filled me.

'Nothing much,' I replied casually. 'I wanted to be alone for a moment.'

'Hope you don't mind me gatecrashing?' he asked. The question was a loaded one filled with double meaning. Not only had he gatecrashed the party, but also my moment of solitude. I knew Ollie and Griff had specifically not invited him, even though they announced said party to the entire dining room, so couldn't dictate shit.

Neither of them wanted him anywhere near me—especially not out in the woods in the dark of night.

'I don't, but I'm sure your brother will have something to say about it when he sees us.'

'He always seems to have something to say when it comes to you, Little One. Don't you see you're trapped?'

'T-trapped?'

Orlando walked towards me. With each step, my heart rate climbed, getting faster and faster to where I thought it would leap out of my chest.

'You know. The way Oliver doesn't allow you out of his sight? Doesn't allow others to spend time with you without him knowing who you're with and where you are? Sounds pretty stifling to me.' His lips grazed up against my ear.

'It's n-not.' I stuttered. Why did Orlando make me revert to my shy, stuttering self? 'Me and Ollie are happy together.'

'Of course you are,' he mocked, putting his hands up in a placating gesture. I'd spent enough time with him, both in disguise and not, to know he was laughing at something on the inside.

'We are.' I grit out, more forcefully than before.

'No need to lie to me,' he said, his tongue snaking out of his mouth to touch my neck in the softest of grazes, but hard enough to make me shiver. My nipples peaked under my dress, and this time, I couldn't blame the weather.

It didn't help that he looked like a carbon copy of my boyfriend—looked like the spitting image of the boy I loved.

Sounded like him, too.

'I'm not lying.' I needed to head back. At least within the party's safety, people would be witness to whatever came next.

Orlando reached out for me.

'I am, am I?' he growled, grabbing my wrist to hold me in place.

'Please Orlando,' I whispered. 'Let me go.'

Twenty-Seven

'I CAN'T DO THIS,' Sky whispered, her gaze pleading.

Her beautiful blue eyes were wide and red-rimmed, tears glistening in the corners, threatening to break free and run down her face.

A face that made me feel more than any single thing ever had before.

'Can't do what?' The words came out clipped. Angry. Did she mean she couldn't talk to me? Couldn't be near me?

My thoughts raced ahead, and the anger crept further in. My vision turned red at the edges; a slow fog, a haze clouding my vision. My judgement. *Everything.*

I pushed her, my hand still gripped around her wrist, until we came to a tree and I used my force to press her up against it.

Her pulse rapid under my thumb, her heartbeat increasing.

It all gave me a sick thrill. A bolt of lightning through my body, sending every nerve ending into overdrive.

I wanted to *destroy her.*

Wanted to plunge my dick so far inside of her she'd split clean in two.

Wanted her to gag and cry and scream in despair.

What would she look like if I ruined her? Cut her pretty cheeks and slashed her throat? Watched as the blood spurted, then trickled down her pale neck.

'Orlando,' she said in a croak, drawing me out of the depraved images in my head. Her tears were flowing fast, and I wanted to lick away each one.

'What?'

'You're hurting me.'

Those words should have had me backing off, stepping away, but instead, I moved closer. Our bodies were as close as they could be without me climbing inside of her chest cavity. Would it be warm there, nestled between her rib cage and her heart?

'Stay still!' Spit flew from my mouth and landed on her face. She winced, and I could see myself in her eyes—could see her reaction to me. And I wanted to stop, but I didn't know how.

I'd never had to stop the beast before. Had never wanted to, even.

Without my brain and heart aligned, I needed to take a step back. Take a breath. Truly think before I fucked things up with her more. Everybody believed I didn't care about my little one. They thought I wanted Ollie's life—which, yes—and therefore wanted Skylar because he had her. Because she belonged to *him*.

It may have started that way, but time changed everything.

I removed my hand from her wrist and brought it up to cup her chin. My lips placed a soft kiss on her cheek.

My other hand, seemingly with a mind of its own, trailed down her body. Breached the top of her trousers. My fingertips played with the lace band at the top of her underwear.

Fuck.

I had to get out of here.

Before I touched her. Before I let the voices in my head corrupt her—and me.

'Little One,' I whispered.

Her tear-stained, mascara-streaked face glanced up at me. Her eyes pained. This hurt her. *I* hurt her.

'Orlando.'

'I'm sorry,' I whispered, my tone harsh, before pulling myself away from her.

I turned and fled.

Running out of the trees and away to another clearing. A place where I could get away from her. Get away from the urges I had. Get away from the monster within.

———

THE EMPTY CLEARING I found myself in was far away from the party.

So far away, in fact, I could no longer hear the thumping bass of the music. I could no longer hear anything once I stopped and took it all in.

Until ...

'Orlando!' Ophelia called, her voice getting louder as she got closer. 'Baby!'

It came out as a whine, her nasal voice sending goosebumps up my arms. I stayed facing away from the direction I could hear her stumbling, hoping she'd get the hint when I didn't answer or turn to face her.

Ophelia spent the whole of last year not being able to tell me apart from my brother, yet nowadays, she knew within a second.

Explain that one.

'There you are!' Her voice was at my back now. Close enough for her to reach out and touch.

'What do you want?' I asked after a couple of minutes. My silence not giving her the hint I hoped it would.

No, instead of leaving, the stupid bitch came closer.

'I've been trying to find you for the last hour,' she said, her words slow and drawn out as if she were talking to a toddler. She'd been drinking all night, and the vodka had finally gone to her head and made itself at home. 'Somebody said they saw you slink off with Skylar the slut.'

The entire sentence ran into one another, her words slurring together, and I laughed at her, all sinister and devoid of actual joy. Not that Ophelia could tell.

'Skylar isn't a slut,' I growled. 'Don't let me hear you say shit about her again.'

Ophelia came into view, her crop top barely covering the girls.

'Oh, shhhhh.' Her pointer finger covered my lips. 'I don't want to talk about her.'

I grabbed her finger, bent it back, and moved it away from me. Her face twisted in discomfort, but she didn't make any noise.

'Why? Because she's more of a woman than you'll ever be?' I asked, wanting to antagonise her. Wanting to piss her off and bring out her claws. I needed a fight, and she'd walked straight into my cage.

My headspace remained fucked, and I was out for blood. Any blood.

'Skylar Crescent is a nobody and doesn't deserve your attention. Let your loser brother have her.'

'You didn't call my brother a loser last summer when you were hanging off him.' My words poked at her. I may not have been there to watch it unfold firsthand, but Leo told me enough about how Ollie acted last summer.

'Well, I've seen the light,' she tittered, 'and I want the sunshine state.'

God, this girl.

'That's Florida itself.'

'Same thing,' she said, brushing my bicep up and down. I rolled my eyes at her flirtatious tactics—ones I wouldn't allow to work on me.

'Either way,' I told her, 'I don't want you.'

'Because of her,' she spat. 'She doesn't want you.'

'I thought you didn't want to talk about her?' I asked, needling her further.

Come on, Ophelia.

Give me what I want.

'All anybody at this fucking school has done since *she* started here is talk about her! She's been the focus of every single fucking person, and I'm sick of it! Sick of her! Things would be a lot easier if she died when you stabbed her. But even that you fucked up.'

The end of her sentence blurred together in my mind, and I fixated on the fact Ophelia believed the world might be better off without Skylar in it.

A lot easier if she died.

I saw red.

My rage hit me in a flash. Every vile thought, every slur she'd said about Skylar, hit me full force until I couldn't hear anything else. Like a loop, her words played over and over. She was still talking, her mouth moving a mile a minute, but I could no longer understand any of the words she spoke.

An animal made a sound in the distance, scuttering through the brush, which caused her to stop talking for a moment. I watched, as if in slow motion, Ophelia turned in the noise's direction, searching for the animal who made it.

I took advantage of her distraction.

Picked up a large branch and swung.

The branch connected with her skull, and a crunch reverberated throughout the area. Ophelia made no sound; the blow knocked her out cold.

Her body slumped down to the ground, thudding as she landed. A sick thrill filled me. A jolt of pleasure that brought a wide smile to my face. I dropped the stick and came to my senses.

I needed to leave. Go to bed and forget this terrible night had even happened.

As I walked away, I glanced back to Ophelia, laying in the centre of the clearing, all peaceful.

Stupid fucking cunt.

She deserved to suffer the way Odette had. The way Olivia had.

Maybe Oralie needed to watch out, being the last one left and all ...

Twenty-Eight

WHAT THE FUCK JUST HAPPENED?

My thoughts swirled around in my head. Twisted and entwined with others until they were no longer decipherable; until I couldn't tell them apart anymore. Couldn't separate the truth from my nightmares and fears.

I stayed rooted to the spot in the clearing, unsure of what I should do, where I should go.

If he hadn't got a grip on himself, would he have gone further? Would he have given in to whatever dark and depraved thoughts swirled in his head?

I'd always let Orlando off—more than I should—but I couldn't deny his actions this time. No writing them off and pretending they weren't heinous.

He assaulted me.

Or at least attempted to. *No*, scratch that, because calling it an *attempt* made it sound as if he were unsuccessful. As if it could only be called assault if some form of penetration or pain took place, which is utter and total bullshit. Anything unwanted, anything that crossed boundaries or went against your consent, equalled assault, plain and simple.

I adjusted my clothing, putting myself to rights again. At least in appearance.

Breathe, Skylar.

Orlando was nowhere to be seen. He'd departed like a man

possessed. Maybe he was, which would explain why he'd acted so out of character. But then again, it wasn't out of character, was it? The boy had an anger problem, one I'd seen the brunt of on more than one occasion.

The fucker stabbed you, Skylar, and you're still making excuses for him!

All I could do was stay put and wait for somebody to find me, because somebody *would* find me. Clo, or Griff, or Ollie, or fuck, even Leo, would search for me. I'd been gone long enough. Surely at least one of them would notice.

What the fuck was I going to tell Ollie?

I couldn't keep this from him—didn't want to keep this from him. After everything the two of us had been through these last months, I didn't want to have to hide anything from him, or to feel like I had to.

Especially after I hid *that* kiss. Look how that had turned out.

How long have I stood here, alone, stuck in my mind?

Time blurred in a haze—probably due to all the alcohol. Would things have gone differently had I drunk less? Did my actions cause people to feel entitled? Ollie, Hawkins, now Orlando. All of them had taken from me, in one way or another.

What made Ollie's actions forgivable compared with the others?

My stomach churned, and I held down the vomit threatening to rise up and out.

Even the drinking hadn't been fun. Now I could drink without repercussions in the eyes of the law, drinking had lost its edge.

Fuck, growing older sucked.

Skylar, stop.

I needed to get my bearings and to figure out what the fuck I should do next. Should I go find Ollie and tell him everything and risk him killing his brother in a rage?

Should I tell Leo? See if he cared enough to jump ship from underneath Orlando's thumb and help us bring him—and all those who wanted to harm me and my loved ones—down?

Did I tell Griff, who wouldn't do much about it but would cheer me up inside?

Then there was Clover. She had a violent streak living within her, bursting to make an appearance. Maybe Ollie wasn't the most likely candidate for murder.

Mind made up, I walked out of the clearing, hoping I headed toward the party and not further into the woods in the direction Orlando fled.

Like Alice heading further into Wonderland, I kept going, hoping I would see a sign in the trees telling me which way to head. Or maybe a great big smug smiling cat.

I saw neither.

The trees were telling me something a lot less *Alice in Wonderland* and more *Snow White* when the woods tried to harm her.

Everything became sinister. Otherworldly. Out to harm me.

'Fuck!' I screamed into the world, nobody around to hear me.

After a few paces, something up ahead came into view, resting against a tree.

Slowly, I crept forward, trying to make as little noise as possible. I didn't want to startle whatever—or whomever—it lurked there.

'Hello?' I called out. If somebody sat at the base of the tree, they would answer me, right?

Nobody wanted to be out here all alone.

It was dark, and getting rather late. Or early, depending on whether you were a glass half-empty or half-full kind of person.

Knowing my wild imagination, it would turn out to be some kind of debris, or maybe a discarded piece of clothing from a student using these woods for privacy.

'Hello?' I called again, louder this time.

I kept walking forward. Kept walking towards what I now could see were a pair of legs and a torso propped up against the tree.

'Ophelia!' Her name ripped from my throat, the force of my shout hurting.

Something was wrong.

Very wrong.

If Ophelia heard me call for her, she wouldn't bite her tongue. The two of us were no longer enemies, but we weren't friends either, and with the way she'd sidled herself up to Orlando lately, it wouldn't surprise me if he had twisted her against me once more.

Either way, she'd never miss the opportunity to tell me to shut the fuck up.

How long had it even been since Orlando left me in the clearing?

I growled out loud in frustration. Pissed I didn't know. Pissed I didn't have my phone on me or even a watch.

My phone had dropped out of my hand during my altercation with Orlando, and I had been in such a daze I hadn't thought to grab it before walking away, and now I didn't want to head back to find it. No chance of finding it, anyway, without a phone to shine a torch from.

How the fuck had this evening gone even worse than I expected? I shook my head, trying to clear the fog settling around my brain.

'Ophelia!' I called again. 'Answer me! A grunt, even. Anything.'

I became frantic again, getting closer to her with each stilted step, every fibre of my being knowing I wouldn't like the sight in front of me.

Have you ever seen the film *Stand By Me*? One of my absolute favourites to the point I could quote every line in time with the characters.

Anyway, there was a scene when they find the boy they went in search of and they get a glimpse of the dead body they'd made the journey for.

Well, Ophelia reminded me of that.

Twisted.

Broken.

And undeniably, definitely dead.

Somebody had propped her up against the tree trunk, her head at a funny angle. This may be the second dead body I'd seen, but it seemed different with Odette. That had all been a blur, one I could barely recall even now the memories of the charity show had returned to me in stages.

Ophelia was different.

Her neck looked like someone had snapped it in anger. Her legs stretched out, pale and odd.

What the fuck?

I couldn't breathe.

Pain shot through my body and my heart tightened in my chest. A deadly squeeze. My vision blurred, the dreaded black spots entering at the edges, making quick work of taking my sight away from me.

The other times I'd passed out were nothing compared to this.

My legs buckled beneath me, and I crumpled to my knees, careful to not fall too close to Ophelia. My hands grabbed the sides of my head, trying to put pressure on my temples to stop the headache from taking over.

I'd never had a panic attack alone, and the thought scared me so much I panicked even more.

Leaves crackled somewhere behind me.

Shit.

A swooshing sound reached my ears, and as I turned to find out where the noise had come from, a sharp pain started on the back of my head.

Then everything went black.

Twenty-Nine

'STUTTER!'

I blinked ... What happened?

Oh, right. I passed out. *Again.*

No wait. My head throbbed, struggling to recall anything. I'd been on the verge of passing out, yes, but then ... then somebody whacked me around the back of the head and I blacked out.

The moonlit night hurt as my eyes adjusted, my head throbbing.

The voice called out. 'Stutter, you around here?'

A drunk Leo stumbled into the clearing, a bottle of jack fixed tight in his grip, and he came to an abrupt stop a metre in front of me.

'Leo ...' I let his name hang in the air, trailing off into the empty clearing.

Wait, empty?

I sat up way too fast, the blood rushing to my head causing me more pain, but I had to see if I could see Ophelia. Had to get her help, and fast.

'Why are you out here all alone?' Leo asked, swaying on the spot, unaware of my despair.

Surely Ophelia hadn't got up by herself and walked away? The girl's neck hung on by a thread.

'Where's Ophelia?' I asked, snapping my head in every direction. 'Have you seen her?'

'Ophelia? Why would I have seen her?'

'She was here.' I pointed to the tree. A dark patch remained where her head had been, but nothing else. Her blood? 'You sure she didn't pass you on your way here?'

'I'm sure,' he said, narrowing his eyes. 'Are you okay? You seem a little out of sorts.'

Did he know? How had he found me? Had he been watching me?

'Are you sure you didn't see anybody?' I asked, choosing not to answer his question. 'Not even Orlando?'

'I haven't seen Orlando all night.'

I scoffed. 'I find that hard to believe.'

'It's the truth, Stutter.' He took a swig from the bottle in his hand. 'The party got boring, so I wandered off on my own.'

'Pity party for one, huh?' My laugh sounded harsh even to me.

God, when would I stop pitying him? Stop wanting to climb inside his mind and find out what went on in there?

Leo didn't respond. He stood there, gazing at me intently, his eyes raking from my head to my toes, searching for something. 'Shit Stutter, you're bleeding.'

My hand touched the sensitive tingling spot on the back of my head and it came away covered in blood. 'S-somebody hit me. I don't know who.'

'Shit!' Leo crouched down to my level. 'Let me take a look.'

I turned my head so he could assess the situation. 'Is it bad?'

'Not too bad, but we need to get you back to school to have it checked out and washed properly. Do you think you can stand?'

I nodded, and he stood up, putting his hand out for me to grab, and I used his steadiness to get myself back to standing.

'Can you walk?' he asked, his tone gentle. 'Here, lean on me if you need.' He wrapped his arm around my waist and the two of us began the slow hobble back to Hawthorn.

'Now you've got me alone. Want to fill me in on everything? For real this time.'

'I've not hidden anything from you.'

'No, but you've not gone into too much detail either.'

'What would you like to know?' he drawled, a playful smile appearing on his face. His smile still turned my insides into jelly. He'd been drinking out of the bottle all evening, so maybe he was a little looser tongued than normal.

'Everything,' I whispered in his ear. He shivered, the hand on my waist tightening a fraction.

'Everything's a little vague, Stutter.' We paused, and he turned to face me, his gaze boring into mine. Goosebumps covered my arms, and not just from the chill of the night. 'Where should I start?'

'How about you start by telling me how you got involved with Orlando?'

Because that was the event this all stemmed down to.

'I wouldn't say I got involved with Orlando. Not like I had any choice or say in the matter.'

'No, I know, but you've never gone into detail about the tasks *The Sanctum* wanted from you and whatnot.' I waved my hand, hoping it came across in the casual way I intended.

'So, I've already told you about how ol' Winnie took me to the woods the day I met Orlando for the first time?'

I nodded, silent, egging him on to continue.

He stopped talking and rubbed his finger on his chin before running his hand through his hair.

'Go on,' I urged, looking around to make sure nobody had stumbled onto our spot in the woods.

'They gave me two scrolls. If I didn't follow the instructions written inside, they'd kill Red.' His eyes stayed locked on mine, and he swayed on the spot. 'You know Red and I grew up together? Guess they knew about my relationship with her and wanted to use it as their bargaining chip.'

He shrugged and took another swig from the bottle. Liquid-courage and all.

'What did the scrolls say?'

'One had the Hawthorn family tree, and the other held a letter, telling me I had to help Orlando Hawthorn take his truthful spot as an heir. To help him in all endeavours, otherwise they'd harm all I love and I would never get to enjoy the perks of becoming a real member.'

He shook his head. His eyes shone in disbelief, one we all experienced when trying to wrap our heads around the whole scenario.

'So, what did you do then?' I asked. 'Freak out about this ginormous secret they kept from you all?'

'Oh, yeah.' He chuckled. 'As soon as my parents arrived home a couple days later, I flew straight to my dad's office and demanded he tell me more about our family tree. Within moments I could tell he knew fuck-all. He didn't know about Orlando. If he did, he hid it well. From then on, I knew I was on my own. I met with Orlando a week later, in the hidden corridors of the school, to talk about what help he wanted.'

'And ...?'

'He told me to go along with his plan to ruin Ollie's life and take back what he claimed was rightfully his. He knew Clover was attending the next school year as a scholarship student, after Ollie and I had rigged it so she could return, so only one option remained for me. I needed to make it clear I gave zero shits about her. If I didn't care about her anymore, then neither would Orlando nor *The Sanctum*. I made sure the entire school turned against her and I abused the power being the head of *The Sect* gave me. I treated her like shit, never wanting her to know the truth; never wanting her to know I did it all to protect her.'

'You pushed her away to save her?'

'I did.' His bloodshot eyes found mine. 'Orlando also knew you were going to be the scholarship recipient the next year. Knew Ollie planned to make you suffer for the sins of your father, and he wanted in on it. Wanted to harm you, too, but worse.'

I shivered. I'd known since meeting Orlando—as himself and not as his brother—he wanted to hurt me more than Ollie ever had, but having it confirmed by Leo, standing in the darkness of the woods, alone, was eerie.

'And to be honest, Stutter, I didn't know you then, so didn't think about you being a person with feelings. All I knew, you were the daughter of somebody hated within our circle. None of us knew what you knew about your dad. For all we knew, you could have come along and acted like an entitled cow who had been denied your birthright. So I agreed to help Orlando in taking Ollie's place when you arrived. Agreed to make you suffer if it meant keeping Clover safe. I regret it now. From pretty much the moment I met you, I wanted out. But you don't say no to Orlando.'

'I get it,' I said. And I did. I understood the dilemma they had placed him in and could appreciate he hadn't known me from Adam. I could've come along and been a spoiled brat, or been a plant of Jacob's. He'd done what made sense to him at that moment, and I couldn't hate him for that.

'During the first year, there wasn't much to do. You weren't here yet, so Orlando stuck to the family mansion on the grounds, mainly.' Leo swigged from the bottle, but when no liquid entered his mouth, he frowned. During our conversation, he'd finished it. 'Fuck,' he cursed, throwing it to the floor. It smashed on impact, the shards of glass flying out and landing on the branches and leaves below us. 'Shit, be careful, Sky.'

'It's fine, I'm wearing boots.' I raised my foot to show him my sturdy boots, and I watched him relax at the sight of them.

'Right. So. Shit-all happened that year. During the summer, though, things ramped up a notch.' He looked off, and I could see the cogs turning in his head. 'Ollie was putting his "revenge" plan in place against you with the girls ready for September, and Orlando had tasked me with letting him know everything Ollie planned to do.'

'And ...'

'And I told him everything.' He shrugged. No emotion attached to his actions because his loyalty lay elsewhere back then. 'He got the idea in his head to mess with you. Pretend to be his brother and tell the girls to do worse than Ollie asked. Pretend to be his brother to seduce you. To drug you. And so on.'

'Right. And I guess he knew when Ollie wasn't around because *you* told him when to strike, hm?'

'Yeah,' he said, sheepish. 'If Ollie was with me, I'd let him know. We had to be careful. Couldn't have Orlando being seen by other students who may then see Ollie elsewhere and question shit.'

'Sounds like a pretty stressful operation.' I let out a sardonic chuckle. I had to give it to them. They'd pulled off some pretty decent black ops shit. Nobody had been any the wiser. I'd never doubted the "Ollie" I spent time with wasn't the real Ollie. Not at the time, anyway. Now I doubted all the shit.

'You've no idea.' He chuckled. 'It gets pretty hard to keep it all straight in your head. I can tell you that much.'

I didn't point out how I too struggled to keep it all straight in my head. 'Then what happened?'

'Huh?' He frowned, his beautiful blue eyes glazed over and bloodshot.

'Well, after school started, you *knew* what happened. You knew who drugged me, drowned me, and stabbed me. How could you stay silent? I thought you felt something for me. We said I love you, Leo.' I ended my sentence in a soft whisper.

'And I meant every single word of it.' He gripped my hand in his, squeezed gently. 'It's complicated.' I could see the stress in his features; sense his inner shame. 'I guess you know I wanted the fake relationship to piss Orlando off as much as Ollie?'

I nodded. Leo had multiple angles. Leo always had multiple angles and overlooking that would be silly.

'I knew Orlando had fallen for you, Ollie too, and I knew both of them were too hard-headed to do shit about it and admit it. Plus, anything to piss Red off worked in my book. Me being unable to be with her didn't mean *Griffin* could.' Leo's hands formed into fists at his sides, his knuckles white.

My stomach swirled in a mix of anger and sadness. Most of this I'd been aware of deep down. Even though I was getting the *true* story, my gut had known the truth all along.

'This is a lot to take in,' I mumbled. 'Maybe we should head back? My head and all ...'

'Fuck!' Leo's eyes widened. 'Why didn't you remind me?' He

turned me around and shone his phone light at the back of my head. 'It's not bleeding, but we should get it checked out, still.'

'Thanks, but I want to get in the shower before snuggling up in bed.'

I gestured behind me to the trees. Back to the sort of safety of the school and to Ollie's arms, where I could lay awake all night processing all the information Leo had given me. From here, we couldn't even hear the party sounds anymore. I wasn't even sure if there *was* a party still happening or if it was late and most people had crashed out and burned.

'Sky,' Leo said, and I froze. He rarely used my name. Whenever he did, it meant something. It was more real than anything else he said.

'Yeah?'

'I'm sorry. For being a part of it.'

'Sounds to me like you had no actual choice.' I shrugged, the last remnants of my anger towards him leaving and fluttering away in the wind. Maybe after so many apologies, he'd worn me down, or maybe I was ready to forgive him and move the fuck on. Either way, I wanted my friend back. 'I forgive you.'

Many people would say everybody had a choice in everything they did. You could choose to be good or you could choose evil.

If somebody threatened your life, or the life of the person you cared most about, are you telling me you wouldn't do the bad thing? Wouldn't harm others to stop others from being harmed?

If you could honestly say yes, then you were a better person than Leo or me. A better person than *a lot* of people.

'Thank you,' he said sincerely, reaching out to pull me into a hug. 'For being you.'

He kissed my head, and like an egg being cracked on it, it travelled down and out to all of my limbs, leaving a warm fuzzy buzzing in its wake.

'Come on,' I said, pulling out of his arms so I could place my arm around his waist. 'You need some sleep. I know I do.'

'Ha!' He chuckled, as if it were a lot funnier than it was. 'I've not slept right in this place for some time, Stutter. Doubt it will change now.'

How odd, because whenever Leo acted as the little spoon to my bigger one, he slept soundly.

It seemed cruel to say anything, so I said nothing at all.

THE TWO OF us began our trek back to the academy in silence, and it hit me during our entire conversation that I'd not once mentioned Ophelia to him. Fuck, maybe she had a valid reason for not liking me. I reverted to such a trash human in the boys' company.

'Leo,' I started.

'Hm?'

'Did you follow me tonight?' I asked, hoping he'd take my question and run with it, rather than me having to go into any more detail. I didn't want to guide him to the answer I wanted.

'Follow you?' He smiled. 'Follow you where?'

'Anywhere,' I answered. 'Did you see me with anyone before ...?'

He shook his head. 'No. I wandered off earlier after ... Well, I wanted to be alone. I didn't know you were out this way, too.'

'I stumbled across Ophelia after ...' Fuck, why was it so hard to talk to him now? A few months back, I'd have had no issue opening up to him and telling him what Orlando almost did to me, but now it didn't feel right to burden him with my shit. He already had enough on his plate. 'She was badly hurt, but when you found me, she'd disappeared.'

He glanced my way, but continued walking, saying nothing.

'Do you think we should tell somebody?' I glanced at him as we walked, trying to see whether his face was as worried or concerned as it should be. I saw nothing more than his usual blank, bored expression. The one he used to give me a lot back when I first started coming to school here.

'I reckon somebody already knows,' he said, cryptic as all get out.

'What does that mean?'

'It means, Stutter, if your good pal Orlando did this, he would've already passed it on to good ol' Winnie. It's rare anything happens here she doesn't know about. You'd be best to remember that.'

'Back when you first told me of *The Sanctum,* you mentioned you thought she was in charge when they recruited you.' He nodded in response. 'Well, it makes sense she'd be high up. She wouldn't have told them about Orlando if she didn't think they'd keep it a secret.' I shrugged.

'Stutter, if I'm being honest, I try not to think too hard about it. Messes with my head.'

I understood, but it still seemed a bit cowardly of him—the one word I would never associate with Leo Hawthorn.

When I thought Leo wouldn't say anymore, and we would continue on in silence, he spoke up softly. 'Was it Orlando who hurt you?'

'Huh?'

'The blood on the back of your head. Did Orlando do it?'

Oh, so he didn't know.

'No,' I told him, wanting to ease his worry. 'Not that I know of. I didn't see who did it.'

But I was covering up the ways Orlando *had* hurt me. How he'd been about to touch me without my consent hurt me.

'Are you sure? You're not lying to me, are you?' he asked as he stopped dead in his tracks.

I stopped walking, too, and turned to face him. Our eyes locked, him searching deep into my soul for the truth.

If I turned my gaze away, or gave even the tiniest hint of distress, Leo would pick up on it. I didn't want to worry him in his current state. I kept my eyes as still as I could. Trying to convey everything in that one gaze.

'I'm not lying to you,' I lied.

'If you're sure.'

I nodded and reached out my hand to take his large one in mine. Our connection flowed from my fingertips into his, and back again. We still had a connection; a deep friendship. I hoped he wouldn't fuck it up by doing something stupid. Something like helping a secret organisation harm me or my family. My newly arrived dad. Fucking hell. As if my mind didn't have enough fighting for dominance already.

'Where's Ollie?' he asked, and I shrugged.

'You're more likely to know than me.' I smiled at him tentatively. I lost track of Ollie around drink number five. Least I think I did.

'I thought he'd be glued to your side all night.'

'We're not attached at the hip, Leo.'

'But you are back together?'

A lead weight dropped to the bottom of my stomach. 'We are.'

'I'm happy for you both.' I raised my eyebrow in question, and he chuckled. 'I mean it. You deserve the best in life, Skylar.'

A happy buzz spread through me. The two of us were going to be okay. I could sense it.

Leo had sobered up during our talk and walk, and was once again able to stand upright without swaying.

'Let's get you to bed,' he said, waggling his eyebrows.

I barged into his shoulder and moved to walk ahead of him. 'You wish.'

'WHAT ARE WE GOING TO DO?' I asked, my eyes widening in Ollie's direction. 'What do you think happened to her?'

'We're going to do nothing.' His hard tone made me blink. 'We're not getting involved this time. I'd much rather find out who hurt you. You're lucky they didn't bash your skull in the way they did hers.'

'We don't know how she died yet,' I mumbled. It had crossed my mind more than once since my birthday party that the person who whacked me around the head likely killed Ophelia. But why had they killed her and allowed me to live? Or maybe they hadn't. Maybe I was meant to be dead, too.

Wouldn't put it past some fuckers here to still want me dead, Orlando included.

'The school has got away with this shit for too long. They won't be able to hush up another one, right?'

He shook his head, more uncertain than I'd have liked.

'Unfortunately, it's in Ophelia's parents' best interest to hush it up.' He winced.

'Shit like this doesn't disappear. Orlando's out on bail. If he did this, it's enough to put him away for life.'

'It does if you have enough money, babe. You'll learn eventually.'

'Oh, wonderful. Once again, my lack of a trust fund is a problem,' I joked, but even I heard the bite in it, so Ollie must, too.

'That came out wrong,' he said. 'I didn't mean it like that.'

'I know you didn't,' I muttered. 'I also know you're a bit of a dick.'

'I know you want my dick.' Ollie laughed and reached out to grab me and pull me closer. I resisted at first. Pretended I wasn't interested. Had to keep the boy on his toes somehow in this constant battle of wits. We may be a couple now, but I didn't want him to stop working for it—for me.

'Oh, sh you!' I laughed, not letting him get a grip on me, but also not getting any further away from him.

Ollie played along a little longer, but then stopped. 'Sky, I think you're joking because your breathing sped up and you're moving away from me but also not, but after everything ... I need you to say it.'

I leaned into his warmth, his heart beating fast under my hand splayed across his chest. 'Say what?'

I rested my head on his chest, and he stroked my hair, sending tingles through me.

'Say you do want me. Say this is okay. I never want you to feel like you've not got a say in anything like this ever again.'

'I—' My mouth opened and closed like a mindless fish, the words struggling to come. 'Ollie, if I ever don't want something to happen, I'll tell you. I promise.'

'No matter what?'

'No matter what. But if it makes it better, you can check in.'

'It does make me feel better, yeah. I never want to do anything you don't want ever again. I'm so sorry for ...' he trailed off, but we both knew he meant the library. The time I'd said no, and he hadn't listened. 'Sky, you mean the world to me.'

'You're not too bad yourself.' I bit my bottom lip, shy but happy he felt comfortable now voicing his emotions. The Ollie of a year ago barely knew how.

'Why thanks?'

I tilted my head up, and he leaned down to press a bruising

kiss against my lips. The butterflies who lived in my belly flapped their wings into a frenzy. One kiss from Ollie and I was ready to rip his clothes off and launch myself at him.

But it wasn't the time or place.

'Ollie,' I said, stepping back to create an inch of space between us. I ran my fingertip down his pec. 'Reckon Winnie's called the police? Would she if she suspected Orlando hurt Ophelia?'

'She has no choice but to, I suspect. She may be in charge of the school, but there's a board she has to answer to and more. Plus, it looks worse for Orlando if she doesn't. Like he has something to hide.'

'So, the police will come here again and question us all?'

'Most likely, yeah.'

'Joy.'

LATER THAT NIGHT, I lay in bed in Ollie's arms, awake, staring at the lamp on his bedside table.

His soft snores grounded me, yet couldn't lull me to sleep because my anxiety had spiked to nuclear levels.

But my anxiety wouldn't allow me something as simple as sleep. Not when so much shit took place in my mind.

My dad's arrival, mixed with Orlando's assault, wouldn't leave me be.

Orlando killed Mr Hawkins for his actions towards me, yet when it came down to it, he had also ignored my pleas, ignoring my lack of consent. I couldn't wrap my head around it. I thought Orlando cared about me, in his own weird and twisted way.

Yes, life had treated him poorly, but poor treatment from others never excused acting shitty towards others. An explanation, maybe, but never an excuse.

Thoughts swirled.

Images of Orlando flashed.

How do you hate somebody when you know you should, but you didn't have it in you to feel so strongly towards them?

Love and hate walk a tightrope together, a loss of balance either way descending you into the madness of one extreme.

And maybe something died inside me the moment Orlando put his hands under my clothes without my consent, because now I couldn't find any emotion for him besides pity.

I pitied him.

No hate. No love.

Instead, a vat of sadness sat low in my gut, twisting my organs and making it hard to breathe, or to relax enough to get some rest.

And whenever I stopped thinking about Orlando, images of my dad flashed in their place. Jacob Cooper was a mystery to me, even if I'd learned a little about him from others, and I still hadn't made my mind up about whether I wanted to spend time with him.

Ollie wanted me to—I'd even go as far as saying he was *pushing* me to—but he also knew I wouldn't do something if I didn't want to and I could see how much restraint he put on himself whenever the topic came up in conversation.

I tossed and turned in bed, careful to avoid waking Ollie. He mumbled, but didn't wake.

I always found it creepy in films or literature when somebody commented on how peaceful a sleeping person looked, like a corpse somehow still breathing, but Ollie also fit the description. His eyelashes fluttered against his cheeks and the permanent scowl he seemed to walk through life with magically disappeared the moment he reached a deep enough sleep to forget about his worries for a while.

'Ollie,' I whispered, half in hopes he'd answer, half in hopes he'd remain asleep and I wouldn't have to voice the things echoing in my mind.

'Mm,' he murmured. His left arm snaked out from the duvet to drape over me, his hand resting on my hip bone.

'Can I ask you something?'

He mumbled some more. I took it as a sign to continue.

Maybe talking it out loud would help me, even if he didn't reply.

'Am I broken?' The words came out stilted. Small.

It seemed to grab his attention. He moved closer and kissed my bare shoulder. 'Broken?'

I nodded, but said, 'Yeah,' in case he didn't see or sense my movement. 'I don't trust my mind anymore.'

'In what way?'

'I can't explain it without telling you ...' I took a deep breath. I hadn't told him about what Orlando had done at my party yet. The right time hadn't presented itself, and with Ophelia's twisted body being found the next morning, well, I had other things to fixate on. 'Something happened at my party, and I haven't told you yet.'

Ollie shuffled up the bed, so his head rested on the pillow at the same height as mine. 'Okay.'

'Orlando ... he acted ... badly?' The disjointed sentence came out excruciatingly slowly, and I still hadn't managed to get across what happened. It came out as a question, my voice going up at the end, and the use of the word badly didn't even cover it. I tried again. 'No, I mean, yes, he acted badly ...' I pressed the heel of my hand against my eye, wanting to relieve the pressure building there. 'He touched me in a way I didn't like.'

'He fucking what?' Ollie growled, rearranging himself to sit up against the headboard, glancing down at me. 'How? Why?' He shook his head. 'No, don't answer if you don't want to. Are you okay?'

'I don't know. Is it bad if I don't hate him for it?'

Ollie cracked his knuckles. 'Not if that's how you feel. Whatever you feel, however you deal with it, is right for *you* and that's all I care about. I care about you, Skylar.'

I swallowed. Yes, I knew he cared, but fuck, it was nice to have it reiterated at a time like this.

'I know. I'm sorry I didn't tell you straight away.'

'You have nothing to apologise to me for.' He stretched out his arm, and I moved closer to his side to snuggle up against his chest. 'I want you to be comfortable telling me things, sure, but I want it to be in your time. Never rush yourself into anything because you think it'll make me happy, or worse, because you think I'll get mad you kept something from me.'

I breathed out through my nose, my body calming down merely from talking to him. It always surprised me when Ollie had the power to make me feel better. A reminder of sorts—one I needed. 'You're the best, you know that, right?'

His chuckle reverberated through his body. 'No, I'm not. I am trying my best for you, though.'

'I know we haven't been a couple again for long, but I want to tell you how much I like you.'

'You don't—'

'I don't have to tell you. I *want* to tell you. They're two different things.'

'Okay, then.' He leaned down and kissed my head. 'I want the record to state I like you a lot. *A lot, a lot.*'

I laughed. 'Thanks for not pushing.'

'Don't thank me for that. I may not be pushing now, but I have been pushing you to spend time with your dad and I'm sorry. I'm not ready to be around him yet, so it's shitty of me to assume you would be.'

'No, you're right to make me think about it. Without you, I'd push it down so far it'd never resurface.' My hand splayed across his ribs, and I dug my fingers in a little.

We both chuckled, and I snuggled in closer to his side. Once more, I found myself falling for Oliver. I'd wait this time before telling him, though. I wanted to be one hundred per cent sure before I blew everything up again.

'I think I'm ready to see him.'

'Okay.'

'You'll come along and rescue me if I need it?' I asked, batting my eyelashes at him. The boy barely refused me anything, so I was pulling out all the stops to ensure he didn't refuse me this. He hated Jacob Cooper. I only hoped he liked *me* more than he hated *him.*

'Skylar,' he said. 'You don't need me to rescue you. You are more than capable of rescuing yourself, because you're strong and beautiful and you take no shit from anybody.'

His words settled over me; a soothing balm to my scorched and somewhat fractured soul.

'I wish I had as much faith in myself as you have in me.'

'One day baby, you will.'

Thirty-One

JACOB COOPER WAITED for me at the entrance, dapper in his shirt and trousers. The fact he'd shown up at all surprised me.

I didn't know why, but I guess I expected him to not show. The fact the man was even walking around this town—this campus—like he'd never left shocked me.

He'd stolen a lot of money, allegedly, and the reactions his name received at the fashion show told me he wasn't well liked around these parts.

Plus, the fact the entire student body had bullied me because of his actions also let me in on his popularity status amongst the elite.

Exiting the doors, I prepared myself for the day ahead.

'Hey, Skylar,' Jacob said when he spotted me. His eyes were the same shade of blue as mine, but they had wrinkled lines at the edges, adding an air of approachability. Friendly. 'You okay?'

'H-hey,' I said, timid, my stutter rearing its ugly head. I knew it would. I'd not been put in a situation like this for some time, and even though my anxiety and nerves had improved, they were still bubbling under the surface. Especially when already apprehensive. And meeting my dad for the first time? My apprehension went into overdrive. 'I'm good, thanks. How are you?'

His smile made my heart stutter. 'I'm good, thank you. Ready to go?' he asked, putting his sunglasses back on. They were black aviators, and they made him even cooler.

On the rare occasions I'd imagined my dad growing up, I hoped he was cool, but deep down I'd assumed he was a low-life. If Cora wouldn't talk of him, well, then you knew he had something wrong with him. She'd married *Andy* after all.

'Yeah,' I replied, rinsing my hands together in front of my waist. 'Where are we g-going?'

He hadn't told me the plan for the day, just that he wanted to talk to me off of school property so nobody would overhear us.

I found that hard to believe. The part about not being overheard. I swore the town of Beurre had eyes and ears everywhere. I hadn't been in town much since starting at Hawthorn, but nothing had changed since the days I went to the local high school and lived on the Hollowdale estate.

'We're going to a little cafe down the way. I used to go there a lot back when I went to Hawthorn. Also used to go with your mother back when ...' he trailed off and I tried to mask my surprise.

Mum had never mentioned him, not once—not until the Mother's Day we spent with Lottie and Leo. I suppose I'd never thought about the things they liked to do together. That they spent much time together, even. Guess I always associated it as a brief dalliance resulting in the unwelcome present called me.

'You did?'

'Yeah,' he said, my confusion lost on him. 'When we first started dating.'

I laughed. I couldn't imagine it. Couldn't see it in my mind. Even in the short time I'd spent with Jacob Cooper, I could tell how different the two of them were. *Are.*

Dad grew up wealthy and his life had been easy—well, maybe not easy, but it had been easier than those who had none.

'Bet you looked a right couple together.' I chuckled. An image of him in an expensive designer suit with Cora standing beside him sporting a large over sprayed bouffant and a skin tight snake print dress entered my mind clear as day.

'We were definitely something,' he said, grinning too. 'Your mother came into my life during my rebel phase.'

'Makes sense,' I said, having already come to the same conclusion. 'Bet your parents didn't approve of her one bit.'

'That's an understatement.'

The two of us were now by his car, a sleek Mercedes that no doubt cost a lot more than any I'd known somebody to own, and he unlocked the doors for us to get inside. It worried me that being stuck in such a small space with him could stifle me, but I had to put on my confident pants and try to dampen my anxiety.

I took my place in the seat and waited for him to get in and start the engine before I spoke again.

'How did you and Cora meet?' I asked once we were on the road heading across town to this small cafe he'd spoken of. He didn't comment on the fact I called her *Cora* and not *Mum*.

'It's a funny story, actually,' he said, his entire face lighting up. Like a creeper, I couldn't take my eyes off his face, watching as his expression changed with each syllable. 'I was trying to escape the life I'd been born into, as you do, and I came down the hill into Beurre to get away from it all. When I was sitting at a bar, alone and nursing a whiskey feeling sorry for myself, this bombshell walked through the door and every eye in the place turned to her.'

'Sounds like Mum,' I said, surprised he'd referred to Mum as a bombshell. A bomb sounded more like it, debris and decay doing its best to get miles away from impact.

'Cora made people take notice.' He chuckled.

'Still does,' I said. I couldn't deny it, no matter how my relationship with her was. These days she came across as more of a caricature of herself, but at the age of eighteen, she had to have been a better sight. 'You should've seen her when she arrived on Parents' Day my first year at Hawthorn.'

My dad laughed, lines appearing on his cheeks, and his eyes wrinkled at the corners—such a human gesture—endearing him to me. Ever since he'd burst on to the scene, I'd been trying to come to terms with his appearance in my life. How it would work in the long run. Would we grow into a relationship, or would he fall off the face of the earth again the moment I got comfortable?

I didn't want to get my hopes up too much.

'I can imagine everybody took notice,' he said, then continued the story, his eyes glazing over slightly. 'So, she entered the bar and came over to me. Asked me why I sat there oozing misery.'

'Sounds about right,' I said. The car came to a stop, and I glanced out the window. He parked the car on the high street, outside a cute coffee joint with sofas and armchairs called The Lounge. Cosy and bright. It also happened to be mine and Griff's favourite spot. 'Me and Griff come here a lot.'

'Really?' I didn't need to know the man to know he was chuffed. 'Me and Damien used to come here. Looks a little different now, I'll admit.' Jacob exited the car, and I followed suit, an odd sensation trickling through me at being out and about with a parental figure.

'The entire town has changed a lot over the years,' I told him. 'A lot of businesses have cropped up, and then disappeared as fast as they arrived.'

'This place used to be up and coming.'

'Well, it isn't now.' I raised my eyebrows, wondering how the town must have been years before. The town had been full of crumbling buildings my whole life, exteriors covered by cracked or fading paint, and an overall sense of decay.

'Still feels like coming home,' he said, his tone nostalgic. 'Suppose I didn't realise how much I missed the place until I came back.'

I followed him into the cafe, and we made our way to the sofa seating area. The moment we were both sitting down, things became even more awkward. The car ride over hadn't been too bad, which probably had something to do with the fact we were both staring ahead, briefly glancing at one another in turn, before our attention went back to the road. Now we were face to face; nowhere to hide.

The waitress coming over made things even more awkward. I glanced at the menu and decided what to order. Cheesy chips and a Diet Coke would be perfect, and right now, I needed some comfort foods to help me with the situation.

'So you have you missed it?' I asked him after the waitress had gone back to the counter. 'The town?'

What I meant: have you missed me?

'There's a lot I've missed,' he said. 'The town, my family, *you*. It's hard though, because this place also holds a lot of memories for me and not all of them are good. There's so much I need to tell you, Skylar.'

The waitress arrived with our drinks, and the two of us fell silent. Yes, Hawthorn may not be a safe place to talk, but the cafe may not be either. Best to be on our guard.

'I don't even know where to start,' he said, bewildered but determined. 'I guess you know about mine and Millie's affair.' I nodded, wanting him to continue. 'It wasn't sordid the way people think, at least not at the start.' He sighed. 'We were together from ages thirteen to eighteen. Thought we'd be together forever, honestly. But then she ended things, and I met your mum ...'

He left the gap in the middle alone, skipping past it.

'After I left your mum, I moved away for a bit,' he said, sheep- ish. I liked how he didn't say "after I left *you*", but we both knew what he meant. 'I left Beurre and travelled; saw the world. Five years later, Millie left me a hysterical voicemail telling me about Damien and Eliza and how I needed to get back as soon as I could. I'd been off the grid and the numbers I didn't have blocked were Cora's and Millie's. By the time I returned, I'd already missed the funerals.'

His entire demeanour reeked of regret and despair. My heart went out to him. Yet, I hated myself a little for having sympathy so quickly. This man left me with nothing—nothing but an uncaring mother and her alcoholic husband—and I needed to remember that.

'She wanted to leave Henry, but we couldn't ...' he trailed off, then changed the conversation. 'What do you know about *The Sanctum*?'

At his mention of *The Sanctum*, my drink had gone down the wrong way and I nearly choked.

'Err …' I paused, unsure what to say. What did we even know? Not much. It shocked me he'd got into it so fast. I respected it, though. I appreciated those who didn't beat around the bush. 'We know they're the adult version of *The Set* and *The Sect* and they rule the underground.'

'That's half of it,' he said. 'They've got a lot more sway, though. Most of the important people in the country have dealt with *The Sanctum* at some point or another. Politicians. The police. Every major business person. All under their thumb.'

'Guess that explains how Ms Hawthorn covered up those murders,' I mumbled, mulling the thought over in my mind, but speaking out loud.

'What murders?' Jacob asked, his brow furrowed.

'Three girls who were a part of *The Set* when I joined school. There's one original girl left now.'

It was the first time I'd said it out loud, and when I did, it hit me how fucked my life had become. Even back at my old school, nothing similar had happened. I mean, there had been some minor issues, like knife crime, but nothing in the way of murder.

I felt so disconnected from it, though. Maybe because someone had also attacked me multiple times and had stabbed me. When these things weren't a part of your life, they seemed extreme and worth worrying about, but now I lived it. Disassociating from it became as easy as breathing.

'And how …'

Once again, we paused when the waitress came over to the table and deposited our food in front of us. The smell of the cheesy chips made my mouth water. I smothered them in salt, vinegar, and tomato ketchup, then watched as Jacob did the same.

We shared a look. *Great minds think alike.*

I waited for Jacob to continue, but he'd taken a mouthful of his food.

'How did they die?' I finished his question for him. Jacob nodded, swallowing his food.

Hm, how did I sum this up? There was one word for it. One word which could answer all.

'Orlando.'

'Orlando?' Jacob repeated, pausing his fork in front of his mouth.

'Yeah. He's Millie's son.' Saying it aloud tasted off in my mouth. 'Well, I know he murdered one of them for sure. The other two ... well, the evidence hasn't presented itself yet.'

'But the one you know about, you have proof?' he asked.

'If being stabbed in the gut in front of the dead body of the victim is proof, then I've got plenty,' I deadpanned.

'What the fuck? Skylar, are you okay?'

'Yeah,' I said. 'Don't worry about it.'

'Don't worry that somebody stabbed you?' He put his fork down and narrowed his gaze. 'Sky ... can I call you Sky?' I nodded. 'Sky, of course I'm going to worry about you.'

I scoffed, not meaning to, but unable to hold it in. 'Of course.'

'I didn't know.'

'A shame in a way, because having you find out about it made up half the motive.' I sighed.

'So Orlando killed those girls?'

'One of them,' I said, but then remembered my birthday party. Shit. 'Okay, definitely two of them.'

'You need to get away from him, Sky.'

'Oh, so you think now you've reappeared, you can tell me what I need to do?' I asked, crossing my arms, raising an eyebrow at him. Giving him a hard time on purpose.

Now he wanted to act like a dad, huh? Not on my watch.

'It isn't safe for you here.'

'You've had no problem with me being here for the last eighteen odd months, so why do you care now?'

'I didn't know you were here.' His eyes widened. 'I thought you were still under Cora's care. Safe, and far, far away from the harm of Hawthorn.'

'Yeah, 'cause I was so safe and away from harm at home.' I chuckled. The man was deluded. Which, yeah, of course he was. He'd gone *off the grid* to get away from his problems. Nobody sane did that shit.

'What's that supposed to mean?' His fingers went to reach out and graze mine, but he stopped himself, instead letting his hand rest in the middle of the table, his raised fingers twitching.

'Nothing,' I mumbled, not wanting to talk about my home life. I didn't want to let him walk into my life and take over, acting like a parental figure.

He hadn't earned the right.

But I hoped one day he might. If he played his cards right.

'Back to *The Sanctum*,' I said, changing the subject away from Orlando and what I needed to do. 'What were you going to say about them?'

'They ruined my life,' he said simply. No embellishments. No dramatics.

A cold, simple truth. *His* truth. One he believed with his whole being.

The question: why?

Thirty-Two

OLLIE and I were huddled together in an alcove, killing time before we headed off to our next lesson, when Leo stopped in front of us and coughed.

'Stutter. Oliver.' He nodded at us both in turn.

'Leo,' Ollie said, his tone making it clear how little he appreciated the interruption. 'What can we do for you?'

'I've got some news you both might find interesting.'

'And that is …' I said, joining the fray. These two weren't fighting, but they also weren't back to being best buddies, either. Which, understandable. Especially now Ollie and I were together *again*.

'There's a meeting of sorts tomorrow evening, if you catch my drift.' Leo's gaze darted around and paused when a large gaggle of students passed, laughing and joking about something unimportant compared to everything going on in our lives.

'Go on,' Ollie urged when the coast cleared once more. 'Spit it out.'

'I'll text a time and a place, but make sure you stay hidden. I'd rather you leave Griff and Clo here, so there's less chance of you getting caught.' Leo's eyes narrowed on mine and I tilted my head in acknowledgement. I would also rather they stay back.

No need for us all to go down with the ship.

'I mean it, don't get caught. I won't be able to step in if you are.'

'We understand,' Ollie said. 'You're treating us like we're stupid, mate.'

Leo's wince my way made me smile. 'Don't worry, Leo.' I smiled wider. 'I know you only think *one* of us is stupid.'

He smiled back. 'All members are required at this meeting, so it's an important one. I'll be in a fuck ton of trouble if they find out I've blabbed to you, okay?'

'Your secret is safe with me,' I said. 'Let us know and we'll be there.'

'Don't let me down, Stutter.'

'Never.'

WHY DID it not surprise me that *The Syndicate* planned to meet in the woods?

The frigid night air chilled my bones as Ollie and I stood and waited for them to arrive. We'd got there early to get a hidden spot, but now all we could do was wait, and fuck me, I hated waiting.

Patience may be a virtue, but it wasn't one of mine.

'Do you think it'll be much longer?' I asked.

We were crouched down behind some kind of rock formation Leo had told us about. I hoped we were hiding on the right side of said rocks, otherwise we'd be revealed the moment they arrived.

'Bloody hope not,' Ollie replied. 'I didn't think it would be this cold after midnight, seeing as it's May. Swear it isn't usually this chilly at night this time of year.'

'Global warming,' I said, the typical response of a Brit caught up in a conversation about the ever-changing weather.

'Must be.' Ollie nodded.

God, what shit small talk. Ollie and I were better than this. I wracked my head for a topic that wasn't boring as fuck, but nothing came to mind.

'What time did Leo say in his text?' I got out my phone to check, as if I hadn't already read the message a gazillion times.

Meeting's at The Rock at 1 sharp, don't be late and DON'T get seen!

Lucky for me, Ollie knew what he meant by The Rock. All I thought of when I heard the phrase was about the wrestler turned actor. Well, technically, I suppose he'd been an actor all along, hadn't he?

'One sharp,' I said. 'And it's ten to.'

'Not much longer.' We went back into a comfortable silence.

The shuffle of cloaks on the leaves came ten minutes later, like clockwork.

Showtime!

Figures appeared, and thankfully for us, we'd chosen the right side of The Rock to hide. Would've been a bit awkward otherwise. I held in my snigger at the thought.

You know, the sight in front of me looked like it had been taken from a movie about a secret society, or the way I imagined an old religious sect would've behaved years gone by when they were trying to eradicate the plague or witches or whatever issue they had.

Leo was right about one thing. You couldn't tell who was who.

They were all hidden by the hood, a black endless pit where a face should be. A shiver ran down my spine. I didn't like this one bit.

My eyes locked on to Ollie's unnerved ones. Nice to see he took it all so seriously. These people were behind a lot of shit, and had known about Orlando long before his reveal, yet stayed quiet for their own gain. But what did they want?

Jacob Cooper had arrived, but so far they'd made no move against him.

'Welcome,' a voice intoned from the group. They were standing in a circle, because, *duh*. The cliches of my life killed me. If anybody else was telling my story, I'd laugh at them. The speaker took a step forward. 'Thank you for meeting tonight on such short notice. As I'm sure you're aware, Jacob Cooper is once more in our midst.'

Murmurs and head nods followed the statement.

'According to certain members, he has returned to spend time with his daughter and will make his way between his base and the school frequently.'

Will he? News to me.

When he left me on the steps of the school after our day together, we decided not to rush anything and to take a break from anything too heavy. I invited him to the school for Father's Day, but there were still a few weeks left.

'What are you implying?' Another voice piped up. A female's. Sounded like Winifred to me, but the wind whistling through the trees meant I couldn't be sure.

'Why move away from our previous methods? We've dealt with Coopers effectively in the past. I don't see why we can't employ the same tactic.'

The same tactic?

Did they mean ...?

My hand covered my mouth, needing something to stifle my realisation. The article headline we found in Hawthorn House flashed through my mind.

A person in the circle stumbled, catching my eye.

Leo.

Even in a heavy cloak with no way of deciphering features, I knew him from his posture. The way he carried himself. All of it.

He couldn't hide from me.

'And what do you mean?' Leo's voice carried through the clearing. 'Some of us weren't around back when you handled the Coopers.'

The group bristled. Fabric rustled.

I smiled.

The other members must be aware of who spoke. Just because Leo had never seen them didn't mean they hadn't recruited him without knowing his identity.

'If Jacob Cooper plans to drive around town in the same vehicle, then things should be easy to arrange. Cars have trouble every day.'

Well, guess my dad will have to hire an unfamiliar car every time he wants to leave his base for the foreseeable future.

Then the implication settled in my gut. Poor Griffin. We'd have to tell him what we learned, but I didn't want to be the one to break it to him. It probably should be me, though. They were my aunt and uncle, too.

'I'll get it arranged,' somebody said.

'Thank you,' the leader replied. 'Next on the agenda, Skylar Crescent. A member has put forward the idea we stop targeting her and spare her if our plan against Jacob succeeds. With her dad dead, she'll be a living Cooper and could one day join our ranks.'

Anger burned. I would *never* join their ranks. They'd have to kill me to keep me quiet about their heinous shit.

Steady on, Skylar. That's what they've tried to do the last two years!

'I say we see how things go with Jacob first before we make any big decisions.'

Orlando.

His voice sounded distinctive, and so much like the voice of my boyfriend. The boyfriend huddled down beside me, seemingly as murderous as the bastards in front of us were.

Orlando wasn't sticking up for me, but he wasn't being a total prick against me, either. Everything about him was such a contradiction all the time, and it gave me a headache trying to keep up with it all.

The rest of the meeting, they discussed mundane things about people I didn't know. During certain sentences, Ollie's eyebrows would climb up into his forehead, so I reckoned he understood a lot more about it than me.

The air turned colder; the night brightened into morning, and my bum became numb.

The crouched position hurt, and I breathed a sigh of relief when *The Sanctum* and their cloaks crunched away, leaving no proof they were even there.

'Are you okay?' Ollie whispered once he was certain they were gone.

'Yeah, I think so. Are you?'

He nodded, reaching his hand out for mine. Mine went willingly, slotting into the spot I now thought of as mine. 'Let's get you back in the warm. We can wait until the morning to talk to Griff and Clo.'

'Sounds good to me.'

Thirty-Three

'CLO, do you think I'm a little too reliant on Ollie?'

'In what way?'

My head tingled as the hairbrush made its way through my lilac curls, and I shivered at the sensation. Clo had agreed to straighten my hair for me and I wouldn't pass up the chance. I'd already made her brush the same spot five times because it felt so nice.

'I don't know. I guess the word I'm seeking is codependent?'

It crossed my mind more and more lately. Ollie and I spent most of our time together, and at first I thought little of it, but now I realised maybe it was too much, too soon. We did this the last time round and then when it turned out he'd betrayed me the whole time, things hurt a lot worse than they would have if I'd kept some distance between us.

Being in love made you do some pretty funny things. Things you said you'd never do.

'I suppose you are,' Clo said, running her fingers through my hair. 'And if I was talking to somebody else other than you, I'd say it was unhealthy.'

'But?'

'But it's you and Ollie, and I don't know, but this shit seems inevitable for you two.'

She stopped playing with my hair and leaned down, turning on the straighteners with a little beep.

'Inevitable doesn't mean healthy,' I said. 'I guess I don't even know what a healthy relationship is. Can't say I've been around any.'

'Me either, come to think of it.' She parted my hair into sections. 'I wouldn't say my parents are healthy.'

I didn't want to startle her by pointing out she'd mentioned her parents of her own volition without being forced into it by somebody else, so I stayed silent and waited for her to continue.

'They're still together because they've got too much history to end it, I think.'

'Sounds a pretty poor reason to remain married,' I said.

Clover seemed lost in her task. She picked up a strand of my hair with her left hand; the straighteners gripped in her right. 'So many people stay married for the wrong reasons. It's weird, but I think the one decent marriage I've seen is the one between Edward and Lottie.'

Jeez! Did Clo feel alright?

Mentioning both her parents and Leo's parents in the same conversation without something setting alight was a miracle.

'Don't think I've spent enough time with Edward and Lottie in the same room to pass judgement on them. I've mainly spent time with Lottie when he isn't around.'

'Lottie's lovely, and so many people think she married Edward for his money, but it's not like that at all. She loves him, you know? Unconditionally.'

'Guess I've never thought about it.'

If I was being honest, I didn't think about other people often if they weren't in my direct eye line. Well, what a lie. I thought about them a hell of a lot if anxiety was attached to said person or a situation involving them. Then I thought about nothing *but* them.

'Edward and Lottie make decisions together. They both love Leo and want the best for him, no matter what. Can't say the same for my parents.'

'All I've got to look at is Cora and Andy, and nobody is ever going to aspire to be like them.'

Clo was around halfway through my hair now, and the repeated motion of the straightener calmed me.

Talking of Cora and Andy, I hadn't heard from Mum since my birthday. Lucky for me that she even remembered it. She called and told me she loved me and wished for me to have the best day and to get everything in life I deserved. The whole time, all I could wonder about was how much she'd had to drink before dialling me. She'd called at ten in the morning …

'Least your mum loves him,' Clo said. 'Even if he is a massive arsehole.'

'My mum's never had the best judgement.' I sighed. 'Sometimes I wonder if Cora acts the way she does because of her life and all that's happened in it, and then when I think about it, I think maybe I'm a little harsh on her.'

'Oh, really?'

'She didn't get along great with her parents, and I think her opinions bothered them. Extremely over opinionated, you know? So she sought out love wherever she could find it. I've always thought that's how she ended up hooking up with Jacob. He was rich and flashy—the complete opposite of a woman trying to escape her life, with barely more than a few quid to rub together.'

'Sounds a little sad.'

'It is a little sad, but I suppose my anger and hatred towards her has always overshadowed everything else. I always got jealous of the girls who had good relationships with their mums and could tell them everything. Go to them for advice.'

'No need to be jealous of me and my mum, then.' Clo gave a small laugh. 'I've never been able to go to her about anything, and when she wants to talk to me, it's to dictate my life or to tell me I'm doing something the wrong way.'

'Are we bonding over our shitty mothers, Clover Luck?'

We both chuckled.

'Why yes, Skylar Crescent, I think we are.'

'I'M PRETTY SURE my dad hid some stuff back from me.'

I couldn't put my finger on why, but something didn't add up. Or maybe he hadn't actively hidden stuff, but chosen to not speak of it, which ... okay. It had been our first time properly meeting and talking and getting to know one another, so maybe he didn't want to bog it down and make it all heavy and miserable and dark.

'Maybe he saved some stuff for next time, in case it didn't go well. To ensure there even would *be* a next time,' said Ollie.

I nodded. Ollie made a good point, as usual. Sometimes I wished he'd be a little less right all the time. His head could do without being inflated even more.

Good thing I loved him, wasn't it?

'Maybe. Do you think I should reach out to him and arrange another meeting?'

'Do you want to?'

I shrugged. 'I don't know. After what we overheard at *The Sanctum* meeting, I texted him a warning, and lucky for me, he didn't ask how or why.'

'How did he reply?'

'He thanked me and said he hoped to see me soon.'

'Will you invite him to Father's Day?' Ollie asked, running his fingers along my shoulder blade. 'If you don't, Winifred will do it for you as an official school invitation or some bullshit.'

'She does have a habit of sticking her nose in where it isn't wanted.' I chuckled, the image of Mum and Andy arriving unannounced at my first Parents' Day here. At the time, I was certain it had been the boys and the O girls who invited them, but maybe not. 'But yeah, I already decided to ask him. Do you think it'll be super awkward having your dad and Edward here too?'

'Undoubtedly.' Ollie smiled, a glint of mischief flashing in his blue eyes. 'My dad and yours will have to get used to spending time together. We're together, after all, and I'm sure there will be events they both need to attend in years to come.'

My heart dropped. Was Ollie hinting at something ...?

I shook the thought away. Focusing on a future which may

never come to pass wasn't worth it. Not yet. Not when we needed to stop those who were trying their hardest to harm us, or worse.

'It might take some time,' I said. 'The two of them don't have the best history.'

'No, but if I can get over it for your sake, then Henry can get over it for mine.'

I'd be lying if I said I wasn't happy to hear Ollie say he could get over his hatred of my father for my sake. The fact he would put something so serious aside to keep the peace made me smile. In his eyes, my dad was one of the many reasons his mum hated her lot in life—one of the reasons she no longer *had* a life.

'I understand if it takes some time,' I said. 'I'm not sure how I feel about him yet, either. It's weird to go from being a girl without a dad to a girl with one.'

'You'll take it in your stride, Skylar, the way you do everything else. Jacob Cooper is lucky you're giving him the time of day.'

Ollie's words soothed me, but they also didn't ring true in my heart. 'I suppose.'

'There's no *suppose* about it!' Ollie kissed my cheek. 'It's within your rights to refuse to see him, yet you haven't because you're the bigger person.'

'Yeah, yeah,' I said, brushing it off. I needed to change the topic. Too much praise so early in the morning would go to my head, even if it came from Ollie. 'Now, what do you say about staying in tonight and not having dinner with the rest of the school?'

'And ditch Griff and Clover?' Ollie smiled. 'I like the way you think, Ms Crescent.'

Thirty-Four

THE NOTE CAME under my door before breakfast.

Skylar Crescent,
Your presence is requested on Saturday night at midnight in the pool
house.
Do not tell anybody.
Come alone.

I read it, then re-read it, until I could recite it off by heart.

My first instinct told me Orlando had written the note and slid it under my door, but I couldn't be sure without either asking him or going to the meeting. Since my birthday, I'd given him a wide berth and avoided him at all costs. He hadn't tried to talk to me or get me alone, either. Which, now I had time to sit down on the edge of my bed and think about it, was pretty fucking weird. To go from wanting to get me alone all the time to not going anywhere near me ... well, it was a little odd, wasn't it?

Maybe remorse filled him after his actions at my birthday party. *Hmm.* Somehow, I doubted that.

The note made it pretty clear not to tell anyone, but maybe I could tell somebody.

Not Ollie though. He wouldn't understand, and he'd force me to allow him to come. Or worse, go in my place—maybe without even telling me.

Maybe I could text Leo? He'd at least be able to tell me whether the note came from Orlando. Suppose it was a trap? Would be silly of me to walk into it blindly.

What to do? What to do?

Not like I had to decide straight away. Saturday was another four nights away, so plenty of time to weigh up the pros and cons.

Right?

———

AT LUNCH, I still hadn't made my mind up about what to do.

At dinner, I was none the wiser.

Same for breakfast the next morning.

No, all I did was replay the note in my mind and think of different ways I could handle the situation. For a brief moment, I thought of telling Griff, but squashed the idea straight away. Griff may be good for a lot of things—plus he was family—but keeping a secret wasn't his strong point. It would pain him to keep things inside, and I wasn't mean enough to make him.

During my free period, I needed to grab some bits for my room, so I said my goodbyes to the boys and Clover and set off on my own.

When I walked alone, I got distracted by the most stupid things. The way my feet stepped against the floor, or a fixed point in the distance, or a cloud resembling a hippo. It meant I entered my own little world, unaware of everything going on around me, oblivious to it all.

A hand gripped my shoulder from behind, and I jumped in the air. Literally, my feet must have made it at least an inch off the floor. 'Shit!'

'Sorry,' Leo's gravelly voice said, calming my heart rate down a fraction. 'I didn't mean to startle you.'

'It's okay,' I said, placing my hand on my chest where my heart lived. 'Didn't hear you coming, that's all.'

'What were you thinking about? You seemed pretty occupied. I called your name twice.'

'Oh,' I laughed. 'It always amazes me how little I pay attention. I didn't hear a thing.'

'Well, now I have your attention. Can I talk to you, in private?' He nudged his head towards an empty classroom and I nodded.

'Where's ...'

'Orlando?' Leo asked. Our telepathy still worked, even though we weren't a couple anymore, fake or otherwise. 'He's busy. Winnie demanded his presence in her office.'

'Sounds serious,' I said. 'How are things going?'

'Do you care?' he asked, sullen, but then he must have realised how moody he sounded because he kept talking before I could answer. 'Sorry, that was shitty of me. I'm good, thanks. Well, as well as I can be with all this crap going on all the time.'

'Feels like there's never any letup, doesn't it?' I laughed. 'The moment I think things will become smooth sailing for a little while, everything blows up in my face, or so it seems.'

'Are you okay?' he asked. It sent a shot of thrill through me whenever Leo cared about me. I doubted it would ever go away, no matter how much time went by.

'I think so. Everything's been a little ... odd.' Why was I downplaying it for Leo's sake? 'No, odd doesn't cover it. Everything's fucked.'

He chuckled. 'Sounds about right for this place. How are Griff and Ollie doing with ... everything?'

'What part? The fact that Griff's parents were murdered or the fact both their parents were mean-spirited bullies who pushed a girl too far one day and regretted it for the rest of their lives?' I crossed my arms. 'They're both dealing with it in their own way. Which means Ollie's not talking about it, but brooding at night when he thinks I'm asleep, and Griff is cracking even more jokes than usual to hide the sadness.'

'Not a surprise,' Leo said. 'They've never handled things in the most mature of manners.'

'I want to agree, but I also know the two of them are struggling, so I want to be kind and give them grace.' I bit my bottom lip and sniggered. 'But yeah, you wouldn't find a picture of them in the dictionary alongside mature.'

We laughed at the boys' expense. Leo ran his hand through his hair, tousling it further. 'Sky, are we good?'

I frowned. 'Me and you?' He nodded. 'Yeah, why?'

'Checking, I suppose. I know I've said sorry and you've accepted my apology, but it's hard to know how to act around you now.'

'I would say act the way you did *before,* but to be honest, I don't want you to go back to treating me like something not worth your time.'

'I could never do that. Not now, I know you better.' Leo's hand hovered in the air between us, wanting to comfort but not knowing how. 'Another apology is on the tip of my tongue, so blink twice to stop it from coming.'

My heart twinged at his hand hovering in the air, afraid to reach out and touch. Bittersweet sadness overwhelmed me. The one way to pause the melancholy in the air was to blink twice, real exaggerated like, to make him laugh.

Blink. Blink.

Leo responded the way I expected, by barking out a chuckle, and the tension dissipated with it.

The note entered my mind once more, and I took a deep breath, knowing my course of action may be foolish. 'If I tell you something, will you keep it a secret?'

'I suppose I deserve your scepticism, even if it is a dagger through my heart.' He playfully grabbed his chest, a soldier wounded in battle. 'What's up?'

'I got a note through my door yesterday morning,' I said. '*Typed.*'

Translation: typed so I couldn't decipher who it came from.

'Saying?'

'Asking me to go to the pool house at midnight on Saturday, and pretty sure we both know who it's from.'

A smile danced on his lips. 'Is it the location or the time giving it away?'

'Bit of both,' I said, a similar smile on mine. 'The real question is whether I should go?'

'What's your gut saying?'

'It's teetering on the edge, changing its mind each minute. I'd love to find out what he wants, and why he thinks a note and secrecy makes a difference to him asking me in person.'

'Ever since your birthday, he knows he can't approach you without issue.'

'So he told you about what he almost did to me?'

Leo nodded. 'He did, yeah. What kills me, Stutter, is the fact we walked back to school together after he did that and you said nothing about it.'

I tutted. 'Let's not make this about you and your feelings.'

'Shit, I didn't mean—'

'I know. I didn't tell you because I hadn't processed it yet and wasn't sure how I truly felt. It wasn't anything against you. *Not that I have to justify myself.*'

'Sky, forget I said anything. I'm acting like a douche canoe.'

'Yeah, you are, but I'll allow it.' His hand, no longer hovering in mid-air, had returned to his side. It took everything in me to stop myself from reaching out and taking his hand in mine. Not in a romantic way, more in a friendship way. Best not to confuse things, though, when we were already in such a precarious spot.

'Why are you telling me about the note?'

'I trust your guidance. Do you think I should go?'

'What does it say, word for word?'

I put my hand into the inside pocket of my blazer and removed the note. 'Here, peep it for yourself.'

Leo took the note, careful not to touch my hand, and read it. His brows furrowed and I couldn't take my eyes off the creasing of his forehead.

'You've already broken the rules by telling me,' Leo pointed out. 'And you haven't told anyone?'

I shook my head. 'Nope.'

'I'm touched,' Leo said. 'Do you want me to hang around in

the corridor linking the pool house to the hospital wing, so if anything goes wrong, I'm there?'

The idea of Leo being nearby to rescue me if I needed it warmed me. How on earth could he be such a good guy but also such a liar at the same time?

'Probably a good idea. What will you do if it is Orlando, and he catches on?'

'I'll bullshit him the way I have for the last two years. He's never caught on before.' Leo chuckled. 'I think you should go.'

'Yeah?'

'Yeah, I do. I wouldn't tell Ollie or Griff either. Nor Red. Seems silly to involve them and cause a fuss for nothing.'

I agreed. I had no plans to tell the others. Fuck, I hadn't had plans to tell *Leo* either. 'Plus, I wouldn't want them to get hurt. What if it isn't Orlando?'

'Who else could it be? Would Ollie do something like that?'

I thought about it. 'Narh, I don't think so. Our history with the pool house ... I doubt he'd put me in a similar position again willingly.'

'Right. I forgot.'

Forgot the time I nearly drowned? Or the time Ollie nearly drowned?

Either way, it pissed me off a little that he could forget either event. They were kind of a big deal.

'Okay, well ...' I trailed off, no longer wanting to talk to him. 'I best be off. Will you spy on the pool house entrance for me so if it isn't Orlando, you can raise the alarm?'

He nodded. 'It's the least I can do.'

'Thanks. I'll see you later.'

'See you later, Stutter.'

Thirty-Five

I COULDN'T TELL you the amount of times I changed my mind about going to the pool house at midnight on Saturday night. At least fifty.

The reason fear hadn't overtaken me had to do with the knowledge Leo would be watching and lying in wait in case anything bad went down. My own personal avenger.

WHAT IF I ARRIVE BEFORE WHOEVER IT IS?

Leo's reply made me smile.

I'LL BE WATCHING, AND IF IT ISN'T HIM, THEN I'LL GET OLLIE

That settled it then. I would show up and hope Orlando walked through the door, and if he didn't, well, I'd cross the bridge when it came to it.

'Why can't I stay with you tonight?' Ollie's pen hovered above his paper. 'I've got used to you being my heater.'

'Oh, so it's nothing to do with wanting to spend time with me?' I widened my eyes and opened my mouth as if in shock. 'I'm a warm body, am I?'

'Shut up.' He laughed. 'You know you're a hell of a lot more than that to me.'

'Pft.' I crossed my arms across my chest, pushing my boobs up in the process—on purpose. Ollie's eyes travelled lower. 'What am I then?'

'You're my girlfriend.' His eyes met mine. 'And if you tell Griff I'll murder you, but you're also my best friend.'

'I'm your best friend?' I tried to keep the wide smile off my face but failed. Something about his words had touched a nerve, in a good way. 'I sort of want to tease you about it, but I won't because you've made me feel good.'

'Tease away,' Ollie said. 'I've got nothing to be ashamed of.'

'It becomes even less fun now you've given me permission.' Somehow, my smile got even bigger. 'Don't tell Clover, but you're my best friend, too.'

'Really?' He dropped his pen and put his hand on top of mine. 'Do you mean that?' The way his tone turned all soft and vulnerable had my insides turning into mush.

'I do,' I said. 'Why would I lie?'

'I don't know.' He shuffled in his chair. 'Maybe for my benefit.'

'No reason to do that.' I shrugged. 'I wouldn't lie to you, especially not about something so serious.'

No, I lie about other things that are probably more important.

'If you're sure.'

'I am.' His hand squeezed mine, and I turned my hand so it was palm up and squeezed back. 'Now, I need to get this essay done before Monday, so if you could keep the distraction to a minimum, I'd appreciate it.'

'Yeah, yeah.' He picked his pen up again. 'So, tonight?'

'I need a night in with Clo. Since everything went down between her and Griff, she's obviously not staying out anymore, so has been all alone. Don't want her to become some kind of ghost haunting the place.'

'I highly doubt Clover would choose to haunt *Hawthorn,* of all places.'

'You speak true.' I pointed my pen at him in accusation. 'But if she did, you would be to blame, and I can't have that on my conscience.'

'We can't have that at all,' he said. 'I could spend the evening with Griff and then spend the night alone, I suppose.'

'You suppose?' I laughed.

'I'm not thrilled about it,' he chuckled. 'But it would do us good to not spend every waking moment together. Or so people would say.'

'Codependency as teenagers isn't a good look.'

'Says who?' Ollie demanded. 'Who's been filling your head with such bullshit?'

'Nobody,' I said, evading the fact it was Clover who said something. Ollie wouldn't take kindly to me listening to her for any relationship advice, seeing as all her relationships had blown to smithereens. 'It's what people will say, isn't it? We're too young to spend this much time together.'

'People may say it, but as long as you don't think it, then I don't give a shit. If we enjoy spending time together, that's all that matters.'

'I agree.' And I did. 'But I'm still staying in my room tonight.'

'Yeah, yeah, I know.' He smiled, the wrinkles at the corners of his eyes making me smile. I loved to see him so happy. It made a massive change from last year. 'Remember, you can sneak into my room at any time.'

'If I miss you that bad, I'll take you up on the offer.'

***

THE POOL HOUSE was empty and dark when I arrived.

The staircase on my right drew my eye, but I couldn't let myself get distracted. Somewhere up there, Leo watched and waited, keeping an eye out for me—keeping me safe. Or as safe as I could be in this place.

The idea Leo still cared about me enough to watch over me was bittersweet. It also gave me hope. Maybe once all this mess was done and over with we'd return to being real friends. Ones who didn't toe the line of a relationship to piss people off.

The pool room was even quieter than the rest of the building.

The waves of the pool reflected on the ceiling; the calm before the storm. I wandered around, taking in the surroundings, hoping Orlando showed soon.

Hoping Orlando actually showed up and not one of those cloak wearing Sanctum members I didn't know.

The door opened, and unlike previous times, I turned to look at whoever had arrived.

'Little One,' Orlando said, closing the door behind him with a gentle *click.* 'You came.'

I stayed put, letting him walk closer to me. 'I came.'

'Alone?'

I exaggerated and turned in a circle. 'Can't see anyone else here, can you?'

'No.' His little smile unnerved me. 'Unexpected, though. Thought you'd rope in my dumb as rocks brother or my even dumber cousin.'

'I didn't tell them a thing about it.' I spoke the truth. I hadn't told Ollie or Griff a thing. 'The note said not to tell anybody.'

'You've never been one to follow instructions.'

'I've also nearly died multiple times, so I'm sure you can understand why I like people to know where I am.'

'You're safe with me,' he said. 'Always.'

My laugh filled with scorn. 'A bit rich coming from you, isn't it? The last time we were alone you tried to ...' I trailed off, unable to voice the word. I suppose if I was honest, I hadn't come to terms with it yet. 'Wouldn't call that safe.'

'Which is part of the reason I wanted you to meet me here tonight,' he said. 'I want to apologise.'

'You could have apologised in broad daylight where there were witnesses,' I pointed out. 'Makes it all a little shady boots the way you always want to hide things.'

'Not gonna lie, Little One, but I didn't fancy getting punched by my brother in front of witnesses.'

'He wouldn't punch you.'

Orlando laughed. 'No need to lie to me. I think we both know how much he'd love to deck me.'

'Can't blame him for it,' I said. 'Plenty of times I've wanted to deck you.'

'Lucky for me you haven't. Even if you'd be well within your rights to.'

'So, are you going to then?' I took a step closer. 'Apologise?'

Orlando took a matching step to mine, bringing us closer together, but still not close enough to touch. I wanted to keep enough distance, just in case.

'I've built it up now, and whatever I say won't be good enough.'

My heart twinged, but I stood my ground. There was no way I was letting him off the hook so easily. 'That's the amazing thing about apologies, Orlando. The ingredients needed to make it effective are the words I'm sorry.'

Suppose he'd never had to say it often enough for it to stick in his brain.

'I am sorry,' Orlando said, his hands wringing in front of his waist. 'I don't think I can put into words the extent I'm sorry.'

'Would it be mean of me to force you to try?'

'I deserve that,' he said, 'and I know you're teasing me, but you're right. I should at least try to explain some things to you—it's why I asked you here alone.'

'Okay.'

'Can we sit down?' He pointed to the seating, and I nodded, following him over there. When I sat, I left space between us. I even went as far as sitting in the row above him, so I had the higher vantage point. 'I'm sorry for how I acted the last time we were alone together. There's no excuse for my behaviour and I won't sit here and bullshit you with a reason for it.'

'How big of you.' I rubbed my knees, hoping to put some kind of sensation back into them. The weather outside may be warming up, but fucking hell, the pool room cooled down when empty, with nobody there to fill it with body heat. 'Because you're right, there is no excuse. I do have a question for you, though.'

'Yeah?'

'What went through your head?' I tilted my head, assessing

his reaction to my words. 'When you pushed me up against the tree?'

'There isn't an easy answer, and the answer I have, well, I'm not sure I want to voice it to you.'

'Why?'

'You'll think the worst of me.'

I chuckled. 'Hate to break it to you, but I sort of already do. Not sure you can sink any lower, in my opinion.'

'Nice to know you don't feel the need to lie to me.'

'I'm trying a thing where I tell the truth ...' A thought entered my mind. 'Well, except for not telling Ollie or Griff where I planned to go tonight.'

'You didn't tell them?'

'Do you think we'd still be alone if I had?' The image of the two of them bursting through the door made me laugh. 'They'd have shown up like some second-rate action heroes ready to rescue me.'

'You don't need rescuing from me.' Orlando's voice was barely audible, and I had to lean forward to hear him better. 'At least, not anymore.'

'Well, what's changed?' Because in my head, nothing had and most likely never would. Orlando didn't know how to change. He'd never had an excellent role model in his life to show him the way of things. No, neither had Ollie, but at least he was learning.

Orlando shrugged. 'I've seen the error of my ways.'

'More like you know you're not getting anywhere in your revenge plot to steal your brother's life, and you never will if you continue to alienate everybody.'

'I deserve Ollie's life as much as he does. A split second decision gave me my life and him his. A fifty-fifty chance and Millie picked me to give away to her sister. It could have easily happened the other way around.'

'But it didn't, and that's not Ollie's fault, no matter how much you want to make it his.'

'Whose fault is it, then? Who's to blame?'

'Millie Hawthorn,' I said. Millie had caused this animosity and hadn't even lived long enough to see how it played out. 'She made the choice to do what she did. Nobody else.'

'No matter what you say, Little One, I still want to see my brother suffer, and *that* I won't apologise for.'

I stood up abruptly.

'Suit yourself,' I snapped. 'Thanks for the apology, but I must be off now.'

'You don't have to leave.'

'Yeah, I do. You can fuck off if you think I'm gonna stay here while you're chatting such shit about Ollie and how you want to see him suffer.'

For the first time, I didn't hold back when speaking to Orlando. Kept nothing inside. He deserved my ire and so much more and I was bored with giving him the benefit of the doubt all because his life was harder than Ollie's. Fuck, my life was hard yet I didn't come to Hawthorn ready to ruin the lives of those more fortunate than me!

No, I came to Hawthorn to improve my life and get into a decent university. Something the bastard in front of me had attempted to prevent at every turn.

'The next time you think of sending a note requesting my presence, know I won't show up, but someone else will.' I moved closer to the door, keeping my eye on Orlando the whole time. 'I understand wishing for a better lot in life, and I understand being mistreated, but you can't constantly weaponise it.'

'Little One,' he called, standing up from the bench. 'You're the one person I can talk to.'

'Maybe so,' I said, my hand gripping the door handle. 'But it doesn't mean I have to listen to it any longer.'

Thirty-Six

AFTER MY EVENING meeting with Orlando, I decided not to tell Ollie or Griff a thing about it.

I weighed up the pros and cons, and what did I gain from telling them? Nothing, that was what.

When I left the pool room, I went to the corridor and found Leo, waiting patiently the way he said he would. I thanked him and he walked me back to my room. We didn't talk much, except for me to tell him what Orlando wanted to see me for.

Now, Ollie and I were in History together, listening to the teacher drone on about some war or other. Well, I say listening, but I took not one word in. My head was floating in the clouds and I'd paid little attention to my classes all day.

'Are you okay?' Ollie whispered out of the corner of his mouth. 'You've not written anything down.'

I nodded my head. 'Yeah, sorry, just living in my own world.'

'Good thing you can share your boyfriend's notes then,' he said with a quiet chuckle. 'I'm gonna think you're using me soon.'

'If I was, it wouldn't be for your notes.' I let out a barking laugh, and the teacher snapped their head in my direction, putting their pointer finger against their lips. Ah, the universal sign for shut the fuck up. We all knew it well.

A knock came at the classroom door.

Mrs Wood called out, 'Yes?'

The door creaked open, and when my eyes glimpsed the person standing on the other side, my heart sank. *Shit.*

Detectives Smith and Saunders were standing there and both of them had dark, serious expressions on their faces. Ms Hawthorn hovered behind them, a smug smile playing on her grey features.

'Hello, Mrs Wood. We're sorry to interrupt your lesson.'

'No problem, detectives. What can I do for you?'

Detective Smith took a step into the classroom, surveying the area looking for something, or *somebody*, in particular.

'Oliver Brandon,' he called out, locking eyes on Ollie in the seat beside me. 'Please stand.'

Ollie pressed a bruising kiss to my cheek. 'God, what do they want now?'

The chair screeched as he pushed back from the table.

'Oliver Brandon, you are under arrest for the murder of Ophelia Rogers. You do not have to say anything. But, it may harm your defence if you do not mention when questioned something which you later rely on in court. Anything you do say may be given in evidence.'

Ollie's jaw dropped, but he remained silent. Knowing these bastards, they'd use anything he said to aid their case, even if it were to say goodbye to me.

He placed his hands out for the detective to put handcuffs around his wrists. The thing that let me know he was pissed? The change in his breathing. Everything else in his outward appearance remained calm and in control. It impressed me. Ollie always seemed to have it together in front of other people, yet behind closed doors he let me see his true self.

CODE RED. OLLIE'S BEEN ARRESTED FOR OPHELIA'S MURDER! CONTACT THE LAWYERS ASAP.

I texted the same message to Leo and Griff, tapping the message out under the table so the teacher wouldn't see. I don't think they'd penalise me at a time like this, but Ms Hawthorn would, the old witch.

My phone lit up in my hand—a message from Griff.

SHIT! ON IT, CLOUDS

I was at a loss, not knowing what else I could do to make things better. Messaging the guys was my only move.

'Ollie,' I called to him as he reached the door beside the detectives. 'I'll get this figured out, okay? Trust me.'

He nodded, his face determined yet grim. I blew him a kiss as he went out of view.

Fuck me, could things get any worse?

'THEY MUST HAVE some sort of proof, otherwise they wouldn't have arrested him,' Griff said. 'We need to figure out what they've got on him.'

'They've got forty-eight hours to charge him,' Clo said, pacing in space between the middle of our beds. 'So I don't think we need to worry yet.'

'Clover,' Griff said, in a tone that made it a clear reprimand.

'I'm just saying,' she said, not sounding anywhere as chastised as she should. 'These detective dickheads have questioned us all plenty over the last two years, and they're as clueless now as they were then. If they can't see the Orlando-shaped criminal in front of their eyes, then nothing we do can change their oversight.'

'I think we should get Leo in here,' Griff said, not for the first time. 'It makes sense to tackle this together. He'll know more for sure. This has Orlando written all over it.'

'I'll send him a message.' I got my phone out. 'Wait, what if he's with Orlando now and he sees it?'

'Well, don't put anything suspicious, so if Orlando sees it, he won't think much of it.'

'Okay.'

HEY, COULD DO WITH SOME OF YOUR SHINING OPTIMISM RIGHT ABOUT NOW IF YOU'RE AROUND?

I pressed send, then threw my phone on my bed like a child. Why was I nervous? Probably had to do with the fact I hated rejection and if Leo rejected me, I think it'd push me over the edge. Especially at a time like this, what with Ollie being arrested and all.

It sounded so wrong in my head.

Arrested.

Not even asked in for questioning like in the past, but arrested.

Leo's knock came within five minutes. He called through the door, 'It's me.'

Griff let out a jovial laugh when he opened the door. 'Of course it's you. The only other person it could've been got hauled off by police a few hours ago. Not sure if you heard?'

'Leave him alone,' I said. 'Leo can't help it.'

Did I even believe my words? Could Leo help being under Orlando's thumb? Probably not if he wanted to keep us all safe. I'd attended a meeting. I'd heard the way they spoke so callously about ending a life. They meant what they said and if Leo didn't play ball; well, I doubted I'd have a beating heart for much longer. Same went for Clover.

'Please don't stick up for me, Stutter. I deserve the shit.'

'You're right, you do.' Clover nodded her head as if it was all decided and we could move on now Leo's shit status had been determined. 'So, what do you know?'

'About ...?'

'Don't act obtuse, it doesn't suit you. What do you know about Ollie being taken in?'

'Since Sky's birthday, I wouldn't say I'm in the fold.' Leo's gaze seared into mine. 'Oh, and somehow they knew I gave you the heads up about going to Hawthorn House while they were out.'

'Reckon they have cameras?' I asked. 'Would make sense, I suppose. At the entrance, at least.'

Leo shrugged. 'Probably. Doesn't matter now. What matters is that Orlando no longer trusts me the way he used to.'

'And who's at fault?' Clover snapped. I rolled my eyes, already bored with having the two of them in the same room together. It got so tedious, their constant animosity. Sure, I understood it, but it didn't mean I had to like it.

'The people at fault here are Winifred, Orlando, and *The Sanctum*. We need to remember and stay united, not divided.' I sat back down on my bed, having stood when Leo arrived for a reason unknown to me. Maybe it was an unconscious want—to hug him and act like things weren't fucked between us. 'And we can all agree it's because of them they've taken Ollie in, yes?'

The group nodded or mumbled their agreement.

'Alright then.' I clapped my hands together. 'Now the question we need to answer is how?'

'Not why?' Griff asked, scooting back on my bed so his back rested up against the wall. Since he and Clo split, my bed was his go to seat these days.

Which left Leo in an awkward position. He hovered in the middle of the room, as did Clover, who had stopped her pacing and looked from left to right. If he chose my bed, it may come across like the three of us were against her, but if he sat on hers, he could end up pissing off everyone in the room.

I patted the bed next to me, making the choice for him. I'd rather Clo be pissed at me than anybody else. Leo came willingly and sat beside me, a large enough gap between us for it not to be improper.

'We know the why,' I said once the awkward moment ended. 'They hate him and Orlando wants his life and blah blah blah. No, the *how* of it all is most important now.' I ran my hands through my curled locks, breaking apart the knots that had formed during the day. 'Where was Ollie when Ophelia left the clearing?'

Blank stares came back to me.

'What?'

'None of us know.' Griff winced. 'He disappeared around the same time as you.'

'Oh.' I shook my head, thinking back to the party, and how we left things before I wandered off. 'So he's unaccounted for?'

Griff nodded.

'Not ideal.' My small laugh sounded false. 'You reckon that's what they have on him?'

'Well, yeah, plus the fact he and Orlando share DNA.'

'But Orlando doesn't have an alibi, either?'

Leo coughed and shifted on the bed, the mattress depressing to the point I nearly flew off. 'He says he was with you …'

'Why haven't the police questioned me about it? Surely they're not taking the prick's word for it?'

'But there's a witness,' Leo mumbled.

'People can't tell the two of them apart most of the time!' I stood up, too mad to stay still, needing to pace to keep the darker thoughts at bay. 'And in the dark in the woods? Per-lease!'

'They were wearing different clothes,' Clo pointed out. She was sitting on her bed, back pressed up against the wall, watching Griff and Leo apprehensively. 'It's not like before where Orlando's worn the same as Ollie to throw us all off. He doesn't have to anymore. He's out in the open these days.'

'Don't I know it,' I grumbled. My head was getting a little dizzy from the small space I had to pace in, but it didn't stop me. 'Let me guess, the witness is you?' Mine and Leo's gazes locked, and he didn't even need to answer, because I could read the truth in his expression. 'Of course it is.'

'I got questioned, and I told my truth,' he replied, tactful as ever. 'I saw Orlando follow you around the time they were asking about. I didn't lie about that.'

Okay, so he had me there. But … 'Why wouldn't you talk to me about it first?'

'They didn't give me time to. Orlando summoned me to Hawthorn House, and the detectives were there waiting for me.'

I scoffed. 'Why would he have given you time to? He *knows* he wasn't with me.'

'In my defence,' Leo put his hands up, 'I thought he *was* with you. I saw him storm away not long before I bumped into you.'

'You were pretty drunk,' I said. 'But it had to be longer than you thought.'

'If I go to the detectives and tell them I've changed my version of events, they'll assume I'm doing it to save Ollie.'

'True ...' I rubbed my temples, the ache setting in. Being a student at Hawthorn was never simple. 'Okay, so they don't know where he was and they may have his DNA linking him to Ophelia. Anything else?'

Leo's face scrunched. Jesus, was there anything more he could add to make it even worse?

'Yes, Leo?' I crossed my arms.

'It may have to do with the fact Orlando told them Ollie would do anything to make him disappear. Everybody knows Orlando is out on bail, so any crime would have him locked up with no chance of freedom until trial.'

'So, they think this is Ollie's revenge?'

'Suppose so.'

Thirty-Seven

'DO YOU THINK KANT HAD ISSUES?'

'Do I think Kant had issues?' I repeated Griff's question, raising my eyebrows in his direction. 'In what sense?'

Griff shrugged. 'I don't know. Think you'd have to have them to become a philosopher, right?'

'He was a philosopher back when things had less explanation than now, but yeah, I'm sure he had issues. The man believed it's always wrong to lie, so I'm sure that caused him some aggro.'

'Clouds, you believe it's wrong to lie.'

'Not going to make speeches or write essays about it, though,' I pointed out. 'Plus, I believe it's wrong, yeah, but there are times where I still do it.'

'Most people lie. Or maybe they hide or disguise the truth to make it more palatable.'

'Suppose you're right.' I guess he'd given me the segue I'd been waiting for. I wanted to tell him the moment I got back from *The Sanctum* meeting, but life got in the way.

Mainly my boyfriend being arrested for something his identical twin brother did and is now framing him for. 'There's something I wanted to tell you, but I haven't known how.'

Griff paused his writing and turned his head. 'Okay ... Nothing too serious, I hope?'

I opened my mouth, then closed it again. *That's it, Skylar. Resemble a fish, why don't you?*

'Sky?' Griff asked after a minute of me being unable to push the words past my lips. 'Is everything okay?'

'So, you know how Ollie and I hid during the *Sanctum* meeting?'

He nodded. 'Yeah ...'

'They said something about your parents.'

'What about them?'

'They confirmed their deaths weren't an accident. I'm sorry.'

Tears flooded his eyes, and he gulped. 'What are you sorry for? Not like you killed them.'

'I should've told you sooner,' I said. 'Things have been busy, but that's no excuse. Ollie and I wanted to tell you together, but we never got the chance.' Tears filled my eyes, matching his. I hated seeing Griff sad. 'I am so sorry, baby boy.'

His voice cracked. 'It's not your fault.'

I pulled him into a hug, ignoring the stares from the other students in the lesson. Lucky for us, the bell rang to signal lunch and everybody filed out.

'Can we stay, sir?' I asked Mr Sommers. 'We'll close the door on our way out.'

'Of course,' he said, putting his things into his briefcase. I sent a smile his way. He was by far one of our nicest teachers. 'Please close the door, otherwise who knows what I'll come back to.'

'I promise,' I said, waving him out the door. I focused my attention back on Griff. 'Do you want to stay here, or shall we head to the dorms?'

'Can we stay here a while?' Griff whispered. His bottom lip wobbled, and the tears in my eyes grew thicker. 'I don't think I'm ready to go through the halls yet.'

'We won't move until you're ready,' I said, pulling him into a deep hug. 'Well, that's not strictly true. We won't move until we get kicked out.'

His chuckle vibrated my body. 'Thanks, Clouds.'

'No problem. I've always got your back.'

'It's nice to have it confirmed,' he murmured, leaning back a little. 'I've always thought something was fishy about it all.'

The freckles on his scrunched-up nose caught the light. Griffin Cooper was a thing of beauty. His picture should come beside the dictionary definition so everybody can witness it for themselves.

'But I never thought I'd find out the truth,' he continued talking, unaware of where my thoughts had run off to. 'I was supposed to die too.'

'There's no way to know for definite.' I gripped his forearms. 'They didn't mention you, plus, they tampered with the car itself so they had no way of knowing who would get hurt.'

'Can't decide what's worse. An attack intended to take us all out, or one where they hoped for one and anyone else was an added bonus.'

I winced. His anger wasn't misplaced, and having nothing to do or say to make it better didn't sit right in my gut.

'I'm so glad you're alive, Griff, and I'm gutted I'll never get to meet my aunt and uncle.'

'Thank you,' he mumbled. 'And thank you for telling me the truth, even though it was hard.'

'I hate that I had to.'

<hr>

'I'll have the veggie burger with chips, please.' I handed the waiter my menu and leaned back in my chair.

The dining room was pretty quiet for a Wednesday night. Orlando and the last remaining O girl were sitting with Cordelia and Celia at their usual table, holding court over the school in a way they seemed to get a kick from.

'What a bastard, sitting up there all smug and smarmy,' I said, bitterness filling my mouth at the sight. 'Acting like he isn't in the process of getting away with murder.'

'He's out on bail for another crime,' Clo said. She got out her lip balm and pouted, covering her lips in the stuff, before putting it back in her blazer pocket. 'Another *murder*.'

'Exactly!' I screeched. Heads turned to our table. A flush

covered my cheeks. Even though since joining Hawthorn I'd come under a lot of scrutiny, and had a lot of attention my way, I still hated being in the limelight. Usually, I had Ollie by my side, which softened the blow a little, but with him gone, things were off-kilter.

I sent an evil glare Orlando's way.

'Stop trying to antagonise him, Sky,' Clo said, handing her menu to the waiter as he made his way around our table. 'He's not worth it.'

'Easy to say, but harder to do. It's like I can't help but think about it all the fucking time. And whenever I try to stop and think of something else, my brain somehow links it back to him, or to Ollie, or to the current situation. Fuck, the other night I lay in bed thinking about cute cat videos, then about cat milk, then about dairy products in general, then cheese, then the word turophile, then the time Ollie joked about my love of cheese the week I learned said word.' I took a large gasping breath, not having taken one while talking.

Griff and Clover both gawked at me open-mouthed, pausing in their actions. Clo had a lip balm halfway to her lips, and Griff was mid chin scratch.

How to explain my brain to somebody who didn't under-stand? Or didn't have the same way of thinking?

'Well,' Clo said, breaking the silence, 'that's a lot.'

'Yep. It's constant. A whirring in my brain I can never turn off.'

'Sounds painful,' said Griff. 'I can always distract you if you think it'll help?'

'I am sort of intrigued,' I said, and I meant it. The idea of Griff attempting to distract me amused the fuck out of me. 'How would you distract me?'

'For starters, I could tell you about the time Clover ...' Griff continued talking, and I nodded in what I believed were the right places, but the words weren't going in.

The side of my head burned; a certain someone's eyes on me, no doubt.

It was hard to ignore somebody when they took up such a

large presence in your day. Every time I walked down the corridor, his booming voice or barked laughter filtered into my ears, or I spotted him standing with the girls all hanging off him like flies on honey.

Leo took the empty seat to my right, catching me off guard and dragging me out of my darkening thoughts.

'Hey.'

'Hey ... You lost or something?'

He chuckled. 'No, funny enough. Thought I'd come and ask you something in person rather than sending a text.'

'Ask away.'

I ignored the disproving stares from across the table.

Leo had come and talked to us when Ollie got arrested and told us all he knew. To me, that meant he was on our side. Even if he hadn't voiced the sentiment yet.

'Will you meet me tonight?'

'Where? When?' I frowned. 'Stop being cryptic.'

'You know where and when.' He got up and went over to the staff table.

I shrugged at Clo and Griff's questioning faces.

Suppose I was off to the secret tunnels at midnight.

Thirty-Eight

LEO OPENED the door to the tunnel the second I knocked.

'Stutter. Fancy seeing you here.'

I narrowed my eyes. 'Yes, fancy seeing me at a location at the time you requested.'

'I wasn't sure if you'd show up.' He shrugged, opening the door wider so I could step inside the small space alongside him. 'We've not been friends lately.'

'We're not *not* friends.' There didn't seem to be a better way to put it. I didn't dislike Leo—I just didn't know if I could trust him. And trust was super important to me when it came to friends and those I let in. My whole life I hadn't had anyone close who wanted to know me, and now I did. Well, it made sense I wanted to trust them.

'But you still don't trust me,' he murmured.

'Are you a mind reader?'

The two of us headed further into the hallway, one behind the other, until we reached the intersection. His shoulders moved from his laughter. 'No. I just know you well.'

'Yeah, I suppose you do.'

My tone didn't hold any of the sorrow it would have a couple of months ago. Things were slotting back into their correct place. When I thought of mine and Leo's brief relationship, I chose to remember the happy times. Not much point in dwelling on the past when so much was happening in the present, right?

'What did you want to talk about?' I asked, crossing my arms across my chest. The stance of somebody who meant business and wasn't leaving the tunnel until we'd resolved everything between us. 'And why couldn't you talk about it while the others were around?'

'Because it sounds silly.'

'Leo, nothing you say ever sounds silly.' Even the thought of it was absurd. Leo Hawthorn was the furthest thing from *silly*. 'You're overthinking it.'

'Maybe, but I didn't want to risk it.' He took a deep breath. 'I know I'm a broken record and I've said it all before, but I can't go on knowing you think poorly of me.'

'Huh?'

Well, that was unexpected.

'I know you said on your birthday you believe I didn't have a choice in what happened to me, and I know I've said sorry more times than I can count, but ...'

'But?' The frown remained on my face. 'Leo, I can't do or say anything more than I already have. I forgive you. I accept your apology. I know you did what you thought was best and tried to change the course of things when you realised you loved me.'

It was the first time since we split up—if you could call a massive betrayal resulting in us not talking for weeks a mere break up—I mentioned the word love. The two of us had tiptoed around it in the months since everything blew up, neither wanting to broach the topic first.

I had loved Leo, and he had loved me. Even if we hadn't outright said the words, we'd made it clear we were falling and if things had continued, it would have been a full-blown love affair.

Fortunately—or unfortunately, I suppose, depending on who you asked—things didn't continue.

'I'm not worthy of your forgiveness.'

'That's a you problem,' I said, gently. 'I can't help or dictate how you feel.'

His responding sigh depleted his whole body. 'I know. It's a hurdle I haven't figured out how to cross yet, but it's one killing me inside.'

'Is there anything I can do to make it any better?'

'You've already done so much. Sky, you're nice and supportive and understanding and forgiving when I deserve none of it.'

'I don't think that's the truth of it. You're making me sound a much better person than I am.'

'Well, that's how I see you,' he said, his eyes kind.

'And I don't see you as harshly as you see yourself, so I guess we're even.' I put his hand in mine. 'Leo, we're good, I promise. So no more apologies and no more tiptoeing around me, okay?'

'Okay.'

'I mean it,' I said, reprimanding. 'And I expect you to help us brainstorm a plan for the upcoming ball.'

'Not sure what I can do. *The Sanctum* will all be there.'

I stared at him blankly. Any second now ...

'Oh.' He laughed. 'Yeah, sure. I'll see what I can come up with.'

'Once Ollie's back, we can figure out our plan of action.' And I meant it, because in my head, no reality existed where Ollie didn't come back. He couldn't go to prison for Orlando's wrongs. He couldn't. 'I don't want to do anything until he's here, too.'

'I get it.' Leo's hand twitched.

'I suppose you know about what our parents got up to while they were here?' I changed the subject, then corrected myself. 'Well, not your mum. She's a sweetheart, as always.'

'She sends her love.' His teeth shone when he smiled. 'I think she loves you and Clover more than she loves me.'

'That's not true!' I chuckled. 'The woman dotes on you. She'd do anything to make you happy, Leo. Wish my mum would act the same way towards me.'

'Cora's a funny one,' he said, and I rolled my eyes. Did he mean funny *ha-ha* or funny *odd*? Both counted, actually.

'I used to hate her so much, but now, I don't know what emotion I have.'

'What's changed?'

'Meeting you guys, coming to Hawthorn, meeting my dad ...

All of it has made me question and overthink about everything. Yes, she's still crap and has a scummy husband, but I think she's trying?' I shook my head, the confusion causing a headache. 'I can't fault her for that.'

'How are things going between you and your dad?'

Leo took his hand from mine and slumped down to sit on the floor, his back pressed up against the wall. I followed him, my aching feet ready to have a little rest.

'Alright, I guess.' I picked at the drawstring on my hoodie, folding the aglet within the cord and then unravelling it again. 'I'm not sure I'll get used to having a dad who wants to talk to me. We've been texting, and I called him one time to warn him to never drive his car anywhere, but it's still early days.'

Leo nodded, understanding. 'It must be weird building a relationship with him now at your age. Fuck, I struggle sometimes with my dad and I've known him my whole life.'

'Edward's intimidating to be fair.'

'Believe it or not, he's mellowed out in the last couple of years.'

'Really?' I tried to imagine an even more intimidating Edward, but couldn't. He had always been nice to me, but I could tell he was a man used to getting his own way, and fast. 'No, you're right, I can't believe it.'

'He keeps calling, trying to find out what I know of Orlando's plans and of *The Sanctum*, but I keep ignoring him. I'm not sure what I'm even allowed to say to him.'

'How come he isn't a member?'

'From what Orlando has said, and let's take it all with a pinch of salt, he left. Didn't want to be a part of it all anymore. Same with Henry.'

'When?'

'Not long after they were recruited. It must all tie into whatever happened when they all went to Hawthorn.'

'But *what* happened?' I sighed. 'I feel like we're no closer to knowing than we were before my dad showed up and we started snooping in houses and infiltrating meetings, etcetera.'

It was all so fucking frustrating!

The closer we got, the further away we managed to slide in some roundabout, twisted way.

Bet Orlando and his wicked mother constantly laughed at us behind our backs. I still didn't understand the dynamic between the two of them—not sure I even wanted to understand—and as of late, Orlando had been keeping his distance from me. No doubt for some nefarious reason.

'There has to be a way for us to figure it out. The article we found in Hawthorn House spoke of a girl dying, right?'

I recalled the article in my mind. 'Yeah, Sandy Parks. It said *The Set* and *Sect* were outside the bathroom she died in.'

'And named our parents as being complicit,' Leo added. 'In case anybody at school didn't know who they meant.'

'If it's anything like now, adding their names wasn't necessary. Whoever wrote it wanted their crimes to be known to everyone. Reckon that's why The Hawthorn Herald school newspaper got sacked off?'

'Must be. Can't have something like that falling into the wrong hands.'

'Like the police?'

'Them.' Leo nodded. 'But also the parents of Sandy Parks. I did some digging, and she was a scholarship student.'

'Sounds familiar, doesn't it? Some jumped up Hawthorns, bullying somebody because their family isn't rich enough for their liking,' I said. My stomach soured. 'They do say history repeats itself if people don't learn from it.'

'In our defence,' Leo said, putting his hand in the air, open palm facing me, 'your family, at least one half of it, is pretty fucking rich.'

'So it was justified?' I laughed, without humour. 'You guys make it hard to forget when you act so entitled and justified in what you did to me.'

'No, it doesn't. At all. And for the record, we are trying to be better. Or at least I am. I'm assuming Griff and Ollie are, too.'

I reached out and put my hand on his forearm, intending it to soothe him. I wanted him to know how much I could tell he was doing all he could to change.

'Forget what I said. It was shitty of me. I know the three of you have remorse for what you did and that you've changed. I'm being sensitive.'

'Well, you do have a lot going on.'

I tutted. 'An understatement of sorts, but it also downplays everything you have going on. How are you? *Really*?'

'I ...'

'We're in *private* private, Leo,' I said with as much emphasis as possible. 'Nobody need ever know.'

He sighed, his body slumping further down the wall. 'I suppose I'm not used to talking about myself.'

'Take this chance and run with it because who knows when you'll get it again.'

He cracked a tiny smile. 'Everything's wrong. Out of my control. Like I'm spiralling and there's nothing to be done to stop it. If I don't do as they ask, they'll hurt you all, and I could never live if they did. If they kill me, then so be it.'

'Don't even joke about that!' The thought alone turned my innards into twists and turns. 'Nobody is killing you anytime soon, Leo Hawthorn. We're both going to live long and fulfilled lives and in thirty-plus years, we'll reminisce back on all this absolute *bullshit* and laugh our arses off.'

Leo didn't seem convinced about the future I painted. 'I hope you're right.'

'When am I ever wrong?' I'd been wrong a bloody lot in the last eighteen months, but not like I was about to point it out. 'Whatever happens, we'll be side by side and face it all together.'

'Is that a promise?'

'No. It's a vow.'

Thirty-Nine

OLLIE

ARRIVING BACK AT HAWTHORN, the thing I wanted most was to see my girl. Hug her. Hold her. Whisper all the things in her ear, and never let her go.

Being apart from her during such a tumultuous time pained me physically.

All because of my stupid fucking *brother*.

The bastard had set me up, probably with the help of his fucking awful mother, and I couldn't wait to see the smug look on his face wiped off when I showed up for breakfast in the morning.

I'd messaged Skylar while in the car on the way back and had expected her to be waiting for me at the bottom of the school steps, but it wasn't Skylar who waited for me.

No.

It was Leo.

I got out of the car and made my way over to him.

'Where's Sky?'

He nudged his head towards the school. 'Waiting in your room.'

'And she's not here because ...'

'Because I asked her to stay in your room and said I'd meet you instead.'

'And you did that because ...'

'Because I wanted to talk to you, of course.'

'Of course.' The two of us walked up the steps in unison. 'But why?'

'I wanted to ask what happened while you were gone. Orlando's been tight-lipped about it all, which is shady enough, and I don't like being in the dark.'

'No,' I said, a tad dry. 'You prefer to keep other people in the dark.'

'Are we still not over that?' Leo asked, and I wanted to punch him in the face—again. It seemed my previous punch wasn't hard enough to make a point. 'I've said sorry.'

'Have you?' I wracked my brain, unable to recall the apology he spoke of. 'Did you speak it out loud, or was it all in your head?'

Leo rubbed his jaw. 'Look, mate, if I didn't ... I'm saying it now.'

'Saying what?'

Leo's shoulders moved with the force of his responding sigh. 'I'm saying sorry, alright?'

Most people wouldn't take his words as an apology, and usually I wouldn't either, but after a night in prison for something I didn't do, let's say I was a little out of sorts.

And by out of sorts, I meant a lot more forgiving and understanding than I normally would be.

On any other day, I'd never let him get away with something so half-hearted.

'Alright. Water under the bridge and all that shite.' We continued walking at a slow pace. 'Not much happened. The police were wankers as usual and kept accusing me of killing Ophelia and had DNA to prove it.'

'So, how are you out here and not still in there?'

'I pointed out how their DNA evidence isn't from fingerprints and without those there's no way of knowing if it was me or Orlando they were after, and seeing as Orlando is already out on bail ...' I let the sentence hang in the air. 'Well, they were uncertain enough to let me go for now. That, and our lawyers got involved and maybe my dad paid money or something.

Didn't stick around long enough to ask once they told me I could leave.'

'But they'll be back?'

'With bells on.' I shook my head, my frustration towards the situation creeping into my mind and getting the better of me. Everything right now was a constant battle. Orlando, Winifred, *The Sanctum*. Even my relationship with Skylar to a degree was a battle, but mainly because I kept opening my mouth to tell her I loved her, but something would come along and interrupt us. 'Wouldn't surprise me if they tried to find a way to take both of us. Or maybe they'll see who offers more money and decide, corrupt bastards.'

Leo nodded, understanding the way the Hawthorn police worked.

Hard to remember a time in my life when people weren't rotten to the core. Maybe they always had been, and I was too young to realise.

But the one person I could rely on to never act rotten was Skylar, and as much as mine and Leo's conversation was important, it still wasn't where I wanted to be.

'Contact your dad and get the best lawyers on it, in case they come for you again.'

I nodded my agreement. 'Already done. Dad's hatred towards Winifred is the strongest it's ever been, so for once he's on my side with no fight.'

'A miracle.'

Leo's dry tone made me smile against my will. It was a miracle. One I doubted would repeat anytime soon.

'A miracle indeed.'

I LEFT Leo at the entrance to the student rooms, the black door at the end of the hallway beckoning me. Calling to me in a way I couldn't ignore a moment longer.

Skylar waited for me inside, which was all that mattered.

Other students milled around, but I ignored them all. Nobody would find my behaviour unusual, because I usually ignored everybody, anyway. It was rare somebody was worth my notice in this shit hole, after all.

Skylar waited for me on the other side of the door, already dressed in her nightdress ready for bed.

She squealed when she saw me. *Damn.* My heart kicked up a notch.

'Yay, you're back!'

She ran into my open arms, and I hugged her tight, breathing in the scent of her. It grounded me, being so close to her. Fuck, I loved her.

I wasn't sure if she also loved me too.

'How was it? How are you? Are you okay?' All her questions ran into one another, coming out in a jumble of gibberish. 'Did they hurt you? Were they wankers? Are you okay?'

'If you'd take a breath, maybe I could answer one of your questions.' I chuckled.

She laughed back. 'Yeah, sorry. I've hated not being able to talk to you. See you. It sucked.'

'It sucked hard,' I agreed. 'But I'm back now and everything's all good.'

'You mean *for* now?'

I nodded. 'For now, yes. I'm sure tomorrow will bring another battle of sorts.'

'It's tiring, isn't it?' she asked. 'Always fighting battles.'

The question was rhetorical, but I inclined my head. Of course, it was fucking tiring. We needed a distraction, and I had the perfect thing in mind.

'Come shower with me,' I said, a cheeky grin on my lips. 'I need to wash the dirt off.'

'I can wait here,' she said. 'No need for me to come.'

'I don't want to leave your side,' I said, batting my eyelashes at her playfully. 'I've missed you, Sky. In more ways than one.'

I raised my eyebrows at her suggestively, hunger stirring in my belly as I pictured myself pressed up against her in the shower.

Skylar smiled and rolled her eyes. 'You just want to see me naked.'

'I'd never turn down an opportunity to see you naked,' I said. 'But I promise it isn't about that.' Then I coughed, unable to lie to her wide-eyed gaze. 'Well, not entirely.'

'Fine, I'll bite.' Her voice was light, but an eagerness lingered in her eyes and the smile on her lips matched mine.

We both stripped on our way to the shower, leaving a path of clothes in our wake as we walked to the ensuite, a sense of ease settling between us again that made me sigh in relief. Our connection grew stronger every day, and I was so fucking lucky to call her mine.

Leaning into my shower, Skylar turned on the water, letting it warm up before getting in. I'm sure she also did this to give me a better view of her bum, which I appreciated. Giving it a slap, I growled instructions in her ear to let me in. She was under the warm water and I was chilly—never a good look.

Sky shivered lightly but obeyed without question, moving further into the shower to make room for me. Honestly, I was just glad I didn't have a huge shower, so there was nowhere for me to go but up against her soft skin.

Her body stayed still as she faced me, anticipation and curiosity on her face as she watched me. Smirking, I pressed a firm kiss to her lips as I reached past her for her shampoo. I continued devouring her lips and tongue as I popped it open and poured it on to her lilac hair, already soaked from the hot water pouring down.

How did I get so lucky?

I ended the kiss and moved Skylar into a better position so I could focus on washing her hair. This delayed gratification would make it better for both of us, so I did my best to ignore my hunger for her pressed against me, focusing on my fingers instead.

'Are you sure you're okay?' she asked, her voice mumbled. 'I should be the one pampering you.'

'Don't be silly,' I replied. 'You're the important one. No matter what happens.'

She reached up and stopped my hands and turned to face me. I bit down the laugh bubbling up at the view of her foamy scalp. She bit her bottom lip and smiled.

'Yeah, yeah, I look funny. But being serious for a moment,' she said, taking my hands in hers. 'You're important as me.' Then she blinked and shook her head, the bubbles in her hair flicking out and landing on my chest. 'To me, you're the *most* important, okay?'

I swallowed. It hadn't got easier to hear nice things from her about me, but I loved hearing them, nonetheless.

'Okay?' she repeated, more forceful, this time. The conviction in her tone made me love her more ... but now wasn't the time to tell her.

My voice broke when I said, 'Okay.'

Sky nodded with determination.

'Good.' She turned around once more, putting the front of her body under the spray of the water. 'Now, get back to massaging my head.'

'Yes, sir.'

We fell into a comfortable silence, and when Sky turned to put her head under the water to wash off the shampoo, she smiled shyly at me. 'You're pretty perfect, you know that, right?'

'You may have mentioned it once or twice.'

I put some body wash on a washcloth and placed it on her body, starting at her shoulders. My hand made a circular motion, sweeping across her collarbone, down each arm and back again, before moving to her breasts. I circled around them first, ensuring everything got coated in soap before moving my gentle attention to her nipples, already gathered into stiff peaks that had me aching to tug at them with my teeth.

Instead, I played with them with my other hand, amazed at how soft and smooth they were with the soap.

'Don't stop,' she murmured.

I hadn't planned to, but hearing her voice the command had

me growing harder. There was something extremely sexy about Sky asking for what she wanted. Demanding it, in fact.

Back when I met her, she would never have uttered such a sentence.

Her newfound confidence was so fucking attractive it almost hurt to watch.

I continued to wash her, turning her around so she could lean back into me as I worked. Soft moans of enjoyment left her lips. 'Mmm.'

In a slow tease, I trailed my hand down ...

I placed the cloth down on the corner shelf and touched her pussy with my right hand, grazing my fingertips across her sensitive flesh, hoping to elicit another moan from her lips.

As soon as I brushed against her clitoris, finding it with instinctive precision, Skylar arched against me, panting with need. 'Ollie.'

I put one finger inside her tight walls, and then followed it soon after with a second, picking up speed.

'Yes?' I bit at her earlobe and moved us so we were both under the warm water, Skylar's back pressed up against the wall tiles. 'Come for me, baby. I need you to fall apart while I hold you up.'

Her pleasure mounted faster as I spoke, using my thumb to rub her clit as I continued to move my fingers. When Sky came, her moan had me nearly coming too. The way she choked back a scream while trembling in my arms was pure heaven.

I didn't give her long to recover, moving her so her tits pressed up against the wall, her head turned towards me, eyes dazed but still hungry. Her back arched; her body ready for me.

'God, you're too damn sexy for your own good,' I growled, thrusting my cock inside, giving her no other warning. She was already slick from her recent orgasm and tight with need. It was a damn good thing I knew how to hold myself off, or I would have finished in seconds from how perfect she was.

As I moved inside her, awed at the way she gripped my cock, she whimpered, a wordless beg for more. For me to give her another release. *Mine,* I thought to myself fondly, grabbing her hips to pull her tighter against me. *All mine.*

Her sounds of enjoyment increased as I moved faster, harder, my breath coming in controlled bursts as I did my best to bring her to climax before I got there myself. Thankfully, as I teetered on the edge, Skylar let out a long, high pitched 'Fuck!'

Her walls clenched around me so hard I wouldn't have been able to fight off my own even if I tried. Grunting, my body released its load, pulsing for longer than I had anything to give.

Flipping Skylar around to face me, I put my forehead on hers, catching my breath for a moment before kissing her adoringly, my hands resting on her waist. She kissed me back, and it hit me like a bolt of lightning that this was the girl I wanted to spend forever with. I didn't know what I'd do without her by my side, and I didn't want to think of a scenario where I would be without her.

I needed to tell her.

And soon.

Forty

THE MORNING after Ollie's return, and our great night of sex and intimacy, a thick, cream card invitation slid underneath his bedroom door.

It read:

Mister Oliver Brandon and Miss Skylar Crescent,
You are cordially invited to Hawthorn Academy's Charity Masquerade
Ball
Date: Saturday 2nd July
Dress code: Formal attire
Masks: Required
We look forward to your presence.

'Fun,' I said, my tone dry, after reading the invitation and passing it over to Ollie. 'Reckon the others have one too?'

'I'd say so. It's odd we're being invited as guests.' Ollie rubbed his chin and my eyes followed the movement, fixated. 'Maybe our parents have paid our fee.'

'Fee?'

'It's a charity event, Skylar,' he said, as if his words were all the explanation needed. Stupid rich-all-his-life bastard.

'And that means ...'

'That means everybody in attendance will have paid an exorbitant fee for their tickets.' He laughed, his eyes wrinkled in mirth. 'I forget how little you know about this life.'

'Oh, ha, ha. Laugh at the scholarship kid.'

He stopped his laughter. 'I'm sorry.'

'I'm teasing you,' I said. 'You're not wrong, in a way. I don't know much about this kind of life. How exorbitant a fee are we talking here? And who would have paid for me?'

'Your dad or mine,' Ollie said. 'No idea of the exact amount, but we're talking in the thousands.'

'The thousands?' My tone was incredulous, because *I* was incredulous. Even after the time I'd spent around the kids here at Hawthorn—and their parents—I still couldn't get over how much money they waved around when it suited them. There were people who lived on the estate I grew up in who had barely enough money for bread and milk, yet these people had never known a day of true hardship in their entire existence. It soured my stomach.

Was I part of the problem? Had I acted grateful enough for all I now had?

Becoming a student at Hawthorn wasn't something I asked for, yet somebody footed the bill for my time here.

'Yep, and the money all goes to a charity of the school's choosing, which means a charity of the *parent's* choosing.'

'Right ...' It all sounded a little dodgy to me, but what did I know? Not a lot, let's be honest. 'So, are we going to go?'

'Yeah.' Ollie threw the duvet off himself and sat upright. 'Somebody has gone to great lengths to invite us. Can't disappoint them.'

'And I suppose we'll need to look the part?' I tried to keep my tone light, but underneath, I was a little giddy. One thing I rather liked about this new life I found myself in was the opportunity to dress up and act fancy. It still made my eyes water to know how much my formal dresses cost, but the moment I put them on, it became easy to forget such a slight detail.

Ollie, knowing me well enough now to see through my bullshit facades, smiled. 'I suppose so. What a heavy task that will be for you.'

I sighed, playing along. ''Tis a heavy burden, but one must make the most of it.'

'Yes, you sound *so* put out by it.' Ollie laughed. 'I'll arrange an appointment for you. We've got a couple of months.'

'Thank you.' I sat down on the edge of the bed and leaned forward to place a grateful kiss on his lips. 'Have I told you how much I appreciate you?'

'You may have mentioned it once or twice, yeah.'

'Good.' The invitation remained in my hands and I couldn't help fiddling with the corners of the card, folding and bending them over. 'Maybe we could use this ball to our advantage?'

'What have you got in mind?'

'I haven't figured that part out yet.' I waved the invitation around. 'But this could be the chance we've all been waiting for.'

'Are you suggesting ...'

'*The Sanctum* will be in attendance, right?' I smiled, the certainty of my words growing. 'So, why don't we make a plan of sorts?'

Ollie moved closer to me. 'We can talk to the others later. See what they think?'

'Don't see why they'd be against it, but sure, I'll message them all in a bit.' I moved off the bed and put the invitation down on the bedside cabinet. 'We didn't have any plans tonight, did we?'

Ollie shook his head, his dark hair ruffled from sleep.

'Nothing we can't postpone until after we meet with them.' His eyebrows waggled, and I laughed at his implication. As if we hadn't spent enough *alone* time together since he got back from prison on Friday night. We hadn't seen anyone since he got back, too wrapped up in each other, but that needed to change if we were to get ahead of the game.

'If there's time. You know we won't be able to meet until much, *much* later. Can't have any eyes on us and we don't want to be spotted by Orlando or Ms Hawthorn.'

'Those two rats will have scuttered back down to the sewers by then.'

The image made me smile.

'We can hope.'

'So, we all got the invitations, yes?'

My gaze travelled across the room, taking in the sight of Clo, Griff, Leo, and Ollie standing in front of me.

Clover had a bored expression on her face, but I doubted it was from being around us—more like boredom from us being targeted all the time.

Griff had his usual cheeky smile plastered on his face, more than ready for the scheming to take place.

Leo, who could match Clover for the most bored expression in the room, stood silently, hands clasped in front of his waist. He wore grey jogging bottoms and a white T-shirt and even though my deeper fondness for him had dissipated, I could still appreciate how mighty fine he looked.

Then there was Ollie, the happiest I'd seen him in a long while, which was an enormous surprise seeing as his week had been more than a little trying.

'To the masquerade ball?' Griff asked, and I nodded. 'Yep. And we all know I don't have any parents who would've paid for my ticket.'

'They were from *The Sanctum*,' Leo said, as casual as anything and bloody hell it made me want to deck him. My emotions were always so up and down where he was concerned, never knowing whether to be happy we'd sorted shit out or mad he was still a vexing bastard on the daily.

'You know this for definite?' Ollie asked, his body turning in Leo's direction.

'I do.' Leo blinked, not one bit threatened by Ollie's stance or glowering eyes. 'They're planning something.'

'Like?' I said, stepping in before Ollie could. 'How do you know this?'

'No idea what.' Leo shrugged, nonchalant. 'I know, because they said so at the last meeting. They want all of us to be there, including the parents. '

'Wonderful,' Clo muttered. 'Assume my parents don't make the cut?'

'No,' Leo said in a clipped tone. 'They don't.'

I rolled my eyes. The two of them could sort their squabble at a later time. There were far more important things to deal with than their shared history.

'Cut it out,' I snapped. 'Bigger fish to fry over here.'

I gave Clo a stern look, and she raised her eyebrows in response.

Yeah, yeah, Clover Luck. Act like you've got no idea why I'm repri-manding you.

I continued talking, giving neither of them time to say anything. 'If they want our parents there too, then something sinister must be afoot.'

'Afoot?' Griff's grin grew. 'Are you well, Clouds?'

'Am I well?' I asked, his change of direction confusing me enough to sidetrack my thought train.

'Yes,' he replied. 'Only it seems you've swallowed some kind of old-timey dictionary.'

My laughter came out as a harsh bark. 'An old-timey dictio-nary? Honestly, Griff, I wonder about what goes on in your head sometimes.'

The word afoot wasn't too old-fashioned, right?

I didn't think so, but then again, maybe it was? Eurgh! Now I wanted to get my phone and search for the origin of the word. I'd have to do it later, if I remembered.

' ... *Sanctum.*'

Fucking hell. I needed to pay more attention to the conversa-tion going on instead of my own mind. No idea who had spoken, but I hadn't heard a word of it.

'Sorry, what?' I asked, my voice sounding loud to my ears.

Griff scrunched his nose. 'What part?'

'Err, all of it?' I gave them what I hoped to be an impish grin.

'I asked whether there's anything we can do if *The Sanctum* targets us at this thing,' Griff said. 'If they don't talk of their plan in front of Leo, then we've got no heads up. Plus, it could be anything.'

'True. However, we could try to use the crowd to our benefit,' I said.

Ollie came closer and took my hand in his. He pulled me to his side and placed his arm casually around my waist. I couldn't decide if it was his version of staking a claim or whether he wanted to touch me and craved physical contact the way I did. I hated how it made me more aware of Leo, though. Like I was rubbing it in his face or something.

I know, I know. It was silly of me to think like that, but I couldn't help it.

There was nothing to do but get over it—and myself. *I'm not special.*

'What you got in mind, Stutter?' Leo said, unaffected by Ollie's new position next to me.

'Well,' I chuckled, 'I sort of hoped the five of us could figure something out together.'

'So, you're hoping to use my brains for your own gain,' Griff said, in between bites of a strawberry cable. It must have been a tough one, as he yanked it with his teeth so hard I thought they would break if he kept going.

'Yep, pretty much,' I confirmed. 'My brains want to sit this one out, thank you.'

'How about Ollie asking you to dance in front of everyone?' Clover asked. 'Once you're dancing, Orlando will butt in, I'm sure of it.'

'Okay ... And then?'

Clo shrugged. 'I don't know. Piss him off somehow. Rile him up. Get him to admit something or reveal *The Sanctum*.' She shrugged again. 'I'm sure you can think of something.'

'It's not a poor plan,' Ollie said.

'It's not a *good* one either,' Leo said.

Clo saw red. She snapped, 'Got a better idea, boring bollocks?'

Which shut Leo right up, because instead of snapping something inane back, he kept his lips pressed tight together in a thin line.

A smile crept on to my lips. I couldn't help it. Sometimes watching the two of them was like watching a train wreck—one you couldn't look away from, no matter how hard you tried.

'Let's be civil,' I said, before the situation could devolve further. I clapped my hands together. 'Let's make a plan.'

Forty-One

THE END OF JUNE ARRIVED. Which meant, you guessed it, exam time.

Finally, we would sit our final exams to determine how good of a life we'd have when we left the halls of Hawthorn.

And I was so ready to ace everything. I'd been studying—somewhat—and I knew I would do better than I had the previous June in my mocks. It also absolutely baffled me to realise it had been an entire year since the failure of those exams. So much had happened before them, but a lot had happened afterwards, too.

It had been an entire year since I had come back to school, revenge plan in hand—a poorly attempted revenge plan that never took off, but we move.

And now my dad had shown up and wanted to spend time together. Get to know me. *What the fuck?*

'Are you nervous?' Griff asked me as we were lining up to enter the hall for our ethics exam. As long as the question wasn't one about a topic I hadn't focused on as much, I had high hopes.

'I am more than ready,' I told him. I put my hair into a high ponytail, meaning business, and swished it in his face to make him laugh. 'I want to be done.'

'I feel you, Clouds.' He nodded, serious. 'Once these are over, we've got the masquerade ball, and then we're scot free. Away from this bullshit, this place, and everyone in it.'

'You think so?' I asked, sceptical. And I had every reason to be.

I doubted Orlando would leave us alone once we left the school. That *The Sanctum* would leave us alone once we were off school grounds. They seemed pretty determined fuckers.

'I know so.' He chuckled. Ms Hawthorn came to the front of the line and gave a speech about the behaviour she expected from us while we were taking the exam. The line hushed. And then it was time to enter the hall.

Time to take my seat and write non-stop for three hours straight.

And then after, I had another four to go. Then I was done.

And a weight lifted.

FATHER'S DAY.

I didn't join last year, seeing as up until not so long ago, my father lived outside the picture, but now I had one excited to attend.

Lucky for me, I wouldn't have to face the day alone with Jacob as my sole company.

Ollie and Henry were coming, as were Leo and Edward. Unfortunately for us all, Orlando was joining them.

Henry's genius idea, apparently.

He believed it would be a great way for both him and Ollie to meet Orlando and talk as a family and get to know one another. As if we didn't already know enough to want to keep our distance from this newfound member of the Hawthorn/Brandon clan.

When Ollie told me of his father's plans, I laughed. Poor Henry. He could act so ... wrong ... sometimes.

'Does your dad think it's going to work?' I asked Ollie, not turning to face him.

I took myself in from head to toe in the full-length mirror in Ollie's room, and fixed some platinum hoop earrings into my ears that Jacob gifted me for my birthday. They were the most expensive gift I'd received—excluding my necklace from Ollie—and I loved them. But no matter how much I love them, and appreciate the present, I wouldn't allow Jacob Cooper to buy me. The man could win me over with his actions and words in the normal way, thank you very much.

'It would seem so,' Ollie replied, coming into view in the mirror image of the room. 'Seems to believe if he talks to Orlando, things will get all cleared up and one day we'll become like one big, happy family.'

'Miracles do happen.'

'Yes,' Ollie agreed. 'And so do disasters.'

I laughed and turned to face the real him. 'Promise me no matter how bad today gets, we're in this together, okay? As a team.'

'You and I are the best team there is.' He came over to me and placed a kiss on my lips. 'You look stunning. This dress is beautiful, like you.'

My dress was another vintage inspired full skirt design, and I loved it. It had billowed sleeves to be worn off the shoulder, and the most striking turquoise check pattern. It complimented my light purple hair really well, and I loved it. It had been a gift from Ollie for today, and I was thankful he had such impeccable taste and knew me well enough to get it right without my input.

I took him in from head to toe for the first time since he got changed and whispered out, 'Fuck.'

He chuckled, and I fake punched him in the arm.

'Like what you see, baby?' he drawled. His top lip curled up, amused by my reaction. The fucker knew he looked good and could turn me into a puddle, and he used it to his full advantage —frequently.

'You know I do,' I said, taking him in once more. He wore trousers teamed with a suit jacket, which he knew I liked, but he'd gone one further. The trousers and jacket were *grey*.

Damn!

There was something perfect about a guy in grey. I couldn't tell you what, just that I bloody loved it. It was a major turn on.

'Are you sure we have to go?' I asked, reaching down to squeeze his bum to pull him closer, so our bodies pressed flush together. Every contour beneath me had me wanting to undress him right then and there. 'We could bail. My dad did a good enough job of it for the last eighteen years, so not like he wouldn't deserve it.'

'We do,' he said. As always, he got a kick out of me, and how much I wanted him. Me wanting to stay in rather than face the music with his dad and brother.

Could you blame me?

'Spoil sport.'

'Come on, you.' He removed my hands from behind him and pushed away from me. 'Henry's waiting for us at the main entrance and I'd rather get there before Jacob arrives.'

I sighed and took in a deep breath, trying to calm down my newly appeared nerves. I'd been fine while I put my makeup on and got dressed, but the closer it got, the more apprehension filtered in.

'Do you think it's gonna be a total disaster?'

'Oh, yeah. Big time.'

I laughed. 'Okay ...' I took one last look in the full-length mirror to check nothing had changed in my appearance. 'I'm ready.'

'Let's do this shit.'

HENRY WAITED for us outside at the bottom of the stairs leading into the main building. He seemed more tired than the last time I saw him, which made sense. The last time we'd seen one another was at the New Year's Gala, and *let's be honest*, a lot had happened since then.

His hair had grown longer and unkempt, but it was also a lot more silver than before.

'Oliver,' he greeted, holding out his hand to Ollie, who didn't take it. 'Skylar.'

He nodded his head at me in greeting, and I smiled back at

him. Since the Orlando shit happened, I sort of felt sorry for him these days?

Yeah, he'd acted creepy towards me, and he had beef with my dad, but aside from that, he was a hurt man who wasn't sure what was what anymore. And no part of me blamed him.

'Hello, Father,' Ollie greeted. Cool as ice. It always surprised me how frosty the two of them were together. I suppose I thought things would improve now they'd opened up a little, but things were the same as before.

I stayed silent, doing my best to not shuffle from foot to foot to have an output for my nervous energy. The tension rose the longer we stayed here, and I wasn't sure if I should make the next move.

Lucky for me, somebody else stole the limelight.

'Hello,' Orlando boomed from the top of the staircase, a wide smile on his face. A smile that put me on guard.

It was the definition of untrustworthy.

The three of us froze, staring up at him. After a beat, I walked towards Orlando, and after seeing me do so, Ollie and Henry followed suit. They shuffled up the stairs slowly, but at least they *were* coming.

'Little One,' Orlando murmured, inaudible to the two Brandon men still making their way to us. 'You look sublime.'

'Thank y-you,' I stammered back. 'You look good too.'

He wore a similar suit to Ollie, but in a darker grey, and I bet he somehow found out what his brother planned to wear and picked his outfit out accordingly. I shook the thought away. Surely he wasn't *that* sad?

'Dad,' Orlando said, holding his hand out to greet Henry when he got to the top. Shock crossed Henry's features in a flash. Maybe like me, his mind travelled back to New Year's, to the time before the real Ollie had shown up. Or maybe he noticed how different Orlando acted toward him when compared to Ollie.

'Hello,' Henry choked out, taking Orlando's hand in his and shaking firmly. 'Good to see you.'

Shit. This was the first time they were meeting, wasn't it? Properly, I mean, and not in some piss-poor showdown.

'Brother,' Orlando greeted Ollie, holding his hand out to him. Ollie recoiled and stepped closer to me.

'Hi,' he said in a clipped tone. I'd never heard Ollie use the word "hi" in all the times I'd known him. It sounded, *I don't know,* weird. Too un-Ollie.

'Well, isn't this nice?' Orlando said, taking each of us in one by one. 'Waiting on one more, are we?'

I rolled my eyes at him. God, he could be such a dick. 'Jacob text to say he was running a little late, so he'd meet us inside.'

Henry's eyes widened, but he said nothing.

'Let's get this over with,' Ollie said, grabbing my hand and pulling me towards the open school doors, not waiting for the other two. Once we were a couple of paces ahead, Ollie whispered, 'Keep an eye on him. I don't trust him one bit.'

'I don't either,' I agreed. 'But there isn't much he can do in front of all these people, is there?'

Wishful thinking and all that. Of course, he could do a lot of shit in front of this many people. There'd been a fuck ton of people at the gala and he still masqueraded as his twin for the entire evening with nobody being any the wiser. He only came clean because Ollie broke free and spoiled his fun.

'Watch him,' Ollie repeated, urgency in his tone. I nodded and squeezed his hand to tell him I understood.

When we entered the main hall, shock shot through me at how unrecognisable it had become.

It had transformed into some kind of lads' den.

There were large screens all along one wall, each one showing a different sporting event. Then, in the far corner, a section was set aside with video consoles and games, and there were already a couple of students playing with their dads in lush—most likely expensive—gaming chairs.

The vibe was so different to the one on Mother's Day, and instead of an Afternoon Tea, today's option was an outdoor barbecue. Which, yeah, probably catered to the dads more than small sandwiches and different flavours of heated water. Heck, it probably catered to half the mums more, too. My mum bloody loved a good barbecue.

Ollie and I stopped once we reached a seating area. Orlando and Henry joined us not long after.

'Shall we go grab a beer?' Henry asked the three of us, and the boys nodded, scarily in-sync.

'I'll stay here,' I announced to nobody in particular. 'Make sure we keep the seats.'

'Thanks, Sky,' Orlando said, acting the perfect gentleman. 'Would you like anything?'

'I'll get you a drink you like, okay, baby?' Ollie said, standing to join them, giving his brother a dark look. He didn't like Orlando addressing me at all.

'O-okay,' I said. 'Thank you.'

Ollie nodded, gripping his hands together in front of his stomach. I sensed his agitation from my seat, but I knew I couldn't go to him. He needed to do this without me.

'Come on, then,' Henry said over his shoulder, as he headed towards the bar on the far side of the hall.

I got comfortable in my seat, watching the three of them walk to the bar together. I wouldn't tell them, but they all walked similarly. It was in the way they carried themselves. Confident. Cocksure. They knew what they wanted and they wouldn't stop until they got it.

'Stutter,' Leo greeted me, taking the seat opposite. His father, Edward, took the seat next to him and I smiled at them both. 'You're looking well.'

'Hey! Thank you. Scrub up pretty nice yourself,' I said to Leo before I turned to Edward. 'How have you been?'

'I've been well, thank you, Miss Crescent. Lottie sends her love. She's rather gutted that she couldn't come.'

'Never had Lottie down as a barbecue goer,' I said. 'And please, I think you can call me Skylar now.'

'Of course, Skylar.' He rubbed his hands together, getting comfy. 'Where's your dad?'

'Not here yet. Henry, Ollie, and Orlando are over there.' I nodded my head towards the bar. 'It's the first time …'

Leo's eyes widened, picking up my thought. 'Yeah, Orlando mentioned he was joining his dad and brother today.'

'What's that little shit doing here?' Edward's jaw clenched. 'My sister mentioned nothing about it.'

'Yeah, but your sister's a bitch,' Leo said, bored. *Ah, bored Leo. How nice it is to see thee.* 'Winnie tells you things only if she's going to benefit from them.'

'Don't talk about your aunt like that,' Edward said, sounding tired. He rubbed his face with the palm of his hand, as if the weight of the world lived on his shoulders. 'She's family.'

'I'll stop talking about her when she stops ruining shit,' Leo mumbled, glancing out of the window.

'Watch your tongue, son,' Edward snapped. He took a sip from his drink, and the uncomfortable tension sitting in the air had me fidgeting even more. 'People may overhear you.'

My gaze trickled back to the bar, pretending not to be paying attention to Leo and Edward's tense exchange. The three Brandon men were making their way back to us, each with a drink in hand. I spotted Ollie had won the battle to get me a drink.

'Here you go, babe,' Ollie said as he handed me a tall glass of lemonade and violet flavoured gin. My favourite.

'Thanks,' I replied, moving on the seat a little to make room for him next to me. He took the spot willingly and slung an arm around my shoulder, pulling me closer. 'You handled that well.'

'Hello, Edward,' Henry said, shaking Edward's hand. The two of them both wore black suits, the epitome of wealthy business executives, and I could see the crow's feet at the corners of their eyes—one of the few features on their faces showing their age.

'Hello, Henry.' His tone hadn't changed from when he spoke to Leo last. Guess I'd always assumed the two of them were friends, but thinking about it, maybe they weren't. They were family, sure, but being family didn't mean you liked one another.

The yearbooks we'd found earlier in the year told us they were pals back then, but a lot had changed in the time since. Edward had lost two sisters, and Henry had lost his wife, who happened to be one of those sisters. Tragedies could change even the strongest of friendships.

'Uncle Eddy,' Orlando said, a wide smile on his face. He brushed his hand through his hair, and I reckoned it was a way to come across as nonchalant and carefree. He was taunting him, though, being disrespectful. Orlando was going to act like he hadn't pulled a *literal gun* out on the man the last time they were in the same room.

Edward's free hand clenched and unclenched at his side.

'Hello,' Edward said through gritted teeth, not wanting to respond to Orlando, but not seeing a way out of doing so.

The tension was palpable, everybody in the vicinity on edge and unsure of what to do and how to act, and the six of us fell into one of the most awkward silences I'd ever experienced in my life.

Forty-Two

THE ROOM WAS a large hub of movement and sound, what with all the other pupils and their fathers dotted around the large hall. It was overwhelming to a degree, but Ollie's hand on my arm reminded me of why I was here.

So when the room went silent, we all noticed straight away.

All heads in the room turned to the door as each person tried to see what caused the commotion. Or at least what had caught everybody's eye.

'Ah,' Ollie whispered beside me, able to see the door better, being taller than me.

Henry's face went pale, the colour draining from it.

Guess that explained who had arrived.

My body moved before my brain caught up with the action. I stood up and made way closer to Jacob, to meet him halfway. Everybody's eyes were on him, and I wanted to show my support. Make it clear he was welcome here—invited.

'Sky,' he said, his voice gruff and filled with emotion. 'Thanks for inviting me.'

He opened his arms, and I went into them, being pulled into one of the tightest hugs I'd ever been a part of. His arms were so warm it made me sweat, but I didn't pull myself away. Most people I kept at arm's distance, but it seemed I'd decided my dad could be an exception to the rule.

'No problem,' I said. 'Glad you could make it.'

'You and everybody else, I'm sure.' He chuckled.

I stepped out of his hug. 'I think some people are turning our way.'

Funny, Sky. Bit of an understatement, too. *Everybody* looked our way, and the hall stayed as silent as when he came in.

'Let them,' Jacob said. 'You ready for this?'

'Ready as I'll ever be,' I said. The two of us made our way back to the table where nobody had moved a muscle. Well, not entirely true. The muscle in Henry's top lip moved, as did the twitch in Edward's eyebrow.

When we reached the table, I took my place at Ollie's side and Jacob sat down in the spare seat next to Orlando.

'Jacob,' Henry said, his tone dark and his eyes narrowed. Edward's expression matched. Both of them were pissed, even though they knew he was coming. I suppose it wasn't easy to be around somebody with so much bad blood swirling between you. 'Nice to see you.'

Slowly, the sound in the hall picked up once again, although I reckoned it was a way for them to hide the fact they were still staring over here. *If I were them, I'd be doing the same thing.* People liked to deny it if asked, but everybody had a nosey streak. It was the reason cars slowed down to bog at a crash on the hard shoulder.

'Henry,' Jacob said back. 'Edward.' He nodded at them in turn. 'Is Griff coming?'

'He's coming any moment now,' I said. 'He made it clear he wouldn't miss the barbecue for no man or woman.'

Jacob laughed, but the others all remained silent, sipping their drinks for something to do.

I got out my phone while the adults glared at each other and tapped out a quick message.

HERC, JACOB'S ARRIVED. YOU GONNA BE LONG? x

His reply was instantaneous.

Be there in ten, Clouds x

' ... had to come see my daughter.' Jacob was finishing a sentence I hadn't heard the start of, but it raised my back up and I couldn't place my finger on why. He made it sound as if he wanted to come of his own volition and not just because Cora had called him and practically demanded it.

'Pretty sure your daughter's been alive for eighteen years,' Leo drawled, contempt dripping from every syllable. 'What made you crawl your way out of the gutter now?'

I covered up a cough at Leo's words. Nice to know he still had my best interest at heart, even if we'd been on shaky ground of late.

'I'll have you know I lived on a lovely island, Leo. Not a gutter at all.'

My stomach squirmed. I fidgeted in my seat, the hem of my skirt becoming extremely interesting, a sense of shittiness creeping in. While he'd been sunning it up on an island, I'd struggled to make ends meet and have enough food to fill my belly. Nausea swirled in my gut, and I had to fight the urge to flee the room.

'Well, while some of us were tanning in the Bahamas, others were working in a supermarket to put food on the table,' Ollie growled, placing his arm around me to pull me tighter.

Jacob's face fell, and he didn't need to say anything for me to know he felt guilty about rubbing his exile in my face. It was as if the two of us had an instant connection. An instant piece of string entwining us together, every thought and emotion clear as day.

I hated it as much as I loved it.

'I'm sorry, Skylar,' he said, his eyes earnest.

I swallowed and mumbled out, 'I know.'

I *did* know, but it didn't stop it from hurting.

'What are you doing here?' Edward said through gritted teeth, having had enough time to collect his thoughts. His face went as red as a pillar box, struggling to keep his calm. He'd already been mad at Orlando's presence, so no wonder this had tipped him over the ledge.

'My daughter invited me.' The word *daughter* went through the group like a shockwave, or maybe it was the word *invited*.

'No,' Edward said. 'I don't mean today.'

'What's so urgent you've appeared out of your hole?' Henry spat, his displeasure clear. 'Millie's death wasn't urgent enough.'

Ouch. Low blow.

Everybody shuffled in their seats, not sure what to do or where to focus their gaze. So sod's law meant Griff arrived right then.

'Hey guys!' he said cheerfully. 'How's everyone ...' he trailed off as his eyes landed on Jacob. He'd known Jacob would be here, but it must be different coming face to face with somebody who was the spitting image of your dead dad.

Jacob's facial expression was equally affected. His eyes widened, and he stared at Griff awed. The first night he arrived, Griff hadn't stuck around long, rushing after me when I fled, so they'd spent barely any time in the same vicinity.

'Griffin,' he whispered, tears forming in his eyes. Tears he didn't wipe away.

'Uncle Jacob,' Griff whispered back, his voice cracking. 'Hey.'

'I—' Griff was at a loss for words, and I couldn't blame him. I hated seeing him so bereft of his usual self. It was super rare for Griff to be at a loss for words.

I moved up in the seat to sit on top of Ollie's lap to make room for Griff.

'Come here,' I said, patting the seat next to me.

In a daze, he stumbled towards me and sat down. I reached out and squeezed his thigh, and he grabbed my hand in his and didn't let go.

For so long he'd gone without family, and now he had a cousin and his uncle back. I couldn't imagine the emotions running through him.

'Thanks,' he mumbled, and I nodded, happy I could be here for him. Could be the support he needed.

'The barbecue must be ready now,' Leo said, drawing the attention of the group away from Griff and Jacob, who were still staring at one another, lost in their moment. 'We should head out.'

Everybody grumbled out a 'yes' and we all moved to stand as one.

Griff kept his hand tight in mine, and we made our way out of the hall to the cooking food. It smelled amazing, but I'd lost my appetite.

Suppose the idea of spending the day with people who hate each other would do that to a girl.

'So, Jacob,' Edward said, holding a pint out for Jacob to take. The gesture seemed friendly enough, but I could see the serpent under it. 'How did you fund your lavish lifestyle? It's been, oh, I don't know ... about thirteen years since we saw you last.'

'Yes,' Henry continued. 'You left a week before your brother died, if my memory's correct.'

I watched Jacob wince, but he stood his ground, not letting the two men walk all over him. 'Unfortunately, *circumstances* prevented me from returning for the funeral.'

Yeah, *circumstances* had prevented him from returning. One of those circumstances being Cora, I assumed. Or maybe me. The others ... well, they weren't clear to me yet, but they would be in time.

'Didn't prevent you from returning after,' Henry grumbled under his breath.

He was talking about the affair Jacob had with Millie for the five years after the twins' deaths. In some weird way, the affair made sense to me. Both Millie and Jacob lost their twin in the car accident—one we were pretty certain wasn't an accident—and they sought comfort in each other.

Plus, Jacob and Millie had been together while attending

Hawthorn together, so I can imagine the bond between them, not to mention the chemistry, already existed between them.

'Things were complicated,' Jacob said. 'They still are. But I knew I couldn't leave Sky here to fend for herself any longer amongst you vultures.'

'How gallant of you,' Edward said. 'And I suppose you made this decision after your daughter had nearly drowned, been stabbed, and whacked over the head?'

The group fell into silence—me included. I hadn't realised Edward knew as much as he did, but maybe Lottie or Leo told him.

Not to mention we all knew Jacob's answer. He'd decided *after* I got hurt, not before. Before those things happened to me, I doubted I was even a blip on his radar while he got a tan and lived his life to the fullest somewhere exotic.

'A pity you've arrived and made her life even more complicated,' Henry said. 'If you cared a smidge about your daughter, you'd have stayed away.'

Jacob laughed. 'Sorry, but am I getting parenting advice from the man who didn't know his wife gave birth to two living twins?'

I winced at my dad's words. Yes, he had a point, but it wasn't the time nor the place to point it out.

Orlando, smug as fuck at how things were playing out, ate his food in silence. To him, we were the entertainment. He loved drama, after all. It surprised me he hadn't yet intervened to cause even more of it.

'Did anybody want any more food?' I asked. 'The coleslaw's banging.'

'No, thank you,' Edward said. The others all muttered similar things, and I shrugged. More fool them.

The pasta salad called my name.

And I must follow the call.

Forty-Three

AFTER FATHER'S DAY, I went straight back into prepping and cramming for my exams.

I spent every spare moment thinking about all the required topics, and when I wasn't thinking about school, I thought about *The Sanctum* and the upcoming masquerade ball.

Jacob texted me Father's Day evening to thank me for inviting him and without putting more thought into it, I replied and asked him to meet me at Hawthorn House the next weekend. Winifred and Orlando were leaving the grounds for a meeting with Orlando's lawyer in London, leaving the place empty.

Jacob agreed to come within minutes of me sending the message.

So for the next week, I knuckled down, attended my exams and worked my absolute hardest to write as much as possible on each booklet. Quite hard to do, to be honest, when all I could think about was whether somebody was going to attempt to kill me and my friends at the upcoming charity event.

'So,' Ollie said, taking my hand as we left the hall after our History exam. 'Your dad's coming tomorrow, right?'

'He is. He called me last night to say he'd arrive around midday.'

Ollie frowned and pulled me into an alcove. 'He called?' I nodded. 'Where was I?'

'Shower,' I said. He'd tried to pull me into the shower with him, but I hadn't wanted to. 'He video called me, which was a first.'

'How'd it go?' His fingers rubbed soothing circles on my wrists.

'Weird. I've never had a relationship with a parent like that. Cora rarely remembers to send a text, let alone video call me.'

'But even though it was weird, it was good, yeah?'

'I'd have told you if not.'

'Would you?' Ollie squeezed my hands in a comforting gesture. 'Because you didn't even tell me he called.'

There was a small amount of reproach in his tone, and I batted my eyelashes in hopes of defusing his mood. Ollie could be such a moody bastard, but more and more, he seemed to be calming down.

'You want the truth?' I asked, moving my arms to wrap around the back of his neck. Ollie nodded, and I moved my hands up the nape of his neck into his hair. 'I had every intention of telling you, but then you came out of the bathroom all mighty fine and wet in a towel and I forgot everything but how much I wanted to kiss you.'

'Well, I can't be mad at you,' he said, although he didn't sound like somebody who couldn't be mad.

I raised my right eyebrow in his direction. 'You sound pretty mad.'

'Nope. How can I be mad when my girlfriend's looking at me like that?' His smile was beautiful. So beautiful I couldn't help but smile back.

'Is it me or is the word mad sounding odd in your head?' I laughed.

Maybe I was the one going mad.

Ollie kissed my forehead with so much affection I swooned. The glint in his eyes spoke a thousand words. 'Where are we meeting your dad again?'

'Hawthorn House,' I replied, like we hadn't spoken of it multiple times since last weekend. 'Leo told me it would be free.'

'Did you want me to come?'

'Do you *want* to come?' I asked back, genuinely wanting his response. I wanted him there, but only if it wouldn't make him too uncomfortable. Or worse, have him start a fight or argument with my dad. 'Because you don't have to if you don't want to. I promise I won't get pissed about it.'

'I promise you, it's fine. It'll be fine.'

He sounded like he was trying to convince himself as much as me. Ollie wouldn't take kindly to me pushing him to admit something he might not be ready to admit yet.

'As long as you mean it.' I scratched my fingers against Ollie's scalp and he let out a moan.

'I do. Now, if you've finished talking about the topic, can we head back to my room?' he asked, a wicked sparkle in his eye. 'There's much more to discuss.'

'Oh there is, is there?'

'Mhm.' He nodded. 'Lots to talk about.'

I moved my face an inch closer to his. 'Yeah?' I murmured, my lips brushing against his.

'Yeah,' he whispered back, his lips touching mine. 'Lots.'

And then we were kissing in the alcove, and I forgot where we were and what we'd been talking about.

'THANK you so much for meeting me here.' Jacob opened the door to Hawthorn House wide, and I stepped inside, Ollie close behind. Jacob turned around and walked towards the sitting room with the gigantic fireplace. 'Leo let me in.'

'Leo's here?' Ollie asked.

It shouldn't have surprised either of us, but apparently it did. He spent a lot of time at the house on the grounds with Orlando and it made sense he was comfortable here from all the summers and holidays spent here as a kid.

'He is,' Dad confirmed. 'Should he not be?'

Jacob's face fell. *Eurgh, damn my heart for sinking alongside it.* He'd appeared so happy to see us—or should I say me—when he opened the door. Yet now his face had fallen like he'd stepped on a bee.

'No, no.' I waved my hand. 'Just a surprise, that's all.'

When we entered the room, Leo was already seated in one of the large leather armchairs arranged in front of the unlit fireplace, a tumbler of whiskey gripped in his right hand.

Something troubled him. I could tell from his facial expression and the slight unruliness of his hair, but I doubted he'd voice it without prodding and poking.

And honestly? I didn't have the strength to try. If he wanted to tell us, he would in his own time, and I had to be okay with it.

'Take a seat, take a seat,' Dad said, ushering us over to Leo. 'Would you like a drink? Whiskey, Oliver?'

Ollie nodded. 'That would be lovely, thank you.'

'Skylar?' Dad asked when I didn't reply. I hadn't responded, too busy taking in the scene, and now my mouth opened and closed like a stupid fish.

'A Diet Coke is fine, thanks.' I took the empty seat in the middle of Ollie and Leo. 'Lots of ice, please.'

'Coming right up!' Dad left the room and the three of us stayed quiet, all glancing at one another when the other wasn't looking. It was pretty comical, to be honest. The three of us were acting like children, but luckily for me, it wasn't awkward.

More like funny.

Jacob returned with my drink and took the last remaining armchair. He placed a tumbler of whiskey for himself on the small circular table in the middle of us. 'Will Griffin be joining us?'

'He's got something on this morning, but he said he'll come by in an hour or two,' I said. 'He can't wait to talk to you more in depth.'

'I'm excited to spend time with him, too. He looks so much like my brother.'

I laughed. 'He looks more like you than I do.'

'I'm sure you wouldn't appreciate me telling you how you've got the majority of your features from Cora?' Dad smiled, raising his glass to his lips.

'You've picked up on things quickly,' I said. 'I've been told my whole life how much I resemble her.'

Ollie reached over and placed his hand on my knee. 'You might, Sky, but that's where the resemblance ends. For starters, you'd never wear your hair in a bouffant.'

Jacob frowned, but the rest of us let out a chuckle.

'Definitely not like the ones she's so fond of,' I said. 'I'm not sure how Mum dressed when you knew her, but recently her tastes have been rather ... eclectic, to say the least.'

Jacob got more comfortable in his chair, a fond smile playing on his lips. 'Any examples?'

'We don't want to scare you,' I said, trying to recall some of her most recent fashion faux pas'. 'But there was a time not too long ago where she wore socks and high-heeled sandals. We were all frightened, yet somehow still in awe of it.'

'Cora brings that out in people.'

We all nodded at Jacob's words. My mum brought out *a lot* in people, usually none of it good. No, often she made people experience despair and hatred.

'It is quite a skill,' I said. 'But enough talk of my mum. There are plenty of better, more exciting things to talk about.'

'I wouldn't say exciting,' Leo said in a dull voice, 'but there are *other* things to be talking about.'

My dad put down his glass and clasped his hands in front of his stomach, resting his full weight on the back of the chair. 'You sound like you have a topic in mind, Leo.'

'There are a few things we think you can shed some light on,' Leo said. 'Things like what happened here when you went to school with our parents.'

'What happened here ...' Jacob trailed off, his brow furrowing. 'A lot happened here if I'm telling the truth.'

'We've got something specific in mind,' Ollie said, joining the conversation. 'A girl died here, in your last year, I believe?'

Dad's head turned Ollie's way. 'Hm?'

'Sandy Parks,' I said. The moment the name hit his ears, my dad slumped in his chair. 'She died in the girl's bathroom.'

'I know the name.' Jacob gave a swift nod of the head. 'What do you want to know?'

'What happened to her?' I sat up straighter in my chair, eager to learn the answer. 'We found some articles upstairs in a locked chest and one of them was from the Hawthorn Herald after it happened.'

'*Ah*, the Hawthorn Herald.' Dad's eyes widened. 'Blasted newspaper. The students who ran it didn't like us one bit.' He laughed. 'Because of all the rules, I suppose.'

'You mean the rules of *The Set* and *The Sect*?' I'd forgotten my dad had been one. Fuck, if he'd stuck around, I would've been a member of *The Set* without question. I'd like to think I wouldn't be as bitchy as them, but who knew? If I grew up surrounded by life's luxuries the way they all had, maybe I wouldn't be any better.

'I do. I'm sure you know them.' His smirk reminded me of Griff. 'Reckon they haven't changed much in the years since.'

'They're still bullshit, if that's what you mean,' I said.

Me and my dad shared a warm smile. 'That's what I mean, yes.' He sat a little straighter once more, and I hoped it was in preparation to tell us the truth. 'Okay. I'll tell you what happened, but I don't want any interruptions until the tale is told. Do you understand?'

The three of us nodded.

'Sandy Parks was a scholarship student here at Hawthorn and the daughter of the English teacher and, for the most part, kept herself to herself. Most likely in fear of what would happen to her if she didn't.' Jacob paused, choosing his words carefully. 'No matter how hard she tried, though, it didn't stop the wolves. Rich kids can be particularly cruel when they want, especially to those they believe beneath them.'

His eyes softened my way, and I averted my gaze, not wanting to see the pity in his. I knew what he meant. It had happened to me not so long ago, after all.

He continued, 'I'm unsure what Sandy did, or what she said,

but Millie and Eliza took offence one day and then I suppose it sort of became open season.'

I gulped at the image filling my mind.

Poor Sandy Parks. I could relate more than the others in the room to what she went through.

'It started off harmless enough,' Jacob said. I winced at his wording. I doubted any of it was *harmless*. 'Mostly words hurled at her in the halls or statements written on the toilet walls.' *Ah*, as I said, none of that could be classed as harmless. I kept my tongue. Nothing I said now could change the past. 'But things escalated in our last year and there was no escape for Sandy.'

Jacob turned to Ollie. 'Before I tell the rest, I want to make it clear to you. I loved your mother, Oliver. Millie is the love of my life and talking poorly of her isn't something I'm comfortable doing. However, in this story, Millie doesn't come out of it smelling the best. I want to remind you she was a brilliant woman and a splendid mother, regardless of what comes next.'

Ollie and I locked eyes, and I reached out to squeeze his hand in mine, hoping my support acted as a comfort to him. Whatever came next no doubt would make Millie come across as pretty evil —a girl died no matter what happened—and Ollie already struggled with the image he held of his mother.

'I understand,' Ollie murmured. 'Please, go on.'

Jacob took a deep breath, steeling himself. 'One day, Millie took it all too far. Told us all she'd planned a prank for Sandy and we needed to work together so she would flee to the girl's bathroom on the second floor of the English building, the way she did whenever something happened. Whenever any of us asked what the prank entailed, she and Eliza did their twin thing and refused to say anything. They'd just smile and act coy.

'So, the day came, and we did what they asked of us, and Sandy fled to her sanctuary.'

'To where the girls waited for her, you mean?' I spat, unable to stay silent. My blood boiled at the callousness of it all—at the matter-of-fact way my dad told it.

'Yes,' Jacob said, his eyes downcast. The shame radiated from him, but I didn't pity him in the slightest. A girl *died*. 'To where the girls waited for her.'

'Then what happened?' Ollie asked, steering the conversation back on track after my interruption.

'I don't know. I know what Millie and Eliza said afterwards, and what Winnie has alluded to over the years.'

'Which is?' I snapped, bored, waiting for an answer.

'The girls forced her onto a chair and convinced her to put a noose around her neck. They kicked the chair away and left the room for a moment, to scare Sandy not to harm her, but while they were gone, they got distracted and returned too late to save her.'

'How did she get distracted?' Ollie asked, confusion swimming in his face. 'Or should I say, *who* distracted her?'

'Three guesses who,' my dad said darkly.

'Winifred,' Leo said, his tone even darker.

'Precisely.' My dad nodded his head. 'Then she covered it up. She hid the truth and made sure the girls never got penalised for their actions.'

'So they'd forever be in her debt,' I said, understanding Winifred's motivations well enough after all I'd learned during my time at Hawthorn.

'Precisely,' Jacob repeated, his eyes softening my way. 'And as the saying goes, the rest is history.'

Forty-Four

ORLANDO

'THE MASQUERADE BALL is in a week. I hope you've been preparing yourself.'

I was in Mum's office, walking close to the walls, inspecting all the photos and trinkets she'd placed there. Didn't want the bitch to think I was giving her my full attention.

But I was.

Because the Masquerade Ball would be when *The Sanctum* arrived and showed their faces. Faces I was still yet to see even though I'd attended meeting after meeting for literal years.

'Preparing myself for what, exactly?' I asked. My tone was petulant, and I knew it would tick her off something rotten.

Winnie needed knocking down a few pegs if you asked me. Nobody ever asked me, though. They barely glanced at me if they could help it.

'As you are aware,' she said, her tone one of ice. '*The Sanctum* has invited your brother and his friends.'

'I think they plan to kill them.'

'Kill them?' I asked, turning to face her. 'Bit drastic.'

'Need I remind you, *you've* also been trying to kill them?' Her lips pursed together.

'I only tried to kill Sky and Ollie.' A memory swirled into my mind. *That didn't sound right.* 'And Griff and Clover.'

'Exactly,' she bit out. 'You *tried,* but you *failed.* Which is why *The Sanctum* needs to step in and clear up your mess.'

'Well, if *The Set* was still whole and not half murdered, then maybe *The Sanctum* would have had others on its side to do their dirty work.'

'Yes, well, *somebody* couldn't stop themselves from killing those girls, could they?'

I rolled my eyes, wanting to get away from her piercing gaze.

My mum blamed everybody else for their issues. For the things in their life going balls-up. She always had.

In her mind, it was Millie's fault. Or Jacob's fault. Or Skylar's fault.

Even *my* fault.

But never hers.

'Why do they even want to kill them?' I asked, for maybe the umpteenth time this year. 'Seems counter-intuitive.'

'Never you mind,' Mum said. 'You can ...'

She continued talking, but I stopped listening. I usually stopped listening whenever she spent forever talking about something I couldn't give zero shits about. Which basically was everything the woman ever said.

'Are you even listening to me?' Mum snapped. My eyes went back to where she sat behind her large desk. She thought herself so important, but to me, she looked like somebody playing pretend.

'Always.' I smiled. 'Not like you give me any choice, is it?'

'When *The Sanctum* arrives, Orlando, you have to do everything I say. Stay silent and follow orders. Don't show me up like you did at the gala.'

'Will you stop going on about the gala?' I shouted, my anger rising. 'I get it. I'm a big disappointment to you and your little society friends. Bore me later.'

'You're right, you are a disappointment to me. So, get out of my sight,' she replied in a clipped tone, dismissing me. I took one last look at her, hoping for some kind of reaction, but she'd already glanced back down at the papers on her desk.

Bitch.

One day, she'd get what she deserved..

A slow, and painful, demise.

––––––––––

'ORLANDO, WAIT UP!'

I found Little One lurking a little further up the corridor, hiding out in an alcove. Had she been waiting for me to leave Mum's office?

Doubtful.

But hope filled me regardless. I hadn't seen much of her since we spoke in the pool house after I'd sent her that note. Any time I caught a glimpse of her in the halls, or the dining room, I had to fight my instincts to not stare at her the whole time.

Skylar Crescent had a hold on me, and it seemed I couldn't do anything to break said hold.

I sauntered over to where she waited for me and she took me by surprise when she pulled me in closer to her body.

'I heard raised voices. Everything okay?' Sky said, giving me a tight hug.

She stepped back, putting a good amount of space between us, and assessed my face.

'Yeah ...' My scepticism rocketed sky high. Since when did she care about me enough to stop me in the corridor and hug me?

I'd only ever had this kind of reaction from her when she thought I was my brother—and only because she hadn't known at the time it wasn't her boyfriend in front of her.

'It sounded like the two of you were going at it.' She shrugged. Her blue eyes were open wide and honesty swam in them. She reached out to rest her small hand on my bicep.

Alarms started blaring in my brain.

What was she playing at? It may be everything I wanted, but I wouldn't be played as a fool. I wasn't a mug, even when it came to her.

'Who set you up for this?' I snarled, grabbing her hand and

pulling it away from me. 'What game do you think you're playing?'

'N-no game,' she stuttered, her face no longer as sure as it had when she called me over. She blinked multiple times in fast succession, and her heart rate increased within the space of a few seconds. 'Am I not allowed to care about you?'

'Not like you have before,' I muttered. I was acting surly, and I knew it, but the roles were usually reversed. Sky usually wanted to know what I was playing at or what my true motivation was.

'I care about you,' she said, daring to replace her hand back on my bicep. 'You may not believe me, but I do. You've done some shitty things and I won't ever forget them, but I've forgiven you for them.'

She shrugged, running her hand through my hair, brushing it back from my face. A tingle ran through me, like a bolt of lightning, and I jolted back from the electricity of it.

I wanted her.

I craved her.

And I'd been playing the long game.

Because I wanted her to pick me. I didn't want to decide for her, which was something I'd considered more than once.

Taking her captive and keeping her locked away until she had no choice but to love me was an image that played in my mind daily.

Huh. Maybe I needed to tell her my overall goal.

'Little One,' I whispered. 'You know what I want, right?'

'In what sense?' She tilted her head, her gaze so intent on me all I wanted to do was kiss her.

But I didn't kiss her.

No.

I had some control over myself still. Instead, I spoke.

'In life,' I said. 'What I want for my life.'

She squinted up at me, craning her neck to look me in the eye. Even though I couldn't hear her thoughts, I had a good idea of what they were. Sky was pretty predictable, even if she didn't realise it.

'I wish I knew.' She sighed. 'I'd help you no matter what it was, you know?'

'I don't think you'd say that if you knew'—I grinned and watched her gulp—'because what I want, Little One, is *you.*'

'Me?' she sputtered, moving back, but not going far, before bumping into the wall at her back. 'What do you mean?'

'I want you to be my girl. Not Leo's. Not Oliver's. But mine. I want to wake up next to you. Watch you as you fall to sleep. Be there when you have nightmares—'

She cut me off in a sharp tone. 'Nightmares given to me because of you! Memories from when you stabbed me. Drowned me. Drugged me.' She poked my chest, emphasising in between each sentence. 'The nightmares would never end if I woke up and saw you.'

What she didn't realise was that a feisty Skylar made me want her even more and showed me the spunk underneath her usual calm exterior, and gave me a glimpse of the girl I wanted by my side forever more.

'Are you attending the Masquerade Ball?' she asked, changing tact.

I frowned. 'Do I have a choice?'

'Guess not.' She chuckled. 'Not like any of us do, really.'

We both fell silent. We were in the same position, but for different reasons. Neither of us had a say in what was to come. All we could do was show up and hope we left intact.

Mother made it clear she expected me to be there. Stay silent, and do as she said. Do as *The Sanctum* said. And for years, I'd allowed her to tell me what she needed from me without ever questioning her motives.

'So, the ball …' she trailed off.

'Guess I'll see you there?' I joked, trying to lighten the dark cloud surrounding us. We both knew we'd see each other there.

'I'll be the one in a mask,' she teased, biting her lower lip. Damn. I wanted her.

'I'll be the one in a tux.' I smiled. Sky laughed. Easy. Carefree.

And it only made me desire her more.

Forty-Five

THE NIGHT before the masquerade ball, the atmosphere between us all was rather sombre as apprehension about the next evening filled us all.

We had a plan, that wasn't much of a plan, but it was better than having nothing.

'Sky,' Ollie whispered and placed a kiss on my temple. 'It's time to get some rest, okay? We can worry more in the morning.'

'I can't help it,' I whispered back, pressing my back harder against his front as he spooned me. 'Every possible scenario and outcome is flashing through my mind and every time it replays, the worse the outcome becomes.'

He placed another tender kiss, this time on my head. 'Skylar, I won't let anything bad happen to you. Ever. You have my word.'

'But what if something happens and you can't control it? I doubt *The Sanctum* will ask your permission before trying anything.'

Which was what worried me most, and what kept me awake well past midnight. There was no way of knowing what they had planned. Leo, who had been told so much over the last few years, was being kept in the dark now. Probably because they knew he'd chosen to talk to us and wanted to be careful in case he was no longer as under their thumb as they believed.

'I know it's hard, baby, but we have to have faith things will work out for the best and in the way we want them to.'

I turned around in Ollie's arms and moved an inch back so I could take his face in. 'Who are you and what have you done with my boyfriend?'

He chuckled. The room was dark, but I could faintly make out his face. His long eyelashes as he blinked drew my attention.

'You make me hopeful, Skylar Crescent.' His top lip lifted into a smirk of sorts. *Fuck, he was so beautiful all the time.* No matter how many times I saw him, I never got bored with the view that greeted me. 'And there's something I need to say to you.'

My mind started racing. Of course, I doubted he was about to end things between us or anything equally as drastic, but my mind didn't always function under the umbrella of logic and fact. My anxiety spikes were unnecessary most of the time, but I couldn't exactly control them.

'What?' His eyelashes fluttered from my whispered question.

'Skylar.' Ollie blinked and placed his hands firmly on my hips. 'I love you.'

I blinked back, so many emotions washing over me. Hearing those three words leave his lips—knowing this time they were real and genuine—had tears filling my eyes.

Oliver Brandon loves me.

And fuck, do I love him, too.

'You do?' I whispered.

'I do.'

A tear travelled down my face. 'I love you, too.'

Ollie blinked, his features relaxing the moment I said the words. 'I want to be cool about this and act like you haven't made my day, but I don't think I can.' His hands, still on my hips, pressed in a little harder. 'I am so lucky to have you in my life.'

'You are.' I bit my bottom lip, stifling my giggle. 'I'm glad you're finally realising it.'

He chuckled. 'You think I hadn't before now?'

My heart beat faster. The *thump-thump* of it registered in my ears, while the rest of the room remained deadly silent. I pressed up onto my tiptoes and kissed Ollie's lips, the taste of my tears mixing with the taste of him.

'I've got a question,' I said. At his frown, I added, 'Nothing too bad, I promise.'

His body loosened under my arms. 'Okay. Shoot.'

'Do you remember when you said to me that our first Valentine's Day together was when you doubted your plan because you were falling for me?'

'Yes?'

'Well, when did you know you'd fallen?'

He sighed, blew out a deep breath, and said, 'It's complicated.'

'Talk to me,' I said, my tone gentle but the words a demand. 'I promise nothing will change for us now. I'm all in, O.'

'You are?' he asked, and I could see the doubt fluttering across his face. His voice was low and gritty, and his eyes were taking all of my face in.

'Course I am,' I replied, certain. I knew it would take some time for him to believe me. For him to understand I was all in now, no ifs ands or buts.

Ollie's eyes were bright blue and shining with love. I'd never seen eyes like it before. My heart swooned and if I'd been standing, I would have gone weak at the knees. 'I'm all in, too. In case you didn't already know.'

I beamed at him, teeth all on show, and his face mirrored mine. It had been nearly an entire year since the events of the fashion show and so much had changed since.

'Believe it or not,' he said, 'I am more than happy I arranged for you to get the scholarship here, because it was everything I wanted but never knew I needed.'

Fuck. I had dropped down dead and gone to heaven.

'You're everything I need, too. Which is why I can't stop thinking about tomorrow and worrying about every single possible outcome.'

'You've got little to worry about.'

'I lost my temper with Orlando the other day,' I whispered. 'I thought it'd be a good idea to corner him and lay the seed for the ball, but then he pissed me off and I saw red.'

'What happened?'

'He told me his one wish in life is to have me.' I scoffed. 'And the fact he can't see shit as it is … well, I couldn't hold my tongue.'

'You think he'll still cut in to dance, though?'

'I'd put money on it.' I shuffled on the bed and raised my leg to drape over his hip. 'If you make eye contact with him, make it clear you're showing me off and rubbing it in. That'll rile him up like nothing else could.'

'Just remember the plan when you spot me acting like you're a trophy, okay?'

I laughed. 'I'll try my best.'

'Make sure you do.' He kissed my head. 'Right, what can I do to make you fall asleep?'

'Well …' I thought about it for a moment. 'You could tell me a story.'

'Any particular story?'

He sounded a lot more into the idea than I thought he would be. I only said it to make him smile, not for him to actually do it.

'Hmm. How about a story about a rich bastard who fell in love with a poor student?'

'Don't think I could do a story like that justice.'

'I'm sure you could. Now, I'm gonna turn around again and you're going to hug me and tell me a story, okay?'

'Fuck, I love you.'

'Yeah, yeah, you mentioned.'

My words may have sounded cavalier, but when I rolled over, a huge smile covered my face.

Whatever the next day had for us, I was more than ready for it with a man like Oliver Brandon by my side.

Forty-Six

WHAT WAS it about rich people and masquerade balls?

I swear every film or movie I loved included one—or at least a large majority did—and here I was preparing to *attend* one. It felt as if I were playing in somebody else's life. Could never be mine.

Ollie had kept good to his word and arranged for Clover and me to go shopping for dresses to match our masks so we'd fit in amongst such extravagance. My dad had offered too, but it hadn't seemed right to accept. We still hadn't known one another long and for all I knew, once this was all done and over with, he may fuck off to an island somewhere, never to be heard from again.

My mask was one of the most beautiful things I'd ever seen, made of intricate black lace, and it enhanced my features in such an artful way it surprised me whenever I glimpsed myself in the mirror.

Something I'd been doing all evening.

I chose my dress to match the mask. It was black as night and covered in tiny sparkling crystals. Every time it hit the light, it shimmered and filled me with such joy I couldn't help but have a permanent smile on my face. It had a full skirt and the lace-covered bodice matched my mask, tight fitting to the point I couldn't wear a bra underneath. Lucky for me, the lace hugged me in the right places, so nothing untoward was on show.

Didn't want to send Ollie into a heart attack anytime I moved or somebody looked my way.

Clo entered the suite and took my breath away. Every time I saw her in formal wear, I was reminded of how stunning she was. She stole my breath away—in a totally platonic best friend kinda way. 'You look fucking amazing, Skylar.'

'As if! Look at you,' I screeched in reply, taking her in from head to toe, my excitement and trepidation for the night ahead getting the best of me. If I thought Clover scrubbed up well during our other formal events, then her current outfit blew all of those out of the water.

Her skin-tight silver dress had a high slit up to her thigh and her auburn hair was slicked back in a high ponytail and showed off her sharp cheekbones. *Pure perfection.*

Both Leo and Griff would be in heaven.

'Okay, okay,' she placated me. 'We're *both* amazing! The stuffy people at this ball won't know what hit them.'

'Not to mention *The Sanctum.*' I giggled.

Ah, maybe we shouldn't have had five pre-drinks each, but sometimes, a little liquid courage was nice.

I'd never tell Cora that. She'd be way too proud that her daughter was following in her footsteps or some shite.

'Are you ready?' Griff called as he entered the room, doing his best impression of a boxing commentator. Jeez, the boy scrubbed up well with his tux all tailored to perfection. Clover gulped beside me.

The attraction still hovered between them both—they'd both admitted as much to me—but neither of them would act on it.

That ship had sailed.

'My gosh,' he said when he saw us both. 'You look outstanding. Beautiful. Perfection.'

Griff's enthusiasm on any day was enough to bring you out of the darkest of moods.

'You are delicious, darling.' I smiled with all my teeth on show. 'We'll be the belles of the ball.'

'What about me?' Ollie asked, entering the room and taking me in from head to toe. 'Am I also a belle of the ball?'

'More like the beast,' Clo said, but unlike anything she would've said last year, she said it with a smile. 'A handsome one.'

'Sky,' Ollie whispered. He came to stand in front of me and brushed the back of his hand along my cheek. 'You are the most beautiful girl I've ever seen. This lace dress should be illegal. I don't know if I'll be able to stop myself from punching everybody who gazes at you too long.'

'Oh, hush.' I laughed. 'Punching people is beneath you.'

'Tell that to Leo!' Griff chimed in and I darted an evil glare his way. We didn't bring up the time Ollie gave Leo a black eye. It was a thing of the past, never to be repeated.

'Maybe if *The Sanctum* show their faces I will,' Ollie mused, as if Griff hadn't spoken. The air in the room soured. Whatever spell we'd existed under for the past few hours had broken. None of us had thought about them all evening, and now, all I could think about was the night ahead and what might happen. Ollie, oblivious to the shattered atmosphere, continued, 'Let's hope it doesn't come to that.'

'Is Leo meeting us there?' I asked. Last I heard, he'd arrive with Orlando. It bothered me, the two of them hanging around together still. Yeah, we all decided it was for the best, so nothing seemed out of the ordinary, but it didn't mean I liked it.

'Yep,' Clo replied and glanced at her phone. 'We should make a move.'

I nodded, and went to follow Clo and Griff, but Ollie pulled me back towards him before I could get closer to the door.

'Wait up,' he whispered. His eyes flitted to the necklace around my neck. It was the one he'd got me for Christmas shaped like the north star, and I loved it. Every time I saw it, I was stunned all over again. It went perfectly with my dress, too. He touched the star. '*This* is going to draw attention.'

'I think this *dress* is going to draw attention.' I chuckled. It felt daring to be wearing something so sophisticated yet sexual. I finally felt my age, in a way.

We were all adults now; time to act like it.

'You're mine,' he drawled. 'That's what matters most.'

Ollie leaned in and kissed my cheek, then his eyes went to my bright red lips.

'That colour on you makes me want to bite them clean off your face,' he said darkly. 'But I won't.'

'I'm glad you can refrain,' I joked. 'Do you think our invitations came from *The Sanctum*?'

'No idea.' He kissed my temple, stepped back, and reached out his hand for mine. 'I'm sure we're about to find out.'

'Let's do this shit.'

Henry, Edward, and Jacob were standing together in front of the silent auction table, acting their usual intimidating selves.

No part of me expected to see those three in one another's company voluntarily, but there they were.

'Hey, Dad,' I greeted him when we came closer. 'Hello, Henry. Edward.'

The three of them looked over at us, and my dad's eyes filled with tears.

'Skylar.' He brushed his eyes, flicking the moisture away. 'You are ... beautiful.'

'Th-thank you,' I whispered. My emotions were all over the place. The man had been gone for the last eighteen years of my life, but he was trying now and I couldn't hold it against him. 'You look great.'

He coughed, and the group fell silent. *Wonderful.* Our awkward display of familial affection had caused everybody to freeze up.

I giggled. These stuffy rich men wouldn't know familial affection if it bit them on the arse.

'Dad.' Ollie nodded. 'Uncle Edward. Jacob.'

It was weird and unusual to see everybody in elaborate masks. Very high fantasy, and very misleading. After watching plenty of films where the mysterious girl was unknown to all because of a mask, I wondered how nobody had known her identity—it always seemed pretty obvious to me sitting at home watching—but now I was living it, I understood a bit more. I barely recognised anybody.

What a mind fuck.

'So,' Griff said, cutting through the tension. 'We all ready for some food, booze, and silent auctioning?'

His infectious smile had me beaming right alongside him. No matter what, the boy made me happy.

'Can't wait,' Clo said, sounding miserable. She'd never been one for parties, and a school sanctioned party was the worst of the worst in her eyes.

'Oh, come off it, Lady Luck. We'll have a splendid time.' Griff grabbed Clo's hand and pulled her in to twist her out again into a spin. Lighthearted and free. 'Okay?'

'Okay,' she replied, still rather begrudgingly, but with a smile of sorts. 'If you say so.'

Edward, Henry, and Jacob stayed silent on the fringe of our small group. They were serious, and their facial expressions told me they were watching out for something. What? Or rather, who?

'Why are you all so on edge?' Ollie asked. Lately, he seemed able to read my mind, and it freaked me out. Maybe it was because we spent so much time together.

'Son,' Henry said, not answering Ollie's question. His eyebrows dipped, and he searched for his next words. 'Was the invitation you guys received for tonight ... unusual in any way?'

'Are you asking if *The Sanctum* sent our invitation too?' Griff asked, no longer joking around with Clover, putting his rarely used serious face on.

'So you got them, too.' Edward nodded. 'As we expected.'

'They invited you, too?' I asked, pinning my gaze to my father. When he'd told me he was coming tonight, I thought little more about it. And when I had, I'd thought maybe he was coming to make an effort now he'd come back into my life. 'Makes sense. I suppose that they'd want all of us here together.'

Well, it looked like we were none the wiser about any of it.

What they wanted. *Why* they wanted us.

None of it.

Leo and Orlando entered the ball and in a moment of déjà vu, everybody in the hall stopped talking and turned to face them to watch as they made their grand appearance. I scoffed at the pageantry of it all.

As if these parents were still happy to let a murderer amongst their midst and their children. It sickened me how money had warped all the people in this room so much they were happy to cover up the murders of innocent—albeit bitchy—teenagers.

'Surprised he showed his face,' Henry mumbled.

'I'm not,' Edward replied, talking out of the side of his mouth. I stepped a little closer. 'Not if he invited us here.'

'You don't think?' Henry rubbed his jaw. Any time Henry made a gesture so similar to one of Ollie's, my stomach flip-flopped, the oddness of it surprising me.

'Maybe. My son has told me a little about what he's been doing these past few years, and I believe there's something not right here about *The Sanctum*. We know they exist, but surely not to keep the identity of a secret heir hidden. When we were members, I never got the impression they'd give a shit about something like that.'

'That was a long time ago,' Henry said. 'We've got no clue what they do now.'

My dad joined in. 'Except for trying to kill teenagers.'

Forty-Seven

THE DINNER TOOK PLACE, and there were no issues. The food was fancy, and I hated it all.

Orlando had been placed on our table and it was as awkward as you'd imagine it to be. Conversation was stilted, but mostly, people were too busy eating to get into it, which I was super thankful for. Food had so many purposes in this life and I appreciated every one of them.

'We can get a pizza delivered when this bullshit is over,' Ollie whispered in my ear during the main course, and I nodded enthusiastically.

He knew how to talk dirty to me.

Once the dessert plates got cleared away, Ms Hawthorn made her way to the centre of the stage, and her appearance made me pause.

She wore an ill-fitting grey dress; the material bunched up around her hips like a dress you'd see in an Edwardian book, and a grey mask which showed the depth of her grey eyes and grey hair she'd pulled back into the most severe bun I'd ever seen her sport. Miss Havisham come to life in front of our eyes.

'The silent auction tables are available along the back wall,' she said, pointing in their direction. 'There are many prizes to be won, and all the money raised is for charity, so don't be shy.'

Some parents cheered, while others politely clapped. Our table had pretty sombre occupants, and we did neither. All of us were either watching Ms Hawthorn with narrowed eyes, or were darting our gaze around the room to seek those who may wish to harm us.

I'd been certain something would have happened already.

Plus, members of *The Sanctum* wouldn't wear their cloaks to a soiree like this. Nope. They'd blend in.

Damn, even the most unsuspecting person could belong to the secret society that had plagued us for the last two years, and we'd be none the wiser.

'Would you like to dance?' Ollie whispered, his tongue darting out and touching my ear, causing goosebumps to trail down my arms. Everything about him—every action, every glimpse, every touch—made me fall even further in love with him. My heart was fit to burst thinking of it; of him.

'I'd love to,' I replied, hoping my smile came off flirtatious, and not like an illness. This casual flirting malarkey had got easier, sure, but it still didn't come naturally to me. It was like I was playing pretend, and not doing an excellent job of it.

'If he sees us dancing,' Ollie whispered. 'It won't be long until he asks to cut in. Bastard won't be able to stop himself.'

I turned my focus to the silent auction tables and nodded absentmindedly. It wasn't much of a plan, but it was something. It also made my stomach flutter funny when Ollie asked me to dance, knowing he asked not because he wanted to but because he wanted to rile up his twin.

'We're off to dance,' I announced to the table. Orlando's devilish stare landed on me, and I tried to keep my face neutral. I turned my attention to Clover. 'You coming?'

'You know it,' Clover said. She stood and pulled Griff with her. He gave a half-grimace, which I supposed could be classed as a smile in some circles. 'Can't let you two steal all the attention.'

We laughed good-naturedly and left the table, while Orlando's stare burned a hole in my back. It was well known now how he wanted to be in his brother's position. Wanted to be the one holding me close, flush up against his chest.

'You reckon this'll work?' I asked, as quiet as I could to be heard over the music. Ollie's azure blue eyes stared back at me, so much love and affection swimming in them, I nearly burst into tears at the emotion he was showing me. So much had changed since we met and sometimes it took me by surprise. 'Because now we're here, it all seems rather flimsy.'

I wanted *this* to be over. And by this I meant all of it. *The Sanctum*, Orlando's bullshit, being at Hawthorn, having to worry about whether somebody was going to make an attempt on my life anytime I left my dorm, to name a few things.

Oh, and I wanted to be happy. Healthy.

And I wanted both of those things to take place far, far away from Hawthorn.

The band played a slow song from their position on the stage, and the two of us waltzed in time to the music. Ollie was such an elegant dancer. It seemed I never had enough time to appreciate his skill before something or *someone* interrupted us.

Within moments, a small cough came from behind. Like clockwork, set to happen.

'Can I cut in?' Orlando asked, falling right into the trap laid out for him.

'No,' Ollie replied.

'No?' Orlando laughed, a deep chuckle making my insides twist. 'And why is that?'

'Do you need me to lay it out for you?' Ollie mocked. 'I rule this school. I rule over *you*.'

The plan was simple. Create a scene and draw all eyes in our direction. Which, knowing Orlando's reaction to all things me, shouldn't be too difficult.

The anger on his face already told me he was putty in our hands, ready to be moulded whichever way we chose.

'*You?*' Orlando scoffed. 'You rule over nothing. You're delusional.'

'I'm the delusional one?' Ollie laughed. Loud. Barking. Attention-stealing. 'You seem to believe Skylar wants to be with a nobody like you. Heck, even your own mother didn't want you. Told everybody you'd died. How does that feel? To be so unloved and rotten, even your mother wanted you gone before you could ruin more lives.'

'You think you're so special, don't you?' Orlando spat. 'There was a fifty-fifty chance of what twin she gave away. I'm sure if she had based it on personality, things would be different around here.'

'Are you questioning my mother's judgement?' Ollie's eyes narrowed on his twin. It always seemed odd to watch the two of them so close together. A mirror image without the mirror.

'*Our* mother,' Orlando corrected. 'And yes, yes I am.'

I rolled my eyes at the pissing contest the two of them had entered. Even at a time like this, they couldn't help themselves. A compulsion of sorts. *Idiots.*

'No. *Your mother* is standing somewhere in this hall.' Ollie made a show of standing taller and searching over the heads of the crowd, seeking Ms Hawthorn. 'No doubt embarrassed by you and the spectacle you're once again making of yourself.'

Orlando stood frozen at Ollie's callous words, flung at him when he least expected it. His face rearranged into something ugly. A sneer on his perfect lips, cold enough to turn my stomach.

He pulled a gun from his waistband and the crowd formed around us gasped. One woman screamed in terror so loud my hands went to my ears involuntarily.

For fuck's sake.

It was like the New Year's Gala all over again. Same position. Same people. Same stupid bullshit.

Yes, there had always been a possibility things would turn violent, but it would've helped us all if Leo had told us Orlando still had access to a *fucking gun*!

It would be nice to work with all the information for once. Was that too much to ask?

I didn't know where to look, or where to turn, but I knew I needed to keep my calm. It would be stupid to ruin things now, not with *The Sanctum* so close to being revealed. Or maybe they'd remain in the shadows and watch it all play out, and decide what to do later down the line when things were clearer. Orlando may not be important to anybody besides Winifred.

Ollie and I stayed where we were. United, hands grasped together, staring Orlando down. Yes, I was terrified—I assume most people would be if they had a gun pointed their way—but something told me I wasn't the one in danger. No, my terror was for Ollie and what could happen to him if Orlando lost his temper and decided killing his brother was worth the inevitable prison time.

Orlando had nothing to lose, after all. He was already out on bail, and it was a matter of time until they arrested him for Ophelia's murder. Which made a guy pretty reckless in my books.

'Do you think that's a good idea?' Ollie asked, his voice a low growl. Nobody liked being threatened, especially in the middle of a masquerade ball.

'I do.' Orlando threw his arms back, an over-the-top gesture showing off to the growing audience. People screamed as the gun in his right hand swung when he moved, sweeping across the crowd. 'Everybody in this room needs to be taught a lesson. For years, they've been allowed to get away with their heinous crimes and nobody has called them out, so it's time somebody does.'

The way Orlando acted so casually while wielding a weapon in his hand scared me more than anything coming out of his mouth. His face told me he wanted nothing more than to shoot Ollie dead. If he was gone, and out of his way, Orlando probably thought he'd have a better shot at taking his brother's place.

A better shot of winning *me*.

But one thing he'd never realised was that I was not some prize to be won. I never had been, and I never would be, no matter what tactics he employed, nor how desperate his actions became.

'You're wrong,' Ollie said. 'The only people in this room who need to be taught a lesson are you and those who go by the name of *The Sanctum*.'

'And what do you know of *The Sanctum*?' Orlando barked. 'You know nothing, Oliver.'

'Maybe.' Ollie gave a casual shrug. 'But there is one thing I do know.'

'And what's that?' Orlando couldn't help but ask and fall into the carefully laid trap of a question. 'Because from the time I've watched you, I've realised you know little.'

Ollie's eyes scrunched at the corners, amusement dancing on his features. 'I know you have no position of power. Not here and not within *The Sanctum* either. You're a lackey for those higher up than you.'

Where the bloody hell were Griff and Leo?

I braved glimpsing away from Ollie and Orlando for a second to search the room, eager to find my friends amongst the masked faces crowding the dance floor. Griff and Clover were behind us, watching it all unfold, ready to back us up with a moment's notice.

Leo stood by our parents on the edge of the dance floor. I caught his eye on my perusal and he tilted his head and gave a little shake. *Not yet, Skylar. Let it unfold.*

I turned away. Ollie and Orlando were still facing off, not having moved a muscle in the brief time I stopped paying them any attention.

If one of them wasn't holding a gun out to the other, I would laugh. The two of them had similar stances. Similar faces. Similar *everything*.

Even after knowing of Orlando's existence for a while, it still unnerved me how easy it was to mistake one for the other—the police had managed it enough times.

'A lackey?' Orlando laughed, matching his brother's deep bark. 'There are many names I'd expect you to call me, but a lackey isn't one of them.'

'Now I know for a fact you are delusional,' Ollie growled, staring his brother down, not letting the weapon faze him in the slightest. 'If you're not a lackey, then have them reveal themselves right now. Demand they show their faces and come into the light.'

Orlando's face soured, but whether it was at the demand or

the realisation he had less power than he'd like to portray, I couldn't be sure.

'You do not give demands around here, boy.' Ms Hawthorn's voice gave me a chill. She always came across as stern and grey, but now, as she removed her grey mask and walked into the centre of the dance floor, I saw cruelty.

I saw a woman who wanted chaos.

Everybody around the circle removed their masks, too, as if the spell of the evening had lifted in her one move. The band had stopped playing when they realised nobody was dancing or paying them any attention.

Nobody in the hall talked. They were all patiently waiting.

'No, you're correct,' Ollie said icily. 'That would be *The Sanctum*, wouldn't it?'

'Oh, Oliver dear. You think you're all so clever.' Winifred smiled. 'But *The Sanctum* won't be showing their faces here tonight.'

Her smile grew wider. Thin lips pushed up and teeth on show.

The cat who got the cream, the canary, and the curious.

What kind of bullshit bomb was she about to drop?

Forty-Eight

'*THE SANCTUM* NO LONGER EXISTS. Or at least not in the way you think.'

'What do you mean, it no longer exists?' Ollie spat. 'We *know* the members are here.'

'One day last week, all the older members were sitting around a dinner table, talking and having a laugh. Then the next, they slumped in their seats.' Winifred shrugged. 'Seems they all drank poison.'

When I looked around to see how the others here were taking the news, I spotted Leo. I hadn't seen him slip back into the crowd. Even he appeared stumped at the announcement.

Griff slumped beside me. 'Now we'll never know whether they wanted to kill me.'

'Oh, you foolish boy.' Ms Hawthorn turned her piercing gaze to Griff. '*The Sanctum* didn't want to kill you.' She laughed again, setting my teeth on edge. 'I did.'

'You did?' Griff answered.

She cackled, evil personified. 'All three of you were meant to die in the crash. I convinced the other members we needed to eradicate the whole Cooper line.'

'You sound like you're in charge,' I said, finding my voice for the first time since Ms Hawthorn entered and became the centre of attention. Hoping my words would stroke her ego to the point she'd answer me honestly without too much thought. 'So why would you kill them all?'

'My whole life, I've had to listen to others. Follow instructions. Sit there, be silent, and do as I'm told.' She locked eyes on each person before moving on to the next. This was personal for her. 'Well, not anymore. I decided enough was enough. I wanted what was mine. What should have always been mine!'

'And what is that?' Ollie said.

'The Hawthorn legacy,' she shouted, her voice cracking. 'The school, the money, all of it! It should have been mine. I'm the eldest and tradition always dictated that the eldest got it, regardless of gender, after an addition a hundred years ago, but no! My stupid parents didn't trust me. Thought I'd squander the lot and fuck it up for everybody. So they gave it to *Edward* instead.'

I squeezed Ollie's hand in mine, my anchor in the tough times, and from the hatred exuding from Winifred's face, we were about to hit some rough sea.

'Then my younger sisters were born, and things got worse. Everybody loved Millie and Eliza. Adored from birth they were.' She took on a mocking tone. '"*Oh, look how beautiful they are. The twins will have everybody fighting over them.*" People wouldn't stop going on about how loved they were. Including our parents.' Her venom surprised even me.

'What did you do?' Edward roared.

'I don't know what you mean,' Winnie said, playing coy. What a bitch. 'If you're asking about whether I killed our dear mother and father, then you would be correct.'

Ollie bristled next to me, the fate of his grandparents settling over us all. Damn, Winifred was even more coldhearted than I thought.

'God, woman, why?' Edward's face melted into one of complete horror. His bloodshot eyes filled with tears. Learning of your parents' fate this way, in front of such a large crowd, was cruel and calculated. Something Winnie took pleasure in.

'An inheritance doesn't exist if people are alive. I needed the

Hawthorn money passed down to the next generation, even if it meant I saw a small fraction of it.' She smiled wider.

'Did it make you happy?' Leo said, watching her with narrowed eyes.

'For a time,' she said, gesturing around the vast hall, 'but like everything else, it goes away.'

'I still have my part of the money,' Edward replied, 'so you must have been doing something wrong, Winifred.'

She cackled with derision. 'I *did* do something wrong. I helped you brats cover everything up!'

'What we did?' Henry looked at Ollie, then Orlando—who hadn't spoken since his mother had taken over the floor, but still held a gun to Ollie's head—and then to Edward. Winnie must be referring to what happened with Millie and Eliza back when they were members of *The Set*. The prank gone wrong; the one she helped covered up as a suicide. 'That was years ago.'

'And I've never forgotten it!' she screamed, spit flying from her mouth. She turned to my dad. 'How do you think Jacob Cooper "stole" Hawthorn money? Because I let him! I shoved it into his greedy grasp and told him to never return, no matter what happened. I wanted Millie's life ruined worse than the way she ruined that poor girl's.'

Jacob stepped forward, having hidden behind the others during the rest of Winnie's speech. His face told me all I needed to know. This was the truth of what happened, and of why he left. Winifred paid him off to leave Millie.

He'd already left me long before.

'And now he's back, ready to ruin everything I've achieved.' Winifred's grey eyes glared at my dad, her hatred for him evident to all.

'I've returned because of your actions,' my dad said. His eyes were sorrow-filled, and I knew he had remorse for his part in everything. For leaving me. For leaving the love of his life alone in a cold world. 'I also left for the same reason I've returned. You told me if I didn't leave, you'd kill my daughter. Now I know you've been trying to kill her the last two years, anyway.'

Winifred shrugged, little care given. 'You'd left her with her shit-for-brains mother ten years before you took me up on my offer.'

The dig towards Cora hit me in a place I never expected—my heart. Yes, I could think poorly of my mother, but having it come from this evil witch was *not* okay.

Winifred also had a valid point. Jacob disappeared from my life within a couple of months of me being born, yet he'd stuck around Beurre for a bit if he had time to have an affair with Millie.

'And you, of all people, know why,' Jacob growled. He moved into the centre of the circle and swept his gaze on everybody watching. 'This woman,' he spat, 'has been threatening our children's lives since they were born. I left Skylar at Cora's, because Winifred Hawthorn told me she'd kill her if she ever stepped foot on Hawthorn ground.'

I gasped alongside every other person in the room watching this shit show unfold. All of this was news to me. Ms Hawthorn had never hidden the fact she hated me, but no part of me ever believed she wanted to *kill* me.

Ollie tightened his grip on my hand, keeping us rooted to the spot, which was as much for his benefit as it was for mine.

Jacob continued talking. 'She threatened Edward, Millie, and Eliza, too. If we ever told the truth of what happened when we were at school, she'd kill our children.'

'But why?' I whispered, confused. It was so extreme. So drastic. Why on earth would this woman want us all dead? Even for her, it seemed *a lot*.

'Why, Miss Crescent?' she asked, her beady eyes locked on mine. 'They killed an innocent girl, and came running to me to help them. Snivelling little brats wanted me to make it all go away. Millie even went as far as blaming me for distracting her.'

Edward, Henry, and Jacob all looked geared up to rush her, but then, as one, they remembered themselves and held back.

God, I'd love to wipe the smile off of Winifred's face.

I *hated* her smarmy smile. The way she took joy in revealing the secrets and lies she'd been complicit in. It made me sick.

No wonder Orlando was so fucked up.

This woman had been his role model. The person to show him the way of the world and teach him about other people's emotions and needs.

For the first time in a while, I understood the full extent of Orlando's childhood and upbringing. Of how twisted his mind was inside—and who had made it so.

It was all making sense why he thought murder to get what you wanted was okay.

'Did you shoot Griff at the gala?' Edward asked, his hands clenched into fists at his sides.

'Yes, yes,' she said, amused. 'It was all me.' Her smile split her entire face in two.

I'd never seen the woman before me. Not the way she acted at that moment, anyway. I'd always found her uncomfortable, and from the first time she laid eyes on me, I knew she didn't like me, but I didn't realise how deep it ran.

She despised me.

She despised all of us.

'Why did *The Sanctum* kill Olivia?' Orlando asked, lowering the gun in his hand an inch.

Winifred narrowed her evil eyes on her son, disappointment oozing from every pore.

Orlando had told me he didn't kill her, but I hadn't believed him. I'd given him a hard time about it, actually. Been a bit of a bitch. Yet he'd told the truth the whole time.

My heart dropped.

'We needed to frame Skylar, and you handed me the perfect opportunity when you took *that girl* back after the gala, pretending to be your brother.'

'Why did you *need* to frame me? It didn't even work. You hushed up the murders with the police. Paid them off. Why do that if you wanted to frame me?'

'Because she wanted it to get back to me,' Jacob said, shaking his head. 'Wanted to torment me and have me believe all the steps I'd taken to keep you away from this life had been fruitless.

If I knew you were in danger, or needed help, then she knew I'd come.'

A gunshot rang out throughout the hall, shocking everybody. My head frantically snapped around, my heart beating out of my chest, searching for the sound. The last time I heard gunshots, Griff and Clover got hurt.

Henry lowered a gun down. He'd fired the warning shot into the high ceiling to get everyone's attention.

'This is beyond ridiculous, Winifred. You've stood before us all and admitted you killed Eliza and Damien. Killed the poor girl, Olivia. Attempted to frame my son and his girl-friend. Corrupted my other son—one you never even told me existed.' He took a deep breath and paused, collecting his thoughts. 'I'm sorry, but you can't leave this room. I forbid it.'

Winifred scoffed. 'You forbid it? Oh, please, Henry. Are you going to stop me?'

If I didn't want the woman gone, I'd be a little impressed. She was being held at gunpoint, yet still acted like it was a normal day —a normal conversation.

A small part of me admired that.

'We're all going to stop you,' Ollie said, moving to join his father, not caring Orlando had a gun trained on him the whole time. I'd never seen Henry and Ollie so united; so in sync. They both widened their stances, a metre gap between them, and stared down Ms Hawthorn. 'Nobody in this room is going to let you leave.'

'You won't get away with this,' Henry spat.

Hysteria settled into her features. 'My whole life I've been overlooked. There was always somebody prettier. Somebody wealthier. Somebody with more brains, or more brawn. Well now, I will win. It's my time to shine.'

It was pitiful.

My feet unstuck from the floor, and I went to move over to where Ollie stood with Henry when Leo grabbed my arms from behind, taking me by surprise.

'Don't, Stutter,' he whispered in my ear harshly. 'He's a big boy. He can look after himself.'

'He wants her dead,' I whispered back. 'We can't sit here and watch this.'

'She wants *you* dead,' he reminded me. 'And has tried to kill you multiple times.'

He was right. She had, and during the course of the evening, had shown no remorse for it. No, if anything, she seemed pretty proud of it all.

I locked my feet to the floor once more, turning my attention back to the stand-off happening in the middle of the room. Everybody forgot the charity effort now. All eyes were on the unfolding drama. Masks off—literally and figuratively.

'You won't kill me,' Winifred cackled. 'You haven't got it in you, Henry dear.'

Henry's face changed in a split second and his intention became clear, the gun gripped firmly in his palm, pointed at his sister-in-law. He pulled the trigger, and after a flash, the bullet found its place in Winifred's chest.

She fell, crumpling to the floor, shock covering her face.

Of all the things she expected, it was never that.

'Mum!' Orlando roared, falling to the floor to put his hands over the blood gushing from the wound. Red stained and covered his hands. The gun clattered to the floor, forgotten.

The guttural sound from deep in his throat rang out and reverberated around the hall, the high ceilings causing it to echo.

The pure emotion gutted me. I wished things were different, and I could rush over to him and pull him close. Hug him tight, until no breath remained in his body.

The room's occupants waited with bated breath to find out whether Winifred had breathed her last.

Orlando let out one last wail. He pushed himself to standing, his angry gaze locked on Ollie like a bull at a red flag.

'You,' he seethed in a low and deadly tone. 'You did this.'

Ollie said nothing. Must be weird to watch an unhinged version of yourself staggering towards you. Leo still had a firm grip on my arm. His fingers no doubt would leave bruises, and I couldn't do anything to stop whatever Orlando had in mind.

I felt lost. Like a weak girl bullshitting herself. One who said she couldn't do anything but could if she applied herself.

I didn't know *what*.

'You will pay!' Orlando's gaze searched the floor. He found the gun and scrambled for it before anybody else could. Once again, he raised it and aimed at Ollie.

My heart stopped beating. The blood in my veins turned to ice.

'No!'

I screamed, my heart threatening to leave my throat. The sickness and nausea swirled around with the dinner and alcohol I'd consumed, dragging me under.

Then everything happened as if in fast forward. Not slow motion, the way things told us life-changing events were.

Orlando pulled the trigger.

Henry leapt in front of Ollie.

Pushed him out of the way.

Took the bullet with Ollie's name on it straight in the heart. The ultimate sacrifice.

My jaw dropped to the floor. My heart was beating erratically, and my vision struggled, those black spots clouding the edges once more. I fought them off. I couldn't pass out now. Not when Ollie was still in Orlando's path of wrath.

'The knife,' Leo whispered in my ear. 'Ollie's unprotected. Go!'

I stumbled forward, tripping on the skirt of my ball gown, as my dad and Edward went to Henry's aid.

How had this night descended into chaos so fast?

We'd known it was going to explode, but we'd been so sure we'd come out on top, victorious.

In a nervous gesture, I brushed the skirt of my dress, checking the knife was still in its place at my thigh. *It was.* Sighing in relief, I scrutinised Orlando, my heart breaking at the sight of him.

Like Oliver, he looked destroyed. The mother he'd been given through some luck of the draw was lying dead at his feet, her blood covering his shoes, his shirt, and his hands.

I was in between Ollie and Orlando, but it was the latter I turned to face.

'Little One,' he croaked out, his voice breaking as much as my heart. 'Don't do this.'

My eyes filled with tears, the gut wrenching emotions hurting me more than anything else ever had.

My hands shook as I removed the knife from the hidden holster on my body and I gripped it tightly in front of me.

'I have to,' I whispered. 'You've left me no choice.'

'Sky,' Ollie said from behind me, taking a step closer, his shoes clicking on the floor. 'Are you sure?'

A tear left my eye and trailed down my cheek. I turned my eyes to Clover. Then Griff. And, finally, Ollie.

'He'll n-never stop,' I stuttered. 'He wants your life. He wants *me*. He always has.'

'Little One,' he whispered, reaching out and grabbing my wrist to pull me closer. 'Do it. It's only fair,' he whispered in my ear. 'It was all me, Skylar. I stabbed you and drowned you and drugged you. I love you.'

I whimpered and pushed the words from my heart past my lips. 'I love you.'

Then I reared my hand back and lunged, the hot sticky blood coating my hand in seconds.

Orlando grunted as I held him up, allowing the blood to cover my dress. I glanced down, the blood on my clothes and my hands settling like a second layer of skin.

Out, damned spot. Out, I say.

It was as if the world had reduced to nothing. No words entered my head. No sounds. Orlando and me, alone. The sins of the past washed away.

My heart pounded in my chest, threatening to leave it.

Numb. Lost. *Whole.*

'Skylar!' Ollie's voice sounded as if it was coming from behind a door. Or a wall. One I couldn't penetrate. 'Skylar!'

His face appeared in front of mine. I watched his mouth move, but the words were still foggy.

'We've got to go!' He shouted in my ear. 'Fire!'

Then it registered. The smell of smoke. The distinct smell of something burning, and then the heat of the air. The physical smoke in the air.

The smoke in my lungs. The black bleeding into my vision.

Then ...

Nothing.

FIRE AT HAWTHORN ACADEMY

A fire broke out at Hawthorn Academy late on Saturday evening.

The firefighters who went to the scene believe the fire started in the school's old hospital wing and spread from there. By the time the fire force arrived, both the hospital wing and the pool house were unable to be saved.
The administration building also suffered some damage.
There were four fatalities and a number more casualties.
Headteacher, Ms Winifred Hawthorn, lost her life, as did her son, Orlando Hawthorn.
His body is yet to be recovered.
Henry Brandon, father of Orlando and brother-in-law of Winifred, tragically lost his life in the same evening.
Their deaths aren't being treated as suspicious.

Epilogue

GRADUATION. A day I never thought I'd see.

Yet here it was and I couldn't be fucking happier.

'You really are so very beautiful, Skylar,' Ollie said, placing a deep kiss on my lips.

'Thank you.' The blush at his words rose on my cheeks. Ollie's praise had always been something I craved, but now, after everything we'd been through, it mattered even more.

My dress, a knee-length 1950s style find with a full skirt and Bardot shoulders, made me feel a million pounds. The moment I saw it at a vintage store in London, I had to have it.

'Shame it'll be covered by a stupid gown for most of the day,' I said, my hands travelling down the bodice, touching the fabric with reverence. 'You scrub up well, too.'

'In this old thing?' he joked, holding the lapels of his suit jacket and straightening them out.

Damn. He looked hot. *Really fucking hot.* Good enough to eat kind of hot, and I wanted to climb him then and there, but I knew my mum waited downstairs for us with my dad, of all people.

Stranger things have happened.

If you told me when I started at Hawthorn that I would finish my scholarship with two parents who cared about me, then I would have told you to stop smoking drugs or whatever you were doing, causing you to hallucinate and alter reality.

The question that had run through my mind all morning left my lips unbidden. 'It's odd, isn't it? That we're here?'

Ollie paused in his fidgeting, and his eyebrows raised, scrunching up his forehead. 'Here as in Hawthorn? Or here as in graduation?'

'Both?' My voice went up at the end so it came out sounding more like a question.

Ollie stepped towards me and placed his hands on my shoulders to ground me. It was something he'd started doing often, and I loved it. I think it grounded him as much as it did me. Something we both needed.

He placed a kiss on my head, before resting his defined jaw there, pressing into my skull slightly.

'Hm,' he mused, taking his time to answer. 'Guess it is a little odd, but I knew we'd get here.' His tone was so confident, I moved my head from underneath his chin and looked up into his eyes in question.

'You did?'

'Sure did. Things were a little hairy at the start of the year, I'll admit. At the start of your scholarship, I *definitely* didn't see us getting here, but even then, in my gut, I guess I always knew we'd be here in the end.'

I hummed, not believing him. 'Well, I didn't.'

'Not that hard, babe. You struggle to see something even when it's right in front of you.' He smiled, hinting at his teasing, and his eyes sparkled at me.

'Hey!' I nudged him with my sharp elbow. 'You didn't know about *him* either.'

Ever since the events of last month, neither of us had mentioned Orlando's name. I couldn't decide if it was a denial, or whether it was a way for us to move on, but either way, he barely came up in our conversation. It was easier to talk about anything else. To move on without the shadow of him lingering over us for all eternity.

'I'd never seen him,' Ollie said, the answer an obvious one in his eyes.

'Oh, yeah, yeah.' I nudged him again, but straight after I wrapped my arms around his waist, so they joined at his back. 'Well, I'm sorry I didn't know you had an evil twin lurking about.'

'You're more than forgiven.' He leaned down and kissed my lips. A kiss holding the promise of *more*.

'Thank fuck.' I bit my lip, once again my dirty mind going back to all the things we could get up to if we didn't have to attend our graduation … 'Come on, my rents are waiting downstairs.'

I unfurled my arms from around him and placed his hand in mine to drag him along behind me. The longer we spent upstairs, the longer we were putting off the inevitable, and I didn't want to put off graduation any longer. I *wanted* to graduate from Hawthorn Academy and get the fuck out of dodge. It was always my plan and to see it come to fruition? Well, victory was sweet indeed.

Graduating alongside Ollie, Griff, and Clover was nothing short of a miracle in my eyes. Multiple events and circumstances over the last two years had made me believe we'd never get to, and now we were able to, I wanted it to be done and over with.

Ollie ushered his hand out towards the door. 'Lead the way, baby.'

He didn't need to tell me twice.

The two of us left Ollie's suite and made our way to the front lawn of the school where the chairs and stage were set up. The weather was lovely, thank fuck, otherwise this wouldn't be much fun. A soggy outdoor graduation? No thanks.

The fire at the Masquerade Ball started in the hospital wing and burnt the building and the pool house down to the ground before the fire could be stopped. It broke my heart to see the hospital wing go. Yes, we had our differences, but it was a huge part of the history of the school and of what it once was during the war.

The pool house could rot in hell for all I cared. Too much bad had taken place there for me to see it any other way.

By the time the fire reached the main building, the firefighters had arrived. They rescued me soon after arriving, but they left Orlando until last.

They never located his body.

It was still surreal, the entire end of the evening a blur. A nightmare I hadn't woken from.

Was I at fault? A murderer? According to the reports, he died of smoke inhalation and it was no fault of mine, but he and I both knew better. He'd given me a choice and had honoured my decision, had honoured *me*.

Our graduation gowns were being held in the hall for us and it gutted me that my gown would cover up Ollie's jacket. The way his shirt stretched across his broad shirt should be illegal. All hard muscles and straining buttons. *Fuck.* Maybe the gown was a good thing after all.

Cora's face split into a wide smile, stretching across her entire face when she spotted me. If she'd given me the same smile a year ago, I'd have wondered what she wanted from me, but now I saw it for what it was: genuine love and affection.

Bloody weird, right?

'Oh darling,' she said, dragging out the word to make it the longest word known to man. 'You look ab-so-lutely ah-mazing.'

'Thanks, Mum.' I still found it hard to act normal around her. Even though we'd sorted our differences, it would be a while before I forgave the past. If I ever did.

'My baby, graduating.' She wiped a tear making its way down her cheek, small flecks of mascara clinging to its path. 'Skylar, I am so proud of you. You know that, don't you, darling?'

I nodded, letting her pull me in for a hug with her outstretched arms. Her perfume nearly knocked me out. It was so strong I could *taste* it.

'Yeah, Mum,' I said. And the thing surprising me the most? I sort of meant it.

'Skylar,' Jacob said, moving from his position off to the side to stand in front of me and Cora. 'You get even more beautiful every day.'

'Thanks.' It came out even more uneven and awkward

sounding than when I answered Mum. Jacob and I were still on uneven footing. Whatever way you sliced it, he had still been absent for eighteen years of my life, and I couldn't bypass that just because he was here now.

One person who wasn't here was Andy. When I was in the hospital getting checked out after the fire, Mum came. She'd seen the fire on the news and called Lottie, who sent a car round for Mum to bring her to me. While there, I opened up about what had happened on the day I left home for Hawthorn.

'MUM,' I said, scared to voice my thoughts, but knew this was my chance to talk to her without interruption. 'There's something I need to tell you.'

'What's up, darling?' she said, interested at what I had to say for once.

'There's something I have to tell you about Andy.'

'What?'

I took a deep breath, steeling myself for the difficult conversation ahead. 'He kissed me, the day I left to go to Hawthorn.'

'Why didn't you tell me before?' she asked, her expression one of genuine shock. She squeezed my hand, encouraging me to continue.

'I left for school pretty much straight after, then I barely saw you without him afterwards. And when I did ... guess I didn't know how.' I tried to shrug it off but was unable to because of being hooked up to the IV still. 'And Andy told me you wouldn't believe me.'

'I'm sorry he made you think that,' Mum said, her eyes shimmering with unshed tears. 'I wish you'd told me, darling.'

Tears leaked out of my eyes, an overwhelming rush of emotion surging through me at her reaction. I hadn't expected her to believe me. Hadn't expected her to be so nice about it.

'I promise I'll do better, Skylar.'

AFTER OUR CONVERSATION, she kicked him out of her house and threw out his stuff. It had shocked the shit out of me. I hadn't expected her to do anything with my words, but I was so fucking glad she did.

'Shall we go get our gowns?' Ollie asked me, stretching his arm out towards me so I could walk into it. I went willingly, a smile covering my face.

'Yeah,' I replied, then looked at both of my parents. 'We'll be right back.'

The two of us went into the main entrance of the school, and those gargoyles were staring at us as we did so. I would miss those pesky little guys.

Clover, Leo, and Griff waited in front of the hall entrance for us, each with a big smile of their own.

'You ready to do this shit, Clouds?' Griff asked me, his cheeky grin covering his face. It had taken a while, but his smile had returned, and I hoped it would be permanent from now on.

'You bloody know it,' I replied. 'I am beyond ready to never step foot across this threshold ever again.'

And I meant it. Even coming back in ten years would be way too soon for my liking. Even without the dark cloud of Orlando and Ms Hawthorn lurking above the place, it still felt wrong. Even if Leo owned the place now.

Didn't have that on my bingo card, that was for sure.

'You and me both,' Clo said, looping her arm in mine and walking us into the hall. The gowns were all arranged on rails behind a desk, and one of the teacher's volunteers helped each of us into a gown in our size. It was meant to be oversized, but this was beyond, and I imagined I looked a little stupid in it. It swamped me and I swore it made me appear shorter.

Clo, who was shorter than me, looked even more like she was wearing a large parachute tent. You know, like the ones we used to run and hide under in primary school during PE lessons?

'We look ridiculous,' she giggled, her smile wild. It was nice to see her so carefree. Now everything about her past was out in the open she'd relaxed a lot.

'We do,' I said. 'Wonder if the boys look as silly as we do.'

'Nah.' She shook her head, her red curls bouncing with the

motion. 'They'll look like some kind of heavenly beings or some shit.'

I laughed at the image she painted in my mind, but I agreed with her. If those boys managed hotness in those tiny swimming speedos, I knew they could pull off graduation caps and gowns. Although Ollie might get a little precious if it messed up his hair.

'I'm so happy we're here, Clo. Together.'

'Me too. And if you tell anybody I said this, I will kill you, but you're my best friend, Sky. My life wouldn't be the same without you in it.'

My eyes welled up, but I pushed it down. 'You're mine. Hawthorn's good for something, ay?'

Ollie and Griff came back into our eye line and a smile came to my lips. As expected, they were gorgeous. Not that I'd ever tell them I thought of the word gorgeous in relation to them. They preferred to be called sexy or hot. Well, Griff preferred to be referred to as a Greek god, causing us all to roll our eyes in unison; a collective unit.

'Hey,' Ollie said, pulling me into a tight hug. His hands travelled south to my bum, and I tilted my head up.

'Hey there,' I replied, the playful smile still firm on my lips. 'Man, when I thought you couldn't get any sexier.'

He chuckled and squeezed my arse. 'Sky, you look beautiful, don't get me wrong, but you do also sort of resemble a yurt.'

'A yurt!' I shouted, chuckling, before schooling my features into a frown. At least he said a yurt and not a regular old boring tent. 'Piss off.'

'You wouldn't want me to go anywhere, would you?' His eyes glinted with humour as he placed a kiss on my lips. I returned the kiss, an enormous wave of love for him rushing through me. It happened a lot recently, and I wasn't mad at it.

I hummed, dragging out his torment. Or at least attempting to. We both knew I was full of it. 'I guess I'd be sad if you left.'

'Come on, fuckers.' Griff called over his shoulder as he left the hall, Clo by his side, the two of them having resolved everything broken between them. They were best as friends and thank fuck they'd realised it. 'We've gotta move!'

'Leggo, baby,' Ollie mumbled, and placed one last kiss on my forehead.

I took a step back and spotted some of my lipstick staining his lips.

'Wait, come here,' I said, and discreetly tried to take my red lipstick off his mouth. 'Apparently, my lipstick isn't as matte as I'd have liked.'

He smiled, and heat prickled inside me. *Fuck sake.* Not now.

'I'd like to see your lipstick smeared somewhere else,' he drawled, a salacious smile on his lips tempting me to ditch this thing and get him alone. I poked him in the stomach to stop this train from derailing off the tracks.

'Ouch!' I shook my hand, hoping the pain would disappear with the motion, but it didn't. 'That hurt.'

'Next time,' he said, amused, 'accept it and move on.'

'Yeah, yeah,' I replied, not able to hide the smile gracing my mouth. 'Let's go.'

'GRIFFIN COOPER!' Edward Hawthorn called out from his spot in the middle of the stage behind a podium. Even though he didn't want to own the school, he was still acting head until Leo took over at age twenty-one. Our class was small, only forty of us graduating, which meant the ceremony would be short, thank fuck. I didn't have the patience to sit through a long, drawn out thing.

Griff strolled across the stage, cocksure as always, and stopped to receive his diploma and handshake from the guest speakers who were here to talk motivational words at us. I cheered loudly, clapping my clammy hands together, happy for Griff.

Edward opened his mouth once Griff passed, and called, 'Skylar Crescent-Cooper!'

I took a large lungful of air and made my way across the stage, tears pricking the corners of my eyes.

I'd done it.

Somehow, I survived this shit show and was getting everything I ever wanted.

'Woo!' Cora called from her spot in the front row of parents. 'You've done it, baby!'

'Well done, Skylar!' Jacob hollered from next to Mum, both of them standing and clapping and making the most noise they could. I rolled my eyes at them, acting embarrassed by their behaviour, but I was thrilled. I'd never had parents who cared. And now, from the disaster I'd experienced here, I had two.

I shook the lady's hand and received my diploma, then stood and posed for the photographer positioned in front of the stage.

Moving back to my seat in the front row next to Griff, I smiled at Ollie sitting on Griff's other side. His eyes were warm as he smiled back at me, and whispered a quick, *Congrats, baby.* I sat down and waited for the next name I cared about to be called out.

I didn't have to wait long.

'Clover Luck!'

Griff and I stood up the moment Clo appeared on the stage, cheering as loud as we could. Her parents weren't here, and if I ever got the chance, I'd give them a strong piece of my mind.

Regardless of what had happened before, they shouldn't be missing out on her enormous achievements because of it. They didn't deserve her.

In the row for parents, Cora stood and clapped as loudly for Clo as she had for me. Lottie Hawthorn stood next to her, cheering as loudly as Mum. At some point, somehow, Mum and Lottie had become … real friends? Yeah, I didn't understand it either.

But they were both happy, so who was I to judge?

It made me so happy to see them embracing Clo and loving her the way her own parents should. Cora had stepped up in such a short amount of time, and yeah, part of me waited for the other shoe to drop, but I hoped that wouldn't be the case.

'Go, Clo!' I called out, cupping my hands around my mouth so it would carry further. 'Woo!'

In my peripheral, I spotted Leo standing with the members of staff, and he clapped as heartily as us. Nothing had happened between the two of them since *The Sanctum* had disbanded and Orlando was no longer holding shit over Leo's head, but maybe one day it would. I wasn't getting involved. The two of them would sort it out in their own time. I sensed it in my bones.

After posing for her picture, Clo made her way back to the rows of seating for students and took her seat. I leaned forward to smile at her, and she beamed back, shaking her head in disbelief.

My eye caught Ollie's as I leaned back and he winked, warming my already overheated cheeks. He moved his arm and placed it across Griff to take my hand in his briefly. After a quick pump, he removed his hand and went back to sitting properly.

Griff chuckled in between us, and whispered, 'Do I need to move?'

I shook my head at him and shh'ed him.

The rest of the ceremony continued, but I didn't take any of it in. I tried my hardest to not cry, but everything was overwhelming, and I was the happiest I'd been in so long.

I never expected to be so content.

My life was more than good. More than great.

It was fucking fantastic!

Afterword

Thank you so much for reading the Hawthorn Academy
Collection.

If you would like to join my newsletter to stay up to date with my
upcoming projects, scan the QR code below.

About Katie Lowrie

Katie Lowrie is a Brit who loves to read and write.

A list in no particular order of her greatest loves:

- Henry VIII and the Tudor era
- Her baby cat, Cress
- Musicals
- Disney
- Cheese

She loves to stalk people online (in a good way) and understands if you do too.

instagram.com/katielowrieauthor

goodreads.com/katielowrieauthor

facebook.com/katielowrieauthor

bookbub.com/authors/katie-lowrie

Also by Katie Lowrie

Hawthorn Academy:

Disorder

Disease

Disturbed

Rebels of Hollowdale High:

Haven at Hollowdale High

Hero of Hollowdale High

Heirs of Hollowdale High

Re-Imagined:

Key of Cunning (**Dark** Billionaire Romance)

Also by K. Lowrie

Model Act

Model (mis)Behaviour

Lanes of Love

Law of Love

www.ingramcontent.com/pod-product-compliance
Lightning Source LLC
Chambersburg PA
CBHW050557170726
48283CB00001B/1